# LAST EXIT

## BOOKS BY MAX GLADSTONE

*Empress of Forever*

*This Is How You Lose the Time War*
(with Amal El-Mohtar)

### THE CRAFT SEQUENCE

*Three Parts Dead*

*Two Serpents Rise*

*Full Fathom Five*

*Last First Snow*

*Four Roads Cross*

*The Ruin of Angels*

### TORDOTCOM ORIGINALS

*The Angelus Guns*

"Crispin's Model"

"Fitting In"

"A Kiss with Teeth"

"The Scholast in the Low Waters Kingdom"

### WILD CARDS

*Texas Hold'em*

# MAX GLADSTONE

# LAST EXIT

TOR

A TOM DOHERTY ASSOCIATES BOOK
NEW YORK

LAST EXIT

Copyright © 2022 by Max Gladstone

A Tor Book
Published by Tom Doherty Associates
120 Broadway
New York, NY 10271

www.tor-forge.com

Tor® is a registered trademark of Macmillan Publishing Group, LLC.

The Library of Congress Cataloging-in-Publication Data is available upon request.

ISBN 978-0-7653-3573-9 (trade paperback)
ISBN 978-1-4668-2614-4 (ebook)

Our books may be purchased in bulk for promotional, educational, or business use. Please contact your local bookseller or the Macmillan Corporate and Premium Sales Department at 1-800-221-7945, extension 5442, or by email at MacmillanSpecialMarkets@macmillan.com.

First Edition: 2022

Printed in the United States of America

0  9  8  7  6  5  4  3  2  1

*To S and C, as we walk.*

*Alma mater floreat*
*Quae nos educavit*

# LAST
# EXIT

## CHAPTER ONE

When the worst of the bleeding stopped, Zelda hitchhiked back to the Bronx to say that she was sorry.

New York wasn't safe for her even then. She crept in sideways, kept her head down, and did not think about possibilities, about spin or rot or all the other ways the skyline might have looked. Those thoughts were dangerous here. But she had to tell Sal's mother she was gone.

Years ago, when Zelda and Sal and the others left to begin their time on the road, she had dreamed that one day she might come back to this city triumphant, to stride down her long boulevards as confetti rained from rooftops and bands played marches. They were young and proud, and they knew that if they tried, they could fix what was broken in the world. It was a stretching early summer then, the glass-walled streets casting the blue of the sky back up so they'd felt as if they were marching off to storm the gates of heaven. They were saviors. They were adventurers. They believed.

Zelda made her way back alone. The 138th Street subway station was a grungy straight tunnel tagged with graffiti in hard-to-reach places, a tired, worn station best used for homecoming, just as it had been when Sal first brought Zelda here to meet her mother, all smiles at her gawping, cornpone girlfriend. Zelda had never left South Carolina before she came north for college. She was used to backcountry roads and towns with two stoplights. More people crouched on New York's few square miles than lived in her whole half of the state, all those lives weaving around and through one another.

She climbed the dirty stairs to a street that had not changed much since she had been what she'd then thought was young. Her mistakes climbed with her. Down on the platform, a girl cried, "Hey, wait!" Zelda almost did. She almost turned, and a nightmare voice suggested that if she had, she would have seen Sal.

She climbed instead, into the wet-dog heat of an August afternoon.

When she knocked on Ma Tempest's door, she heard the old woman wailing upstairs. So, she knew. A premonition, a dream, or just word traveling fast. Ramón might have called her, or Sarah, or even Ish. Zelda knocked, and kept knocking, and no one came. She bruised her knuckles, broke the scabs on her fists, and left bloody prints on the olive-painted door. Her heart was a hairy, howling thing too large for the cage of her ribs. She had lost Sal. She had lost Ma's girl, her favorite and firstborn.

She had gone off onto the road with her lover and their friends and ruined everything. She wanted to kneel at Ma Tempest's feet, bow her head to those thick sandals, and let herself be beaten until blood flowed from her back and the white bones lay bare. The bloodletting might relieve the pressure in her chest and quiet the voice inside, repeating: *It's your fault.*

It was her fault they'd left in the first place, and so was everything that came after, and the fact that Sal was gone. After all that, to need punishment or absolution from Sal's mother, now, was a crime greater than any she'd committed in those road-bound years. Except, perhaps, for stepping out on the road in the first place.

But she had nowhere else to go.

So she stood there, a tired woman in her midtwenties, sobbing bloody-knuckled, slumped against a door on a sidewalk in the Bronx. The most natural fucking thing in the world. Dog walkers took no notice. Trucks rolled by on the Cross Bronx Expressway. A cop car blared its siren at her once and she jumped, turned, glared. They drove off snickering. A bodega cat sauntered out and sat across the street to watch.

She kept knocking. This had brought her across ten states, straining to outrun the shadows on her heels. After Montana, there had been nothing left for her in the world except for this olive door. If she could look Ma Tempest in the eye and say that she was sorry, that it was all her fault, if she could take the blow across her cheek, then she could go and find a cozy little hole to die in. Or she could leave—walk out into the Hudson and never, ever come back. There were pills she could take, needles she could slide into veins, and if all else failed, there was good old legal booze. She could rot her liver and die jaundiced, miserable, screaming. That would be worth it. That would be right.

One conversation, and then she could go away forever.

So she knocked, and sobbed, and felt the steel in her spine bend.

The door took her weight.

It opened. She stumbled, caught herself.

A girl waited inside. Skin Sal's own deep brown, hair in puffballs. Cheekbones that with another ten years' growth could mirror Sal's, and big, dark eyes blinking behind glasses mended with masking tape, lenses thick enough for Zelda to see herself in the reflection. Not a sister but close to it—a cousin Ma had the raising of. June. Zelda had met her when she first came to visit during college. She was barely walking then.

June stood straight, silent, with the uncanny stillness of a child watching an adult (which Zelda had never, before this moment, felt herself to be) lose her shit.

Zelda trembled to see her, this girl who might have been her Sal long before it all went wrong.

Just say it, she told herself, just say, *She's gone,* or *I'm sorry,* or anything with an ounce of blood in it.

But before Zelda found her voice, June said: "She doesn't want to see you." Precise and clipped. Zelda reached for her—just to touch her arm or the black hand-me-down Wu-Tang T-shirt—and the door closed in her face and left her out there on the sidewalk alone, with tears stinging her eyes and snot running down her nose and blood on her knuckles where the scabs had opened, and the sky uncaring and perfect blue, solid as a dome overhead.

She forced herself away from the closed olive door, away from Ma Tempest, as untouchable as the past.

Since she had not apologized, she could not now disappear to die.

So she took her first step away.

﹡

Every year she came back.

Every year she'd failed a little more. Every year she'd gained a scar or two. Road dirt worked into her skin. Every year the country grew a little darker.

She'd been told, back in college, that she and her friends were going to save the world. She'd been told they would seize its reins and turn it toward truth and light. No one said it in quite those words, no one would be so gauche, but the intent was there. You, they said, are special. You will help the planet, you will guide the nation.

They'd been out in the world a decade now or nearly, those bright young things—the fuckups like Zelda and the ones who got it right, the polished and prepared debate-team children, the masters of the college political union. They'd been out there in the world for ten years, and somehow there was less truth each year than the last, and the light was dying.

Even in the years of hope, she'd seen it. In the great cities of the coasts, there was a sidelong wariness, glancing out of the corner of the eye at something not quite there, a high-pitched laugh of desperation, almost a scream.

And in the heart—on the long open roads—the tension grew. Small-town cops dressed in black now and sported rifles like the ones they might have used before they got kicked out of the army, in one of the smaller stupid fucking wars. She got their sidelong glances—head to foot and back up, lingering along the way—a woman traveling alone, ratty and ragged. Their fingers twitched when they looked at her. The small-town diners and truck stops got hard, and they'd been no easy places before, America always quicker to call itself friendly than to make friends. The smiles, when she found them, seemed shallow and fragile. She felt hated there, in the dark that seeped through the fault lines in those lips.

Heat lightning flashed, silent in the gathering air.

The world moved on. Or had it always been this bad, and she just never noticed before? Facebookless, lacking mobile phone, and with no internet but the public library, she was left to feel out the moment on her own. Those false smiles soured and became the baring of teeth. Cop cars on grim city streets slowed when they passed her—the eyes behind the windows covered in dark glasses, reflective like the nighttime eyes of monsters.

Every year she came back and knocked on Ma Tempest's door until her knuckles bled. The door never opened. The Bronx changed with the years: coffee shops opened and the young rich, or at least the young not-quite-poor, filtered in. But the important details did not change at all: the blood, the olive door, her memory of June's dark eyes.

﹡

The tenth year after she'd lost Sal, Zelda was living in the back seat of a hard-used Subaru in a small town in Middle Tennessee, waiting for the end of the world.

It might happen any day. She worked as a checkout clerk at the local Walmart and slept in the parking lot with the other losers and retired mobile home people, and every day she felt the rot gather, the wet foul heat of it, the summer heavy as a guillotine in this time of change. She had followed the rot here across three states, guided by the hackles on the back of her neck, by yarrow stalks and the faces of upturned tarot cards. This was the place. There was a mystery here, and she would solve it, or she would die—which would solve one mystery at least.

A boy—eighteen, nineteen, in a black T-shirt, with a homemade tattoo of Thor's hammer on his wrist, always staring at his phone—wandered up and down the fishing aisle. She'd pass him sometimes as she restocked. While she was around, he never, ever looked at the guns one aisle over.

Sometimes he'd glance at her, though. Never quite brave enough to match her eyes.

It might be him.

Or: Mona, her sometimes partner in the checkout line, her eyes deep-set and red, her shoulders down, her face bruised sometimes, or her wrist. She offered Zelda weed, and they smoked out on someone's back forty under the stars, and Zelda coughed because it had been a while since she last smoked and when she remembered just how long and whom she'd been with, she began to weep and passed it off as more coughing. Mona wasn't from around here either, she said, by which she meant she was from East Tennessee, Smoky Mountain country, not used to flatlands or the local flavor of dirty strip mall. When she worked her lighter, the spark caught reflections of something jagged in the depths of her eyes.

Mona's husband drank and stayed up late into the night, typing on the internet and watching videos about how she was the root of his problems. He'd been a good man, she said, when they met, and he still was, just confused. Zelda said she didn't care what was in people's hearts. You only had to watch their hands.

Mona said that she had a secret place, a clearing in the woods out back of their small house, where she'd go when it got too much. She'd pretend that no one could find her there, and she'd lean against the rough bark of one tree and talk into a cleft, tell the dark space her fears, and sometimes, she said, she thought it whispered back.

It might be her.

You had to be lost to let the darkness in. You had to lie awake turning and churning around a coal in your stomach, body aching and mind alert to the whispers behind the door. You had to need something you couldn't imagine, need it more than life or sanity, you had to pray not to some airy aftermath god of smoke and cloud and resurrection but to a grotesque wriggling belly-deep god of Now. No one comfortable could muster that razor need. But you never knew who was hungry. Or sick. Or curled around a fishhook of what he thought, or the TV said, the world denied him, or gave to someone less deserving. Everyone else was less deserving.

So where would the end begin? Where would the rot break through, and who would call it?

She never knew. She envied movie detectives the clarity of their cases. In real life, you never know what your problem is, unless someone loves you enough to tell you. Philip Marlowe just had to drink and wait and not even hope—sooner or later, a beautiful blonde with legs long and bright and curved as the swell of swift water over rocks would stride through his door, of all the doors in the world, with a mission. Zelda would never be half so lucky, with the mission or the blonde. And she was running out of time.

Every morning she crossed off another day on the calendar hanging in the Subaru, one day closer to Sal's birthday, one day closer to her date with that olive door. One week left, and the drive would eat most of that if she wanted to do it safely.

She could give up. She didn't have to sneak a third of the way across America and through the black hole orbit of Manhattan to stand on Sal's mother's doorstep and knock and fail for another year. This was her life now, had been for the better part of a decade: wandering alone, haunting back lots, shoring up the sandcastles of the country as they crumbled. Give up what was gone. Take the L.

She considered it, drunk, for the better part of an hour. Then she went hunting.

It was harder to do things this way than to wait for the rot to manifest. First she had to build spin. She circled the small town in her Subaru, to the extent there was a town to circle. There was a town square, at least, a city hall in red brick and a movie theater built in 1950, where she'd spent some of her spare cash to watch a forgettable action picture starring a guy named Chris. The other buildings on the square were shuttered and empty, except for the attorney's office, and there the curtains were drawn. Vacant storefronts sported peeling decals: COLE'S HARDWARE, a liquor store, a pharmacy with a punning name, all gone now.

The buildings in the town square had been built to last three hundred years. They would stand while the stick-and-board houses she drove past rotted to dust. But they would stand three centuries empty. Why build anything to last when the whole country lived on borrowed time?

She drove circles around the city hall, drinking the strangeness of the shuttered place. The sun glanced off windows as haunted as Mona's eyes. Turn and turn and watch it, feel it—suck the spin of the wheel and the suchness of the passing world down into the pit in your heart, where it gathers like cotton candy around a carny's wand. She listened to the wheels of the Subaru on the seams of the road. And when the spin churned inside her, she popped the glove compartment without taking her eyes off the road, withdrew a handful of yarrow stalks, and tossed them onto the empty passenger's seat.

The yarrow stalks told her that she'd almost missed the turn.

She heeled the car hard right, felt it tip, and slid through a narrow gap in the wide-open gulf of the two-lane road, onto the right track. Hunting.

She had worked out how to do all of this way back in college, had perfected it on the road with the others, and with Sal. Driving by yarrow stalks and by the transformations in her head, Zelda remembered other cars and other worlds, lifetimes ago: Ramón's black Challenger with the red racing stripe, Sal in the passenger seat, the two of them blissed out and talking math as they slipped from streetlight to streetlight and all the darkness of the world rolled over Sal Tempest's skin. They had dared each other out into the deep, like girls at summer camp, not realizing just how far either of them would go to please the other, until the lake's depths yawned bottomless beneath and they'd both lost the strength to swim for shore.

Just a little further.

><

That's what Sal had said every time Zelda balked—those full lips parted slightly as they curled into a smile. Just a little further, her hand on Zelda's wrist, cheek, thigh, drawing her after.

Zelda had never known anyone like her when they met. It had been orientation week of Zelda's freshman year, at, of all the absurdities in retrospect, a Christian Fellowship mixer, one of those ploys the campus evangelicals used to rope in faithful who might otherwise hear the siren song of the convulsive drunken rest of the campus. Zelda went because she'd promised her mom she would—Zelda, who'd come to campus book-smart and quiet and careful, a little South Carolina Lancelot, armored with purity and hair clip and sensible skirt against the corruptions of the northern school to which her parents couldn't bear not to send her.

To the collar of her unremarkable blouse she'd clipped the enamel rainbow flag pin she took from the alphabet soup alliance table at the activities fair that afternoon when she'd thought no one else was looking. She went to the mixer because she'd promised Mom, and she wore the pin because she'd promised herself.

Surely, she thought, heart in her throat as she walked down York Street to the events space where the Fellowship met, one gothic pile down from the campus newspaper, surely it would be different here, surely the Fellowship would get it, at least the other kids would—she still thought of herself as a kid then. Surely this was a small concession, set beside her willingness to come here at all, to keep her feet on this particular path when she'd left North Bend and family and church behind.

And yet.

One thing to tell herself this, and a whole different thing to grip the wrought iron handle of the great, heavy wooden door and pull with her legs and back until it begrudged her entry. To stride into the brightly lit room with the yellow walls and the punch bowl on the table in the rear right corner and all the kids in polo shirts. That heavy-bellied man with the bouncing step would be the pastor, turning toward her like an artillery battery. She already felt as if she'd walked in naked with a fanfare. How could she have been so *dumb*? She knew the rules. You never showed anyone else your soul, not even a piece of it, or you would give them something to pray against. Of course it wouldn't be different here. The rules didn't change in adulthood, no matter what anyone said. You kept your surface clean and tidy, made yourself look like everybody thought everybody else was supposed to look. You mowed your lawn so no one thought to look in your toolshed. And now here she was, exposed to the withering heat of the pastor's kind smile. She might have run, but there were other kids between her and the door already, the congregation extending amoebic pseudopods to draw her in, digest her.

Anyway, she'd promised Mom.

The pastor knew his job. He welcomed her, offered her punch, a name tag—made a joke about the princess being in another castle that confused her too much for her even to pretend to laugh. Pastor Steve was his name, but of course he wanted everyone to call him Steve.

"And where are you from, Zelda?" Pastor Steve asked.

Where, indeed. The world was small, smaller still with a name like hers, and in that moment as she met his eyes, the part of her brain that calculated fast but figured people slow churned away. There were only so many churches in North Bend, South Carolina. One might without trouble call them all, if one were a youth pastor wondering whether the new girl with the rainbow pin might have worn one at home or whether her family knew, or cared. She had meant to contain this small experiment, this small moment of rebellion—to test herself, to masquerade as the kind of person who would wear the pin not just on trips to bars in town but to *church*. And now the mask might glue itself to her face. She imagined the phone call soon to follow, and Mom on the other end of the line.

Her mouth went dry and her tongue was too large to fit her mouth. The room with the punch bowl seemed too bright and inhuman and close. Cheery faces pressed in to crush her as the floors and ceiling opened out to infinity and down forever. She felt herself begin to fall.

"Zelda!" A voice from out of sight, and then a girl dawned through the crowd—tall, sharp, and dark, her hair in tight braids back from her face. Her arms flung wide and she embraced Zelda, firm and warm, and Zelda's own indrawn breath caught her speechless. The girl smelled of sandalwood.

"Sal," Pastor Steve said without a trace of chill.

"Zelda's a friend from back home," Sal said, turning around to face the pastor, arm still around Zelda's shoulders. "Grew up down the block. Ma asked her to meet me here—that's okay, right? All who are hungry, let them come and eat." She had a brownie from the snack table in her free hand. She took a bite. "Though I guess that's the other guys."

"Will we see you at youth group?"

"Expect me when you do." She saluted with her brownie hand, two fingers to the temple like a Girl Scout. "We'll get gone, Pastor. I'm sure you have fishes to multiply."

And, arm still around Zelda's shoulders, Sal drew her from the room into the dark, down York Street with the tall castle walls of the residential colleges to their right. Loping beside her, Sal chewed, swallowed. Zelda watched the muscles of her jaw and neck. Sal tore off the part of the brownie she'd bitten into, offered Zelda the rest, and asked questions. "First week's rough, but you'll get used to it. Where are you from, really? What's your roommate like? Don't worry, at first it seems like half the kids here are from Westchester, but they're just, you know, different. And there's plenty of the rest of us around. We just don't talk about high school as much. You learn the patterns, anyway. I'm still getting used to the guys who wear their shirt collars popped."

The voice that had frozen in Zelda's throat when she faced Pastor Steve babbled now like a spring brook, answering, and Zelda felt herself melt to Sal's side, though she had to stretch her legs to keep pace.

Cars rolled along Elm past the Au Bon Pain where the woman stood selling roses, and somewhere some orientation group raised a cheer loud enough to make Zelda flinch. Sal pulled away, looked at her. Zelda felt her departure as if a magnet pulled them together.

"Thank you," Zelda said.

"You can't leave everything behind," Sal said, as if she hadn't. "I made the same mistake when I showed up. Spent half the year wrestling with people who wanted to save my soul."

"Did they call your church?"

"They tried. Turns out my pastor's cooler than I thought."

"Why did you come back?"

"Brownies." She finished her half. "And to rescue young ingenues." Gesturing with her chin to Zelda, grinning.

She'd learned that word her second day at college. Her roommate was into musical theater. "I'm hardly."

"Oh." Sal appraised Zelda: her sensible blouse, her skirt past the knee, her long hair gathered back. "I must have been mistaken. You're clearly piratical. Scourge of the seven seas. I came back," she said, "to spike the punch bowl."

When Zelda laughed, she realized it was the first time she'd really laughed since she came to town, a laugh untainted by confusion. "You didn't."

She took a flask from her inner jacket pocket, unscrewed it, upended the last drop into her mouth. "Either it was me or the miracle at Cana."

"So—what now?"

"I thought I might show you around. But with you being so piratical and all, you obviously don't need my help." She grinned, mocking, inviting. The light did interesting things to her silhouette. She must have noticed Zelda's sway toward her as she drew back; she turned away slow enough to torture.

"Wait."

Sal stopped at her word, one eyebrow raised.

"What if I'm a pirate," Zelda said, "in *disguise*?"

"A ruthless killer, faking innocence. A murderer in a french braid." She flicked Zelda's hair.

"I'm here on a mission. I feel naked without my cutlass. I spent hours staring into a mirror, practicing how to flutter my eyelashes." She demonstrated, and got the hoped-for laugh. Sal took her arm again.

"Come on, Captain Kidd. Let me show you around."

All night Zelda followed Sal from courtyard to courtyard, skimming the edge of parties—peering through astronomy club telescopes on Old Campus at the moon when it peeked through orange sherbet clouds—a pitch-perfect mock ingenue. Playing that role, she had the freedom to ask the questions she'd not felt comfortable asking before—where people came from and what it meant, what Westchester was and what Stuyvesant might be, where power lived on campus, how that power worked. Zelda had never been around class before, not this flavor of class, anyway, which the kids (she wasn't thinking of them as men and women yet) pretended didn't exist, even though it was obvious that some people, like Zelda, were working in the library, and some people, like her roommate, would spend Thanksgiving break in Switzerland. Sal knew it all, and liked sharing what she knew, with cutting asides that made Zelda laugh. Zelda wondered, while they walked, at the depth of Sal's insight, and wondered also if this girl was lonely: watching, judging a world with little place for her. After a year of study, in self-defense, it must feel good to share what she'd found with someone else.

After hours of wandering, Sal led her up the stairs of the A & A Building, floor by floor to the rooftop deck and then to the fence that separated the lower deck from the true roof. Just a little further. Sal's eyes sparkled with reflected streetlights and the few stars that pierced the orange shell of New Haven sky.

Zelda lay beside Sal on the pebbly roof and pointed up into the swirls of yellow, purple, pink. "A comet!"

The warm length of Sal twisted against her as she raised her arm to point at another patch of weird and mottled sky. "Spaceship. Aliens."

"Looks like a plane to me." She nestled into the hollow of Sal's arm. Where Sal pointed, Zelda could almost see the ship—curves of crystal and translucent metal, impossible to build, a gross affront to aerodynamics, useless to imagine anything like that leaving a planet's surface, a perfect rose in the sky trailed by—

"Rainbows," Sal said. "That's how you know they're aliens. Like in *E.T.*"

"I think that's a dragon over there."

"Dragons don't come north of Pennsylvania," Sal said. "Everybody knows that."

"Not me." Zelda didn't have an accent, but she could put one on for effect. "I'm just a plain, simple country girl, on mah own here in the big city."

"This isn't a city."

"I can't see but three stars. That makes a city."

"You forgot the comet. And the spaceship."

"And the dragon."

"I said, no dragons this far north. They don't like the winters."

"What about Viking dragons?"

"European varietal. Hardier. Your American dragon is temperate."

The colors turned in the sky above, and on the street below, the Christian Fellowship stumbled from their orientation mixer, warbling hymns, drunk on the Holy Spirit and the contents of Sal's flask. Zelda found herself on her side. Sal's chest rose beneath her tank top, and fell. Her hoodie's wings spread out beside her on the roof. She wore a gloss that gave her lips the shine of still water, a pool where a big cat might kneel to drink.

If you'd asked Zelda hours ago, she would have said that of course she'd kissed people before. But now, searching back and comparing each of those moments to this one, she found only memories of being kissed, moments where kissing had happened to her. And this, what she thought this might be—there was nothing passive in it, nothing of the pawing pro forma junior prom date with Billy Klobbard or the deeply uncomfortable truth-or-dare with John Domino. She wanted to do fierce things to this woman, and that need, owned fully for once in this strange place, scared her.

Sal was watching. "It's okay to ask, you know. If you want something."

"May I?" Zelda's lips pursed around the *m*.

"Have you ever done this before?"

She would not lie. "Not . . . as such. Not exactly. No." The shame was real. She felt it color her cheeks.

"I should not take advantage of an innocent." A dare, an invitation. Sal's hand on her side, on her hip.

She had a vision then of the two of them perfectly alone in the center of a vast and hostile universe, these few square feet of pebbly rooftop the heart, the city and that sickly melted-candy sky just a shell, and beyond that shell an immense and profound darkness, a writhing night full of blades and fangs and needles pointing in, the cosmos a trap and her the mouse creeping, whiskers atwitch, toward the trigger. And she prayed to a god she was no longer certain she believed would listen: *Let me have this.*

"I'm not an innocent, remember? I'm a pirate. In disguise."

Sal's face eclipsed the trap of the world. She was smiling. "Come on, then, Captain Kidd." Her breath warm. "Just a little further."

✦

Zelda drove Tennessee back roads, following the yarrow-stalk map.

There was more witchiness to her current lifestyle than Zelda liked to admit. She'd worked it all out on paper from first principles back at school, theorems building on other theorems. First you gathered spin, accumulated history and memory, possibility, strangeness, dredged the depths of your soul for everything you did not know was true. Then you held it inside, let it charge you and change you. You gathered uncertainty until what might be bloomed into what is. There was mathematics under the magic, and stranger parts of physics, but every time she practiced her art like this, she felt the math give way to a deeper dream logic of chance, memory, and regret.

It never should have come to this: her, alone, on the road. She should be driving with Sal right now. Instead of this beat old Subaru, she should be driving the Challenger Ramón had built in his uncle's garage, she should be trading barbs and theories with Ish, bobbing her head while Sarah made up lyrics to sing over radio jazz. They should be young and unafraid. Somewhere back up the road, they still were, and even though in all of Zelda's travels she'd never been able to turn back time, when she was on the hunt like this, charged with spin and open to every possibility, she sometimes thought, *knew,* that if she only turned the next corner, she'd find them all there beside the parked Challenger, Ish cooking while Sarah picked out a song on the guitar, and she could warn them all. Or, if causal laws forbade her from changing the past, she could at least pause at the foot of the gravel path to watch them, an older woman they might barely recognize, weeping before she went away.

She would never hurt her friends again. That's what she told herself, every time. If she had a second chance, a third, a ninth, she'd do it right.

The Subaru slipped into a long gravel driveway. Her hand found the parking brake on its own. At the top of the hill squatted a small yellow house. The sun was setting and the porch lights flickered on. A screen's uncanny blue flickered through the living room windows. This was the place.

She knew this driveway, this hill, those squinting angry windows.

When she picked Mona up for a late-night rendezvous, she stopped at the foot of the driveway so Alan would not hear the engine.

So, the rot was here after all.

She wanted to leave. Sometimes the detective knows the answer to the case, but turns away. Lets the crook go. Works on anything else. But the yarrow stalks had drawn her. And that olive door was waiting.

Wind blew an earthy scent from the trees—green and growth and rot and behind those, a silver ozone smell of sour moonlight.

She stepped easy, left the gravel for wet grass. She took no weapons with her, save the spin coiled around her heart. If she lost control, there was nothing a knife or gun could do to save her.

The rot felt her approach. It curled back and drew the forest around itself like a quilt. Hiding, yes, but also daring her. I have made this place my own. Come after me. Step out into the dark.

There were ways to hunt carefully, to approach sidelong and slantwise, so even spiders would not feel you drawing near. But those ways took weeks, and she had to leave tomorrow. Which meant ending this tonight.

She entered the forest.

She walked slowly, on the balls of her feet, testing the ground as if it might break. There was a chance she'd not be noticed crossing the lawn, so she spent a little of her spin to make that chance the truth. Soft breeze ruffled tall grass around a rusted lawn mower propped up to show its blades.

The sun vanished. The sky grew deep and orange. Sal used to sing "Mood Indigo" at sunset when they camped. But she had lost Sal and now she was alone.

The forest, seen from the driveway, had been simple Tennessee scrub, dense with brambles and young trees. Now, as she stood at its mouth, on its lower lip, she stared into a gullet lined with teeth. The rot on the breeze had deepened. She smelled carrion, spilled meat, and opened guts.

When Zelda was eight, she had lost her dog. They had five or six depending on how you counted—but Goof was hers, the one who ran to her when she came home from school. The Tuesday he didn't come, she thought little of it, but when two more days passed and no one had seen him, she packed herself a bag and set off up the mountain, looking. Maybe he was hurt, or stuck. Maybe he'd taken something down up there and was dragging it home inch by inch. She thought, in the simple way she had that made her so good at math, the trick of thinking not in gulps but step by step, that to find him, all she had to do was climb the mountain behind their house and come down in a spiral, covering each foot of ground. She took salami from the fridge, and a flashlight.

The sun set while she was on the mountain. Her parents and her brother climbed up to look for her, but they did not have her careful mind and she hid when she heard them coming. If they took her down the mountain, she'd lose her place and have to start her search all over. She crouched in the hollow of a rotting log, breathing low, and when a grub fell from the pulped wood onto her cheek and bounced off, leaving a wet smear behind, she did not squeak.

Her family gave up the search. She did not.

When the moon set, she heard something else looking for her. Quiet steps in the dark, a rustle of leaves, a caustic ammonia stink. Kids at school said there were mountain lions in the hills, but kids at school said a lot of things. Whatever it was, the silence came closer. Her hands slipped on the heavy flashlight. She imagined how teeth would feel in her arm.

What would it feel like to be swallowed? Could some part of you be aware?

The smell and silence neared.

She found the flashlight switch, swept its beam through the dark, and saw— movement, a nothingness departing, perhaps a wake of wind.

There, between a tree and a rock, she saw a swollen mound that she knew was Goof.

His belly was puffed up with decay and his tan fur was torn where scavengers had found him, and there was blood. Grubs churned in his wounds. Her clearest memory was of that flop of ear inverted, trailing in the mulched leaves. He hates when I do that; he shakes his head and yowls until the ear sets right again. And in Zelda's mind as she looked, *hates* became *hated*.

Her life was different now. So was his. Every moment they'd shared, rolling together in the grass, her hands trailing over his head in her lap as she worked out sums or puzzled over the whirling shapes of helicopter seeds, was infiltrated, overturned, by this ending in the trees. It led here—this weight of skin and bones, this smear on the rocks, this churning stench. All of it inevitable. He'd run out here, smelling a challenge, and in the dark he found it, and made an end.

She could not change that. She felt baptized by the putrid flesh, by the needle tooth marks on bare bone where his meat had been gnawed away. They crept in, even into her moments of joy, and changed her life so it was not what she had thought.

But kneeling there with her dead friend's head staining the knees of her overalls, she felt something tear-hot and firm as a blade inside her. It did not form. It had been there always, and only now did she reach for it. This would not be her story. The carrion eaters did not own what they devoured.

She took off her jacket. Her hands squelched into his fur when she lifted him, and muck and shit came out. In her backpack of supplies, she'd brought a spool of parachute cord because of what Sam Gamgee in *The Lord of the Rings* said about rope. We'll want it if we haven't got it. With the rope and two sticks and a knife and her jacket, she made a sling, and used her backpack straps for a harness, and together they started down.

At first *down* was all she had to go on, since the moon was set and the stars confused. The small sounds of the forest bowed when she passed by, out of respect, perhaps, or fear. When first light threatened in the east she knew what direction east was, and shifted course. Goof's stink filled those hours of descent. In school later she'd read *Karamazov,* read about the monks trying to hold vigil over their great Elder Zosima and deny that the man's corpse smelled, because he was so holy, and she'd know what they were about.

What she was doing was right. That rightness should have made it okay. But still she gasped him, rotting, into her.

Her parents found her at dawn in the backyard beside the chicken coop and a mound of fresh-turned earth, two sticks at its head tied with paracord as best she could into a slanting cross. Dry-eyed, though there were tracks of tears down her cheeks. Her hands black with gore and a spade between her knees.

They hugged her—gingerly, she noticed, around the stains. Made the sounds she expected, *love, dear, don't you dare,* rarely congealing into sentences. She'd buried her jacket with him. She said she'd lost it. Father commented on the cost of getting a new one. She stayed in the shower for what felt like days, scrubbed herself red and raw with every soap she could reach, even Mom's special one that looked like a seashell and was never used. Scrubbed beneath her fingernails, and the pads of her hands and feet.

When she stepped out of the shower that first time and stood wrapped chin to shin in one of the good fluffy towels that smelled of chemicals that smelled like lavender, and stared into her own large and open black eyes in the mirror, home and safe, she drew a breath and smelled the faintest hint, the slightest airborne suggestion, of the body cavity of her dead dog.

The next thing she remembered, she was bent over the toilet, retching because there was nothing left in her to come up.

In more than twenty years, she had not forgotten that smell, and it was that same stench exactly that blew from the wood behind Mona's house, through the darkness and past the trees like broken teeth.

She drew a staggered breath and stepped, hunter soft, into the shadows.

Her sneakers sank into the mulch, came out wet and stained. Cold wet wind bearing that same old rot whipped her jacket around her, raised dust devils of powdered leaves, then, on her next step, stilled. She walked through the cloying stink. She breathed it.

A branch snapped behind her.

Even though she knew better, she looked over her shoulder.

The trees went on forever. There was no driveway, no small yellow house. This was no scrubland forest. What if the old primal wood, the wall of green that European explorers found after their illnesses scoured the continent, had not vanished, had not been burned or cut clean but curled into a tight ball and hid, a vastness of forest lurking hungry as a tiger in shadows, waiting for a moment's inattention in its prey to spring? That old forest, Zelda knew, would hate her.

In the black halls of the trees, something moved. A suggestion in the shadows, and large.

The rot was hiding, playing off her fears. Move on.

Soft feet padded near. Branches rustled in the still night. Her breath crept up from her belly to her chest, until she panted, in and out, in and out, through her open mouth. Goof had climbed his mountain alone and found something sickle-clawed and silent in the depth of night. He thought he was ready. So did she. Now at the end, they were both alone.

The silence gained a new depth. That rasp might have been two branches struck together—or fur bristling against bark. Was that the click of a claw?

No path lay beneath her feet. The sour moonlight smell was gone. She walked alone beneath mad stars, pursued by something she dared not turn to see. If she did turn and look, she'd make it certain, make it real, that beast in the trees. But if she did not look, she could walk, and spend the spin she'd gathered in her chest into the soil, to will this forest otherwise.

The branches grew so close above that she lost the sky. In that unsure, step-by-step dark, she saw the mountain lion in her mind, as vividly with her eyes open as she would have if they'd been closed: no healthy beast but a rot-mad one, smearing foul black blood on the branches it passed, claws finger-long and curved, its shoulders bunched with muscle and its maw spittle-flecked. A bright pink tongue tested air between the spire teeth.

It reached for her now. It had been waiting in this memory forest for her all these years, knowing one day she'd return without the protection of Goof's sacrifice. Two paws, each the size of her face, stretched down, down, from the dense branches, hooked claws turned inward, and they would catch her cheeks like fishhooks and drag her up by her jaw into the trees and teeth.

Something brushed a lock of loose hair by her left eye and she almost looked. But with a cry and a final burst of will—this was not happening, the lion was not there, she was not about to die—she spent her spin in warding, and staggered through.

She stood, blinking, in a sunset grove.

Her shirt was soaked with sweat. Her knees shook and her heart throbbed in her ears. Her hands found her thighs. She gasped like a deep-sea diver surfaced on scant air, tears hot in her eyes, too scared to let them fall.

Details of the clearing filtered in slowly: purple sky, few stars, sun declining, and far off to the north, the contrails of a passenger jet. To her left, through a football field's worth of scrub trees, slouched that mean yellow house. The smell: burnt meat from a neighbor's bad time with a backyard grill. Beneath that: ozone and sour silver. Spoiled moonlight. She had come through. The rot was here.

It wasn't much of a grove, all things considered. Just a roundish gap in the trees. You'd have to have a powerful need to use it as a gateway, as a door.

Mona's need was powerful. Zelda felt the rot here: the hurricane weight of the ending world. There stood the cleft tree, the darkness inside razor-edged, untouched by sun. The rot was small, but Mona fed it secrets, and it grew.

Zelda padded toward the tree.

Within the crack in its bark she glimpsed something breathing, small and fierce as a cornered rat. It shrank back into its hole, its final refuge now that she'd breached all its other walls. She reached into the crack.

"Zelda. Don't."

Mona stood at the clearing's edge, flour on her hands, hair frizzed out. The door to the yellow house was open behind her. She reached for Zelda, trembling.

"You can't," she said. "Please. Zelda, it *listens* to me." Such hunger around that word, *listens*. She'd known Mona for less than two months. Long enough to tell how rare that was in her life. How long had she been drowning here?

"It's young now," Zelda said. "The first crack in the wall. Your need calls it. But it will grow, and listening won't be enough for it anymore. It will eat you up and then you'll be gone, as if you never were."

"Is this what you do?" Her cheeks were wet. "You go around and take away the last thing people need?"

"It will eat you, Mona. It will carve you open and wear you out and eat other people too. It can't live in our world. Not like you want. It can't help you. But I can save you."

"Zelda, no—Zelda, please—god*damn* it, Zelda, *stop!*" Shrieking, she ran for her, clawed at her arms, her face, too late.

Zelda reached into the crack in the tree.

Needle teeth pierced her palm, and whiplike barbed-wire limbs circled her fingers. The rot-thing bucked and writhed. She hissed from the pain, felt her grip go slick with blood. Her stomach churned. Mona's nail scraped her eyelid, gouged her cheek. But Mona worked the checkout line, and ten years on the road had left Zelda hard and strong.

Once, she had not been used to being hit. Once, the feeling of something alive burrowing into her hand would have done more than hurt—it would have sickened her, made her scream. But she had been walking in the dark for a long time now.

Once, a friend screaming, begging her to stop, would have made her open her hand and fall to her knees.

She remembered: on her knees on the black-flower road, her hand around Sal's, as dark limbs pulled them apart and a mad smile played across Sal's face. *It's beautiful.*

Zelda tightened her grip on the rotten thing in the tree. It cut her, but she held it, this alien that Mona's need had invited in, this monster that would consume her from the inside out. All the spin she'd built observing, wandering this stretch of country, remembering, turning and turning around that town square—all the possibility of the road—she spent it in one fierce breath.

I deny you, she told the rot that was eating her hand. I deny your power. You are not a thing. What reality you've clawed for yourself already, from my friend—I take it back.

It wasn't hard. Like breaking a heart, or a rabbit's neck.

She closed her hand—a killing grip—felt a squeal, a pop—and then she held nothing at all.

The clearing was still. Stars emerged from a darkening sky.

Mona knelt, weeping. She clutched Zelda's thigh like a tree in a flood. She always had a spine, an inner rebar that showed only when she was so tired she forgot to hide it. Most days she was all smiles and bright teeth and self-effacing humor, a master of the tricks you used to hide integrity and self-regard when the people you called friends and family would tear you apart for having any. But let a dirty old man in line spit in her face—one had, once—and the steel showed.

Mona had known, whatever happened, that there was this grove, and this crack in this tree, where a growing monster waited, swelling with her need of him.

And then came Zelda. Her friend.

"He listened."

"I'm sorry."

"Go away."

"I just—"

"I don't care!" She pushed back from Zelda, scrambled to her feet—slapped Zelda across the face. Her hand came away smeared with the blood her nails had drawn. There were deserts in her eyes. "Just go. Now. I can't look at you anymore."

She'd heard those words enough to know when they were meant.

Zelda's hand slid out of the crack in the tree. Liquid shadow dripped from her fingers, smoked beneath her gaze—an impossible substance, a bit of elsewhere. Soon it was gone. Blood remained. Her wounds were painful but shallow. She'd not lose much feeling in the hand. The thin oozing lines and the puncture in her palm would heal, and the scars they left would be thin and pale on her tanned skin, like all the others. People assumed she had a cutting problem, when she let them close. They were not altogether wrong.

Mona's back was a wall, a cliff. She was safe, she was broken, and Zelda had broken her. She was shaking, and if Zelda were a decent person—the kind of person who would not do what she had just done—she might have tried to touch her one more time, to reach across the gulf and offer some comfort to the woman she'd sat and stared at stars with, give up all pretense of justification and try, for once, to help.

But she had set off on the road ten years before, like she had set off up that mountain chasing Goof. When you began a work like that, you had to take the answers you found: the bodies, the pain, the long-gone friends. You lived with what you found.

She limped away as Mona wept behind her. Steeled herself with memories of why she was here, of what she walked the road to do. There was a wall to the world, a wall made of thorns, and someone had to guard that wall.

She'd dreamed otherwise once. She'd dreamed of changing things. She'd dreamed of the crossroads. But all those dreams went smash.

She flexed her hand. Blood stuck to blood in her palm, tracing the scars across the lines of her life and heart.

The weight began to lift—the summer storm pressure, the suffocation. Air cleared, cleaned with every step she took. She felt lighter and more sure. This, at least, she let herself enjoy. She was guilty of so much, but this was *why*, the moment when her road sense told her that, for now, the world's end was paused. For now, the red clock on someone's wall stopped ticking down. And for a few weeks—maybe even a month—she could find a quiet park somewhere to camp, or a shit job that paid on time in cash, and just survive, without hurting anyone.

With every step down the twisting driveway to her car the sense of doom would ebb. It always did.

But it ebbed slower this time.

Surely, she told herself, this is an illusion. I can still hear Mona crying. This town, this job, got its hooks in me and I'm holding on to the feeling like a cold woman holds on to a blanket as it's slowly pulled away. By the time I reach the car, it will be gone, and I'll feel fine.

She reached the car. Fished for her keys.

She did not feel fine.

The weight was not so heavy or immediate as it had been in the clearing. She had won, if you called this winning. But there was something else wrong here, something vast and pervasive, a distant cataclysm that had been obscured behind that small, eager bit of rot in the trees.

Focused on her hunt and the Xs on her calendar, she'd mistaken a sunshower for the oncoming storm.

Zelda settled behind the Subaru's wheel. She was so tired, on a level NoDoz and coffee could not touch. Once she'd had the will to change the world, with her friends at her side and her lover at their head. For ten years she'd been drawing from that well. Now, when she threw the bucket in, it struck and scraped the bottom, came up mucky. But still—go on. One step at a time. What else could she do? What else was left?

The sky was a star-dotted shell. Sunset underlit the clouds in blood and fire.

All that endless space, she knew, was the painted backdrop of a stage, billowing, crinkling, tearing as an immense jagged Thing pressed against the cloth. A giant monster prop from another play, it seemed at first, until you realized it was not a prop at all. The world that seemed so still and sure was not.

Zelda gunned the engine, squealed out onto the narrow road, and drove hard north for New York City, ahead of the storm.

⤝

Zelda scuttled into the city like a rat.

Sal told her, on their first visit, that Penn Station had been a palace once, a rival for Grand Central, towering vaults and high windows, cathedral architecture. Then the world moved on. By the time they tore it down, the walls were coated in pigeon shit and the windows tarred with nicotine smoke, and with the rise of the automobile, no one used rail anyway. (Except, of course, for the trains of food that kept the city alive day to day, and for the people who could not afford to drive or park, and and and.) The old Penn Station was a place for gods to saunter in, but when it died it died, and no gaggle of nostalgic protesters could save it. Like the country, the city killed what it thought it didn't need, fast, and mourned in self-indulgent leisure.

Now Penn Station was a labyrinth. Zelda's first computer game, on a machine old even when she inherited it from a kid who'd moved away, was a text-only thing where you tried to guide yourself through a maze. If you entered the maze without a map and other tools, the computer would describe every room with the same sentence: "You are in a maze of twisty little passages, all alike." Zelda used to have nightmares about that maze, about turning and turning deeper underground, the road ahead looking just like the road behind, her torch guttering low. Penn Station was that, only with fluorescent lights and thousands of other people who were all lost too.

Posters on the walls advertised the City's plans to rebuild the old Penn Station, a new palace; those posters had been there for a while.

She'd hated Penn at first sight, but these days she found it comforting. Here she was lost like everyone else. She could pretend she'd come from anywhere and was bound anywhere else—a poor poet maybe, back from abroad; a graduate student on her way to a conference where she'd meet a lover she saw only at these sorts of things; someone dangerous and desirable with a fencer's grace and the eyes you got doing hard work under the sun. Someone who hadn't stepped off the path into the dark.

Someone who wasn't back in New York for her girlfriend's birthday to try, again, to apologize.

She climbed the stairs and left the garish twisting paths behind and found herself, for all her fantasies, in Manhattan again, pinned to reality like a butterfly to a board.

Ads everywhere. Fifteen-story musical ads, ads in white for the latest piece of pocket glass to solve all your problems and tell whoever cared to ask exactly where you were at all times, ads for television shows she didn't watch and clothes she didn't wear. Full-length ads in bus stop awnings featured a man in a thin black suit cautioning citizens to do their part "to protect the safety of our region," whatever that meant. Two men in fatigues with automatic rifles flanked the station's exit. Zelda wasn't sure how the rifles helped protect the safety of our region, exactly. The men watched the crowd with lidded eyes and the dry contempt of the heavily armed. Zelda recognized that look. She saw it in the mirror.

A briefcase man jostled her. Two women in bright pants cut across her field of vision, talking loudly in Portuguese. Three teenage girls, short buzzed hair, one of them dyed rainbow, another with heavy gauges in her ear, marched past bearing protest signs scattered with glitter. Zelda felt a stab of wonder at the rainbow girl's laugh, so pure, so unbruised. One of the men with the rifles studied the teenagers as if they might have bombs hidden in their bras. Christ.

There were too many eyes on her, too many cameras, this ground too known. The city in its millions crushed in. This was not her place.

She hated coming back to New York. New York City was the world's least magical place outside of Disneyland, if you did not know it well—each street corner shot in a thousand films, each bench memorialized, no angle new. She did not know how to find surprise here, could not wish herself otherwise. The city had been hammered into its present shape by old gods, all its spin juiced and spent in their service. Blame Moses or the street grid or Giuliani, but New York settled on her like a lead blanket.

That was why she snuck in on the train. Leaving the car in Philadelphia made it easier to hide. Her spin did not belong, here, and the city seemed to know it, to fight back like a body fought a splinter. The last time she tried to drive in, a semi jackknifed into her on the New Jersey Turnpike. The time before that, heading south from Maine, her brakes failed just outside of Stamford. It was safer to creep in, to make yourself small. To play into the story the city told about itself.

She cut west to Eighth, walked north past porn shops and liquor stores and nothing storied, nothing famous. She stopped at a convenience store and bought a pack of mints she didn't want from a clerk watching acrobatic porn on his phone, and asked if she could use a sink. She filled her water bottle, conscious of the close quarters and his sweat and his eyes on her ass, aware, as ever, of her knife in her pocket if she needed it, and thinking of the ways she could make him bleed.

At least New York relieved the weight of the storm. It had chased her all the way north, the sense of impending doom, only to recede when her train crossed the state line. The storm wasn't gone. But the wall was too thick here for her to feel it, the city too sure of its own reality to let in nightmares. A child, or Zelda herself years ago, would have relaxed. Now she felt as if she'd seen a man walking toward her on a dark street with a tire iron in his hand, and the single streetlight had just gone out. The man was still there. Nearer, and more deadly because he was unseen.

But she owed Sal's family an apology, and after Mona and the grove, she owed herself some pain.

The 3rd Ave–138th Street subway station had gathered graffiti tags, been washed clean, then repainted over and over in her visits here. At this moment it was clean again, a canvas. Late-summer heat lay heavy on the Bronx. Every time she emerged from the subway here, no matter how little time she'd spent in Manhattan first, the size of the sky stunned her. When she was younger, she'd felt free when she crossed the river to the boroughs, with their broad streets and low roofs; now she felt exposed. The storm drew near. She'd almost died three times on the road north and bore bandages beneath her clothes to signify. NoDoz buzzed in her veins and bad cheap coffee gurgled in her belly.

But this was the day.

Some of Brooklyn was seeping north into the Bronx now. She passed a white couple wearing good clothes working in a community garden by the highway overpass—she knew it was a community garden because there was a sign. There were coffee shops with reclaimed wood tables, infiltrating.

She walked east, then north, past the police station. It had always felt like an occupying fort up here, bastion of some foreign power on a distant shore—now safe for the colonists to arrive.

Maybe it would turn out differently this time.

She was bitter. She was hot. She was scared of what she'd left behind, of what waited for her in the sky beyond the city limits, of what she was about to do. She stank of the road, and the scabs on her hand were healing more slowly than they had when she was younger. She had sweated through her shirt.

A few more steps, that was all. Fail again, then go back out into the world and—well, fail some more, if it came to that. Don't let that stop you.

She stood before the olive-green door, without having registered the intervening space, or time, or years. She had always been here. The couple from the community garden drifted past, walking their dog. It was safe. A cop car rolled past again. Ten years and she'd never left this spot.

Raise your hand. Clench it into a fist. The scabs pull—there's blood already and you haven't even knocked yet. They won't talk to you. You try anyway. This is not for them—it's for you. Penance matters. If you stand here until it feels okay to knock, you'll never knock and never leave, and the hurricanes and the snows and the cold north wind will find you here, hesitating. Just knock. You owe her that much.

She did.

This time, it was the first knock that left blood prints behind. She made ready to try again; remembered singing in church as a child, *Knock, and the door shall be opened onto you.*

She knocked.

And the door did open.

She almost fell—again. Ten years and that door had only opened once.

The girl wasn't Sal. Her neck was too skinny, her figure lean—but her eyes were the same, and her cheekbones, and that was the nose Zelda had kissed. There was an open hole in Zelda's heart, and the vision of this girl rushed in to fill it, the suction of Zelda's need so strong that for an instant everything that didn't fit was forced into the contours of the hole, limbs squished and skin pulled like Silly Putty, until what remained was almost Sal. Close enough for Zelda's mouth to go dry, close enough for her hand to reach out, close enough for her body to quake with all-over hope and panic and fear.

But that was wrong. The girl wasn't Sal. And with that second denial, her brain had space to work and remember that time did in fact exist. Given that, she removed impossibility to solve for what remained.

"June," was the name that found her lips. June, grown without her cousin, without her friend, into an echo in Zelda's eyes.

"Ma's not home," June said. Sixteen maybe or seventeen now, fastest kid on the block, steel and defiance salted with quick, taunting humor. Did she remember the cousin whose footsteps she was running in? After ten years, what could she remember? Maybe, at least, that day Zelda stood on this same doorstep, younger and more raw, and always, still, at fault.

Don't screw this up, Zelda. Don't lose this chance. You've known all along what you had to say, and she needs to hear it as much as anyone.

"I—" She made it halfway.

June stepped out and shut the door behind her with a click.

She stood so close Zelda could smell her—cardamom and flowers and girl. Unblinking. She must have spent—months? Years? Waiting for this. Talking herself up to standing eye to eye with the dragon that came for her cousin. Well, not quite eye to eye. June was taller. Zelda's neck got that same crick it used to have when she looked up at Sal.

"I want to know," June said. "Everything."

She should have seen this coming. Should have quit this yearly ritual, must have suspected that the girl growing up in the absence of a cousin closer than a sister, in that house with its many candles and its carved driftwood religious statues, would not mourn forever. Sooner or later, she'd want answers.

"Please," June said. But the word was a demand.

Ten years ago, Ma Tempest had wept upstairs. She was cursed with girls who wanted to take that one step further, and cursed with Zelda, who could not bear to stop them.

So she looked up at June, despite the crick in her neck, and said: "Let's walk."

# CHAPTER TWO

The Bronx had been a pleasant place to walk before Robert Moses got his hands on it. To hear Sal tell the story, Moses had been the king of New York roads, a child of wealth who burrowed into government and, once he chewed through its outer shell, established himself in its rib cage, a sort of parasitic pontifex for a new Rome. As Detroit churned out cars, roads were built to match, and bridges, massive spiderwebs linking Manhattan and its nearby islands to the shore—chaining them down in case they should float away. But roads and bridges brought fumes, noise, great stanchions to block light and starve the streets, so Moses built and anchored them in places too poor, too Black, too distant from power, to stop him. Take a friendly neighborhood of parks and sidewalks and second-floor walkups and build a six-lane highway down the middle, and watch it wither, as if the bridge towers spread roots to suck up life and give it to the cars.

Some communities endured, rebuilt. Most failed. Over time, other people, new and hard and desperate, moved into the husks of dead neighborhoods, settled and built lives where they could. The expressways and bridges still cast their shadows, and would as long as New York was New York. Build a road and change a city. Lock it into your vision. Every car driven over asphalt is a prayer to gods the builders choose.

That's the story Sal told. You could still walk, though. You just needed courage, and a guide.

June matched Zelda's pace, hands pocketed, shoulders up as if walking into a cold wind. She had a swift loping stride, bobbing her head to a rhythm Zelda could not hear. She kept her hair buzzed short as a shadow on her scalp, and a stud gleamed in her nose. A line of muscle worked in her knifelike jaw. This was June's city, but now that the girl had asked her question, she did not know where to go or what would happen next.

Zelda steered them toward the Willis Avenue Bridge and otherwise kept quiet, leaving it up to June to find her own path through the silence. When she didn't, Zelda, gently, tried. "What do you know?"

"Some of it," quick as a breaking branch, and after that the fall. "You learned something in college. Some secret. Some kind of . . ." Saying the *M*-word made some people laugh as if they couldn't believe themselves, made others grave. June was the second type. "Magic. You could go places, do things. She'd come home with gifts." Her hand darted to her neck, fished past the cross on its bright chain to something heavy dangling under her tank top, pulled it out. Glittering metal, a disk of sun in her palm. Zelda saw the print: a snake rearing, a pyramid, a stylized man. "It's Aztec, or something like it. Gold. I looked up the writing. That says it was minted in 1927. But not with our dates. With theirs."

They'd found that coin in a distant rotting alt, a landscape of glass and blood. Fleeing the carnage, they stumbled on a walled estate that had been lush and green before the power died and toxins fouled the wells and soil, some rich man's island he'd hoped would save his family from the end of the world. Guards dead at their posts, dogs in their kennels. Ramón and Sarah had tried to bury the dogs.

In the big house they found a bed, and on that bed a body, teeth yellow, eyes long since picked clean, every bit of meat reclaimed by scavengers, just a skeleton lying on rotted silk in a halo of gold coins.

They reached the bridge. Narrow sidewalks flanked the road, built more to scare people away than to provide a true footpath. Concrete rumbled underfoot with traffic. The sidewalk, just broad enough for two people side by side, was separated by a knee-height railing from the road. A heavy truck full of BROADWAY MEAT rushed past, drawing such a wind in its wake that Zelda staggered.

She stopped at the railing and leaned out, the Bronx on her left and Manhattan on her right. To the south, brick walls gave way to spires and glass. June had let the silence grow again.

She was good at waiting. Zelda had given her too much practice.

"It's not magic," Zelda said first. "It's just . . . possibilities. The world isn't always certain. We think it is, we're taught it is, but there are moments when you don't know what's going to happen next. You come to a road and you cross, or don't, or turn left. In that moment, there's uncertainty. Back at school, Sal and I, our friends, we found some tricks. Operations we could perform. Ways to gather that uncertainty, store it for a while, and use it. I figured the math out. Sal was the one who suggested the observer-dependency."

"What, quantum stuff?"

"Kind of. But also . . . it's like, when you're walking in a new place you've never been before. Paris. You ever been to Paris?" A flat what-are-you-talking-about stare back. "You turn a corner, and you don't know what's there. Could be a circus. Could be a Roman arena. Could be an alleyway or a statue of Saint Michael or a church. You don't know. Anything."

"But that's just because you don't know. The people who live in Paris know what's supposed to be there."

"But you don't. And if they're not looking, you can change things. Here. You got a quarter?" June frowned, checked her pockets. Washington's head winked silver. "Flip it." Zelda called heads while the coin was in the air. Anywhere else in the country, she could have shaped its fall with a breath of will. Here, she had to focus. The spin she'd gathered on her drive surged against the world, and the city.

In June's open palm, Washington looked up out of the corner of his eye. "Luck."

"Try again."

She did, three times, and each time Zelda called the toss in the air. She felt a thrill, showing June this shred of power—it made her feel like some old wizard come into Hobbiton from wandering dark places, as if she knew what was going on, as if she weren't just someone who had fucked up her life and her friends until nothing was left but the road. So she missed the turn in June's eyes from wonder to panic, the rising anger.

"What does this have to do with Sal?"

"This is why we went out. This is how it started."

"Quarters? Coin tosses?"

"Think bigger."

She shook the coin between them. "This is a trick."

"You have to believe it, if you want to know the rest."

Lips thin, pale, eyes narrowed: "You're saying this is what she—what she died for?"

Using all the will that had driven her through the last ten years of grinding loneliness, she tried to keep her voice level. She almost managed. "She's not dead. You know that."

"Then where *is* she?" The six-year-old who answered the olive door had not cried, but she'd been weeping all this time somewhere inside, and a crack in the wall of June's face let her peek out now, through a single line of tears, a twist of that familiar lip.

"You have to believe," Zelda said. "If you don't, I could tell you the stone truth and you wouldn't hear. And I owe it to Sal to make you understand."

"Then tell me!"

"I'm trying." She was almost crying herself now. "But it hurts. I've been carrying this for years. Why do you think I keep coming back?"

"This isn't about you, Z. This is about how you lost my cousin. You owe me the truth. I don't owe you shit."

Zelda had said worse to herself so many nights, in parking lots and cheap hotels. It wasn't nearly so bad as she'd expected to hear it out loud. She'd carved away the meat and vital tissue June was aiming for a long time ago. Her barbs just rasped on bone. "Toss the coin again."

"You're fucking with me."

"How? Am I holding that quarter? Did I give it to you? I'll turn my back if it helps. It is a trick, but I told you how I'm doing it. You have to accept that, for the rest to make any sense at all." She should have stopped there, it would have been enough, but it turned out there were still vital bloody bits down near the bone, organs Zelda had not yet culled, and June had hurt her there, and she was tired and cruel enough for spite. "Except maybe you don't want to hear. You had your suspicions, enough courage to go against your ma and open that door and ask me what happened. But really you're just a scared kid."

"*Fuck* you." And June threw the quarter into the street.

It flashed silver in the flat light, spinning, and bounced off the window of a taxicab speeding by northbound. The driver honked. A fat man in a black suit reading in the back seat looked up, shocked. The quarter arced back, bounced off the bridge railing, and landed on the sidewalk between them, rolling on its edge. It settled slowly. June crouched to watch it land. Zelda did not need to look.

Heads.

June peeled the quarter off the sidewalk and slipped it into her pocket. Arms crossed on the railing, she leaned out, her head over the drop to the water. When the rage passed, denial faded with it. Her whole body softened. A rat forced to swim too long gives up, goes limp, and floats in hope some luck will carry her to land before she dies. That shake of her head and shoulders might have been a laugh.

There was a small vicious part of Zelda that wanted to wait for June to admit it out loud, to say uncle. Mercy won. She spoke softly. "I started small, like this, with coin flips and cards. But if there were other possibilities, other ways things could go, where were they? A coin might flip heads or tails without changing the course of history, but not always, or forever. And some changes do make a difference—a plague coming this year or that, a storm, a weakness in a blood vessel in the brain. Was there a world where history turned out different?"

June frowned. "So we're somewhere else now, is that what you mean? Somewhere that coin only comes up heads."

"No. Nobody cares about that quarter, except you and me. The world heals, covers the bruise. But there are some changes too big to fold into the world we know. We went looking, and found them. The other places. The alts." Easier to say than she'd expected, after all this time. "We started in college—Sal, me, some of our close friends. A road trip across . . . everywhere. At first I thought I'd find . . . it doesn't matter what I thought I'd find. Dumb kid stuff. A better world."

June looked over slowly. "Did you?"

"We found . . . something. Broken worlds. One after another. Beautiful, some of them, but sick. Burned down to the bone. Places where life was cheap and death caught you slowly, and took its time. But we never found anything better."

"Impossible." That was not the only word June spoke, but it was the only one Zelda understood.

"I'm telling you the truth."

"You're saying this is the best chance we've got?" She hit the railing and it echoed hollow. "This world? Shit, you must not be living in the same one as me. With the kids in cages and the machine gun cops? Forty blocks that way across town, there's the one playground Robert Moses built for a Black neighborhood. One and only. To get there, you have to cross Riverside on a narrow bridge, and when you're there it's covered in wrought iron monkeys. The planet's half smothered with its own pillow, we've got Nazis on our streets. I'll be lucky if this city hasn't drowned before I'm forty—and what you've got for me is, this is the best we could do?"

She was breathing hard when she was done.

Zelda did not have much room for gentleness now. "I'm not saying it's so. Just that we never found anyplace better."

"What is any of this good for, then? Flipping quarters when the whole goddamn world's on fire?"

There it was, in those burning eyes, in the tears she would not shed: the hunger and the fury she'd seen sidelong on Sal's face so many years ago, when they still had a chance to turn back. She should not answer June. She should just be a pathetic old road witch, a failure, and let the conversation end. But memory was a hook, and a part of her was still young, and remembered what they had been. "Sal said the same thing. So we went further. There's a crossroads, far out in the alts beyond our highways. A place where worlds meet. We thought that, if we got there, we would have the power to change everything. Fix the world. We tried."

"What happened?"

"We found the rot."

"Rot." Bitter, skeptical, and slow.

"There's an edge to what we can imagine, and something lives out past that edge, beyond the walls of our world, beyond what we think's possible. It's old and hungry, and always looking for a way in." Silence. "When we tried for the crossroads, it fought us." She unwrapped the bandage on her hand and pushed up the sleeve of her flannel. The scars started on her palm, rough and angry, red, and worked up her wrist, up her ruined forearm—slit and furrowed and melted flesh. June turned away, shuddering.

Sometimes Zelda forgot how this would look to someone so young. When she was June's age, she had not believed scars were real, beyond cosmetic markers of badassery in books she read. She did not realize quite how much they hurt.

"The closer we came to the crossroads, the more rot we found. It was like there was some wound deep down, some pit in the heart of the world they bubbled from. We thought maybe the rot was what was wrong, with our world, with all of them. Maybe if we got to the crossroads, and stopped it, things would get better." Zelda had been the one to think that. Sal didn't agree. "We tried." They had fought so hard, in the final weeks. If Zelda paid attention, maybe she would have seen it in time. "But in the end, I wasn't strong enough. And I lost her."

"You're lying."

She was not. But she'd stopped short of the full truth.

She remembered the black-flower road, the road through the sky to the crossroads, and she remembered a mad smile, black lightning reflected in black eyes, Sal suspended over the infinite pit as whiplike legs of shadow caught her and drew her, laughing, down and out into the dark.

And Zelda, weak and shattered and, at last, at the end of things, alone, tried to pull her back.

She'd screamed Sal's name as blood dripped from her arm and slicked their clasped hands. Trying to hold on. Flaying herself against the fierce bands of the wind. Sal, her mouth gaping and many-tongued and fanged, pulled her down. *Zelda. It's beautiful here.*

"She fell. Out of any world like ours, into the rotten places, where the angles don't meet like angles should, where down isn't down and corners don't match. I tried to save her. But—you remember. She was so strong."

It sounded lame—a therapist's excuse. There was nothing you could have done. We have to accept that sometimes the world is beyond our control. We can't make people anything but what they are. Honeyed nonsense.

"I failed," Zelda said. "And she's out there now, past where alive and dead have any meaning, way out in the dark. The others gave up. They left. For a while

I hoped that someday I would find her, if I went far enough, fast enough. But every time I tried, it . . . hurt things. The rot seeped in faster. These days, it's all I can do to seal the cracks, and new ones form faster than I can fix the old. The country's crumbling. And that's the whole story. I loved her, I had her. We tried to do something great. And I lost her."

She leaned against the rail by June's side, deflated. Cars juddered over pavement seams behind her. The wind was heavy with oil and salt. Across the river lay Queens, across the other river, Manhattan. They were between spaces, balanced. She remembered stars moving in the orange sky over the A & A Building, the heat and warmth of her lover by her side, possibility spreading from the hand that rested on her belly. Her cheeks were hot and wet. She had felt that night as if she could fall up into the sky. But she had spent so many years falling down instead, without hitting the hard dead stop she knew was at the bottom. She had told the story now—that was one less weight she'd carry until she died. One more line crossed. Maybe that meant the hard stop was coming soon. She'd welcome it.

She had done her best. Told the truth, even though it was of no help. Now all she had to do was speak the final words, and walk away.

"I'm sorry."

Nothing changed. She tightened her stomach, dragged the back of her hand across her eyes, and raised herself to go.

June's hand trapped her wrist, tight as a steel cuff. Her eyes sharp—an eerie echo in light brown of Sal's eyes, black. "Show me."

"I can't."

"No. You talk this game about secrets, magic, weird coin-trick shit"—the quarter tapped against the rail—"you tell me my cousin's out there, lost, that you lost her, and you expect *sorry* to be enough?" The bridge stank of exhaust. Off to the south, the sun was burning through the cloud layer. "I want to see them. The alts. The other worlds."

"You're not listening."

She'd said it as calmly and patiently as she could, but the words were a spark and June was ten years of gasoline soaked into a girl's body. "You don't get to tell me that!" Her grip was so tight Zelda fought back—her fingers tingled, numb, blood-hungry. "She left us. I loved her and she left me. Ma lights a candle every night and prays to any god she thinks might listen, and tells all her friends her baby will come home someday. She was what Ma had left from all that love she and Pop shared, and whatever Sal saw out there, whatever kept her ass on that road, she left Ma behind, and she left me. That's not magic. She made a choice. I got to know what she chose over us."

The wind could not fill the gap where her voice had been. The city was gone now—only June and Zelda remained, and June's hand on Zelda's wrist, and the pain.

Ramón had told her once about a thought experiment, one of Einstein's. Imagine you are in a room. Imagine the room starts falling an infinite distance, through emptiness. It never will hit ground. How would you know you were falling?

Perhaps you would start to float. The furniture might lose its association with the floor. Pens and pipes might rise from the tables where they lay.

Very good. Now: Imagine it's just you, alone, in a vast and angry cosmos, falling forever. How would you know? What's the difference between floating and falling, when there's no bottom left to hit? No arms to catch you, and no pavement to pulp yourself against?

Just you, and forever.

The hand on her wrist did not let go.

"She left me too," Zelda said.

"She left us for you. First. Show me why. Wouldn't you want to know, if you could?"

There were so many reasons to say no. Start with: It's close to impossible. There was no city so sure of itself as New York—no city so markedly single-minded, locked into form, stamped with street grid. The skyline was high, imposing, known. Growing up in the mountains far away, raised to distrust any population of humans counting more than a few zeros behind the one, even so, she'd reached New York on her first trip to find its whole skyline carved behind her eyes. Everything here was recognition. She did not have the spin. Even if she was strong enough, there was still the gathering storm, the weight of the ending world, the rot that had chased her all the way from Tennessee. How could she bare Sal's cousin to such a threat? She had made so many bad choices in her life, but this one, at least, she could reason clear.

And yet.

*Wouldn't you want to know, if you could?*

For all that responsible ponderation, the fact remained: she had known this might happen, hoped it would, from the moment June stepped out the olive door. Why else lead her there to the middle of this bridge, neither one place nor another? Why tell her the story at all? She could have lied. Zelda wanted this—wanted to share the truth after so long, and especially after Mona. She wanted to see the spark of wonder in June's eyes, and by its light to know that when they set out to save the world, they had not been any more foolish than any other band of bright-dumb kids might have been in their place. Teetering on the edge of gray jobs in gray buildings, they had seen adventure, a chance for change, and reached for it.

June stood behind her. The sun on her skin sifted through the shifting clouds. The breeze carried the scents of distant sea and nearby oil.

"Close your eyes," Zelda said.

"I want to see it happen."

"That's the problem. You want to see, but you know this city, and that knowledge locks you into place. Close your eyes."

She looked, first, deep into Zelda's own. Whatever she found there, she obeyed. She looked so innocent with her eyes shut.

"Take your hand off the rail." Good. And now—she hadn't done this for its own sake in so, so long. Hadn't taken anyone with her since Montana. And never here, never in New York.

Start with the water, if you have water to work with. Its reflections hold so many colors and shades of light—let them dapple, gather, guide. Fill yourself with uncertainty. The next place your gaze falls, let it brighten, let its reflections clarify. Don't focus on them, don't decide what sort of world you're slipping into. Just follow the water as it blues, as its surface eases, gentles—undisturbed, here, by wakes, by ferries, never rainbowed with oil slick.

"I smell—" but June cut herself off.

"Say it." The water trembled as reality, or something like it, pushed back, the greatest city in the world elbowing itself into Zelda's imagination, a bull-shouldered jowly man in an ill-fitting suit, don't you know who I am—"Tell me."

"Cedar," she said. "Marsh smells. Mud, dirt, rushes. It's . . . raw." With each word, the resistance fades—June a partner now in the journey. Each detail dripping implication.

They were in-between now. Zelda's spin picked at the lock of the world, building on suggestions. Yes, rushes half glimpsed out of the corner of her eye. Yes, campfire smoke on the breeze, rising from a wooded farther shore, between burnt-out ruined buildings long overgrown with vines. The street grid and concrete pylons remained, anchoring them home—but the story those pylons told, the world they required, was like an annoying voice speaking loudly in another room.

Now: *decide*. This is real. That line of smoke reflected. Those ruined towers. That blue-green water, bulging.

A dolphin broke the surface of the Hudson.

June's hand drifted out, searching for a railing that was no longer there. Her arm hovered in midair, like a conductor's before the downbeat.

She opened her eyes.

Tall trees and sloping boughs and marshland walled the river, and beyond them rose skeletons of buildings, naked girders clutching at a clean sky. Manhattan lay beneath a shroud of vines, its skyscrapers listing on cracked foundations, the ruin of a long-dead city.

"We can't stay here," Zelda said. "We're exposed." The hulk of a treaded war machine rusted to their right. The bridge itself was cracked and potholed so badly the water showed through in places, robin's-egg blue. "There are people here, still. Or things like people. It's been a long time since their world ended."

June was smiling. Fierce and hungry and full of awe. Wide-eyed, and too young to know regret. "Can we keep going?"

"What do you want to see?"

"More." She sounded far away. "There's something in the air—"

The world flicker-shifted beneath June's hunger as she drove them deeper into the alts, into the depths of possibility. The sky darkened, purpled, grayed. The river muddied and dried up, baring bones and cracked mud. Gnarled trees curled on the opposite bank, and the bridge shook underfoot. Clouds boiled out of the gray sky, crackling with lightning.

Zelda felt them slipping, down, down. The farther you went from home, the easier it was to take the next step. Huge naked forms shambled across the ruins of New York, bleeding ichor. They were past the edges of the firelight now. The things that lived here could kill them with the simple closing of a mouth. She tried to slow them down, but they were tumbling downhill into the weird. Zelda pulled against June's grip on her wrist—and cut herself on fingers that were now blades.

Black lightning licked the earth, and gouts of ebon fire gnawed at the dry trees. Almost-human voices screamed in terror, pain, exultation. Wild flutes rose on the wind, shrill and alien, as the midnight clouds funneled up and bulged and stretched a tongue down toward them, long and black and winding as a road.

"June. Stop."

"We're almost there," said a voice that was not June's, a hungry voice, old and ragged round the edges. "Just a little further."

Zelda felt as if she had been plunged into an icy lake, too shocked to swim, her chest too tight to breathe, as she sank, desperate and drowning, into the dark.

She recognized those words, and that voice. She had not thought she would ever hear them again. Years ago, as her despair burned itself to grim and comfortable ash, she had decided she did not want to hear them again, that hearing them would be wrong, a crime against the world. That voice was lost, gone. The words did not belong anymore to the girl she'd kissed on the roof of the Art and Architecture Building, when they were kids and there was nothing wrong anywhere except the few inches and layers of clothing between them. They belonged to the long black-flower road, to that once-familiar mouth limned with teeth, her geometries strange, her clawed hand tearing Zelda's wrist, before she fell.

Zelda's skin felt so tight, as if moving would burst her and leave her guts and lungs and heart to tumble out in a squishy, useless pile, her skeleton exposed. She turned to face June, with the same reluctant eagerness she had felt as a child when she'd fallen from a tree, felt her bone snap, and, before the pain hit, lifted her arm to see how it had changed.

The girl by her side was an eclipsing moon, and behind her rose a shape vast and many-angled and writhing, a sun made of shadows. Blades bubbled from her skin. And the voice that wore June Tempest like a glove was a voice Zelda had not heard in ten years, save in her own nightmares, and in those aching parking lot moments of loneliness when her hand sank beneath the waistband of her jeans. . . .

"Sal."

It could not be her. She let go, she fell, she was gone, and Zelda could not save her.

"I missed you, Captain Kidd." The voice slithered down her spine like a snake, squeezed. She was sinking. They were sinking. Light failed and the tornado road reached down. "You look just like I remember."

The years and scars and the many miles of bloody road between them could not stanch the shameful fierce bubbling well of surrender in Zelda's stomach and further south, the need to throw herself between those lines of teeth, to let those thorns pierce her and twine her bones and grow out the hollows of her eyes.

"This isn't you." She was crying. She could not breathe. Sal's grip on her wrist was strong and saw-toothed, and blood slipped down her skin as she pulled away.

"It's been me all this time. I couldn't let you go." Her voice was made of whispers and mad flutes, the chorus from beyond the crack in Mona's tree, the voice of the edge and the end of the world. The weight of the storm. "Where you are, it's so small, it's hard even to imagine. Zelda, I have so much to show you."

"Sal, let her go. Sal, Sally, *don't*." She yanked against the knives that held her. Skin tore. Zelda fell free. Landed hard on crumbling concrete. Get up, she told herself, and again, get up, cursing in every language she knew, lashing herself with loathing, cradled around her wrist. That's not Sal. It's not her. It's a trick. It's a lie.

"You don't understand," Sal said through June, and that inhuman face seemed for a moment sad. "You're kittens raised in a bottle called America. But I can show you what I've seen."

June stepped off the bridge.

She did not fall. Black fires claimed the farther shore, their smoke rising higher than any tower toward the horror of the sky. The tornado road reached down, and June, step by step, climbed to meet it, her gaze fixed on the sky where—oh God, Zelda heard herself praying for the first time in years, the Our Fathers slipping from her like blood from her wrist—where the black lightning cracked and gathered itself into eyes, eyes she knew, eyes the size of moons in a face of cloud, staring down, staring in.

No. She could not let this happen again.

Spin quickened in her gut—all the ways things might have been, all the mistakes she might have made—and as June stretched out one foot toward the tornado road, Zelda jumped.

The river beneath boiled with saw-toothed and tentacled beasts. A thorn wind blew her back. But ten years ago in an upstairs room behind an olive door, Sal Tempest's mother was still crying, and Zelda would not give her further cause.

She caught June in the air and pulled with all her weight and strength and spin, and more than a little prayer. June had drawn them far out into the beyond, but in a sense they were still in New York, indomitable New York, and there were no ruined bridges here, there was no shattered sky. She used the weight of that certainty, of street grids and bridges and Moses, she dug her fingers into June and wrapped her legs around her and believed, as fiercely as she could, that they were home.

And then, with a thunderous sound as though the sky were a sheet of thick paper suddenly torn—they were falling.

Zelda flicker-stepped from alt to alt in the chaos as they spun, remembering home, remembering the color of the sky—no, not quite, yes, there—remembering skyline, forcing the water that peculiar sick and silted shade of green, smudging clouds with smog—almost there, almost spent—forced her weight against thrashing June, shouted, get your feet down, tense—

With a feeling like a key turning in a lock, they were home.

And then the river hit them.

The Hudson—the real Hudson—was rank and gritty-slick. This water would give you cancer, would make your hair fall off and your skin crack and bleed. She embraced it. She bobbed to the surface like a cork, flailing, blinked burning water from her eyes, saw overhead, relief, a smudged blue normal sky, at least as normal as skies got these days. Empty of storm, of eyes, of the tornado road, and Sal.

Treading water, she scanned the river. "June?"

She saw only green, and far away to the south, a ferry.

They'd fallen into the same place, feet down; she'd kept her safe. She had to be here.

But—thoughts coming too late: Could June swim? What if she'd gasped as the river hit, breathed a lungful of water, went down? "June!" Zelda treaded higher in the water, scanned the low waves.

Nothing. Jesus God. She couldn't stop losing her. "June."

Something grabbed her leg and pulled her under.

Her gasp was a mix of air and water, a convulsive swallow of a tea of eight million humans' waste, and that roughness in her throat made her whole body want to turn inside out. But she couldn't fight and throw up and not drown all at once, so she clenched her stomach and reached blind around her in the murk.

The thing that caught her had long strong arms with human joints, fingers even, and it was not battering her so much as pulling, down, down, climbing her body like a rope. Long bony knees found Zelda's stomach, and churned bubbles from her mouth. Zelda fought through that grip—found a face, a neck with a cord around it, and a coin dangling from that cord.

She forced her eyes open under the burning water. There, weakening now, eyes panic-wide, was June. Innocent, and desperately scared. And, in her fear, about to drown them both.

In that dark and toxic green, Zelda grabbed the back of June's shirt, anchored her, and hit her once—hard—in the face. Pain cut through the fear, and awareness followed pain. Zelda's knuckles ached. June went limp, Zelda pulled the back of her shirt and swam up, against deadweight at first, then, as June understood and weakly began to kick, rising faster.

They breached the surface with newborn gasps, coughed the city from their lungs, and swam for shore.

When they collapsed on the concrete bank, at last, Zelda let herself throw up, great heaves into a bush in a cement planter until she was wrung out and shivering. June just lay there, still, tank top plastered against her skin, her eyes open to the blue. Saul would have looked like that on the Damascus road.

Cameras must have caught them falling—boredom is the best kind of surveillance, and there was a lot of that in the faceless apartments that fronted the river. There would be citizen journalists soon with their Twitters and their Instagrams and cops soon after if they weren't lucky. She should run. To linger was a mistake.

Zelda sat beside the girl on the concrete. Her hand found June's; the girl's fingers twitched, then closed hard. Zelda wondered how much she was hated, behind those brown eyes. But at least June was alive.

She remembered looking into another sky, in another city, with someone else beside her.

June was breathing fast and shallow and her open eyes were bright. God, Zelda, get it together, this girl doesn't hate you. She's afraid. She needs your help. "It's over," Zelda lied. It was never over. It was barely beginning. "You're safe."

"That was her."

She shook her head. Unable to speak. Unable to frame the possibility. Her breath was sick and sour.

"When it, when *she* looked at you, I felt it, Zelda." There was an intimacy to her voice when she said Zelda's name now, which had not been there before. An echo of a long-gone caress. "She's coming home. For you."

"I know," she said, her voice hollow. She'd known, when she begged the others to stay beside her, back in that Best Western parking lot in Montana, she'd known. That's why Zelda had wandered this rotting country's rotting roads like a bit of trash circling a drain. Sal's not dead. Just gone.

But she had forgotten that gone was not the same thing as over.

After everything, there was still a place inside her that bled when she heard her name in the thunder's voice. Even on that bridge, a part of her wanted to kneel before the monster in the sky, to run after Sal into the jaws of Hell. More than all the monsters out beyond the crossroads, that was what scared her.

"It's not just Sal," Zelda said. "The face in the sky. It's the rot. She's bringing it all home. I felt it. I didn't know." Because she could not bear to know. "Maybe it's her, or maybe they're using her. Or maybe there's no difference, out there."

June brought her back to the world. "What are we going to do?"

"You are going to do nothing. Stay in New York. It's safe here for now. The wall's high. This place knows what it is too much for her to reach you without my help." She'd known the storm was coming, and still she'd let June egg her on, let herself get carried away. Too late for all of that now. There would be time enough for recrimination on her journey west. "I'm going to stop her."

"You can't."

"Not alone." Those eyes, that storm-cloud face, like an angry moon about to crush the city and the world. "I need the others. Together, maybe . . ." She trailed off.

"What happened to them?"

"We grew apart."

Saying it like that, she could hide, she could pretend—that growing apart just happened, that it was no one's fault, that there had not been a moment in a Best Western in Montana where they all turned their backs and walked away and left her weeping and alone. That they weren't right to leave. "But this . . . they'll listen." She said it to herself as much as to June and she was not sure to which of them she was lying. "We can fix it. Together." She'd said that back in Montana too.

But this time it would be different. There was the enormity of Sal in the sky, of the storm, of her black lightning eyes. She was coming home as the end of the world. This time they'd understand. The flicker in her heart at that thought—it had to be fear. It could not be happiness. Could not, after all this time, be joy. That would be sick, that would be wrong.

She missed them all so much.

She stood, and held out a hand to June. "Lie low. Stay in the city. Stay out of the shadows."

"Where are you going?"

Don't tell her. What she doesn't know, she can't pass along.

But she was Sal's cousin, and Zelda had failed her too. "I'm going to get them. Ramón. Ish. Sarah."

She could still speak those names. They were names, that was all.

"Penn Station first," she said. "Then west. To where the country stops."

"Zelda," June said as she turned to go. "I saw what's beyond the storm. Just for a second, before you tackled me. It's—"

"I know."

"Beautiful," she said, and Zelda climbed away.

# CHAPTER THREE

June caught up with Zelda halfway to the 138th Street station. The kid called after her twice, but the first time, she just said "Hey!" and Zelda could ignore her, since that *hey* could have been meant for anyone. The second time, June called her name, but there were the video games, of course, and in a city of eight million people, there had to be at least one other Zelda.

She did not want to talk to June.

Her head was full of visions of the tornado road, of the face in the sky, and her body was full of memories of Sal. She was dripping wet, her clothes soaked through, her backpack heavy. She had three thousand miles of road in front of her to be afraid and alone, and after that she had to reach the crossroads. She never meant to hurt June. But she had given in, had taken her across the border knowing what waited out there. A second later and June would have been lost, and all for, what, for Zelda's own satisfaction? "Just a little further." One more of Ma Tempest's children claimed by her silly, busted quest. Better to go. Better to disappear.

June caught her at the subway stairs. Grabbed her arm and spun her round and glared at her, fierce and dripping on the pavement. "You can't just show me that and walk away."

"You saw that thing. You're not safe with me."

"That thing is my cousin."

"I know who she is!" Zelda was shouting. A switch had been thrown inside her, and the anger gushed out. She'd been holding it, she realized, even longer than June, and behind the walls she'd used to dam it up, the anger had grown sick, stagnant, and full of pus. "I have to stop her."

"Not alone."

"Yes, alone. If the others can't help, or won't. It's my fault."

"Bullshit. Sal always did what she wanted."

A kid with a backpack and a stocking cap shouldered by, glanced out the corner of one sullen eye at Zelda, soaked. She felt cold all of a sudden, and weak from the swim and the spin she'd spent. June's glare did not ease. Why should it? Zelda had almost killed her, and now Zelda wanted to leave. "She's not the only one."

At that, June did smile, soften. "Lot of that going around."

She felt seen and did not like it. Below, a train arrived. Southbound. "That's my train."

"You don't have a place to go. Do you? Like, a place where you live."

"I live on the road." She did not feel ashamed, she told herself. "It's safer that way."

"Come back to Ma's."

"I can't." She had wanted to, for ten years, but once the offer was made, how could she accept?

"Ma's out all day, at her sister's. You need a shower. Clean clothes. You gonna get on Amtrak looking like you just took a bath in the Hudson? Shit. They'll throw you in jail on general principle."

Zelda felt the road-hunger, the ache to be anywhere but here. Three thousand highway miles alone. That was what she needed. That was what she deserved.

"You saved my life," June said. "At least let me do you some laundry."

✳

Behind the olive door, a stairway she remembered climbed to the third floor, where there were two apartments. The one on the left was Ma's.

June ushered her in. The same tall wooden carvings occupied the entryway—rough-hewn Indians with cascading warbonnets, bears with paws upraised. Memories rolled over Zelda as she stepped through the heavy bead curtain. The air here had a weight of woodsmoke and sage, the metallic tang of turmeric, Sal's mother always midway through mixing up some concoction for some client who couldn't strictly speaking pay. Witchcraft worked best through barter, was what she said, with a big laugh. With Ma gone, the smells were echoes. Buddha's hand twisted on a piece of twine hung from the kitchen ceiling, drying beside other fruits and roots and bits of power. It was the same, just smaller. The spices, smells, and smoke all fading.

June tossed her jacket over a chair back to dry. She filled a glass of water, drank, as if the room were not full of ghosts. As if Zelda could not see herself, younger and unscarred, seated at the card table by the sink, listening to Ma's long stories, half sermon and half spell and half conspiracy rant, while Sal's long fingers crept spiderlike and secretive to Zelda's hand under the table, then climbed to her thigh. As if what they had been here—young, brilliant, in an angry yearning crush of love—were not carved into the space, an architectural feature like an arch or a whispering vault.

June, she realized, was talking. "What?"

"Water," the girl said with an eye roll, and offered a glass. "What do you have that needs cleaning?"

Zelda opened her backpack, took inventory, as automatic as an old soldier stripping a rifle. The pack's waterproof lining had held up. First aid kit, clothes, tools, all in their ziplocks. The lockpicks she unrolled to dry, the knife she flicked open and closed again, testing the hinge's grease. "Just these clothes." One second later: "You have a washer?"

"And dryer. Church took up a collection when Ma's knee went bad. Saves her the walk to the laundry. I told her I'd do it after school, but she doesn't let anyone wait on her if there's something she can do herself."

Thinking of Ma Tempest hurt was enough to chase the memories away. Back when Zelda first visited, the woman had been aging like a tank—rusting in places, but unstoppable. Years had passed since then. Zelda's own scars hurt her in the mornings, and her knee ached if she spent too long walking on concrete. "I'm sorry to hear that," Zelda said, and June said, "Towel," holding one out. "I guess you remember the way to the bathroom."

She did.

Zelda passed her already-mostly-dry clothes back through the cracked-open door and stood in front of the bathroom mirror while the water in the pipes knocked itself up to hot. The river had left deltas of grime on her arms and belly, a long strand of weed wrapped around her neck. Her eyes were wide and there was a shadow of her, younger, in the mirror.

Two carved masks hung on the wall behind her, and another statue stood on the toilet tank. Sarah had visited this place a few times. What had she thought of all the cigar store Indian stuff? She never said, which said a lot by itself. Ma claimed the carvings had religious significance, but how exactly, she'd never made clear.

Zelda's eyes were deep in the mirror. She fell into herself.

Ten years alone on the road were nothing set against that shape in the sky. She had dreaded this moment ever since she lost her. She must have known, somehow, deep down, that this would happen. That was why, when the others left her, having lost the faith, she'd kept driving, walking, training. Yes, someone had to fix the cracks they'd made, but there had always been more to it. And here it was: Sal, and the end of the world.

So why was she excited?

Steam closed the mirror's eyes.

The shower embraced her. The pipes knocked and spoke as she remembered, just before the water veered hot or cold, giving her spare seconds to lunge aside to avoid being scalded or frozen. You showered here with one hand on the tap, riding it the way Ramón used to ride the shifter in his Challenger as they barreled down Highway 80.

Mud and sludge and road dirt that had nothing to do with the Hudson melted off her. Ten years couldn't melt away so easily. Not even with June singing to herself on the other side of the wall, "See-Line Woman" out of tune, as Ma used to.

Zelda realized she was crying.

She could not do this again. She had tried before, and lost everything. Ten years of free fall, and all she had at the end of it was this life of halfways and in-betweens. She had her freedom—sure, and she'd wanted that once. Secrets and truth. To understand the shape behind the curtains of the world.

What had they been, after all, back then? A few kids in an old car who thought they could change the future if only they wanted hard enough.

She knew secrets now. What use were they? She had her freedom and she had power of a sort, and it was good only for parlor tricks and saving the lives of people who had little enough left to live for. Back then she'd run after knowledge as if it could solve everything—heal your cuts and bruises and fill the hole inside you until at last you could speak the right true answer to the Question of the world, and it would unknot and no kid would ever have to be gunned down in the streets with a fucking toy gun in his hand again. But you could find an answer and speak it and no one would hear and it couldn't change any damn thing. She'd not understood this about magic, back when she started to look for some: magic was a slow sort of suicide. You pushed on that gap between the way the world was and the way the world could be, until, if you were strong and smart and pure and very lucky and very dumb, one day the gap grew teeth and opened its mouth and ate you.

Once she'd been young and brave enough to thrust her hand into the nation's heart, thinking she could fix it. That lost her Sal, and every friend she'd brought along for the ride. The world did not notice.

What if she just stayed here? Well, not here exactly, in the shower, someone would notice, but somewhere quiet where she could draw a nice bath, sit down with a glass of decent wine, and wait for the end of the world? At the rate things were going, Sal might not even make it in time to matter.

Zelda was ten years older now and not ten easy years either, and the country she'd set out to save had spent so many of those years demonstrating at best indifference toward, and at worst loathing for, her and her friends. And Sal—if that even was Sal in the sky—the thing she'd become, or by which she'd been eaten—she sounded just as sure, and just as fierce.

Ramón had once tried to explain his comic book collection to Zelda. "The X-Men, you see, they're low-key the best allegory for political change I can think of, but not the way people usually mean. See, Professor X and his mutants, they set out to prove to the world of normal people that mutants are basically helpful and good, that they don't deserve all this hate and fear. Meanwhile his enemy, Magneto, he thinks, that's a waste of time, humans will always hate us, so we just have to get as much power as we can, so we can rule them, or protect ourselves. At the beginning, it feels like of course the X-Men are right and Magneto's wrong. But if the world ever really came to terms with mutants, there would be no more comics. So instead of this big assimilationist message each individual comic tries to pitch, over the years, you see Professor X and his students just saving everything again and again, and every time what the humans do is say thanks, maybe one or two people learn the error of their ways, but a few years later, they're right back to Mutant Registration Acts and genocide robots. And you gotta figure that after all of that, even Prof X starts to feel real tired."

He'd been pulling comics from boxes as he spoke, with a half-eaten Twizzler jammed into the corner of his mouth, where an old movie star might have held a cigarette.

She was tired. And nothing seemed simple anymore.

June was singing "Fast Car" now. Her voice was higher than Sal's, smoky, with a roundness on the top notes when she let herself go. A teapot screamed and the song cut off. Sal never made tea, didn't like it, asked always, what's the point?

June was not Sal. They weren't even twins. They were cousins. That seemed so simple and obvious to say, but looking into her eyes, Zelda almost forgot.

She heard a knocking in the pipes; while she was still reaching for the handle, cold water hit her in a rush, and she felt again the full-body shock of her fall into the Hudson, that moment of searching for June. Certain she'd done it again—walked out into the depths with one of the Tempest girls and come back without her.

She turned off the water and stood, dripping, in the tub, shivering and alone with the masks watching from the walls.

Wrapped in a towel and only a little red-eyed, she emerged minutes later, barefoot, her hair dangling loose at her shoulders. June was drinking tea, and she offered Zelda a mug. It tasted thick and sweet, with a fierce punch of spice. Zelda didn't ask what was in it—Ma mixed her own blends and kept them in a big tin over the fridge, changing the mix each time according to some witchy logic she'd never shared with Sal, promising only, *You'll know when you're older.* There was orange peel in there, and cloves, and something that made her throat tense up, like betel nut. June set a plate of round flat cookies down beside the mug. "Digestives. Ma's cousin started her on them a few years ago. She can't stop. Anything that tastes so little like food, she says, it's gotta be healthful." Her imitation of Ma wasn't good. Sal's had been like hearing a recording.

They're not the same. They're not. Zelda took a biscuit. It did not taste like food.

June watched her. In the closet, the washing machine buzzed. June changed the clothes to the dryer, pushed the button that brought the rumble. She resumed her post at the counter beside her tea, watching Zelda, ten years and a storm behind her eyes.

What more could Zelda give her? "I've told you everything." It wasn't much of a lie. There was more—but what she'd said contained it all, folded up like one of those tiny foam pills you got in dollar stores, the ones that, when you dropped them in a glass of water, bubbled and unfolded into some monstrous neon approximation of a flower, or a wide-eyed drowning face. I had her, we tried, and I couldn't keep her safe, and I lost her. That was all that mattered. But the girl was leaning against the counter, watching clothes roll in the dryer, and Zelda could not speak.

"I'm going with you," June said at last.

"No." Fast as a reflex, as if she'd put her hand to a searing stove and drawn it back only to watch the blisters form, the skin crack, fried nerves singing with pain. "You can't. I won't let you."

"She's my cousin."

"She was. She's not herself anymore. She's been gone for ten years." She held the mug of tea between them as if it could shield her from the weight of June's gaze.

"I know. I've been here the whole damn time. Maybe there's some way to get her back."

"It doesn't work that way." Even she could hear the bitterness in her voice. She was raw, and trapped, and naked under this bath towel, and inside her, not too deep, there was a bleeding hungry part that clung to the memory of that face in the sky, and wished beyond all reason that she'd lunged not to save June, but to reach the tornado road.

"How can you say that?"

This had been easier back at school. You just said, Kant, and half the people in the room groaned and half nodded, but they all got it, and those who didn't at least pretended, too scared of being the slow one to ask what you meant. "There's possible, and then there's . . . what's beyond possible. There are worlds so different that our fundamental categories break down. Time. Math." June's eyes tightened. Zelda groped for words. It had been years since she last tried to explain this. "Look. You and I, we live in the same world."

"We don't, though," June said. "You're, like, fourteen years older than I am, you can fuck up coin flips with your mind, you went to Yale and I'm failing math, you're from some South Carolina shitheel and I'm from the *greatest* city in the world, I'm pretty meh on the whole sex thing and you are thirstier than the French Foreign Legion, and between the two of us I got, like, ninety-five percent of the melanin. And I speak French."

Zelda blinked. "Wow." Also: "We didn't have French where I went to high school."

"What'd you have?"

"Koine Greek. So we could read the New Testament."

"See? We do *not* live in the same world." The dryer rolled. Outside, a cat yowled in heat.

"We're bringing different perspectives to this conversation. But we're experiencing it in the same order, in time. Because if we didn't, it would be, um, impossible for us to think like people do. And most people have some basic, common points in how we make sense of the world."

"Memory's different, though."

"But we both experience linear time the same way. And space."

"All of that's relative, though, isn't it."

"I thought you said you were failing math."

"Math's not physics."

"Just you wait."

June laughed at that, sang Zelda's words to an unfamiliar melody.

"What did I say?"

June blinked. "I didn't think we were having *that* different a conversation. You don't get internet when you're monster hunting? Or Broadway?"

"No."

Now it was June's turn to say, "Wow," and: "So, what, no Facebook, no Twitter?"

"Nope."

"Shit, you don't know how you lucky you are. The world's a fuckin' *mess*."

"It's rotting," Zelda said simply. "And it will rot faster as Sal gets closer."

"My cousin's not a Nazi."

"Of course not." She breathed out, gathered her points in her mind. This was going in directions she hadn't anticipated. But she needed June to understand what was happening, why she couldn't come along. "Relativity means that time and space work differently depending on how the fabric of space-time gets bent—but everyone in the same place experiences the same time. Those categories don't exist, out where Sal is. Time goes forward and backward at once. Everything shifts into everything else. You can't depend on any truth. Just power and pain."

"You sure you're not talking about Twitter?" She caught Zelda's expression, held up a stilling hand. "Fine, sure, I get it. I felt that thing inside me. I saw it. I'm just saying—I don't know how 'fundamental' any of this stuff really is. Ma talks all this witch stuff about Men and Women, you know, capital letters? And, like, half my friends are neither. Maybe it's not as weird out there as you say. Maybe we can save her."

"I want to believe it's possible. But if you're going to come with me, you need to know that it might not turn out like you hope. I've seen what the rot does to people."

She'd said the crucial words, and June was all at once smiling, as if the words that came after didn't count. "I can come?"

You just almost-worse-than-died, Zelda wanted to scream at her. But of course she didn't understand that, not really. A gun, or a cop, those meant something. Sal in the sky, the alts and the rot, they weren't real to June yet, they weren't her nightmares. Adrenaline still burned through that sixteen-year-old circulatory system, and she was no stranger to pain or anger or fear, but she was still learning about scars. "I don't think I can stop you."

"Damn straight. Try to skip out on me, and I'll chase you right across the country."

"You should shower first," she said. "And pack."

June's eyes narrowed.

Zelda frowned. "What?"

"You're gonna run out on me while I'm in the shower."

"I am not going anywhere with someone who smells like the bottom of the Hudson. And once we hit the road, it might be a while before we get another chance."

"Yeah, but none of what I just heard was, 'No, June, don't worry, I'm not going to run off and leave you soon as you're not looking.'"

"I don't know why you think I would."

"I think you got facing-up-to-your-mistakes problems. I think you've been coming back here every year of the last ten and you still felt some simple apology would square us. If I had money, I would not put it on you sticking around."

"Harsh."

"Tell me where you spot the lie."

She crossed her arms, leaned back. Why couldn't Sal have had a pushover cousin? But if June really wanted to join Zelda on the road, she'd need that edge, that combination of conviction and skepticism that let you do real work.

She wondered for a moment if she should change her mind.

June didn't move during that pondering silence. Her arms were crossed too. Zelda wondered if she'd mirrored her intentionally, and if so, why.

"June. I will not run off and leave you as soon as you're not looking."

She said it with the confidence she used to step into another world, and June, after a second's judgy hesitation, believed her. She grinned, open as a child. She still was a child, Zelda reminded herself. She was younger than they had been when they started. If not by much. "So, what do I need?"

"I'll write a list. You shower."

While June was showering, she did write the list. Ma kept scrap paper in a cookie tin and pens in a tiki glass on the counter beside the old rotary phone. Zelda grabbed one of each at random and found herself writing a road adept's packing list on the back of a decommissioned library card for *Demonology*.

There wasn't much to write. She'd winnowed down her essentials through the years. You never needed as much as you thought, if you traveled smart. The more you brought to the road, the less the road could wear you—and you wanted it to wear you, you wanted dust in your mouth and dirt in the pads of your feet, you wanted that faint engine grease smell and the crazed hard skin as if you'd spent too long in an oven. You wanted the country to shape you like a key to a lock, so you could feel what it was, what it could be. What it could have been.

So: two pairs of pants, three shirts, socks, material that dried fast. Concentrated multipurpose soap, stuff that wouldn't kill fish if you had to bathe in a river. Pocketknife. Parachute cord ideally, but any rope would do. Toothbrush. Zelda had her own water filter. A first aid kit. Needle, thread. Lighter. Dryer lint for fires. Zelda had a magnesium block and a flint in her pack, but if you used those all the time, you got lazy. She had an extra sleeping bag in the Subaru. Waterproof bags for everything, good thick ziplocks would work—so you could hike through a rainstorm if you had to.

Compass. Straight razor. Map. Notebook, pen, a book, a deck of cards for when you got bored. Tarot cards if possible, because you never knew when you might need advice.

June, still shower-damp, scanned the list. "I'll need to go out to get some of this." A glance at Zelda, suspicious. "Come with me."

"My clothes are still drying."

"I'll wait."

"We don't have time to waste. If I wanted to run, I would have left while you were washing up. I told you. We're in this together."

Her eyes did not un-narrow. "I'll be back by two." She found her coat, and a bag, and left, locking the front door behind her.

Zelda paced the apartment, alone, inside for once. It had been a while. The place was small, and without realizing it, she found herself in Sal's room. June had taken it over, the floor now a swamp of clothes, the bed a tangle of black sheets, protest signs taped up on the wall: NO KIDS IN CAGES, bars and a face staring out. LOVE IS LOVE in rainbows over the bed. REFUGEES ARE WELCOME HERE, in white on black board, with a painted dove. BLACK LIVES MATTER.

There were sketches, too, held up with thumbtacks—young people mostly, a large-jawed girl glancing over her shoulder, a boy slumped against a charcoal suggestion of a brick wall, his legs splayed, looking down at his crotch—dead, asleep, waiting for a miracle. They were bold, swift, drawn with a hunger for shape and shade, as if the whole world were slipping away from her and these people might slip away, too, and all June could do in that failing moment was grasp them with her eye and heart and fix them to paper. A girl shouting, her hair shaved close, a megaphone raised. A crowd holding signs, conveyed by charcoal waves, like an ocean in a storm.

These were June's friends, her memories—people she could not give up or leave behind. June's soul was naked in these pictures, and Zelda should not be here, seeing them. But she could not look away.

Most of the kids Zelda met these days, she met on the road. There were so many kids on the road, and they seemed so young—drifting from flophouse to flophouse through the hollowed-out country, carrying mementos of long-gone families and foster parents, sharing details on new scams and boltholes by text on burner phones charged in libraries. Some would make it. Some were already hooked, on pills or meth or dreams. She passed through their camps like the Ancient Mariner, escaped alone to tell thee—they were teenaged, but not teen-agers exactly, not as she'd been. They didn't have the luxury, or the obligation. They were wild in a country that hated wild things. They were nothing like June's life, either, with Ma, with friends, with the world ending.

Would that be June's life, out there in the wind?

Zelda should have left already.

But she kept looking from drawing to drawing, not knowing what she sought until she found it near the bed, unfinished or abandoned. Abandoned, she thought. There were smeared streaks through the charcoal. Maybe dew from a glass had collected on the artist's hand and fallen to mar the picture—and June could not abandon what she'd done so far, nor make herself finish it now that it could not be perfect. It could have been dew, from a glass.

Two women sat on a bed, in this room, by the window. Back then June's own bed had been shoved in the far corner. In the picture there was a dark girl, hair in braids, high cheekbones and fierce, eager eyes, leaning in, leaning forward, toward another girl, shorter, rounder, and, in the artist's imagination, more beautiful than anyone Zelda had ever seen in the mirror. Her mouth half open. Their hands propped them up on the bed, their arms crossing like bridge cables, the shorter girl's knee up, the other's hand resting on her thigh.

Just a moment, abandoned, of two women in love, at ease, in the late after-noon, as June had seen them or remembered them. Had it really looked like this, from outside? It must have. Might have. Moments vanished into the past like stones into a pool, and while their passage left ripples behind, even the rip-ples someday stilled and left the surface unchanged, placid and glassy as if there had never been a stone in all the universe.

If you remembered something hard enough, could you make it true? Could you remember a moment into being?

She'd known enough people down south who tried. Hell, this was America, after all. Revisionist history was as much the national pastime as baseball. Rap-ist slaveholders became civic saints. Men who fought to keep people enslaved, who insisted slavery was the point of the war, lived to see their own children and grandchildren proclaim slavery had nothing to do with it at all and much of the nation convince itself they were right. This was little league by comparison.

But it was still wrong.

On Zelda's first visit, June had slept in Ma's room. That night—the door closed, Sal's hand between her legs, her mouth on her neck—Zelda could not contain the gasp, the moan. The walls. The walls were thin. She had to keep her breath, her voice, to herself. "They don't care," Sal whispered, but Zelda felt so hemmed in, people above her and beneath, her every breath overheard, as if she lay before them on a stage, but she could not stop or ask Sal to stop, she wanted it so much, her body pulling them both down, down. If she could open her skin down the middle and pull Sal inside her, she would have, felt her surging against her ribs and from the inside, unable to escape—but she could not ask for that, did not know what it even was, so she lay pinned beneath her fear, silent. Furious with the world. With herself. Afraid.

She'd grabbed her discarded shirt, stuffed it in her mouth, bit down so hard her jaw hurt and she clenched into a C. Sal's eyes went wide, her hand stopped, she drew back. Zelda felt as if she had thought she was falling into a bed of leaves, but the leaf pile covered a mine shaft and now she was tumbling down and down as the light receded, thinking: I have made a terrible mistake. That was how it felt, to see Sal's eyes when she pulled back and did not understand.

"Can you just, just—hold it there," she said in the dark, which was not really dark, there was no dark in this whole city, and in the silence, which was never silent. "Over my mouth." Sal crouched over her on the bed, striped with shadows, her skin lit by neon outside the window, still wearing her unbuttoned shirt, shadows flanking the muscle and swell of her stomach like arrows pointing down. She was larger than Zelda, stronger, and one year older, which had seemed an impassable gap of sophistication and experience until that moment. But in that not-silent bedroom, falling though still, Zelda realized for the first time how young they were, both of them, and how dangerous were the weapons pressed against their skin. Sal watched her, wary. Zelda might as well have spoken in tongues.

"I don't want to hurt you," Sal said.

How could she explain it? Someone, somewhere, probably had words for this sort of thing, magic formulas to trade—she'd glimpsed the edge of that world in web searches for dog collars and the gag reflex, accidents she told herself at the time, on the school internet—but they scared her. She wasn't that sort of person. She wasn't any sort of person at all. "You won't hurt me."

"I might."

"You won't." Angry, she curled into a ball, hugging her knees and digging her nails into her arms hard enough to mark the skin. She wanted to crush something, to hurt herself. Not to explain. "I need you to. I shouldn't need you to, but I *do*. Don't be so fucking gentle with me. I'm not making sense." She was crying and she didn't know when that had started, and now everyone could hear, just as they'd heard her before. And Sal sat there large-eyed and tried to understand. She reached out, gently, her hand on Zelda's shoulder, as if Zelda were made of fine-spun porcelain, to break at a breath. Zelda wished she were made of something so airy and brittle. She wished she would shatter. She caught Sal's hand at the wrist and stared at her, into her, breath molten in her throat.

Fear in Sal's eyes was new, and a little pain. "Z. Please let me go."

Zelda pulled back from her, from herself, to the corner of the bed. "I'msorry," all one word at first, then, "I am sorry." Halfway out of bed now, one foot on the floor, her hair ragged around her face like a ghost woman's, her guts all teeth. The room seemed brighter, her eyes wider in the dark, pupils filled with night. "I'm wrong."

"I don't think you can be." Sal spoke slowly, as if finding her way through a thicket where venomous creatures lived. They'd grown up, both of them, in thickets like that, learned when they were young where the thorns were, lost enough blood and then forgot it all and just figured the stooped-over way they walked was natural. "Not about yourself, not about this. I'm just . . . not used to it."

Meaning: this wasn't how Zelda felt when they were at school. But school was its own place, wasn't it, like the mind in Milton, a special bubble full of weirdos like her, like Sal and Ramón and Ish and Sarah, a few fake Gothic buildings surrounded by magic rings and wards, unreal and untouchable as fairyland. You could be someone there you hadn't been before. You could expand to fill the space you'd cleared when you set your old self on fire. You could buckle a mask to your face and melt your face to fill the mask.

At school she could be an eager prodigy from someplace no one had ever heard of, and that was enough. You were the jokes you made, the points argued in class, the parties you threw or went to, and how you dressed for them, and whom you spent time with when you weren't working, and nothing else. Some people were more than that—the girl whose family name was on the library, the screenwriter's kid, the president's daughter, the boy who sold his dad's coke to the improv groups—but you could start fresh and start here. You left the outside world behind and sank into the dream the campus dreamed of itself.

But Ma Tempest had welcomed them into her home, made them dinner, showed Zelda the tiny workshop where she carved her statues and made her magic. She let Zelda say as much or as little as she wanted. She hovered near Sal, asked her about classes, whether she went to church and if so who with, made needling little childhood jokes, was a mother. If Sal, bold, unstoppable force in tight pants, Sal who feared neither priest nor deacon and who had never lost a fight, Sal whom Zelda had never seen without a comeback or a plan, was also and inescapably someone's daughter, then that meant Zelda was, too, that no matter how she tried to shuck it off, she carried everything she'd come from on her back like a snail. Here in this room, unseen and intangible as God and all his angels, hovered her own mother and father and Pastor Steve and everyone she let herself believe she had escaped.

She tried to explain. The words jammed together in her month. She said *I* five times, and *you* six or seven, and each sentence started before the last one finished. The only thing she was sure she'd said, after a confusing ten minutes or forever burning with shame, naked except for socks, was: "It doesn't feel the same."

"You're scared."

"I'm not! Aren't you?"

"I've brought girls home before."

"How many?" was the wrong question, but she'd asked it anyway.

"A few." As if it didn't matter. The answer, or the fact she asked.

"I haven't."

Eyes narrowing, a calculus behind them. Where was Zelda going with all of this? She knew so many bad ways this conversation might end.

"At school," Zelda said, "you're you. And I'm—I'm being someone new. Or I'm being me differently. It's stupid."

"It's not stupid."

Couldn't she stop being so damn understanding for a minute and let Zelda flay herself? "I'm going to explode. Just burst into a million splinters. Into stars or coins or I don't know. I need you to hold me together. Hold me down. Please."

Sal crawled toward her across the bed, tentative when Zelda would rather she marched, would rather she grew forty feet tall and lifted Zelda clutched in her fist like a toy.

She did grow as she neared. She filled Zelda's world, which folded into the curves of her.

The hunger ached. You could hurt me, she wanted to say. You could crush me, shame me, be my queen or my god. Capture me, own me fully and take away the life I've known. "Just—" She twined her leg through Sal's. Years later she would wonder which of them had trapped the other. "Put your hand over my mouth."

Sal bit her lip when she was thinking, when she was worried, and Zelda had never seen anything so rare or so sexy. "I can do that." Large eyes darting around the room. Thinking. She picked up her shirt, still wet from Zelda's mouth, and offered it to her. "Hold this tight in both hands, over your head. If you let it go, I'll stop."

A bargain. Safety. Zelda didn't want it. She needed to be out of her own control right now, in this room that felt too real. There were so many eyes behind the shadows. But she took the shirt, wound it around her hands, pulled it tight, and stared up at her: defiance, need.

Sal's hand over her mouth tasted of vanilla and coconut from her hand cream. She pressed tentatively at first, exploring, uncertain even though they'd slept together before, off in the dream they shared. Even that touch was electric. She bucked, fought—Sal almost pulled away but Zelda caught her with her eyes. *Don't you dare.* Her nails bit into the palms of her hands even through the shirt she held. She felt a stitch in the seam give. Don't stop.

Sal was scared, she realized then—of her. And angry. She welcomed it. Battering them both. Her breath hot against Sal's hand, her body slick. Her shoulders and back ached from pulling at the shirt, her forearms cramped. Her hips bucked. Sal's fear and anger and need echoed Zelda's back at her and built, and built, and for a moment, she was held, and for a moment it was all right, and she burst into the void and screamed into Sal's hand and was gone.

When she found herself again, Sal lay limp beside her, breathing hard, tears on her face, and when Zelda touched her, her lips twitched almost to a smile, though her eyes stayed fixed on the sky beyond the ceiling. Zelda kissed her tears, her lips, her neck, her chest, and down. Sal petted her, caressed her, lightly, as if holding Zelda down had wrung all the strength from her.

This dream would not last. Zelda knew it then. The four years would end, and the world after that. Any idiot could see it coming. They were at war, and wars were not kind to dreamers or to dreams. She wanted to shelter in Sal, but no body could hold her or guard her, and what could she offer Sal in return? Life was real and they would die. She worked between her legs, caught her thighs with her fingers, heard a gentle breath of life.

Why was the world like this? And could it be better?

When they were both done, aching, tear-wet, Sal said, I love you, and Zelda kissed her, and thought, I will find a way.

They'd gone back to Ma Tempest's apartment many times, but those two girls, scared and desperate and dreaming, madwomen clutching each other as they drowned—those girls were the ones June had drawn here, on this bed, watching each other with simpering and easy love, like characters in a kid's cartoon where all you had to do was talk your problems out to fix them. Zelda hadn't worn her hair that way since freshman year.

That was what June thought she was heading into. A lover's quarrel maybe, some kind of story with easy endings, not one where people fell and broke and hurt each other. She thought this was an adventure. She thought she could save Sal. Or Sal and Zelda both. That there was something left to save.

Zelda checked her watch. June hadn't been gone for long. There was still time. The dryer wasn't done, but close enough.

She packed quickly. She'd had practice. She filled her water bottle from their sink, stole some granola bars and ground coffee from the cabinets, and considered leaving a note for Ma, but decided not to. She'd come here to apologize—but it didn't seem right to apologize to Ma, not now that Sal was coming home.

Her shoes were still damp. They'd dry when she started running.

She hefted her pack, adjusted the straps. The statues glared at her. She felt guilty. Of course she did. *But, hell, statues, what do you want? For me to take June along, drag her into the same mess? Sure, if Sal comes back, she'll be in trouble sooner or later—but let's say I can stop her. What do you think that's going to cost? I'm going to die.*

That was it: she was going to die. The others who'd made the first mistakes by her side—Ramón and Ish and Sarah—they might join her, help her. But June deserved her own life, not the echo of her cousin's.

Zelda remembered the look on June's face as she walked into the sky. Something like ecstasy.

She was making excuses. She was good at it. She'd had practice.

She took the drawing off the wall and folded it in quarters, with a crease between her and Sal, over their clasped hands. She slipped the paper into her jacket's inside pocket, then slipped out the window and down the fire escape.

As the Bronx settled over her like a wet, microwaved blanket, she told herself she was doing the right thing. Sal would never have wanted June mixed up in this. If she did, she would have told June the whole thing herself. (Of course, June had been a child then. But she was still a child. Just taller. Two years younger than Zelda herself had been when she found the road.)

Wrought iron dug into her palms. Her calluses flaked rust from old metal. She dangled from the fire escape, let herself fall to the pavement, landed in a crouch.

She pulled her hood up, stuck her hands into still-damp pockets, and walked toward the subway, toward Sal, and most of all, away.

She was just crossing the Graham Triangle, feeling the knot between her shoulder blades untie, when she heard a familiar voice behind her shout, "Zelda!"

Stupid. Should have taken the long way round. Made for the Willis Avenue

Bridge rather than the subway, avoided large open spaces with clear sight lines. But if Zelda's luck were any good at all, she would never have had to learn how to make her own.

June was crossing the triangle in the opposite direction, carrying two tote bags of the supplies Zelda had hoped it would take her longer to assemble. She'd stopped halfway across the street. She didn't know what she was seeing. She'd been so ready for a mission, for a quest. When life didn't work out that way, she teetered like a car that took a hairpin turn too fast, skidding on two wheels.

June was younger, stronger, she had longer legs and fewer injuries. But in one respect at least, Zelda had June beat: she had more practice at leaving.

She ran.

June wasted breath calling after her—a mistake. Zelda found her speed and opened up distance as fast as she'd ever run from spike-haired *Mad Max* rejects in any broke-down rotted alt. Faster. She wasn't running for safety this time. She was running for her soul.

There wasn't a walk sign on Rider. She lunged out into traffic. Cars roared toward her, around her. She darted between them. Exhaust fumes and the burnt rubber stench of brake pads seared her nostrils. She trailed horns and curses. She did not die. She did not die some more.

When she reached the sidewalk, gasping, she wasted a glance over her shoulder—June with tote bags sprinting after. God, but the kid could cover ground. But she waited for the cars to pass, chose her moment, while Zelda charged ahead.

The next two streets had walk signs, worse luck—she heard June shout her name again, wasted breath. When you were sixteen, you could afford to call out while running. June was gaining and Zelda had only the barest shape of a plan.

She'd meant to hop the subway and disappear into the crowd. But the timing was tricky. If the train came too soon, June would see her get on and catch her. Too late and she'd be stuck on the platform. She was doing the right thing, but she didn't think she could convince June of that. In some cities, she could have tweaked the timing of the trains, but she'd spent too much spin today, and she had no way to gather more until she left New York.

Her lungs were full of acid and her legs were made of lead, and the girl chasing her was bold, fit, sixteen, and furious.

Zelda was out of good options. Might as well focus on the bad ones. As per fucking usual.

Ahead, Third Ave–138th Street. "Welcome home," Sal had said the first time she led Zelda up the stairs. People streaming out—three teenagers with backpacks, loping, joking; a young man with a kid in a sling; an old man in a three-piece suit, a rolled-up dirty magazine sticking out of his jacket pocket—train brakes squealing. Bad sign. She grabbed the railing, cornered hard, took the steps three at a time past teenagers and dad and the man in the suit, who cursed after her. Swiped her card and hit the revolving iron gate as June apologized her way down the stairs after her.

The platform was empty. The train was gone.

She stopped at the downtown side, hands propped on her thighs to keep from falling. Dizzy with her own breath. The air down here tasted of garbage and clay. A rat ran along the tracks and disappeared into the darkness. Far away, something large and made of metal growled.

"Zelda, stop." June stumbled through the gate, breathing hard, shining with sweat. "Zelda, you said I could go with you. You promised." That last word ached. What else had the world promised June? What other promises had it broken? She was so tired of running.

"She promised me too," Zelda said. Promised that they'd stay together. And what had Zelda promised in return?

June understood. That understanding worked on her like a chisel, hollowing her out. Zelda caught a glimpse of the face the world would carve from June's in another ten years, or twenty.

"I want to go," June said, as if life could possibly be that clean, that easy. "I want to help."

"You don't know what happened. What we were. What it was like."

"So *teach* me!" The growl neared. A train screamed in the underground dark. June stepped forward, one hand out. "You're not the only one who loved her. You're not the only one she left."

But Zelda's heart was a trap, was a pit lined with thorns and teeth pointing in, and if she forgot that for an instant, if she let Sal's little cousin force her to care about someone else, to see herself as some kind of mentor or responsible adult rather than the universe's most colossal fuckup, if she believed the lie of that charcoal drawing in her jacket pocket, then she'd break herself to pieces and break this girl too. She had a fate to meet, a fate she'd stumbled away from years ago. It was a bad fate. But it was hers.

Just a little further.

She jumped onto the tracks.

She landed in the muck between the rails and ran into the darkness, into the growl of the oncoming train.

June screamed after her, the words lost in echoes. Zelda ran until the dark crushed her in its teeth.

Nine million people lived in New York, give or take. More had seen its skyline on television, had read descriptions of it in books. Its avenues were cataloged, its street corners canonized. The subway, too, was known. But all those people, all those stories, also knew: there could be anything in the subway tunnels. Mutant turtles. Giant alligators. CHUDs. Beasts. Labyrinths and lost temples, palaces and lakes. Anything at all.

She ran toward the train.

She ignored its voice, ignored June's cries. Focused on the clay, the musky smell of river water. On her footsteps, echoing forever.

She almost wanted it not to work. Wanted the city to hold her here until the train crushed her into salsa. She'd failed so much and left so much else behind. How perfect and easy to end here, spared Sal, spared one more journey into the country's sick heart and one final failure.

But that would be an easier end than she deserved.

The train roared and rumbled closer now. It shook the ground beneath her feet. She might not even feel it. An instant, that's how long an ending takes. It would be easy, brave, tragic, almost kind.

So, of course, in the instant before the train, her spin found purchase and the world opened and closed flicker-step fast, and she landed on her knees, weeping in undercity dust, surrounded by skeletons, somewhere altogether Else.

# CHAPTER FOUR

Zelda walked through the underworld alone.

Her flashlight beam found skeletons clutching the rails or one another, ribs tangled in embrace. Scraps of cloth hung from dead arms. She tried not to crush the scattered finger bones underfoot. Sometimes she succeeded. In America, you never could walk without stepping on corpses. Sarah had taught her that. In some Americas, the truth was more literal than others.

You went to a new America like a cop to the scene of a crime. Not just any crime, but one of those real charnel houses, where you had to bring in cold, dead-eyed techs to pick apart the meat and molars on the floor and tell how many bodies were there. Everything was wrong. A child's plastic teething ring glittered undecayed beneath a skeleton's hand, but she did not see a child's skeleton to match it. A memory, maybe, dragged down here as the crowd rushed in to escape—what? Not a gas attack. Anything heavier than air would be worse belowground. Not a flood. Human violence? Riots? Invasion? Bombs?

You'd never emerge in an America that killed you at once. To cross into an alt, you had to see yourself inside it—and human minds did not like to envision worlds where they could not exist. So they'd walked nuclear glasslands without dying of radiation sickness. They never turned left into a city flooded with hydrofluoric acid. They had found plague lands, Americas where the groundwater would poison you or drive you mad, they'd found death cults aplenty and all manner of aftermath. You might fall to your death, or catch rabies, or a bullet. But you were safe in the instant of your crossing.

At least, that's how they thought it worked. It was always possible, Ish had pointed out, that they were just blind lucky.

(That's what spin was, Ramón said back. You were lucky, until you weren't.)

After you came through, you asked questions. Once in a while, you had enough evidence to work out whys and whats and wherefores. Sal always wanted to find some fix, someone who could be saved, some answer. But there was little justice to be done. Sometimes they'd find people to help, but helping survivors did not bring back what they'd lost. The most you could do was witness.

The tunnels were larger than the ones back home. Her footsteps echoed.

She had been an idiot. If she'd died, if she hadn't found a way out of the city before the train hit her, who would stop Sal? June would have done just fine on the road. Zelda could have used her. She wanted to spare her, to spare Ma. But what did that matter, against Sal and the end of everything? Small, to compare the life of a family with the life of a world.

The problem with trying to be a hero was that much of the time, you sounded like a psychotic narcissist. And vice versa. Anyway, the world was doing a good-enough job of killing itself without any help from monstrosities Outside.

She had to focus. She had tickets on Amtrak out of Penn Station this afternoon, bound south and west, back to her Subaru and the open road. There would be time for second-guessing on the highway. For now, she had to make her train. Which meant navigating a dead subway system over and through these bodies, and finding a soft place to climb out and back home. Before Sal—before the thing that wore Sal's face, that used her like an anglerfish used a lure—smelled her through the alts and chased her down.

So, first: Where was she going?

Forward. Away from June. Just march and tell yourself: She would have died if she came with you. You saved her life. That's something. Let it be enough.

She fished her compass from her pack. The needle spun, glinted under her flashlight. It settled at last pointing behind her. The tunnel led south. As long as it did, she would follow it and hope it was uninhabited. Hope it wasn't flooded under the river. (There would be a river here. Every alt had the river, or the place the river used to be.) She couldn't guess when she might find an exit. All this place shared with the New York she'd left behind was a stretch of tunnel.

She walked south.

Something scurried in the black behind her.

She spun around, aware all of a sudden of just how many things could live in a down-below space like this. Dark, warmer than the outside world, and damp. She'd joked about alligators in the sewers, but there were rats—clever and kind when they weren't hungry, but they could eat through steel, crest over people like a wave and leave nothing more than bone behind. There would be stranger things than rats down here, in the depths of this dead world. But she did not know them yet, so she imagined rat teeth, white and wet, and small, red, hungry eyes.

Her flashlight swept the tunnel. Empty. Train tracks ran off into the shadows, the gap between them damp. Bones everywhere, ribs jutting up. Teeth knocked free of jawbones lay like gravel between subway ties. The metal glinted, the water was flat and muddy dull. She heard a drop of water fall from a great height into an unseen pool.

Nothing moved. What had she heard?

A mouse. A rat. Some bones she'd jostled as she passed, settling into a new position. Whatever it was, it had stopped. The light scared it. If there was an *it*.

*Calm down. This isn't anything you haven't seen before. Just dead people. Tunnels. You know how this goes.*

But back when she was used to this kind of mess, Sal had been there, Sal and Ish and Ramón and Sarah. Together there was nothing they couldn't do, no one they couldn't beat. Even running from monsters was fun when you had friends to do it with. The horror set in when you were alone, without anyone to make you brave, without anyone to help you pretend death was one huge joke. No one to say, I've been down here before. I know the way out.

Something wet touched her cheek.

She screamed, spun, flailed out with the flashlight, caught nothing. Her ankle turned in the muck and she fell hard, hit her shoulder on the rail, bit her lip as her head bounced off a tie.

The flashlight went out.

She swore. The curses echoed in the perfect darkness of the tunnel. She'd seen where the flashlight fell. More or less.

Unless she'd turned around as she pulled herself to her knees. Her breath sounded so loud. Had she turned as she fell? She tried to remember. Tiny lights danced before her eyes in the dark. Your mind could not bear an absence of light. It imposed patterns on blackness. She'd read about that back at school. Colors came from nothing. Come on. Focus. You didn't hit your head *that* hard.

The flashlight had fallen to her left. She had not turned when she rose to her knees. It would be there.

Her hand found water and mud and, groping in horror in the dark, at last, the knurled metal of the flashlight's grip.

Panting, desperate, she lurched to her feet and turned the flashlight on.

Or tried.

It didn't light.

She heard the scurrying again, closer. Louder. And in many places at once. It was a harsh sound, like nails scraping the inside of a casket. She slapped the flashlight twice, three times. She'd bought it from a military surplus store in Tennessee with a Vietnam-era jeep on bricks out front, from a gawky auction hunter with a peppery goatee who followed her around the store asking too many questions about where she'd come from and where she was going. Waterproof, he'd said. Used one just like it myself. She didn't ask in what war so he didn't have to lie about it. She'd hoped he wasn't lying about it being waterproof.

More scurrying. It was a mouse. It had to be. Just a mouse. Believe in the mouse. Forget that when you stepped into an alternate New York just a few hours ago, the sky boiled into the shape of your ex-girlfriend, and she said she was coming back for you, and that had been on a bridge in plain view of the whole damn Bronx, and this was a forgotten tunnel in the dark. Forget that Sal—this thing you can't stop calling Sal even though she's gone, devoured, digested in one of the many bellies of an incomprehensible beast that lurks out past the edge of sense—forget that she has your scent. Know: it's just a mouse.

She slapped the flashlight so hard it made the small bones of her hand hurt, and tore her scabs. The bulb flickered. The scurrying was close now, loud beneath the rush of her own panicked breath. She turned, blind, at bay, and shook the flashlight one last desperate time.

And the bulb lit.

The scurrying stopped.

Bones cast shadows in the flashlight beam, down the tunnel until the light gave out. She saw no trace of movement. No jawbone teetered, disturbed by passing feet or a flicking tail. The puddles between the train tracks lay murky and still. Her breath echoed over the dead.

A cold hand closed around her heart. She knew what she *should* do next, but she couldn't bear to. If you didn't look, if you left the page unturned and the secret undiscovered, surely you'd be safe. If you don't open the closet, neither will the monster. All you have to give in trade for your survival is the knowledge that the monster is in the closet, and your hand is always inches from the door.

She looked up.

The ceiling was studded with jewels.

Then she raised the flashlight, and the jewels boiled away from its beam—flowed down the sides of the tunnel wall like a flock of starlings, that same blooming, writhing jellyfish motion composed, on closer look, of simple, single points.

Some of the jewels fell, tumbling, their clawed legs dislodged from the brick. Two splattered against bone or rail. A third landed on the back of Zelda's wrist.

The jewel was a beetle the size of a half-dollar, with a smoky iridescent shell and delicate legs. It clapped its long mandibles twice in the air. It chirped. Then, with terrifying speed, it buried its mandibles in her arm.

She screamed. The pain, burning through her forearm, almost made her drop the flashlight, but sheer will and terror kept her hand clutched around the metal. She had a vision of what would happen if she dropped the light, of beetles closing around her like a fist, shredding her flesh in the dark, and here in a tunnel it would all be over, in some backwoods alt without friends or backup and with no one left but June to know that Sal was coming. All of that for nothing. All the road she had walked and all the people she'd hurt, all those ten long years seeking forgiveness for her sins. That vision kept her grip tight for those agonizing quarter seconds before her free hand tore the beetle from her arm and flung it away.

Her arm burned. Blood slicked her grip on the light. She was breathing rabbit fast, her chest tight, her eyes wide, her scream's echoes buzzing in her ears. And that buzz was real—the beetles on the tunnel walls flicking their wings and casting reflections like moonlight on the swells of a cliff-walled bay.

They scurried down the walls away from her flashlight beam—toward her.

She ran.

Her flashlight beam fell on a writhing carpet of beetles over the tracks ahead. They surged away from the light, scrambling over one another to make a lane as narrow as the beam. She sprinted down that path and heard the buzz and scurry behind as beetles closed over the tracks, chasing her. She was faster, but there were so many of them and they were so close, their buzzing and scurrying inside her bones, and the *click-click-click* of tiny hungry jaws. They smelled her blood.

She ran down the path her light made between the mobs of bugs.

She had lived through worse, she told herself. It was even true. Chased three times by dinosaurs, countless times by subhuman irradiated mutant weirdos, by robots, by the rulers of the Green Glass City, and that one time by the Gun Cult on Meriamne's World. But they had been kids back then. They hardly knew what pain was yet. Born in soft peacetime afternoons, in the heart of an empire, they'd taken the prospect of risk, of death, for a kind of game. They had learned the truth at Elsinore.

She'd lived through worse. That didn't mean she would live through this.

There had been a logo on that beetle's back. Distorted, as a tattoo might be if the person who wore it gained forty pounds—but too self-contained and geometric for natural coloring. Someone made those beetles. Someone had chased people down here into the dark, and loosed the beetles to feed.

She was tired. No, *tired* made it sound as if you wanted to go to sleep. She wanted to spit out her lungs. Living on the road wore you hard, but it didn't keep you in hell-sprint-from-beetles shape. For years she had been careful, which meant lazy. She stayed away from the alts—from just this kind of mess. She walled these border worlds out so no one could stumble into them. Of course, there was only so "in shape" you could be for something like this.

A beetle fell into her hair, and she slapped it off before it could do more than cut a small line in her scalp. They closed in. Jaws snatched at her shoes, tearing canvas and rubber. She risked flashing her light back behind her—the carpet of beetles that was chasing her halted, while ahead others crunched like the bones beneath her feet. When she cast the light back in front of her, the lane she ran had narrowed to the width of a garden wall. She trampled bugs as she fled.

Her arm was on fire. Her arm was numb. Her hand slipped on the flashlight. And her legs weighed more with every step.

Ahead—she had to be imagining it—she almost wept—would have wept if she'd had the breath to weep—the tunnel widened. Ahead, she saw a shimmering light.

Chest heaving, she forced herself faster. The flashlight guttered. Bugs buzzed. Hungry chorus. Somehow, she crossed the distance and burst out of the tunnel into a cavern.

Not a cavern. A station.

It had been gilded once. The paint dulled and chipped with time, but mosaic tiles still clung to the high vaulted ceiling, a night sky with constellations she did not recognize. And there, at the apex of the vault—a skylight, its stained glass shattered. Beyond that skylight . . .

Blue.

Blinding. Her eyes watered after so long in the dark. A pool of sunlight fell on the broad platform between the tracks.

Bugs poured out of the tunnel after her.

There—a ladder up to the platform. She dropped her flashlight into the tool loop in her jeans, or tried. It slipped out of her numb, bloody fingers, and bugs swarmed over it when it landed. Shit. There wasn't even time to get angry at herself for dropping it. She could hate herself later, if she lasted that long.

Get to the light.

Her right hand would barely close on the ladder's rungs. Fortunately her left and her feet could do the work. She hooked her right wrist behind the rungs for balance, and in three hard jerks she lay on the platform, gasping.

Behind her, bugs spilled over the platform's lip, tumbling over other bugs, quicksilver, hungry.

God.

You can do it. A few more steps. Don't think, don't feel. If you let yourself feel right now, you're dead and this is all for nothing. Feeling is for later. Go.

Just a little further.

With a roar wrung from her belly, with a burst of strength from her legs and her good arm, she launched herself off the concrete, a scuttling crablike lunge, more pounce and fall than sprint. Her ankle turned on her third step, another spark of pain. There was buzzing, clicking all around. But she could *see* the circle of light. She would not be some near case, some Junior Great Books tragedy.

Almost there.

She gathered her screaming body, leapt—and fell.

Rolled.

She came to rest, sobbing, in light.

A scuttling ocean of bugs surrounded her, but they stayed just outside the sunlit circle's edge. Zelda lay panting there. The throbbing pain in her ankle eased. The bite in her arm felt like someone had cut her open and sewn coals inside.

She might have died just now.

She might still die, just now.

When Zelda first set out on the road, she would come through scrapes and realize, days later, joking about how drunk she'd been or how near the car had come to spinning out, just how close she had been to being dead. The older she got, the nearer the realization came to the event. Now the one ran on the other's heels. Someday the awareness would eclipse the moment, and then it would happen. It wasn't all that different from slipping into the alts. You had to see a possibility to embrace it. And when the possibility of death closed out all others—well, there you were.

She was spinning off. Vagueing. Disassociating, was that what Sarah called it? You played games with concepts to protect yourself from where you were, the feelings you felt. Walk back into your body. Start with sensation. Live here now, you useless, overeducated mess-person. Find a path that will keep you alive until later.

Pain in the arm. A stitch in her side. Hell, more like a spear in her side. The world flexed around her with the urgency of her breath. Queasy. Tears on her cheek. Concrete pebbles pressed into the side of her face. She tasted copper. When had she bit her cheek? Or her tongue? When she fell. When she landed.

She was staring, she realized, into the blank eye sockets of a skull.

Fine. With her good hand, she pushed herself up. She sat in a pool of light. The skylight above was a deep thick well cut through rock to the surface, its sides overgrown with moss and ivy. The light would move as the sun moved, and quickly. Direct sunlight kept the bugs away. So, once the sun passed the well's edge, she would be stuck down here with the bugs and her skeleton friend.

Something tugged at the toe of her right shoe. She kicked by reflex, felt a weight that should not have been there fly off into the dark, saw a glittering iridescent parabola as the bug sailed off from her shoe to splash into the others. Sitting up, she had shifted to bring her foot into the shadow. Or the sun was already moving on.

There was a hole in her sneaker. Her foot was bleeding. She hadn't lost any toes. Yet.

Get your shit together, Z. You don't have much time.

The subway platform was ornate and ruined and covered with bones. On one track rested the gleaming chrome hulk of a train that belonged in a Norman Rockwell painting. Its windows were busted and the sides streaked with a substance that might have been rust. All these skeletons had been running from the surface. They'd come down to the tunnels to die.

There had to be stairs. An elevator. A ramp.

There was—behind her. A winding iron stair with thick iron cage walls, rising to the arched ceiling. The cage should keep the beetles out. It looked like a deeply impractical way to enter a subway—there must be elevators somewhere, wider stairs—but maybe a long-ago architect thought winding staircases looked cool. Anyway, she didn't see another option that wasn't crawling with bugs.

The bugs covered the platform now, a quivering, rolling surface like a pond's in high wind, pushing over and through one another to reach her, only to fall back, hissing, as they edged the circle of light. Their hisses, the click of their mandibles, the tick of their claws filled the cavern. They were hungry, desperately hungry, and a carpet of them lay between her and the stairs and, maybe, safety.

There's your problem, Z. Figure it out.

She realized then: She would not let herself die here. No matter how bleak it seemed, no matter how her arm hurt or how little daylight she had left.

She had run from June to save her. But if she didn't make it out of this tunnel, no one would face Sal. One day the sky would rip open, and that would be it for June, and Ma Tempest, and all the rest. She would have left June behind for nothing.

Christ, she hated New York.

First things first: the wound in her arm.

It did not look good. The ragged edges of the bite oozed blood. Around the wound, her skin was puffy and red. Closing her fist hurt and took the kind of concentration she normally associated with trying to cut a deck of cards using just one hand. Her dad had taught her emergency first aid for rattlesnake bites, you cut the skin and tried to suck the poison out, but the Boy Scout manual she carried in her pack had a big red X printed over its diagram of the procedure. The risks were greater than the risks of the bite.

Sunlight glinted off a tiny silver speck caught in the wound. She found her first aid kit, sterilized her tweezers with her lighter flame, and, biting down on a folded belt, drew a small curved sliver of mandible from the bite. When it was out, she sagged, breathing heavy. A rope of spit dangled from her mouth. The pain lost some of its urgency. She could make a fist without wincing, much. It was a start.

She splashed iodine on the cut and groaned as it bubbled. Gauze next, first to mop up the blood, then for the bandage. She threw the dirty gauze pad to the bugs. They scrambled over one another, savaging themselves for a snap at it, and she heard herself laugh. They were just dumb creatures. They could eat her, sure, but they were puppets to their hunger.

As if she wasn't.

Bandaged, she surveyed her surroundings again. The circle of sunlight was an oval now, tracking in a direction she figured was east. Faster than she expected. The winding stair remained bug-free. Her skeleton friend lay still beside her, bones gnawed, grinning.

"You're a model of perseverance," she told the skeleton. It did not respond.

She needed light. She needed a path to the stair.

Her lighter wasn't enough. She could make a torch—but her clothing was quick-dry stuff, designed to wash in a rest stop sink, dry overnight, and wear the next morning. It would melt before it would burn. The same went for her towel and her backpack. Even her still-damp jeans had been at most introduced to cotton at some point in the manufacturing process. There was an essay here, if she survived to write it, on flexibility and design and repurposability, a *Seeing Like a State* sort of riff. But she'd have to think of a new example. Her present circumstances weren't exactly relatable.

Vaguing out again. Focus.

Gauze would burn too fast. Her candle wouldn't give enough light. Coat the gauze in wax? No time. Paper, same problem as the gauze. Magnesium shavings from her fire starter would flash, not hold a flame. The thermal blanket, too, would melt before burning. She should have a cotton T-shirt in her pack just in case. Something to add to June's list.

She missed the kid. It would have been wrong to bring her. But what right did Zelda have to leave her behind? Zelda might have caused this mess, Zelda and Sal and their whole generation, but June had to live in it, just as she, Zelda, had to live in all the other messes older generations left. Simple wars weren't. Deferred costs could not be put off forever. It didn't matter if it was your parents or your grandparents or theirs who wrecked the climate; you still faced the hurricanes.

The light was passing. She didn't have time. What she had was a bunch of stuff that wouldn't burn, and a bunch of stuff that would burn too quickly, and some bare gnawed bones and a circle of sunlight, and a turned ankle and a messed-up arm and—

And. Ah.

There was the answer—and that familiar feeling that you were a little clever, and a lot of an idiot for not having seen it before.

She unfolded the thermal blanket. Its reflective foil caught the sunlight. She lifted one side. It wasn't a mirror or a lens, but it cast a dim light into the bugs— and the bugs gave way. Clearing a lane to the stair.

Multipurpose items. This would do.

Now she just needed a way to prop up the blanket.

That, at least, was easier. She looked to the skeleton. "Sorry, friend."

Lashing femurs and humeri together with parachute cord from her pack, she made a loose rickety tripod and a frame from which she hung the blanket. By the time she was done, the oval of light was stretched and narrowing—but it should be enough. Just. She tied one end of her remaining parachute cord to the corner of the blanket. That way, she could adjust the angle of the light, if she had to.

The bugs gave way before the reflected light, grudgingly, all the way to the winding stair. Her skeleton friend's skull grinned at her, but the grin had an accusatory edge, which she had to admit was fair.

By way of apology, she took the skull and nestled it inside the tripod she'd made from its body. She patted its cheek, or the place where its cheek used to be.

Then she squared her shoulders, hoisted her pack, and limped onto the path of sunlight.

Step by teetering step, she walked between the hissing, angry, hungry bugs. She felt an unfamiliar sensation rise in her, beneath the sticky weight of fear and guilt: confidence. She could do this. She was doing it.

Not just surviving, as she had for the last decade, following her calculations and yarrow stalks from town to town to heal the ten thousand little cracks their failure had left in America. Not keeping low, scraping together part-time drifter's jobs, meeting again and again the migratory hordes of seventysomethings trying to stretch their social security to keep the camper in gas another month. Not treading water. Not hiding.

She was fighting back. She would spend herself, her spin and blood, her nails and teeth and dignity, to beat this thing, so people had a chance to go on making their own mistakes. So Mona wouldn't have to turn to monsters to find someone who might listen.

The beast beyond the edge of the world, the beast that took Sal and wore her skin, had finally followed her home. So Zelda would stand against it face-to-face, even if it towered dark and godlike in the sky. She would demand answers and she would get them. Or she would die. One way or another, this whole life of secret wars, of running and hiding and quivering beneath the memories of her mistakes—it would be over.

Her foot landed earlier than she expected, on cold metal. She stumbled, and caught herself with her good hand. The wrought iron staircase rang and shivered. Dust drifted down from the steps overhead.

She'd made it.

She looked down at the parachute cord and remembered reading *The Lord of the Rings*, which she checked out of the school library for weeks at a time. She remembered Sam's elven rope that untied itself by magic when Sam said *namarie* to it, which was goodbye in Elvish. She'd carried this cord for thousands of miles, and now it would end here. Stupid to feel bad for a mass-produced bit of nylon rope. But it was her rope. It had helped her bear all that crushing weight and weakness, so she could do what had to be done.

"*Namarie*," she said to the rope. And because the world was not magic, its knot held tight.

She let it go, and climbed. The stairway's cage door swung shut behind her.

Rust flaked and fell from the steps. Her footfalls rang through the empty station, over the dead bones. Bugs buzzed in answer. Far below now as she climbed and climbed, the oval of sunlight drifted east, narrowing through the middle and stretching into a long thin line, before it vanished. The silver tide closed over her bone lattice, her cord, her skeleton friend. Her tripod teetered, and toppled.

For a while the reflected light let her see the sea of bugs below, the iron stair around her, the glinting remnants of mosaic constellations overhead. Then even that glow failed and she was climbing, climbing, alone in the dark forever. She breathed dust. The air grew thick and heavy like it did before a storm.

She heard footsteps behind her, on the stair.

An echo, she told herself.

Someone back there in the deep started whistling, low and only roughly in tune. But she recognized the sound, even recognized the mistakes. That was "The Impossible Dream," from *Man of La Mancha*. Sal used to whistle that song that way.

Sal couldn't reach her in New York. The world was too thick, too observed, too known. But this was not New York.

She climbed faster. She would face Sal—when she was ready. Once she walked the trail again, and reached the crossroads, and could set things right. Not here, in the dark, bleeding and spineless, where all she could do was die.

Echoes—her own breath in her ears, that slow-tempo whistle—told her she'd climbed out of the cavern. There was rock on all sides of her now, or concrete. This could be any tunnel anywhere. And at the tunnel's end, soon, there would be a door.

Her groping fingers found it, a metal slab covered in flaking paint. There would be a latch—yes, there. It moved. She pushed—but the door did not open.

Stuck.

The whistling neared.

With a cry, with the heat of her will and spin, she threw herself against the door. Rust cracked. Hinges screamed.

Zelda tumbled, blinking, into unbearable light, into the hungry brown-gray concrete hole of a New York subway station, her New York, next to a half-disassembled MetroCard kiosk that a woman in an MTA uniform was frowning into. She turned over to look at Zelda, too confused to be angry.

"Sorry." Zelda waved her bloody hand, laughed. Try not to look too crazy, Z. "I got a little turned around." The door closed behind her, revealing a big DO NOT ENTER sign. "Other side was blank."

The MTA lady shrugged and turned back to her machine, as if Zelda, bloody, grimy, and giggling, was maybe the fourth-weirdest thing she'd seen today.

Zelda limped for the surface and the rest of her war.

＞—

After the tunnels, New York by day seemed muted and unreal. She stopped on a park bench to nurse her ankle, and the light, the grass, the shining buildings, blared around her. She felt like an actor on a children's theater stage, a real human amid primary colors and big paper props. How could this be whole and real, and the dead tunnel and the bodies and the beetles just a might-have-been? But she'd seen enough of the world to know that this city was by far the bigger miracle.

The bench hurt. She looked down and saw ridges welded into the metal—you could sit here for brief rests, but not long enough to recover. She cursed and pulled on her shoe. What did they call it in the magazines? "Oppositional architecture." Fuck.

A dirty guy in a tattered heavy flannel coat sat on the grass nearby, and at her curse he laughed and raised a Nalgene bottle in a toast. The liquid inside was clear, and she could smell the fumes. It wasn't paint thinner but only by a bit. She fished in her pocket—seven bucks left. She was done with this city. She limped over, sat down beside him, and set a five on the grass.

He said thanks, and, "Headed south?"

"West." She didn't know him, but he recognized her road-worn look.

"Watch yourself. Gets mean out west."

"Mean down south too. And here." She nodded back at the bench.

"Different mean," he said. Shrugged. "Still warm here for another month."

"When you leave, watch out. There's a storm coming."

He humphed into his Nalgene, waved with his fingers, and she staggered away.

She limped across town. Spin seeped into her. She looked at the city like a stranger, a ghost, bright and glowing without a trace of substance. She drifted into streets against the walk sign, heard car horns blare as if they were far, far away. Eyes drifted from her, refused to focus. Sal's whistle on the dark stair echoed in her ears, clearer and louder than the banker screaming into his cell phone, more real than the Times Square tourists shouting after their kids as they sprinted off to chase a fake Mickey Mouse. Dirty, bleeding, she was the kind of person the city cared about only if she lingered.

She crawled into Penn Station, as always, like a rat.

As the roof closed out the sky, with the weight of Madison Square Garden overhead, she felt a quick stab of terror, eased it with deep breaths. These lights would stay on. There were few flesh-eating beetles here. None, probably. The bright lights made an artificial day, and people of every description flitted around her, darting from the latte line to the sandwich shop, and always, always, checking their phones to see where they were, to remind themselves where they were going and why they were scared. In the last few years, as she spoke with people in gas stations in that way you did when you were traveling alone, she'd found this once-placid country growing into an uncomfortable awareness that things could change, violently and fast—but few people seemed to understand just how violently, just how fast. There was nothing special about this place. It was a country brave as a child who'd never broken a bone. The rot worked its way in.

Whistling.

The 3:15 south to DC by way of Philadelphia was on time, half an hour out. She limped to the women's restroom and washed the blood off her hands as well as she could. There was no soap here—all the dispensers either empty or out of order. She used a drop of Doc Bronner's from her pack, then drifted back to the main arrivals hall, a heartless high school gymnasium with a big black sign that announced the track numbers of the incoming trains at the last possible minute. As soon as a track was listed, a tide washed through the crowd, everyone bound for that train trying to be first in line for the escalator down to the track. The tides buffeted Zelda left and right. Men in camouflage stood by the walls, bearing automatic weapons. She had so little spin left, had gathered only shreds on her walk over. If they tried to shoot her, she'd be hard-pressed to make them miss.

She had a mission. She owed it to June. To everyone she'd betrayed to get this far. To Mona and, more than any of them, to Sal.

When her train's status switched to APPROACHING, she spent a trace of her remaining spin and walked without looking to gate 7W. She fished her journal from its plastic bag in her backpack, and took from the journal's back pocket the ticket she'd printed out on a library computer in West Virginia. The conductor scanned it without looking at her face. The line of passengers behind Zelda almost bowled her over as she descended the narrow escalator. She took the steps as fast as her ankle allowed, hobbled from the escalator to the train, and collapsed in a window seat.

She wove her legs through her backpack straps in case anyone tried to steal from her while she slept, and let herself sag against the window, her cheek puddled on darkness and her reflection. Her breath misted the glass. Tears welled in her eyes. She had not realized just how tired she was. Just how much she hurt. In that quiet moment as the train filled around her, she let go, stopped kicking to tread water, and sank.

The seat beside her was still empty when the train lurched into motion. A true miracle, one she hadn't even spun for. There were always better seats, it turned out, than the one next to a dirty crying woman with torn clothes and a bandaged wrist.

She almost wished—not that anyone would sit next to her but that someone she trusted would. That Ish or Ramón or even Sarah would just so happen to be on this southbound train. As long as she was dreaming, why not Sal? Sal as she used to be, searing and bold, who never took anyone's story at face value, Sal who laughed and would not back down.

She'd been right to leave June behind. That was the good, hard thing to do. But, God, she could use a partner now.

Someone sat beside her, saying nothing, and Zelda huddled closer to the window.

They emerged from the tunnel into dazzling light, and there was the city, just and pure and shining in its most perfect aspect, the city whose subways ran beneath the water table and would flood if the power went out for long, the city whose food supply depended on a single ailing underwater freight tunnel no government could find the political will to fix, even back when governments were still interested in fixing things. The city that stared so often into its own reflection that it could believe itself a fact of the universe, like gravity, and forget the tremendous monumental will, the million pyramids' worth of collective effort it took to keep the place itself day by day.

Arrogant. Naive. A kid sister who didn't understand why you warned her to be careful.

She would throw herself in front of trains to save it.

She sat straighter and watched it recede.

"So," June said beside her, "what's next?"

# CHAPTER FIVE

June remembered Sal and Zelda, and loved them, but love, she said, was not the same thing as trust. So while Zelda showered, June had looked through her bag until she found the paper ticket folded in the journal behind the maps. Just in case.

June nudged her own bright yellow backpack with her sneaker toe. "Couldn't find everything you asked for. But it's a start. And I was in a hurry."

Zelda couldn't speak. All her words lay entombed somewhere back under Penn Station.

It felt the way pastors she had liked told her miracles were supposed to feel: an inevitable and unearned grace, perfect as a puzzle piece or the punch line of a good joke.

June was still a kid. She wasn't used to silences yet, to words so deep-rooted that to say them was to tear open the black, damp surface of the earth. Zelda saw her read the silence as anger and disappointment, and rush to fill the gap.

"I won't let you do this alone. She's out there, and if there is a chance to save her, I have to try. You need my help."

The words had a suspicious polish. She must have practiced this. They'd already had this fight in her head.

"This is my world, too, Z. I know it's ending. Every year the summers are hotter and the storms are worse. If there is something I can do, you have to let me. It's like you think all of this is on you because you failed, but that's some wrongheaded, individualist horseshit. This is not just your problem and it's not just your fault and you won't fix it solo. We got to do this together."

She finished, bare and honest, and Zelda felt so unworthy of this girl that she almost missed the moment when June's conviction began to wilt—when she realized she'd jumped on the Amtrak with a woman she barely knew, a woman who ran in front of a train to get away from her. Seeing that wilt hurt more than the beetle's jaws hurt in her arm.

She hugged June close and tight, so sudden she drove the breath from the kid's chest. It was easier to do that than to speak. June sat frozen by the speed of it, and by disbelief—until she sagged into Zelda, hugged her back, soft at first then desperately tight, tighter than when she was drowning in the Hudson.

"I'm sorry," Zelda said. It was easier without ten years of run-up. Then, something like reality asserting itself: "What about Ma?"

"She'll understand."

That did not seem likely. "What about school?"

"What about it?"

Fair.

"You best have some money with you, though," June said. "Spent what I had on this ticket."

She thought of the couple bucks in her pocket and the small roll she'd left in the rattletrap Subaru in the Philly lot. "We'll get by," she said. For the first time in she did not know how long, she meant it.

---

June stepped onto the platform at 30th Street Station in Philadelphia with more ceremony than seemed proper—a glance behind her, a close of the eyes, a whispered prayer, and a taut breath as though she were about to dive into deep waters. A large woman with a briefcase shouldered past her, too locked on her cell phone to glower effectively.

An outlandish possibility occurred to Zelda, chilling in its implications. "Have you ever left New York?"

The confused, cock-headed reaction almost relieved her, until June said, "Why would I?"

Well. Everyone started somewhere. She shouldered her bag—winced at the pain in her wrist. Once she was back on the road, her spin would take care of the infection—probably—but it hurt like a bastard and she'd need that arm for driving. "Well, don't gawk. We have places to be."

June gawked, following her, taking the city in—the station that wasn't Grand Central, the buildings too squat and too far apart to belong to her city. They built with different rules here. June studied the place without awe and with only a little fear—a hunter in an unfamiliar forest, seeking patterns she could use.

"Where's the Liberty Bell?"

"Across town. We're not going."

"This *is* my first time out of New York, you know."

"We have a job to do."

"But we're not exactly on the clock, are we?"

"Outside of the fact that if we don't win, we die and so does everyone else, no. We are not technically on the clock."

They'd been walking through the parking garage, winding up levels. At last they reached the Subaru. Zelda opened the door, threw her backpack into the passenger seat, slapped the roof and felt it firm under her palm—real and solid. She'd been swimming in dark water, and this was land.

"Zelda."

June stood across the car from her, by the passenger seat, which was full of Zelda's bag.

"Sorry." She got in and tossed the bag into the back seat, where it landed in a jangle of loose change. "Habit."

But June, she saw, hadn't been bothered about the bag in particular. Zelda considered the car in its altogether. Scraped paint, dented sides, patches of rust, a chunk near the rear left taillight kept on with duct tape.

Zelda tried to take care of the Subaru. She did. But the car looked like what it was: a live-in beater owned by a woman who'd been on the road for a very long time, a station wagon that had been, occasionally, mauled by dinosaurs. She did her best—cleaned the upholstery with good soap and a toothbrush to get the hard-to-reach bits, vacuumed and buffed and polished, but the fact remained that most American cars stood idle 90 percent of the time and were not built to be full-time living-slash-interdimensional-exploratory vehicles. She didn't mind the Subaru's appearance any more than she minded her own. She had grown accustomed to it: her weapon, her tool, her home. "It drives better than it looks."

June's glance said, I hope so. She added aloud: "You don't think we're coming out of this alive."

Zelda could lie. But the steering wheel was under her palms, and what was the point of the road if you lied to yourself while you were on it? "It's a long way to the crossroads. You saw what's out there. There's still time to turn back." If that was enough to scare June off, she wouldn't be here anyway.

June got in, shut the door. When it didn't latch on her first try, she slammed it shut. The slam faded, leaving a high ringing note behind. That was the sound of your brain working, someone had told Zelda once. Or it was tinnitus. Or the voice of angels in the ether. "I'm driving to my death in a broke-down Subaru."

"You're being driven. Technically. *Can* you drive?"

Again, that what-do-you-take-me-for look, which Zelda figured meant "no." "I want to see the Liberty Bell."

Zelda turned the key. Her heart eased as the engine churned. Under the car's hood, cylinders compressed aerosolized gasoline until it exploded, driving the car forward. Strange that hundreds of tiny explosions a minute could sound so soothing. She felt warm in here, safe inside this bubble of aluminum and steel, behind a four-chambered artificial heart.

"Let's go," she said, and they went.

—

They sneaked in to see the Liberty Bell by riding the wake of a Scandinavian tour group. The only other guests in the small museum were a field trip of grade school children running around tackling one another as their teacher tried to guide them through the exhibit. While most of the kids played tag, one large, dark-haired boy in glasses methodically circled the room, reading every plaque.

The bell hung just off the ground, from a wooden crosspiece. It was always larger than Zelda expected, even though she'd seen it many times. On stamps and postcards and in history books, you lost a sense of scale. The real thing became a shadow of the icon. But the bell had been cast to ring and ring loud, and it was cast large.

Its crack always looked fake to her, because it looked just like the crack in the pictures.

Sal had insisted on visiting every time they passed through Philadelphia. She liked the crack. "It's a good reminder," she said, and each time Zelda had asked her, "Of what?" she got a different answer. There were too many stories about the bell, and most of them were false, or mythical, which wasn't the same thing. Did it ring for independence? Maybe. It was that old, but there were no records of it having been rung on that occasion, and its bell tower had been all rotten through in the summer of 1776, so, maybe not. Did it crack when it rang for the death of John Marshall? For Lafayette? Or just when some enthusiastic bell ringer struck it wrong on a Tuesday or let a kid try ringing it, thinking, What's the worst that could happen? It wasn't even called the Liberty Bell until abolitionists started calling it that, to shame Philadelphians who weren't doing enough to free people from slavery.

The bell was like the country—when first cast, it sounded lousy when struck. You had to recast it again and again to get something that rang well. And then, of course, it cracked. But it was still here.

June punched her in the arm. "Selfie?"

Zelda half turned into a camera flash. June laughed at her face in the photo on the phone.

"You'll have to throw that out."

"The photo? It's not going on the gram or anything."

"The phone."

It disappeared into June's jacket before Zelda could blink. "No way."

"It's the only way. Give."

"You're kidding."

"To gather spin, you need uncertainty. You can't know exactly where you are—you have to let yourself discover. And you can't let other people know where you are either. The more people are looking, the less you can change."

"I won't tell anyone."

"Doesn't matter. That thing talks to the internet a few hundred times a second. The GPS chip you use to get directions tells Google right where you are. With one of those things in your pocket, you're always under surveillance."

"I'll turn it off."

"Doesn't work. The chip can draw power as long as the battery's connected, and you can't take out the batteries anymore. Did you ever wonder why that was?"

June drew back, one hand on her jacket pocket over the device.

"So I say, let's go stop monsters from beyond the edge of the world, and maybe die, and you're fine with that, but I say, ditch your cell phone, and all of a sudden we have an issue?"

"What are we even trying to do here?"

"I'm sorry?"

"What happens next? How do we stop her? What's the game plan?"

"You need to know that before you give up your phone?"

"You've never had one, have you?"

"I don't see what that has to do with anything. You left Ma with just a note. Why is this such a problem?"

"Because Ma's right here." Tapping the phone. "And everybody else I know too. You want me to disappear."

"I don't *want* you to do anything. I wanted to do this on my own."

"That's not happening. So tell me the plan."

A group of tall blond women with a long selfie stick took a photo with the crack in the bell.

"Unless you don't know. Is that it? You don't have a plan?"

Zelda closed her eyes, pinched the bridge of her nose. She hadn't wanted to have this fight in public. The sky felt heavy. Somewhere, a raven croaked. They were too far south for ravens, she'd thought, but she'd never been a bird-watcher.

Blood drummed in her temples. No—that wasn't inside her. And the sound wasn't drumming. It was footsteps.

She opened her eyes.

June stood taut and angry before the crack in the Liberty Bell.

There was something behind her.

From the crack in the bell, long, spindly arms unfolded, as many-jointed as insect limbs. Hooked claws at their tips dripped shadow.

The tourists laughed and took another picture. The schoolkids tumbled. Only the boy in glasses stopped and stared, ashen with horror.

The rot should not be able to break through here. This place was known. Recorded. But the bell people thought they knew it wasn't the real bell. This was the real one, nestled inside the stories like a speck of sand inside an oyster. And a crack was a crack was a crack. Under the right pressure, any one could open.

"June," she said calmly, "walk toward me. Please."

The teen didn't move—frozen by the thought of what might be behind her, or by her read of Zelda's expression. The limbs kept unfolding, joint after joint, their barbed tips bent tenderly in. They dripped ichor that burned the concrete floor where it fell. And no one noticed. The Swedes took another picture—the flash cast more shadows from the solid blackness of those limbs. A girl ran past, her jacket flaring pink behind her, tied around her neck like a cape. Only the kid with the glasses saw—not what he was supposed to see, but what was really there. His hand stretched out, trembling.

June seemed many-handed, like the goddess statues in museums. She flowered with arms.

The flower closed.

Zelda was faster. She shoved June out of the way and dived across the railing, into the arms' embrace. Her hand darted into the crack in the bell. The darkness burned cold. Her fingers closed around something wet and slick and round on the other side of the crack, cased in wriggling dark.

The arms seized her. She heard a bell—*the* bell—ringing, muffled and grotesque.

The arms did not carve her. They wrapped her in a gentle, bladed embrace and drew her toward the crack. She caught herself against the bell, pushed back with all her strength, bleeding as the arms cut her, and she tugged on that piece of grit, the hidden secret. She was not strong enough. Her cheek pressed against hot hard metal.

There were whispers all around, beneath the thundering peals of the bell, voices from beyond the crack. She could not understand them, could not let herself understand. Screams of flayed backs and dying children. Choked gasps of plague. And beneath all of that . . .

Sal's voice, as if heard through a pillow.

Just a little further.

If she let go, she might be able to save herself. But the crack would remain.

It would grow wider. People disappeared all the time. "She just fell through the cracks," they said when it happened. They said that about her already.

As the shadow pulled her in, she pulled back. Wet tendrils stretched and snapped. The bell rang, louder, clearer. The footsteps neared. She was so tired. The wound in her wrist was open again, burning and bleeding.

She kept her grip. She could not afford to lose. She was losing.

Arms circled her in the dark, human arms warm and strong, and in spite of everything, as she felt them tighten around her waist, she thought, *Sal*, and was happy.

Spin rushed into her, wild and uncontrolled but spin all the same, a certainty about what was and an openness to what might be. The shadows parted. With one final tug, the thing Zelda held tore free from its fleshy mooring and she fell back to the brick plaza, gasping, sweat-slick, her arm coated in gore: her own blood and a thick purple ichor.

The claw-flower shriveled. Her brother had thrown a spider into the fire once, and it looked like that as it died, frantic, pathetic. She'd burned herself trying to fetch it out again. She reached for it, unsure what she meant to do— feeling dirty, not triumphant—almost said, I'm sorry.

The bell tolled one last time, loud, high, deep, angelic and clear. She was crying. That sound came from a world she'd never seen, could barely imagine. A world worthy of redemption.

The tourists heard it. They stopped to look. The kids fell silent. The teacher caught one of the two she was chasing; the girl in the cape stopped, stared. Her cape billowed behind her in a wind Zelda didn't feel, and she looked almost invincible.

They hadn't seen her struggle—but they heard the bell, and when they turned to look, they saw it.

The crack had been there, deep and real and old.

Now it was gone. Or filled. It looked like glass but it held the light too long, and split it into too many colors. Rainbows shimmered when she moved her head.

Someone was crying. There were questions in Swedish. People stared in awed silence.

Zelda stumbled to her feet, trusting—no, not Sal's arms. June's. Her eyes wide. "What did we do?"

"I don't know." The ichor steamed off her hand, but the blood remained. There in the center of her palm, red-slick and dull but there all the same, lay a dark iron ring, sized for her finger. Something deep in the pit of her stomach lurched and turned. She needed to throw up. She swallowed hard.

Had she recognized it, on some deep level, by touch? Why else had she clung so desperately to it? Why else had she pulled it from the crack?

This was the point where someone on TV, or in the bad movies she saw in theaters when she had the cash to pay, would throw the ring away, would collapse sobbing and scream at everyone else to leave her alone. She never had that kind of courage. If you showed people what you were so openly, so boldly, it gave them something to use against you. If you told them to go away, how could you know they'd ever come back?

She screamed inside her own head. She told herself to go away. She was good at that. But even in her innermost heart, she could not throw that ring.

"Let's get out of here," she said, and June, for once, listened. She helped Zelda walk. Security guards had come, drawn by the tolling of the bell, and even though the cameras wouldn't capture Zelda's face, she'd learned the hard way that it was best for a woman whose permanent address had out-of-state plates to be somewhere else when people in uniform started asking questions.

As they slipped through the crowd, she saw the kid in the glasses, stammering, pointing toward her as he told the girl in the cape what he'd just seen. The girl watched Zelda in awe. She waved—then she was gone, and they were back out in the late-summer heat, on the road. With her ring in her bloody hand, firmly in her pocket.

"You can't drive," she said later.

June looked out the window. "You say that like it's a bad thing."

"It's not a helpful thing."

"Neither was building a transportation infrastructure that depends on burning a nonrenewable resource to dump a few billion tons of $CO_2$ or whatever into the air every year and letting your economy and way of life get so tied up in it that you spent most of the twentieth century toppling every democratically elected government within spitting distance of that nonrenewable resource to assure your supply. And then when that didn't work, you plunged the country into two decades of war without an exit strategy. But you don't see me complaining."

Zelda stitched through traffic onto the freeway. Her head ached. Her wrist pulsed in time with the ache in her head. The world was leaching colors. She still didn't know how that crack had opened in the bell. What had happened when it was sealed. There was a ring in her pocket that should not exist anymore. She just wanted to pass driving duties on to a more or less normal teenager licensed to operate a moving vehicle. Instead she was engaging in a political debate on the subject.

"Most of that," she said, "happened long before I was born, and the other half got started before I could vote."

"You didn't stop any of it, though."

"I tried." She slipped past a big rig, kept her eyes on the road. In the Northeast—or wherever Pennsylvania was—you couldn't gather much spin on the highway. Trees ran right up to the edge of the road. Out west there were deserts, broad stark landscapes, scrub brush, and Judas pine. This country kept its secrets hidden. Not that highways were good for gathering spin at the best of times, too flat, too measured. They were built so you could drive the same way everywhere, built to let people drive without surprises, because the human mind wasn't made to handle surprises at eighty miles an hour.

Still, she gathered what she could, drinking in the shadows under the trees, the long unrolling road.

"And it keeps getting worse."

Zelda ignored a pickup truck with three Confederate flag bumper stickers and a quote from one of those Spartans who died protecting their repressive slave state from an arguably less repressive slave state. Great political models. She'd once tried to argue in middle school that she'd rather have been born a Spartan than an Athenian because the Spartan women, the aristocrats anyway, ran shit when the guys were off to war, while the Athenian women were kept so cloistered that Aristotle could be wrong about how many teeth girls had. But at least she hadn't put her middle school classics opinions on a bumper sticker.

"You're right," she said. "It keeps getting worse."

They didn't talk about the Liberty Bell. And, thank God, June didn't ask about the ring. Zelda kept her mind on the road, on the opening distance, on the space she was creating between them and Philadelphia.

"Sal knew how to drive," she said after a while.

"She learned before she went to college. Before she went away. One of the ladies who goes to church with Ma, her son was a roadie for a touring act, small-time, whistle-stops, shit towns, the kind of bars people go to get knifed. Sal went with them—they could barely pay, but it was one of those things where she carted speakers around and they gave her driving lessons. She figured she was going to this big school and everyone else would show up with cars or knowing how to drive or shit like that, and she didn't want to stand out just because she didn't."

"She never told me that," Zelda said. "She told me about the trip, but never that that was how she learned to drive."

"You think she'd tell you? She loved you, Z. She wanted you to think she was perfect. Wanted you to feel that you could lean on her. That she belonged."

"She did belong. She grew up in New York. She knew what it was like up here. I might have been going to an alien planet when I showed up at school."

But she'd jumped onto that planet's surface with both feet, hadn't she? Never looked back. Learned the language, flattened her accent, paid attention to the kind of jokes people told, learned what not to say. She'd wanted inside that fairy-land, that magic circle, so badly, because there were people there who didn't hate her, who could talk the way she needed to talk, who understood. If they knew she didn't belong, if they smelled her home on her as something more than a gentle, sexy, not-quite-affected twang when she was drunk, wouldn't they recoil from her just as she recoiled from the phone when her parents called, or worse, her pastor? Sal had been a master of that magic circle. The sorceress of those castle dorms. But then, a sorceress did not belong either.

"I'm just saying. To her, you fit."

⇒

"Here's the plan," she said later, in a Walmart parking lot at dusk, while water boiled for freeze-dried rice on a camp stove on the blacktop by the Subaru.

"First, we're going to send some letters. I can't do the next part alone. I'll write to the others. Then we'll go to Montana and wait for them."

"Why Montana?"

"That's where we washed up last time. After it all went wrong. Seems fit to start there. Pick up where we left off."

"Then what?"

"Then we hit the road."

She felt so tired. In a rest stop, she'd scrubbed the blood from her hand and tried to clean her wrist. Red lines stretched from the cut. Its edges were ragged where she'd torn them, reaching into the crack in the Liberty Bell. While she worked, she'd felt eyes on her—a sallow lady in a black T-shirt with bags under her eyes, paying Zelda the wrong kind of attention. There was a time when Zelda would have tried to ignore her, but that didn't always work these days, and when it didn't work, you were truly fucked because if you ignored your surroundings, you didn't know what was coming before it hit you. She shot the black T-shirt lady a smile, an acknowledgment without friendliness. Some people read nice as "weak." But the glance, the smile, covered the once-over she gave the lady. No gun, at least. Not here. Not that a gun was the only sort of danger.

She'd been cornered in a restroom once, in Dayton, by two women whose problem with her seemed to consist of the fact that she kept her hair short and didn't want to answer their questions. They'd punched and kicked her, and she'd almost let the situation get out of hand. They weren't possessed by anything more than normal hate. They were no cracked windows in their eyes, no shadows in their mouths.

She'd killed before, in self-defense and in defense of Sal, and wept after. But she wasn't supposed to do that here. You didn't just break someone's fingers in a US public restroom, didn't drive your knuckles deep into their neck and feel their windpipe give way. It took her until the second slap to find a nonlethal out, to grab one woman's arm and pull her off-balance, shove her into the other— watch them fall and squawk while Zelda got her fists up. "Come on, then." They didn't. She backed up slowly, and once she was out of their sight, she ran to her car and left. Cowards hated nothing more than proof of their own cowardice.

The lower half of the black T-shirt woman's face grew tight with decision. She walked over. Zelda tipped her bandages into the trash. Time to go.

"Hey." Thick fingers touched her shoulder. She twisted, hands up, sliding out of the woman's grip. The woman drew back fast, as if she'd reached to pet a dog only for fangs to snap shut a half inch from her fingertips. Tense, they breathed together, eyes wide open staring into eyes.

Someone flushed a toilet.

The woman's voice was soft. "I just wanted to ask if you were—okay. If you needed help. I mean. You look rough. I've been there."

God. She let her breath out, tried to force her body into some posture of ease. "I'm okay." She wasn't. "Cut myself working." Working on what? Z, you've been at this ten years and you can't even lie right.

"Is he . . . ?" The woman trailed off, but that last word contained too much of a life story. Her eyes were green, Zelda saw now. Some of the roots under the blond were brown, and some were gray.

"There's no he." In case she'd seen them arrive: "Just me and a friend. We're traveling. To Cleveland."

"The Rock and Roll Hall of Fame?" She was testing.

"Sure."

"If you need a place to stay." She reached for her pocket, slowed the motion when she saw Zelda twitch. Her business card was crumpled at the edges. First Christopher's Church. No denomination. "We have beds."

She wondered how hard up she looked. No, that wasn't right. She knew. She just tried to forget. "If I need a bed, I'll find you." She could still sound polite. She knew the woman had seen her glance at the card, recoil at the cross.

"Come as you are."

That snapped a Nirvana song to mind, and the way she imagined it might feel to press a shotgun barrel between her teeth. She'd had a gun barrel in her mouth before—only for a second, until Sal killed the man who held it.

Zelda had been ready to fight this woman. As tight and ratfuck angry as if her back were up against the wall. She'd been wrong this time, but you couldn't judge decisions by their outcomes. She'd been right before. "Thanks."

"Say Cassie sent you. They'll call me."

There were small circular scars on the inside of Cassie's wrist. Cigarette burns, maybe. Old and long healed, to the extent things like that ever healed. "Thanks."

She found June by the register, paid with forty bucks from her dwindling roll, and was gone.

Even now, parked in a Walmart lot so big you could have played three football games side by side with plenty of room on the sidelines for bored moms and coaches and cheerleaders, she felt boxed in. Her head hurt. The wound in her arm throbbed. But she owed June a plan.

"We tried to reach the crossroads last time," she said again. "To get there and fix things. We failed. You see how that turned out." Her fingers closed over the ring in her pocket. It wasn't a lie. "So we have to try again."

"Why didn't you try again last time?"

She swallowed. *Let go of the ring, Z.* Her fingers uncurled. "We had been trying. This was the closest we ever got. When it failed, we had different ideas about what we should do next. And they left me."

That last sentence hung between them.

"You think they'll listen now."

The water boiled. Zelda knelt, tore open two freeze-dried packets of Rice-A-Roni, tipped them into the pot. She stirred with a titanium spoon from her kit. Camping food always made her expect to hear camping sounds, but there weren't many crickets in a parking lot. Just cars on the highway and that weird blacktop dead air echo. She knew it too well. June hugged herself, in spite of the humid weight of late summer. She was looking for corners, for shadows, as though they were bedded down in an abandoned house.

"The others will know something's wrong," Zelda said. "They can feel it. They'll come."

"I can't feel anything."

"Of course you can. Doesn't the world seem . . . weak to you? Thin, fragile? Like a shell we're trapped inside—a shell that might break at any moment? And you don't know what's on the other side, what you aren't seeing even as it opens its arms and reaches out?"

"That's not magic. That's just, like, life."

"It's not magic. It's spin. Uncertainty, change. We gather it when we don't know where we're going, or why. When we're open to what might happen next. Everyone alive does this. Anyone who doesn't is dead, even if they don't know it yet. You used spin to pull me away from the Liberty Bell. And Sal—out there beyond the edge—she's gathered a hurricane's weight of it, and now she's bringing it home. That's what you feel. The storm against the wall of the world."

There were no cricket sounds at all now, and even the distant highway noise had dwindled, died, left them alone on the vast and quiet blacktop. Silence had an ocean's depth, and they fell into it together. The gaps between the few stars visible against the parking lot lights yawned wide. When Zelda looked into them, she felt the vertigo of falling up.

"So, how do I use it?"

"You start by learning to drive. Tomorrow."

"No way."

"It works better if you can control how you're moving. On foot, on horse, behind the wheel."

"You've ridden a horse?"

"Sure."

"You're gonna get us picked up by the cops. Black girl with no license, driving out in the sticks. Not a place I want to be."

"Where we're going," Zelda said, "there won't be any cops."

"Well, now I'm paying attention."

She laughed dryly. Fished into her pocket and took out a small black book. "Here. Happy birthday. Copy your numbers down. Ma, everyone you care about, anything you'll want to remember. No phones starting tomorrow."

"You're still on about that."

"It's a hold the world has over you. Locks you into place. Mail it home, if you don't want to break it. I've got some bubble mailers in the trunk."

"Z, you got some of everything in that trunk." She took the book, flipped through it, frowned. "You got a pen?"

Zelda passed June a ballpoint and, a minute later, a bowl of Rice-A-Roni. She'd eaten way too much of this stuff on the road. Less than a dollar a meal in bulk. But it had been a long day, and her stomach growled at the smell.

"Nobody's gonna come for us here?"

"What, in the parking lot? Not as long as we don't try to start a union or anything. Walmart's nice about people camping in their lots overnight, long as we clean up after ourselves. Most of the campers are old white folks with RVs, but we should be fine. Surprised there aren't more here, to be honest. I only see three, four." She pointed with her eyes and jaw. The camper was obvious, and there were two gangly men with matted hair and worn clothes smoking, leaning against the hood of the grimy blue station wagon. That Corolla, probably—it had the right odd overstuffed look and the profusion of bumper stickers and the desert grit ground into the body. And there was a white-haired couple in well-worn suits circling the parking lot, walking with intent but no purpose. No gyms on the road. You got your exercise where you could. "More like that out here every year. Old folks without savings, bit of social security if they're lucky. They keep moving. Seasonal jobs all over to keep gas in the tank. Bit of food. It's a fine life if you don't need much, until you get sick."

"Don't the old ones have people?"

"Not the ones on the road. And no one has as many people as they used to." She sighed down into her shoes. "Back where I come from—I mean, I could have stayed if I didn't mind drowning. There wasn't anything to do, you know? Any upside. Anything you could feel good for doing. There were jobs at the super-market. Driving trucks, that's still a good one, until the robots take over. Some kids, their families had land. But the rest of us, if we want to work and get paid enough to get sick someday in this country, we have to go where the money is, where the jobs are, and our families can't follow us there, not with how much those places cost, you know? So you have people getting old at home, and their kids maybe miss them, but if they go home, they don't have a job anymore.

"Meanwhile there aren't enough nurses to go around. I read a couple weeks back that there aren't enough in Maine even to cover the full-time care the government's willing to pay for. So you're growing old, and even if you have friends, they're growing old, too, and what are you going to do, remind one another to take meds for the rest of your life?" She dug a spoon into the pan and filled her mouth, which was dry from talking. Dumb to say so much. Everyone knew this stuff, didn't they? Except, looking up at June's wide eyes, the city girl chewing over what she'd just said, maybe everyone didn't know. That had always been one of her problems, even at school: assuming wrong. Figuring that everyone knew the axiom of choice and no one had ever heard of *Star Trek: Deep Space Nine*. "And," she finished guiltily, "some of them are just on the road because they like it."

"What about you? Do you like it?"

She breathed over the rice in her mouth and swallowed when it was cool. "I have friends who stayed home. Some people I knew in college put down roots as quick as they could, dug their fingers into the dirt so hard they got bedrock in their cuticles. I'm glad I've seen what I have seen. The country is always dying. The one that was here when I was your age doesn't exist anymore, except in the minds of people who remember it. But when you wander, you see the bones of the thing. I've seen rivers flood and high plains come back to life after a storm. I stood on a mountaintop and watched the moon eat the sky. I've never once wished I had not done those things." She ate more, in silence. The food lay heavy in her belly. "But if Sal were still here, and if she asked, I would find a small place with her somewhere we could afford, and set fire to my car and bury my keys and sit on the front porch hand in hand with her and wait for the end of the world."

But you *had* that chance, a voice in the back of her mind raged. You held it in your hand, she offered you everything you'd never dared to ask, and you threw it away because you were scared. The ring pressed against her thigh through the jeans. She remembered leaving Sal bleeding in the Challenger in Elsinore, and leaving that ring, too, in her hand, before she turned back to the breaking tower and ran for the crossroads. She had her chance. She made her choice.

"So why don't you stop?"

She looked up fast, startled out of memory. "She's gone."

"You could find someone else."

As if it would be so easy. As if she could just pull the world over her head like a quilt. June knew what a hole Sal left in your life. The sky was still there, and the road and the mountains, but the shell of the world was thinner, and days lost their weight.

There had been others, bodies passing in the night, people bent and aching with need and ready to pretend for a few hours, as she was ready, that their need was so general just anyone with the right kinks and curves would cover it. They served, and she served, for the moment, like tarps served to cover a pit. But you couldn't build on that.

She almost said all of that, and more, compressed into three words. *I love her.* But just in time, she saw the hunger in June's face and understood the cunning of this girl who had waited so long to ask her that question outside Ma Tempest's door. Zelda had slipped into seeing her as a vessel to be filled.

There was that drawing folded in her jacket pocket. That was a story June had lived by. Her older cousin's love that drew her to the road, destroyed her, made her a legend. June was hungry for that story. Even though the story was deeply, deeply wrong.

So she said something else that was also true.

"When we tried to walk the trail before, when we failed, when I failed and Sal fell, there were consequences. We'd built so much spin, we were so close to the crossroads, and when we slipped, all that power . . ." She spread her fingers. "It busted out. It cracked everything. Hairlines in places, huge gaps in others. Like you saw with the bell. And rot spread through them. Rot and whispers. If you've felt like there's poison in the well in the last ten years, like time was spinning too fast, you're not wrong. It wasn't because of us, but we were a part of it. The rot was there before us, but we made it worse. The others decided they couldn't go on. I kept going. Someone had to close the cracks. I've done that for ten years. For what it's worth." She did not want to think about what Sal had said back on the bridge, through June's mouth. *It's been me all this time. I couldn't let go.* She knew June remembered it just as well as she did.

Zelda swallowed her last bite, tipped some water into the pan, swirled it around, and drank the remaining scum of rice. Waste not. She cleaned the pan with a rag from her pack. June hadn't moved. "That's why they'll come. Because they know I've been out here, alone, and they're guilty."

Zelda wrote the letters that night after dinner, on a book over her knee as she sat on the Subaru's hood, while June copied contact info out of her phone.

She felt the weight of everything she had once been to these people, everything they had once been to her. How do you start a conversation like that up again? How do you break ten years' strained silence, get through all the weeds that grew there? Any letter that said a fraction of what she owed each of them would be ten pages long and still too short.

So she wrote a few lines, the same few lines, to each.

She's coming back. I need your help.

Let's meet where we split up.

An address. That, at least, came easily.

She signed each one: *Love, Zelda*. Because after all of that and everything, it was still true.

She addressed them: Ish Colby, San Francisco. Dr. Sarah Masters, Kingston, Virginia. Ramón Espina, c/o Angelina Espina, Los Angeles. And then it was done. Stamps applied. Her mouth tasted of envelope glue, stale and sour.

June was humming a song. "See-Line Woman" again, but slow, off-rhythm. The sound opened like a corpse flower in the empty parking lot. The sky bloomed overhead, stained violet with streetlights, but behind that violet there was black, black forever back to the beginning, and only this frail guttering light against it, this circle of the world humans could know, puny when compared with all they could not comprehend.

Math would not touch what lay beyond the light. Math was a prisoner feeling her way around the dark cell where she was chained. You could learn about the cell, but it would not let you out. Physics didn't help either. It was no accident the numbers and equations for problems about the size and shape and speed of humans were easy, their exponents whole numbers, their concepts amenable to common sense, but as you moved into the realm of things much larger, smaller, faster, even slower than us, the laws tangled into weirdness. The mind has a shape. Some things don't fit inside.

All they had was this small circle of light, and the light was strangling itself. That had started long before she hit the road, but the fact remained. The world was withering.

Beyond the shell of the sky rose dark fractal clouds. The tornado road. Sal's face peering in.

Zelda's heart beat countertime to June's song; her skin seemed too tight and the wound in her arm pulsed with her heart and the ring burned against her thigh. The sky lowered and the parking lot curled up around her like the fingers of a massive hand, its fingertips mountains. She was falling up, unmoored from the earth and the hood of her Subaru. She was limp in the sky. She had not moved. Her breath was fast and wet and her blood rushed in her veins and there was a coal in her arm.

She looked up into Sal's enormous eyes.

The letters slipped from her lap and spilled over the Subaru's hood. One landed on the pavement. Ramón's name, staring up. She reached for it but her movements felt slow, as if she were forcing herself through water at a depth light could not reach, where only monsters lived, unseen long sharp things that you knew existed only from the tooth marks they left on the whales they did not kill.

Her hand shimmered in the streetlight, in the starlight, and the asphalt breeze on her forehead felt too cold.

I'm sick, she thought, falling.

I can't be sick. There's too much to do.

They need me. She's on her way. We don't have time.

"Z?" That was June, looking up, over. Zelda tried to answer, but only croaked.

She stood, realized she couldn't stand, swayed and fell back onto the car hood. A long way off, June was rising, nearing. But she would never make it. She had to cross half that distance, then half the distance again, and half of that, forever.

The world was a drum and its drumbeats footsteps and up there far away was a face made of stars. The wind whistled "The Impossible Dream." She opened her mouth to call Sal's name, but shadows rolled in through her lips, and she was gone.

# CHAPTER SIX

A serpent gnaws at the roots of the world.

Far down, where even light gives up, in the dark, below the trash heaps of history where skeletons embrace, so wrapped together in the muck and jumble no one can pick out whose bones belong to whom, there stand great crystal columns, burning with heat and slick with slime, that keep everything we see and know from collapsing into the fire.

The serpent lives down there.

Think as big as you can, and it's bigger. It casts glaciers of grit off its scales as it slithers. It shoulders mountains of rock from the cavern's roofs and sides. It stinks of sweat and rot, and its scales are streaked with the mud through which it crawls. Behind glittering mad eyes, a brain of unimaginable girth grinds knowledge. It knows we're up here, drinking coffee and wondering whether it's okay to turn the AC down one more degree—sure, it's speeding up the death of the planet, but it's hot *now*—and comparing our dreams to our college roommate's social media feed and feeling some bleak nameless yearning too vague and embarrassing to turn into a poem because who writes poetry anymore, really. The serpent knows that we, whatever our faults and however much we hate ourselves, are not where it is, covered in muck, winding through the rot of history, baked by fires no one who wrote about Hell in any scripture could ever have imagined. It knows we are not continent-vast and hungry. It knows we do not feel the weight of the world pressing on our backs.

It knows.

It knows, and it's pissed.

So it curls around the crystal pillars and tightens. It strains. It lashes them with acid fangs, spreading corrosive green through the roots of everything. The roots are strong and the world is heavy, but the serpent does not tire. It has been down there as long as we have been up here, and it knows the only difference between us is chance. It has spent history building up a vast and justified store of hate.

Hate lives in the body the way love does, or fear. It curdles in old, torn muscles poorly healed. It congregates in fasciae. It taints blood. We say there is no measure to our hate—but there will come a moment, if we hate enough, when hate fills us from our toe-tips to the trailing ends of our hair, when it drips from our eyelashes, when hate alone sustains. Most people die before they reach that limit, but the limit does exist. The body can become saturated and preserved entirely with hate.

So imagine, then, the serpent. Bigger than big. A heart as many-mansioned as any father's house. Imagine just how much hatred it can hold, how immense are the oceans of rage it has accumulated century by century, drop by drop, while it thinks of all of us up here.

It will never stop. Would you?

It has been gnawing for so long. No matter how big those pillars were back at the dawn of the world, no matter how deep those roots or how strong, it must be getting close. Doesn't the ground under your feet feel thinner than it used to? Don't you sometimes take a step only to realize the sidewalk isn't where you thought? You stumble, catch yourself, call yourself clumsy, laugh it off, but that wasn't your fault. The ground wasn't where it was.

Because the serpent is winning.

It's winning slowly, but someday it will snap the world's last root, and you will fall and fall, and if you survive the whole way down, you'll find those fangs waiting for you, and the brimming ocean of hatred within that mouth.

A serpent gnaws at the root of the world.

You know this. I know this. But we forget, most of the time. You have to forget, to live anything like a human life. You make yourself forget.

Ish Colby never forgets.

He was a child when he first met the serpent—ten years old and battle lines drawn, waiting for his bullies in the shadow of the trees at the edge of the playground, with a half roll of quarters clutched in each pudgy fist. Hidden by thornbushes from the teachers who did not understand, and who, if they did understand, would not have cared. For a while he'd convinced himself the serpent was under only *his* feet, that if he became someone else, if he ran far enough away, he could escape. The serpent would not follow.

An understandable mistake. He did run. He made it to college with only a few scars and none that showed. He met a girl with a funny name, a girl he would have followed into fire, and they went out with their friends on a grand adventure only to find, after all their wandering, the serpent.

What were you supposed to do, knowing that? Your childhood fears were real. Your world was doomed. What next? Roll back a generation or two, and you'd find the answers other people dreamed up when faced with the prospect of global annihilation—drugs, sex, checking out, various forms of music as primal scream therapy. But they didn't serve.

So. He built systems. Waterworks for his fear.

Now, in his mid-thirties, he woke up at five o'clock every morning. On this particular day, he woke at 4:55, from dreams of teeth and a road that was a tornado and a face hidden behind the sky as if behind a curtain. He would recognize that face, he knew, if he put out his hand to part the curtain. But when he tried, he found himself stuck to a bed, drowning in his own sheets as the sky flowed into his mouth.

Then he was awake. Alone.

He breathed fast and shallow, from fear, yes, but also to remind himself that he could, in fact, breathe. His bedroom asserted itself. Pale and spacious, modernist clean, the air light with a fake lemon chemical smell. The maids had come yesterday while he was out.

Simplify, he was always telling his people. You could do everything, but you had to do it one step at a time. His room was bare. He owned ten versions of the same three outfits. After Series A, he'd hired someone to help him shop, and come away with a bright and sunny wardrobe, bold patterns, on trend. After a year of feeling as though he were wearing someone else's skin, he'd decided that grays always went with other grays and returned to basics. Good jeans. Gray hoodie, gray blazer. Black underlayer. He'd seen a man sleeping in the doorway opposite his building wearing a shirt he was sure used to be his, that same salmon color with the tiny blue fish print.

A serpent gnaws at the root of the world. Once you understood that, you saw the tooth marks everywhere.

Ish slept naked—simplify—with workout clothes folded on his nightstand. He dressed in two pulls, took a fresh pair of shorts and shirt from the ones folded vertically in the nightstand drawer, set them on the nightstand for tomorrow, and straightened the bedsheets. One thing at a time.

Next door was another bare, lemon-scented room, weights racked, with a reinforced floor. Three bottles of room-temp water waited on the shelf beside the door. He drank two, hung himself from the pull-up bar for a minute to stretch out his lumbar spine, then did a warm-up set, then Gironda squats, eight sets of eight reps with thirty seconds' rest between each one. It's not working if you don't feel half dead by the time you're done. Never be comfortable. If you're comfortable, you should be lifting heavier. The pain is not without its compensations. Over time, you get used to feeling like you're about to die. You're on a first-name basis with the sense that your heart's about to pop like a teenager's zit.

He showered. He examined his body in the full-length mirror as steam devoured it. His softness had melted away years ago. When he started working out, at first he'd seemed to thicken, his shoulders broader, his shirts looking as if they'd shrunk in the wash, his pants tighter through the leg. Then came the strength—noticing that things he used to think were heavy weren't anymore. And then the muscles erupting, rising peaked and immense as whales from his skin.

Dress. Downstairs. He poured premeasured smoothie ingredients from glass jars in his freezer into the Vitamix, added a spoon of vegan non-soy protein powder. Always add more liquid. He had been on an oat milk thing for a while before he decided he might as well have added a scoop of oats and water to the blender. So he went back to almond milk, which was bad for the environment, but, hell, there was a serpent gnawing at the roots of the world: What could you do?

He drank another bottle of water while he blended his breakfast, and then he drank his breakfast.

Whose face had that been beyond the sky? Ish tried to remember. Let it be a blank signifier—anyone's face, or the face of death, or the face of climate change. Maybe it was the serpent's face. Serpents and women were often linked, in mythology. Zelda had told him that. He tried not to think about Zelda these days.

After breakfast he sat on the living room floor, breathed fake lemons in and fake lemons out, and meditated until the company car came.

On the drive to the office, he read emails on his tablet and reviewed the global exchanges. He'd chosen his neighborhood for its convenience to mass transit, but the demands on his time were such that the car and driver saved him several hundred thousand dollars a year. He had to arrive rested. Ready. Every night he wrapped himself up carefully for storage, like an action figure in a box, and every morning he unwrapped himself, pristine. When he looked in the mirror these days, he could see himself only in a bit of panic around the eyes.

He reviewed orders and requests from their partners back East. Their friends with the three-letter acronyms did not sleep—as far as Ish could tell, they persisted on a diet of caffeine and self-hatred, as Ish used to before he understood about the serpent and the long, long drop. The sun never sets on the American Empire. There are exceedingly normal and apparently human beings of all shapes and sizes and shades of skin, all around the world, who, every day, send little letters home. The occupants of the dingy offices in Virginia, who clock in at 7:00 a.m. to read the little letters those exceedingly normal beings send home, have been drinking government coffee for three hours before Ish checks his email.

Ish sees only the crises, the problems that none of the exceptionally competent people who work for him can solve. By the time he reached his office, he had solved two. San Francisco is beautiful and makes its own kind of sense. He can breathe the sea from his office. This is where it's all happening—the end of the world. He came here once when he was a kid and never wanted to live anywhere else. This city remembers earthquakes in its bones. That keeps it honest. It knows the serpent's there.

Across the street, the doorway stood empty. He wondered what happened to the man in the salmon shirt.

The rest of his day was classified.

He'd founded the company after he left the road. He never wanted to take it public. That was more common these days than he'd been led to expect when he was growing up: limited liability companies being what they were, you as an individual founder could get almost as disgustingly wealthy by making your own fish as tasty as possible and waiting for the pike to come along, as you could by growing into a pike yourself. But after a certain point, you stopped being edible, started being a rival. He'd reached that point five years ago.

Well, he hadn't. Lidskjalf had. (Nobody could pronounce the name who wasn't Norwegian or a very specific sort of myth geek, which was the point.) A certain kind of miraculation—the process of attributing human traits to abstract entities—was not only expected in his industry, but encouraged. After all, information wanted to be free.

He had not gone public, had resisted many pushes and calls to do so, to accept this bid or that, had fought the board and won, had chased away investors, even ones who didn't have shadows gathering behind them, who didn't represent mysterious mob-tainted repositories of immense wealth. He had done all of this because he understood Lidskjalf's true business, and its true clients, while the board understood only the value of their investment, managed over a brief span of decades at most. Often their horizon was even more limited—which he might understand intellectually but could never, as his father would say, grok. Consider life from the vaulted perspective of the corporation, the true corporate person. Apple Inc. wants people to keep buying Apple products not just for ten years but forever—wants people orbiting Tau Ceti as disembodied minds distributed through a thousand robot waldos to tab idly over to the App Store and update *Fire Emblem Heroes*. For a being in that blessed state, not bound by time and death, limitless as human desire, surely the long view was more important than this afternoon's share price.

But, of course, corporations were not people, really. They were made up of people, striving, hungry, limited, scared, desperate for one more million dollars to throw between their throats and the jaws of time. They did not even understand why they were so afraid.

His board—for all his efforts—was full of just this kind of person. They were afraid, which was good. But they did not know what they were afraid of. They assumed it was death, old age, poverty, terrorism. They understood those things. So they did not look further, and as a result, they did not understand the business they were in.

Ish understood.

And his customers—the nervous bureaucrats, the governments with their fat thumbs, even the goons in the White House—understood. Any system that could create and concentrate such wealth as they enjoyed was by definition highly ordered. Order tends to chaos over time. The most cutthroat victor of capitalism understood in his dreams if nowhere else that there are always more losers than winners, and the losers are hungry and must be fed.

There is a serpent that gnaws at the roots of the world, and one day we'll all fall down.

The Lidskjalf was the seat where Odin sat in stories, the high throne that oversaw the world. For the world needed overseeing. You could not stop the serpent. But if you could see the whole world at once—if you could peer through the camera eyes of four hundred million phones, if you could hear through the ears of fifty million personal digital assistants planted in everyday appliances, as if you needed your refrigerator to tell you who won last night's baseball game, anyway if you could track the whole world through the ubiquitous GPS tags most people didn't realize they wore at all times—apex military technology turned consumer staple—if you could see it all, you could find the moments when the world lurched, when the ground caved in, and stop them.

There were limits to this strategy. His customers had their own preferences. They believed certain groups threatened them more than others. Strangely—not all that strangely—they did not seem to be motivated to use the ubiquitous surveillance magic to stop racist idiots with guns from shooting up schools or garlic festivals, even when those idiots went on God's own public internet to brag about their plans beforehand. Far more important to keep tabs on the daily habits of people who protested the latest pipeline, to watch key actors in the last three marches on Washington, or to follow everyone who ever shook hands with Greta Thunberg. Far more important to find people who Shouldn't Be Here according to this or that racist's opinion and make sure they weren't.

None of them understood, even when he tried to explain.

The serpent doesn't care what languages you speak, what god you claim to pray to. Nothing you do can appease the serpent or bend it to your will. It can't be yoked or bridled. It's not a forest fire in the wild, chewing up dead bush, leaving rich ash behind. What the serpent eats is gone. If you speak to it, if you think it calls you friend, remember—the serpent is older than you and far more cunning. When it finds a weakness, it devours. And there are weaknesses everywhere.

But working with these people let Ish do what had to be done. So he worked. It was not pretty or noble. It never was.

He left the office long after dark, and in the back seat of the car he closed his eyes and let himself feel. He did this every day. It was not meditation; it was almost the opposite. To live as he did, he had to practice a certain compartmentalization, a certain division of self. Competence—the efficient exercise of his capacities—required a level of focus and conviction that fatigued the thing that, in private and just between ourselves, let's for the sake of argument call the soul. You had to will the path you walked into being.

To will the path. He remembered her saying something opposite, when the world was young and so were they. "What if we let ourselves discover? What if we see what *might* be there rather than what is? Don't jump from sense experience to meaning. Follow sensation down. Or not down but out." They'd been sitting on Cross Campus, the lawn the bright green of college memories—it really was that color somehow, somehow the landscapers made it happen. Sterling Library towered overhead with the rampart walls of Berkeley College to either side. And there she was, her hair in a French braid, her shoulders bare, her eyes shining—that mind he was always racing to keep up with, its pace so swift and beautiful that even when she was wrong, even when she'd missed some crucial contradiction, he wanted to break math rather than point out her error. He'd managed to point out those flaws only because he knew that if he tried, ever, to humor her, and she found out later, she would never trust him again.

"But we don't know what we'll find. It could be something . . ." He trailed off not because he didn't know how to finish his sentences but because he could not bear to. They could find something awful, something horrible, something with bright teeth and acid for blood. He knew they would. But when he sat cross-legged with Zelda in the sunlight, with her braid trailing over her shoulder and fire in her eyes, and heard her joy in this discovery, this theory that so far departed from any of the subjects of any of the classes they'd taken together—well, he couldn't bear to say what he was thinking, to be the wet blanket.

She was already running ahead. "That's what I mean! It could be *anything*."

So at the end of the day, he sat in the back of the car and let himself feel. The leather seats opened beneath him. Small muscles in his forehead, shoulder, and jaw unclenched. There were holes in the world, and since he was part of the world, there were holes in him too. He remembered the tornado road and the face in the sky. He remembered five people on a highway, so long ago they were washed of color and even shape. Ramón, Sarah, and himself behind. Zelda ahead, receding as he reached for her, and ahead of her always, Sal. And ahead of Sal—the serpent, its mouth, the forked road its tongue. Waiting. And no matter how he screamed, Zelda would not hear him, and no matter how fast he ran, his lumbering slow frame could not catch her.

Time went on, but it never went away. History was still there inside. The world grew from a sapling, and each year its new bark enclosed the past, and past horrors remained to knot and gnarl the future.

When the car stopped, he opened his eyes and found that they, and his cheeks, were wet. He dried them with a handkerchief.

The night was damp and cool, which shocked him. The summer had been hot, the hottest on record. This felt almost like the old city, the one he'd first seen through a ten-year-old's eyes. Somewhere not far away he heard music, horns, cheers. He'd chosen this neighborhood for its robust street culture as much as for its transit access, but he never spent much time on the street.

The building across the street from his condo had a huge mural of a Day-Glo rooster painted on the side, crowing, one spur up in challenge. Every few days he forgot it was there, glimpsed it out of the corner of one eye while turning, and jumped.

Cynthia was waiting for him inside.

She sat on the kitchen counter, wearing a black silk robe and the kind of heels no one wore if they meant to walk outside. She'd poured herself a glass of wine and was reading a thin black paperback with a red circular logo on the cover that he did not recognize. She must have heard the door close, must have seen him come in: her peripheral vision was fantastic, she could walk through rush hour crowds while reading and not jostle so much as a shopping bag. He was standing right there in the kitchen door. But she turned the page anyway, languid, at ease.

Only that slight smile as she read, the flick of her tongue-tip at her front teeth, betrayed that she was aware of him at all.

His breath did not reach his chest. For these few seconds, poised in the doorway, the world was as shallow as it seemed to be, and made of rock all the way through. There were no deep caverns, no serpents and no flames, and he had never stood in the shadow of the trees at the edge of the playground with angry tears in his eyes and a half roll of quarters in each fist.

She knew what she was doing. She turned the page again. Her smile a hair's breadth wider.

The world was, in that moment, a very simple place.

He liked her so much—and she knew it, and was so good at using her knowledge—that it was a problem. He could not afford this sort of thing. But that was fine. That was why he had his system.

The citizens of Florence (Sarah told him once) had a problem of their own, way back in the eleventh century or so, before the Medici. They won a rebellion against their noble class, chopped off the tops of their towers and ran the surviving scions out of town. But after you killed all your aristocrats, how did you run your city? The civil society aspects were easy enough, guilds handled most of that anyway. The nobles hadn't been load-bearing. Their intrigues were a drain on the system, that was all. But without nobles, how did you command an army? Or a police force? What man-at-arms would serve a tanner, or a dealer in cloth?

The solution, it turned out, was simple. Northern Italy was awash in poor cadet nobility, the hungry second through tenth sons of great houses. All you had to do was find someone with the right pedigree and recruit them to lead your armed forces, organize your militia, and so on. Give them a nice, recently vacated palace—once you wash the blood off—and pay them to serve the people.

Now, anyone with a grasp of history could spot a fatal problem with this plan. What happens when your hired commander, this hungry noble sellsword, remembers that he's living in twelfth-century Italy, and that half the cities he knows are ruled by mercenary captains who seized opportunities less perfect than the one he's just been handed, and made themselves dukes? He's living in a palace now. Why shouldn't his children live in one, and their children to the hundredth generation?

So, at the end of each year, the tanners and dealers in cloth would kindly escort their hungry young man to the city gates, hand him a bag of gold, and banish him forever from Florence, on pain of, well, quite a lot of pain, and death sometime thereafter, once they got bored.

It was a good policy. It didn't save Florence forever, but it did ensure that when Florence found itself under something not altogether unlike a dictatorship, it was not some jumped-up foreign noble but a Florentine, one of those dealers of cloth, with a Florentine's fine sensibilities with regard to maintaining at least the appearance of republican virtue, who did the dictating.

Ish Colby had heard this story and thought: That makes sense.

Love was complicated. It hid behind lust and comfort and friendship and fear. Love was a story you told yourself to explain why you kept doubling down on questionable decisions made when your oxytocin levels were through the roof.

Love was, he thought sometimes, a field as green as a memory, and a thick braid falling over a shoulder, and an eager voice so impatient for you to catch up with her argument so she could tell you the really, really *interesting* part. . . . But that thought slipped away in the thinking, like a star system through Grand Moff Tarkin's fingers.

And if you did love someone, what then? There were so many ways to hold yourself down, to break yourself for someone you loved. A feeling that deep: You'd change your life for it, wouldn't you? You'd give up everything. You might even blind yourself, for a while, to the single truth you knew above all else: there was a serpent gnawing at the roots of the world, and one day it would win.

Now, sex—sex was easy, and sex, for him, was needed. But sex, even very professional, very careful sex, could lead to love. And sex, in his experience, was, at its most professional and careful, never quite professional or careful enough. It was like coding in that way.

Besides, working with professionals opened you up to other risks. Bribery, blackmail. You never could be altogether certain whom someone worked for.

So: his system.

There were people he met in the course of his everyday life who found him attractive, whom he found attractive. They had careers, as he did. They understood something about what he needed to be, about how much energy or how little he could be expected to have at the end of the day, or how much time.

These people didn't have much more energy or time themselves. The end of the world kept everyone busy.

His arrangements started with a meeting, maybe two, careful and evaluative, fencing more than courtship, to determine fit. Cynthia had taken him climbing. He was not a climber. He had dislocated a finger on an overhang, and (she'd been an EMT in college) she looked him flat in his eye before she set it, and told him not to flinch. He flinched. She laughed. That was a fit.

Then they discussed terms.

It would last for one year. They'd meet on a rough schedule with randomness baked in to achieve the intermittent-reward magic that really fucked up those rats in the psychology experiments. Within the bounds of the system, with its safety to guard them both from decisions they'd later regret, the idea was to feel drunk, desperate, addicted, not like you were calling an Uber. To make your life a little more like a slot machine.

There were a few tawdry additional specifics, more for the sake of form than anything else. Games they both liked, and how much they liked to play them. He liked silks, she liked black. He liked ballet heels; she couldn't walk in them, but could gesture in that direction. She enjoyed power in the room—whichever of them happened to have it in a particular game didn't matter. And then, of course, the usual protocols: safety, words and checks and balances. Accountability.

And the capstone of the system: money.

Quite a lot of it, and he let himself be negotiated upward. In escrow, to be released at year's end. The money's existence, the nature of the exchange, to be a complete secret, with various NDAs and provisions on that score. She could use it however she wanted—donate it all to charity if that made her feel better. One of her predecessors had. It was enough to fund a start-up, buy a house (even here), to fill a small bag with gold and drop it in the Bay for some lucky future treasure hunter.

But she had to take it.

And when the year was up, they'd go their separate ways. They'd be nothing to each other. Polite if ever introduced at parties. No rules, no ties. That was what the money was for, that was what it bought. It turned a relationship into an exchange, something clear, and severable. Once it changed hands, the relationship was a transaction, and the transaction was complete.

Sometimes he made the pitch and people turned him down, walked away, called him all sorts of names. Sometimes they even stayed away. But most understood—enough, anyway. And the ones who did understand were more likely to be the people he was looking for in the first place: the ones who knew the advantages of clarity.

He walked toward her. She turned the page again, the rasp of paper loud and new in the silence of the kitchen.

Her outstretched foot stopped him, the toe of that violent-heeled shoe pressed into his stomach. She still hadn't looked up. They understood each other. Her neck was arched and long, her hair short and severe and black. The diamond stud in her nose caught the light. She had asked, when they discussed the contract, why he'd been so specific with regard to braids, and his partner not having them. "I haven't had hair that long since high school."

He had not explained.

His hand circled her ankle and he squeezed, then shifted her leg to one side so he could draw closer. She made a sound when he tightened his grip, a low hum like a generator in a science fiction movie. He felt a thrill of pride at winning a sound from her at this stage in this particular game. He needed her because she reminded him that he existed. He needed resistance, something to push against or into, something that would stand. She would play immovable object.

She turned the page again.

Her leg curled around his waist. The spike of her heel dug into the small of his back. His hand climbed the swell of her calf, the thigh, her muscles long and smooth and cable-sure, her body a blade in black silk. Then she flexed her thigh and drew him in—wrestler-fast, so his hands shot out to break his fall against the counter, flanking her hips. His chest trapped her arm and the book against her. Her other hand found his wrist and closed around it, tight. She was strong. He let the pain register, let it make him gasp.

Their faces were inches apart. Her lips were rich. She was perfect. But once in a while her eyes looked black in the light and had that same daring gleam he remembered from a bright grass courtyard long ago, and he felt a stab of guilt, and wondered if, for all his care, he was only fooling himself.

"I was reading," she said, and the voice was utterly her own and reminded him of no one else but Cynthia. He breathed her in, that slight hint of san-dalwood and smoke, and believed that time was real, that the past was past, not prologue, that this now was all there was. "A story. About a samurai who sneezed during his master's birthday party."

"How does it end?"

Her nails found his wrist. She kept them short so she could climb, but she used temps some nights, for effect. She studied him in more than the usual way lovers studied lovers, seeking new tricks to surprise or delight or challenge or ease. She studied him the way he imagined Genghis Khan studying a walled city. What are these defenses set against me? Who raised them and why, and what would it take to take them down?

He was safe. He had a system. The system worked. And, trusting his system, he could enjoy the danger. This was just another sort of game.

"I don't know how it ends. Someone interrupted me." She slid her hand out from between their bodies and placed the book facedown on the counter, spread to mark her place. Well, nobody was perfect.

"I could go."

"Can you?" Both her legs were around him now, her hands cuffing his wrists.

He was stronger, but there was leverage to consider, and skill. And the fact that he did not, really, want to win. She dug her heels into his back—the points hurt—and kissed him with a growl in her throat, and he leaned into it. He fought one of her arms, twisted it behind her, and in a tangle they were both on the counter. It wasn't comfortable. Comfort wasn't the point so much as finding something firm to hold her against, as he was held in turn. There was so much to fight, to ache against as they shifted position, found grips, escaped. The world collapsed to bodies pressing, tense, relaxed. There was no road, no face beyond the sky, there was no cavern beneath the earth.

He pressed her down to the countertop, savoring the look in her eyes, the defiance, the joy in the struggle, and even then the Genghis Khan trace of contemplation, her dedication to his undoing.

Her shoulder was pressing her book flat. She might not care, but he did. He slid the book out, closed it—"You lost my place." "Fight me."—and he saw, at the edge of the counter, a letter.

He recognized the handwriting.

A serpent gnawed at the roots of the world.

In his distraction, she threw him, trapped his arms beneath her thighs—and before her mouth could close over his, he looked her in the eye and said, "Red."

She went slack at once, slid off him. "Did I hurt you?"

His breath was too fast and his heart ran as if he'd just finished wind sprints. His chest was a cage, and the animals in it hammered against the bars, bruised and bloody and terrified. Teeth broke on steel. "It's not me." He tried to stand. The room swam.

"Jesus, Ish, when was the last time you ate?"

"I'm doing IF."

"Fasting. You know, when I was a kid we just called it an eating disorder." She'd hidden her purse behind the counter. "Protein bar." He tried to turn, tried to look at her, but the room's walls were too close and if he moved, the floor would fall away. He ate the bar. He tried again, opening the wrapper first this time.

She was back, with a glass of water shoved at his chest. "Drink."

"Easy for you to say." That sentence took three tries. He wasn't coming off well. He drank, spilled a little, and mopped his mouth with the back of his hand. Cynthia was an arm's reach away, watching him, hugging herself, her mouth half open. "You're pale," he said. "Don't worry about me. I'm fine."

"I'm pale? Ish, you look like a ghost."

"Like I've seen a ghost. That's what people say."

"Can you breathe? How's your heart?"

God, that was something people their age needed to start thinking about, wasn't it? Not many, but you never knew it was you until it was. "I'm fine." He wasn't. "Just a surprise." He tried to drink more water.

"It's empty."

"I noticed." Easier to look at the bottom of the empty glass than at Cynthia, whose face he could read, in this moment, more easily than he had been able to in the four months they'd been together. He felt his careful system trembling. She'd found no hole in his defenses, no weakness in his walls. But he wanted her to understand, in this lonely moment as his heart refused to calm, as his fingers shook and the apartment gaped around him like a maw. The floor could fall out from under you at any time. He knew that. He knew that.

He wanted to tell her about the Challenger and the black-flower road and the face beyond the sky. He wanted to tell her about the thick braid on Zelda's shoulder and a green the color of memory. He wanted to tell her that her eyes were a mirror he couldn't bear to look within. He wanted to betray himself and fall.

His hand shook as he groped for the letter. He tore the envelope open. Inside, where there should have been ten years of his life, there lay a single folded sheet of paper.

"Old school."

He looked up. "The oldest."

The letter was not long. He memorized it before he set it down. He tried to tell himself that he'd expected this. They all had. But they'd lied to themselves, like you did to survive. You tried. You failed. You lived with failure. In some ways it was easier than success.

"You can tell me." She was closer to him now, and her touch on his arm was not a game, not a hook, there was no word he could say that would slow her down or stop her. He might tell her to leave. He tried to imagine doing so. For all they'd done to and with each other, he'd never felt closer to her than at that moment.

He could tell her what was wrong. But he could not tell her to leave. "I have to go away." He heard himself as if he were already gone. "For a while. I owe some-one."

"Who? The Mafia?"

His laugh was a little too loud. "Friends. From college."

"Some of that weird Skull and Bones shit, huh? No, I'm sorry. I've got secrets too."

"Maybe you'll tell me about them someday."

"We can trade. When you get back."

"Sure."

She looked as if she'd lost a book she was half done reading. "You don't have to go, if you don't want to. She can take care of herself. Whoever she is."

"It's not like that. They— I owe them. It's complicated. I promise."

Her head cocked. The rest of her body was still, except for the pulse at her throat. Deep forests got that way when a predator passed by. He'd hidden from a dinosaur in one, once. Sal had saved his life by drawing it off. "Ish," she said, "what are you promising?"

Even he didn't know. But that question sure scared him. "Just . . . don't go anywhere. While I'm gone."

He didn't sound like himself, even to himself. He was falling.

"I won't," she said. He'd never asked her for that kind of assurance before, not for all the contracts they'd signed. But he was asking for something else now. "Here." More water. "What about tonight? Can you come upstairs?"

He drank, he nodded, he followed her. She laid him down in his own bed, drew his hands over his head, closed the cuffs gently around his wrists. They at least would keep him there, kept him from falling. She held him tight, then loosely, as they drifted off to sleep.

When she woke up, the cuffs were open and he was gone.

# CHAPTER SEVEN

The day before he left, Ramón Espina took his boyfriend to Dodger Stadium, to visit his great-grandfather's grave. He didn't tell Gabriel about the grave, only woke him with tickets in hand. Asleep, Gabe looked like a god in marble, one arm cast across his eyes, his other hand draped over the sheets. Ramón wondered at the unthinking art of him, which, seconds after waking, transformed into a goofy corn-fed smile—when he saw Ramón kneeling over him with the tickets.

"Where did you get those?"

"My secret," he said. "Unless you have other plans?" He raised an eyebrow, made as if to throw the tickets over his shoulder—but Gabe caught his arm and pulled him down. It was hard to kiss while you were smiling, but they managed. They had to stop to move the tickets safely to the bedside table. In Gabriel's arms, he could forget about the letter his uncle had handed him last night, when he picked Gabe up from the garage after work.

The morning was skin and sex and tension and blue skies and sunlight through the bedroom window, and when they were done, Los Angeles was waiting for them, his city, his world, perfect as ever. If he'd lived anywhere else, he would have thought the weather was the city's way of tempting him to stay. But no. Los Angeles just got up every day and put her face on. You couldn't trust appearances in this city, a beautiful face did not mean a beautiful mind or a beautiful heart, but it was honest, in its own way. Most other places in America sold you a story and expected you to believe it was true. Here, everyone was in on the joke.

"You okay?" Gabriel asked on the way down to the parking garage.

"Just thinking."

"You were quiet last night too."

"Working a problem. You know."

Gabriel gave him that curious-bird look he had, slightly unsettling, utterly lovely. He wasn't dumb, though that was a mistake too many of Ramón's old classmates made when they drifted through and slept on the couch or met them for drinks—there were books Gabe hadn't read, and jokes he didn't get because he hadn't read those books, but he was good at games and puzzles and every time Ramón walked him through a proof, he followed each step and asked the right questions without prompting.

The world was clear inside Gabe's head. When he wanted to do something, he asked himself if the doing would hurt anyone, and if not, he did it. He didn't worry. If one approach didn't work, he tried another. If they ever tried to break into a bank vault together, Ramón would be bent over the stethoscope with six manuals open around him on the floor and a set of drills, and Gabe would walk up to check if the door was really locked. "Want to talk it through?"

He felt himself deflate. "Right now I just want to drive. And watch a game."

Gabe kissed him, then slid into the passenger's seat.

They were driving the Camaro this month, sporty and yellow, lots of ponies, Gabe's restoring work. He'd grown up with a wrench in his hand on a farm full of rusting equipment, and when he moved to LA to try to make it as an actor, or at least as a man, the one part of his old life he didn't want to leave behind was the magic he could work with his hands and a toolbox on a piece of ancient rusted junk.

Like Ramón.

Well, he shouldn't be too hard on himself. A piece of ancient rusted junk like Ramón had been when they met, three years ago. After the shit went down, after Zelda lost it and lost Sal and lost everything, he'd drifted home and got busy wrecking himself. Found a shitty, soulless, high-paid number muncher sort of job, and disappeared into it. There had been bad relationships and not-so-bad ones, there had been mistakes made, and there were two years he remembered mostly as a blur of drama, drugs, and bad decisions. He'd cleaned himself up after waking on the beach one morning at dawn, curled up and salt-caked with no clue how he'd come to be there. His mother welcomed him home and took him to Mass the next day.

The Sunday cookouts and block parties, the dancing, the drums, he'd been afraid of coming back to them because of how normal they'd feel, and how normal he wasn't. But after a few weeks of living day to day and drinking lukewarm water and eating rice, he went to Tío's shop, where he'd first worked on the Challenger back in high school, and asked if there was anything he could do around the place.

Tío hooked him up with tools and space. Ramón had wandered dumps and junkyards until his knack led him to the remains of a beautiful Mustang, still bearing traces of its original robin's-egg paint job. Restoring it was a simple task, something he could see through to the end. He could not imagine a future for himself, but he could imagine a future for the car.

It came together slowly because he wanted to do it right. He took the whole thing apart. He cleaned it, sorted ruined parts from the ones that would still serve with careful tuning. He tested each piece, every inch of hose, he held one screw at a time up to the light.

It was a kind of therapy, he realized halfway through. He'd raise a screw and turn it and turn it, looking for flaws, and in his memory he was turning each of them in turn.

Zelda: Zelda who'd come to him in the first few bitter weeks of spring semester their freshman year with a ream of formulas and proofs she wanted him to help her check, and oh yes, also can I borrow your car; Zelda in Montana, tear-streaked and bloody and desperate after all the others had left: You have to help me. You have to understand. I did it for her.

Sal, brilliant and strong and full of faith, Sal who used to wake him at four in the morning to walk out up East Rock and see the sunrise. Ish lumbering along after them both, and Sarah, Sal's friend first and at the end, and the first to leave that Montana parking lot. They'd all fit so perfectly together. They'd worn one another, stripped one another clean. He couldn't do anything about that. He told himself he couldn't, because otherwise he'd spend his life trying.

He could still fix a car, at least. That was real. The old skills came back. As the weeks passed, he eased into the work, so the car no longer stood for anything but a car, and he was just a man working while other men worked.

That was a good thing to be. He even started to notice them after a while, the other men, to listen to baseball games with the guys while eating the peanut butter sandwiches he'd packed, asking after Daniel's kids or José's rottweiler.

And there was this one guy especially.

Tall and lean and blond and actor-handsome, the way people who didn't live in LA tended to think humans weren't, not really. They figured it all was done with makeup and style and money, but it wasn't. The light that reflected off his face seemed to have a deeper, softer texture than real light, like someone had smeared the lens with Vaseline. At first Ramón thought he was a vision, a figment of his imagination. A guy like that couldn't possibly be working here. Then he realized as the days added up, that he had things the wrong way round. What if the world he'd imagined he lived in, where men like this weren't possible, was in fact the fake world, and he was only just now realizing it?

Real or not, one day the man with the golden hair walked up to him at closing time, toweling off his hands. He'd missed a streak of grease on his cheek. Ramón would have personally murdered anyone who pointed that out to him. Ramón had said something dumb, like *Long day,* or *You going home?*—something forgettable and unforgivable.

"I figure that must be good to drive." Gabe had nodded at the car. The motion changed how his sweat caught the light, and Ramón found himself thinking of stained glass windows.

He didn't remember what he'd said after that. *Excuse me?* maybe. His memory of this moment was entirely outward-directed. They'd laughed about it since.

"You've gone back through that engine about a dozen times." He had an unhurried drawl, his vowels bowed just a little too long. His voice didn't sound like it had anywhere to be. "I bet she's ready for a spin."

Oh, that voice did things to him. Nuestra Señora la Reina de los Ángeles del Río de Porciúncula, take care of your boy. "It's been a while since I did anything like this. The car, I mean." God, after all the worlds he had seen and after all the chaos he had instituted in the last seven years, he could not be *blushing.* "I don't want to get it wrong. I'm Ramón." His hand was dirty, he realized as he thrust it out. Before he could pull it back, Gabe caught it with his nice newly washed hands. Which settled it. Gabe could not be imaginary. The hands were real. The bones were long and fine and his grip was firm. For all the calluses and muscle, he felt gentle.

"If you'd not mind and all, I could help you check her over. I'm sure she's fine, but another pair of eyes never hurt."

No, they didn't, he thought. Especially not those eyes. A smarter man than Ramón would not have answered: "I don't want to bother you."

But Gabe was Gabe: no drop of anxiety or doubt. "No trouble at all. Just because I get paid to work on cars doesn't mean I don't like it. So long as there's good company."

It took him a few seconds to parse this, and after that to say: "I'd love that," then try to cover, because *love* was a strong word, but Gabe was already walking away with a "Great, I'll see you tomorrow," before he could even start to worry.

They drove the Mustang for the first time together. After seven years, Ramón had forgotten how good this would feel. His hand worked its magic on the shifter, and the road spun into his bones. They had all found knacks on the road, and this was his: he always knew just where things had to go, and how to get them there. The Mustang slipped through traffic into the spaces where other cars weren't. Red lights turned green for him. He sank into the road like a fish into a stream. Gabe whooped in the passenger seat. Wind rushed through the open windows, their own private waterfall.

They kissed at the end of that drive, in front of Griffith Observatory with the whole city laid out below them, like the biggest cliché in the known universe, and he loved it, this moment here one giant middle finger to college, to what he had been since, to the giant Unpronounceables lurking beyond the borders of the sky. Go please yourself with your own tentacles. Poison the world if you want, eat the ground out from under my feet.

I won't do your work for you. I'll stand here in the sun and be in love.

And here he was, three years later, driving Gabe through the city, a whole man, a happy, healed man in a world falling apart.

He felt guilty some mornings when he woke up next to Gabe, guilty for how much magic he'd gathered here in his bed, set against how many people were suffering. He knew that someday there would be a storm after the calm. It could take many shapes: a government knock on the door, a horrible mistake on his part or on Gabe's. But he knew it would come. Monsters never died. They only slept awhile.

They found a parking space right next to Dodger Stadium, thanks to Ramón's knack. It was a bright gold day, and the ballpark was a massive contented humming beast. You could forget in traffic—especially in the stop-and-go mess even Ramón could not route past, the last two miles up Chavez Ravine—that there were people in all those cars, millions and millions of real human lives stitched together into the name Los Angeles. And then you got out of your car, and there was a man with a big mustache hammering on the relish dispenser without luck, there was a kid balancing a pyramid of Dodger dogs with ketchup as she trailed her mom through the crowd, there were three big burly teenagers trading jokes as one of them tried to corral the other two into a selfie frame, there were the San Gabriel Mountains, and there was his city.

Oh, and sure, there was a national anthem too. He'd gone to a game in Boston once, and the anthem was sung by a high, beautiful, police-choir tenor. The next Dodger game he'd come home to, the anthem was sung by the LA cast of *The Book of Mormon*.

It was a good game. Ramón got a Dodger dog and they sat high up and cheered; Kershaw was pitching well, Turner put in a two-run homer, everyone agreed that MLB had to fix whatever was wrong with the ball, they wondered whether

Jansen would close the game without giving everyone a heart attack. Ramón marked the plays in his own notebook. Gabe teased him for that. Couldn't you just look things up online? But it kept Ramón's head in the game, and his mind worked differently with a pen in his hand. That was when he had the flashes of insight, most often wrong but occasionally, occasionally right, that would fuel hours of growling at MATLAB on his laptop at home, long after Gabe had gone to sleep. If he didn't at least try on his own, the numbers didn't dance.

He wondered what Zelda would have made of that. One of their first real arguments back in college had been about observer-dependency and quantum mechanics. She'd tried to explain her concept of spin—sense experience without decision. He'd been the skeptical one.

They were sitting in an alcove on a shortcut from the math building to Timothy Dwight College, which had the best dining hall on that side of campus. Ivy covered the walls and the gates to either side, and a small statue of Mary faced a bench. When Zelda found him, he'd been praying about some shit he was going through at the time.

Freshman year was a mess for a relatively brown, relatively queer boy without much money. There was a trick everyone else here seemed to have, of taking things for granted. He'd expected to have to fight for recognition and respect, but instead he found himself just assumed away. His classmates seemed to figure everyone was like them, everyone went skiing over the holidays and if you weren't, you must have a good reason, like you were going to Europe or you had opera tickets. There were advantages to that kind of presumption—if you wanted, you could just bluff them. He'd tried that, and to his surprise it worked. But with every passing week, he felt more like he had glued a mask to his face.

So he'd been praying about that, until Zelda plopped down beside him on the bench to make a truly absurd claim about quantum physics.

"Observer-dependent effects don't work that way," he said. "The structure of the experiment determines how we perceive the wave function. There's nothing special about consciousness."

"But we don't know the results of the experiment until they've been observed." She'd been after this idea for the better part of a month, crazed, writing-on-walls-in-pencil kind of stuff. "Look, we have two major philosophical positions about math, right?"

"Um." His mind was still half full of the question he'd been asking the ivy-covered and ill-attended Virgin. "Sure?"

Her look said, *You're usually faster than this.* Her mouth said: "Does math relate to things out there in the real world, or does it only relate concepts in our heads to one another? If it relates to real things—how? Oneness isn't something I can just point to."

"What about atoms?"

"Come *on,* man, atoms are made of quantum and subquantum stuff, which isn't even *stuff,* really. Even electrons are probabilistic."

"That doesn't mean they're imaginary, just that they're indeterminate."

"What I mean is that, if we had a different conceptual framework for math, maybe all of that would make sense intuitively—maybe we could interface with probabilities down at the base level, rather than having to break through our intuitions of oneness."

"What about singularities? A lot of oneness there."

"Ramón, do you really think ancient Greek geometers based their reasoning on black hole astronomy?"

"Singularities exist, is my point."

"And they're less singular than you think. They decay, they live and die. They're close to a real physical example of oneness, sure, but again, if we had different core concepts, maybe we'd see those when we looked at black holes. But math has to be more than something inside our heads. Doesn't it?"

"I mean . . ."

"Sure, we're mapping the contours of our underlying conceptual frameworks from first principles, but we don't just make those frameworks up. We extract them from the world and our sense experience. As we see more and more things, we form intuitions about thing-ness. The proof process tests and verifies those intuitions, and from it we derive new concepts, which feed back into our intuition. The mind feeds back into the physical world, too—through observer effects and physical action." She glanced at the statue of Mary, as if suddenly worried the Virgin might be listening. "So what if, using a different conceptual framework, on a deep level, we could feed something else out into the world?"

He'd been supposed to carry the argument forward, to follow where she led. What he said instead was, "You know, Sal is worried about you."

They'd had a fight. A bad one. But even so, he'd been the one she came to when she had her breakthrough and needed a car.

Ramón had two older sisters, but he'd never had a brother before. It took him a long time to realize that was what Zelda was. And until yesterday, he'd not had a word from her in years. He knew she wasn't dead. She'd been raw and torn when he left her in Montana, and nobody that far gone could die. The world was cruel. Every world they'd ever found was cruel. So she wasn't dead, because dead would be too easy. She was out there like Elvis was. Ada Wang, passing through LA for Comic-Con and in search of a place to crash, claimed she'd seen Zelda coming out of a men's room in Boston's South Station one winter, all bruised and cut up as if she'd been in a fight. Chuck Viswanathan ran into her outside a Starbucks once. Zelda sightings even made the class notes pages of the alumni magazine. Somehow she was the one the legends circled around. Everyone knew better than to ask what had happened to Sal.

Ramón had made his decision before he opened the letter. He hadn't told Gabe yet. He'd have to soon. Because he was going.

But there was one thing he had to do first. It was the reason they were here, at Dodger Stadium, on a day that made him want to curl up inside Los Angeles and never leave. The ball cracked off the bat and the crowd cheered.

He'd been putting it off for years. And if Zelda was right—he might not get another chance. He closed his eyes to Kershaw and the mountains and closed his ears to the crowd, and asked the blackness beyond the world a question.

The answer surfaced in his mind as if it had been hidden down there since the instant of his birth. Maybe it had. Plato said that was how math worked—but then, when had Ramón taken Plato's word for anything?

He tapped Gabe on the shoulder. Gabe was leaning forward, elbows on his knees, rapt, fingers laced—he was a drama fan, bless him, here not for the averages and the strategies but for the overwhelming *now* question. What happens next? The world could end during the pitcher's windup, and he'd never notice. "I'll be right back."

Gabe nodded, sure, sure, put out his hand to touch Ramón's waist as he edged away, and that light touch was almost enough hook to keep him there.

He left Gabe's hand, and the game. They'd be here when he came back.

He walked through the stadium unseen. Not invisible—just using his knack to slide from blind spot to blind spot, the same way he stitched together insignificant openings in freeway traffic. The spin he'd gathered at the game guided him, told him when to go, when to stop, when to turn.

He found a door marked AUTHORIZED PERSONNEL ONLY, but when he tried the knob, it was unlocked. Concrete steps led down into the bowels of the stadium. He wasn't supposed to be here. Far below, big machines churned. There were security cameras, of course, but the people who watched the cameras had holes in their attention, too, gaps a careful man could move through. The spin in his bones told him how to stop, and when to start, and how to move.

At the bottom of the stairs, there was a door. He opened it, found a concrete hall beyond. The machines grew louder. Far above, the crowd cheered. He imagined Gabe cheering, too, golden and happy, not even remembering Ramón. It hurt to imagine that, but it hurt less than imagining trouble on that young god's face. To imagine that Ramón might make him regret, even for a moment, their time together.

He followed the hallway to another door. Behind he heard whirs and clicks and the rumble of great revolving drums. This door wasn't open, but it had one of those old-fashioned metal-button keypad locks. He closed his eyes, pressed numbers at random. The lock clicked. He opened the door.

"Ramón."

His hand froze on the doorknob. He'd figured all the angles, worked all the numbers out in his head. And he was an idiot. "Gabe. What are you doing here?"

It was an absurd question. "Following you."

Following. Blundering down through all those careful gaps Ramón exploited, like a rhinoceros chasing a lizard through a forest, crashing trees every which way. Still, they might have a few minutes. If they were lucky. He grabbed Gabe's wrist, pulled him into the machine room, and shut the door behind them. The machine noise drowned out Gabe's startled squawk. He shushed him, held him close. Gabe was warm, and confused.

"Ramón, what's going on?" He knew to whisper, at least.

"The cameras can't see us here. Six inches that way and they can."

"How do you know that?"

"How do I know where holes will be in traffic? How do I always get a good parking space?"

He didn't get it, yet. In the machine room's red lights, he looked younger.

Ramón was two years older, but the gap between them stretched and contracted like an accordion. Some days it barely existed, and some days Gabe seemed centuries his junior. The difference was more of distance than of time. Gabe had crossed half the country to reach LA, but Ramón had crossed so many worlds he stopped counting. "You have a knack, you said."

"I have a knack." He tried not to let his own panic show through. As a quick excursion, in and out, he'd justified this trip to himself. No one would ever know. But Gabe changed all of that, and he didn't want to get Gabe in trouble. "It's better than I usually let on. We need to be over by that pipe in ten seconds, okay?"

Gabe nodded. He was listening. Even if he did look as scared as Ramón felt on the inside. "And—now."

Ramón swung Gabe like they were dancing, down in this hot room of churning machines. Plumbing, he guessed, or part of the HVAC system—Tío would know. Ramón's acquaintance with the practical world began and ended with cars.

Their revolution came to rest. Ramón's head fit neatly in the space above the swell of Gabe's chest and the plane of his jaw. He never wanted to leave. So Gabe, of course, pushed him back. "What's going on here?"

"I had to see for myself," he said.

"The plumbing?"

"My great-grandfather's grave."

Gabe blinked. Beautiful, uncomprehending.

"There was a town here once. Not a big one, a few houses and fields—people who wanted to live and have children who lived. It's a good place, don't you think? Hills with a view. A little valley. Until the city needed public housing. And then, when they decided they didn't need public housing—a stadium."

"I didn't know. Jesus."

Ramón still half expected his mother to appear when anybody took the Lord's name in vain like that—expected her just to take shape in the shadows between two banks of pipes. "I don't even think about it when I'm here, most days. But—my knack tells me where things are, or where they used to be. And I had to see."

There wasn't anything to see. He hadn't expected much, and he had told himself to expect still less, but there was still that little kid in you who thought maybe I'll be able to feel something, maybe for a second I'll be able to peer behind the curtain.

Weird how you could feel that way even when you knew what was behind the curtain, even when you knew that the things waiting there had teeth.

The room was red, and as damp as rooms ever got in Los Angeles. There were pipes leading nowhere he could see. Signs on the walls identified various machines with unhelpful strings of letters and numbers. Many small hand valves and toggles were posted DO NOT TOUCH UNDER ANY CIRCUMSTANCES. Some controls blinked inside a locked wire cage.

It was utterly normal. No bodies here, no graves, no epitaphs or dates. The people who were here, who had been here, just vanished, leaving a hole walled with concrete and warning signs. There wasn't even a crack.

This place was not forgotten. This place was itself a sort of forgetting.

Was that worth saving?

He remembered the ruined cities they'd driven through, the fur-clad shrunken echoes of human beings who lived in the shadows there, hiding from the light and from their ancestors' bloodthirsty machines. He remembered the Green Glass City. He remembered bodies thrown to pigs, remembered twisted skeletons in rusted camps. There were ruined cities here, too—hell, his cousin María had received a uniform and her college tuition in exchange for going to the other side of the world and ruining her share of them. And there were fucking rat bastard camps just down the street, and bloodthirsty machines, and the whole world was choking on its own breath, and the rot was everywhere.

And Sal was coming back.

She always said: "We do what we can." When they were on the road together, he'd thought that meant, "Even small things are worth doing." Later he realized that what he'd first thought was a comforting slogan was actually a challenge. What can you do, really? Look at the world and ask yourself what it needs. Then look at yourself and ask, What can I give? What sacrifices can I make? Whom can I help? There's always a tank rolling down some street. You can't do everything—but that doesn't forgive you for not doing what you can.

Gabe was watching him the way he'd watch a dog that started growling for no reason.

"We should go," Ramón heard himself say.

No one caught them on the way out. They watched the rest of the game, and drove home after under the blanket of haze and light and the few dozen stars that made it through all of that. Jansen made the save, though he loaded the bases to do it. Nothing was ever easy.

"You're leaving."

Gabe had that long-cold-tunnel voice, the end-of-the-road sound. Ramón glanced his way. He was staring out the window at the hills beyond the glass.

"There's a bag in the trunk. And ever since that letter came, you've been so nice."

"I'm usually nice."

"Not this nice. You're nice the way you'd be nice to someone who's sick. And I'm not sick. What you did back there, knack or not, that could have gone so wrong. It was last-ditch, leaving-town stuff. So you're leaving. So don't. Stay."

"I won't be gone long."

"I can hear the 'I hope' you ain't saying."

"I do hope."

"There any room for me where you're going?"

Ramón shook his head. "It's . . . unfinished business. From before."

"Must be some kind of unfinished business, if you're not sure you're coming back. Were you a spy? A crook?"

He felt a sudden lurch, that Gabe was ready to believe anything of him, that they could be so strange to each other all of a sudden. Even if it was his fault. But Gabe, he realized, was joking. "Nothing like that. I was a kid, and I made a promise. That's all. Have you ever closed a door you don't think you'll ever open again? You forget it's there, you wallpaper over it, you move a bookcase in front of it, and then one day someone knocks."

"And I can't come."

"I made mistakes before I met you. Those aren't your mistakes."

"And here I thought I was the only mistake you ever made."

"Don't think that. Please. Don't. You're just about the only thing in this life I know I've done right."

"So why leave?"

"Because I used to be young and a special kind of dumb. My friends went too far and so did I, because I wanted to live in a world that worked the easy way it did inside their heads. We did some crazy things. We lost someone. I've never come to terms with that, not really. It chased me into the hole I was in before I met you. Now maybe I have a chance to bury it. Fill the hole in. Pour concrete. And come home."

"Okay," he said, not like he believed it. "Will you call?"

"I'll call. It's just a week. Maybe two." He didn't know that. But this—the force of the five, no, four of them back together—it couldn't last for long. Too much blood under the bridge.

They made love that night, eager, fierce, and sad, defying jerks and a broken world and their own bodies, and time.

The next day Gabe drove him to the garage. He didn't need to be asked. He knew Ramón did not want the Mustang.

Ramón's father had died in a car crash while Ramón was very young. It was a mechanical failure, ugly—a bad, closed-casket sort of death. After, his mother made a vow that their children would not drive any car they had not built themselves. It was a stupid vow, but she made it anyway, and as a result, none of the Espina children would ever have driven if not for their uncle.

He was a mechanic, and he taught the two older girls the way a bored piano teacher might help a student compelled by parental mandate to learn "Claire de Lune." He built their cars himself, made sure they understood every nut and bolt and joint in case their mother quizzed them, swore them to secrecy, and said nothing more of the matter.

But Ramón wanted to do it himself and to know what he was doing. To hold the whole system in his mind, the way he could hold a problem in math. He wanted to fall in love. He wandered used-car lots and dumps and followed up on listings in the back pages of newspapers until he found the One. A 1969 Challenger with the broad gritted-teeth grille. Ground down by time, its engine a mess, a total rebuild—but he dreamed about it for a week after he first saw it, and when he made it back to the dump and found it was still there, he'd put down half his savings from the pizza gig and bought it on the spot.

He resurrected that car. It took months to do it right, hunting down the proper parts and tools, the right paint, the right upholstery. By the time he was done, the Challenger might have been an entirely new machine. But it ran like a river, and sweet as wine.

It purred, it stretched, it roared. It was a jungle cat. It was a *destrier,* one of those fanged warhorses from his aunt's far-future books, eight feet tall at the shoulder and fire-snorting, zero to sixty at the flick of a rein. It was his baby. At the christening, Tío played "One Piece at a Time," the song that, Tío said, converted him to the church of Johnny Cash, and toasted with the good bourbon—on condition that Ramón wouldn't drive for at least two hours after and would never tell his mother.

Ramón toasted, poured out the bourbon rather than drinking it, and went for a drive, full and free in the gleaming LA night. He drove for hours. When he was hungry, he stopped at Du-par's for a slice of lemon meringue pie and coffee and drove more. He twisted up the roads of Griffith Park, he traced the river's concrete turns. The blacktop belonged to him and to the Challenger, and the blacktop ran on forever.

He'd left that car wrecked and burning on a roadside in a distant impossible place, where the sky was on fire and the ground a pane of cracked glass. Its paint bubbled and ran, like the jelly of a burst eyeball weeping down a cheek. Its leather and metal curled, the anatomy he'd worked so hard to frame transformed back into a wreck, its soul gone out in a column of thick smoke. He'd tried to chase Sal and Zelda down, to stop them before they reached the crossroads. The Challenger tried with him—and when they failed, they failed together.

As he watched the Challenger burn, through tears and the foul smoke, he'd thought: This must be how God feels when he looks at the world. After all the trouble we took to build you, after all we've been through together, how could I let it come to this?

Years could pass in the blink of an eye and leave you more or less unchanged. But some instants were a dentist's pliers. One wrench, and just a bloody gap remained. As he stood by the roadside in the smoke and knew that he'd lost, that their lives and this moment on the road were over, he had, for the first time in years, a vivid memory of his father. Not a picture-book memory or a story his mother or his uncle or one of his many aunts told him, but a man larger than life by his side, with big mustaches and full cheeks and a hard, kind face, staring with him into the smoke. He'd been immortal, and then he was gone. For a few months, a year at most, they'd been immortal too.

And now they were . . . whatever came after that.

He'd thrown himself away. He'd flown across the country helping people make bad decisions and he'd been well paid for it. He'd crumbled and rebuilt himself and now he was here. In all the months he'd worked in Tío's garage buying junkers and fixing and selling them, he'd never once looked at a Challenger. That was a bloody gap he was not yet ready to tongue.

Then, six weeks ago, an old gray lady with a voice like raw leather brought one in to sell. Tío had almost turned her away. But Ramón had just finished a project, and that grille kept grinning, and he thought, What's the harm?

Now Gabe helped him roll back the cover and there it was.

Blacker than black with a bright red racing stripe, its smile wide and vicious and toothy. Those bug-eyed headlights glinted gunslinger steel at a sweating, unready world.

Back in school he'd read Plato, writing about Socrates. The old man claimed he had a daemon inside him, an inner voice that told him where to go and what to do. The problem with inner voices, Ramón had thought, was you couldn't tell the difference between the ones that knew what they were talking about and the ones who just wanted to fuck you up. Inner voices could disguise themselves. Pride might wear Generosity's face for a while, selfishness could masquerade as altruism, laziness as kindness, fear as good common sense. You didn't know what things were until you saw them in the world.

Twice in his life now, Ramón had taken his daemon and made it into a car.

I was not gone, it whispered to him as light reflected from its hubcaps smiled half-moons on the pavement. I don't disappear, I don't fade, and I never die. Sometimes people turn from me because they're not ready to follow, because they can't bear the truths I tell, the prophecies I speak. No one wants to see their country really: what it is under the pavement and the paint, what it is you're driving over when you drive to the end of the goddamn line, because if you saw it, you'd tear your fucking eyes out and rip your belly open with your own hands. But once you sit behind this wheel, once you hear the highway song, you've had the taste of it, and not all the coke or fucking in the world can beat that peculiar flavor. You thought I was dead. You just couldn't follow where I was riding. And now you've brought me back with your own hands and sweat, like last time, only now you know what I am, you know what I want, and you have maybe the first infant's goddamn inkling of what that's going to cost.

We are gonna ride through shit and fire to the end of the world.

Come on, kid. Get in.

Gabe's hand was around his wrist. "You're shaking."

Because you're afraid. Of how right it felt, of how much you like this pretty little life you've built here while you thought you were ignoring me. You think an empty room is the worst you'll find out there? A black road runs from the West, buddy, bringing War, and that is you. A road is a cut and what will you find when you peel back this nation's skin but blood, oceans of blood. Your city and your baseball team and your boyfriend are huddled together in the center of a tiny balsa wood raft, trying not to rock the boat as the blood waves rise and rise. Let's get a-moving, son. She's come back with fire and lightning. She's there beyond the sky. And this time, you best not wuss out when you ride to meet her.

"Ramón?"

He grabbed Gabe, pressed him against the car, and kissed him savagely, hungrily, gulping him down, feeling the sudden pressure of his hard-on through his jeans. The car was real. The road was real. But this—the teeth and flesh and naked need, the taut power of his arms as if he could break their skin and lock their ribs together—this was also real. This would bring him home.

"I love you," he said. "I'll be back."

When he read his aunt's books as a kid, he'd thought the ones with magic were silly. How strange to live in a world where words or will could change the nature of rocks or the course of weather. Now that he was grown, he knew better. Not all words had power, but if you said the right ones at the right time, you could change things far more durable than mountains. He saw a new motion behind Gabe's eyes, deep and unguessed in the silences of his soul.

"Okay." He believed it. And so did Ramón.

His taste remained when they slipped apart, an echo of Gabe in Ramón's nerves, in his mouth. Let it be. Let it stay.

The Challenger's door opened. It closed. The seat curled around him like a tongue.

"Let's go."

He jammed the key home.

The Challenger laughed deep in its throat, then roared. And he was gone.

# CHAPTER EIGHT

Sarah Jaye Masters crossed into Montana, furious.

She'd started off mad, back in Virginia, when she saw the envelope her daughter brought in with the rest of the mail—"Letter for Mommy!" She got angrier when, against her better goddamn judgment, she opened the letter and read it rather than feeding it straight to the shredder. The sheer presumption. The bullheaded, blunt-minded raw *Zelda*-ness of it all, sending a letter instead of an email or a phone call, choosing the route of most resistance and, as usual, not bothering to think—to acknowledge that maybe there were other things going on. That maybe there were reasons old friends might not want to hear from her, that she was asking them to—no, not even asking them, assuming that they would—set aside their whole lives, lives she did not even acknowledge might not be entirely their own to dispose of, to help her. And the worst part was that Sarah knew, she *knew,* she would go.

But there were certain kinds of deep bone-rage she'd promised herself when she was six that she would never show, not where any child of hers could see. Let alone Susan, so blinking and earnest and bright. Alex, the younger, might handle it—devious and wily since he was born, a snatcher of snacks and a teller of tall tales, with his own share of anger—but a promise was a promise, as she told them most every day. Especially when you shook on it. And she, age six, had shaken hands with her own reflection.

So she took that anger and swallowed it down into the gnawing pit of her stomach, where she kept the rest of her everyday rage. When Susan asked what was in the letter, Sarah smiled and said cheerfully that it was from an old friend with an unreasonable request. She filed it in the drawer with the lock and ran down her half of the school-day morning checklist to be sure she hadn't forgotten anything, while Susan helped her track down where Alex was hiding today.

That was one real advantage to parenthood, she'd decided, set against the sleepless nights, the anxiety that plagued her first years with each kid. Before she had kids, there was nothing to check the inside of her own head. Feelings could run forever in the infinite plane of her mind, building momentum, growing as they trampled other feelings into themselves. When she was younger there had been days when she could not eat, could not sleep, could not go outside or pour herself a glass of water for the pounding hooves of rage and sorrow inside her skull. The only solutions she'd found that weren't pharmacological involved blistering overwork, the kind of fierce grind that took her from army base schools to the Ivy League and then to medical school, even with that weird unexplained résumé gap of those two years when she'd been on the road with Sal.

Then the kids came along. Now the stampede might thunder through her body—but Alex had managed to lock himself in the linen closet while hiding, hoping he could escape the school bus. The stampede had to wait.

Evan drew him out in the end, which was only fair because it was Evan's *Calvin and Hobbes* strips that had started the whole problem in the first place. At least that's what Susan said to rile Evan up. It didn't work. It made him feel sheepish, but they both knew the issue had deeper roots than a comic strip. (Though Evan's own parents claimed he and his sister never fought until they started reading the Berenstain Bears.) They had one kid who was sweet, level-tempered, curious, and possessed at times of a deep Wednesday Addams sort of melancholy, and one kid whose heart and head and body galloped in different directions at top speed. Sarah only had to watch Evan, coffee in hand, leaning against the door with the same gentle curious expression he used on students who tried to BS their way through seminar, ask Alex how he planned to learn to fly rockets if he spent the next ten years in the linen closet, so patient even with five minutes until bus time, to tell who took after whom.

They made the bus. Alex raced Susan and was beating her down the yard until he tripped, theatrically, and came up rolling and laughing with leaves in his hair, beside the giant pumpkin balloon he'd begged them to set up for Halloween even though Halloween was still more than a month off.

The bus left with both kids. (They watched to be sure. Alex had played technicalities on the general concept of "waiting for the bus" before. "I waited for three *whole* minutes!") Evan's hand rested on Sarah's waist. The beard the kids couldn't stop teasing him about was soft against her cheek.

The street was empty. The house was empty except for them. And without anything to check it, the stampede surged through her heart.

"Good kids," he said.

"I will keep them." She took his coffee cup from him, set it down on the counter. She thought about the letter. No, *thought* was too weak a word for what she was doing about that letter. It throbbed like a peeled thumb. She curled around it, around the anger. Hoofbeats.

She grabbed his jacket, slammed him against the wall, covered his lips with her mouth. Her fingers dug into his arms. She wished they could dig through his sleeves and his skin as well, through his flesh to that unmovable skeleton or whatever there was deeper than bones in him that let him move so gently through the world. Maybe his marrow was the secret. Maybe if she cracked his bones one by one and sucked them dry—

He tensed under her, pushed some space between them. Like strong magnets slightly parted, they shook, his arms trembling, just strong enough to give her space. "Time." The word more breath than voice. "We have work."

"Later," she said, and the magnets clicked together.

They made it to the living room, closed the blinds, knocked over a lamp but didn't break anything. There was a lawn mower running next door. Her nails dug into his back. He was nervous at first, afraid of hurting her, he always felt that way when it was like this, when she was so much larger than her skin and she needed to be everything in the world, to hold it all back with the fierce tension of her arms. He was what she needed. He was a good man and they deserved each other. They had worked so hard.

She gasped with the fire of it.

Why couldn't it all just go away? She walked a warding circle around her house every day. She said her blessings and she deployed her knack. She turned away all harm, with utmost care. Her knack still worked, though she hadn't been on the road in years. Susan had fallen from the Grants' tree house at their son's birthday party and limped away with a sprain that healed in two days. Alex's tumble on the front lawn hadn't broken a bone. He'd wriggled through a dog door to the basement at Evan's sister's house and fallen face-first down a flight of stairs to a concrete floor, and lost only a baby tooth that he could already twist with his tongue. She kept them safe. The world was ending, sure, but not here yet, and anyway, wasn't it always? Her mother and her grandmother and her cousins back on the reservation had known that long before Sarah and her sister, growing up on a succession of army bases and coming of age fluent in English, German, and army brat, had figured it out. Surely this was the trade: she'd failed her best friend. The hungry nation took that from her. Didn't it owe her this? Why hadn't her knack kept that letter away?

It tried. The envelope was water-stained and crumpled and torn in places, and there were big tire tracks along the back, and drops of something that might have been mud, or blood. But Zelda had always been stronger. Sarah hadn't even been strong enough to save Sal in the end.

She pounded Evan's back with her fists. She trapped his legs with her own. Her teeth were a cage for her breath. A million hooves thundered in her chest. If all her arts were so much dry grass, if her knack could not save her family from this, maybe her heart would burst right there like a ripe fruit dropped on pavement from a height. Maybe it would do her that kindness.

She was being unspeakably, horribly selfish. She had a duty. There was no sense asking, Why now? when you might as well ask, Why not before? But if you couldn't be selfish in your own damn living room with your own damn curtains drawn and your own damn nails digging half-moons in your own damn husband's back, then exactly when and where could you be selfish?

She broke, and so did he. They lay side by side, gasping, nameless. Somehow they had ended up on the rug. The edge of the glass coffee table cut across her view of the ceiling. A clear dark line, and the world on either side more or less the same.

"What happened?" He was a good amateur detective; he'd been in the kitchen when Susan handed her the letter. He didn't need to ask. But he was a better husband than a detective, and in ten years, they'd learned what space to allow each other, how to let feelings unfold and reveal themselves at their own pace.

"Zelda wants to get us all together." There was no helping the scorn with which she said that name. "She thinks Sal's coming back." He knew the whole story. How could she not tell him? She'd even showed him the map she kept on her travels, marked with other worlds and the turns that led there. All the many roads they'd walked, and stayed lost the whole time. "I have to go."

"You don't." When was the last time he'd contradicted her so flatly? She turned to him in shock and they almost bonked skulls; he'd rolled over to look at her, his eyes big and as open as they were the first time she took him north to see the aurora. He was so earnest that it scared her. If she let herself be that open, one moment was all it would take, one moment and all this light and kindness would break like a candy shell between vast teeth.

But he wasn't her, and didn't know what she knew, no matter how he tried to understand. They had different lives. "You are right," she said. "I want to go." Also not quite true. "I do not trust her to get this right by herself."

"How long?"

She did not know.

"I'll call my mom. We can get Char in to help look after the kids for a few days too. We'll be fine. The hospital—"

"Weekes owes me. I have leave banked. A lot of leave."

"You need to do this?"

Meaning, even if he'd never say so out loud: Are they worth it?

And she remembered her roommate, her friend, who came back glowing and grinning the first week of sophomore year with a dance to her step, six hours after she'd left for forty-five minutes to troll the Christian Fellowship orientation mixer, to sit star-eyed on Sarah's bed while Sarah sat at her desk, working, until at last, she could not bear it and turned and asked—"What?"

"Tell me I can't crush on a freshman."

"You should not crush on a freshman."

"I *know*. Goddamn, I am the worst." But she sounded pleased with herself.

"She barely knows who she is yet," Sarah said, as if any of them knew. "You will get hurt. Both of you. You remember what we were like."

"Shit hot and awesome?"

"We have different memories."

"You're right. It is a terrible idea. No matter how cute she is. Or smart."

"Nobody is smart freshman year."

"Well, we weren't. It's a terrible idea. Almost . . ." Grinning so big Sarah could see it in her peripheral vision. "Immoral."

And Sarah remembered, much later, a parking lot in Montana, all of them together, except of course for Sal. Zelda stood there torn and bruised and bleeding, her skin raw, an articulated wince. Sarah looked into the hollows of those eyes Sal loved and said—You lost her.

She had walked away. She had kept walking away for years. She'd been halfway through medical school and a year into Evan before she managed to walk toward something again.

Was there a word in German for the feeling where you blazed a trail through dense woods only to find yourself right back where you started?

Pop would know.

This time at least she could do things differently.

"I owe it," she said, "to Sal. And to you. And to the kids."

"You think it might be that bad."

He knew the story. He believed. But he had not lived it himself, not the loss and the rot, not Elsinore and not Montana. There was still that space between their worlds. She loved him and she hated that space, and she hated Zelda for making her feel as if she were already gone. "Yes."

She left the next morning.

In their Highlander, with her suitcase in the trunk, she tightened her knuckles on the steering wheel and felt her anger, hot and tight and swollen. She tried to focus on the wheel, the gray dawn, the engine's roar, the road ahead.

She had always hated the road.

The road was Zelda's place, and Ramón's. Even Ish loved it, though he would never admit that. Not Sarah. For her, the highway was the long black tongue of a monster with a mouth that gaped as wide as this stupid enormous country, that never had been hers.

She had been born on base in Okinawa, her father a full bird colonel from a three-generation military Lakota family. Grandpa had fought in the Battle of the Bulge and taught his sons to salute as soon as they could stand. Sarah and her sister had grown up on a chain of bases in the almost-peacetime between the end of one forever war and the beginning of another; they understood the rules of survival too well to stick together in public. They supported each other in secret, like guerrillas. When others could see, they scattered. They moved. They were always moving.

At eighteen she knew where to score good weed and better theater in Berlin, she knew how to curse in Japanese, but still she did not know how to deal with the sheer brutal scope of the continental United States and its vast silent spaces. It pissed her off, from sea to shining sea. Or rather, it scared her, and *that* pissed her off.

It hadn't always. She'd grown up with flags everywhere, learning Founding Fathers history on base. To her, America was a myth, a dream, a story people told, and like a lot of first impressions, she had not realized just how right that one was until it was too late. She had visited home, of course. She remembered climbing buttes on reservation ground with her hand in her grandmother's one cold dry Christmas. She remembered mangling the words of a song in a language that should have been hers, while her sister, Ruth, two years younger, never dropped a syllable or fumbled a consonant. They lived stateside every few postings, for brief stretches. But Pop kept them away. She didn't understand why until later, when she hit the road.

Pop had fought for this country, and so had Mom in a sense, and so had all the beautiful, broken, uniformed boys and girls she'd grown up idolizing on base. But it was not her country. She knew it only through bad history and untold stories in languages Pop had not wanted her to learn. You had to work to know this place as it truly was—she'd had to work, in her own heart, to peel back the skin of what she was taught. To excavate.

But on the road, it all seemed easy. You didn't have to dig, to ponder, to confront or question or even think. Just open up the throttle and roll on at eighty miles an hour forever. Blink and you've crossed the Mississippi. Blink and you're at Devils Tower, or Manassas. You could roll through towns as easily as you could list their names, and if you moved fast enough, you'd never ask yourself what those names meant, where they came from. The road had a honeyed voice. It sidled up to the bar beside you and made you feel as though you had something to prove. As though you were the one who was wrong.

She hated the road. But she loved Sal. So she went. And here she was, ten years later, making the same mistake.

She wished she still had the letter, so she could crumple it in her hand.

She'd expected the anger to ease once she left the cul-de-sac, but like fuck it did. If anything, as she pulled onto the interstate, it burned hotter, as if she'd swallowed coals instead of two ibuprofen. How dare Zelda send that letter? How dare she presume Sarah would show up for this stupid last-stand mess?

How dare she be right?

DC traffic always was a monster, but in the last three years, the monster felt more venomous than usual. You sat on a Beltway that might as well have been a parking lot, breathing dead dinosaur fumes while you looked around at cars and drivers and wondered who they were, and what they'd do when the chips were down and the knives and flags came out.

You tried to guess based on scowls, but the Beltway made everyone scowl, and anyway, she'd been in college when she lost the pleasant illusion that people who thought it was okay to kill children with high-altitude robots, to torture human beings without cause, to contribute to the general creeping death of the nation or the planet, were fundamentally unhappy people. You could grow humans however you wanted, like kittens in bottles, so long as you controlled what they saw—and people were all too happy these days to give their eyes away in trust. By itself, that wasn't altogether surprising, she supposed. So much of being a certain kind of American—blithe and faithful, cheerily persuaded of your ultimate justice—depended on a cognitively expensive unseeing. Ignoring the evidence of your senses. Believing the world otherwise.

No wonder people looked at their fucking phones in grocery lines, or even behind the wheels of their land boats. Looking anywhere that wasn't curated for your convenience involved so much unseeing it wore you out fast. If you let someone else tell you what the world was, you could relax, happy, confident, assured. The monsters you supported were out-monstering the monsters you didn't. The world was just. Hooray. Relax, like, comment, subscribe.

Anyone could be a collaborator. Anyone could be a monster, fully fledged or in embryo. Maybe everyone was. (That was one trick of monsters, convincing everyone that they *were* everyone.) Or no one was a monster, and she was here on the Beltway tensing up, expecting to be mobbed by a bunch of drivers who were really too intent on their taxes/mortgage/kids/breakfast/morning meeting/how-much-they-hated-the-last-six-episodes-of-their-favorite-television-show to realize she existed.

She was nervous. Well, why shouldn't she be? Cars were dangerous. Back in the turn of the last century, when cars showed up on city streets, editorial cartoons raged about how many kids they killed. "The Modern Moloch," one caption read, under a picture: mouths of fire, pyramids of dead children. These days you were barely a citizen if you didn't routinely get behind the wheel of a two-ton death machine that could in a matter of seconds hit speeds no land animal on earth ever reached until 1900 or so. This was normal. There was, it turned out, a number of dead children that a country could deem acceptable.

She'd known that in theory, but she only understood quite how fucked up the whole thing was when her kids started walking outside the house. When suddenly you were counting on not just your babyproofed living room and your furniture anchors and the straps around the fridge to keep your toddler safe but a handful of social conventions, luck, lines of paint, and a three-inch curb. Not to mention, of course, the common sense and vigilance of a tiny human who still thought investigating power sockets with her tongue was a good idea. Just that, between your kid and every mouthbreather in the greater DC area with a license.

When she started talking like this at home, over wine, with friends around and the kids safely in bed, Evan could usually coax her out of it. Not with logic, since her logic was goddamn impeccable, but with his cool confidence that they would take care of Susan and Alex whatever happened. And besides, he never said out loud—she had her knack.

Sarah took a deep breath, and channeled calm, focus, center.

The woman in the Buick to her right was staring at her.

Not a normal sort of fuck-you-watch-the-road stare. Eyes wide and fixed, bugged out, like a hunting dog on point.

Sarah was not having this shit, not today. She shrugged at the woman in the Buick and turned back to watch the road and the black van in front of her, the one with military police plates.

But the feeling of being watched, that back-of-the-neck tickle, didn't fade. She wasn't going to give the lady in the Buick the satisfaction of acknowledging her, so she looked left instead, to the fast lane, which was just as stopped as the rest of them.

She looked left—into another pair of staring eyes.

The man in the Jeep, in his big bomber jacket, glared at her over the rims of his aviator shades. Not so crazed as Buick lady, but piercing, pointed. A killer's expression.

She was seeing things. Bad dreams, stress. All sorts of explanations. But, no, Buick lady was still there, staring, and so was the big, blotch-faced man in the Jeep. And behind him, also in the fast lane—stern sixtyish woman, eyes flat, judging. And in Sarah's rearview mirror, a father, two kids, one still in a booster car seat, craning their necks into the shifter well. All watching her.

When she was a kid, there'd been a run of car commercials about a well-meaning, bedraggled office dad who left his coffee mug on the roof of his car as he drove to work. Pedestrians and passing dogs and other drivers rubbernecked to marvel as the coffee cup remained in place, thanks ostensibly to the power of all-wheel drive, hydraulic suspension, antilock brakes, and other features the ad thought were very cool. Pop said it was glue. Maybe Sarah had left her suitcase on the roof. Maybe she was just paranoid.

But her suitcase was in her trunk, her day bag was in the passenger's-side footwell with her purse, her coffee mug was in the cup holder, and everyone on the Beltway was staring at her. Opposing traffic, too—eyes flashing past, the suggestion of turned heads behind dark-tinted glass. Engines growled. Roared. And in their roaring, she heard a deeper pulse—like footsteps, coming closer.

Something was awake, aware, and interested.

The engines were deafening. The footsteps close.

How much damage could these cars do, if they rammed her from a dead stop? She imagined the Buick ramming her into the Jeep, the MP van slamming into hard reverse. The car would twist and buckle and crush her, aluminum struts shoved into her gut, through her legs. She'd had nightmares about car crashes after Ramón told her what happened to his father. She'd never known anyone who died in a car crash before. Not in a normal, civilian kind of car crash. She'd been lucky. Her friends and family too. A knack before the knack.

The traffic was starting to move. The cars two layers ahead, who'd turned their motors off, coughed back to life. The Buick woman's eyes were black. So were the Jeep man's. The black of the inside of a tunnel before you saw the head-lights of the oncoming train.

She'd turned her radio off, but the display was on.

LAST CHANCE.

They could see her. Whoever they were, whatever this was, they could find her through her knack, through the wall she built between herself and all forces that wished her harm. Zelda had all sorts of cute names for this kind of shit, but whatever this was, it hadn't been able to find her before. Why now? Why here?

Her purse buzzed.

Fuck. Of course. Ten years ago, she would have remembered that her phone was in her purse. Back then, they had tricks to get around the trouble of phones and spin. She'd been fond of mailing her phone to herself at some campground where they'd booked a spot, or care of a friend they planned to visit. Ish, natu-rally, thought this was overkill. You just had to take out the battery. But these days, she didn't have to think about her phone. Remembering it was like re-membering your arm.

The cars ahead were shifting into drive, creeping forward. Not much time. Once they reached highway speeds, whatever was about to happen would hap-pen fast. The Buick and the Jeep and that weird wasplike Civic to her right rear were angling their wheels toward her, like filings drawn to a magnet. Two-ton explosive filings.

Shit.

She dug through her purse, found the phone. The buzz—a text message from Evan, supportive noise, call me when you get there, love you, not in this alone, it would all be very kind and meaningful if she weren't about to get pancaked—and a fundraising text.

The text read: ALMOST THERE.

The MP van growled.

Her phone didn't have a battery she could take out. When the fuck did these things stop having a battery you could take out? When did she stop noticing?

When it didn't matter anymore. When she left the road.

The cars two ranks ahead pushed forward. The frozen traffic thawed into a river of metal and glass. The footsteps, the heartbeat, they were louder than ever. The first steps of the stampede.

"Sorry, Evan." She wanted to text him. But there was no time. This might not even work.

She opened her door. Horns blared. Engines roared. On the other side of the median, cars rushed past. It struck her, as it always did when she stepped outside her car on a highway, just how big the road was, how fast the traffic, how intense the smells of exhaust and asphalt and oil were. Freeways, Ramón once told her, were built to look normal only if you were inside a car, traveling at freeway speeds. Those dotted lines that divided lanes, he'd asked her: How long do you think they are? She'd guessed four feet, five, but based on the fact that he'd asked the question at all, she imagined most people guessed low, so she doubled that and said eight.

The real answer: fourteen.

Don't trust freeways. They're built to lie to you: to tell you that you're in control, that you can handle these speeds, that strapping yourself into a box with wheels that runs by blowing itself up in a controlled manner sixty or so times a second is at all a sensible thing to do. When you understand that it's not, when you understand that you're living inside a murder machine, you'll treat the road with the respect and suspicion it deserves.

Yeah, well. She'd grown up on bases, but when Pop took her home to visit family, he took her to the reservation. She might never have felt like she belonged, might not have known what to talk about, or how not to talk, but she had some sense of what it was like to live inside a machine that was trying to kill you.

She threw the phone.

It sailed over the hood of the Jeep, over the median, into traffic. She saw it bounce off a Mercedes, spin, fall. She couldn't hear the crunch but she felt it, felt her world become marginally less certain as that pair of eyes, at least, snapped shut.

Horns blared behind her, and all around her, engines roared, people were staring, one of those kids in the back seat in her rearview mirror was aiming a phone camera at her out his open window. But they were staring normally, the way you'd stare at someone who just did something mind-numbingly stupid on a highway. They'd call it road rage, if people still used that very nineties word, or stress-induced psychosis, because of course there was something wrong with you if you got uncontrollably furious while stuck in an aluminum bubble in a concrete prison surrounded by death machines driven by maniacs. Surely anyone normal would be able to handle that for an indefinite amount of time. That was a reasonable goddamn thing to expect.

But their stares were normal, and as traffic lurched into flow, their cars didn't slam into hers, and she didn't die.

She eased into the flow. When she hit her classic rock preset on the radio, Sting sang: "I'll be watching you."

I fucking bet you will.

Once she cleared DC, she kept off the interstate. It had been years since she did this sort of thing without a GPS, but the muscles were still there.

She ran out of road memory in Kentucky, and stopped at a gas station to buy an atlas. Had to look to find one, and when she did, it wasn't one of the bullet-stopping phone books she remembered—did they even make those anymore? But the densely folded laminated maps in the wire rack that used to hold paperbacks, between the *Penthouse* shelves and the chewing tobacco, would serve.

There was no one at the cash register. She stared up into the reflective dome that hid the camera. Shrugged. She'd read that they might start replacing tellers with robots at stations like this. Could you hold up a robot? Maybe they were betting on the fact that people would feel too stupid to try. Would you pull a gun on R2-D2? "Your money or your life!" *Beep doop-doop de de* WHEEE!

"Hello?" She leaned over the counter. No one here. The BACK IN FIVE sign stood next to the take-a-penny-leave-a-penny bowl. She tried to remember if there had been anyone at the register when she came in, but she had been too intent on the drinks cooler and on looking for maps to notice.

The door chime rang, but when Sarah turned to look, she couldn't see anything except a bobbing white Stetson hat, the kind of Day-Glo white that hats only were in movies. Even under these bad off-green gas station fluorescents, the hat seemed to shine, pure and merciless.

The drinks cooler opened, shut. The air conditioner rattled. October and still this fucking hot. It would get worse before it got better. If it got better. As her paperbacks said when she'd been a nine-year-old reading under covers with a flashlight so Dad wouldn't see: the world moved on. Everything moved on. Except Zelda.

Sarah checked her watch. It had been at least five minutes. When she'd pulled into the parking lot, did she see someone there, on break maybe, smoking a cigarette? He—she had a vision of the sort of person she expected behind a register like this, an unfair vision involving certain standards of shave (poor), skin condition (ditto), gender (male)—might be in the bathroom jerking off, for all she knew.

The hat bobbed up the aisle, paused, turned, walked back. She still couldn't see under the brim of that hat. The shoulders were broad but the man was scarecrow lean, and he wore a bolo tie—she didn't think anyone east of the Mississippi wore those if they weren't a Boy Scout or a poseur, but whoever this guy was, he didn't walk like he was either.

He stopped at the peanuts. Waited. Moved on. She hadn't heard him take anything. Hadn't heard him take anything from the drinks cooler either.

She felt a chill. Looked down at the counter between her hands.

When she entered the gas station, she had turned right. Stopped at the cooler for one of those sweet milky coffees she never drank when she was at home. Felt hungry, skipped the candy aisle, grabbed a bag of peanuts. Then she wandered back toward the door, remembering that some places used to keep maps there.

The cowboy turned on cue, right and then right, back toward the door, his steps measured as if he were tracing a deer through a thicket, following bits of hair, footprints, drops of blood.

She'd been halfway to the door when she saw the wire rack of maps out of the corner of her eye.

His bootheels stopped clicking. Leather creaked as he turned. Back toward the cooler. Then left. Toward the magazine rack.

She leaned across the counter, to see the security monitors. There he was—tall, flannel, slim. But the monitors did not show his face. He left footprints as he walked, as if he'd stepped in something dark and wet.

At the wire rack he paused, ran his fingers over the maps. Turned the rack. Just as she had. Sank into a crouch. She'd found the map she wanted at the bottom.

There was something wrong with the monitors. They were black and white, the paint-factory explosion of the candy aisle transformed into a stark noir vision, like something out of *They Live*. Her floral print dress was a test pattern.

But the cowboy was in vivid, brutal color. And his footprints were blood red.

Sarah opened her purse, tore through the jumble of receipts and Post-it notes with crossed-off or abandoned to-dos. Found her wallet and the folded fifties she'd drawn from the bank before she left Hammond—remembering this much at least, that credit worked fine at home, but you needed cash on a quest.

The cowboy rose from his crouch and walked down the aisle toward her. His bootheel clicks came faster. She had a sudden mad urge to stay, to turn around at the last minute and see his face so she could spit in it. But she could not imagine him having a face. In her mind, when she turned, there was nothing under that hat at all. Not even a skull, just a deep sucking blankness, a bottomless pit where a being should be, and if she slipped, she'd tumble down and down—

She slapped a fifty on the counter. "Keep the change!" Scooped peanuts and coffee and map into her purse and ran for the door—lunging blindly out into the heat as the cowboy rounded the shelves behind her.

She hit something, felt arms around her—and screamed, high and tense, a sound that hurt her throat on the way out. She dropped her weight as Mom had taught her: make a shape with your arms to create distance between you and the person grabbing you. If they're bigger than you, you might not get another chance.

But this person wasn't bigger. She wasn't a cowboy with an empty face. She was a teenage girl, South Asian, in a uniform polo that didn't fit, with the gas station logo on the breast. Staring at her, wide-eyed. "Ma'am! Ma'am, are you all right?" Formal, spooked.

"There's a man," she said, "back there."

But there wasn't.

No hat, no man. As if the ground had swallowed him up. As if he'd been a bubble and just popped. There were bloody footprints on the tile—but they melted away one by one, unwalked, as she watched. Then they were gone.

"I'm fine." She couldn't even convince herself. "I left money on the counter." The girl had dropped something when Sarah ran into her. She knelt, picked it up—a decayed paperback with a broken spine and a cutout on the cover in the shape of a dog's open mouth. "Sorry." The girl was still staring at her, as unsure of what to do as Sarah was. "I heard he does not remember writing this one," Sarah said as she handed the book over. "Because of the drugs."

"Oh. Thanks?"

Before Sarah could be any more of an idiot, she left.

She kept to blue highways when possible after that. She paid cash and stayed off interstates. The rules for magic—Zelda hated when she called it that—weren't all that different from the rules of being a spy. The tradecraft montages in spy movies left out how goddamned annoying the whole process was, though, the annoyance spiked with terror, because if you fucked up any of this fiddly, nimminy pimminy nonsense, you were dead. She hadn't missed that part. She hadn't missed not knowing what was going on, what was coming after her.

She didn't like Indiana, so she pushed on through into Wisconsin, and when she was too tired to drive, she pulled into a gravel lot shaded by trees in Devil's Lake State Park, south of Baraboo. Whose word was Baraboo? Maybe it came from Barabbas, but why would you name a town after that guy? Strange settlers, slapping names on things because they sounded cool, or because they'd heard someone indigenous once say that word in the vicinity. Most of the people who could explain were gone.

She'd taken her family to the UK last year on summer break, one of those things where *probably* the whole world wasn't going to fall apart and *probably* England wasn't going to convulse itself into some kind of Alan Moore comic book police state, but you never did know, so why not take the kids to London while you could? Susan wanted to see Tintagel because of King Arthur, so they'd gone, and hired a Cornish guide to tromp them along the soggy coast, and every time the guide pointed out some undifferentiated hillock and told them its name and a story about it, she remembered her aunts and uncles, and their stories about the rocks and rivers and skies of a place from which they'd been chased by men with guns, a place stolen from them because there was gold underground.

There were no streetlights out here in Devil's Lake State Park, and the stars were fierce between the bare clutching fingers of the trees.

She thought about the cowboy.

They'd seen things on the road, all of them. Not just the rot. Visions crept into the corners of your eyes when you weren't looking. That was the whole point of the road: to see possibilities, dreams, the monsters that were under your bed, the skeletons in your closet. But those shadows had not followed their road-weary band home.

Maybe it was Sal's fault. If she was on her way, she'd be bringing all manner of monster along, that whole many-angled crew.

The cowboy had been here, and then he was gone, leaving ripples that faded as she watched. But she didn't think that human shape was the whole of him. If she were a fly, the cowboy was a carp's gaping mouth, and below him, out of sight, there wriggled the rest, shimmering and huge. Then, snap, and she was gone, and the pond lay smooth again. Gone without a trace.

There was something comforting in the prospect of what came after that—nothingness pulled over you, closing out the sky and the bloody earth. No demands anymore, just a painless blank. And then you'd fade.

Sal was fading already, though not from Sarah's mind. They'd fought for each other since freshman year, they'd raised a snake together in their dorm room closet, they'd held each other crying after lovers turned bad, or love did, though Sal had done most of the holding once she found Zelda. Those roots ran too deep to wither. But at reunions, and when she met other people from her class, she found Sal fading from their stories, becoming "your roommate," a half-remembered dream. Maybe that was racism, or magic. Or maybe it was just that she wasn't around anymore to talk herself into being. Maybe that would happen to Sarah: the jaws snapping shut, and then inch by inch she'd slip away. You know, that premed girl, the swimmer? Didn't she live down the hall from you? What was her name?

Sarah's family would remember her. But she'd be so easy to write out of college memories, because memory was just a kind of story, and whose story about the Ivy League featured a Lakota military brat on work-study who shelved books in the library three days a week? She wasn't a stock character, wasn't campus scenery. She'd just been there, like Sal, like Zelda, like Ramón. She'd never cared about secret societies and never took her nose from the grindstone and she swam every morning. But she wasn't *supposed* to be there, and supposed-to-be was how histories and memories were made.

The names slipped away and the ripples faded.

Sal had asked her, after they escaped that godforsaken gladiatorial arena mess six weeks after graduation, What do you want from this? Why are you here?

They were sitting on a cliff that should have overlooked Boulder, Colorado, but instead overlooked a crater of glass and twisted metal studded with skeletons on spikes. The sky was beautiful and clear, the woods flush with mostly nonmutant wildlife. The stars would have been spectacular if the crater had not glowed at night. Ish claimed that background rad levels were reasonable and the light came from a kind of land-adapted phosphorescent algae. Anyway, it was beautiful, the way vampires in some books were beautiful: lush and dead and deadly.

"When we look at the alts," Sarah had said, "we see what matters. What change is possible. Like looking under this"—she pinched her skin—"to see why it moves like it does."

"Skin's important too," Sal had said with a half smile, knowing they were both in on the joke. Their hands laced and they sat quiet.

Memory was strange. Had she, at the time, felt the overwhelming unspeakable love and anger she felt now, looking back? You idiot, it's not curiosity that brought me out here, it's you, that's all, you and the fact that I love you, not for sex but with my bones and all the marrow in them and whatever's behind that too. I'd pry myself open and give it all to you if you asked. I never knew what a friend was before I found you. And you and Zelda have this twisted beautiful mess of a thing and you won't stop racing, racing, racing to the end of the world, and someone has to stop you from running off the edge, and who's that gonna be if not me? So just slow down and let me hold you back.

Had she felt all of that back then and been too chickenshit to say it? A decade weathered you, and if you were lucky, when it was done, you knew the shape of your own skeleton underneath. If she had known then why she was on the road, she might have been brave enough to say it. Maybe that would have made a difference.

She woke to a loud tap on the window, to darkness and then out of that darkness a face white as the moon, inches and a pane of glass away.

Sarah screamed and grabbed for her purse—and the face's eyes went wide and it recoiled, stumbling back, vanished. She breathed fast and heavy in the dark, scrabbled for her keys, found them, missed the ignition twice—*there.*

The face returned, and with it a hand, just as white in the dark, holding a Maglite. "Ma'am?"

Her hand froze on the keys. Her breath tasted foul in her mouth and strands of hair cut into her cheeks. He was wearing a deep brown windbreaker, park-service-like, but sometimes those militia weirdos liked to look official. But he wasn't wearing a white hat, or boots like the cowboy's, and his face was a boy's face, stunned and a little ashamed. They looked at each other in the light in the dark, breathing.

"Ma'am, you can't park here." His voice was muffled by the glass. She turned on the battery so she could roll down the window. His hand hadn't strayed to his gun when she screamed. She liked him for that, and hated that that was something to like him for, that she could be so easily bought. Oh good, he didn't threaten *my* life for no reason, this time. Must be the car, or the dress. Or my makeup's still in decent shape. Or my skin's just light enough. "Not overnight. It's posted."

With the window rolled down she could hear him better, and the night behind him. Tree frogs and crickets, a shrill cicada-like thrum, almost a heartbeat. Gun or no gun, he seemed small in the black. A kid with no idea what great pressures gathered above him. A fly on a lake. "I'm sorry. My phone broke. I couldn't find a hotel."

"There's a Super 8 up past Baraboo. Back up the road and left. They'll have space there or they can find you some. But we can't have people park here overnight, ma'am."

No, of course not, can't have people sleep on public land, that would be an invitation for people to just move around the country, living, without paying anyone for the privilege. But you didn't say things like that to boys with guns, and anyway, hell, he probably half agreed with her, did anyone go to work in a park because they wanted to harass people trying to catch a nap? He had his orders.

"I'll call," he started.

"No thanks. I can find it on my own."

"It's no trouble. It's not exactly a busy night." Half grinning at the absurdity of it all.

He raised his phone.

The screen light pushed back that circle of darkness behind him—and revealed the broad brim and horned peaks of a bright white hat. It glinted off the gold rings on the white clawed hands of outstretched scarecrow arms.

Those arms closed around him. He screamed. She turned the key, let the engine roar, ground gravel. Sarah swore and desperately wanted to pee, to throw up, to get this whole world in her rearview mirror. Thin fingers punched through the boy's brown windbreaker and the uniform shirt beneath. Blood welled around bony knuckles. The hat lurched down, the brim covering that young face, contorted now in terror. The boy's screams died with a crunch. A red-black bib spread from his neck. The cowboy's hat rose. She did not not *not* want to see what was underneath.

Her wheels found traction, squealed, and he was gone.

She did not stop in Baraboo. She didn't stop in Wisconsin. She didn't stop when the sunrise found her in Dakota. She drove and drove and the worst part was that she couldn't tell herself she'd imagined it, no, it wasn't a fucking dream, horrible things just happened, fucking cowboys appeared out of the dark and ate people and had no face. If this were a dream, she'd have been swimming now or flying in space or fucking someone she hadn't seen since high school in Germany, not driving down back highways past closed restaurants and decaying barns, trying to keep to the speed limit, forcing herself not to throw up, because then she'd have to stop. Her hands a ten–two death grip on the wheel.

In South Dakota she scanned gas station newspapers, saw nothing about a murder or unexplained disappearance among headlines about either the president's or Congress's high treason depending on who owned the paper and what they wanted their people to believe. Maybe they hadn't found the boy yet. Maybe Baraboo news didn't leave the state, or there was no one local to report it anymore. Or maybe the carp's mouth had closed, the ripples faded, and he was just . . . gone.

She drove past the reservation turnoff, apologizing in her heart to her sister, and to her uncles and aunts and her many cousins. She drank bad coffee for hydration and 5-hour Energy to keep going, and when that started to make her shake, she found a truck stop and a big tired skeleton wearing a John Deere hat and a three-hundred-pound human suit, and swapped a fifty for four pills that would keep her awake past Billings, and probably not give her a heart attack.

"You know what to do with those?"

It was the only time in her life it would have been appropriate to say, *Trust me, I'm a doctor*, but she didn't say that, because she didn't want him to know.

This was Zelda's fault. She must have opened a door she should have kept closed, and let monsters loose.

The letter said nothing about a cowboy. But if Sal was coming back, maybe things would come before her. Pilot fish. John the Baptist. Something.

She remembered the hat descending like a jaw, the pop and crunch as the boy's skull broke and the squish of gray matter underneath, and she had to pull over and sit and breathe until her stomach settled.

It started when she left home. It was following her. It wanted her because she was running to Zelda, because she was on the road. It wouldn't go home. It wouldn't find Evan or Alex or Susan.

She told herself that.

At the next gas station, she asked to use their phone, and wondered where all the pay phones had gone, wondered whose job that was to go around the country gutting all those boxes. "Mine's busted." This cashier looked a lot closer to the one she'd imagined in Kentucky, suspicious, narrow-eyed. She put a twenty on the counter. His face crumpled, confused. Then he shrugged, took the twenty, passed her the phone.

It rang and rang. She counted, watching the door, watching the aisles for the hat. The phone had a grimy yellow cord, curling round and round. She found her fingers twisting through it as if she were fifteen again, nervous. That might have been the last time she'd held a phone like this.

Where the fuck was Evan? Three rings, four. She checked the exits again, the aisles, felt the cashier's eyes on her neck, then her shoulders, the small of her back—she checked over her shoulder, and he was looking at his phone again. Or else he'd never looked up and she imagined the whole thing. She didn't think so.

Six rings. Seven. Imagine the cowboy in your living room, sitting in the chair by the window where you and Evan fucked before you left, before you left him because of some damn letter, who *does* that? Imagine the cowboy's red hands, dipping into the shirt pocket where he keeps his smokes. Imagine the slump of his shoulders under flannel after a hard day's work. He shifts one boot to relieve a cramp, and the saturated carpet squelches beneath. He unwraps the pack. Cellophane crinkles as he balls it in one hand. Alex had toys that did that when he was a baby, bits of fabric with crinkly plastic inside, or foil, to crumple in his soft tiny hands. *Had,* because he wasn't a baby anymore, not *had* as in he wasn't—as in *nothing,* eight rings, nine, why wouldn't Evan answer the god-damned *phone.* It just rings and rings as the cowboy taps out a cigarette, raises it toward that unseen mouth.

No click, but a change on the line. The ring cut off. Evan's voice: "Who is this?"

Of course he didn't pick up. He didn't recognize the number. "Evan! Evan Evan Evan."

"Sare? Sarah? Hey! Hey, I'm sorry." All the annoyance and the sleepiness gave way at once like a switch had been thrown. Maybe it was a switch. Evan was a morning person, she always envied that about him, the ease with which he opened his eyes and just did the day. But of course he'd close down if he thought this was some donations call, but also you couldn't not pick it up, be-cause maybe— Well, you wouldn't want to think the end of that sentence, but it had been a day since you spoke to your wife, since she left under mysterious cir-cumstances. You'd answer the phone. "Are you okay? The call didn't go through last night, 'out of service' it said, I figured maybe you were . . . somewhere else. I bet they don't have cell service." He laughed and his laughter was good.

"I had to throw away my phone." It didn't even feel stupid to say.

"Throw away? Babe."

She liked when he called her that, it was so dorky, so eighties, it felt as though they were back in a place where all you had to worry about was the looming threat that some idiots in a dark room would flip a switch and end the whole world all at once and there was absolutely nothing you or anyone could do about it. You know. Clean. "I had to. I'll explain. Do you see the kids?"

"Sare, it's eight in the morning. Susan's asleep. Alex is helping me make pan-cakes." Behind his voice: "Mommy? Hi, Mommy!" She imagined Evan pointing to the phone and mouthing *Mom.* Her whole body thrummed like a plucked bass string. What was she doing here?

"But can you see her?" The cowboy sitting on her bed in that pink-purple room Susan helped them paint—she'd chosen the color because she thought it was "autumnal," which was a word she'd been very proud of knowing how to pronounce, and Sarah hadn't had the heart to tell her she thought the color looked more like spring. What she meant by *autumnal,* it turned out, was that purple was a Halloween color that wasn't orange or black.

The cowboy, settling onto her bedspread, tests the bounce of the springs and the texture of the cotton. Callus ridges on his fingers rasp over fabric.

A pause on the other end of the line. Muttered conversation. In a reflection in the gas station window, she saw the cashier, definitely staring at her this time. Sweating, uncomfortable. She turned back to face the counter. The cashier was looking at his phone again, scrolling through pictures of women in tight gym clothes. She put on a fuck-you sort of smile.

Over the phone, a door hinge creaked. No screams. It closed again. "She's sleeping. Babe, what's going on?"

"I don't know. Just, until I'm back, can you—not use your phone? The landline should be fine. The internet, maybe. Just, no cell. Don't let the kids use it either."

"Is there something—?"

"I don't *know.*" The cashier glanced up at that, and she waved him off, no, it's fine, go back to your yoga pants, I don't need help and especially not yours. She made her smile a wall. "I think there's someone following me. Through the phones. Looks like a cowboy. Big white hat. Just, if you see him, you and the kids, get away. Okay? Fast as you can. Tell me you'll do it, Evan."

"I will. Are you . . . safe?"

No. Not even a little. "I hope so."

"Come home."

God, but she wanted to. This had been a mistake back in college, but in a just world, college was a time to make mistakes that didn't chase you for the rest of your life. She had joined them on the road, back then, because Sal was going, and while she liked the others, she didn't trust them. You couldn't judge decisions by their outcomes, Ish always used to say. Maybe he still did. "I will, when I can. I love you." Meaning I love you, and meaning this conversation's over.

"Alex wants to talk."

"And I want to talk to Alex." They talked: Alex explained how pancakes worked, and the plot of his cartoons, and how he was going to make a new cartoon show and everyone in it would be ninjas and also sharks. It was so normal, so real.

The door chimed.

She jumped, turned, tangled her arm in the cord. But it was only a mom and three adorable pudgy pink-faced girls, each smaller than the last but otherwise identical, like a walking array of Russian dolls. Kids were like that, really: their own people, sure, but also some part of you you'd kept inside a hard shell, suddenly released to the world, exposed.

She had work to do. Ended the conversation as fast as she could without being rude: I love you, Alex, and Evan, and tell Susan I love her, too, when she wakes up. A tight thank-you to the cashier and a swish out the door, and open road from there on into Montana.

Fuck this. Fuck jumping at shadows and fuck cowboys everywhere, and fuck

Zelda for getting them on the road in the first place and fuck Ish for never helping Sarah stand up to her, not once, and fuck Ramón for that car and for the voices he heard when he was driving it. And fuck herself, too, for not seeing how wrong they all were when there was still time to make a difference, for not admitting that they weren't a bold party of adventurers or a ragtag band of anything much and there was no ineluctable fucking *ka* or destiny dragging them along. They were just kids trying to beat the world, too dumb to know that the world beat back. That was the lesson she should have learned from history, from the family songs she was never taught. The cowboys never finished with you. They just kept following.

Well, if that was how it was gonna be—she'd end it. She'd spit in that unseen eye.

The Best Western looked just as she'd remembered. Ten years gone, yet the same yellowed walls, the same vast black parking lot, the same eerie flat horizon and the same sky far, far overhead. She tried to spot the others' cars, but even though the lot was spare, nothing jumped out at her screaming Ish, and there was no Challenger. Of course there wouldn't be. She'd been there for the crash. Her knack was the only reason they'd survived it.

But on the walk to the lobby, she did pass an utter wreck of a blue Subaru, its windows grime-caked, its body a lunar surface of craters, dents, and pockmarks, its rear seat folded down to make room for an internal frame pack, a folded tarp, a shovel, a roll of rope. Zelda and her rope. The shock of recognition was so great Sarah almost turned around, got back in her car, and drove home. It felt like seeing someone you knew from PTA meetings at the supermarket, times a million. In the proper surroundings, she'd know what to do, what to say, but here, out of context, anything could happen, and anything was terrifying. So she curled around her solitude like a lion around a wound.

Stupid. She didn't even know for sure that this was Zelda's car. But it was the car Zelda would drive, if she had never changed. If she spent the last ten years on the road waiting, searching for Sal. Instead of—stopping. Finding a life. Building one for herself. Understanding that time was a pool of unimaginable depth and that you were a bug lighting to drink from its bright surface. Knowing that the fish wait beneath you. Trusting that this time you'll be lucky.

Back home, Alex was writing a cartoon about ninjas who were also sharks.

Sarah clutched her coat closer against the cold, and marched on into the lobby.

There, sitting in a big low chair with cracked blue upholstery, legs crossed, sketching by a vase of plastic roses—there was Sal.

Sarah stopped. The lobby's revolving door slowed behind her. Music played on invisible speakers, an old alt-rock piece she'd first heard on base radio in Japan when she was ten, played soft as suffocation.

This girl wasn't Sal. She was younger, leaner, sharper. But there was a Salness to her eyes and cheeks and shoulders.

The girl didn't look up as she approached. How long had she been waiting here?

"June?"

A kid, maybe six, who wanted to ask her everything about Japan and Germany, in that kitchen with the creepy, carved, stereotype Indians. A kid, wide eyes, eager, unready. She looked up from the sketchbook—confused at first. Who's this lady? Recognition came like an echo. "Sarah?" As if she didn't trust her own mind. Good instinct.

A nod was the best she could do. She wanted to apologize but she did not know for what.

Before she found her voice again, June was up and across the lobby, and hugging her so hard she couldn't breathe. She wasn't ready. June's shoulders shook. She gasped into Sarah's dress, made high mouse sounds. Her cheeks were wet. This, Sarah could do. You held the girl and loved her, and didn't leave. "It's okay, kiddo."

When June peeled away, her eyes were red and wet. "I'm sorry. I just." With one shuddering breath, the little girl receded, closed inside a thin shell. You built them layer by layer. "I sent the letters. You're a doctor?"

She nodded—not yet ready to close the doors the first sight of her had opened, not ready to be the big Russian doll again. She'd been so angry for so long. "Where's Zelda?"

"Sarah—Z's sick."

# CHAPTER NINE

Zelda walked through bright green fields on a path made of black flowers. Ahead of her at the top of the rise, a woman stood, tall as a cliff and black as the blossoms of the path. Waiting for her.

Zelda's feet were bare and she wore a long white dress. Beneath the black flowers, the earth squelched between her toes. Her feet came up stained, as if she'd been trampling grapes to wine, but the stain was the wrong color and the hem of her dress went red where it trailed over the flowers. The red climbed her. It clung to her ankles and her calves.

In her clenched fist she held an iron ring.

She climbed the slope. The road was pulling her along, or else the woman, the sky, the horizon, were all advancing toward her, even though they seemed to be standing still. Every step Zelda took had a terrible momentum and seemed to drag her forward faster, though the mud held her feet and the flowers were screaming.

There was no sun in the sky. The woman blotted it out.

She ached for her, and she was very much afraid.

"There's another way."

The voice was a whisper on the wind, a ghost of whiteness and steel seen out of the corner of her eye. She turned to look, but the ghost was gone, and only the black-flower road ran behind her, until it vanished in the press of green.

But her feet kept walking and her dress grew heavy with blood. Her legs tangled and she fell, down through the flowers into the mud that stank of iron and felt spongy like wet flesh, falling as she reached for the woman who was a tower who was the sky.

She woke with a spasm and a gasp, coughing hard. She felt like she'd punched herself in the stomach. Something smelled acrid and gross and she realized it was her.

Scratchy sheets, a coarse blanket. The motel room. She'd woken here before, hadn't she? Many times. It was a fixed point in her soul. Everything in her life had happened in this motel room. She'd only imagined otherwise. She'd spent thirty years sweating into these sheets and waiting, not to die but never to have been at all. The galloping horses in that shitty mass-produced print, they had been gods before God was. They had been running forever. Burning the painting would not kill them. It would only set them free.

A cold cloth on her forehead. "June." Her voice was cracked and dry. She'd never used it before.

"No."

Zelda knew that voice, and *she* didn't belong in the timeless hole of this room. Zelda's eyes snapped open, focused.

"Your fever's high but not dangerous. Your arm—how old is the wound?"

"Sarah." She glowed in the darkness. Seemed to, anyway. She looked exactly right and not at all how Zelda would have expected, both at once. Rounded, fuller and more firm. Hoop earrings under black hair streaked with white. A turquoise bracelet and a floral-print dress. A fact of the universe. A line from *King Lear* chased around the gummy inside her head. Kent: You have that in your countenance / which I would feign call master. And when Lear asked: What's that? Kent answered: "*Authority.*" There were tears in her eyes, as sudden as if she'd been slapped. "Sarah, I missed you so much."

Her lips became a thin line. "How old?"

From the other side of the bed, June answered. "Week and a half."

"It should be worse."

"I've tended it. I tried alcohol, peroxide."

"Any medicine?"

"Some Tussin for the cough. Tylenol. And these." She shook a rattling bottle. "Ma calls them 'cure-all.' I took some from her desk before I left."

"What's in them?" Sarah took the pill bottle, which was unlabeled, popped it open, smelled the contents.

"She said High John the Conqueror root, when I asked. I think she was joking."

"Sarah," she was babbling now, couldn't stop herself, "I hoped you'd come but I've been hoping for a long time and I'm so, so sorry, and I'm happy to see you." She was drunk on something, and she was desperate. Her mouth was sock-dry and sticky, as if she'd breathed in some of that bloody earth while she was drowning. But she could speak now, after ten years. She'd tried to speak before, but Sarah had not wanted to listen and anyway she, Zelda, had said all the wrong things and here, now, in the sight of the horse-gods, she would get it right.

Sarah was looking at her as if there were a big spider on her face. Sarah had always been afraid of spiders. She killed them every chance she got, even the nice ones. One big smack and it was over. "This is your fault, isn't it."

"It's Sal." Strange to say her name as a present word, as something relevant to this moment rather than to some scarred-over long-ago past.

"The cowboy, I mean. The white hat, the people staring on the freeway. You started something."

Zelda didn't know what she meant. That was fine. There would be time now. She was here. "Sarah, she's coming back."

Sarah had lifted her bag onto the bed, opened it, rifling through tools. But when Zelda said that, her nostrils flared, she breathed deep and sank forward. Long hair fell across her face and hid her. Her shoulders shook once.

"Sarah?"

"Don't you start. Don't even try. I can't, Zelda. Not after what you did to her."

"Z? What's she talking about?"

"Do *you* want to tell her?"

"I told her."

"You told her that you left? You told her that the whole damn thing was your idea? That you were the one who had to keep running? That Sal wouldn't have been out there at all if not for you?"

"I told her. Sarah, we did it all together. Sal and me and all of us." But there was more, wasn't there, more she hadn't told. The ring in her pocket. Where was it? She wasn't wearing her jeans. How did she get here? Who took off her jeans? The ring was somewhere, it had to be. She was holding it in her hand. No. That was the dream.

"That's what you thought. That's what you always thought." She drew herself up, turned back. Her eyes were glittering black stones. "I swore an oath, Z. Not to you and not to her. There's something in your arm. I have to get it out. I assume a hospital's out of the question?"

She nodded. No clue how many warrants might be out in her name. And she didn't want to let whatever was inside her arm out in a hospital, under the care of a doctor who didn't know how the world really worked.

"Then we'll do it here. Old style. June, you'll have to hold her."

"What are you talking about?"

"It's fine," Zelda said. "It's okay." It wasn't. She was bracing herself already, remembering deep backwoods Olympia, Washington, where the forest was on fire and Sarah had given her a belt to bite down on before she pushed the barbed arrowhead through her arm. Surviving these things didn't make them okay. It just let you know that you could survive them. The memory of pain screwed deep down into you, it lived in your meat. If you'd never hurt before, you didn't know how bad it could get. "Listen to her." And, back to Sarah: "Do your worst."

She'd hoped for a grin at least, but Sarah just slipped off her bracelet and rubbed her hands with disinfectant gel.

⟫

It would have been very wrong for Sarah to use an operation, even a relatively minor one like this, to exact revenge. Her professional ethics were clear. You gave no more pain than you had to. You treated the patient in front of you, the human being, without thought to what they'd done to you or to your friends back when you all were idiot kids with unformed prefrontal cortices. You were, in the moment you practiced your profession, the heir to everyone who'd come before you who ever looked at a person suffering and thought, maybe there's something I can do, every shaman and sage back to Asclepius and the Yellow Emperor and the Sky Herself. You were not a woman in her mid-thirties bearing a ten-year-old grudge.

Still, she had expected to enjoy it more.

June held Zelda down while Sarah sanitized the equipment. "Give me some credit," Zelda told her. "Wait until she starts, at least."

A needle, thin tweezers, a candle just in case. The candle didn't need to be sterilized, of course. "You got this from the rot?"

"From a beetle in some alt." Zelda waved imprecisely. "Nowhere you'd know. Nasty flesh-eating guy. There were a whole lot of them. Rot tore the wound open later."

"You'll have to take an antibiotic for the infection. Don't trust this one to spin."

"Even with you around?"

"My knack works off chance and odds, just like yours. You want to know what the odds are that you'll shrug off a blood infection if this goes bad? And you're assuming I don't want you dead." But she felt herself smile at that, dammit, felt even her stellar mass of anger fade into a shared joke. Zelda smiled up at her, through the haze and pain. She looked like a much younger woman than Sarah felt. Shouldn't the road have worn her hard? The needle and tweezers would be sterile by now. "Nice Subaru, by the way. Evan and I were thinking about one. How's it drive?"

"Fine. Nothing special but I haven't needed anything special until recently. The trunk isn't as large as you might—"

*Think* was almost the last word. It got halfway out her mouth before the needle dipped into the nasty raised flesh of the arm. The vowel rose in pitch and Zelda's gritted teeth robbed her of the ability to frame consonants. June bent over her, holding Zelda's shoulder to the mattress, while June's knee pinned her forearm in place.

Back before anesthetic, surgeons used to compete on speed. A man (and they were all men back then, at least all the white ones were) who could amputate a limb in fifteen minutes was assured a good practice, a professional reputation. It was grotesque. People died. But there was an efficiency of technique you learned when you didn't have any other choice. When Sarah took her practical classes back in med school, her teachers had assumed she had EMT experience, or army. They weren't altogether wrong. She'd been EMT designate for five people on an absurd and dangerous road.

There was a little threadlike black whatsit in the wound, and because none of their lives had ever been easy, it was moving. She grabbed the tweezers.

Zelda made a high sweet sound. June watched, sickened. Zelda's eyes were so wide and so trusting. No trace of doubt that Sarah would fix this, because Sarah was her friend, and friends were omnipotent. Sarah would make everything okay.

She wished she could.

Sarah's tweezers snagged the little black whatsit's tail before it could burrow deeper into Zelda's arm. Three terrified nights across country, coffee and pills and those horrible energy shots to keep awake had left Sarah a rattletrap echo of the self she'd left behind in Virginia, but she still had the touch. Just pull it out slow and smooth, because this thing is a fine filament and you don't want any of it to break off in there. That's it. Nice and easy.

Zelda hissed as the last of the whatsit twisted free. It wasn't much thicker than a hair, iridescent black, but it thrashed, tracing small cuts along Sarah's hand. She fed it to the candle flame. It shriveled to ash and smoke, like everything else.

Zelda slumped back. Breathing deep.

Sarah spread more antiseptic on her hands. The cuts burned, which was fine. Bandaging Zelda's wound took hardly any thought. June watched her from the shadows, green. Sarah had seen that expression on students before. You might know in theory that the body was meat, but it still messed people up to see it treated that way. People liked to think people were people.

And then there was the wiggly black whatsit, that thread of rot. June wasn't used to those, either, yet.

"She needs rest," Sarah said as she closed her case. "And I need catching up."

~

"So she collapsed in the parking lot," Sarah said when she got the story straight. "In Pennsylvania."

A nod from June. They were perched by the window near the elevators, Sarah's eye on the door to Zelda's room. Below, the road made a long gray line through two halves of dry nameless country.

"And you can't drive." She kept going without waiting for the next nod. "But you decided, rather than calling for help, rather than asking someone what to do or going to one of the other road people in the parking lot who might have had a tow hitch, you decided to drive yourself. Even though you didn't have a license. Good thing Zelda was driving an automatic."

"There's two kinds?"

June had to be fucking with her, and Sarah decided not to dignify it with notice. June was a kid still, in most of the important ways. She could imagine Susan doing the same in a pinch, or Alex for the hell of it. "There must have been a better way. One cop, that's all it would have taken. Not to mention the fact that you probably have a missing person notice out on you."

"I left a note for Ma."

A note! She tried to imagine Ma finding that note, tried to imagine the overpowering rage and dry-mouthed terror it would wake in her. She was surprised she hadn't passed newspaper headlines about how New York had been destroyed by a ten-thousand-foot-tall grandma. Notes. Alex left notes. *Mom I borrowed the lawnmower thanks love Alex.* "Zelda was barely conscious. Babbling. Sweaty. You tried to cool her down, you ransacked her first aid kit for drugs, but you didn't know what was wrong, what you should do. So you, again sensibly, suggested a hospital. You got out your phone to call one. Even though Zelda had warned you not to use the phone. And that was when you saw him."

"I'm not sure."

"This is magic, June. We're long past 'sure.' Trust what you saw."

"Zelda said it wasn't magic."

"Zelda's sick on a bed in that room, and Zelda is the god-queen of rationalizing her own bad choices, and what on earth do you think is going on here? If she's afraid of calling it magic, do you think that says more about reality, or about her?" Defiance in June at that, a tensing of the shoulders, a lowering of her head as if to charge. June had chosen her loyalties, chosen them deep. Just like her cousin. And Sarah wouldn't lose her again, wouldn't lose this piece of her, all she had left. "I am sorry. Zelda and I have been fighting about this for a long time. That does not have anything to do with you. You called the hospital. You looked across the parking lot. And you saw—tell me again."

"I saw a man."

"Yes."

"A man in a white hat."

"Yes."

"I couldn't see his face."

"No."

"He was so far away. I see well, real well, things most people can't. But I can't see that well. He was forever away but he looked so clear. Like, one time after church we went to look at birds, the youth group did, and if you look through the right end of the binoculars, everything is bigger than it should be, but if you look through the wrong end, it's tiny but cold and dead clear. There were little red stones in the stitching on his boots, and his nails were even." She shuddered. "I didn't see his face. What's it mean that I could see the stones on his boot, but I couldn't see his face?"

"I don't think he has one."

"You saw him too. You asked Z about a cowboy. She didn't see him. She was flat on her back. But you saw him and I saw him."

"Then Zelda slapped your phone out of your hand."

"When I looked up, he was gone. I reached for the phone again. But I could see him in the reflection in the black, like he was up in the sky. So I pulled away. I left the phone there. I could hear those bootheels click-click-click across the lot, but it was also like they were behind me, like anywhere I looked he'd be coming at me from behind. I hauled Z into the Subaru. She was clammy, sweaty, sick. I got the keys from her jacket, gunned it. I didn't realize it was in park. I yanked the shifter but it was in reverse. I panicked."

"Somehow you made it to the road, without crashing. And the cowboy . . ."

"I could still see him, ahead of us. In the streetlights. Like, we'd pass him and there he was at the next one. So I shouted to Zelda, 'Z, we got to be somewhere else,' and I don't know if she heard me, but I remembered what it felt like when she showed me how to get to other alts, on the bridge, and I figured I could just *do* that. I've never felt so awake. There was the night and there was the road and there were houses in the trees and a deer on the side with those bright-sky eyes and headlights coming at me and something was burning 'cause I left the parking brake on. I just—pushed. I forgot everything but the deer and the sky and the burning smell and the road, and I—I jumped it."

"And you were somewhere else."

"Z must have helped me."

"Maybe," she said, meaning no. "It's easier once you've done it. The first time, it's impossible, because you believe it is. Your brain tells you there's nothing out there but this." She pointed out the window at the gray-gold flatland and the concrete ribbon and the gray-gray sky. "That's why Zelda needed the math, I think. She believes in the world, but not as much as she believes in math. If math told her this wasn't all there was, if math told her there were other ways it might have played out, she could let go of common sense. You think I understand all those proofs, the ring theory and chaos and whatever? I believe what I see. I have a brain built for organic chemistry. I like flash cards. I work with bodies because bodies, June, are right fucking here, and there is a lot going on inside them but most of what I care about breaks down to membranes, fluids, tubes. Mechanics. I only passed Multivariate Calculus because Sal sat up late with me every other night for a year while I screamed at my problem sets. Zelda tried to talk me through the strange attractorness of it all precisely once and my eyes glazed over harder than they have glazed in my whole life, and I have been on a serious morphine drip. But when she showed me, I could make it work. Congratulations, kid, you have the knack."

"You said something about a knack in Z's room."

"She did not tell you about those? No, I guess not. There is the knack in general, of being able to go out on the road in the first place. Then, each of us had *a* knack, something that stuck to us when we came back. A trick. I think it depends on why we travel. For Z it is a matter of chance, of options. For Ramón it is about the road, about knowing where to go and how to get there. Ish, he always had to know things—what was around the corner, what was coming next. And me . . . I want things to be okay, I guess."

"What do you mean?"

This was a distraction. But she had to learn sometime. "Do you smoke?"

"Cigarettes?" She made a face.

"What I mean is, do you have a lighter."

"Oh, sure, yeah. Z made me get one of those." She fished in the bag where she'd stowed her sketchbook, came up with a bright blue Bic with a Spider-Man mask on the side.

Sarah snatched it from her, sparked it until it caught, and, bored already with the conversation she was about to have, stuck her middle finger in the flame. Her pink nail polish glistened orange.

And the flame went out.

June blinked. "Huh. You're—"

"Wrong. I am . . . not like the whole Bruce Willis movie thing."

"*Die Hard?*"

She grinned. "Well, yeah, maybe that one. I am . . . resistant. As long as I have spin, things turn out okay for me, and for people close to me. Physical things. Bullets miss. Fires go out. I do not have any control over what happens to keep me safe. It might have been a gust of wind just now that blew out your flame, but I think what actually happened is, your lighter just happens to be broken." She tossed it back. June tried the wheel three times without success. "It helps."

"Will I get something like that?"

Oh great. She was excited. "If you make the mistake of hanging out with us too long. Have you ever started to shake your leg, only to find it will not stop? Or maybe you were making a sound with your mouth, talking in an accent, something you barely noticed doing once you were in the groove. When I first got the knack, sometimes I would slip through just walking in the woods. You blink and you are somewhere else. You have to want to be here, after a while. And that is hard. It gets harder every day." Pause. "Because of the news."

"No, I got it."

Sarah felt herself smile. God, it was almost like talking to Sal, or Ramón, or Ish. She'd have to be careful not to make that mistake. June was faking older than she was. Susan did that all the time, but it was easy to catch because she looked eight on the outside. June wasn't Sal. June was a kid. She shouldn't be here at all. If Sarah were the decent person she liked to pretend she was, she'd be sending June home right now, while there was still time. But June had seen the cowboy, and she had the knack, and whatever the first of those things meant, the second meant that going home wouldn't save her. "So you slipped through."

"Slipped through," she echoed. "It sounds easy when you put it like that." She ran her knuckles across the glass. "Was it like that for you? You just fall through and it's . . . different?"

Sarah waited. That wasn't a question, really. After a while, June spoke again.

"The forest was on fire. There were big black birds circling overhead, when they beat their wings you'd see rainbow patterns reflected on their feathers, like the colors of oil on a rain puddle. I felt cold all over, wide open, just me and the fire. And then something ran out of the woods, trees crashing. It was a bird, I think, but like nothing I'd ever seen before. It was bigger than the car and it had these *teeth* and there was a strap on it like for a saddle. I almost went off the road, but I kept driving. I'd have hit it if it hadn't run away. It hit me with its big tail, caved in the rear door. Still can't get it open. I drove. I left them behind. It just felt so lonesome over there. The roads ran and ran. And Z was out. She couldn't help me."

"It hits everyone differently," Sarah said. "The first time."

"How did you feel? Your first time, I mean."

"Angry, I suppose."

"Why?"

"It is a long story." But June might as well hear it. "It was back in college. Zelda wanted my opinion on the alts, on their, what did she call it, their historicity. Points of divergence. I was the closest thing our little group had to a liberal arts person, which tells you . . . something. I took history classes because I'm good at remembering things and because I always did like a good horror story. When she gave me the pitch we had a fight—I thought she was joking with me, that she didn't respect me, or Sal. So she took me across into the alts. No warning. On foot. It was the first time she'd tried it that way—not driving, just stepping from one world to another. The car makes it easier. Gives you a focus."

"And you were angry because she was right?"

"That is part of it. I was angry because she did not ask first. Maybe she did not mean for it to happen. We were fighting in the cemetery, and she was still learning how all of this worked. We stumbled into a wasteland sort of alt, full of carnivorous lizard-monkey things, and the sky was orange—anyway, we stumbled across, and she could not get us back."

"Shit."

"As I am sure you can imagine, I was pissed."

"What happened?"

"We both died, obviously. You have been talking with a ghost this whole time. Roll credits." June looked more puzzled than amused. Well, you had to amuse yourself before you amused anyone else. That way, at least you knew one of you was having a good time. "We hid out in—do you know what Skull and Bones is? It is a secret society, I mean, they call it secret, but everyone who gives a shit knows who's in it, because the campus humor magazine makes a list of everyone tapped for membership each year. Some kids who want to feel important, and don't mind tying themselves to some grade A questionable historical shit. They used to claim they had the skull of Geronimo. Like, the actual human skull of actual Apache leader and genocide victim Geronimo. Definitely a cool thing to have. Neat collector's item. But anyway, the societies have these buildings with hardly any windows where they meet up, they call them tombs because everything has to be goth-but-make-it-prep with these guys. We holed up in that version of the tomb, once we cleaned the rot out of the casket in their secret chamber, where they kept *their* version of Geronimo's skull. Took us three days to figure out how to get back home. Zelda thought it was fun, when we were not imminently about to die. I did not see it that way."

"But you got out."

"We got out." She'd lost it at the end, in that dark room that stank like burnt rubber from the corpse of the creature that had been lurking in the coffin. She, Sarah, had thrown the skull at Zelda. This isn't real. This is a bad joke. This is your sad vision of an adventure. There's nothing true here. It's all dead weight and bad dreams.

But dreams, too, were real.

"We worked together. Eventually. We found a way out." Squeezed tight side by side in the coffin, the lid shut over them both. Breathing into her face. Realizing, as lizard-monkeys pounded on the coffin lid, that Zelda was afraid, too, trembling, that she did not know what she was doing and that she needed help. And that Zelda wanted, more than anything, to go back to Sal, to be with her this close and closer, even though and because she was afraid. She needed it so deeply that she found herself tracing the outlines of a concept beyond the word *love,* which for her was a totem you brought out to parade before your parents and your family, a magic word you spoke to resolve the plot of Disney films, not that strange enormous knot of sex and death and poetry and hunger, the churning engine under the skin.

The lizard-monkeys battered the coffin lid, they stank of piss and shit and all-too-human sweat in matted fur, and Zelda and Sarah lay there in the black, together, and hitched through.

The battering stopped. The smell faded. They were alone in the coffin. They heard voices, not shrill animal voices but real human ones, bored and tired.

"Yeah, man, I thought this Grand Strategy class was gonna be great, but it turns out it's, like, eighty percent about trying to milk the professor's political connections."

"Well"—a higher voice, tired, superior—"what did you expect? That's what so much of this amounts to, a chance to make the right sort of friends. Of course, some of those friends will be older, we can't all do everything from the ground up. If that were possible, we'd go somewhere else and save," a pause the length of a drag on a cigarette, "a *lot* of money on tuition." All this posturing was undercut by the smell of some deeply unexcellent weed.

Welcome home. Huzzah.

Beside her, Zelda almost laughed, just one little panicked snort, but it was the kind of laugh that would start an avalanche, even if Sarah thought the whole secret society thing was a few steps removed from LARPing, she did not want to be found here. She imagined the *Daily News* story afterward, pictures of her and Zelda on the front page, and she, Sarah, who had just wanted to keep her head down and learn how to be a doctor, would be the base-brat scholarship kid who sneaked into the Skull and Bones. So she clapped her hand over Zelda's mouth and held it there.

There had been an extremely awkward span of interrupted sentences—

"We can't, I mean, not in here—"

"—don't be such a goddamned *boy* about this, come on—"

A thud on the coffin lid. Buckles unbuckled. Zippers unzipped.

"—don't think, I mean, are you—"

"—thinking is rather beside the point, now, do you want this or—"

A gasp, a hiss that might have been a yes.

"—now, get down there—"

"But if someone comes—"

"—well, yes, that is somewhat the idea. Well. *Yes.*"

Sarah tried not to laugh, but if she failed, the sound was lost under the animal noises that followed. Not altogether unlike the lizard-monkeys' sounds, come to think.

While that seemed to go on forever at the time, it likely hadn't stretched more than fifteen minutes or so. At last they were left, Sarah and Zelda, in the coffin, alone.

They sneaked out into a room that did not look at all like the room on the other side.

There was, however, a skull.

The other skull, from the other New Haven, had come through in the coffin with them. So, while Zelda was heading for the door, Sarah switched them.

She showed Zelda after they sneaked out, once they were safely seated in a booth at Yorkside with a big cheesy pizza on the table between them. She pulled it out of her oversize purse and set it beside her beer.

The dam burst then. The terror of their last few days and the extreme strangeness of the coffin faded, and they were shaking with laughter, holding each other, drawing confused looks from the nearest five tables, not giving a shit, home at last. I knew it, Zelda said through it all, her face wet, her arms tight around Sarah's shoulders. I knew you'd get it, I knew you would.

She was wrong. Sarah did not get it. Never did. But Zelda did not yet understand that you could love someone and not agree with them.

That night they both went home to Sal—who was drawn, scared, angry, and trying not to show it, three days without a roommate or a girlfriend. When the shouting and the hugging were over, they showed her the skull, and Sal decreed, We're driving this out west come spring. We're taking it home.

That was the first trip they'd taken together. A beginning and a seed of an end, in that coffin.

"Kiddo," she said.

"I'm not a kid."

"June. You could leave. You should. We started this. We have to finish it."

"But you didn't."

"Excuse me?"

"Start it. You and Z, you both go on like whatever's wrong here must be your fault, just because it happened while you were watching. You found the rot, you didn't make it. At least you tried to do something about it. Maybe it worked and maybe it didn't and maybe you made mistakes. But you tried. Lots of people never get that far."

"We just did what anyone would do, if they knew what was out there."

June's answer was an extremely flat gaze. "Sarah, everybody knows the world's ending. It's been ending. It's been *ended*. And most people don't do shit."

She couldn't argue with that. She had lived it. The world ended and you kept going. Her family never talked about that at the dinner table. Maybe people in other families did say the quiet bit out loud: Pass the corn, do you ever think about how we're living after the end of the world? But you did not have to speak truths to know them. The real stayed real in spite of you, and you lived as well as you could in spite of it. That was a different kind of American dream, maybe—or American waking.

June rolled into the silence. "You want to protect me, 'cause you've been fighting all of this for a while and you're tired and you don't think you made a difference, you took your L and it hurts. But you have been doing something, because I'm here and your kids are here in spite of the whole lot of people in this world who don't want any of us to be anywhere, who want us to have never been at all. You've been holding on. Now you've got me. You and Z keep thinking this is some kind of action movie, like one dude crawling around in the air ducts is gonna save the day. This can't be that. It's an Avengers movie maybe. You need a whole pile of people to make this thing happen."

One part of parenting that Sarah was still working out was what to do when your kids saw the world more clearly than you did. It didn't happen as often as kids' books would suggest. You listened to your kids, sure, but most of the time they were wrong. And then, when you weren't expecting it, they dropped something on you with the hard ring of truth. So you breathed deep and said, as she said now: "Okay. But we have a whole lot of getting ready to do, if a big purple guy's about to show up and unwish the world."

"We're still missing a couple of guys, aren't we?"

"Don't worry about Ish and Ramón. They'll be here. The catch with Ramón is, he likes to make an entrance. This one time, we'd been imprisoned in a mine—except for him, of course, because he always slips away somehow, because that's his knack—and the mine was flooding, and we're busy trying to climb above the floodwaters, when all of a sudden that asshole breaks open the wall, like, what are you all doing down there, only of course he forgot to bring a rope, and Zelda said—"

"Sarah? What's that?"

The road was twisting. It was a long straight asphalt ribbon through the blank gray country under the blank gray sky—and it rippled, pulsed like the skin of a crawling snake. It might have been a mirage except the air was very dry and cool and there was no sun.

That was the trick of magic. You had to trust your own eyes. Not your judgment, which would tell you, oh, you're feeling faint, the sleep deprivation and drugs must be ganging up on you, but your eyes, which were honest, and said: There's something off about that road.

She hadn't often watched others hitch when she wasn't doing it herself, but she knew the feeling from within, pressing yourself against the chain-link fence that was the world until your flesh bubbled through to re-form on the other side. Only one of them could do it that fast.

"That," she said, "is Ramón."

Imagine that real and unreal are different ends of a ribbon. Twist the ribbon. Tape the ends together. Cut the ribbon down the center. Throw it into an autoclave, turn it on, and watch the ribbon bubble and burn and melt. It looked a bit like that.

There was no Challenger on the road.

Then there was.

And it was on fire.

# CHAPTER TEN

The road came back so fast Ramón didn't have time to get scared.

A roar and a scream of tires and he was moving, unstoppable. Shift gears and grind that pedal to the floor and hear the big cat wake and stretch and yowl and roll, under the hood where your heart lives. Los Angeles was a thicket he prowled through, traceless, a beast that made the lesser beasts fall silent and slink away in fear—and then he was out between the hills, out on the long, long line into the desert, past date palms and withered trees and flat black barren country, out where the knife of his wheels could carve and carve.

He did not stop. His few necessary pauses, for gas, to piss or shit or feed, were just hitches in stride. On the road, gravity went not down but forward, pulling you into the wasteland, bottomless, the falling world where anything could happen.

He had missed this, in the kind of dreams that, when you woke from them and realized you'd been dreaming, you gave thanks to the mad bloodthirsty god who made this world that those at least weren't real. Those vivid spasms of imagination where you fucked someone you shouldn't, killed the president, set the whole Valley on fire, and just-kept-at-it—in those hot bright demon dreams he had missed the wheel between his hands, the asphalt sliding past at ninety miles an hour, the welded sense that he was completely out of control and completely under control at once. He had missed being not himself.

Except, the Challenger said, this *is* you. You know the end is coming, you knew it before Zelda took you out on the road in the first place, you knew history was a butcher shop and the future would be worse. But oh, that's a hard thing to know. Can't drink a beer and set your hand on the inside of a pretty man's thigh if you really *get* that, can you? Hard to watch the ball game, even assuming you can sit through all the military shit and the fan two rows back shouting slurs down at the field. You know. So you got an obligation, don't you, to get mad, to set it all on fire? This right here is where you put everything you don't want to feel, so you can love your boy and go to Mass with your mama and enjoy sunsets and long walks on the beach. That nice boy, he's not you. He's the you you wish you were. You have another self. A hidden, honest self. The self that wants to burn it all down. For ten years you've kept that curled up somewhere and now we're back together again and let's fuckin' roll.

Spin ran lightning through the wheels. The sky was rainbowed in hellfire. And as the 15 opened under him, the world changed.

A pile of bodies smoldered out in the desert as tall, many-legged machines scuttled against the horizon and drones filled the air. The desert greened and tall, choking trees climbed toward the wide sky, and heads stared from spikes that flanked the high clear road. A leather-winged circling beast swooped toward him, claws outstretched. He flickered away before it could strike, and into a dead dry-baked land studded with bodies on crosses. Another flicker-step and the whole plane of earth, as far as he could see, was a writhing carpet of what at first looked like worms, but he had the lurching certainty the worms were in fact the wiggly arms of some single large and hungry thing slavering below the horizon. One of those tendrils stretched toward the road. He swerved and ran it over.

He had chased this feeling with drugs and bad decisions. He fled from it by burying himself in cubicle nonsense and money, in consulting and finance—all that shoveling of snow. He tried to disappear in spreadsheets and slide decks. It almost killed him. He tried to forget.

Zelda had told him in Montana: We can't walk away from this. We have a responsibility. We can't forget. She'd also said, when it was just the two of them, at the end: Don't leave me.

He had tried. He had left. And now he was coming back.

People saw him and fell silent. They watched him and they watched the car as if they both glowed. Stares followed him down gas station Quik Mart aisles. They drew back tight with fear, though when he looked at himself in the mirror, he seemed unchanged.

*Beware! Beware! His flashing eyes, his floating hair!*

Two big men jumped him in Barstow.

They'd been filling their truck across from him, they'd sauntered over all *what you looking at?* They were shadows. They thought they were good men. They thought he was an easy target. He'd met men like these before. His knack hummed in his blood. If he wanted, he could have left. He could have drifted past them like a spirit or a god. They could lay no hand on him.

He remembered the bodies on crosses. He remembered walking away from Zelda. One of the men asked, with a drawl and a sneer, So where'd you steal that car?

He did not drift past. He let the other big man sidle into position behind him, the one with the hat, who should never have tried to grow a mustache. He let them trade a look, let mustache grab for his arms while red cheeks went in with a fist. Ramón stepped in, slid to one side, let the punch hit mustache in the gut.

His knack was finding where to be, and when. You looked for gaps and filled them. Fingers in a throat. Heel to the inside of a knee. You applied a precise square inch of the crown of your head to a cheekbone, or to teeth. You put your feet just so and two hundred fifty pounds of dipshit missed you and hit the gas pump hard.

This is where it all ends up, the Challenger said. This is the river delta. You know there's blood beneath the surface, and that's the truth, and that's what they see on you, what they smell. That's what they cannot abide. The truth of it. They close in, bristle up, try to force you out so they can turn away. But you've seen deeper and they cannot touch you, these miserable fucks staggering in a dark room full of broken glass and knives. They put out their hands to feel their way and end up with rusted nails through their palms. Don't turn back. Give them hell.

When they were down, Ramón bent over mustache and picked up his hat.

It was a Stetson, black, with a wide brim. It sat slantwise on his head. He studied himself in the Challenger's tinted window. The hat and his eyes were black and deep as the road.

In the reflection he saw, just for an instant, a tall man in a white cowboy hat. When Ramón turned, he wasn't there.

He felt cold then, in the gas station over the two unconscious bodies. He felt seen. Someone was looking for him. They had glimpsed him and passed by, only to realize they'd missed something important and turned back. Hot plains wind blew over the asphalt, whistled through scrub brush, ruffled the back of mustache's bloody shirt. Ramón had been breathing hard with the weird hot joy of the fight. Now he breathed hard with the cold tight fear of a crouched mouse that smelled a cat. Filling his lungs. Stocking his blood with oxygen. Ready to run.

The gas pump printed his receipt. He tore it off and drove. He left the hat behind.

He saw the cowboy again on a billboard near Vegas, the white brim of his hat pulled low to hide his face, scarecrow shoulders sharp under the red flannel shirt—but he blinked and the hat was black now, the shirt, too, the anatomy underneath less bitter and knifelike. But he had seen the cowboy. He was certain— though he could not see the cowboy's face—that he was smiling.

He drove faster.

His knuckles bled onto the steering wheel. But the blood did not stain and the wheel never got sticky. The leather drank his blood the way thirsty ground drank rain.

He saw the cowboy in the driver's seat of a big rig that tried to draw up on him from behind, but he drove faster—tearing around pickup trucks, grinding through traffic. As the big rig faded in the rearview, he saw the driver wasn't the cowboy anymore.

He wasn't going mad. The cowboy was there, was real. Crazy people, of course, insisted on their sanity.

Don't believe it for a second, the Challenger said. No one in this country knows what they're talking about. The real horror is not that you're losing your shit but that in a world where you tell people that burning oil's poisoning the planet and they respond by burning more oil, a world where lies turn true when you say them loudly and people clap, all of a sudden you've gone sane.

He drove through the night, and when the sickle moon rose over the desert, it was as white as the cowboy's hat.

He'd never seen many hitchhikers on the road and they were even more rare now than he remembered. So when he saw a man on the roadside north of Bountiful, wearing good jeans, with a leather suitcase by his side, Ramón slowed. When he saw who it was, he stopped.

Ish Colby stood there, Ish still broad-shouldered under his black T-shirt but otherwise changed, hardened, his fluff rendered away, his arms still big but carved now, his jaw sharp, and something haunted in the hollows of his cheeks. A sign in his hand: MONTANA. Black block letters.

Ramón rolled down the window.

He'd seen Ish in articles on the kind of websites where he didn't spend much time if he could help it, and he was surprised how much Ish looked, in person, like the man he'd become for the press. Every time he saw those pictures, Ramón had felt a shrinking sort of embarrassment, as if there were something he should have done.

Ish looked out of place on the roadside in the heat, sweating. Ramón wondered just how long it had been since Ish last had to sweat. He wondered when they'd gone wrong, the two of them, as if there were just one moment.

The Challenger purred. It wanted to run. It was not built to stand still. Ish bent at the waist, leaned against the car door on his large crossed arms, and cast a long shadow into the leather darkness. "Hey there, stranger." With a wry smile because, God, wouldn't that be easier? If they were strangers? "You going my way?"

They stopped for lunch at a roadhouse just south of the Utah border, a cramped place with big boxy televisions showing sports recaps with the sound off, and those tall old urinals that went all the way down into a little depression in the floor because you couldn't count on people past a certain minimum of drunk to aim high.

He ordered a beer and a cheeseburger, and Ish ordered two grilled chicken breasts and a salad without dressing, and a lemon.

He looked so different now.

When they'd met, freshman year, there had been a full round honesty to Ish Colby. They'd both been lost, wandering around campus in those first weeks, auditioning for plays even though neither of them had ever acted before, for singing groups even though Ramón only sang in church and Ish only sang in the shower, for improv comedy though neither of them exactly knew what that was. When they crashed out of a Duke's Men audition together, Ramón finally introduced himself.

Ish was a big dude, with the slouch and self-shyness a lot of big dudes had if they weren't pulled into football or something else where their bigness had a place. It hadn't occurred to Ramón—he was, not to put too fine a point on it, short—that this was sort of fucked up, that if you were big, the only way you could fit into the world was to use your bigness to hurt people.

Not Ish. He sloshed around under shirts that were too large even for him, and while he apologized a lot with words, the thing that confused Ramón most was how his body seemed to apologize for itself. It was like his elbows couldn't lock. He held drinks, books, bags of M&M's, close to him, as if he had *T. rex* arms, and his gestures, though expressive, stayed tight to his body. There was something powerfully charming, powerfully sweet about that. He was funny, too, in a weird sideways fashion where he'd make a good joke or drop a reference that was extremely on, then apologize for it, then explain it, or start to, even if everyone in the conversation had laughed already. He thought, he explained when Ramón asked, that people were laughing only to be polite.

He'd come from a professional family—engineer dad, mom a nurse, two older brothers and a sister, their young lives spent moving around the South. Three natural athletes, three social geniuses, and Ish, who liked books and read Dungeons & Dragons manuals and imagined having people to play with. He'd run a game for his sister and the middle brother once, or tried to, but his brother had been more interested in tavern wenches than in fighting the Dark Lord Zarathul, so his brother and sister ended up in a fight, and that ended with Coca-Cola spilled on his notebook of meticulously hand-drawn maps.

There had been other fights, too, when he was growing up. He never talked about it. But after week three, when they'd failed out of everything they'd tried, Ramón suggested they show up for one of the twenty or so martial arts classes around campus, and that was his only suggestion Ish ever shut down. He'd thought he had a sense of the guy by then, goofy and smart—though everyone was smart here, so smart Ramón quickly stopped using that word to describe people. At any rate, he'd figured Ish for goofy and smart and kind of a go-along, but the shutdown on his Wing Chun Club idea wasn't a half-measure thing, no trace of apology. Just a flat no. And: "Let's try something else."

That, Ramón later realized, was when he'd started thinking of Ish as his friend.

They kept failing together. Pretty soon they made a joke out of it. There were all sorts of groups on campus that were just body-hungry. The *Daily News* always needed people who could write a sentence, the Model UN society badly needed humans to throw into the maw of the high school model UN they held every year, and there were affinity groups and gaming groups and the bridge club, and the lovable goofs who got together on Cross Campus every Saturday to hit one another with foam swords. But there was something fun about crashing out of auditions and wandering off after to get pizza and laugh about how much they'd sucked.

Ramón suspected Ish was botching some of those tryouts on purpose. He knew *he'd* done that, anyway. There was something nice about abject failure in this place where so many people took things so seriously all the time. The fake-ancient ramparts of the old residential colleges—"They washed the stones with acid during the WPA to make them look older," a girl told him as they were passing Calhoun College, hushed, as if that were the scandal, not the fact that the building was named after a slaver and a defender of slavery. The fortress tower library, arrow slits and crenellations on dorms built in 1935, the stained glass and the crests, maybe it was all just Oxford envy, "fake it till you make it" with a medieval edge, but it also felt suspiciously like the leading questions professors asked—architecture that gave you a context, that guided you toward thinking of yourself as a person who might find a place in these hierarchies of power, secure enough that you'd not dream of rocking the boat. So long as you took yourself seriously. So long as you saw yourself the way they saw you—so long as you agreed to matter in a very specific way.

Three weeks in, he could feel that identity congealing around him in class, in his meetings with TAs and with the master of his college. (There was a master!) They coated you with authority, layer by layer, like shellac. You didn't notice at first, but as it hardened—it could take years to harden, you might be halfway through your career before it set all the way—you found your chest too tight to breathe. Even one month in, he saw some kids cracking behind their eyes. Some of the spasmodic, desperate first-month drinking, the nights when he'd found himself holding the hair of a future Supreme Court clerk back from her face so it wouldn't fall in the toilet bowl while she threw up, was just the natural result of kids who'd spent ages twelve to eighteen with schedules packed from 5:00 a.m. till midnight, now suddenly released under their own cognizance in an alcohol-rich environment. But some of it had deeper roots. It was terrifying, to smell the rest of your life—and your death too. You'd leave some of your estate to the university, of course.

In the middle of all of that, Ish and Ramón reveled in failure and experiment. You might have to approach your classes, your professors, your work (which in those first few weeks dropped the prefix *home-* and became just *work*, like the kind you meant to do for the rest of your life), your relationships with the same total focus Hannibal Lecter brought to supper, but by God, you could fail out of an a cappella audition, you could make a fool of yourself on a stage and call it a day.

It lasted for that first glorious month. Then the plays and films and groups had their people, the rushes were rushed, and he'd sat across from Ish at one of the chessboards in Ish's college common room and Ish had asked: "What now?"

And Ramón moved a pawn.

"I don't know how to play. I mean of course I know *how* to play but I don't *know* how to play. You know?"

"Me neither."

Ish's big grin at that, the endless ease of his laugh as he reached out, all the way out, one great big arm extended lazily to its full true length as if that were the most natural motion in the world, and moved his knight, they were as clear a message as any angel in his mother's books could have delivered through a burning bush. We can do this. We can get through this and keep our souls. Together.

His beer came. The televisions showed a receiver tackled from two directions at once, and the stretcher after, the blood leaking through face guard bars.

"What day is it?" Had he slept since he left LA? The road did that to him, and the Challenger. For that matter, what day had it been when he left?

"Sunday," Ish said.

"Absent friends," he toasted automatically, then realized what he'd said, the specters crowded round those words. But he kept his glass raised. Ish met him with the water. It was bad luck to toast with water. That was one of Sarah's superstitions, wasn't it? She collected traditions, rituals. You never gave someone a knife. You never bought yourself a tarot deck. You never went back to your house after you left, to get something you forgot. Ish had asked her once if she believed in all those little rules—and she said, with a roll of the shoulders as if ducking out of a heavy coat: Of course not. But I do them. That's better than believing.

She'd taught them the naval round of toasts too. Not exactly a superstition, but one more thing she carried with her. And now, he carried it.

"Why did you come?"

The question caught Ramón by surprise. He had answered Gabe when Gabe asked. But Ish didn't need to hear about duties or about debts, or about Zelda—least of all about Zelda. He knew all of that. But still, he wanted to know why Ramón was going back.

He did not look Ish in the eye. There was a whole bar to notice. Two men in big red hats playing *Raiders of the Lost Ark* pinball against the wall by the door. A woman slumped against the bar with three empty beers in front of her, nursing a fourth. A light flickered overhead. The bartender was cutting lemons. It was that kind of afternoon, stale and heavy. He wondered what industry they had up here. If there was any, or if there was just ground, hard-baked to stone. All of this used to be underwater, he thought. All of this still was underwater.

The beer was deep amber and too sour. He looked all the way down into the glass. "Who doesn't want to save the world?" He laughed as if he had said something funny.

In freshman year, he'd shared few classes with Ish. He'd spent the summer before school working and paging through the course catalog, not looking for the cool classes about Roman erotic art or the structure of propaganda or new topics in black hole research, but the ones he thought would get him where he thought he wanted to go, which was, generally speaking, "up." He was vaguely aware that there existed a stratum of human who drank nothing but coffee, who wore suits to work and complained about how many airplanes they'd been on in the last month, who got email in their pockets and made presentations to clients and saw the insides of their beautiful minimalist apartments maybe once or twice a quarter, and had salaries that made anything his mom had ever earned in a year look like a rounding error.

He wanted that. All of that. The money wasn't a reward you got for the rest of it—the money and the airplanes and the never sleeping and the stress all came in this weird glorious box, like chocolates with bourbon filling. Most people he knew half killed themselves working and barely had enough to die on. If you were going to kill yourself anyway, why not get something out of the deal?

So he'd taken the applied math and econ courses, chose classes that would help him tell a story of himself as the future-brain who'd make you and your people a billion dollars with a *b*. Ish, meanwhile, dived into the theoretical end of the pool, math so pure some of their classmates might try to cut it with a razor and snort it. There were advantages. They compared notes, worked on problem sets together, and found that most of the time they would spot their own errors while they explained to each other where they'd gotten stuck.

One day Ish had come into the college library, whumped down into a seat across from Ramón, leaned onto his massive elbows, and sighed. He twisted a mechanical pencil between his fingers so the eraser ground into the middle of his forehead, where a third eye would open if he had one. The eraser left curls of gray rubber on his skin. Outside, blue sky soared over the residential battlements of Saybrook College, and the trees of the courtyard were a painful gold, the kind of sepia day that conjured admissions-brochure photographers, that made kids write home with pen and ink and maybe enclose a leaf by way of proving, yes, I am here, yes, it is magical, yes, it's worth it. But in the library with its dark wood and leather and its old, old books, sat Ish Colby, anguished as a Michelangelo, trying to erase his own forehead. They had not known each other long, though in that seafloor vent of pressure and heat and the collision of strange forces called freshman year, having known each other since orientation week made them old war buddies. He had never thought of Ish as beautiful before. He set down his pencil with a sense of foreboding.

"In my class," Ish said.

Ramón waited.

"There's this girl."

And, oh, the relief he'd felt then. A girl! Bubbling up inside him like a spring, for all the anguish on Ish's face. A girl! Girls were easy.

Ish, waving his hands, blushing, stammered to clarify. "No, no, it's not . . . like that. She's in my number theory class and we've been going to coffee after it and she's so smart."

"Ish," he'd said with a spread palm indicating the college library, which had cost no doubt an unimaginable sum to furnish, and which he might have gone his whole career at school without noticing, because the whole place looked like this. "Ish. Everyone's smart."

"Not like her. I thought we were just talking about math. We were at first. When it started, I mean. But we've just been talking about anything too. Where she comes from. What we want to do. This place."

*Jealousy*: an ugly word. Misleading too.

In a month he'd been through two dirty campus flings and one very long sweet kiss, peach-schnapps-flavored, on York Street while a cappella rush groups surged around them. He wasn't lonely. High school had been furtive at times, but bubbling in its own way, suffused with possibility, opportunity. Some nights Ramón felt as if he had swallowed a gallon of those microorganisms that glowed in Caribbean harbors after dark, that his skin was radiating the joy he was uncovering inside him. But that was love, sex, passion. It was a whole different sport from loneliness. You didn't (he had thought, young and stupid) sit across the table from Michael, whose kisses tasted like peach schnapps, and help him through the confusion of this first strange year.

Friendship wasn't some ranked or exclusive thing. What idiot would think of it that way? But still the thought of Ish sitting down with someone else, confessing his innermost thoughts to a person Ramón didn't know, raised uncomfortable questions. Were there things Ish couldn't tell Ramón? If so, what? Had he sent some signal, flashed some colors, indicating Ish couldn't trust him? Or—were these things Ish didn't think Ramón would get? Things he didn't feel safe enough to share?

Ramón felt ashamed of those thoughts. He couldn't have articulated them even at gunpoint, and when, writing in his journal much later, he realized what he was feeling, he'd stared at the page as though he'd found a spider drowned at the bottom of his coffee. At the time, he felt only a sort of heart-sourness, a readiness with cutting words.

"And she's pretty," he'd slid into the pause Ish left between them.

"I can't get her out of my head. I've heard people say that before and I've said it, too, but only because other people said it. I keep thinking about—the way she looks when she thinks I'm wrong. I'm wrong a lot."

"So you want to sleep with her."

"No, no, no, I mean, yes? I don't know! She's . . . I don't want to make it weird, I don't know what to do about this—how to talk to her, what happens after that, I could mess up everything. But I can't not."

"You are asking extremely the wrong person for advice on this subject."

He shrugged. "I mean, women are people."

"Yeah, but, like. There are differences."

Ish went red all over. "I've never been any good at any of this." With a desperate help-me sort of look that made the vinegar bubble off Ramón's heart. But Ramón still didn't have much—or any—of the kind of experience Ish needed.

So he went to Sal Tempest.

He'd met Sal in week two at an LGBT et cetera mixer, in the odd atmospheric way he met people at those things. She'd been singing "Miami 2017" on karaoke when he showed up, brought down the house, back when 2017 seemed impossibly far away. Later, she'd been dancing with an intense girl with French-braided hair and a bright blue dress, a girl who when they weren't dancing lingered near the drinks with the discomfort of the not-quite-out-even-to-herself, but when they were dancing she moved with Sal in total fixation, as if something undeniable were forcing its way out through her body.

That night he'd ended up in a small circle with Sal sharing side-eyes as a trust fund Marxist insisted that class solidarity was prior to all other forms of identity politics, and after a fierce argument that in a kung fu movie would have turned into a three-location fight scene, they'd ended up leaning out someone else's dorm room window sharing a joint and swapping favorite Fugees lyrics. If Ramón's big sister had been on campus, he would have called her in to help Ish, but she wasn't, and Sal had felt like family. So he asked her.

When she finished laughing, she said, "Sure."

The point, Ish said—he spun words around himself in those days, sentences wrapped him like Wonder Woman's lasso—the point was not to practice pickup lines but to practice this specific thing. How do you tell someone you really do like as a friend, that you have other feelings for them, too, and would like to explore those if at all possible or mutually amenable. Having told them, if the answer was no, how do you go on being friends, or anyway not being weird at each other.

Sal, meeting Ish, thought the whole thing was a bad idea, and said so. You confessed your feelings because you wanted to change things. If you didn't want things to change, you held those feelings close as you held your cards in a poker game. Why do anything, why come to school or uncap a pen or leave your house, if you didn't want to change the world? But—she emphasized—but, she would help. For the experiment.

To see if it could be done: to change something and not change it at the same time.

They practiced under the bright gold leaves. That was the only way to learn. Ish refused to give the real name of the subject of his interest, in case any of them knew her in another context. Sal rolled her eyes, but said it was his game, if he wanted to play it like that. He called her Alice, and confessed his love to Sal-as-Alice over and over that afternoon, while leaves fell and their ciders grew cold.

Sal could have acted onstage if she'd wanted to. That shouldn't have surprised Ramón. Their whole lives were acts, especially in this place with its Bushes and its Vanderbilts and its expansive definition of whose families were "middle class." But Sal had a talent for it.

When Sal laughed off Ish's confession, Ish believed it, felt himself crushed. When she went still and twitchy and asked him, full eye contact, why would you tell me that, he wanted to shrivel down to a worm and hide in a sidewalk crack. When she said, of course, me too, I can't believe it, I've been trying this whole time to work up the nerve to say something—there was, in that moment, joy. She switched from the one to the other in the space between sips of too-sweet cider. She'd give notes, then gesture with two fingers, quick, come on, hit me again. Ramón tried to stand in for Sal when Sal got tired, but he couldn't stay light about it, couldn't stay loose or in character. He kept thinking, how would *I* respond?

Ish's first few tries were awful. Ramón didn't know much about chatting up girls, but you probably weren't supposed to go bright red, hyperventilate, stick your fist in your mouth, and walk away. But Ish and Ramón were good at failing by then, especially in front of each other, and he did get better. He turned around, breathed deep to cleanse himself the way Ramón's sister did after yoga, and got right back to it. By the end of the day, he was able to look Sal in the eyes, get shot down, take that, and move along.

"If she's mean about it, she wouldn't be a good partner anyway. But you do this thing where you're trying so hard with the eye contact it feels spooky, like you're a Terminator. And—take this how you take it, but when you feel burned, you get angry around the eyes. That's something you need to be honest with yourself about. You need to beat it."

"I'm not angry at you—at her—I'm angry, I mean, I'm disappointed and angry with myself."

"It doesn't matter. You know how careful people have to be around angry guys? Especially woman people. I just met you, and I feel it. Even if y'all are friends, she's known you maybe two months and that is not enough to know whether a dude is gonna be a problem. Do you understand?"

"So what am I supposed to do with my feelings?"

"I don't know, manage them? It's what everyone else does. How long on average do you think I go, in hours, without feeling seriously throat-punch furious about something? If you are not good at the mask, start small. Just—look down. That's right. Look at your shoes, bite your lip—let your body say 'sad,' and put the rest of those feelings somewhere else. When you can, you look up and you smile."

By the end of the afternoon, they had Ish in something like shape. "You've been graduated," Sal pronounced, and knighted him with a gold-leaved fallen branch. Next came sinister phase two of the operation.

That's what they called it, though there was nothing sinister, or even elaborate, about the plan. The sitcom versions of the three of them, Ish observed, would have come up with something much more fun. And worse, Ramón pointed out, which settled the issue.

The stage: a Halloween party before the big symphony orchestra show. The booze and the costumes would lend the evening an air of misrule. Halloween was a night when everything mattered and nothing did, when students all around the world channeled and cathected abstract concepts, nightmares, personal horrors, and collective unease through the concentrating power of fishnet tights, pumps, and booty shorts. If you couldn't fess up to an uncomfortable attraction then, you were hopeless. Might as well wall up your tongue.

Ramón wanted his first Halloween in college to be a stunner, so he planned for it, planned to make boys faint because all their blood had to go somewhere other than their brains. He'd been to big parties in LA, so he didn't expect to be wowed himself tonight, but he wanted to practice the art of wowing. Your first big night was a chance to make a new impression, to show everyone what lay under the nice clean polished rock—the mud and the muck of you, the fertile dirt.

He'd sifted Goodwill and the salvo store every afternoon, and in the second week he found them, the grail in thigh-high black leather, boots with heels he could sway in. Dr. Frank-N-Furter might be an obvious choice, but, shit, in these boots? For ten dollars, he would be a black hole on the sidewalk. Not even light would escape him.

On the night of, the costume came together, like the waters came together on the second day of Genesis. A snap of elastic, the tights against his legs, the shorts popping. The girls who loaned him the makeup screamed when he dropped it back by their suite and they saw what he'd done with it. He couldn't master that Tim Curry smolder, but every time he looked in the mirror, he saw a fox-in-henhouse grin. Big and toothy, the last sight some poor slow diplodocus saw before the *T. rex* mouth came down. He wanted to tear his own meat off the bone.

God, yes—feel uncomfortable, feel afraid, feel like you don't belong and everyone here knows, feel like you're letting down everyone who ever expected anything of you the other 364 days of the year, but tonight, here and now, let yourself be something totally else. Be surface and show and sashay, be everything they're afraid to be and do, make them stare and master them when they do, leash them through the eyes.

He descended in triumph to the street.

He owned Old Campus and Cross Campus, owned the slutty ghosts and the twenty-seven dime-store Indiana Jones, he owned Doctor Manhattan and the Ghostbusters and the Blues Brothers and six presidents of the United States. Catcalls, whistles, open stares as people he knew from class recognized him, cried out—he blew kisses, waved. Greek gods, mostly naked for all the October chill, lounged around the Women's Table passing a horn of plenty of something purple, and Apollo reached for him, Apollo who was on the lacrosse team and just a week ago had seemed untouchable as Betelgeuse.

Ramón writhed out of Apollo's arms and trailed one nail down that sculpted biceps, teasing, *later,* and when Apollo drew close to breathe *where* into his ear he answered *find me* and twitched off past the Frankenstein's Monster juggling fire. He owned the gods and he owned the goddamned university. He'd help his friend with this one simple thing and then he would take this whole town and juice it like a grapefruit.

When he found Sal, she was glaring hard at a brick wall outside the college that was hosting their party. She was trying not to cry.

His glamour wilted. He wobbled in his perfect boots.

He had a choice in that moment. The thing he'd made himself, that he needed so desperately to be right now, the god that was riding him, did not know what to do with a crying friend. He realized a lot just then: that she was his friend; that even though she seemed tower-strong and mighty, a landmark, she was in fact younger than the youngest of his sisters; that even though she was his friend, even though they'd shared joints and Fugees lyrics and moments of true and righteous side-eye, she felt at least as out of place here as he did if not more and just fronted harder to compensate; and because of that and the strangeness of this place, they might spend years or more side by side without ever knowing each other, without being able to put down the weapons and shields they carried day to day. The God of Fishnets and High Boots did not know what to do with Sal, and Ramón could choose to be that god, or to help.

He said her name and, softly, set his arm across her shoulders.

"You look beautiful," she said a minute later, when her voice was almost steady. It occurred to him that she had a great deal of practice hiding anger but much less hiding this. Whatever this was.

"You too." She did: she was going for a Puss in Boots thing, emphasis on the boots, though hers were brown. The floppy Spanish hat, cocked right, would slant rakishly over one eye, and the sword swung from her hips, the belt snug against her orange body stocking. "Is that a real sword?"

She kept her eyes wide as if closing them would squeeze the tears out. Some kids from the Precision Marching Band marched past across the street, playing "With a Little Help from My Friends" and dressed like the cover of *Sgt. Pepper's.* When they were gone, she was herself enough to try a grin. She'd drawn whiskers onto her cheeks with silver eyebrow pencil. They twitched. "A gentleman never tells."

She talked like that, he'd understand later, like a Musketeer in a book, when she wanted to be in control and didn't think she was. She talked like that often. "What's wrong?"

"Can't you guess? 'And I awoke and found me here, / On the cold hill's side.'"

Because they were friends, he said what he'd come to believe were the most dangerous words on campus: "I don't get the reference."

She sniffled, laughed into him. What an absurd place to be, and what absurd people to be there. "It's Keats. 'La Belle Dame sans Merci.' He was our age when he wrote that, I guess. A little older?"

"Girl problems?" Too general. "The same girl I saw you with?"

"Zelda. She's worried. She's not . . . comfortable. Being forward. In public." The stress on each word made it obvious she was quoting someone a bit more recent than Keats. "Kissing. Specifically. She's from, you know, down south. It's harder for her, I guess. But it can't be about that with her, because she's not afraid of *that*, you know, she doesn't care what other people think. Or so she says." Her hands rose, and she let them fall. "Sarah told me. Don't crush on freshmen. No offense."

"I'm not your type."

"She is." Like someone reading their own death sentence. "I thought it would be fun, you know? And if it wasn't anything, I'd just roll on, do whatever came natural."

"But it is something."

"Don't you go talking all sage like I won't be holding your head over a toilet six weeks and two boys from now, my god." She straightened, shoulders back, recovering some grace in the arc of her spine. She was cool like that. A cavalier, a hero, the person she tried to seem. "I'm fine. If anyone held me to account for half the dumb shit things I've done, you don't want to know how long I'd be gone. Now, let's go and see your Young Werther through the night. Shall we proceed, Your Doctorship?"

Ish was in the courtyard, beer in hand, awkwardly held as if he did not know what it was for. He waved with the beer hand, spilling some. He was dressed as a movie Dracula, high-collared cape and evening wear and slick hair and all, which wasn't how Ramón would have chosen to dress for a serious discussion of feelings, or for attracting a potential romantic partner. He had a banjo strung around his body, under the cape. Ramón wasn't sure how that was supposed to play into the costume either. "Wow! Rocky! Hey, check it out! I'm Béla Lugosi!" Waving the banjo.

"Isn't it pronounced like *bella*?"

"No, see, there's this famous banjo player, Béla Fleck, and he says it *Bay-la*."

It would have been rude to ask, *There are famous banjo players?* So he let Sal handle this.

She saw the cue. "You ready for Alice?"

"I asked her after class if she was coming, and she said she planned to come, so—"

Ramón saw the change in faces, Ish's and Sal's, both fixed like the arms of an angle on some unseen vertex near the door behind him, and from Ish's excitement and fear, Sal's trepidation, he understood the cruel joke of the situation. Behind him he heard laughter, no one he knew, and it was the old blind god's laughter in his ear, the breath hot and hungry and dense with desire. You don't ride *me*, boy. You don't dig your knees into my flank and tell me to go, you don't pull your reins against the corners of my mouth. I'm the one on your back, I'm the bit in your mouth and the spur in your side and don't you forget it. Turn, boy, turn and see.

He turned. And he saw—the girl with the braid from the party, but there was no braid anymore. She'd cut her hair short, like there were black flames rising from her skull. She wore jeans, boots, she had painted herself green and drawn on Frankenstein's monster stitches in eyebrow pencil and pasted bolts on her neck, and here in the throng of drunk gods and bad jokes, she was dressed like a self she'd never been before—and as she marched toward them, all those other creatures became shadows her own self projected out, bad echoes of worse dreams, and the only real things in the world were this girl and the woman she was marching toward.

Sal had time to open her mouth but not time to decide what to do with it. The girl's name slipped out, and then Zelda hit her like a wave, and shut her mouth with a kiss, and all the gods and demons cheered, and the old blood-hungry voice in Ramón's ear just laughed.

Sal stiffened, unsure for the first time Ramón had seen her. Then she made her peace with it. Her eyes closed. Her head bent down.

And Ish—they would laugh about it later and he would play Ramón the Weezer song "Pink Triangle" and pretend that was that. But while the gods cheered, Ish looked down at his feet for a long long time, and when he looked up, he was smiling.

Ish never told Zelda. Ramón didn't think so, anyway. What would be the point? And Sal was merciful. She sussed it out, the secret of Alice, and thought the whole thing was fucking hilarious, and kept quiet. After a few months, they were all friends—Zelda helped Ramón understand the axiom of choice long enough to ace his final, and helped him get over Apollo when that time came, and Ish and Sal swapped music. What did it matter, a two-week passing puppy crush in freshman year, back when they were all still trying on faces for the mirror?

Then Zelda showed them all what she'd found.

Ish had taken a bullet for her on the road. People used that as a figure of speech, but he'd really done it. He'd gone, alone, through trackless wastes to look for water. Once, he'd offered to let a bandit chief cut off his left hand to save them, though circumstances intervened before the bandit followed through. Ish understood the dream of the crossroads. The power to fix things. He believed in it right up to the end.

And then they stood in a parking lot in Montana, under the broken sky at the end of the world, and Zelda was bleeding.

Sarah left first. Ish drew back when Zelda reached for him. After all her talk about saving the world, now she wanted to break it open, to go out after Sal, even though they knew she had fallen, even though they knew what the rot did to the people it grabbed. Ish wanted to help her. But he couldn't. He'd seen the rot.

Ish pulled away. But he watched Ramón out of the corner of his eye. If Ramón stayed, if his best friend and the girl he loved—the woman he loved, now, a threshold had been crossed in shadow and she stared back at them from the other side of it, scarred, scared, bloody, no longer young—if they were both on the road, then of course Ish would join them, and there were only two ways that could end. They'd get Sal back—and Ish would find a way to die in the process—or he'd sour. There were too many chances on the road for him to say something that would tear open their tight silence. Ramón did not want that either.

Ramón had believed in love. *Believe* was the right word for it. You didn't have to believe in something you'd been through yourself. (At least, that's what he had thought at the time. He needed a few more years to understand that you could be something and doubt it at once.) He'd passed through many valleys he called love at the time. He'd been used, smothered, strangled. He'd hurt and been hurt, he'd blinded others and been blind himself. But he believed in Sal and he believed in Zelda, and if he, Ramón, had been alone with Zelda in that parking lot, he might have gone. It would be worth a try.

But he couldn't let them kill each other.

So he had left, to save all their lives. To save Ish. For all the good Ish had done since then. For all the monsters and spies he'd helped scare good people into staying quiet, for all the kids his programs and apps and Lidskjalf had helped cage. Ish had spent his career since Montana being the biggest and smartest scared little boy in increasingly richer rooms of big, scared, smart little boys. Ramón had saved Ish for VC meetings and newspaper photos of him shaking hands with evil men in bad suits.

When the letters came, he'd known Ish would drop everything and go to her. The whole mess, wound up again like clockwork. And for that reason as much as any other, he knew he had to go.

He could have said that, in this dirty bar at the northernmost extremity of Utah. But if he'd been the man to say the words the moment needed, the last ten years would have played out differently, and everything would be easier. Or at least, it would be hard differently.

So instead, Ramón said: "Who doesn't want to save the world?" And, still not looking up: "You're looking good."

"I had to do something to get my mind off of it all, after. I just started picking up heavy things, you know. Putting them down again."

"You've done a lot of things."

"I used what I had. My knack. Just like you do."

"Well, I didn't use my knack to lock up innocent people. Kids."

He expected Ish to flinch at that. How often did Ish have this argument? Daily? "Lidskjalf is a tracking algorithm. That's all. Predictive analytics. With a little extra juice from my knack. We don't make policy. Everyone makes it sound like I've built the One Ring."

"When you sell it to fucking Sauron, I can understand the position."

"These people aren't Sauron. They can't find their asses with both hands. We know what we're giving them. We have it under control. And they had what I needed. Money, you can find money anywhere. I needed access. Data."

"Bullshit. You didn't have to work with them."

"No. You're right. I could have just sat back and waited for the ground to open under us. Tried to forget it all. Worked in a car wash."

"It's not a car wash. And don't think you can out-mean me, man. I've been mean a lot longer than you."

For a moment, then, Ramón saw his anger. It billowed up through his body—but he shook his head, folded it, put it away. He seemed smaller without it. "She needed help."

"She didn't ask for it."

"Of course she wouldn't." He sounded tired. "But she was out there, trying to close the cracks one at a time, by hand. I couldn't be with her. But I could help. Close them in my own way. Stop them forming." He'd folded the straw's paper wrapper into a perfect square, each crease flattened with his thumbnail, and tucked the torn end into the folds so it was invisible. "You can find anyone through their phone, Ramón. How many kids' rooms have smart microphones these days? Alexa, tell me a story. The phones, the mics, the satellites, they all watch. Fewer dark corners where wriggly beasts can hide. No more secrets. No more monsters under the bed. I helped do that."

"And obviously it's made things so much better." Inwardly, he reeled at Ish's vision. To gather spin you drew uncertainty, as a spinning magnetic field quickened current in a wire. Less uncertainty made for less spin. Fewer cracks. Fewer people falling through them. It wasn't impossible. But would that be the only effect? Could you damp uncertainty like a vibration on a string—or was it more like pressure, which built when it had nowhere to go? "You did all of that."

He nodded.

"Fuck."

"I think that's why it's taken Sal so long to find her way back. Or maybe I'm just fooling myself."

"What's going on, Ish? What happened to you?"

He folded the square of straw into another square. "I came home, and looked around. We worked as hard as we could, and the world got worse. I'm scared, Ramón. I'm scared all the time. Sometimes I think it must have been this way forever, everyone scared all the time, and maybe we grew up in one of the few moments in history when a few people weren't. So it feels worse for us. But that's what happened."

Ramón couldn't keep watching the top of Ish's head as he stared down into the table between his hands. He had to do something—he wanted to scream at him and he wanted to cry. The jukebox started playing Tears for Fears. Ramón did not like eighties music, hadn't heard this song since his last Safety Dance at school.

When he looked at Ish he felt the room collapsing, no larger now than their table, the two of them. He made himself breathe, made himself look away. The bartender slicing lemons in deliberate rhythm. The pinball blared and flashed and one of the men in the white hats cursed while the other reared back laughing. Just the same.

Wait. Had there been a jukebox before? There must have been. One was playing now. But he had not seen a jukebox when he entered, when he scanned the room. You had to know the exits when you were on the road. When you were doing . . . whatever they were doing. Sarah would have called it magic, and Zelda would have argued that it wasn't magic really. But there had not been a jukebox before, he was about 80 percent sure, and there was a jukebox now, a big cherry-red cabinet with neon and the kind of pages that flipped with a low thunk when you pressed the heavy Bakelite buttons. The kind of jukebox that belonged in this kind of place—except it had not been here.

And there, at the jukebox that shouldn't be, stood the cowboy.

His back faced them, the upside-down smile of his shoulders, jeans drooped from his lean hips. His boots were leather, dark red and high, and he smeared the checkerboard tile when he tapped his foot to the music. Like the boots weren't red really. Like he'd stepped in something that would not wash off.

The men at the pinball machine had been wearing hats before, yes, but their hats had been red.

One finger on each of the cowboy's long, white, liver-spotted hands was raised. His perfect, blunt nails glinted as he shimmied, left and right, to the music.

"We have to go." Ramón pushed back his chair, stood. The cowboy paused.

Ish said, "What's wrong?"

Ramón gestured with his head to the jukebox that wasn't, to the cowboy revolving toward them on his heels. His boots left wet half-moons on the tile, red reflecting neon lights.

Ish looked, looked again, paled. He stood, too, fumbled in his pocket, dropped two twenties on the table. The bartender didn't look, as if they were not there, as if the cowboy wasn't either. Maybe they weren't.

Ish could see him, though. That meant something. Ramón had been worried on some level that he was making the cowboy up, that the rush of spin and the Challenger's knifelike wheels carving the freeway open had torn open the dungeon holes of his own brain. But Ish could see him. They were in it together. As if they'd never left.

Ish said: "That guy isn't there."

The cowboy faced them. But he had no face, no eyes, though Ramón felt a gaze pierce him, knew those eyes were steel blue, could have drawn the face exactly. He saw the features clearly with his heart, but his eyes saw only the hat tipped low. Only the harsh line of the cowboy's jaw cut out from underneath the brim.

"He's there," Ramón said.

"But he's not. There's no one there." Ish retreated, one thick hand raised toward the cowboy, fingers spread, as though they were in a game and he meant to cast a warding spell. His knack was a kind of foresight, a trick of memory. He knew where people were. He knew where they were going. But he didn't know the cowboy. "Exits?"

Ish really was out of practice. "Kitchen," Ramón said. "Behind the bar."

The cowboy tapped the beat with his toe. He walked toward them, but his steps were unsteady. Feeling his way through the dark.

The men at the pinball machine weren't laughing anymore. Their feet tapped in time with the cowboy's. No other part of them moved—the one still bent over the pinball cabinet, the other frozen with his beer half raised to his mouth. But they were both staring at Ramón, at Ish. Their eyes were wide.

*Everybody wants to rule the world . . .*

"Kitchen," Ramón said again, and ran.

He hit the swinging door hard, knocked the waiter with their food back into the prep cook and both of them into the sink. Ramón's cheeseburger and fries landed splat on the floor. Ish's chicken breasts bounced. Ish hit the door a second later, and one of the pinball men hit Ish from behind. Clawed fingers caught at Ish's neck. A thumb fishhooked his mouth. The second guy, diving for Ish's knees, took him down.

Ramón pulled the second guy off Ish by the shoulders of his denim shirt; the guy came up with furious speed and slammed Ramón to the dirty tile floor. They rolled in cheeseburger grease and fry mash. Growling, the guy spidered Ramón's body, pummeling him, but Ramón got his arms up and most of the blows glanced off. Ramón heard, closing in, the *tap tap tap* of the cowboy's boots.

The denim shirt guy's full weight was on Ramón's chest, pinning him down. He'd caught Ramón's wrist in one hand while the other pressed his face into the floor. Ramón's cheek crushed his fallen cheeseburger. There was meat juice in his eye. His other eye, open, showed him the guy's face, a red-pink monkey-cage fury mask. Whatever color his eyes once were, they were now that piercing, range-covering cowboy blue.

*Tap. Tap. Tap.* Bootheels slow and metronome sure.

A knack wasn't a song you knew how to sing or a combination you could spin for a lock. It was like breathing.

The knowledge bubbled inside him like the answers for tests used to—the openings, where to go, and how to get there. He could not see. He did not need his eyes for this. He pressed up, through the stink of meat and spilled beer and fry oil, past the flailing arms that held him down, slipping through weak points in grip and guard just as he slipped through traffic. He found his hand on the other man's cheek, easy as a caress, and his thumb hooked at the eye socket to gouge.

He froze.

While they were on the road, he'd done a lot of things he did not think about much anymore, except when the nightmares woke him sweating. He had not even felt bad about them at the time. Looking back, that was the worst part. They had been kids and they had been heroes. That's what they told themselves.

That short, quick scrap in the gas station—they'd started it. They weren't ridden by some fucked-up cowpoke who wasn't even there. And he'd finished it clean. It had been a long time since he hurt someone in a permanent sort of way. Not since Elsinore.

His hesitation, in the end, mattered more than his reasons.

The attacker batted his hand aside and clawed Ramón's face. Ragged nails bit skin. And though Ramón was not in the Challenger now, he heard the Challenger's voice. The god he'd built with his own hands shook its shaggy head. Boy, you know the rules. Quarter and mercy ain't how you live to shit another day. If you don't take, you gotta give and if you don't give, you gotta take. I thought we were on the same page about that. But you got your eye in the hamburger now, and that tap-tap-tapper, he's gonna be here for you soon, and he gets it like it's been got. Real shame. I thought we were on to something. I thought you might go all the way this time.

A hammer in the shape of a human fist rose, and fell. The guy on top of Ramon went down like a cow out of a slaughterer's chute.

Ish stood over him. His bulk closed out the light. His shoulders surged and ebbed with the weight of his breath. He stretched out one hand to Ramón—all the way out, like the gesture was easy. His knuckle-skin seeped blood, but his grip was firm as he levered Ramón to his feet. The other pinball guy lay in a puddle of dirty dishwater, under a sink with a fresh, skull-shaped dent. His hat was red again. Ish's shirt clung, dishwater gray, to his body.

The hulked-up action star Ish looked like these days would have filled the silence with a quip. Actual Ish said, "Um," instead.

They ran past the recovering waiter and cook, out the side door, into the dark, past another cook smoking on the back steps, and piled into the Challenger. The engine roared, yowled. The roadhouse front door spilled light onto the parking lot, and the cowboy stepped out. Gravel ground like teeth under his boots.

Don't stop, boy. Don't ever stop.

They fishtailed gravel across the road. The Challenger's wheels cut in, cut deep, and they were gone.

# CHAPTER ELEVEN

**S**arah reached the parking lot running. June had been on her heels at the staircase but Sarah had lost her somewhere, outpacing the kid with raw panic.

The Challenger had skidded off the road and toppled the ENTER sign at the mouth of the parking lot. Its wheels dug deep muddy arcs through the grass. That car should not be here. It was a ghost. Sarah had pulled Ramón from the wreck of it in a toxic alt, dragged him by the armpits through shattered windshield glass while he fought to get his hands back on the wheel. She'd thought she would never see it again, and never would be two days too soon. But here it was, roadside, burning.

Fire clung to the car's skin in patches, black and tarry. It had not reached the gas tank. There was time, if she hurried, to save him again.

The air stank of pitch and sulfur like a frontier preacher's Hell. Ramón lay still, his head against the window, superficial lacerations and contusions about the face, a swollen eye, bleeding from his temple. Sarah saw his chest move.

Smoke stung her eyes. She wadded her hand in her coat, tried the door. It was stuck. She wrapped her coat around her elbow and swung. Window glass shattered in. Ramón pulled back, blinking. His eyes wouldn't focus. Mild concussion? She hoped it was mild. "No, no." She reached past him for his seat belt.

Which was when she saw Ish.

She almost didn't recognize him at first, the new planes of his face like cliffs worn from a gentle hillside by the long action of a river. But he was there, with blood on his shirt and an arrow in his shoulder.

Some justice in the world, at least.

She was a professional. You helped the patient who lay before you. There would be time for feelings, for memory, for collapse, after the work was done.

"Can't stop, can't stop." Ramón was reaching for the wheel, for his keys. His feet stretched toward the gas pedal. No spinal injury at least. It had been a long time since her ER training, but it came rushing back. His black eyes, wide open, locked hers. "We have to catch her."

He was not here, not now. He was on another road, in a distant alt, ten years ago. She wrapped her arms under his armpits and turned his body and lifted—a single motion, and his shoulders were out the window. "Kick. Ramón. Help me." The last words worked. His heels dug into the seat cushion and they were out on the grass, tangled together.

A piece of glass had cut his arm through his red shirt—add that to the list of things she'd deal with when there was time. No big pieces embedded, and the blood wasn't spurting. It could wait. They'd both had worse. He was groaning in pain. They hadn't had worse recently.

"Don't be a whiner."

He cut off, laughed. "Ish. He's inside." The cut or the fall had brought him back to the present. Poor guy.

"On it." Up and around the car. She left Ramón in the grass, for now. The flames spread. Paint bubbled. Scars of silver metal glinted through the black. Maybe this door would be jammed shut, too, and she wouldn't be able to fit him out the window. She'd known he would be here. Ish. She'd told June as much. But there was knowing, and then there was seeing him again. How could any of this still matter, after ten years? Whatever was between them, it had been a mistake. And mistakes were no reason to let someone burn to death in a car, especially when they had been her mistakes in the first place.

He might be poisoned. Nothing she could do to save him. A girl could dream.

The door opened. Ish slumped out into her. He was denser than she remembered and the impact jarred her. He gasped when the arrow moved. He had headlight-blue eyes, just as she'd wanted when she was a kid. Before she realized why she'd wanted them. Those eyes were open now, staring up. "Sarah." She'd forgotten the way he said her name. The surprise.

"The seat belt's jammed. I have to cut it." She had a knife in her purse. He'd bled onto her dress. Well, if it stained, at least it was a floral print. Big, bright, brassy colors. Should blend right in. Her blade gleamed orange with reflected flames. "Hold still."

Every time she had to saw a seat belt off someone, she asked herself, in the blur of the moment, why they made the damn things so hard to cut. He leaned against her as she worked at the strap; the profusion of muscles under his shirt confused her. That wasn't the body she remembered.

The strap came free. The fire was spreading. "Need your help, big guy."

Three, two, one, lift, and they stumbled out into choking smoke. One of his legs buckled and she bent under his weight. She needed help. Where the hell was June? The girl had been only a few steps behind her.

"Get down!" There—the kid's voice.

She ducked, closed her eyes, stopped breathing as a fire extinguisher's gray fog rushed over the Challenger, smothering the flames. More bursts followed. In between them, she saw June standing like a knight in paintings, one fire extinguisher under one arm, another at her feet just in case. Must have grabbed them from the hotel. Sarah felt a swell of—not pride exactly, there was nothing proprietary about her relationship to June—but a swell, at least, of recognition. This was something Sal would have done. And she would have looked like that while she was doing it.

They staggered through gray and black to the stretch of grass where she'd laid Ramón, far enough away that he'd be safe so long as the gas tank didn't explode. When Ish hit the dirt, the arrow twitched in his shoulder and he howled. Ramón had recovered enough to raise himself on his elbows. He squinted over with his half-closed eye. "Don't be a whiner."

Ish laughed, though the laugh made him wince. Those two, of course. Some things, even if they changed, they also came back around.

"The car." Ramón tried to stand, slipped.

"I'm on it." Sarah took the second fire extinguisher from June. Their injuries could wait. She felt spin flow out of her, as if she were a mountain weeping rivers into each of them, rivers that were wishes. Stay whole. Don't let that arrowhead twist into something vital. Contain the bleeding. That is not a serious concussion. The organs might be bruised but nothing's ruptured and they will recover. Her knack worked beneath the level of will. She'd left pieces of her heart in both these men. It wasn't just an oath that bound her to keep them whole. It hadn't been just Sal she was trying to save, when she set out on the road.

She pulled the pin on the extinguisher and aimed for the base of the flames. Sal—no, it was June, it was June who smiled and gave her the thumbs-up. June who circled the car with her, putting out the burning pitch and the cinders that landed in the grass. The girl was steady, confident, and brave, and working with her in the billowing gray, Sarah felt an intimation of her own future—what it would be like to work next to Susan, to set up camp together, build a lean-to, paint a room. Someday Susan would be as much Susan as June was June now. If Sarah and Evan didn't fuck her up on the way.

Circling the car in opposite directions, they met at its hood—in front of the massive grimacing grille, two women in a cloud.

The old demon car was safe, was mocking her with its melted and buboed paint job and its spans of bare metal—look, you even saved *me*. June panted, sweating from the run and the fire's heat. She glowed with accomplishment. It wasn't panic that had let Sarah outpace June on the sprint down. The girl had gone for the fire extinguishers.

Bootheels clicked on asphalt.

Sarah went cold and still.

It might not be him. It did not have to be him. Many people in this country wore boots. But would any of those people saunter up to a wreck like that, the way a man might saunter up to a deer he'd shot through the lung?

She was scared. Hearing things. She had come two-thirds of the way across the country without sleeping. But June heard the footsteps too.

"Sarah. Sarah, it's him. Sarah, look."

It might have been a trick of the light on the interstate through the haze. Or it might have been a tall, thin man in a big hat. Walking slow and easy with his hands in his pockets. He was a ways up the road, but his footsteps seemed to come from everywhere, closing in on all sides at once. She was the deer, her lungs filling with blood.

He wasn't here, not yet.

She felt him rise, felt him gather himself and swell toward the surface of the world.

"What is he? Sarah?"

She shook her head. "Don't let him in."

"I'm not *letting* him."

"He's not here. He's looking for a door. And we're giving it to him. Our fear gives him shape. Keep him out." His bootsteps cracked like gunfire across the dead flat land. "See the road. The sky. Listen to my voice."

She reached out blind, found June's hand, gripped it hard and focused on the girl's skin, on the long bones of her palm, like Sal's, focused on the smell of her and on the smell of burnt paint and of fire extinguisher foam. The road was black, recently repaved. There had been potholes here over the winter, water seeping down to freeze in the asphalt and explode, but the county must have had money to fix them, and now the road ran straight on forever into sunset. The world was complete. It did not need a scarecrow cowboy in a bad white hat.

*I deny you. I cast you back.*

He was a suggestion in the air, a mirage in smoke and extinguisher fumes, there and gone at once. But the footsteps came closer.

You know I'm real. Deny me all you want, wad up your sense of true and tell yourself history ain't never happened and that we're all just folks now, but you do know that I am here, that I have been here as long as this has been America. I'm realer than any of you, and I ain't nothing you got rights to cast out.

The voice bubbled up inside her head. She felt sick, hollow, as if she were just skin wrapped around a gaping hole. His footsteps were hammer blows. Worse. In medical school she'd studied at a bar one block over from a construction site. They were building a high-rise and when those huge cranes drove the piles down through layers of incompetent earth to bedrock, they rang so loud her molars hurt. Like that.

His shirt pulled its redness from the earth, his hat its whiteness from the sky. Step by step. Closer. Three wet footprints trailed behind him. Four. The hat brim was a smile wider than his unseen face. She could not deny him. How could she? She was filling him in. Because he belonged.

A hand slipped into her hand. Callused and dry and scarred, real as the road. She looked to her right. A second or a lifetime ago it had seemed impossible to look away from the cowboy, and now she did it without trying.

Zelda's face was bright gold, glorious and true, as if there were no haze or smoke, as if the sky overhead were blue and the honest sun shining. She looked wan, she looked older, she looked bedrock sure. Sarah remembered then why she'd left, and why she'd followed. Remembered wanting to hate her and remembered laughing with her after Yorkside, with New Haven streetlights in her hair.

Spin flooded into her.

*I cast you out.*

The road was real and black, the horizon flat, the sky tall.

The cowboy, for now, was gone.

Zelda's knees buckled. Sarah reached for her but June was there first. They did not fall. Ish and Ramón lay moaning but safe. Across the parking lot, the lobby door of the Best Western swung open and the kid from the front desk stumbled out, his phone in his hand.

---

Sarah, as the one among them who wasn't passed out and who could do the most reasonable impression of an upper-middle-class authority figure—Sarah, at any rate, was the one chosen by silent ballot to make nice with the desk kid, whose name turned out to be Sean. The fact that she'd voted for herself didn't make her any less frustrated at being, as usual, the responsible one.

Sean was gangly, awkward, eager. He really thought they should call the police, that was what the police were for, wasn't it? Helping people when cars crashed and folks had arrows in them and that sort of thing? She drew him back into the lobby, where he was comfortable, where there weren't burned cars and people bleeding. He wore big glasses and nodded when he talked, as if the words he spoke pulled him forward. A clunky laptop sat behind the desk next to the hotel's ancient blinking PC. She couldn't resist a glance at the screen—it wasn't showing porn, to her mild surprise. He was writing fiction. Some jobs, she supposed, gave you the downtime.

"Sean, it's fine. The car is fine. No one's on fire. No one's been seriously hurt."

"Ma'am, that big fella, I saw he's got something sticking out of him. He needs a doctor."

"I am a doctor, Sean."

"Ma'am." He looked doubtful, then ashamed of feeling doubtful. Not wanting the argument. "Are you, can you help him? Are you that kind of doctor?"

"Do you want to see my student loans? I'll take care of my friends, Sean. We've come a long way and we can handle ourselves. But if you'd like to help?"

He wasn't breathing fast anymore, wasn't sweating. He was taller than she'd realized, with that slight hunch tall men sometimes had, the gentle ones anyway—a curved posture, not quite a slouch, softening their height. Lending a hand was something he could do. He was here, after all, to help. "Yes, ma'am. I mean, yes, Doctor."

She decided she liked him, and when she smiled—she didn't, often, and especially not when she was being professional, because to a certain kind of person a smile meant exploitable, meant pushover—he broke into beaming, goofy relief. She sent him for clean linens and a teakettle for her room, and only when he asked which one was hers did she remember she hadn't checked in yet.

By the time they did the credit card dance, the others had maneuvered the Challenger into a parking space, with June and Zelda pushing as Ramón steered. Ish could stand, at least, and walk with help. Nothing structurally wrong with his legs or his balance. He wasn't losing much blood, and he'd always been good with pain. But they had to deal with the arrow. She grabbed his other arm.

"Second floor. Come on. I got a room."

"Big spender." Through gritted teeth.

"Don't worry. You're paying."

He did not laugh at that, since laughter would have involved movement and more pain. But he hissed in a rhythm. To be fair, her joke hadn't deserved more than that.

Sean brought the towels himself, which surprised Sarah—maybe they were shorthanded or maybe he just wanted to help personally. He was waiting when they limped in from the elevator, his arms piled with fresh linens, an electric kettle teetering on top of the stack, trapped with questionable effectiveness under his chin.

She opened the door for Sean and directed him to spread towels two thick on the bed. "That looks like— Is that really an arrow? I should, I mean, at least tell my boss. . . ."

There being no time for an elaborate cover story, she settled on a certain sort of truth. "This is all a mistake." Ish groaned when she laid him on the bed. Pain softened his face. Around the eyes he still looked like himself, which was hard, because it forced her to remember that he really had looked like that, big and open and kind, when he saw his first dinosaur on the road, or under the gold-pink rings of that alt with all the chewed-up moons. She hadn't imagined it and she had not been blind. Blind would have been easier. It made life so simple to believe that you had been a moron at twenty-two, mistaking shadows on the cave wall for the fullness of a real bear, a table, or a lover. Sure, your prefrontal cortex wasn't jelled yet, some basic circuits of risk analysis weren't in place—but you were still yourself and even the mistakes you'd made, realized, remedied, and repented did in fact belong to you. You might try to cut them off, but then they hardened and ached like the stump of a limb. "A big old mistake."

"I take exception," Ish said, "to your—"

She poked the flesh near the wound. For purely diagnostic purposes. "Don't you start. Thank you, Sean." As he left, June came in with Sarah's bag, retrieved from Zelda's room. "You've been wonderful."

June left. The door closed. They were alone. She considered the buttons on his shirt. They were mother-of-pearl, not plastic. She drew her knife and cut the shirt off.

"So," Ish said after a while, "how's the family?"

"Somewhere else."

"You look—"

"Stop it." Scars dappled his chest, his arms. Of the five of them, he and Zelda had been her most frequent practice dummies, Zelda because she ran into trouble, and Ish because he ran after her and did not have Sal's coordination or practicality. "You did it again, didn't you."

"They caught us at a gas stop. Siphoning some big Soviet war-wreck in Wyoming. They were aiming—Ramón didn't see."

"And you did not trust his knack. I have seen people miss that boy with a bazooka. So have you."

"He's my friend." Simple as that. He'd said as much for each one of those scars. A knife at Antietam. Large snake at Crowheart Butte. His skin was an atlas of the country, Burlington to Buras-Triumph, Decatur, Jacksonville, Jasper. Clarkesville, Gatlinburg, Platte, Olympia, Cheyenne. Some of the scars she didn't recognize. Tectonics under his skin had skewed once-clean lines and stretched the seams she'd sewed. "How bad is it, Doc?"

"You'll live," she said, without *more's the pity.*

"I just wanted to—"

"Don't."

"I just—"

"Do not."

"To apologize."

She squinted her eyes shut. Her nails dug into his chest. Some memories she wished she could amputate, cast off, hurl into Mount Doom with Frodo's ring. She tossed a washcloth in his face. "Bite down on this. You know the drill."

"Some reunion. We should have done this years ago."

She went to work, and he bit down and could not speak, which was some mercy at least.

---

Together again.

The hotel conference room was as normal as a knock-knock joke. An indifferently watered plant grew in one corner, and the back wall sported a photograph of a man, dressed as George Washington, riding a bicycle near Devils Tower. The lights were demon-green fluorescent; the table was laminated in a fake wood grain. It occurred to Zelda that there were some people who had seen more fake wood-grain pattern than they had seen actual grain on actual wood, who had seen more camouflage prints than they had seen actual shadows on actual leaves.

The men and women around the table were not the ones she had dreamed about, the friends she had remembered. Ish, with his arm in a makeshift sling, wore his body like clothes now, not like flesh. Sarah was more solid, more real than she had ever seemed back at school. She was bluntly, simply, there. Her hair grayed in long thin lines, and she wore makeup now, just a touch, giving her face the crisp finish of an edited sentence.

Ramón. Thinner than he had been. More haunted. A cup of coffee near one hand, half finished. He flipped a pen over his knuckles, caught it, flipped it again. He didn't look at her. She wanted him to look at her.

What must June make of them? To her they would be a child's memories, checked now against the real world. They would not be men and women transformed overnight into odd impersonations of themselves.

Zelda's dreams sometimes felt like this, feverish and desperate, weighed down by silence. She had stood in front of each of these faces a thousand times in memory or in those vicious, almost-waking nightmares, the kind where, in the moment you realized what you had to say, your eyes opened and the chance was gone.

"So," Ramón said, "do we use Robert's Rules or what?"

Ish: "I left my pig's head in San Francisco."

"Isn't that supposed to be your heart?"

"That too. Organ-storage-locker situation."

"It's a conch shell anyway," Sarah said. "In the book. The pig's head's on a stick, they pray to it. And Zelda has the conch shell, if anyone does."

The voices were different, older, but still theirs: the capping and the echo, the ease with which the words were spoken, because they didn't much matter, because the things that mattered most did not need to be said here—you belong, or you're worth it, or I'm here if you need me. These were her people. Her friends remained inside these bodies like a tree's youth preserved inside its rings.

So she said thank you, instead of I missed you all and I'm sorry and this is all my fault and I told June I knew you'd come but I was half fronting and half hoping and I had no right to expect it, and I don't deserve this, and I love you. "It's been a long time." You could go. You should go. Look at you with your lives and some of you have families, you made worlds for yourselves and what right do I have to ask you to leave them? "None of us wanted this. I sometimes thought, I hoped, that someday there would be a Fourth of July and a nice green lawn and fireworks and we could all sit and talk and somewhere there would be music." Eyes opened. She shrank in the sudden quiet. But now that she'd started, she could not stop. "I know it ended badly. But. You're here, and I— It's water, that's all. Water, and I've been thirsty a long time."

"Tell me about the cowboy," Sarah said into the uncomfortable silence.

Zelda had felt the change in her bed, in her fever swoon, felt it in her dreams. She walked the road of black flowers and heard a voice behind her. But Sal was a tower on the horizon and she could not turn, even though she knew she should. The dream gulped her uphill. Behind her she heard footsteps, boots, in mud. A hand settled heavy on her shoulder and she woke in fear, alone, and heard the footsteps and ran toward them. She said: "I've never seen him before. There was someone after me in New York, but I thought it was Sal. I never saw them face-to-face."

"What about the rest of you?"

"I saw him on the road," Ramón said. "On billboards. In rearview mirrors. He showed up in a roadhouse, chased us away. It was like he was . . . inside people. Where did you see him?"

"He chased me through Kentucky. He—" When something scared Sarah, she got angry. Her jaw worked, her lips paled and pursed. "He *ate* someone. A boy. A young man, I mean. The hat just came down like teeth. I heard him chew."

Ramón tapped his fingers on the table one-two-three-four and again. His voice soft. "We ran from him at the roadhouse, cut hard into a wasteland. Same one from Barstow, you remember, wrecked tanks everywhere. Only this time when we stopped, there were people waiting for us. Things that used to be people. Ditch-eyed neo-Confederate froth boys, battle flag and gimp masks, you know, those assholes. But they were wearing white hats, and he was with them. On a horse—I've never seen a horse like that before. They tried to shoot me with an arrow. Ish took it instead." Ish looked embarrassed—that at least had not changed.

"We ran for the car. Made it out. But he was right behind us. I could hear those hooves over the engine. I've never heard anything that loud. We opened it up." She heard the change when he said *we*—he wasn't talking about himself and Ish anymore. He meant himself and the car. "We charged from alt to alt, hitching fast. Places where the road ran melting through lava fields. He was gaining on us the whole way. I didn't want to lead him here. So I pushed hard out, like the swerve we did with those giant bats near San Diego. Somewhere the sky was on fire and the ground flowed and spiked beasts shouldered past mountains. The air burned my throat." He coughed, winced. "I'd hoped we lost him. Guess not."

"He has to be rot. I mean, doesn't he?" Ish spread his hands at the empty table—look at the evidence. "If Sal is coming back . . ."

"She is," Zelda said. "Don't you feel her?"

"I saw the cowboy."

"I saw Sal," Ramón said. "I think I did, on the horizon, on the road. She was—big." His face twisted as if the word tasted wrong.

"This cowboy isn't Sal." June stood, started pacing, looked from each of them to the next without seeming to find what she was looking for. "Does he seem like her jam? Does he feel like a guy she'd fuck with?"

"She's not herself anymore," Zelda said.

"You recognized her voice, Z. You saw her in the sky. You think some sorry old monster out there could fool *you* into thinking it was her?" The others, except for Ish, looked at her. "I'm just saying."

Sarah frowned. "The cowboy—he chased me through my phone, Z. He almost ate June through hers. That's weird. That's not how the rot works. It needs soft places. Phones should make it weaker. They freeze possibilities. They report back to the server. They make sure Ish knows what I ate for lunch."

Ish laughed and she glared at him, and Zelda saw, then, the first real difference between this guy and the one she had known: now he had learned to hide the quick blink of his shame. "That's not what we do. I mean. That's part of it. But we try to keep track of people so they don't get lost. So the rot doesn't get them. We try to make the world stronger."

"What a world to be stuck in."

"Do you see any better options? Maybe I should move out into the wasteland, retire, have a couple kids and raise them as well as I can before we all get eaten by cannibals?"

Behind the umbrage, she saw the same old Ish—trying. Angry because he didn't know how, or what he was supposed to do. "Could something have changed? Can the rot spread through phones?"

"I don't know," Ish said. "The internet has its own uncertainty. It's not as subtle as the physical world, not as high-bandwidth, but there are cracks. Corners where no one looks. The rot could gather there. Then there's social media, destabilizing reality on a personal level. All those conspiracy theories, anti-vaccine propaganda and vampire cabals and all that bullshit, they create weird semi-local bubbles of consensus, so everyone you talk to on a regular basis on Twitter or whatever believes they're living in the world where the conspiracy is real, but no one else on your street does. When people don't agree on the world they're living in, reality, or what we think of as reality, gets . . . thinner. Maybe that's a part of it." He shrugged. "Just a guess."

"The cowboy isn't Sal," June said.

"Maybe not." Zelda remembered that voice behind her on the black-flower road, the total confidence and snide slant of it. "But he's after us, and he's bad news. If they're not the same problem, we have two problems. We have to outrun them both."

"Where?"

She had known this question was coming. She should have been ready for it. She was ready, really, for the question and for June to ask it, but she was not ready for how she'd feel when Ish and Sarah and Ramón looked at her without Sal among them, knowing what she would say, having grown so tired of hearing the words when they were on the road, knowing what they meant, and how slim were their chances of success. But they had come anyway. Her mouth was dry. She failed three times to open the lid on her water bottle. Managed it. Drank. She was weak, she always had been, but she found the strength to say it. "The crossroads."

Ish did not move. Ramón did not move. Sarah leaned back in her chair, screwed her eyes tight, raised her hand to her temple, and said, after a long exhalation: "Fuck."

They drew back into themselves. Ish stared down into his crossed arms, Ramón into his coffee, then up into the drop ceiling. June looked at them in confusion, trying to gather what she could from faces abruptly closed, but she was too cautious, or still too in awe, to ask the questions she was framing. Back in Pennsylvania, June asked if they would come, and Zelda said yes. But she had not asked, what will they do after that, and if she had asked, Zelda would not have had an answer.

"I thought," June said tentatively, "that you never made it there before."

Zelda shook her head. "No. But we don't have a choice. She's too big. We need power. Leverage. A place where spin gathers and concentrates, where the world can change. We'll go. Stop the rot. Save the world."

Sarah frowned. "Wall it off, you mean."

Zelda felt the shame again, of that night in Elsinore, of the ring in her pocket. "You saw the cowboy. The rot gets worse every year. You can see it in people's eyes. On the news. The world's hollowing out."

"Zelda, the world's been ending for hundreds of years. Ask anyone who was living here before white folks. There used to be so many people in this country that when most of them died, their escaped livestock became those million-head buffalo herds people tell stories about. None of this is new."

"But it is getting worse."

"We tried," Ish said. "We tried for two years. Three, if you count summers."

Sarah's eyes were still closed. "I have kids, Zelda. They're waiting for me."

Zelda focused her attention on the table beneath her hands, on the air freshener and stale coffee smell, on the smooth and normal surface of the world, rather than the serrated wire in her heart. "You can go. You should go."

Sarah's eyes opened then. Her stare was as flat and skewering as ever. Worse, in a way. She had practice, from being a mom. "You don't mean that."

Zelda had no answer. She really did not mean it. She had no right to ask Sarah here in the first place, and Sarah knew that, but Sarah had still come. Zelda had a sudden terrified sense that, whatever the others did, Sarah would stay. She should never have sent that letter.

The clock ticked.

Ramón had finished his coffee. He stared down into the watery dregs in the cup. "We never got close to the crossroads. When we went right for it, we almost died. When we tried to go around, to find a path or a gate or a road or whatever, it didn't work. The closest we ever got was Elsinore, and—" He cut off. Didn't want to finish that sentence. "What makes you think this time will be any different, other than *because it has to be*?"

"Because it has to be."

He set the cup down and nodded. But he did not leave.

She was out in the middle of the frozen river already. Turning back was as much a risk as carrying on, so she carried on. "We don't have time to waste, not with the cowboy after us, not with Sal on the way. We have to go as hard as we can. So we'll start at the Medicine Wheel."

"No." Ish did stand up. He turned his back, clenched his fist, then let it go and turned back to face her again. "Sal almost died in there. We can't—"

"I know. I pulled her out." She'd been the one to run in after her, and snatch her half frozen from the claws of the storm. "And she was okay."

"Only because of you."

"It will give us answers, if we can stand the storm, if we can ask the right questions. It might get us to the crossroads. At least it will show us the way."

"Or kill all of us, and then Sal breaks through anyway."

"We'll do it together. You and Ramón can find the path, and Sarah will keep us safe. I think we can make it. And it's the better way."

"That means," June said, "that there's another one."

No one else answered the question June hadn't asked. They wanted Zelda to be the one to say the words. It was only fair. She wondered if traitors ever said that, in the old times, before they were drawn and quartered, or if a witch who really had sold her soul would say it at the stake. "The other choice is, we go to the watchtower at Elsinore, deep in the alts, where the princess waited, where we made our last great attempt and the rot broke through. The place where I lost Sal."

Sarah said nothing.

"If any of you has a better idea," Zelda said, "I'd like to hear it."

She scanned them one by one. Ramón. Sarah. Ish. Loyal Ish, at last. She wasn't sure what she had hoped for. More than this would have torn her heart open. They still meshed, they were still who they had been, only with a few more scars, kids, memories. They fit so well she wondered if any of them truly understood what they had done, or what was happening to them now. Had they come together by accident, in school? By tricks of room draw and lottery, of course selection, of parties they'd not skipped? There was a clockwork fit to them. She felt uneasily as if, were she to turn fast enough, she might glimpse the clockmaker's retreating hand.

None of them said yes. They did not place their hands in the center of the table, all for one, one for all. But no one left, either, and their silence, their continued presence, the ticking of the gears, was enough. Ramón was about to speak.

There was a knock on the door, and it opened.

Zelda recognized the young man from the front desk, but it was Sarah who knew his name, Sarah who stood. "Sean. What is it?"

"Excuse me. Um. There's someone downstairs. On the phone? And he wants to talk with you."

❧

The lobby was empty and bright.

Beyond the plate glass doors lay Montana, soaked in darkness that burgeoned and grew and teemed. Out there, things rushed, crept, slithered, ranged, hunted, lurked, and whispered. This was a darkness that had friends.

Outside the plate glass doors stood a young man in a white hat.

Sarah had never known his name. His face was still that earnest full moon. He still wore his park service windbreaker. The legs and ankles of his jeans were wet, as if he had walked a long way through mud. Footprints glistened redly on the asphalt behind him.

His hands hung unnaturally still at his sides. There was dirt under his nails. His palms were smeared red. Those full lips twisted into a soft mean smile.

He wore the hat. Or the hat wore him.

What she could see of his hair looked slick and heavy. Dried cracked lines of blood ran down his temples.

"Doctor, ma'am." Sean offered her the phone. And the boy, the man, the ranger outside, whom she'd left in the cowboy's arms, raised his fist to his ear, thumb and pinkie outstretched, and shook his hand.

The phone rang.

Zelda was with her, and June. Zelda hissed when she saw him, as if she had seen a snake.

"That's the boy I told you about," Sarah said. "The one who got eaten."

He shook his hand once more, and again, the phone rang.

"Sean. Do you see him?"

He looked over to the door, jumped. "Shit! Ma'am. Sorry. He wasn't here a minute ago. I should—do you think I should help him?" That tone of voice saying I don't want to.

"No," she and Zelda said at the same time.

"I think," Zelda said, "he's past any help we could give him."

"He's bleeding."

"No." Sarah reached for the receiver. "He was bleeding. That's over now." She lifted the receiver to her ear, watching the figure outside the door. "Hello."

"He says to tell you that you've made him walk a long, long way."

The ranger's lips moved, and she heard his voice on the other end of the line, tinny and far away. He did not have a phone that she could see. He was just speaking slow and even, like her kids spoke when they were half asleep, when she asked Alex what he wanted to wear tomorrow and he answered, *airplane.* Half here, and half gone.

"Put him on speaker," Zelda said. Sarah's finger found the button. She did not look away from the door.

"Not that he minds the trip. He told me to tell you that. He doesn't bear a grudge, you understand. But he has a job to do."

"Who is he? The cowboy. Who is he?"

"He's . . . necessary? That's what he says."

"Tell him to let you go."

The moonlike face tilted and crinkled, puzzled. "He says we're friends now. And we got work to do together. Us too. You and me."

"Go away. We don't want you here."

"You tried that, ma'am. It worked a little, because he doesn't quite know how to be here yet—how to have a body. How to be in one place, not in every place. But in the meantime he's got friends to speak for him. Lots of friends. They're on their way. Some of them are already here." Truck lights burned in the parking lot behind him, and shapes unfurled from the flatbeds and from the cabs—fat shapes and thin, men and women, moving heavy, their features lost in the dark, their hats all phosphorescent white. "And he's coming. But you got a chance, if you listen to his offer."

Sarah was about to scoff but Zelda asked: "What's he offering?"

"We don't want this, Miss Zelda. He doesn't enjoy it, being so . . . in one place. And he respects you. But he wants to be sure."

"Say it."

"You come out here, Miss Zelda. Out here to dance with us. The rest can go. Except—" and here the moon face looked troubled. "Except for the girl. He needs you both. I'm sorry, but that's the way it has to be."

"Doctor? Ma'am? I really think you should let me call the sheriff. He'll sort all of this out." Sean sounded so confident. Maybe he even believed it himself.

But Zelda—weak, bandaged, road-worn—marched up to the glass. Sarah had been watching her while the ranger boy in the white hat gave his ultimatum— watched her consider it, with everything and the world at stake. Give herself up for her friends. Well, she'd made so many wrong choices—why not choose right at least once?

But when the white hat asked for June, she went cold and hard.

"You tell that guy in the hat to stay the hell away from my people. That I will find him wherever he hides, and bust his teeth in however many mouths he has, as a lesson to all his squamous buddies as to why they should stay the hell away from me and mine."

The ranger slid his hands into his pockets and investigated his sodden shoes. "He did think you would say that. But he figured he owed you the offer. After so long an acquaintance and all." He looked up with a smile. "At least you know you had the chance." And he tipped his hat.

Then he collapsed. Even through the thick plate glass door, Sarah could hear his skull thunk off pavement. She ran to join Zelda at the window—and stopped. There was nothing she could do, and she had known it all along. No living body's limbs would arrange themselves that way.

June was steps behind them. Zelda turned, tried to stop her, but the girl stared down, and so did Sarah. This wasn't her fault. It was the cowboy's fault. But she was a part of it.

The top and back of the ranger's head were gone. White ridges of broken skull jutted through the skin. The braincase was a hollow wet bowl, off-yellow in the lobby light that filtered through the window. Scraps of gray and white tissue clung to the sides. Sarah's practice seldom called for autopsies, but she had performed them in school and now those memories all rolled back. A professor had once told her: Once the skullcap's sawed off, you deliver the brain from the skull, like delivering a baby.

The hat lay where it had fallen, upside down in a pool of blood, still white.

"Doctor, ma'am. Is he—? I can't— Aw, hell. I got to call someone. Who do I call?"

No one. It was a dream. It had all been a dream since Virginia, since the

Beltway. Just phantoms in a dying woman's head. Maybe someone had crashed into her after all. Maybe she'd been launched over the median and plowed into by an oncoming semi. But that was wrong. This might be a dream—but it wasn't her dream. White hats bobbed out there in the night. They were still coming in—one truck at a time. "It does not matter," she said. "They are already here." There was a two-tone sheriff's car parked in plain sight.

"I gotta, ma'am, he's *dead*."

"He died a long time ago." Not long. A day, maybe less. But they'd known this, too, on the road. One day could last forever. Ten years could vanish in the space between breaths. She had a family back East. Susan. Alex. Evan. And she had a family here.

Her hand drifted out and found Zelda's. It wasn't a grip. They didn't have strength to spare. Just—contact.

It was enough.

Sean, fumbling, drew his phone. June slapped it out of his hand. It clattered on the tiles. "Hey! You want to let them in here? Pay attention, man. He works through phones."

"There is a *man* right there with *no brain* in his head, I do not know what in all hell is going on, and I am supposed to call the nine one one in the case of a medical emergency which I do believe this constitutes, and I cannot afford a new phone, thank you very much."

Sean bent, reaching for his cell phone. It buzzed. Unknown number. He pulled his hand back as if it were a hot stove.

A phone rang. Not his. The desk phone. She heard more rings, buzzes, calls, from the floor above them, from the halls behind. Every phone in the place, ringing at once.

Ramón was drinking from the minibar in Zelda's room, with Ish, both doing their best not to talk, when the phones rang. He reached for the handset by the bed automatically, but before he could pick it up, Ish put out his good arm and stopped him.

It wasn't just the room's phone ringing. It was all the phones. Ramón heard them up and down the hall—a chorus of speaker trills and ringtones.

Their eyes met. He wondered what his own looked like. Ish's were wide open and his pupils were tiny pinpricks ringed with gold.

The television clicked on.

The screen was the empty blue of a dead channel—but there was a shape inside that blueness. A form dimpled it, approaching through the fake sky. He saw the outline of a hat, the slope of broad thin shoulders, and from the speakers came a sniff, long and deep, like a hound following a scent. He'd never known dogs growing up, but Tío had been hunted by dogs twice, and when he was drunk he told stories. Out in the alts, Ramón had been hunted too. He'd never been able to talk about that with Tío—how could he explain? It wasn't just the sound of the dogs that got to you, or the smell, but the feeling, the sureness that someone out there, some being with teeth, cared about you.

The cowboy was a clear shape in the blue now, closer step by step, all form without lines or colors, like a Magic Eye picture.

"We should—" he started, and Ish finished: "Go."

Ramón scrambled for the door, his legs unsteady. It was Ish who grabbed Zelda's backpack from beside the bed, Ish who reached the door first. Ramón wasn't used to his friend moving so fast, with such conviction. Ish had always thrown himself in front of danger—but when there wasn't a clear threat, he tended toward decision paralysis. Not now. He pulled the door open and gestured for Ramón to go first. You could take the boy out of the South, but not the South out of the boy. Ramón went through without questioning.

The hall was longer than Ramón remembered, in both directions. Closed doors stood in rows like soldiers at a funeral. Behind each one, a phone rang.

"The stairs," Ish said. He looked as if he'd glanced into a mirror and seen a skull staring back. "Where?"

Ramón limped down the hall, Ish by his side. A light blinked over the fire door at the end of the hall. The phones rang louder. Or maybe that was just his panic. There was nowhere to run. The knack never left him, but fear clouded it. They were surrounded. They were walking not down a motel hallway but along the closed lips of an enormous, cruel face. It smiled. And soon a continent-sized tongue would slip out and gulp them down.

They had almost reached the stairs.

A door opened. Someone rushed out.

Ish was there first—a blur, even with his wound. He slammed the figure against the opposite door. A skull rapped against wood. A woman's voice swore loudly.

Ish had her by the throat with his forearm, pressing her with his bulk against the door—her brassy hair in curlers, blue eyes staring through the eyeholes of one of those Korean beauty masks. "What the hell are you doing? Get off!" She made to knee him in the groin, but Ish let her go, pulled away before she could connect.

"He didn't mean—"

The woman slapped Ish. "Who does that? Jesus! What the fuck is going on, with those phones? Who do you think you are? What goddamn video game do you think you're in? I was trying to watch my shows, and now all of a sudden the TV ain't working and I'm being assaulted in the hallway and all these *phones* just won't stop *ringing*—"

The door behind her opened, and there was a tall man in a white hat, his arms outstretched. Ramón lunged for her, but too slow. Ish would have made it. The hat descended with a fierce and bone-deep crunch.

Ish grabbed Ramón's hand, pulled. They barreled through the door to the stairs and down down down. On the second floor, they met a man in a white hat, walking up. Ish did not blink. He kicked the man hard in the chest and the man fell back down the stairs, landed hard, went limp. The hat lay over his eyes.

"Ish!" When Ish rounded on him, Ramón did not know what to say. Fear raged on Ish's face. Ramón could tell it was an old fear. How long had Ish felt it? Long enough to harden him. Terrors Ramón had spent years trying to forget had callused, inside Ish, into something like conviction. Christ, maybe that man had just been wearing a white hat.

"We don't have time," Ish said, and ran.

They met Zelda, Sarah, June, and the guy from the front desk—Sean, that was his name—coming up from the ground floor. "They're upstairs already," Ish said. No need to explain who *they* were.

Zelda backed up, let them into the lobby, slammed the door. "Outside too. Between us and the cars."

June: "Why don't they come in? Are they being polite?"

"They're waiting. Waiting for *him*." She turned his way. "Ramón, is there a way out?"

He closed his eyes, listened to his knack. He felt a vibration there—he'd mistaken it earlier for his own heartbeat, but it was too regular, and stronger each time it came: footsteps. "Haven't found one yet."

"Can't y'all just make one? Z, you ran toward an oncoming subway train. Can't you just do that again?"

Zelda was thinking too hard to talk. Sal used to joke about the smoke that came out of her girlfriend's ears. We'll have to buy carbon offsets for your thinking cap. But someone had to say something, and Ish was breathing too hard, and Sarah was too spooked, and that left him. "Not with people watching. And those guys in the white hats do count as people. Did she really run toward a train?"

"Yeah."

"Risky."

"I thought it was nuts, but I don't know how y'all's magic works. So."

"Magic?" Sean was not handling the situation any better than Ramón would have expected.

"It's not magic," Ramón said automatically—as did Zelda at the same time, without breaking her concentration.

"Not the best use of our time, guys," Sarah said. "It's magic."

"If she ran into the tunnel, she did it to get out of sight, into the undefined. This was in New York? It's hard to hitch through in New York. I never would have tried a subway tunnel, but it could work. If you were desperate." He was babbling. Outside, white hats bobbed in the dark. "What was she running from?"

"Me," June said.

"Can we turn off the security cameras?" If Zelda had heard them, she'd ignored them.

Sean shook his head. "People are trying to kill you, and you want to turn *off* the security cameras?"

"It's a simple question."

"I don't know. This sort of thing is not exactly in the manual. I don't think the controls are even here. The cameras, it's all outsourced. There's somebody watching, far away, and if they see any problems, we get a call."

"That is stupid."

"Saves money," Ish said. "No need to pay one guy to sit around eating doughnuts. Plus you can leverage analytics to identify exceptions and surface them to human operators. The head count savings alone pays for the system in a year."

Sarah's eyes narrowed. "Is this *your* company that's fucking us over right now?"

"Not mine, no. This sounds like a Liao Industries thing."

"Great."

"We just sublicense their surveillance analytics technology."

"Jesus."

"So we kill power to the building," Zelda said.

Sarah's turn to frown. "Can we? If he knows what's going on, he'll be down by the breaker already. Or one of his hats will. If there even is a way to kill the power."

"I tried to call the sheriff," Sean said. "It didn't go through."

"Way to be a Karen."

He looked at June. "Pardon me?"

"That is a hell of a thing to be able to assume. Something's wrong so let's call the po-lice."

"Who do *you* call when things go wrong?"

"Not the guys with guns and anger management problems."

Sarah set a hand on June's arm—she shook it off, glared at Sarah, at Sean. Nothing was ever easy. "Z, you got any ideas? There are a lot of white hats out there."

Zelda raised one finger. "The weather. Cloudy?"

"Overcast," Sarah said.

"This is taking too long." Ish was searching the lobby—stuffed chairs, ferns, front desk. "Do you have a fire axe?"

"Um." Sean stepped back. "Is there a fire?"

"We'll have to fight our way out. We need weapons."

"Are you—? I *know* these people."

"You don't. Not anymore."

"I can talk to them. They're not—they're not bad people. Not like you're thinking. I don't know what those hats are. They are not themselves."

The elevators, Ramón realized, had all been called up. They were beginning their descent. "Zelda. We're running out of time."

Her eyes snapped open. "I have a plan."

"Is it a good plan?"

"Do you remember Cairo?" She pronounced it *Kay-roh,* like Illinois.

"No. Zelda, no. That didn't even work then."

"It'll work now. And I don't see any better options."

Sean again: "Excuse me? What are you talking about?"

"Sean. Can you get us to the roof?"

# CHAPTER TWELVE

Storm clouds lowered over the Best Western and the empty country around, great gray masses of night. Zelda stumbled under their weight. The emptiness danced and the horizon swayed. June was there, under Zelda's arm, holding her up. The cut in her arm burned. She had kept it together for the meeting, in the lobby, in their flight to the stairs, but there wasn't much of her left to keep. Her legs could barely hold her. Still weak from illness, she should have felt smaller all through, but instead, she felt too big for her skin, like a snake about to molt.

She would have prayed if she still believed in a listening god who might have pity or mercy or a sense of humor. Even now, Zelda was enough of a church kid to argue with herself about theodicy. Why would God let bad things happen? And when you were omnipotent and omniscient, what was the difference between *let* and *make*?

Sometimes she got real tired of the inside of her own head.

She was trying not to think of the dead boy, of the inside of the skull smooth as licked ice cream, or to think of Sarah's face, the cool still judging expression she had when things were very bad and she told the squishy human bits of her to go away somewhere they'd be safe.

Below, the white hats ringed the building like mushrooms. Mushrooms, rings, fairy circles—those were good omens in a way. Places you went when you had to be somewhere else.

"What's the plan, Z?"

The plan, June said, so sure there was one, so sure it all added up to something and Zelda wasn't just fucking this up as she went along. "We need to lose them. We need to be unseen. But we can't do that while the power's on, and they control the power."

"So why are we on the roof?" June asked, and then: "Oh." Her voice went small, and she looked up. Into the clouds.

Sarah leaned over the edge. The whitecaps were closing in. Beyond them the road stretched hungry and forever until the darkness ate it. Clouds flickered overhead. "I can't believe we're trying this again."

She looked so much like herself. Ish had surfaced from the sea of his own body—all his strange edges laid bare—and Zelda was not sure how she felt about that. Ramón looked leaner, sadder. Sarah, though, Sarah had never looked this much like herself at school or on the road. The slight rounding of her lines, the bright print of her dress, even the thin fine streaks of gray in her hair fit her better than any campus org T-shirt or Goodwill treasure ever had.

Sarah had never approved of Zelda. She'd never been mean about it or snide, but she held back and gave Zelda and Sal space, and watched. Suspicious, maybe, the way a good belay partner was suspicious of the mountain. They were friends. They were. But without Sal, the gravity was off and everything was weird.

"Hey," June said, "don't sweat it, I can't believe half the shit I've seen in the last week. You want to help, or stay here and wait for them to catch up?"

"Help."

Zelda held out her hand.

Sarah's palm was soft, her grip sure. "I'm so tired." The words slipped out of her like a splinter. "I didn't remember this part of it. It all felt normal back then. Zelda, we were kids. We can't do that again."

"What we tried last time didn't work," Zelda said. "So we might as well try something different."

Ish said: "They're coming in."

They were. Flowing across the parking lot, all together in a flood. The plate glass doors burst under their weight.

"Must have smelled us up here," Ish said. "Or maybe there are finally enough. We could wait till they're all inside, climb down behind them. Rope?"

Zelda frowned. "With your shoulder?"

"I'll stay. Hold them off."

"You're really looking for a chance to check out quick." Ramón grabbed his arm, pulled him back to the line. "If we're doing this, we do it together. You opened the letter. You showed up. Let's get it done." He took June's hand, held out his to Ish. "Come on, man. I need you around to save my ass."

Even then, Ish balked. That was the part of him Zelda was not ready to see—it had been submerged before, like the propeller of a great ship, the alien screws and monstrous chains that, because they were hidden from view, did not have to pretend to be human scale. There was so much fear in Ish. Fear that gathered power to itself as if power would be a salve and comfort. Fear that, under pressure, could burst through the crust of him like diamonds shooting out of pipes in the earth. His knuckles had been bloody when he reached the lobby. There was blood on his shirt.

She understood. She remembered that night in Elsinore, the screams and the walls sprouting arms, remembered the courtyard, the black iron ring in her hand. They had so much in common, in a way, she and Ish: southern families, histories of shame and violence, math, the same kind of fantasy books, power and control—she hadn't realized in all their wandering until this moment that they held their fear in common too.

"Ish," she said. "Let's go."

Something passed across his face just then that she could not read, whole paragraphs in a gibberish alphabet. The sky flashed overhead. With a growl, he grabbed Ramón's hand.

Spin rushed through her, from Sarah to Ish and back around the circle. Waves built, crest adding to crest and valley to valley. So long on her own, she'd forgotten how it felt, the tension of possibility, the branching infinite paths of the four of them together. Five, now, with June. Each gathered spin in their own way, because each saw different details, different possibilities. This, Sal had proposed, was the reason for their different knacks. What you found became who you were. Who you were shaped what you found. For ten years she'd been stuck, seeing only through her own eyes. And now that was over.

"Sean." Sarah offered her hand. "Come with us."

The kid shook his head. "I got to stay, ma'am. Doctor. They don't know what they're doing. They don't know what it is that's got them. If I can help—"

"You can't," Zelda said.

"I got to try. I can't let them all end up like that ranger. Maybe I can buy y'all a little time."

Zelda felt him slip away, back toward the door that led down from the roof. She felt the white hats boil up the stairs toward him, felt the guests in their rooms, all refracted through Ish's knack. There was Sarah's, overlaid—the currents of risk and disaster in red relief parted around them by the tiny breathing space Sarah's knack assured. Ramón's, too—paths led from the rooftop, gaps in danger, safety in motion, out, to the road, to the alts. The Challenger burned bright on the rim of her awareness and she heard it speak, its words muddled as an echo of a whisper, but its tone fierce, urgent, ready.

There were paths they could walk. Above them stretched the sky.

She gathered all their spin and reached—up.

<hr />

Sean closed the rooftop door behind him, locked it, and locked the dead bolt too. Then he unlaced his boots, slipped the left one off, and, judging aim, brought its steel toe down hard on the head of the key where it jutted from the lock. The leather tore. Footsteps climbed the stairs, lots of footsteps. They didn't sound like normal people. No shuffle, no groan, no heavy breathing, no taking the stairs two at a time, no chitchat. They had the silence of people ashamed to be here, people with a dirty job that someone had to do.

It scared him. He didn't think of himself as a guy who scared easy. He liked monster movies, he liked it when things with knives for fingers came at the hero out of her bedroom closet. When he went to church with his family on Sundays, he wasn't afraid of Hell in the way he figured the preacher probably hoped, not the way his older brother Earl was, but in a kind of Halloweeny way instead, thinking about big black shapes with wings and eyes of glowing white, about flames as tall as buildings and a snake that could eat the moon. Hell reminded him of how roller coasters had made him feel when he was a little kid, as if the world were ending and he'd never get enough.

But he had seen Earl in the parking lot with a white hat on his head. And that made him feel a different kind of way.

Now, what was a guy to make of this? Of the dead man with his brains scooped out, of the parking lot full of—full of Earl and his friends who worked out on the range together in season and worked at the drugstore when the weather got bad, of Deputy Ross in the sheriff's car, of Tammy, whom Sean had crushed on hard back in high school, and whom he saw sometimes at the truck stop where she waited tables, which wasn't on his way from home to work but he sometimes pretended it was.

Something had them. They weren't part of it, he told himself. They weren't volunteers for whoever was on the other side of that telephone line. He knew these folks and he knew they would never say, just give us the woman and the girl and we'll let the rest of y'all go. That was what bad guys did, and they weren't bad guys.

He told himself that. And he knew he was telling himself that. Which bothered him, because if you were telling yourself something, didn't that mean you had to be told? And if you had to be told, that meant you didn't know it already. That you thought it wasn't so.

He hit the key again with his boot, and again his aim was wrong. He dented the door. What kind of guy couldn't even break the head off a key when he had to? He'd seen people do this in movies. Or they swallowed the key, but that never seemed right to him. A handcuff key maybe, but not this big honkin' rusty old thing with the snaggle teeth and the broad blade. That would just be asking for you to get your gut torn open, by the key or by the guy who was coming up behind you.

In fact, Sean thought, with a wacky kind of laugh in the part of his brain that didn't think this was really happening—not that it was all a dream exactly, but a kind of show, that someone would walk out of the wings in a tuxedo like that guy he'd seen in the dinner theater *Our Town*—in fact, that would make a good scene for the book he was writing, which he'd titled *Fear* to give himself something to write at the top of page one. A bit for the helpful side character, the guy with the crush on the lead girl who never once said anything about it even though he wanted to before they were never gonna see each other again—though she didn't know that, of course—that guy could lock the door she'd run through and swallow the key and think he was so clever, and then the monster (he didn't have a cool name for it yet) would just grin knives and gut him and take it.

*Sean,* said a voice behind him that wasn't Earl's, not Earl's normal voice, not the voice he used at home or when he and Sean were watching football together, or at their mawmaw's funeral. But he had heard Earl use that voice once, down at Jake's Taproom, when someone Sean didn't recognize came up and asked Earl a question Sean couldn't hear, and Earl got real stiff and looked at the guy the same way he'd look at a rattlesnake, and told him to leave, like you'd tell a snake to git. *Sean,* Earl said in that voice. *Turn around. Don't make it be like this.*

The footsteps were still coming up the stairs. They hadn't reached him yet. "You ain't him. And you ain't got the right to tell me nothing."

He hit the key again. The head bent, but did not break. He realized then that he'd done this wrong. He could have given them the key, on the roof. But that would mean he wasn't coming back, that Earl and all of them were gone, that they'd been got by their hats and by whatever story the hats made them think they were part of. He was coming back. He would talk Earl out of this. There was still time.

He realized he was telling himself that too.

*If you ain't scared, Sean, what you doing trying to break off that key?*

There was some humor in the voice, that loose joking-with-himself kind of twang. That wasn't from the cowboy hat. That wasn't the voice of something that made a ranger kill himself just to make a point. That was Earl. Not rattlesnake Earl either. Just Earl himself, like he was after church on Sunday.

Sean turned around.

There his brother stood, three steps below him in the stairwell. The stairs behind him were empty. Sean couldn't hear the people climbing anymore. Like they were sound effects, and someone had turned them off.

That happened to him in a haunted house once, at Halloween. A speaker fault, a crash, a spark, then—nothing. No sound, no static. The lights flickered. Ghouls jumped out from behind corners in total silence. Hands rosé from coffins. He'd gone in alone because the other kids were afraid, but he hadn't been afraid until the sound went off.

Earl wore a white hat.

He looked the same. No weird eyes, no black veins around his temples, nothing. The stairwell lights made his hat look a little green, like it was sick in a cartoon.

*See?* Earl said. *It's just me. This ain't the fight you want to have, Sean. You got more waiting for you on the other side of this. A whole life, even. You got books to write, man. And someday you're gonna work up the nerve to ask Tammy on a date, take her to see one of them good movies, not the mess you're always trying to get me to watch. What a man has got to look forward to, you've got. Don't throw it all away.*

"Are you trying to scare me, Early?"

*No, buddy, no. I'm just trying to tell you that you got the wrong dog in this fight. Those people on that roof, you don't know them from Adam. They are drifters, Sean. They are criminals and they do not belong here. It's not their place.*

"They came," he said, "into my house. My place of business. And while they are here, they are under my protection."

*Sean, buddy, you are the night manager of a piss-mattress motel chain on account of nobody else in this county gonna pay you to stand around doing nothing while you type up your demon books. You think you are some kinda hero all of a sudden? Shit.*

*Shit* had two syllables the way Earl said it.

"They're my guests," he said. "And what about you, Earl?"

*Me?*

"Why didn't I hear you come up those stairs? What makes you and Sheriff Ron and the rest of them care so much about some drifters all of a sudden? Didn't you see what happened to that kid in the parking lot?"

*He was dead already, Sean.*

"Yeah, and who all killed him, Earl?"

*You got this wrong.* Earl took a step forward. He left a red-brown footprint on the concrete stair. *There's good guys in the world and there's bad. And sometimes those of us that's good, we got to stand up and stand together and protect what's ours. Do what needs doing. You and I might not like it, buddy, but that's the world we live in.*

Earl's hair looked wet where it curled out from under the hat. "Earl, can you take that hat off?"

*I don't want to. This is a badge, an honor. When it's done I'll take it off. Bury it maybe. But what they're doing out there, what they might do—he told us and I can't even conceive it. You know what's howling out there in the dark? You know how easy it could eat us all? Just one big snap and we're done. He wants us to live to see glory.*

"Who is he to you, Earl? Is he your brother? Do you know him, trust him? Have you ever seen his face?"

A cloud of trouble crossed Earl's features, and after that cloud a trace of dawn. That light, that confusion, glowed to Sean's eyes like gold in a riverbed.

"You're all wearing that hat." He pressed his advantage. "You're all taking the word of a man you don't know, not like you know each other and not like you know me. I never asked you much, Earl. All I'm asking you now is to take that hat off and if you then say to me, 'Sean, I want that door open,' then I'll listen."

*Sean,* he said, *what does a hat have to do with all this one way or the other? We're just wearing them so we know who to trust.*

"Then take it off."

*You don't get it, bud. You always been a little odd for someone from around here, and we all respect that. I been there for you in ways you don't know, to make sure folks respect it. Because you are one of us. Whether you feel you are or not. But that feeling sneaks in your heart, tells you no one gets you, that there's no hope for trying nothing. It puts you on the wrong side. If you'd just listen, you'd know that you ain't so different from us. Your shit's got the same stink to it and your boots got the same blood on 'em. You accept that, you join in, and all of a sudden, man, it all gets easier.*

*You get what you want, because you ain't afraid of it anymore. We got the whole world, buddy. We got Tammy, little Tammy down there at the truck stop with those round juicy thighs I know you been thinking about, under that skirt she wears to work. Just give it up and open that door. You can't imagine what's possible if you belong. The world ain't like your demon books, and none of them on that roof's gonna give you a second thought where they're going and why should they? You ain't on their side, really. You're on ours.*

*We got a game to watch on Sunday and you got books to write and Tammy's right down there in the motel parking lot feeling flush just thinking about you being a hero right now. She's glowing on the hood of that Dodge and you, you're on the wrong side. But only by accident. By mistake. So why not step over. Just turn that key.*

Earl looked as sincere as he ever looked on Sunday. Sean wondered what it was that Earl heard when the preacher was talking, and whether it was the same thing he, Sean, heard. You could ask the same question, couldn't you, about the Pledge of Allegiance, or the Declaration of Independence, or a Kenny Rogers song. You could sing along in church and then you could kill a man for looking different or because somebody told you to, and never feel the two didn't go together, because in your mind they did. He'd thought that church was for good people, but maybe there were two nations in the church—or more—and they sat and smiled and they sang about the God of Wonders Beyond Our Galaxies, but they had different wonders in mind, and they prayed to different gods no matter that they used the same words.

Earl wasn't one of those. Earl was a good guy.

"I got one thing from those demon books," Sean said. "I learned how demons talk."

He struck the key once more with his boot, and the head cracked off and the blade, too, inside the lock. Behind him he heard a hiss that did not come from any human throat.

He felt Earl's arms around him like a hug gone wrong. He fought. The arms clung tighter.

They weren't alone in the stairwell anymore.

The others crowded shoulder to shoulder, staring up, eyes tight, judging. Sheriff Ron was there. Tammy was there. The hats bloomed like caps of poison mushrooms. The air went sour with their breath.

And *he* passed through them, shoulders above even the tallest, but so thin he seemed like a breeze might blow him over. Always starving, he was. They bowed out of his way like new wheat under the farmer's hand. His footsteps rang. The hat hid his face, though he was taller even than Sean. The bolo tie swayed as he climbed.

Sean fought, even though he couldn't win. Earl had his arms behind his back, and Earl was a veteran and a black belt badass in dirty tricks from the dojo of Jake's Taproom at closing time, and Sean had never been the fighting kind. But he tried, as those boots tolled up the stairs.

The cowboy stopped two steps below him. Their heads were even. Sean tried to look away, but Earl's big callused hand clamped his jaw like a steer's and forced him against himself, until he was looking straight at that downtipped brim.

The cowboy raised one knobbed and gnarled finger and tipped up his hat so Sean could see his face.

The stairway lurched. It stank of breath and bodies, as if all these people Sean knew and loved had spent their whole lives eating corpses.

He panted. He drew that rot into his lungs.

And he spat in the cowboy's face.

⊁

The sky was gathering.

Wind whipped Zelda's coat and swayed her on her feet. If not for the hands that held her—June's, Sarah's—she would have fallen. Sickness made the world raw. The first drops of rain on her cheeks felt heavy enough to bruise.

She poured spin out and up into the clouds. The hotel was full of cameras and cell phones, microphones and gyroscopes, all pressing against her, watching. But they were not pointed up.

The clouds were close and tall beyond all scale. They crashed together, reared apart, billowed and bloomed. The black and gray yielded colors, lit from beneath by the parking lot and from above by the flicker-flash of high-up lightning. She'd seen *National Geographic* pictures: in the stratosphere the lightning looked like jellyfish, it schooled and danced, and in those flashes, the clouds were iridescent green, purple, blue, were bloody red and all the colors of a coral reef. Air hung upon her heavy as a coat. The lights bared pieces of the clouds' holy anatomy, God performing the dance of veils—a height and scale she could only imagine falling through, ten years' solid and unbroken fall before the final stop.

So close.

"Hold on tight," she said. "If we're separated, make for the Medicine Wheel."

"Got it," June said. "Where's that?"

"South. And west. It will draw you, when you're close. Just . . . hold on."

June's hand tightened around hers. "I read somewhere the inside of a lightning bolt is hotter than the surface of the sun."

Zelda couldn't answer.

"That's pretty hot."

Another raindrop, another bruise. They were all falling, the raindrops, tumbling from high clouds to smash. Thousands. Millions. Like graduation: you gathered yourself and fell. She remembered when she was a kid, watching the World Trade Center on television. Watching the flakes that fell first, that were people tumbling—only living beings fell like that, trying to fight it the whole way down. Raindrops just went.

"I guess I am asking—have you done this before? You have. Right?"

"No."

"Okay. Good. That's great."

"We tried it once. Sal's idea. Didn't work. But I think I know what we did wrong last time."

"You think," Sarah said.

The sky flashed so bright it revealed the whole flat country all around in noontime clarity. When the flash died, Zelda plunged, blinking, into total darkness. Small hairs stood up on the back of her neck, on her arms. Thunder growled—not a single sharp crack but a roll, immense and all around, a terror felt in the bones and gut more than a sound.

She heard a scream behind her. She remembered Sean.

And then, in the darkness after the lightning, in the silence after the thunder, there came a voice.

———

To Sarah the voice sounded like a key in a lock:

"I know you never wanted this. You're here for friendship? Your friends will leave. They left already. And you know the truth, more than any of them—you know there's no way to run, there's nothing out there but the end. A few words that make people feel sad when they read history books. You made your peace. You got your family, your yard, your boy and your girl, even if you do wake up in the middle of the night sometimes knowing just how tiny your dream is when the chips are down. You belong on my side. You made the deal. You belong to me. So stop this now. Go home. Your kids are hungry and they need you. Let go of her hand and open the door."

She thought of Sal, and of how Zelda had looked when Sarah plucked that black squirming thing out of her arm. How she'd felt when the cowboy marched toward her down the road. She clutched June's hand tight.

June heard:

"You're not supposed to be here, girl. You're not part of this. But you've been noticed now. And you know what happens when the eye's on you. And all of that for what? For the truth? You've known the truth. For Zelda? Ask her sometime what really happened the night she lost your cousin. None of these fine folks will go to bat for you. They'll let you down. You walk out there and you're just another missing girl. You stay here, you play nice, and there are all sorts of deals we can make."

She thought about a drawing she had taped up beside her bed, and gripped harder—Sarah's hand, and Zelda's.

Ramón heard:

"You don't want this. You talk a big game in your head about being honest, you hear that dumb damn voice in your ear about where the real blood is. But you ran last time, kid, when things went wrong, you ran as far and fast as you could, into a soft, fat job. You shoved your head into the sand. That's what you do when the pain comes—you knuckle under and let go. You get right the fuck out of the way. You ain't confronting shit. And none of the rest of them is any tougher than you. You really trust them to back you against me?"

He remembered a morning on the beach, and waves against the sand. He remembered Gabe, on the hill in Griffith Park. He held on.

Ish heard:

"You know me. You know what I want. And you'll come to me sooner or later. You'll call me when you're ready. But you could stop pretending now, stop thinking this might all work out. You're sentimental, but I know you from the inside. I know what you need."

The rooftop felt thin underfoot. He was sweating and his heart was doing its triple-beat trick. There was a serpent who gnawed at the roots of the world. There was a serpent. There was a serpent. He clutched Ramón. He tried to remember a time when he did not feel so afraid.

And Zelda heard, at last, her hands rain-slick, her eyes open and stinging:

"You heard me first. We breathe each other's air. You know I'm right. And you know you're weak. Just give them to me. You lost them long ago. They moved on. They're not yours and they never were, and neither was she."

He was right.

His voice was a slither on rocks, less a sound than a memory of other sounds. The words were true. She'd been on the road so long, she was worn down too far, to lie to herself. She was weak. She was the reason they'd all split up. She'd failed Sal. She was a bear trap wearing person clothes.

But spin filled her—not the power of what was, but the power of what might be.

Clouds boiled overhead. Their shapes massed and smoothed into the geometry of a human face. Cheekbones high as mountains, eyes deep as starlight. Full lips with a contrail smile. A face pressing against the clouds from the other side, like a body against a sheet.

She stared up into Sal's lightning eyes.

"Z." June's voice.

Charge built, possibilities gathered. An orchestra bowed and breathed crescendo. She'd known this might happen, that this much spin channeled in one place would thin the world, open the door for miracles and sendings from the place beyond the shadows where Sal walked.

Sal was haloed in spider legs and black lightning, and Zelda had never seen anything more beautiful.

"Z. I can *hear* her."

Something immense struck the door behind them. The hinges bent. The metal frame buckled and dust sifted from concrete. Another blow came, harder. No convincing now, no wheedles, no game. Denied, the cowboy turned to force. She heard them, the many who made themselves his limbs, surging like a flesh tide against the door. She imagined the door torn off its hinges, their small circle dragged apart, imagined fingernails tearing open her cheeks, boots on her knuckles, the smell of their sweat as they ripped her hair from her scalp and pulped her eyes in their sockets. She did not imagine this because she was afraid—though she was afraid. Terrified. Her whole self curled into a tiny rodent in her chest, its heartbeat rapid as a trilling tongue. She imagined this because she knew these people, because she knew how they were—the kindness and the welcome smile so long as you remembered forever and always to submit. And if you refused—there was nothing worse than refusal, and no quarter would be given. You were an animal. You were cast out. You did not belong.

She knew Sal. But that face in the clouds was not her. It was larger and more awful, more awe-ful, than Sal had ever been. The wind howled shrill and high, like a madman's pipes.

The door buckled. Its hinges burst.

Zelda reached up to the sky and called the lightning down.

Lightning starts with two surfaces, distinct in charge, positive and negative, like the two poles of an immense magnet: the clouds and the earth. When, finally, the difference in charge is so great that it can overcome the resistance of the air between soil and sky, a spark rises. That first spark is a bridge—an explorer. Others follow. They strobe back and forth from the heavens, millions of volts in moments. If your eye could split the hundredths and thousandths of a second, you could see it, a god or djinn gone dancing. The center of that dancing column was, for an instant, hotter than the surface of the sun.

For Zelda it was light, blinding light, and a crack as if the whole world were a ship and its mast had gone.

She could not see into the heart of the building beneath her, to watch circuits pop and burst and wiring melt as the lightning coursed down every path save the one it was supposed to travel, the short easy road to ground. Cameras burst like pimples. Phones died. She could not see any of this, but she felt the rooftop sway and give, its solidity unsure now that the cameras and security system were blind.

The thunder said: *I missed you.*

There was a darkness in the heart of light, and in that shining darkness they slipped away.

***

The door burst from its frame and rolled to a rest on the empty roof.

The cowboy walked out. His feet crunched gravel.

Below him, alarms rang, sirens wailed. The hotel was on fire. The fire department would come. Maybe on time. No concern of his. He did not need these people. They had almost served their purpose.

He raised his face to the sky, and his hand trailed down to the holster at his hip.

But the face in the clouds was just clouds again, drifting and torn by the murderous cold wind.

Rain lashed him. He smelled smoke.

He tipped his hat to the storm, walked off the edge of the roof, and was gone.

## CHAPTER THIRTEEN

Zelda showed Sal the alts for the first time in the spring of freshman year.

She took Sal back up to the roof of the Art and Architecture Building, where they both lay in thick coats on the pebbles of the roof, beyond the chain-link fence that was supposed to be as far as they could go, and there they shivered, stared up into thick smoggy clouds as Zelda pressed her heart against the eggshell of the world, and willed, move, move. All her practice with Ramón, dodging dinosaurs down cracked echoes of I-95, seemed less real than this frozen rooftop, because Sal felt more real to Zelda than Zelda felt to herself.

The clouds above billowed and changed, orange and pink, charged with steam and with the lights below. Sal lay beside her, hand in Zelda's hand, watching her sidelong more than she watched the sky.

Humoring her.

*Please*, she thought. She might have prayed.

Please. I found her here, or she found me, and I've been chasing her ever since. I feel like my body's about to split at the seams and unfold like one of those paper fortune-tellers we used to make in school, open and close and open and close to see whom you'll love, where you'll live, how you'll die. What's inside me is so much more than my skin can hold. I can't speak it, I can't sing it or write it or weep it. I have to show her.

Because she's slipping away.

I can feel how much I'm not worth her, how little I understand her. I know this can end. It will end. It must. I'm not a kid, I'm not a child, I know we met in a fever in the first couple weeks of my first year away from home, and she was so much deeper than beautiful and I was so hungry, and I know how that story ends. It doesn't have to end like that. There must be exceptions. Outs. But there is a thing I do not understand between us, a silence that grows and grows. She's cool and strong, she's not scared out of her mind, and I *am,* and I'm not worth it, I'm not enough, not brave like she is.

Back on Halloween, I put on my face and marched to meet her and I kissed her in front of God and everyone, and to get there I had to cry so hard in the bathroom stall that I felt like I was going to throw up. I can never match her. I can never be like her. She needs someone to walk beside her and I need her to be one step ahead, and as big as the sky.

But this—I found it, with all the coagulated force of this thing inside me that I cannot name, and I will show her, and she will understand.

Please. Let her understand.

Their breath rose up like smoke. She clutched Sal's hand so tight it hurt.

The clouds—parted.

Zelda had grown up under stars like fields of wheat. She could count all the stars she'd ever seen above New Haven on her fingers. She had never seen stars like these before. They wheeled. They danced. There were other moons in the sky, before they changed and fell away.

Sal gasped as though Zelda had just torn off a bandage.

Her eyes glittered wet in the shifting lights, and strange.

"What is this?" Sal asked, and though later Zelda would chatter about manifolds and indeterminacy and possibilities and paths not taken, build a whole intricate palace of words like wards against the unsure heart of this rooftop night and this other sky, in that moment she could not speak.

Sal could see the alts.

But she could not step through.

They spent the spring exploring. Hand in hand with wandering steps and slow they made their way through campus past ghosts of ruined cities and swamps where streets should be, in the months when the sooty drifts melted and the first snowdrops slipped through gaps in the bare cold earth.

In the Challenger, Sal saw the dinosaurs outlined against the sky, smelled their big rough feather-stink on the wind, but when she tried to touch them, she just felt empty air. They drifted through the lumbering beasts of the road as if they were fog. The first time it happened, Ramón almost swerved them into a tree, trying to avoid a wreck with a phantom. But they had not hitched through. They were just gunning it down Connecticut back roads the whole time.

Sal was the only one with this problem, and it vexed her. Sarah fought all the way, but once she knew the alts were there, she could slip through as easily as Zelda herself. Ramón was the most natural of them all, used to the highway and the view behind the wheel. Ish learned the knack only with great reluctance, unwilling to cede her argument, unwilling to follow where she led, always dragging her into the weediest of implications. She had to wrestle him into dreaming, into seeing otherwise, by sheer irrefutable mathematics. Things could be otherwise. So where *is* otherwise? Where does it go?

But even he could pass through. Sal could not.

Zelda tried everything. She explained the math of the proof she'd found, explained why what she did was possible and what mental transformations would help her gather spin. Sal did not just follow, she suggested refinements besides. They chased each other through the math in the small hours of the morning, when Sarah and Sal's other suite mates were asleep.

Zelda made teas of various herbs to promote vision, she found the best weed on campus, but Sal remained rooted to the earth. She wondered, she posited, she argued, but she could not budge. Yarrow stalks did not avail. Neither did tarot cards or castings of the *Yi Jing* or readings of the zodiac or Hermetic chants. Sal remained herself. A bit more annoyed than usual, especially after Zelda's ill-fated experiment with acupuncture.

"Maybe," Zelda said, one night in early spring, seated cross-legged on Sal's bed with her notes spread in front of her, "we could try fasting. The heightened mental state could pull you over the edge."

Sal was turned away from her, silhouetted against the screen of her janky, old, duct-taped Dell. She was clicking through something Zelda could not see. "My mental state does not require any heightening or tightening or loosening, thank you very much." *Click. Click.* Scroll.

"What about Transcendental Meditation? Or we could ask Ma if she has anything that could help."

"We are not asking Ma about this." Scroll. *Click.* Scroll.

"She might know something. It's all useful, you know. Each experiment refines the theory."

"Why do you need this?" Scroll. Scroll. "You can do it. Maybe I just can't. Maybe it doesn't work for me."

"It will."

"Why does it have to, though?" *Click. Click.* "You don't know what you're doing. Maybe it works because of the math, or maybe it works for some other reason. You didn't know any of this was possible six months ago. Maybe it's not *for* me, what's out there. Why is it so important to you? Why do you need me to do this?"

The bitterness of that question caught Zelda, curled her fingers into fists on her legs, curled her toes. Her notes, which had seemed so clear and precise and logical before, proofs drawn up like troops and tanks for parade review, blurred and scattered, routed in chaos. She tried three times to frame the word *because,* and gave up. "Why don't you want to?"

*Click.*

"What are you looking at?"

"Naked human pyramid."

"Fine. Don't tell me."

Sal shoved herself back from the desk so Zelda could see, and jabbed a finger at the laptop screen. "Some place called Abu Ghraib. The soldiers over there are torturing people. It's really bad. You . . . You don't have to look." She reached to close the computer. Zelda stopped her.

She did have to, and she did look, even though looking made her feel sick. Leaning across the bed, she clicked down. Down again. Some of the photographs she did not understand then, seeing them for the first time. Some of the photographs she would not understand for years. "Jesus Christ." That was blasphemy where she came from, but she did not mean it blasphemously. Even a curse could be a prayer. "They'll . . . Someone will . . ." Words did not finish themselves. "They'll stop this. They have to."

Sal's eyes were on her, not the screen, and they were flat, and deep, and Zelda's mouth was very dry. She thought, If the world is a test, I've just failed.

Sal closed the computer. Stood. Looked down at Zelda for a long silence, like a god might look on her creation. Then she stretched out her hand, open. "Come with me."

⟡

Bundled into coats against the affront of freezing April, Zelda followed her through the Cross Campus slush and across the cold concrete plaza in front of the cubic spaceship of the Beinecke Library. Zelda expected they'd keep on straight to Woolsey Hall, always bright-lit white marble, a glaring place without shadows, but Sal turned right instead—toward Woodbridge, the building Zelda rarely remembered was even there at all. She'd had to check the name on the plaque. There weren't classes here, or events. It was just the place the university was run from, where the board met and where the president's office was. She remembered reading about protesters in front of Woodbridge in the sixties.

Sal led her around back, held her ID over the reader box, and the light buzzed green, which it should not have done. This was not a student place. Zelda looked a question at her, and she shrugged with a sly grin that lightened the storm clouds of her face. The sky was flat as rock above. "You coming?"

She settled the door closed behind them without a sound.

Zelda had never been here before. She was never supposed to be here. Neither was Sal. No one was. At least, no one they knew. The carpets were thick and the silence rang. It was late, even for them, even in those days when they'd thought midnight was the early evening. She was used to indoor lights on campus being automatic, motion activated, but those sensors were on timers, and since no one was supposed to be here, the sensors were off. She felt as though she had slipped backstage. Outside, spotlights cast the steam and smog in rainbow colors and students sang or fought or laughed or argued about philosophy or politics or sex, brilliant young things, beautiful, on a thrust stage before backdrops painted to suggest a campus. Here there were shadows and the movements of great machines that made the colors and light, but were not light, were not colorful, would crush her if she fell into the teeth of their gears.

Sal led her down halls and through a heavy door.

In the room, tall chairs gathered around a long, polished wood table. The carpet was plush and deep, the kind that ate sound. The room looked like a caricature of itself, too *much* to be real: this was where Decisions Happened.

"Where are we?" A whisper sounded like a shout.

"It's where they hold board meetings," Sal said. Her gaze lingered on the table, as if she'd say something more, then she turned away, to the wall. To the painting that hung on the wall.

It took Zelda a long time to realize what she was seeing. It wasn't instantly tritone abhorrent like some demon or Lovecraft monster, so that her mind refused to wrap around it. It wasn't so visceral as those photos on Sal's laptop. More like the opposite: it looked like any number of indifferent pieces of portraiture Sal had shown her in the British art museum across the street from the Starbucks back when they started dating. Absolutely mediocre, absolutely normal, nothing for your brain to grip.

There were four men in wigs gathered around a table, and a child beside them. The four men around the table were white. The child was black, and he had a collar locked around his throat.

"That's the guy," Sal said, pointing to the paunchy seated white man. "They call him the founder, but he didn't dig any foundations or lift any rocks. Just packed up a bunch of his old books and sent them over. That's all it took to get a place named after you back then, I guess. The kid doesn't get a name."

The silence rang like a Tibetan bowl. The empty sound gained depth and weight, and seemed more real than the walls, more real than the world outside, more real than anything she'd ever known except for Sal and that painting. Zelda did not know the right thing to say. If she waited until she knew the right thing to say, she would be waiting until the end of time, and she had to stop the silence before it broke her bones and Sal's and shook their brains to jam. "I heard about this."

Sal nodded. "Everyone does. It gets around. People talk. Do you remember who told you?"

"No."

"But you knew it was here. That's how it works. They don't put it on display. I wonder if they—the president and all of them—if they even really think about it. Maybe they don't. Maybe they don't even think. Maybe *it* thinks about *them*. It doesn't want to be out there, visible. People would see it and raise a fuss and it doesn't like fuss. It wants to be in here, where all the decisions get made, out of view. It wants us to know it's here, and it wants us not to be able to do anything about it."

Zelda tried to hug her. It was like trying to hug a statue. She kept her arms tight anyway. She could not bear to let her go.

"You don't get it, Z. What you've found out there, it doesn't matter. You can't run from this. It will follow you. And even if you escape for a while, it will be right back here waiting. You want, what, to disappear, somewhere it's just you and me and our friends forever, where we can have adventures and nothing hurts? It doesn't work that way."

Sal's eyes were wet. Zelda held her tight, and the tighter she held her, the more rigid her body felt, more fact than flesh, unable to yield in front of this monstrous normal thing. Zelda was crying. She could not breathe.

A light out in the hall clicked on.

The edges of the closed doors burned gold and cast the room in deeper shadows.

She heard heavy footsteps drawing near. Men's voices, gravelly, tired. Keys jangling from belts. Janitors, or security.

Sal looked at her then. Those wet, bitter eyes went wide with shock. Zelda realized what had happened, without needing to ask, which was good, because there was no time to ask. Sal had counted on whatever trick she had used to get into this building to also hide their presence here, long enough for them to get out. She hadn't counted on security.

What were they going to do? Fight? Run? They could break through the windows. Or just climb out. People did that in movies, didn't they? What if these were campus police? Would they shoot? Were campus police armed? Why didn't she know the answer to that question?

She knew, suddenly, why she did not know the answer.

She understood the edges of what Sal was trying to show her, and she thought, If we're caught here, what will they do to her? And she thought: I can't let that happen.

The door to the boardroom opened.

Her arms were already around Sal, but now she *pulled*.

It should not have worked. You had to have uncertainty to pivot off, some corner where you did not know what lay around the bend. But she did not know this elegant room, with this painting on the wall, even though it stood at the heart of a place she thought was hers. She did not know her school, she did not know her country. She did not know anyplace, really. She was blind. And the least her ignorance could do was help them, now, wrap around them and pass them through to somewhere else.

They landed in the ashen ruins of a room that had once been elegant. Now crumbled brick and snapped steel rose from ashes to a starfield sky. Far away, a great cat cried itself king of the ruins.

She was on top of Sal, breathing hard, slick with sweat. She started to roll off. But Sal's arms were around her, drawing Zelda to her chest, holding her. Just that. Not a pillar, not a statue, but a human woman in the dark.

She did not move. She did not want to spoil it. All she could do was spoil it. That was all she was good for.

But Sal was holding her, and she was laughing. "I will admit," Sal said, "I did not expect this."

They were quiet for a long time in the ruins, cheek to cheek, heart to heart, their sweat cooling. It was warmer here. Global warming. Maybe the seas were higher. The ice caps melting. She remembered Waterworld, the city below the ocean. Remembered a *Teenage Mutant Ninja Turtles* comic she'd read off a wire rack once in the Piggly Wiggly when she was ten, the Turtles time traveling to a drowned Manhattan. She remembered where she was, right now, her face nestled beside Sal's, their breath in time, neither one speaking.

"We can change things," she said.

The stars reflected in Sal's eyes. Her teeth were bright in the dark. "What do you mean?"

She had not meant anything when she said those words. But now they were said, she could see the thoughts behind them, surfacing from the ocean of her mind, like any proof, complete and glistening and too pure. "The alts are infinite. Anything we can dream of should exist, out here. Somewhere. We just have to find it. So there's a place, there must be, where we can change how the world works. Fix things. Make them right."

It was one thing to hold the idea in her mind, and another to speak it out. It was too big to say. But Sal caught it from her and followed her thinking through. "A crossroads."

"And we," Zelda said, "will get there."

## CHAPTER FOURTEEN

When Zelda woke up, she thought at first that she was still there, in the burnt-out wreckage of some decayed alt's Corporation Room, with a lion roaring far away and Sal beneath her with stars in her eyes. Where she was smelled of elsewhere, of alts: that clean, strange air, the grass that was not the grass of home, weird dirts and pollens like alien spices, and the faint sweet edge of rot.

But this place was not that place, and now was not then. Her body hurt too much for her to be that young. She wanted to burrow into the memory, to breathe Sal one more time, even knowing everything that would come next. But if she wanted to burrow into the memory, that meant she knew it *was* memory. So she opened her eyes.

She lay on a rooftop, concrete pebbled and cracked by who could say how many winters, beneath a sky the color of cedar hearts, and split, to the south, by an orbital ring. She tried to guess how vast the ring was, that she could see it in daylight, even if from planetside it looked no thicker than a string you'd tie around your finger so as not to forget. The mind boggled. This world must have been advanced once. And then it fell.

Well, join the club.

Rising, she took inventory of her aches. Must have pulled something in her hip, running up the stairs to the roof; she was out of shape because of her illness. The cut Sarah had made in her forearm throbbed, but the good kind of throb, the healing throb. For now.

There were other aches than physical. Sarah. June. Where were they?

She pushed herself up. The roof was crumbled and studded with rotten X-shaped bars the right size to hang people on, like Saint Andrew. The manacles that dangled from the crossed bars were empty, rusted through, and there were no bones, which did not mean there never had been. Even bones decayed, if you waited long enough. Critters gnawed and stole them. You came from the ground and the ground took you back.

She was alone.

She could not be alone. She had held on to the others as lightning fell and the world opened. She had clutched them tight as they tumbled into the alts. But the wind between the worlds had taken her, and taken them, and they were scattered. She had lied to herself if she thought she could gather them like reeds and bind into a staff, make of them something to challenge the world. Who was she to gather them, after what happened last time?

June. Ish. Sarah. Ramón.

They came back for her, and this was what she did to them.

They were fine, she told herself, out in the alts. Just scattered. All she had to do was find them. They would be safe. But there was a crouched, gnomelike fear in her: You'll never see them again, you failed, you failed, all you do is fail. In ten years, she had grown so used to the gnome's voice that she no longer heard it, but she responded anyway, like a woman who had lived by train tracks so long she no longer realized when the train went by, but still raised her voice to talk over its roar and screech. They are fine, she told herself. She knew, deeper down, that she'd never see them again.

*I will find you,* she promised, though how she meant to do it was still a mystery.

A groan drew her attention to what she'd thought was a pile of rubble at the foot of a rotting cross—but some of the rubble turned, and a limp arm lolled out, a face paled by dust. Ramón.

She ran to him and knelt over his body, reviewing his black T-shirt and his jean jacket, his face so like the face she remembered, the skin just starting to crinkle around the eyes. Her hands hovered, scared to touch him, in case she hurt him worse than he was hurt already. But she saw no blood.

He blinked then, and his eyes were as big and black and honest as ever, taking her in, and the sky behind. His nostrils flared. Smell was a powerful gateway to memory. Zelda had been told that so many times she gathered that it was probably true for most people. She had never felt that way. Then again, if you needed a gateway into memory, that implied you left memory at some point.

She watched his mind work, watched understanding rise one long and awful limb at a time from the deep water of his mind. The smell of the place fired circuits in his brain that he had not used in a long time, that he had, she hoped, tried to bury beneath other, happier memories.

He had tried to save her at the end. He gave up everything. He had built his Challenger with his own hands, and when it all went wrong, he drove into a lava field trying to catch her, and Sal. Even when he left her, in Montana, she never blamed him. The others, from time to time, but never him.

There it was. The slight widening of the eyes. He was back. He understood. "Did it hurt this much, back when we were kids?"

"Probably." She offered him a hand. The cut on her arm tugged as she pulled him up, but the pain was worth it. "We didn't realize, or we didn't care. Come on." He staggered up, leaning on her without a hint of macho bullshit. He'd never been bothered by things like that. She said: "We're alone."

He didn't shout at her, didn't curse, didn't tell her how worthless she was as a guide to this mess of a world, which shocked her before she remembered that the real Ramón, the man standing beside her, was still, whatever he'd become since, the half-honed, half-weakened product of the boy she had known, and that boy would never do those things. He was not bent that way. She had spent so much time with the knives inside her own head that she put those knives in others' hands, and especially in the hands of her friends.

She had known them for six years, and they had since been apart for ten.

He closed his eyes, breathed, tensed, exhaled, went soft again. Soft like a whip was soft before the crack. "Okay."

"We'll find them," she said, all of a sudden certain this was true. She had pulled others out of worse spots than this, had rescued hitchhikers and truckers and high school kids who'd drifted into alts only to be captured by fairies or imprisoned for gladiatorial games. She had ten years of practice at this sort of thing.

He tried to stand on his own and almost fell. She caught him. He smiled at her. *Thanks.* "Do you know this alt? I don't, but . . . it's been a while."

She pointed. "I think I'd remember that ring."

He looked up, and over, and his body as much as his voice said: "Wow." Even in his awe, his brow furrowed. "How do you think they even *made* that? Is there that much steel on the whole planet?"

She knew, *knew,* that he was trying to run the numbers in his head. Estimating planet radius, what's a stable orbit, okay, give the ring a minimal thickness, just enough for a habitat, say ten meters, and how broad. Grind out the internal volume, figure about half of that's air . . .

"Asteroid mining," he said, "I guess. A lot of asteroids. But even if you got enough metal, you'd have to smelt it, work it. Up there." He looked around as if for pencil and paper, then realized, again, where he was. That was a durable, bulletproof habit. Back home you always assumed there was scratch paper around. A napkin, even. You had to bring your own paper with you, out here. God, she loved him. Again, he said, "Wow."

"Did you ever come back?" There were so many more important questions now, but that one slipped out. She wondered if that had been one of the attractions of the alts, one reason the quest held them as long as it did: there was always something practical to do, some warlord to overthrow or escape, some monster to trick, some prince to rescue. Your feelings could wait.

What did she expect him to say? *Of course I did? I only left you for ten years because of a mistake?*

"No. I found other ways to get lost." He sounded as if he were surprised to hear those words out loud. And then, coming back to the moment, to her: "What's the plan?"

"We'll meet the others at the Medicine Wheel." She had expected his frown and pressed on in spite of it. "It's still the easiest meeting place, even if we don't want to go inside."

"I can find them," he pointed out, "once we're on the road."

Of course he could. "Do you know if they're together?" She didn't ask *if they're okay. Okay* was not a thing you asked for or expected, on the road. It was a thing you cherished when it came, like good weather.

That faraway look he got when he consulted his knack—that hadn't changed in all this time. "Not from here. I need a car."

She remembered too late that his new Challenger was back home, with the cowboy and the white hats. "I'm sorry we couldn't bring yours through."

"I'm not." That was too fast, and from the look of him, he had not expected to say that either, and having said it, was not sure he agreed. "I mean. It's . . . it's okay." He read her expectant look, and went far away again. He pointed off down the ruined highway. "There's a car that way. A working one. Not far."

She drew her monocular from the inside pocket of her coat, adjusted for focus, scanned the horizon, saw a smudge. "Camp smoke. Could be exhaust. About ten miles off. Think you can make it?"

"And when we get there, what? We ask the postapocalyptic crucifix randos very nicely to lend us a car?"

"The crucifixes are rotten. These probably aren't even the same people."

"Yeah. These guys probably killed and ate the crucifix guys."

"That's the spirit." She slapped him on the back, hard, because that was part of the joke, and found herself, to her own surprise and in spite of everything, smiling. "Come on. Just like old times."

# CHAPTER FIFTEEN

June looked up and she thought: Dandelions.

If you picked a fistful in the rush of early summer and blew with all your might so the seeds burst out above you, carried by the wind off the river high and all around until you stood inside a snow globe, only the snow was rising, not falling, and you felt like you were rising, too—that's how the stars looked overhead. So deep, so dense, so different. Not just points of light against black. She saw clouds of light, grades of brilliance and distance. The stars had colors, too, like rainbows. And wherever she looked, the ghosts at the edges of her vision suggested that farther out, in the deeper dark, there were more.

Some of those ghost blurs were galaxies. She knew that from school. And some were tears. Because as much as she saw up there, it didn't match what she'd seen in the sky over Montana, on the other side of her cousin's lightning eyes.

To think of Sal was to think of Zelda, too—and with that thought, June realized her hands were empty.

"Zelda?" She sat up.

She was on top of a small bare hill surrounded by a field of tall grass. Then darkness out to the horizon. She could tell what was earth and what was sky because the earth had no light in it.

She was alone.

Zelda's hand had been in hers until it wasn't. Two weeks of traveling together—most of them with Zelda sick, half conscious—should not have left her feeling so naked with the other woman gone. But she had carried Zelda in her head since she was a little girl, carried the memories of her, and the way that had Sal looked at her, thinking, Maybe someday someone might look at me that way.

When someone looked at you like that, their look was a string tied around your heart. You could fall but she'd catch you, the person who looked at you that way, even if you were hanging over the Devil's own pit and all you had to hold on to was the strength of her gaze.

Zelda was gone. June was alone in the dark, in the alts.

She should be afraid. People were supposed to be afraid, when they were alone in the dark, in a place they did not know, with no phone, no friends, no backup. Maybe she was, somewhere deep down, below the wonder.

She shuddered, not from cold or fear so much as from the vastness of it all, the wasteful roll of earth out to the horizon and beyond. There was so much country, so much more land than she ever could have imagined back in New York, where the culture changed from one street corner to the next. She knew how big the world was, of course. The mute facts of its size were grade school stuff. But knowing a number was not the same as feeling the breadth of space. You could fit her whole city in the land she now saw with her naked eyes.

And it was empty.

Even back home, so much of it was empty. Vast stretches of highway ran through trees and mountains, and that was all you saw. Then you came to the Great Plains, the waving wheat, the corn seas, and there were deserts somewhere. Three hundred million humans in this country—another figure that didn't break your mind until you tried to accept that every one of them was as real as you, as real as your best friend—but they vanished like a drop of oil on the surface of a lake.

On her ride across the country and through the alts, with Zelda hallucinating in the passenger seat, June had glimpsed people, not close, as shadows flitting through trees. She kept her distance and they kept theirs, fading back and away, their ruins more present than their selves. The alts were ghost towns. The snap of a twig here echoed like a gunshot.

But at least, back then, she'd been with Zelda. Now it was just her.

How could she have let go? So stupid. There had been a wind between the worlds, and the lightning flash was so bright and sudden, and her hand was empty as an echo.

No use cutting yourself over it, June. Time to move.

She stood.

Night breeze whispered through the tall grass.

The best thing to do when you realized you were lost, she'd read somewhere once, was to stay put and wait for people to find you. But that assumed some things, didn't it? Like, it assumed there were people who weren't lost. What if everyone was lost, and just sitting around waiting until people found them? In life, she was coming to suspect, you never knew if you were the one who was lost or the one who was supposed to go looking.

Okay. She'd made it across country through the alts, dodging dinosaurs—at the wheel of Zelda's Subaru, but still, she'd made it. She could find the others. Sarah had said, once you got the knack, it was so easy you could sometimes slip through alts without noticing, even on foot. And if she didn't find them that way, she could set off on her own for the Medicine Wheel, where the worlds touched. South, and west, Zelda had said. It will call you.

That was something like a plan.

June took her first step in this new world, under the bright moon and the dandelion stars.

The grass bobbed around her, waist-high. The edges of the blades were gray brown as if they had cut someone and the blood dried. Maybe they cut the earth, coming out. In health class, she had heard a baby tore its mother's flesh sometimes, as it was born—just ripped the skin it wriggled through. When she'd learned that, her insides curled up into a knot and her thighs got very tense and her stomach tight and hard as a walnut shell, and she couldn't look at herself in the mirror naked for a week. She liked her body and her body scared her. Bodies were facts, like history—something you were given and learned to live with.

But not out here. Not in the alts.

As she walked the grass, she tried to make it change.

The stars remained stubbornly fixed overhead. This world was real as real. It smelled of earth and growth, which meant it smelled, she was coming to understand, of shit and death. Grass blades scraped the backs of her hands. Again she heard that whisper she'd taken for breeze, but if there was a breeze, it was too far away for her to feel. She thought about snakes, about the size of snake that could hide in grass like this. She was very cold. The hill where she'd hitched through rose behind her, tempting.

Why not go back? Wait to be rescued?

She didn't know what she was doing out here. She had hitched through the alts once, in terror, with the cowboy after her, and made it home by luck. What she had done once, Zelda and the others had done hundreds of times, until it was natural as breathing. They had lived this life for two years. They had their knacks, and their scars. When Ish came out of the stairwell, back in the hotel, with blood on his knuckles and on the front of his shirt, she had seen the others notice, and say nothing, as though this were something normal in their lives, something they all expected.

She was a guest among them. Zelda's student, maybe even an apprentice. But out here, alone, she was just herself.

They saw her as a civilian. Even Sarah, whom she liked, who was kind and generous and who, unlike Zelda, actually explained this shit straight out so you could understand, rather than wrapping it up in weird metaphors—even Sarah looked at her and saw a kid. The kind of teenager they made TV shows about, who lived in some suburb somewhere with yards and worried about cyberbullying and proms and varsity squads and shit like that.

They didn't know her, really. They didn't know where she was from or what she'd seen or how she felt when she walked home at night. They'd never stood beside her at a protest, they'd never seen a mounted cop's horse's hooves wheeling overhead, ready to plunge. They didn't know how pepper spray felt in your eyes and the back of your throat. They knew Sal, so maybe they had some idea of what they did not know, but they'd all been young in a gentler time. And they'd all met at that big school, where they spent so much time trying to front to one another like they belonged and like the most, what, salient fact about their lives was who got selected for this program or that society. Sal had more fronts than the Second World War.

They did not know June, and she did not know them. She did not have their skills, their knowledge, their weird comfort with violence. To her, the life they lived was the life that ate her cousin—it had never been a game, never an adventure. She had not spent years on the road, but her whole life had been off the map. That had to count for something.

Focus on your breath. Think about Zelda.

Zelda understood, and Zelda was the best of them. The others had left the road, while she had walked it for ten whole years. They looked at her with respect, even awe, the kind of respect and awe you had for the half-toothed guy on the corner with the veteran patch who got holy drunk on Fireball and spent all night in shouting arguments with God. You never heard God answer, but you could fill in what She was saying based on his replies.

One night June had been up late talking with LaShae about her latest breakup, and Talks-to-God guy started in on the corner, and they decided to play a game where they'd each write down what they thought God was saying back, and compare. When they showed each other what they'd written, it was word for word the same. She had burned her paper after. It didn't feel right to save. People shouldn't listen in on conversations, even if, in a city, you couldn't help it. Even conversations with God.

Z's old friends had moved on. Even Sarah had. They had seen all of this, other worlds, faces in the sky, monsters you could fight and sometimes beat, unlike all the other monsters June knew—and they'd gone home. And they thought Zelda was the one who'd made a mistake. The one who'd missed a turn, taken a dead-end exit to nowhere.

Zelda kept faith. She kept to the road, anyway. And so had Sal. The fact of Sal's fall meant she had the will to go there, out beyond the edge of the firelight circle, where people were changed. Maybe the darkness got her and maybe she'd never come back. But at least she hadn't flinched.

June wouldn't flinch either.

The first step, Zelda said, was to turn your gaze outward.

That wasn't how magic usually worked in her books. You closed your eyes, let go, found your center, all that Jedi stuff.

Zelda said, This isn't magic.

Sarah said, Of course it is.

Again she heard the whispers. This time they were louder—and she knew they were not the sound of the wind in the grass.

Your mind turns back on itself when it seeks certainty. Turn it out into the world instead. Ask unanswerable questions, find no answers, ask again. Don't stop. The mind is a prison, its blocks built of what you know. Turn your focus elsewhere. Into details. Into the world as it's given to you. Light on a leaf. A shadow's curve. The fade of color from the back of your hand to the palm. The click of insect wings at night. The stars one by one giving way. Don't know what you'll see before you see it. Don't decide what it is. Let it tell you. Let it lead you somewhere you don't expect, somewhere you could never imagine.

Spin trickled into her like water over dry lips.

Long black knives of cloud cut across the sky. The moon seemed to glow more brightly as her eyes opened to the dark. An unseen hand stroked the leaves of grass and set them bobbing in soft, shimmering waves, silver, gold, and rose, and she thought: We read the unseen from the seen.

She walked through the depths.

The moon cast her shadow, and the shadows of the grass, upon the ground. The shadows sang of secrets, with high eerie voices like the notes of a glass harmonica.

People looked around at the shit of their lives and dreamed magic would find them. They wanted God to speak to them. But when you met those who really did hear—who were broken open and pulped by the Word the way you'd have to be, because anything that wouldn't pulp you wasn't the Word—when you met some-one who heard and was uprooted by the hearing, who changed their life and let their whole world go smash, you felt awe. Respect. But you also felt a kind of pity. You shook your pockets for loose change you could drop into their bowl and before you went to sleep at night, you prayed, God, save me from God. I want to be burned but not consumed. I want to stay a sturdy little wafer, a cup of too-sweet wine.

The moon felt bright as day. She could see colors by it. Any moment now, she thought the shadows would give way, fade, but that was wrong, wasn't it? That wasn't how shadows went away. You could never burn hot or bright enough enough to burn the shadows out. Even atom bombs only burn shadows in.

She realized she was crying. Her cheeks were wet. Her breath came in deep, full draws, as if she had just run miles.

Those shadows held a secret.

She reached for them and they reached back.

Every moonshadow in the waves of grass out to the horizon stretched to-ward her. They twitched, uncurled, lengthened, put off new shoots as whip thin as centipede legs. They dragged the grasses with them as they moved, a ripple against the wind. She heard a high, rich, distant music and voices whispered in a nearby room in a tongue she did not know, many tongues and many voices.

She called the shadows and they came.

In Philadelphia, the shadows had opened like this, like cracks, and stretched out long thin arms. But there she had been afraid. Hadn't she? Zelda had been afraid.

June had not called the shadows then. She had asked Zelda to take them to the Liberty Bell because Sal used to tell her about it, way back before—because Sal visited it every time she set off cross-country. Standing there, June had stared into the crack in the side of the bell and wished, and prayed, for Sal to come back.

She reached out one trembling hand. The sky seemed close and thin as tissue paper. What kind of shadow might America cast? She could almost see her face. She could almost speak her name.

*What do you want?* the shadows asked.

She answered: Take me to my friends.

The night closed around her like a hand.

When she'd run from the cowboy back in Pennsylvania, she had felt the change, like when the Subaru hit a curb at speed, but as this darkness closed around her, she slipped through it like a fish through a stream. The grass knelt back into the earth. Mountains breached the horizon, then settled. Stars danced. Step, and she walked through a desert, through the rib cage of a great skeleton, bones three stories tall. Step, and she strode down the main street of a fungus-claimed clapboard town. Step, and her heels crushed leaves of crystal. The alts smelled of ozone and cinnamon, of woodsmoke and oil. They were suggestions, a voice whispering in the back of her mind. It's your walking through that makes them real to you. You could go further. Further than they ever dreamed.

June remembered those stretching insect legs, and the shape of Sal in the sky, and could not imagine what lay behind them, or beyond.

The shadows whispered: Try.

She heard a voice, out there in the shifting worlds. Sarah's voice, indistinct and far away. She turned and the shadows turned with her.

She saw them. On the other side of the darkness, they were clear and small.

Sarah was arguing—with Ish, she saw now, the pair of them pacing under a full moon on an alt of scrub grass and mesas. June could not make out their words through the whisper of the shadows. Sarah's eyes were wet and she looked angry. June wondered what she was angry about. They felt so far away—but she had to find them, had to find Zelda. They had work to do.

She put out her hand. The world parted like a curtain.

Sarah saw her first. And though June could not hear her voice, she saw the shape her lips made: "Sal?"

June tried to speak, but her voice was a crash of surf and screams. Cracks and wriggling shadows dripped from her outstretched hand.

Ish was on her before she could try to speak again. His bulk slammed her to the hard ground. She lost her breath. Moonlight glinted off his wide staring eyes, cold and pure. His nostrils flared. He stank of fear and anger; his big hands pressed her arms down, sought her throat. One fist went back. His knuckles were still torn, bloody. She fought him, tried to buck him off. He was so much bigger than she was, so much stronger, but she fought anyway and she almost won. One of her hands slipped through his guard, caught his biceps.

But her hand was not her hand—its fingers were too long, too sharp, were unfeatured black like the inside of a closet or the gaps between the stars. He bled from her touch.

June screamed and let him go, in horrified recoil more than mercy. In that instant, his clutching, blood-slick hand found her neck. Spots danced. He squeezed. She fought for breath.

There came a distant roar of a voice heard through water. She was coughing, was free. She drew heaving, ragged gasps of air. Rolled over, kitten-weak, on the dry grass, on the dusty earth. Her shadows were just the normal moonshadows now, her skin her own, not that beautiful, bladed, horrifying thing she had seen. Ish lay on the ground, curled around the wound she'd left in his arm. In his eyes she saw terror, and—what was that? Recognition.

Sarah knelt between them, parting them, hands out, her commanding cry of *Stop!* still echoing through the dry night of the world. "It's her," she was saying now, softer, ragged, though he had already seen. "It's her."

Before June could speak, Sarah's arms were around her, crushing, and warm.

━━━━━━

Sarah fixed them up with gauze and alcohol from Zelda's knapsack, a splash from the plastic bottle for disinfectant and a swig from the flask for sleep. June glared at Ish the whole while. He said "I'm sorry" and winced as Sarah wrapped his arm. The cuts June had made there were too clean and deep and thin for her blunt ball-player's nails, for any human nails she'd ever seen. It looked like a hand made of broken glass had seized his arm. Lucky, Sarah said, they weren't so deep. Lucky.

"When you came through, you didn't look . . . like you." He fumbled the words. "There was rot all over you. You had too many arms."

She kept glaring. He didn't return the glare. Sometimes when people did that, it meant you'd scared them. Sometimes when people did that, it meant what was inside them was too naked for their comfort, and they didn't want you to see.

"You did look . . . different," Sarah said. "I couldn't see your face at all. Just darkness, straight through. Like the night was moving."

"You said, 'Sal.'"

Sarah, at least, looked back at her. "I thought you were her. You looked like she did, up there in the sky. Like the rot does when it takes someone. Then you . . . turned human. How did you do that?"

She didn't want to tell her, with Ish sitting there. But he had said he was sorry. "I listened to the shadows. I asked them to lead me to you. They did."

"And then they let you go." A patient voice, kind.

June felt the shadows' absence as if she'd just taken off her coat in the cold, only the other way around. This warmth she'd let in, it stifled her. She shuddered. "They didn't *let* me go. I just left."

Sarah looked to Ish. "Is that possible?"

June felt a stab of jealousy. *Don't look at him, look at me.* She wanted to be sitting back near the window in the Best Western again, not out here in the dark. "What do you mean, 'Is that possible'? What's he have to do with what's possible?"

"He knows the math." Sarah returned the unused bandages to Zelda's pack. "That should hold, if you are careful," she said, nodding at his bandage. "Which means it will not."

Ish grinned at her. Must be an old joke between them. "We aren't the ones who get to say what's possible. The world does that. We have theories, that's all. Principles. We think they're right." Ish weighed her with his eyes. She could not see their color in the dark, could not remember how they had looked under the fluorescent hotel lights a million years away from here. "The rot doesn't let things go. It eats them."

"This doesn't feel like rot," she said.

"It wouldn't, while you're in it. There's a fungus called Cordyceps that lives in ants, and off of them. When an ant's infected, the fungus makes it want to climb to where it can overlook the colony. Then, when the ant's in position, the fungus sprouts from the back of its skull and bursts spores all over the other ants below, infecting them too."

"What does that have to do with me?"

"How do you think the ant feels, as it's climbing?"

"I'm not infected. I hitched through, just like Zelda taught me." But Zelda hadn't mentioned voices, or shadows, or Talks-to-God Man. She didn't even know about Talks-to-God Man. She had talked about whispers through the cracks in the world, about them being beyond the edge, incomprehensible.

The whispers hadn't felt that way to June.

She didn't say any of this. She didn't want to be some zombified ant, not owning even the thoughts inside its head. She didn't know if ants thought. Then again, she wasn't sure that *people* did. "I came looking for you. And you jumped me."

"I'm sorry. I said. You got me pretty good, if that helps."

"A little."

"We all have knacks," Sarah said. "This might be June's."

"Using the rot?" Ish's face got an expression June recognized from Zelda, and she wondered which of them caught it from the other, or if this was the kind of thing people wired like them just did. It reminded her of when LaShae tried to teach her video games and she got to a bit where the game wouldn't let you go forward yet, no matter how hard you pressed the controller—until something changed in the game and you rocketed into new possibilities. Generally when that happened, she died horribly and fast.

Ish was running possibilities in his head. "I don't know. It would be like . . . dividing by zeros. Some people think you get infinity when you divide by zero, but you don't, because zero is nothing, and infinity times nothing is still nothing. The rot is just chaos."

"It is not total chaos. Sal is there."

"Something's there. Shaped like Sal because it wants to be. Do you really think that's her?"

"Our knacks don't make much more sense than this," Sarah said. "They're shaped by what we need. What we want."

"So what does she want?"

They were talking about her as though she wasn't there. She wanted them to see her. She was part of this now. She was on the road alongside them, out here beyond the edge of the map. She should have shut up, maybe, but she could not just sit here and let herself be talked about, let herself be the threat or the mystery Ish saw, or the kid Sarah saw, when they looked at her. Simple as a dare, she told the truth. "I want my cousin back."

Ish tested his arm again and winced. "That's what I'm afraid of."

⟶

The night was getting on, and they needed sleep. They'd set off the next day, seeking a ride first, then Zelda and Ramón, or, failing that, the Medicine Wheel. "She'll go there," Ish said, even though he'd argued that they shouldn't try it, back at the hotel. That, June thought, was why he was sure.

Zelda's knapsack held a one-man tent, tight and tiny as a cocooned caterpillar when folded up. Unfolded, it would barely fit June and Sarah, "if," Sarah said, "you don't mind being cozy, kiddo."

June, raw and cracked and shaking, did not even mind being called *kiddo*. Ish offered to take first watch, and sleep outside, and good riddance. The tent was just large enough for them. They fought over who would get the thermal blanket for a while—June really wasn't cold and anyway Sarah was the one wearing a dress, she should take it. Sarah claimed she was used to this sort of thing and there was no sense in June starting the next day cold and tired. Finally they called a truce. It covered them both barely, but it crinkled when either moved, so June tried to tell her body to just lie still, the same way she tried to tell her body not to exist sometimes, when the wrong sort of people were watching her.

Sarah shifted, rolled onto her side, shifted again.

"Do you want my jacket?" June asked.

"No."

"For a pillow, I mean."

"Good night, June."

Sarah smelled a gentle kind of nice June could not place, like she imagined the homes she saw on TV smelled, the kind with big spare rooms and maybe the people who lived there paid someone to come in every couple of weeks to wipe things down. Nestled next to her, even though June was (she realized, to her surprise) the taller of the two, she felt as if she were small. She told herself it was mom energy—that weird I-got-this grounding aura all the moms she knew seemed to project, either because they genuinely did got this or because they didn't have any other option so they sure as hell had better get this got, whatever *this* was.

But there was more to it, she thought as sleep weighed her down. Something eager as a puppy's tail. Sarah had sat across from her by the window in that Best Western as Zelda lay asleep, and crossed her legs in that fine floral print dress, and looked at June as if she had just as much of a right to be there as any of them. Maybe that was it.

Sarah had seen Sal when she looked at her. Maybe that was the shadows, but it wasn't only the shadows. They all saw Sal, because they needed to see her— they needed her not to be gone. So they painted her into every canvas, like the Goyas June had seen at the Met—they all had the same light, that light which, whatever it was meant to be, was not the light of God. She didn't blame them. She should have but she didn't. She did the same thing. When she looked at Zelda, she saw a woman ten years younger, less worn, less hurt. A woman from a drawing she'd hung on her wall.

They all had something broken in them, these people she held in her heart the way some kids held the X-Men: her cousin's friends.

A few years ago, June had messed up her knee playing basketball, and the doctor gave her all these exercises to do and said, If you don't do them, you'll get better but you'll get better wrong, so your knee doesn't quite work the way it should, and you won't notice until maybe twenty years down the line you've worn off the cartilage in your kneecap and you need a cane to walk. June, thirteen, tried to imagine the shape of *twenty years down the line*. The only images she came up with were something like *Fury Road* only with less desert and more drowned cities and a bunch of men with guns running around talking about how the late frost meant global warming was bullshit really. She couldn't imagine having a long or happy life in place like that if she couldn't run. So she did her exercises every day, three times a day. She'd been the only thirteen-year-old she knew who did stretches and warm-up before a pickup game.

When she looked at them—at Zelda, but at Ish and Ramón and Sarah, too—she saw how you looked when the cartilage started to wear out. She didn't know if that was from what had happened to them, or if the world just did that to you, seeped out what you'd been and left holes behind.

She tried to make herself sleep. She told herself again and again that she was in fact asleep, that she was unconscious, that she was sinking through the tent into the earth. It didn't work at home either, when she lay awake watching shadows trail gentle fingers over her drawings. A shadow's was the only touch that would not smear.

But sleep wasn't something you did piecemeal. An extra few minutes of lying to yourself wouldn't make you 3 percent more asleep. You were, or you weren't. She'd tried to explain this to Sal once, and Sal had said that was how some people in Northern China in the Song dynasty thought enlightenment worked, and it was in fact how infinity worked in math. You were never 98 percent infinite, you were either infinite, or not. Which didn't help June sleep at all.

The sky hung huge and alien up there and the earth ran on forever and totally unknown down here and the tent was snug and warm as a mouth. Where had she been, as she walked through shadows? Was that where Sal was? Did she hear those voices too? Did she know them?

The word *rot* did not feel right in her head.

When she felt like this at home, spinning out of control as she lay dead still on her mattress hoping sleep would find her, her not-quite-dreams a flipbook of crisis, of melting glaciers and confused polar bears wondering where the rest of the iceberg went, of angry white boys with guns and riot gear, of bugs dying, no more bugs even, that feeling you got when you were rolling downhill and you realized you were going too fast, that you'd missed your chance to stop with grace and now the best you could hope for was to jam your hands into the dirt and only snap a couple of fingers and pop your wrist—when she felt like this at home, she would get up, turn on the light, and sit at her small table, drawing until her fingers were bright with pencil lead.

She heard a whisper.

Not whispers—not the voices through the cracks. Just breath, formed into words she did not know, words so strange to her she could not tell where one stopped and the next began.

Among those words, she heard her name.

"Sarah?"

The whisper stopped. She could not tell whether it was over or interrupted. The silence ran between them. "I thought you were asleep," Sarah said while June was still thinking.

"With cowboys after us and Zelda gone and with us being on some whole entire other world? I notice, for instance, that you are not sleeping." She breathed. "You said my name."

"I was praying. That is not the right word, I think. It is the English one."

"Huh."

"A blessing. My father used to say it. He didn't teach us. He was like that. I don't really know what it means."

She tried to ask the right question. "Where's it from?"

"Here. Well. About a hundred fifty miles south, back home. Snake River territory. That's not really where it was *from* either. The Black Hills, if you go back further. My sister would know more."

"I didn't know you had a sister."

"I do not talk about her much. Pop was in the army. We moved a lot. My sister and I . . . Families on base handle it in different ways. Some kids hang together, when they move that much. Us? We split up to survive. To live our own lives. She went back—" June heard her almost say *home,* then retreat from the word. "She went back to Dad's parents, to Snake River, when she was old enough to make her own choices. Lives down there. Married. Kids. Three nieces, two nephews. We're closer now than we used to be. I went to them, after . . . after we all split up the last time. She picked up the pieces of me and put me back together. Sewed me with sinew and patched me with spit." A big rough breath, a sigh. "We try to be close. It's funny. She was always the one who hated going back to visit. She and Pop used to fight all the time."

"They got over it?"

"Heart disease," she said, a minute later. "He passed five years ago."

"I'm sorry." Words felt too light, too easy for the subject. Some things you should have to scream, but you could only say, *I'm sorry.*

"He got to see Susan, and Alex. Just. You can't ask for more than that." A pause. "I mean, you can."

June felt her own ache, her own missing persons. "It hurts, though."

The silence was the hardest part of this conversation, every time: when people remembered Ma Tempest wasn't your real mom, when they wondered what to say, when they looked for the door in the conversation marked Exit. "You were so young."

"Daddy got sick." She didn't want to know whether Sarah was the kind of person who, given the opportunity, would ask a question like *Was it violent?* or even just *How?* She hoped she wasn't. She liked her. "He just . . . got sick." She had practiced saying it like that, abrupt, final, to cut off the next question about her mom. "Susan and Alex. They're your kids?"

"Yes."

"I heard their names in there too. With mine."

Her yes came guilty, grudgingly.

That yes stung. Of course Sarah sees you as a kid, June told herself. What do you think you even *are*? She knew you when you were six. She's Sal's friend. She has two kids of her own. She has been all over the world and outside it and back. You saw her stare down that cowboy and sew up Zelda's arm on thirty-six hours of NoDoz, and she still smells nice as a maid-cleaned house. Who do you think you *are* anyway, to be seen as something other than a kid these hurting folks, these heroes of yours, will have to carry cross the finish line?

Well, she told herself: Zelda brought me out on this road. She tried to skip out and I ran her down and I've saved her life twice. So maybe there is some puppy-crush flavor to what I am feeling right now—maybe. But I am here because I fought to be. And I am gonna save Sal. I am gonna save them all.

"Tell me what happened," she said. "Why you set out. Tell me about the crossroads. I deserve to know."

It sounded too much like begging for her taste. If you weren't a kid, you wouldn't have to tell people not to treat you like one.

She remembered, then: she never had to tell Zelda.

Sarah let out a breath she might have been holding for ten years, and said: "I never should have gone along with it. I really do believe that now. But we all had our reasons. And we were just smart enough to be a very special kind of dumb."

They set off after the thaw, looking for the crossroads. When the elms budded and heat shaved the dirty, sandy snowdrifts down to speed bumps, they were ready.

Zelda spent the last weeks in a frenzy of preparation. She and Ish closeted themselves together to grind through proofwork and models, and laughed about how normal they seemed—in coffee shops, their tensor diagrams and scrawled notes didn't look all that different from the mounded note cards of some kid's history paper. Maybe, she pondered aloud one afternoon, as she came back from the counter with a fresh mug of hot chocolate, they were all trying to find the crossroads too. Maybe every one of these projects had deep, world-shaking import, maybe they would all flower and sprout, maybe they were seeds spreading tiny threadlike roots to crack concrete and burst water pipes and sip the world.

Or maybe people just liked to look busy.

Ish had saved her time and again throughout the process, because he did not believe. He did not need alts or elsewheres, did not seem to want them, though he laughed, as they all did, from the holy joke of seeing a live dinosaur. Back at the start, when she was fresh from that first visit to New York with Sal, the concept newborn and wriggling in her mind, she had said to him, on Cross Campus, There must be other paths within the manifold, all the other ways it could have gone must have wound up *somewhere*, he asked, Why? Why could this not be the only way? And what makes you so sure that, if you do step outside this world, what you find won't eat you? And anyway, observer-dependencies really do not work like that.

Without his headwind, she would have had nothing to tack against. She might have wasted four years wandering through campus and the math department building on Temple Street in a fog, wanting the alts to be there, wanting this not to be the only world there was, and missing the flaws in her work. You could want all you liked, but *doing* made the difference.

Every flaw he found in her arguments drew her deeper into the effort. This had to be more than perfect. It had to be right. Her proofs collapsed from notebooks to pages, to a single page, to the back of an envelope. She wrote it once, in permanent marker, on the back of a broad dry leaf. Then she crumbled the leaf and ate it.

But no matter how elegant her work became, she'd go back to him, bang on his door at four in the morning, and they'd sit beside each other at the Yankee Doodle counter because that was the only place that was open. They'd glare at her notes and at each other like lovers in a fight until they found some flaw, or worse, some flywheel or lemma her argument required, the proof of which itself would earn you a Fields Medal.

In the end, the math of it was a perfect gem in her mind, an unsayable purity. To whisper it would be to hammer the acid-washed university and its elms to paste, to blast her fellow students beyond the edge of the world.

The next day, on the road with Ramón, she hitched through.

Preparing for the crossroads felt altogether different. When she told Ish about the idea, he brightened. He'd never thought about that possibility—of feedback, of a control surface to the world, out there in the alts. Was it Aristotle or Archimedes who said, Give me a lever and a place to stand and I can move the world? Spin was a lever. This could be their place to stand.

She'd been afraid at first that his excitement would disturb the alchemy of disbelief that led to the initial breakthrough, but she shouldn't have worried. He stayed after her like a hound after a fox. There were two ways to approach God, the mystics said, the *via positiva,* seeking what God might be, what attributes such a being as God might have, omniscience, omnipotence, and so forth, and the *via negativa,* approaching through what God was not, that was to say, anything bounded, created, anything with a limit. You found God by holding up every gnawed and browning apple core and saying, Not this. You stared at every pretty face until your heart ached, and then you imagined those lips and cheeks melting, the eyes shrunk like raisins in the skull, bones peeking out. Not this. Not this.

Just a little further.

They were all eager, and they were all afraid. It began as a wonder, as a test. How fast can you run, what can you see? How wide might you open your eyes?

Sal went with her every step of the way, and it was Sal who made the final leap. What they found in the alts, the roads they drove and the seas they sailed and the wind that whipped them on, would be shaped by their own imaginations, their own sense of what was possible. What stories were planted so deep in their minds that they did not know they were there? What dreams would shape their path? Sal added, to their two-in-the-morning waking conversations about lemmas and theorems and alts and spin, Percival, and Psyche, and notes she'd copied from the little black book Ma Tempest kept on the shelf in her workshop, diagrams and names none of them recognized, unfound on the internet, only hinted at in dusty books in Sterling Library. This was a quest. To begin, they had to know what questing meant.

Zelda felt like they were racing side by side—united in this, grasping for the future, together. Nothing could stop them. They would change the world.

And so, with their math and their magic and their young and eager faith, they gathered together one night in spring, in an uneasy circle around the Challenger in the Temple Street garage: Ish, Ramón, Sarah, Zelda, Sal.

They fixed it in their minds. Around them, the world changed. They began.

And what happened then?

Well, best beloved: they failed.

# CHAPTER SIXTEEN

J ust like old times," Zelda had said on the rooftop of the ruined hotel, or
castle, or whatever it used to be. They picked their way down, sliding along
scree slopes and spotting one another, seeking handholds where rusted rebar jutted from rotting concrete. Having found their way to level ground,
they set off over the blasted plain. Ramón thought back to those old times and
wondered if she was right.

After that Halloween when Zelda had kissed Sal in front of God and everyone and went from being the mysterious jagged chick Sal was dating to being
a person he understood entirely too well, he began to notice her everywhere:
at dining halls, on Cross Campus at midnight, around the math building. He
liked to think that they had been destined to meet even if it hadn't been for
Sal. They might have shared a dining hall table or a study group and become
lifelong friends. Given their comfort with math and their general respective
feelings of wonder and confusion at the place, at the audacious fake Gothic
theme-parkiness of it all—given all of that, Zelda and Ramón were close as the
flip sides of the same sheet of paper. They would have run across each other
sooner or later.

Or, she'd pointed out, they could just as easily have spent four years on campus breathing each other's air, and never spoken once.

He tried to keep his distance from her at first. He really did. He was friends
with Ish, and Sal, and the Ish-Zelda-Sal situation seemed like a December sky
before the kind of thunderstorm that flooded streets. He'd heard enough horror
stories about freshman-year relationships to develop a healthy caution around
a fling that, two months into fall semester, had already left a friend crying
through her Halloween makeup. But Sal seemed happy. And weird as it was, Ish
seemed happy too.

Still, he tried.

But Zelda kept crossing his path. He'd find a mostly empty table in the Timothy Dwight Dining Hall and sit chewing over the crossword and his grilled
chicken breast—the guy who ran the grill was the best on campus—anyway,
he would sit down in peace to try to think of a six-letter word for "help" that
ended in *r*, and look up fifteen minutes later to see Zelda at the opposite corner
of the table, working the crossword, too, trying to remember whether Gaddafi
had two *d*'s and one *f* or the other way around, and did it start with a *K* or a *Q* or
what? And he'd ask her for help, and she'd say, "Succor," then double-take and
claim she'd been there for a half hour without noticing him and ask, half joking,
if he was following her.

He asked her, years later, whether those meetings were really accidents, and
she'd said, Most of them, and then after a pause, Well, I think I thought they
were back then. But I knew you were friends with Ish, and Sal.

I was in awe of Sal, he said. Not quite the same as friends.

Well, who wasn't? Outside of Sarah. I mean, we weren't in anything together, you and me, we weren't in the same college, but there were these threads. Connections. Bread crumbs. And if I was paying attention—and I was paying attention to everything back then, though maybe it was the wrong everything I was paying attention to—I would have known where you ate lunch, where you walked and when. Not, like, scheme-ily. Just deep down.

Oh, so you were *sub*consciously stalking me.

God, I sound like such a weirdo.

That was the bond, more than either of them would have admitted at the time. They knew it was weird for them to be here, Ramón a first-generation college student, and brown, Zelda from a family of bookish zealot weirdos up a gravel road in South Carolina, neither of them with any money to their names. They didn't doubt they were smart enough or good enough or anything like that—any fear Ramón had of being outclassed intellectually vanished his first day of Political Thought, when the professor asked the class to point to Athens on a map and no one else could find Greece. But there were things they didn't know, things the kids who came from prep schools with names Ramón could tell he was supposed to recognize *did* know, and seemed to have learned without being taught.

For example: if you didn't know what to write for a paper, you could just go ask the teacher, and they'd walk you through the whole thing. Or: if you were going to be late on a project, you could ask for an extension. Zelda didn't believe him when he told her that, so she'd tried with a complexity theory project she was working on, a big final project sort of deal no one could possibly offer an extension on since the due date was the last day of the semester. But when she asked, the professor chatted with her about the topic, suggested an additional angle for her to explore, then, apologetically(!), said he could not offer her any more time than the end of the *next* semester, but after that she might consider applying to these three fellowships to fund future work. Ramón had been waiting outside the math building, ready to collect on the five bucks they'd bet on the outcome of the meeting; when Zelda emerged, swearing and pink with rage, he thought she was going to deck him.

You mean I could have been doing that this entire time?!

You never know until you ask, he said. And I was too scared to ask.

Who the hell told you?

Nobody. I heard some guys talking about extensions in the dining hall. Thought I'd try it out. I was madder than you when I found out.

I'm not sure about that.

In that way, without fanfare or declarations of blood-brotherhood, they discovered that they had each other's backs. It wasn't the same kind of losers-club bond he felt with Ish. Ramón and Zelda could go days or a week without seeing each other; when their paths did cross, it felt like an easing of the guard, like two old kung fu masters who met in a wood might decide to share a glass of wine and talk shop, because they knew things the pampered merchants of the city did not understand.

But Zelda was different with Sal. That worried him. Sal was bold; she threw parties and got her friends to act in plays, she circulated petitions to end the war, to end wars, to end prisons, she wrote poetry the literary magazine rejected and then she posted it all over campus, and when they were together, Zelda played the bright-eyed ingenue, awed and in love, Sal's biggest fan, running beside her step by step. It seemed an act, a mask, a role. He'd been in relationships like that before, and they ended badly.

Sal loved high places, and she collected keys. Or people who would serve as keys. A friend of hers in the Guild of Carillonneurs—a carilloneur being a person who played a carillon, and *that* being something like an organ but with bells and high up in a tower, and hammers and levers instead of keys, even more foreign to Ramón than an extension on a paper—had traded a tour of Harkness Tower, where the carillon was, for some favor, the details of which Ramón had decided were best left a mystery. Known, they could be either tawdry or boring. Unknown, they could be magical.

The tower was the tallest building on campus, a pinnacled clock spire, and from its height, he could see down into Old Campus and out over the Green, across to Sterling Library and the bright fields between two halves of Berkeley College. The height dizzied. The wind was so strong it took him three tries to light his joint.

They'd passed it back and forth without talking for a while. Up here, they weren't quite out of the fishbowl, but they'd scooped themselves above it. You could find privacy on campus—people would give you space in study carrels or the library, or in your own room, but even the walls were watching. You didn't notice the pressure, not all at once. It accumulated like snowflakes. Here, what you did mattered. If you went to the right classes and knew the right languages, you'd get a call from CIA recruiters, that was the story—and like any rumor, that one traveled not because of its particular truth but because of the larger and more general truths it suggested. Your classes matter. Your run for student body president matters. Your college paper byline, your ill-considered op-ed or Dean's Office–funded literary magazine, they make a difference. People notice. The kind of people who grew up to be the sort of People whose job it is to Notice Things. But you didn't feel that pressure at first, because it gathered flake by flake.

Sal looked different up here. Tighter, despite the weed. Tired, too, unexpectedly. But then, she had a year on the rest of them, one more year under the snow. He'd never realized she was wearing armor before. She made it so finely that it seemed at first glance to be her skin.

"You're friends with her," she said. "At this point."

There was only one Her for Sal back then, only one person the pronoun, introduced alone, might mean. He had lines when it came to this sort of conversation. Confidences he refused to betray. He considered the great distance below them and the even greater distance above, and how the whole winter universe seemed to be a globe of gray crystal, and how back home in Los Angeles right now, the skies would be blue and the hillsides yellow green and thirsty for December rain.

"Is she okay?"

That was not what he had thought Sal might ask. The concern on her face cut him in a way he was not ready for. A friend who'd been stabbed once said you didn't feel pain at first, just as if you'd been poked really hard. You noticed when your lung collapsed, though. "What," he said, "does okay look like?"

"I don't know. She loves what she sees, and that makes me want to be who she sees when she looks at me. She tries to keep up with me and I run faster to keep up with her. She's perfect. I brought her home to meet Ma."

"Big step."

"Yeah, well. You know, man. Second date, moving van." She waved off smoke. "She wanted . . ."

"What?"

"Wanted me to—take over. To take charge. It was a lot. I shouldn't be telling you any of this. It's not fair. To her."

"Sounds hot."

She did laugh at that.

"I think," he said, then: "Do you want to know what I think?"

She took a drag, held it in, and swept one hand over all the Kingdoms of This World beneath the great gray crystal sky, which he took to mean that she offered him these and asked only for this one small truth in trade.

"I think." Ash fell onto High Street. The wind carried the sparks away. Back home he would have worried about fires. Here the roads were gray-brown slush and the sidewalks were lined with four-foot-tall snowdrifts coated black with coal dust and the sand they spread to melt the ice. He still felt the dart of fear, when he mislaid a spark. He pictured a wall of fire and smoke beyond the Holly-wood Hills, the Griffith Observatory burning, all of it his fault. You dug irrigation ditches in your soul to channel your fear, to guide it to useful work. But the ditches remained even when the fear was gone—and some part of you kept shoring up those ditches and maintaining the waterworks in case and until the fear came back. Because the fear had to come back. Because you had built so much of yourself around it. This whole time he'd kept silence. The height said, You're not supposed to be here. He said: "I think we talk about love wrong."

"She's never said it." Sal snatched the joint back. It was almost done. Just an ember now. "That word."

"It doesn't matter."

"It does to me."

"I mean it doesn't matter for what I mean. We talk about it like a binary, you know, a one or a zero. Love or not."

"I know what the fuck a binary is."

"But in English anyway you don't say she's landed in love. You say she's fall-ing. And when you're falling, it doesn't stop. You just keep going, faster and faster, toward whatever it is that's drawing you down. And if there wasn't any-thing to fall through, like in a vacuum, you'd keep falling faster and faster for-ever."

"We're not in a vacuum."

"No. There's air here. But we don't notice most of the time, because it doesn't move very fast. But think about that. All your life, you breathe the stuff and take it for granted, assume it's there when you need it and won't impose otherwise, but now you're falling faster than you thought possible, so fast the air itself is like this great big hand pushing you back, trying to slow you down. Maybe you just want it out of the way. Even if that means you can't breathe anymore. Because the air's between you and what you're falling toward, because you want it that much. Even though you're starting to do the math in the back of your head about how far you've fallen and how fast you're going and what will happen when you hit."

"A horse," she quoted, "splashes."

"Yeah."

"I'm not some slab of rock," she said. "Passive, down there, waiting for her. I'm in . . . Sarah tells me I'm being an idiot, letting myself care this much. Just take it as it comes, she says. If it hurts, walk away. She doesn't know her own mind and you can't make it up for her."

"I think Sarah's wrong."

"She's not, often."

"Look. I think Zelda knows. I think she's spent her whole life watching herself in the mirror. Being what she needs other people to see. Do you think that quiet loving family with the pastor who checks up every week would have let their girl go off to the godless heathen school if they didn't trust her to walk in the light of whatever? She knows the consequences if she's not what she has to be, so deep she can't put them in words. All of a sudden she's rushing down and she doesn't know how to stop and if she did know, she wouldn't. She needs control. Either she needs it, or she needs someone else to have it. Because she's spent so much of her life trying to make things okay, and now all she sees when she looks down is . . ."

"Splash."

"I think so."

"So why can't she tell me?"

"Would you tell this kind of stuff to the supercool extremely wonderful sophomore with all her shit together that you still can't believe you're dating because what could she possibly see in you anyway?"

"I might tell it to my scared and extremely fronting girlfriend who spends, you know, half her time trying to get herself kicked out of school because that way she's the one who controls whether she's a fuckup and a failure. Who feels it every day—this gathering sense that I shouldn't be here, that I have to be something else for them, something nicer, something more . . . flexible."

"I don't think she knows she's dating that woman yet," Ramón said. "You might try telling her."

He did not know if she ever had. He hoped so. It might have helped for Zelda to hear that there were limits, that Sal couldn't make everything okay and neither could she, that *okay* wasn't, that what they did have in this mess of a world was each other, and that was for real and always even if people were weak and life got in the way. That was all you had: small people trying together. All the acid-washed buildings, all the debate societies and right-wing boys wearing seersucker in November, all the pomp and most of the circumstance, were just ways of shouting into the void, Hey, we're here! We exist. There were so many ways to do that, and most of them didn't involve joining the goddamn CIA. You could start by finding someone you loved and holding hands.

He missed Gabe.

He hoped Sal had trusted Zelda enough to have that conversation. But either way, not so long after that afternoon on top of the clock tower, when the sky was still blank gray and the snowdrifts muck black and he had not seen the real sun, unveiled, in sixty years, Zelda knocked on his dorm room door in spite of not having an ID that would have let her past the building's prox card readers. Sal had passed this on to Zelda already: her trick for opening doors.

Zelda's eyes were bright and her smile belonged to a maniac. I've found something, she said.

I've found something, and I need to borrow your car.

She didn't know how to drive stick. But she was a fast learner, and he needed the road after so long away from it, needed to leave the fishbowl, needed to feel the engine roar in his gut. He could barely hear the car's voice back then, but he missed it when it was gone.

She explained the theory of spin in terms another theorist would have grasped, manifolds and transpositions, decay and topology and a host of quantum semi-gibberish. He knew, more or less, what she wanted to do, but figured even if she wasn't totally wrong, any effects would be minimal, or willful sampling error, just like the eighties parapsychology studies with the cards and the electric shock.

But it felt good to roll the cover off his car in the Temple Street lot. He still thought of the Challenger as *his* car back then, as if the lines of possession went that way. Felt good to find the road again, and to teach something so second nature to him and so alien to the dorm halls and wizard school cosplay of college, to talk U-joints and transmissions and show her the scar on his left hand from working the engine. It was stuff he didn't tell even his hookups back then, since it was a way weirder hobby in this environment than Magic: The Gathering, and he wasn't interested in boys who wanted the rough guy from the wrong side of the tracks who smelled like engine grease. It was always easier to see through your friends' problems than your own.

He did not know how to talk to her about Sal, or what she needed, but it felt good, and bright, and a bit like coming home, teaching Zelda to drive stick. Until the day she took a turn that did not exist, and the sky opened blue above them and the ground spread green on all sides and waved with ferns in the swamp-breath breeze, and they had to break hard to avoid hitting something he was more or less positive was a triceratops.

⟫

Ten years had passed between them, and they had ten miles now to walk through poisoned fields that had once, he thought, grown corn. "It shouldn't be this barren," he said, not sure whether he was referring to the fields after all. "Even without farmers, there should be something wild. Grass, even."

"Back home, the big seed companies sell corn with pesticides coded into the DNA, corn that can't be used to grow more corn, so you have to buy another bunch of seed next year." He knew this. After he came back from the road, when he traveled around the country delivering PowerPoint presentations to people with too much power and not enough point, he'd advised a company with that business model. At the time, he had been too burned out to care. That was how they got you. "Whoever built that ring in the sky must have figured out the same trick."

"I'd hope whoever built that ring in the sky would be smarter than that. Or wiser."

They were about the same height, but her stride was longer, faster. She spent a lot of time on her feet, he imagined. When he saw her the first time back in Montana, still dizzy from the Challenger fire, he'd been shocked by how like herself she looked, as if she'd stepped fresh from his memories. Now, as they crossed the open plain, he could see the weariness and the scars. She carried her shoulders lower now, not because she was less tense but because she'd had to work harder for longer and that forced her into a certain crumpled efficiency. "You've seen as much as I have. Do you think that's likely?"

"I haven't," he replied. "Seen as much."

"You have. Trust me. It's the same out here as it is back home. Just more."

"After . . ." He could not quite say, *After I left*. "Once I washed myself off, once the cuts healed, I got drunk. Then I got high. Then, after the crash, I got a job in finance, until that made me feel too filthy and I quit. I've been in LA ever since. I haven't seen much in ten years, I think. The bottom of a lot of glasses, the inside of a bunch of conference rooms, and Tío's garage, and Dodger Stadium. You've been on the road this whole time."

"It's just the road. You know how it is."

"Not like you do. I hear stories."

That hitched her step. She glanced over her shoulder. "About me?"

"Of course about you. Janice Ao says you saved her from something, she wasn't specific but it sounded like rot, in South Station in Boston, back in 2012. Danny Cohen ran into you in a coffee shop in Seattle around Christmas three years back. Luke Ngobe says he stopped to listen to some buskers in Atlanta, and there you were, singing along."

"He didn't come up to me."

"He wasn't sure it was you at the time. Didn't want to get it wrong. But he said he was pretty sure. I didn't know. You don't sing much."

"I don't sing well, you mean. But when you're on the road, you have to amuse yourself somehow." She walked in silence, hands in pockets. "They told you?"

"Posted about it. Online. There was a Facebook group. There probably still is, but I quit the internet a while back. My point is, people tell stories."

"Those aren't stories," she said. "Janice's is a story, I guess. But it's nothing special. There was rot. I dealt with it. She happened to be there. It was bad luck, that's all."

"People wonder about you."

"And Sal."

It wasn't a question, but: "Yeah."

"And when they wonder, what do you say?"

"I don't."

They did not speak for a while after that. It had been a long time since he walked this much. He ran, back in LA, and he hiked trails in the San Gabriels, but it was always the kind of thing you did on purpose, the kind of thing that brought you back to where you'd parked your car. You got dressed for it, you chose the right shoes, you took a water bottle. You didn't just pick a direction and start walking because you had to get from here to there. Around mile three, he felt a twinge above his knee, and wondered if he'd messed up his squat form back home, if he was imbalanced somehow. Or maybe he'd pulled something running from the cowboy last night. Probably the cowboy.

"I've been doing the same thing every year," she said out of nowhere. "Since you left. Driving the road. Sealing cracks. Digging out the rot. I go to a new place, I meet new people, I solve their problems, if I can. If I'm lucky, that's the end of it. If I'm not lucky, I pick up a scar or two. When it's done, I move on, find a place to rest and heal, save a little money. I cast yarrow stalks to learn where the rot will show up next, so I can be there waiting. These days, it's more a question of where the rot isn't than where it is. We're like a raft on a sea of it. That's not something to tell stories about. I don't know what it is."

"To a lot of people, it would sound like an adventure."

"You know better, though." Without a hitch in her stride, she dipped down, found a rock, and threw. It arced ahead of them, landed, rolled. In fifty feet they came to the rock again, and again she picked it up and threw. "It's plumbing. It's what plumbing would be if the plumber first broke into your house and screwed up your pipes and then, when there was shit everywhere, offered to fix it."

He wondered if she really thought that. "Tell me about the last one you fixed."

She rubbed her arm. "I don't want to talk about the last one."

"The one before that, then."

"Michigan." She could smile still. He saw a trace of grim pride. "Something whispered in the lake. There were these men who went down to the shore at midnight and sang to it, and it got big. Bigger than usual. I followed stories of mermaids, of mouths in the sea wide enough to swallow boats and lined with diamond teeth. It had many children and many arms, and at night, even in winter, people would walk naked into the water, slip beneath its surface, dive down. It was clever. It didn't take locals often. I don't know how it found people, but it found them in their dreams, and spoke to them with a storm voice. I snuck past the singers. I fell into the water. I closed it."

"You don't sound happy about that."

"It's not a happy thing. The rot calls to people who need it. Who need there to be something else than all of this. And then it eats them."

"And you win every time?"

She shook her head.

"What happens then?"

"The gaps grow. People disappear. Whole towns just fade away. People forget they were there. They tell stories about how some of the towns on maps don't exist, because mapmakers made them up to protect their copyright, or whatever. Some of those stories are even true."

"That was a story you just told me," he said. "About the mermaids."

"It only sounds like a story to you because it's not your life. It is mine."

She had a right to the edge in her voice. It was not his life, because he left, with the others, and his leaving had made their leaving possible, and then she was alone. He had done that to her. He had done that to save Ish, to save himself, and to save Sarah and even in a way Zelda, too, but intent did not change the fact. "It sounds like a story to me."

"You tell me one, then. About you."

"I don't have many stories."

She glared at him.

So he told her the first story that came to mind, which was the story of how he met Gabe, working on the car, about their drive together up to the observatory and about the kiss and the rhythms of their life together after. She asked questions here and there. He heard sunlight in his own voice, pure and gold and sweet.

"But you came back," she said when he was done. "Why?"

There were so many answers to that, and because the Challenger was not here to taunt him, he could not say which one was the bare and honest brutal truth. So in the silence of that flat place, he said the words in his heart. "Because you're my friend." She did not speak, and he felt exposed and afraid. "And there's that whole 'end of the world' thing. I don't want that. The world is where I keep all my stuff."

He said that part wry, like a joke, and she laughed at it, or it sounded something like a laugh. She choked and turned away. He remembered Sal on the Halloween sidewalk, dressed like Puss in Boots, and remembered Zelda's head held high and defiant as she crossed the courtyard full of monsters to kiss her. He laid his hand on her shoulder and squeezed so she felt him, and was surprised when she hugged him, tight, for the space of one ragged breath.

She backed away, her arms still clutching his. She was strong, and her eyes bright. "You don't hate me?"

"Of course not." He had expected to. Together they had failed, and she failed most, and that made him feel ashamed, and shame was a door to hate. He had expected to hate her, or to hate this, to hate being back out here in the shit he had been running from since college and maybe all his life, to feel that hatred with the Challenger's true and evil drug-sweet certainty. But here, under this impossible sky, with that ring far, far overhead, he did not. "You showed me my first dinosaur."

She smiled at that briefly, and let him go. "Come on. Let's go steal a car."

※

This was Ramón's first raid in a while. Zelda tried to take it slow.

They lay in wait below the crest of a hill a half mile off as the sun declined, watching the cluster of hide tents and barbed wire and tank traps through Zelda's monocular. Ramón had suggested, on the way, that they just walk up and ask if they could borrow a car, rather than stealing one. She'd not not argued, even though she thought it was a dumb idea. Sooner or later, he'd remember how things worked out in the alts.

When they drew near, they saw the skulls on stakes near the tank traps around the camp's perimeter and heard the screams from within.

The tattooed and fur-clad guards posted at the camp's edge behind the tank traps stood rigidly at attention, as if they would be gutted for the slightest dereliction of duty. They glared out at the open plains in stock silence, spears raised. On closer examination with the monocular, she saw their lips were stitched shut. That, in her experience, was not a good sign. There were in theory an infinitude of alts, so surely there was one where people stitched their underlings' mouths shut for good-guy reasons, but she hadn't found one yet. She wondered how a guard with a stitched-shut mouth could raise an alarm. Bells, maybe.

Zelda and Ramón did not speak. He did not need to be reminded of that, at least. They ate protein bars from her jacket pockets to blunt their hunger, and washed them down with the last of the water from her canteen, which barely took the edge off thirst. She watched him out of the corner of her eye and tried not to feel any of the things she was feeling.

She had missed him so much. With Ramón here, she could tell herself that they were not scattered throughout the alts because of her poor planning and frantic execution. They were only temporarily inconvenienced, like people on adventures in books. June would take care of herself. Sarah and Ish would be fine. They would meet again—at the Medicine Wheel, where all worlds touched. They would walk the path together and make the world right and whole, the way they had failed to do before. It was fit and meet that they should do this. It was a thing that was right to want, a thing she had been justified in asking. With him beside her, they were ten years younger, proud in the fullness of their strength.

But they had not taken the same path through those ten years, had they? She thought back to Ramón's story, to the Kansas boy and their kiss in Griffith Park with the sunlight in their hair. In spite of everything, he had found a form of ease. Maybe it could have been like that with Sal, if she had been brave enough. They had been kids and idiots with their spines and blade edges pressed into each other's soft underbellies, but if they had grown together, if they had had time, they might have come to understand the pain they caused and been able to tell the difference between that and the love they shared. That was something she had cost herself and the world, that bit of love. Every love denied was a price too high to pay.

She knew that, and yet she had called Ramón away from his young man, called Sarah from her family, back to the road, back to the undone task. And they came.

What had she called Ish from? He had always been the closest of them to her—she felt most comfortable with Ramón, she loved Sal, she had an uneasy truce with Sarah for Sal's sake, but Ish was the one who felt as near as an echo.

Regardless: What right did she have, to bring them here? She had told June, *They will come*, and she had believed it, but lying in front of this camp with the skulls on posts and the guards whose mouths were stitched shut, she realized that under everything, she had hoped she was wrong.

But they still came.

She thought about the others he had mentioned, about Janice and Luke and David—imagined being seen in passing, in busking groups, in coffee shops, in bus stations, crossing and recrossing the country. Imagined people noticing her, caring how she was. How long had it been since *she* cared?

The screams stopped around sunset. The guards retired and a new band of stitch-mouthed men replaced them. Fires crackled. Inside the camp, she heard chanting, and over the chanting a high voice wailed a threnody or dirge in a language she felt that she had once known in dreams. Night fell. Stars glinted behind slashed clouds. In the dark, the eyes of the skulls glimmered, and they revolved upon their stakes, keeping watch.

It had been years, she realized, since she last did something that felt this *young*. She'd carved away rot down back roads all across America, but breaking into a cultist camp to steal cars from under the watchful eyes of skull sentinels, that was strictly pre-twenty-five territory. Ramón should stay behind. He was out of practice. She could get him once she'd found the car. That was the only way that made sense.

She turned to him, mouth half open, but he had already risen to a crouch. "Come on," he whispered. "I know the way."

⋆

Ramón had missed this. Not the pants-shitting terror of the situation, of course, but once they started moving, that wore off. The worst had been lying on the hillside, listening to the screams. He'd always had a vivid imagination, and being forced to listen, unable to see what was happening or do anything about it, was like being tied up, unable to leave, the way a horror movie in a theater felt. You couldn't stop what was about to happen, and you couldn't exactly climb over everyone else to get out.

Once you got moving, you saw your options. When you had options, you had a measure of control.

And once he got past the terror, he couldn't deny the thrill.

His knack sang inside him, charting paths. He studied the camp. Those skulls looked freaky with their glowing eyes, and he did not like to imagine how a needle piercing his lips would feel, or the glide and rasp of thread dragged through his skin, but with all due respect to the hardships of the postapocalyptic wasteland, this camp was easier to sneak into than the basement of Dodger Stadium. The skulls could see through their glowing eyes, but they weren't cameras, there were no keypads to sort out, no motion detectors, and while he had no doubt these guys were great at gutting rivals and playing Thunderdome, they weren't exactly a trained security force. Also, there were fewer people here, and more shadows to hide in.

"Let's go," he said, and she followed him.

He slipped them through the night, into a gap between tank traps and barbed wire, in the moment when one guard scanned left and a skull scanned right, and then they were among the tents. His heart was in his ears. He heard deep, heavy breathing nearby. Someone snored. They slept early here, which made sense. Light was expensive. What did they use for fuel, anyway? Not a lot of trees around. He drew a breath, then wrinkled his nose, recognizing the smell. From orbital rings to dung fires in, what, a hundred years, two? Shit.

Then again, climate change was coming, back home. After it changed things, he wondered if their postcataclysm remnants would have anything so cool as watch-skulls.

He had spent ten years being careful, ten years using his knack for nothing more adventurous than dodging traffic or sneaking past a rope line into a movie premiere. Ten years trying to be normal. Now he wasn't. He was weird again and good at it, invisible, careful. And he was not alone.

Zelda could have made it into the camp without him. She moved silently in her thin-soled sneakers, knew how to blend into the shadows, where not to set her foot. He didn't have to tell her when to freeze. Together they were ghosts. Her knack worked around the edges of his, or vice versa, sliding chance into more comfortable paths, easing restless sleepers back to their pillows, encouraging roused drunks to lurch the other way for a piss.

He smiled at her in the dark, and his smile widened when he saw her reluctance to smile back. Why worry? She had been right: just like old times. Everything was going so well.

At the heart of the camp, a large dung fire had burned down to embers. Its off-black light glistened from the chrome of bikes parked around the edge, from the matte black paint of a giant, monstrous Frankencar at the clearing's far edge, resting before what he assumed was the tent of the headman or high priest. The vehicle was made of chopped-up bits of cars, trucks, tanks, even a missile platform. The bikes and the Frankencar were threatening, they were decorated to be threatening; weapons of war and honor, marked by the blood of the glorious dead, chariots with which to storm the gates of heaven, or something similar. He'd heard a lot of talk like that, traveling, from this sort of gang.

There was a dead body on an altar beside the bonfire.

That wasn't why he drew up short at the clearing's edge. Nor did the bikes or the Frankencar impress him, though it had been a long time since he saw bodywork that self-important.

Beside the altar, streaked with drying blood, crouched the Challenger.

Its hood was up, its windows down, its sides scrawled with flames in vivid, dripping paint. But it was unmistakably his car, the one he had driven into the Best Western parking lot just yesterday, or a lifetime ago. He recognized the fire damage, the arrow scores. Its teeth were bare, grimacing. The scars and bubbled paint leered at him. The broken window winked.

Come on, boy. You thought you'd get rid of me that easy?

He did not know how it had gotten here, or why. He stumbled into the light, spellbound, all stealth forgotten, drawn toward the Challenger by a force beyond his control.

Across the clearing, the headman's tent door twitched, and a pale figure appeared, pointing. A piercing voice cried out in alarm. The camp boiled to motion around them.

He and Zelda shared a glance—and sprinted toward the waiting car.

The Challenger ran like a dream.

They screamed out of the camp onto the open road with hell and all its angels following. The buzz-saw bikes came first, stitchmouths astride them, their hook-tipped lances couched, and behind them crested the mass of the Frankencar. Its great tires chewed crumbled pavement, its exhaust pipes gouted pillars of smoke laced with fire, and in its driver's seat, behind thick plate glass scavenged from some long-dead war machine, sat the pale-faced priest, his bloodshot eyes wide, his mouth red with paint or blood.

Ramón had never felt this alive.

That's it, boy. The car spoke to him. He had dreaded its voice as they crossed the plain together, but he had missed it, too—its wisdom, its confidence as total and crushing as the teeth of a bear trap around his leg. That's the truth, it said. You are pursued. They are after you. When they catch you, they will kill you. They will sink their nails and knives into your skin and peel you back until you're red and raw and wriggling just like them. It will happen when you are not ready. It will happen sooner than you think. It could happen here or it could happen back home—the truth does not change with the setting. It will happen. But, for now, we can run together.

Beneath his tires, the road was cracked and painted with dust. He learned it with his bones. He ate it up and drew it into him. Beside him, Zelda whooped like they were kids again, and maybe they were. People don't grow up like trees do, they grow callused, they grow accustomed—to faces, to the rhythms of morning, to the inside of their own heads. But no one, not even him, not even the stitchmouths after them, was callused to this, to the rush of it, to being chased, to fighting back. You trained so your body moved without your needing to tell it every little goddamn thing, so your hands and feet did their dance on the clutch and shifter and wheel, but part of training was that you did not let yourself grow dull to this, you did not let habit lull you to sleep. You cut your calluses off so you stayed alert, sensitive, stripped-nerve raw. Awake.

You've been asleep, boy, asleep so long. This is what's out there. This is all there is. Wake up. See the road. See those bikes coming up behind you, their lances out.

He couldn't slip out into an alt and away while they were after him like this, watching him, intent. They had tried when they were kids, in similar circumstances, and either it didn't work and drained you, or worse, they followed you through, the prey scent so loud in them that they ignored the changing skies and earth and even gravity. He needed a place to hide. To be unseen.

Alt-Montana was still Montana here. The lightning strike hadn't taken them far enough into the alts to give them mountains. The blasted plains stretched moonlit ahead, flat save for rolling hills, no buildings to hide in, no tunnels.

You don't have many options, boy. Lose them. Kill them all, if you can. Or you drive them out of gas, you run until those little chop-shop buzzbikes melt between their thighs and sear their balls off, until that ungainly scrap-lump hill on wheels behind you rattles itself to pieces. Or you find out how sharp that high priest's teeth really are, when they're buried in the meat of your thigh.

Drive.

He could barely believe the Challenger ran at all, after the arrows and the fire, let alone that it ran so well, but the engine purred, then roared. Gears shifted smoothly. It was a perfect instrument.

No scars can stop me, boy. That sleek black, that chrome, the nice clean bodywork, that's just war paint, that's leather and black lace, that's piercings and decorative chains, that's to get you in the mood. The real power lives deep. You got to go down to find it. You got to go where the blood is.

The bikes came up fast.

Six of them. Beetle black, they gulped the road with their wheels and shat tornadoes. The riders wore spiked, bleached leather and helmets the color of bone.

His cheeks would split if he smiled any wider. The whole of him would split at the seam and spill out and leave only the smile at the wheel. His engine roared. They fanned out. Smaller engines, lighter bodies even with their armor plating and those stupid amateur-hour drag-inducing spikes. They couldn't pace him long without melting the dirty little engines on those postapocalypse specials. But they didn't have to pace him long—just long enough to lance one of his tires, for a hooked spearhead to split his brake line.

Come on, come at me.

Two of them popped wheelies and charged, their engine noise a high whine, some awful nitrous mix in there, a speed burst that wouldn't last long—but long enough for their purposes. He didn't give a shit. As they came up, he cut left, then right, felt the dust and gravel of this shitty back-alt road give under his tires, fishtailed off—and his rear bumper kissed the left bike in the side.

The bike flipped, skidded, sparked. The five stitchmouths remaining veered off to avoid the twisted screaming metal hunk that used to be one of them. One misjudged the distance, hit the fallen bike, went down back wheel over front, sparks and screams and the crack of a popped helmet. Then the priest's wheels caught up with bikes and riders alike, and crushed them.

That maneuver had cost Ramón speed, momentum, control, balance. He spun the wheel, let his hands and feet do their dance, got it back. But the other biker who'd come up to flank had all that time to get into position.

His lance burst through the passenger-side window, past Zelda, its hook aimed for Ramón's throat. He flinched away—bad move, a flinch can kill you when you're doing ninety-plus down shit roads in the dark. Zelda didn't flinch. She grabbed the haft of the lance, pulled, twisted. The biker lost his balance, bit pavement.

His weight and the weight of his falling bike, transmitted through the spear, slammed Zelda's face into the dash. She cursed. Blood ran from her nose. She shifted grip, hefted the spear, grinned at Ramón, bloody as the pale priest.

She gets it. Of course she gets it. She never left. She never went to sleep. You know the car, boy, but she knows the road.

He had expected, after so long, to feel something when the bikers died. But that was another thing he remembered from before: a kind of brutal simplicity. They are trying to kill us. We have to stop them. That kind of thinking could warp you, but it wasn't wrong.

Three bikes left. They were more careful now. They knew what they were facing, not some terrified runner, not some sheep, but someone who knew their game, could play it better. The Challenger would win a collision through sheer mass. He could keep them back with that threat—but each time he tapped the brakes or swerved, one of the three seized an opening to slide into spear range. They played with him, too, one darting too close only to peel off while the others took advantage of his distraction. A lance hook caught the Challenger's side and screamed through bodywork, and while he shook it off, Zelda shouted a warning—another had used his slip of attention to slide close enough to aim for a tire. Zelda stabbed that lance away with her own; the stitchmouth tried to catch her lance haft with his hook, and because she did not want to let go, because she always had been stubborn, and because Sarah had sawed through the passenger-side seat belt to pull Ish out, Zelda almost tumbled out the window. Ramón grabbed the waistband of her jeans and tugged her back inside. In a just world, that biker would have tumbled, but there was no justice, there was just the road, and he slipped back out of striking distance, waiting.

The priest did not need to swerve. He did not need to brake. That giant hunk of engine had all the power he needed to catch them, pulp them. You couldn't bring that monster up to top speed fast, but he would get there.

Options closing, boy. It's just you and them and the road, here in the deep of night, in their own country. They know you've got no choices. They can ride you to death, until you're out of gas and they can kill you slow. This is their road, and knack or not, you're just a guest on it.

"I can't shake them here!" he shouted to her. "We need to hitch."

He couldn't. Not with so many on his tail. Not after so long. But Zelda had spent the last ten years on the road. He was good at this, but she was better.

"On it."

Simple as that. They almost caught him when the road doglegged left, one biker revving up for a hit at the engine, another clawing at his undercarriage, their whines high-pitched and vicious. Something tore under the car; a hood wound gouted steam. He twisted the wheel, got balance back. Steering heavy all of a sudden. Couldn't afford another pass like that. He glanced at the rearview and saw the priest had not bothered with the dogleg, just hammered right through, his tires flattening the earth, his shovel-blade bumper uprooting a small tree, to burst back onto the pavement. Unstoppable.

"Get ready!" Zelda cried, and with a lurch, they hitched through.

There were no stars. The sky was underlit by fire. To either side of the road, bare rock cliffs cracked and fell away and tumbled into the magma heat of lava fields that stretched to the horizon.

What the hell had she pivoted off, to get them here? The sound, maybe—the great growling engine sound of a world rending itself apart.

The open-oven air crackled in his lungs. It stank of metal and lightning and sulfur. A lava plume erupted and he floored the accelerator, darted underneath it; it fell across the road behind them. The stitchmouths dodged but not fast enough. Lava caught one in the helmet. With a scream and a spasm he cut left, plowed another off the road. The third, veering to evade, didn't notice a deep crack across the asphalt; his wheel caught, his bike bucked, and he vaulted over the cliff's edge into fire.

Zelda screamed in triumph, which would have been a nice thing to feel. He wished he could have felt it. But even as one part of his brain did the math—no bikes left, just them and the priest—he saw the sky.

Clouds of dark smoke rushed toward them across the charcoaled earth, born on volcano wind. The billowing black waves rose to a crest, tall as the sun and firelit. That crest had a woman's shape.

Eyes of lightning. Tornado legs.

He knew her.

Sal, drawing the lava storm behind her like a bridal train.

The Challenger laughed.

"Zelda!"

"I see her."

"Zelda, what do we do?"

"I can take her."

"You can't *take* her! She's the size of the goddamn *sky*! Get us out of here!"

"I'm trying!"

Something near Ramón's head exploded.

The priest had caught them. Drawn up alongside. He leaned across the passenger seat of his monster car, a huge and heavy handgun in his reedy fist, and he was grinning blood. The gun's barrel smoked.

But he'd missed. Not because of Ramón's knack. Ramón hadn't known he was there, hadn't been trying to dodge. The priest just—missed. So he was still alive.

Ramón knew the world did not work this way, but his memory insisted that he had seen the bullet pass in front of his face.

The priest jerked that monster car sideways; those dumb spikes on its hood tore into the Challenger's body. Metal screamed. His steering column bucked. Something was very wrong. Smoke billowed from holes in the hood. But the Challenger felt weightless around him and free, as he'd always dreamed it would back home. At this speed, time stood still. There was no road, there were no wheels. Just—peace.

He missed Gabe.

He was back where it all made sense. Here on the road, with his life at stake and the world, too, and some storm-cloud monster marching toward him wearing his old friend's face. This was it. This was the real, this was the pulse-pounding truth of the moment, this was the blood-honesty that lay behind the pleasant lies of easy Sunday mornings and Dodger tickets and Griffith Park.

So why did he feel like a shadow here? And why did it seem that the only memory in his life with color was back home, in LA, waiting?

The bubble in which he had not realized he hung suspended burst. The steering wheel kicked in his hands. He smelled ozone and rubber and sulfur and steel. Tornado wind roared in his ears. He could not breathe. He had something to lose. And here he was, losing it. The priest driving him toward the cliff's edge.

You can't stop him, boy. Lie to yourself all you like, but you know that's true. You can't stop him and you can't run from him. He's got his eyes on you and he does not look away. He had the will to sculpt the ruin of his world to make it fit his sickness. And you, you miss your boyfriend.

His hands and feet did their dance. The blades and spikes screamed pieces off the Challenger but they pulled away from the Frankencar. Sal approached, her footsteps lightning and thunder. Cracks spread in the sky like the cracks in his window. He could beat this. He could beat them all at their own game. He just had to wake up. Gabe, and Los Angeles, and Griffith Park, that was the dream, that was the sickness and this was the real, this road under his wheels, this fire to the horizon, this storm-cloud hand reaching down for him.

Zelda was shouting at him. "Ramón! Turn right!"

There was nothing to their right. Just a high cliff and, hundreds of feet down, fields of roiling lava, and within the lava, great jewel-mouthed creatures surfacing like whales.

He could do this. He could win.

"Trust me!"

His grip tightened on the wheel. Lightning crashed and fire rained down around them and Sal bent low and reached for them with storm-smoke fingers. Another lava plume showered the road, splashing the priest's car. It burned, but it did not melt. Wreathed in flames, the pale priest raised his gun.

Wake up.

Zelda grabbed the wheel with both hands, and pulled.

They slipped off the road. Over the edge. He felt truly weightless now. No time to scream. He could not see the priest anymore.

Which meant, he realized, that the priest could not see them.

They landed like a hammer in the parking lot of a 7-Eleven overgrown with luminescent algae. The Challenger hissed and pinged as it cooled. Its hood was torn. Ramón did not like the steam and the smoke, he did not like the sluggish steering or the human-shaped blobs of algae that dotted the parking lot.

But they were alive.

He sagged back into the seat and did not realize for a long time that he was laughing, or that Zelda was, too, slumped against him across the shifter. Laughing was part of it, anyway. They had been young once, full of certainty and joy, bound for a good war. They were not anymore. But they were still here.

She somehow had enough spin to hitch through, away from the priest, the lava fields, and Sal. He did not ask her if she had known that it would work, because he did not want her to lie.

They had made it. That was all that mattered. Sal and the cowboy were behind them, for now, and their friends ahead.

Then Zelda said, "Look," and pointed up.

Above them in the night, he saw thin lines fanned out from the place where the storm that was Sal had been. They bisected stars, they spread across the moon, blacker than black, and they moved when he wasn't looking.

There were cracks in the sky.

Again.

## CHAPTER SEVENTEEN

The first time they tried to reach the crossroads, back in college, they had left at sunset. That was the plan. You drove through the dark, found the crossroads at midnight, and came home by morning. Changed.

They thought it would be that easy.

It almost worked out that way.

East Rock watched over New Haven in the predawn chill. It was used to watching, beyond time, mute and stark, suffering wind, rain, and prying roots. It waited with the patience of stones. If it spoke, it spoke in tongues of continental divorce.

A cliff thinks in eras. Centuries might pass unnoticed, while instants bring change.

A road, purple gray and lined with holdout snowdrifts, wound up to the cliff's edge in the deepest dark, on the morning of their failure. It was empty. Then, like fabric giving before a needle, it was not.

The Challenger rolled to a stop on shredded tires and screaming, sparking rims.

Ish felt numb. The world was slippery. Slick. He wore his flesh bunched up and awkward, like a suffocating coat. He wanted to peel it off, peel himself down to the skeleton, break the skeleton open to let whatever was under *that,* desperate, dying, out.

Ramón fumbled with a blood-slick hand for the shifter, for the parking brake, for the key in the ignition. The Challenger sighed onto its axles. The engine pinged and hissed and popped. His forehead met the steering wheel. His shoulders shook.

He was, Ish realized, crying.

They had set out from the Temple Street garage. They followed Sal's direction, and Zelda's, followed the plan. Worlds flickered around them like an optician's lenses. Focus on the road. That's what Sal said. Make it real in your minds. The place where we can fix things.

The landscape cracked and fire flowed. Great metal centipede-bird things swept by above, with eyes of fire and claws like scythes. Sal sat in the passenger's seat, watching the road with a gaze like an icebreaker's prow. Keep going, we're almost there. Zelda's hands clutched white-knuckled at her shoulders.

And then he saw the crossroads in the sky.

Now, at the edge of East Rock, in the smoking Challenger, Ish tried to reach for Ramón. His right arm would not move. He looked down and saw his hand clutching Sarah's, their fingers laced. He was aware of her nails digging into his skin, of his into hers. He didn't know who was crushing whom. Their eyes met.

He did not remember ever looking in her eyes before. He did not remember ever looking into anyone's eyes before.

She was Sal's friend. He barely knew her. She was a year older, elegant, traveled, athletic. She didn't, he thought, like him. But now, after tonight, after what they'd seen, she understood him more than his sisters did.

He told his left hand to reach for Ramón's shoulder. It obeyed. Squeezed. Found itself clutched in turn.

The air in the car stank of ozone and sweat and fear.

"Sal," Zelda said, "I think I'm going to throw up."

Sal opened the door, stepped out, turned back, popped the seat forward. She moved with the precision of a satellite bound past Jupiter—each movement perfectly controlled because any slip, any mistake, would be disaster.

Zelda staggered past her, fell to her knees in gravel, coughing, heaving with breath. He should go to her. He had never told her—he had never told her anything. And then out there in the alts, in the sky, Ish had seen . . .

They were real. The crossroads. They shaped themselves from the blood aurora, impossibly far away, inaccessible as the moon. But he knew them. He saw them, beautiful and strange, twisted as a Möbius strip, and he knew that they belonged to him—to the five of them squeezed into the Challenger. The power to change things. To make them otherwise.

And then it went wrong.

There were cracks in the sky, in the road. Shadows reached through them. They tore gouges from the pavement, they scraped the Challenger's paint.

He knew those shadows.

He was back in their embrace again, beyond the edge, beyond reason and authority, in the shadow of the trees.

*What do you want?* Was that the shadows' voice, or the voice of the crossroads? Was there any difference?

Stop it, he had begged, stop it, stop, let us go, let us be, let us go home. Let us be safe.

It was not a prayer. He knew better than to hope for those to be answered.

Ramón's hand found his now, and moved it from his shoulder. He helped them out of the car. Ish couldn't let go of Sarah. The light felt too bright. He'd been curled up like a fetus. He might have spent that long in the darkness too. With slow wandering steps, they joined Sal at the edge of the cliff, not looking at one another, each waiting for the others to speak.

No one wanted to say the truth. *We failed.*

"What was that?" Ramón asked.

No one answered. But none of them said, *I don't know.*

Ish found his voice. "It was waiting for us."

Sal pointed with her chin to the east, to sunrise and the ember-fringed horizon.

The sky went on forever. Ish knew that. Behind the blue, there was black, and the black stretched out past stars and galaxies to the beginning of time.

And yet, on that morning, the sky looked like an eggshell.

Behind it, something moved.

It—whatever it was—struck once, with a crack like thunder.

He fell to the ground with a cry, one hand up to guard his face. Sarah helped him up. She watched the sky—face fixed, ready to fight. As if they could fight that thing.

The strike did not come again. But the form was still there, roiling and more massive than clouds, made of shades and swollen nothings. And there in the blue, he thought he saw the tiniest crack.

"What is it?" Sarah asked Zelda.

Zelda looked gray and shaken. "It's real."

Sarah: "So what the fuck do we do now?"

Zelda did not answer. Sal said: "We try again."

## CHAPTER EIGHTEEN

Ish woke on cold earth that was not the earth, from dreams of the serpent beneath the world and the shadow beneath the trees. He had slept too long. He should not have slept at all, should have woken Sarah for her watch, but he needed time to think, to turn over in his mind what to do about this girl who was almost Sal, who seemed to think there were battles here to win and princesses in towers to save.

He was slipping. Too used to his bed. To Cynthia. He thought he had kept in better shape than this—but he had lost some of the old road skills, the asphalt wisdom. Zelda would never have fallen asleep. He would have to do better.

At first he lay without moving on the hard ground, listening, eyes closed, not sure if he was still dreaming, or what had woken him. Nerves? Pain from his hand, or from the cuts the girl had left in his arm when she emerged from the alts like a monster from the sea?

Then he heard the creaking of the sky.

Years ago, before Cynthia, in one of the few lulls in his work during which he'd been able to squeeze in a trip where no one could reach him save by satellite phone, he had flown to the Arctic, to walk on an ice field in spring, knowing that there might one day be a time in which this was not possible because there would be no ice left. Surrounded by glaring white to the horizon, his eyes stinging with the ghosts of the sun, he heard an awful, deep and eerie sound, the world's agony. Then everyone had been running to the plane. They had been safe, but did not know that until later. The icebreak was half a mile off.

Now he heard that same bone-deep creak, from overhead.

Without lights, the eye adjusted to the dark and unfurled the jeweler's carpet of the sky.

It was cracked.

Hairline fractures haloed the stars. Thin, jet-black, spiderweb lines crossed the dusting of galaxies. And at their heart—

Ish scrambled to his feet, shouting Sarah's name. She fumbled from the tent, June with her, and together they stared up into the absence that was Sal.

※

The cracks were still there at sunup, thin black jagged hairlines, razors across cloud and blue. They did not widen. They did not fade. Their insides wriggled at the corner of Ish's vision. He turned to June, and there might have been a trace of glare in his eye, because she glared back. "That's not me."

"Do you hear them whisper?"

Instead of answering, she hoisted a pack.

There was nothing to do but set off.

They had been walking in silence for the better part of the morning when Ish realized someone was about to die.

His knack didn't work like radar. There wasn't some video game heads-up display in the corner of his vision blinking different color shapes and lights, convenient and well defined. Even Spider-Man seemed to get more precise information out of the wiggly lines around his head. Ish just remembered things, the way he remembered that he'd left the bathroom light on, or an email unanswered, or what was left in his pantry. Where things were. What might happen next.

They'd had a flat, easy walk today, which made him nervous—you could see far in this kind of terrain, which meant whatever was out there could see you. He itched for hills, for cover. They weren't moving fast enough. Sarah's shoes weren't right for walking and by the time she said something and Ish offered her the canvas high-tops in Zelda's bag, she'd already worn herself a blister.

His shoulder and arm ached, but if he didn't think about them, they remained aches, not wounds, not weaknesses that would haunt him for the rest of this trip. He'd spent years working so he'd never have to come back here. Years training so that when he did, he'd be ready.

But you never were ready. Life was just learning that lesson over and over. Barely on the road and you slipped right back into your old bad habits. Jumping in front of arrows.

He tried not to look at Sarah as they walked. When he looked at her, he felt something tight and sour underneath his heart. She looked good. Years had rounded and smoothed her like a river rock. He remembered her quiet and steady and new-molted at school. To grow, a lobster had to give up its old armor and leave the husk behind, had to scuttle into the world soft, weak, and wary. Without risk, you did not grow. He'd learned that from her.

She had found a larger shell since, and as far as he knew, called this size and shape ideal. The ring she wore was a simple band inlaid with small stones. He had never realized he wasn't married. Strange to put it that way, but in his life, realizing he wasn't married would be like realizing that the sky wasn't green. You never thought it could be green, so it never occurred to you that it wasn't. Most people he knew tracked their various multi-partner situations in shared online calendars, or slipped from thing to thing because the internet made it all basically frictionless and everyone knew more or less what they wanted and who had time to waste on inefficiencies? They didn't marry.

He did, in fairness, know married people, but they were usually the sort who could afford their next divorce. He'd heard a VC once pass on a company because the founder liked her wife too much. If you thought about it, the market was all about meeting needs efficiently: food, drink, social contact, sex, shelter. You filled your needs with as little risk as you could manage. That's what everyone did. That's why his system worked, with Cynthia.

So while of course he knew that he'd never said "I do" or signed a paper in city hall, let alone gone through the whole priest-*Lohengrin*-rings-banquet

LARP, he'd never thought of himself as unmarried, because he'd never thought of married as a category that applied to him.

And here Sarah was.

He had to stop thinking about this. It made his head hurt.

They could be seen for miles on this trackless plain. He considered snipers on that ridge, or locals slithering on their bellies under cover of tall yellow grass. He felt an itch between his shoulder blades. You could feel it sometimes, when someone looked at you and wanted you dead. But you could feel that same sensation on random Wednesdays, at two in the morning, in your own bed in an empty house with the door triple bolted, the window glass bulletproof, and the alarms all silent.

The world felt thin. That was the problem. The wide-open hairline-fractured sky, the glacier-scoured plain—it was hollow, like an eggshell with the insides out. It should not be this dry, this dead, this unreal.

And then there was the girl.

Zelda trusted her. Even after everything, that almost settled the question. But Zelda had trusted Sal too. And Ish had seen June walk out of the shadows, boiling with rot. He bore the tracks of her claws in his arm.

She had said she was sorry. Sarah was right—a person's knack could take many forms. Maybe it could channel the rot. But no power was truly neutral. Everything you used bound you. He knew. He had made too many deals himself to think that what June was doing now could possibly come without a price attached.

For quiet hours he'd watched the hills approach and hoped that when he reached them, the prickle between his shoulders would ease. At least there would be cover there.

But when the hills drew near, he knew that someone was about to die. Not in front of them. In the valley past the hill. There were others there, dead already. Knowledge flitted in and out at the edge of his awareness—shadow certainties, echoes, television-static dreams. But he was sure about the dead, and the dying.

Sarah was a doctor now, and she'd been Sarah all along, so he didn't mention the dying man. It wasn't their business. He steered them quietly away. Maybe this was wrong, maybe he was breaking some code of the West, but no one had consulted him when they wrote that code, and anyway he had to get back to Zelda. They had a mission. A world to save.

June looked around, as if startled out of a dream. "Do you smell that?"

"No," he said, too fast.

But Sarah scanned the trees, pointed. "Smoke."

"We should keep going," he said. Sarah frowned at him. Zelda would have understood. Priorities. "There are dead people over there. Something killed them. Something dangerous."

"You didn't say."

"There's nothing we can do." He did not mention the dying man. There was nothing they could do about him either.

"We need supplies. A vehicle. Water." She had already turned toward the hill. "We'll be careful. Is anyone alive down there?"

Asked directly, he knew better than to lie. "One. Far gone. Too far to help."

But she was already running, with June running after.

Ish followed, tight as piano wire. The hillside was covered with low scrubby trash pines. He didn't know the names of trees back home and he surely didn't know their names in this shitty dried-up alt. The pines were too whippy and low to offer cover, but high enough that he lost track of Sarah, then June. Branches slapped his face, dry needles scraped his cheeks. Brambles tore his pants leg. He saw Sarah—then she was gone again. He *knew* where she was, but the knowledge felt fuzzy, half static. If there had been a HUD in his head, it would have been glitching out. He glimpsed something bright through the trees—the floral print of her dress, or the sky? The smell of pine choked him, and there was smoke, too, and something most people he knew would have mistaken for burnt meat. They would not have been wrong. Just not altogether right.

He ran through a spiderweb and swiped, coughing, at his face—felt the dead-leaf weight of the spider on his hand, fat and old—threw it off to one side and heard it smack a tree. Blinking webs from his eyes, he saw, thought he saw, beyond the trees, the flash of a white hat.

He froze.

Sarah and June crashed on ahead. Apart from them, the forest was quiet. There were no birds. He had not seen one since they came through. Heard nothing but insects. Ten years in San Francisco had left him too much of a city boy to notice that until now. On alts where people had all killed one another off, poisoned the skies and glassed the deserts, the birds came back fast and in shocking numbers.

But not here. He heard only the *tick-tick-tick* of insect legs.

Breeze shivered through the dry pines.

He couldn't call to Sarah and June. Whoever was listening would hear. He crept forward, walking on the balls of his feet, bent low. He took his small knife from his pocket. No good unless he could get up close. These pines hadn't dropped any branches worth using for a club. He crouched. Found a rock a little smaller than his fist. The dirt got under his close-cut nails.

All at once, he told himself. Don't think. *He* won't. Just do what you have to do. You're ready. Go.

He burst through the trees and found—nothing.

The dead land mocked him. Insects. Dry earth. Whispering needles and scraping branches. Ten years waiting for the monsters to come. Ten years training. And here he was, with a hole in his shoulder and a rock in his hand. An idiot jumping at shadows.

At least Zelda wasn't here to see. But—she would understand. He had to get his act together. Figure his shit out. Be worthy.

He had seen the hat through the trees.

But he didn't know where it had gone. If it was ever really there.

Where was Sarah? June? He couldn't hear them in the bush. Only insects. Pines. Whispering.

He knew they'd stopped at the ridge. But why? His knack wouldn't say. Details slipped out of his memory. He opened his mouth to call for them, stopped himself.

He had seen the white hat. The cowboy followed rules. Back home, it needed phones to see through. What would it use out here? Could it use a name? Could it follow a smell?

Not even the insects were clicking now. His own breath was the loudest sound in the world.

He heard a voice cry: "Ish!"

Sarah. He ran.

⎯⎯⎯⎯

They were dead, in the valley. The lucky ones.

They were dead, and they did not belong here.

Sarah held out her hand to stop June from entering the circle of burnt wagons. When June tried to ask a question, Sarah raised a finger to her lips, shook her head. That wasn't how you lasted, in the alts. You watched. Kept quiet. Waited.

She stepped softly between the fires. June followed, her eyes open as an owl's. Good. She was learning.

When Sarah reached the first body, facedown, a woman, she stopped. Blisters oozed on the blackened skin. Her shirt and flesh had melted together in places. Polyester. The ground beneath was blood-damp and boiled with worms, drinking. Sarah had seen worse.

Not in a long time.

You never knew how you'd handle your first whiff of burnt flesh. She wondered sometimes, when she saw students fresh off their first bad ER shift, which was worse: to be horrified in the moment, to run off and throw up and feel shame in your toilet stall, or to realize that night as you lay down to sleep that something in your past or blood or heart had prepared you to see people as meat.

June did not throw up. She followed.

A low moan rose from the center of the camp. Sarah didn't lead them there at once. The US military wasn't the only group to use the double tap—you bombed a place, and then when people showed up to help, you bombed it again. It would be strange to lay that sort of ambush out here, in the middle of nowhere. But you never knew.

Back home, Alex would be hard at work on his Halloween costume. He did not commit well, her son. He wanted to be Iron Man, then the Hulk, so he'd paint the Iron Man armor green, or paint himself green and wear the Iron Man gloves. She'd bleached the tub three times last year trying to get the green paint off. Evan had got him into monster movies this summer—the old Universal films were pretty safe for kids, which said more about what counted as safe for kids these days than it did about the movies themselves. She expected he'd end up as a sort of Wolf-Dracustein with mummy robes under his cape. A Costco trip for gauze, or else they'd just use toilet paper and hope it didn't rain. Susan had chosen her costume in midsummer and refused to tell anyone what it was, because that would ruin the surprise.

She'd be home for Halloween. She'd be home. This was just a trip. Making amends. Another adventure she'd never tell her kids, another nightmare she'd never share with her therapist. These things happened and you closed the book on them and put it away.

A boy—maybe eight years old—lay on his back beside one of the Mylar wagons. His eyes were gone already. She had seen no birds to take them. The birds might hide by day. If so, from what? Or else the killers took the eyes. But why? Another entry for the book Evan was always telling her she should write. *Annals of Shit I Wish I Hadn't Seen,* volume 5. Still: Why only *his* eyes?

In a full circuit of the wagons she found no signs of life. Eighteen bodies, men, women, children.

"This is wrong," she said softly.

"You think?" June croaked. Sarah held her hand out between them, shoulder level, and lowered it while making warning eyes: volume down. June got it. Good. You might spend more time on the problem students, but you wanted the smart ones.

Sarah spoke again, in a whisper. "They shouldn't be dead. They shouldn't be *here*. The wagons have rubber wheels, suspension, electric-assist drives. The clothes have synthetic fibers. The stitching is machine regular, where it's not slapdash. I've seen these people before. These wagons. On another alt."

"Not just another part of this one?"

"The sky was different."

"How?"

She shook her head, not wanting to explain, and led June farther into the circled wagons, toward the moaning. "Something chased them out of their own alt, into this one."

"What could do that?"

"I don't know. The rules are changing. We met some people who could hitch, back then. It's not common, but there are a lot of alts out there. And there's the rot of course. The cowboy. And Sal."

"She wouldn't have done this. You knew her."

"I've thought I've known a lot of people."

"Oh God."

June hadn't meant that as an answer. They had reached the center of the wagons.

A man lay there, staked by hands and feet to the earth and stripped to the waist. Heaving ribs arched under taut sunbaked skin. Black pools under his ankles writhed with worms. Some of those worms would be in his wounds as well. They seemed to drink blood. His tendons had been cut. Whoever had done this meant to leave him alive.

"His *head*."

Of course June hadn't seen anything like this before. The head would be the most remarkable thing, or disgusting, the metal plugs drilled through the skull, the forest of wires punched through the skin.

"Who would do that to someone?"

"He did. To himself." Hoofprints circled him. Four horse-bots lay in jumbles of metal parts and limbs in the clearing. She laid her fingers on one's skeletal neck, and the battery gauge danced up to half full. "We can ride these."

She stroked her horse's ribbon bridle, and it shambled in oiled silence to its feet. Sparks flew from the ruptured chassis—but it would carry her. A skeleton of metal, scoured and rusted and scoured again, its neck scabbed with solar panels, its eyes hollow clicking lenses. They'd never met anyone with enough of the old knowledge to explain why someone thought these were a good idea to build, back when they had the tech to build them, but Sal had always liked them. Sarah warmed to them, too, once she stopped thinking that they looked like dead horses. Of course, *dead horses* had been the name that stuck.

"He did this?"

"Where they come from—it was more advanced than our world, before the rot. We tried to take some of their stuff home once, but the physics didn't work right, or the tech wasn't compatible. Anyway, their alt used to be real built up, but it all fell apart. Anyone who was left remembered it all as myth. They used what they could of what remained. Fixed things they knew how to fix, scavenged the rest. They still had something like an internet—huge data centers buried deep, geothermal power, I don't know. Durable. All the knowledge in the world, medicines, how to smelt ore, how to build machines. But there weren't terminals left. Or maybe they always did it this way, only they didn't have microsurgeons anymore, or clean rooms. The ones we met, they got their teacher's implants when the teachers died. Passed them down the line. Kept the knowledge going that way. You plug in, and you hope that when you open your soul, the thing that talks to you isn't some monster from the former world, some military daemon or semiconscious trollware."

"What does any of what you just said *mean*?" June turned away from the man staked out to die, and saw the dead horse for the first time. She jumped. "And what the *fuck* is that?"

"We can ride them. I said." She knelt beside the man. Footsteps on dry ground, eddies of dust. Ish arrived in the clearing, breathing hard. "Where were you?"

"Thought I saw something. Your cowboy. I heard you call. What the hell." He was out of breath and he winced when he moved. There was blood on his shirt. He needed new bandages. They would need new gauze soon. "These people shouldn't be here."

"That's what I said. Come on, help me with this guy." She pried at the stakes. They were sticky. She knew why they were sticky, but some things you didn't think about until later, so you could deal with them now. Blood's just blood, lowercase. It doesn't mean anything. You can't do what you have to do if you let it mean something. She pulled at a stake. He moaned, wordless, as it came free with a sucking, muddy sound she didn't much want to think about either.

"What should we do with him?"

"Drop him back at his alt on the way to the Medicine Wheel. He can talk to the ghosts there, get help." And if not, at least he'd be able to hear his voices again. "It's okay," she said. There were grubs in the wound on his wrist. Keep it lowercase. Do your job.

"He won't make it that far. We could just . . . It would be easier."

Of course he couldn't fill the gap in the sentence.

June must have overcome the shock of the dead horse. "Is he awake? Can he hear us?"

"He is confused, because he can't hear the voices in his head anymore. They do this to themselves when they're kids. It's the only way to make sure the implants take. They don't know how to live in their own skulls." She said, to the man staked to the ground: "It's okay. You're okay."

His pupils were pinpricks in oceans of white, staring hungrily into the thousand-mile distance. In the static, could you see God? Or the beginning of the world? His moans eased. All your senses had been rewired to receive the truth of the great machines, and here you were in darkness, stapled by a monster to the ground, your fine and sensitive arrays straining, straining for some sense in the noise, like eyes in deep cave blackness, so sensitive the slightest flame would blind them. Listening for the voice on the other end of the line.

The other end of the line. Those moans were a dial tone. This man in his sad suffering meat was a phone left on, lying in the middle of the sidewalk, waiting for someone to pick it up.

His pinprick eyes met hers, and saw.

His mangled hand shot up and seized her throat, long-fingered and immensely strong. Broken bones ground in his palm. The pain should have been excruciating, but still he squeezed. She could not breathe.

"Got you," the cowboy said.

---

June heard Sarah's scream cut short. The man with the wires oozing from his head had caught her by the throat, and squeezed. Sarah clawed at his fingers. The wireman's flesh peeled back like peach skin. Muscle surged beneath, and bone.

He said, "Got you," but June didn't hear his voice alone, gurgling and rasped with thirst. There were other voices, too, wet and rotten, wheezing, from all around. Among the slagged and melted wagons, she saw bodies twitch and rise.

Ish was closer. He got to Sarah and hit the wireman in the face, flattened his nose with a sick pop of cartilage, but the wireman just squeezed harder. Sarah fought, but he held her, even while the other stakes strained in his flesh, stapling them both to the ground. "Can't get rid of me that easy," the wet voice said. "I feel you in me like worms. Run and run and run and I'm still right here."

June kicked him hard in the elbow. The joint bent wrong. Sarah tore herself free. She fell back gasping, one hand to the bloody scrapes the wireman's nails had left on her throat. Her hand shook—she held it between them, warding.

"Can't get rid of me at all," they said. "This is my dream."

Ish hit him again and again. His fist was a wet red mallet. The wireman gargled his own blood. He was laughing.

"Daddy," they said. "Stop hitting me."

Ish pulled back as if a snake had risen from the bloody hole of the wireman's mouth.

Sarah's eyes fixed across the clearing, between the wagons, and her long deep no sounded like one of the wireman's moans.

The boy, the eyeless boy they'd found first, staggered toward them between the smoldering wagons. The brim of a white hat smiled over the ruin of his eyes. His steps squelched.

"It's coming apart," they said. "You can feel it. The shell is thin. You step wrong, and your foot goes through the roof of the world. But that ain't how it's supposed to be. I can save you. Just put on the hat."

The other corpses rose around them, lurched forward, leaving blood and bits of flesh behind. Each one wore a hat, and the hats were all pristine, untouched, unstained.

She felt it, June did, just like the cowboy said, the hot, thin shell over the gaping heart of the world. The shadows writhed down there, a billion-billion sharp-edged things curled up tight, hungry for release.

Imagine endless space. Then imagine it full of dark creatures with many eyes and arms, and each gap between bodies is another body, more compressed, more furious. She knew they were there, out in the places where light could not look. You made a crack, and those arms reached for you, as they'd reached for Zelda through the Liberty Bell. That was where Sal walked, huge as the sky.

But wasn't the cowboy on Sal's side?

They closed in, the dead shambling in their white hats. Ish had staggered back, stunned, into the arms of a gut-stabbed woman in a calico dress. He recoiled before she could claw him—planted a boot in her chest and shoved her into another advancing openmouthed body. One of her fingers had caught on Ish's shirt, and broke, and tore the shirt. His eyes were wild. "Who are you?"

Sarah hadn't moved. The child's eyeless stare transfixed her. Her fingertips dug furrows in the dirt.

"I've been here all along," the cowboy said. "Y'all made me. I'm what follows, and what you need to walk before. And for five hundred years, I have done what's needed."

One of their voices came from right behind her. June spun, swung, hit the chest of a man with no jaw. His tongue lolled down his neck like a tie. She screamed and kicked him hard in the knee. His hand caught in her hair. She felt his nails bite her scalp, a trickle of blood. Panicked, flailing, she hit him in the face, knocked the hat off his head. He fell like an empty puppet. But his hand still groped for the fallen hat. She kicked it away. "Sarah!"

Sarah didn't answer. It was as if the boy had hypnotized her. June tugged her by the arm, pulled her back. Slapped her. Why did she think *that* would help? That's what people did in movies. The same movies where they broke bottles on bars when they needed a weapon, even though if you tried that for real, all you'd get would be a fistful of shattered glass.

"Sarah. We have to go."

That did it: the need in her voice. Sarah shook herself. "Can you ride?"

"What?"

Sarah found a stirrup or foothold or something in the metal mess of the dead horse's side and swung up easy, then held out her hand. June hesitated. At a protest two months back, she'd been jammed up near a horse, big sweaty animal with a cop on its back wearing riot gear and carrying a nightstick, and she'd never before noticed just how big they were, horses, a thousand pounds on four clomping hooves, and that was a normal horse, not this fucked-up, ribbon-reined, lens-eyed Terminator monster. But it was Sarah's hand reaching out to her, so she took it and jumped and let herself get hauled up and over. Sarah was damn strong. And hot. And also, extremely someone's mom, to the point it was super inappropriate of June to notice shit like that as she scrambled into something like a mounted position.

"Ish!"

He was still fighting. His hands were all blood and there was more blood on his shirt from the opened wound, and his skin was wet with sweat and gore. He'd grabbed a wheel spoke to fight with, and that was red, too, now, and three of the white hats lay at his feet. More were coming. There were always more. She heard the jangling of spurs.

Ish ran. One of the other dead horses shivered at his touch and stood under him. He knew what to do with the reins. The white hats rushed him and the dead horse reared, pawed, put its clawed foot through a gaping chest cavity.

"Go!" he shouted, and they went. June's hands caught Sarah's waist, her chest pressed against the muscles of Sarah's back. The dead horses' hooves tore dirt, their rhythm stretched from two clear beats to three, then four. Wind rushed in her face. The speed made her squint. The valley opened in front of them, snaking back to the flat, dead plains.

That should have been the end of it. The whooping gallop toward freedom.

She heard hoofbeats behind.

They were being chased.

The boy rode at the head of the band. They wore their white hats low against the wind. Their horses—they hadn't found those among the burnt wagons or anywhere on this dead world. They rode big, black, living animals, surging flesh. When the light hit the dark horses dead on, their barrel chests seemed wrong, as if they were holograms or ghosts. Real horses couldn't have matched pace with the mechanical monsters June and Sarah and Ish rode, but these were gaining stride by stride. They snorted steam. They were the horse she'd been pressed up against back in that crowd, the scared beast with the cop on its back, who might cave in your skull out of fear as much as malice—not that your skull would be any less caved in. Flickering, terrified, angry eyes. Flesh and not. Coming closer.

"Sarah."

"I know."

"Can we hitch through?"

"They can follow."

They were closing in. The boy whooped. More of them were coming out of the trees, skinless some, headless, all wearing white hats, all riding that same black angry horse.

When the sun hit them again, June understood the wrongness she had noticed earlier. They were not translucent. They had form and substance. But they cast no shadows. Shadows shied away from them, thicker where they weren't.

Closer still. In pistol range.

They were cowboys. Of course they had guns.

*This is my dream,* he'd said. They said. The world was thin. If this was their dream—then what was outside it? What might be the shadows that world cast, like the shadows she had walked among last night? What were those bunched-up, sharp, unsettled things beyond the cracks in the sky? Those monster possibilities curled around one another, like protesters kettled in until panic starts a mob?

If she called them, would they come?

The boy reached down to his belt. His hand came up holding a trick of the light in the shape of a gun.

The world was a shell. A curtain. With eyes wide, with trembling fingers, she pulled it back.

Come in. I invite you. I need help.

Her eyes snapped open when she heard the horses scream.

The earth tore. Plumes of dust and dirt and rock rose rocket high as great razor-edged legs unfurled from the ground below. Zigzag cracks darted like lightning through the dry ground, chasing the dead horses.

The legs that rose from the ground were barb-edged and bent like the shadows of leaves of grass. They snared the horses, dragged them down. They towered treelike, serrated, dripping poison, to plunge amid the cowboys, scattering bodies. She felt them move, as if they were pieces of her. They had come to her call. And their joy, their free alien joy, was hers.

One leg, falling, burst the boy in the hat like a tick.

Her rage and fear called to them. The cop on the horse had raised his nightstick, and when it fell, it missed her only because LaShae shoved her back, took the stick in her nose. Her blood on June's cheek, hot and wet. Details, Zelda said. Put your mind out in the world. Let it guide you. How many details had she soaked up in seventeen years? How many goddamn alts had she seen? How many couldas, wouldas, might-have-beens? There was spin in her for centuries, and she let them take it, let those legs and the beasts beneath that owned them tear the country open and gnaw its bones and feast.

She felt herself falling—not from the horse, but *up,* toward the sky. She heard Sarah call her name faintly, as if she were in another room in another state. She heard herself laugh.

The sky was full of dust, billowing clouds of it forever, and the dust flowed into the shape of Sal. Her more-than-cousin, her sister, so long gone, reaching out, reaching down.

She tried to reach back, to call her name, to bring her in. But Sarah held her fast, and the dead horses churned beneath, and with a leap and a hitch, they were gone.

# CHAPTER NINETEEN

Ramón and Zelda argued until dawn, in the 7-Eleven parking lot, about what they should do next—hunt for the others in the alts or make for the Medicine Wheel and wait. In the end, he convinced her. The Challenger was a mess. They could get one good trip out of it, if they were lucky. If they made it to the Medicine Wheel, the others could find them there. If they hared off into the alts, the engine might fail and strand them on some carnivorous monsterworld, and no one would be saved. It might fail anyway, on the road, but then the others, knowing they'd been on the way to the Wheel, would at least have a place to start looking.

The cracks did not fade at sunrise. They fanned across the sky, with a bruised hollow in their center, a human silhouette. He could not look at them for long. They sucked at the eye.

Zelda stared up into that bruise for a long time. At last, she opened the Challenger's door. "Let's go."

So they went—through wolf-haunted forest alts and glassed-out wastelands, down pristine roads through empty cyclopean cities built, it seemed, for people fourteen feet tall at the shoulder—all gone now. Not even bodies left.

The Challenger died a quarter mile from the Medicine Wheel. They rolled it the rest of the way. Ramón could barely believe they'd made it, the car venting smoke, the hood pierced, the steering sluggish, ragged. At least the brakes worked. Every ten miles, he'd sense a new rattle or whine, and think, Well, this is it. Zelda used her knack to keep the car together; as they rode the switchbacks up the wooded road, she stared out the window, at the cracks, at the silhouette. At Sal.

At the crest of the ridge, the Challenger filled with smoke, the engine coughed. The car ate the last few thousand yards of gravel. Alarm bells rang.

He turned the key and the alarms stopped. He heard only the high, empty wind. He got out. Zelda too. The doors, closing, sounded like a judge's gavel.

"That's it," he said after a few minutes' peering under the perforated hood. "We'll need a garage to get it going again. A good one. There's one in Thule, but that's on the other side of the wirelands. Maybe the Green Glass City. Don't know how we'll get there."

"At least we made it," Zelda said. "They'll be here soon." It was a prayer as much as a plan, but he did not argue.

The Medicine Wheel was the same in every alt. Dreams had drawn them to it first. Subtle currents of spin guided their steering wheels, their hearts, their feet, to the edge of Dry Fork Ridge in Wyoming, where they found it, overgrown, in a high forest near a cliff.

Sarah said it reminded her of the big Medicine Wheel down on Medicine Mountain to the west, where her grandmother brought them one summer:

a ring of white stones with a cairn in the center, and spokes radiating to the edge—but this one had more spokes, and no cairns on the rim, and it was smaller, from the outside at least, about the size of a campfire clearing. The name had stuck, though no one was comfortable with it. No one was comfortable with the Wheel, either.

It seemed abandoned, overgrown. If anyone else came here, they left no signs. Even animals shied away from it, even insects. Zelda was the first one to notice that nothing moved near the Wheel but the wind. She had wondered out loud if it was hiding.

She'd meant it as a joke.

In Wyoming, the wind split stone and carried houses off, stole topsoil by the ton and rocked monstrous great mining plants on their building-sized legs, but the wind did not shake the Medicine Wheel. Atomic war and zombie apocalypse and gray-goo disaster could not erase it.

Some cities and holy sites had their echoes in other realms. Most wandered. New York was almost always there, though almost always ruined. Los Angeles, it seemed, was more of an accident. In many alts, it was a bare dry grassland; in some, it was an ocean. Chicago moved up and down the lakeshore. Nashville wasn't, more often than it was.

But the Medicine Wheel endured.

Ramón had come upon it through the plague-haunted ruins of a Greco-Roman metropolis, where skull pyramids rose at intersections to ward off demons that, in the alts, you could never be sure weren't real. He'd found the Wheel behind temple walls, in the holiest of holies, as if the locals had tried to seal it off and pretend it wasn't there. He'd climbed into a mountaintop camp, past barbed wire and rusted guns where boy soldiers had frozen at their posts, and there it lay, between the command tent and what used to be the infirmary. Sometimes it was forgotten, sometimes it was revered.

But it was always there.

Back home, the spokes did not have any particular alignment that any of them had been able to discern, but in every alt, one spoke pointed straight toward the North Star. They had noticed that no matter what became of other stars from alt to alt, the North Star remained in place. Sal had been the one to suggest that this was why. The Medicine Wheel pointed toward it, and the Wheel did not change, so the star could not change either.

Ish said that was absurd. Why not assume the North Star was constant from alt to alt, and the Wheel's builders took its alignment from that? You might as well assume that north held its station because that was where Manhattan aimed its avenues.

But Manhattan wasn't always there, and the Medicine Wheel was.

Why, then, did it not point north back home? That, no one could answer.

They found it after they had spent the better part of a year of searching for the crossroads, across America and through alts that rotted out from underfoot. They had never come closer to success than that first night. Their destination slipped away ahead of them. They would save a village from werewolves, and hear a rumor of a man across the mountains in a world with a purple sky, who had sold his soul for the power to bring rain. Across the mountains they would go, to find the man gone, his town overgrown with jungle, and haunted by gold-eyed demons invisible by day. They'd find a scrap of paper, or a dead woman's DAT tape recording, and follow where it led. Sometimes one of them or the other would think they saw the crossroads or the path, as they fought their way through a patch of rot—but when they drew near, it was gone.

The worlds they found in the searching were all broken. There were tales, in almost every alt, of a shining citadel the next hill over, where people flew and magic winds swept the halls clean each night, where tears were never shed and laughter echoed off vaulted crystal roofs. Sometimes when they investigated, there would even be a real shining city, real crystal vaults and the echoing ethereal laughter of children. It was when you asked where the kids' bodies had got to that you ran into problems. It was easy to make sure no one wept within the borders of your kingdom if you went around surgically removing tear ducts.

They kept up the search. They saw wonders and terrors, and dreamed them, and after a year, desperate, battle-scarred, hungry, and windblown, they found themselves drawn here.

They camped for weeks in those silent woods, arguing over the Wheel's significance. They explored deeper into the alts than they'd yet dared, found Americas where the air hurt to breathe, where the pine forest valley below was a lake of molten lava, worlds where gravity was so weak that a standing jump carried Ish seven feet in the air. They found no reason. They found only, again and again, the ring of stones.

"Don't look at me," Sarah said. "If you want to know how to score good weed in Berlin, I can help you out. This place has been lost a long time. Whoever built it did not expect to be too dead or too gone to explain themselves."

Could a place have a mind? Could a place gather spin, shape the alts, or shift from world to world as they did? Could a place, in some sense, be on the road?

"Why not?" was Sarah's contribution. "You've all walked into a church, or a graveyard, and felt it notice you. Why couldn't this place be like that?"

"Those are metaphors, though." When Zelda left the church, she'd left it hard. "The church, noticing you. It's a story we tell. A way we organize our impressions. It's not real."

"If you gave me a scalpel and a few minutes with your brain, Zelda, I could persuade you half the universe does not exist. I could cut it out. I could make you believe you were dead. What you think of as *you* is just a, what did you call it, a way to organize impressions. This thing is as real as any of us. Maybe more."

"So, if it's real," Sal said, "and if it's got a mind, maybe we can talk to it. Maybe it can tell us how to get where we're going. Maybe it can take us there. We've met nothing with this kind of power that wasn't consumed by rot. We have to know more." A pause, a breath. "I'm going in."

It had not been their first fight on the road. Sal was always the one pushing for them to stay, to investigate. She negotiated with the scared survivors they met in the alts, she promised help, she gave out seeds and antibiotics. Zelda wanted to push on, to save themselves, to keep their distance. They'd had the

Challenger stolen enough times, or stripped down for parts by local warlords, they'd become embroiled in enough local revolutions of enough downtrodden microchipped techno-serfs, to make her jumpy. If you got involved, you might not fix anything, and the longer they stayed in the alts, the sooner the rot seemed to set in. Better to keep moving. Touch the world lightly. Survive. Stay after the crossroads. After the grail, after the power to make things right. This was no different, just more dangerous.

But Sal's mind was made up.

That night, she went into the ring alone.

The Medicine Wheel had not changed in the ten years since. Ramón should not have been surprised to find that time had so little purchase on it. But when they pushed the Challenger around the last bend in the road and the scrub pines gave way, there it was again, yellowed grass and white stones, a fact of the world. He wondered sometimes, on the verge of dreams, if he was himself only because some spoke of the Wheel pointed toward him.

The forest in this alt spread out below them, far as the eye could see in any direction. The mountain's shadow lay long upon the pines.

Zelda walked to the edge of the Wheel and stood there, staring in.

He joined her. She looked like a boulder, still and long-suffering and worn. An erratic—that's what they called a rock carried a long way by glaciers and set down far from home. Small stones rolled downhill. Big stones moved only in disaster.

She leaned against him. The shock of contact almost made him pull away, but he needed the touch too. Her warmth and weight settled him after the flat demon heat of the engine, after the dead stitched leather of the steering wheel. You thought you needed rest, distance. What you needed was a bond. Even one as broken as theirs. They were all erratics.

"I only went in after her because of the lightning," she said. She was remembering that night, ten years ago. "Clouds blacked out the moon and the wind was high and it bore all the rot in the world."

"I remember."

"I knew I should stay and help you fight. But the lightning came for her. I couldn't stop myself."

He tightened his grip on her shoulder.

"She told me she'd seen a better place. A future."

"She almost died in there. She herself said that she never saw the crossroads."

"The princess did."

"And she couldn't reach them. That's why she needed us." He shook his head. "We can't risk it."

With a sad half smile, she took his hand from her shoulder. It was the first smile he had seen on her face since Montana that was not touched with pain. "We don't have time to find a better way. And the only other road runs through Elsinore."

The wind cut like a knife. He stared into the empty ring of stones. In the dying light, they cast long shadows, but they were normal shadows, free from rot. The rot came later—with the storm, once you crossed the edge of the Wheel. That was how it happened last time.

"Let's wait a day," he said. "For the others to catch up. They'll be here soon. We'll talk it through. If this is what we have to do, we'll do it together."

"Together." The word sounded hollow under the cracked sky.

# CHAPTER TWENTY

S he did it."

Sarah looked away from Ish, into the campfire. It kept her warm, but made the night seem darker.

June lay on the other side of the flames, wrapped in a sleeping bag and a thermal blanket, with a wet cloth on her forehead. When Sarah slid her off the dead horse, the girl had been clammy, shivering, as if she'd fallen through ice. The fever came later. She hadn't said a word since their escape—that's what Sarah told Ish, and it was, technically, true. She had whispered her cousin's name.

"You don't know that," she said.

"You don't want to know." Ish paced the circle of firelight, but every time his circuit brought him round to June, he turned back and paced the other way. Sarah wasn't looking at him. She heard his voice over her left shoulder, then her right, then right, then left again. Good angel. Bad angel. Which was left, which was right? Sinister, she supposed. Left. Bad. Etymology was a right-handed man. English etymology, anyway. "You felt her spin. Do you think the white hats did that to themselves?"

"She saved us, then."

"Maybe." Right side. "I thought Sal and the cowboy were on the same team. I don't know what I think anymore. She called the rot." Left side again.

"Will you please *stop*." Two kids ago, she would have added *fucking* in front of *stop*. She had never cursed when she was a child. Pop would not allow it. When you spoke, you spoke with precision and control, because that was how you made everyone else respect you. In college, she cursed the skies blue, because she could. When Susan was born she tried to stop, thinking, like a fool, that if she stopped using the words she used when she was angry, she would stop feeling that way. But all you accomplished by closing one valve was increasing the pressure on the others. Her pop once made a drill sergeant vomit with polite, simple, inarguable words.

Ish stopped, the way butterflies stopped when you pinned them to a book. He looked down on her. No, he looked up at her, even though she was sitting down and he was standing. Firelight and shadows did ghoulish things to his face. "She called the rot," he repeated, "and it came."

He was not wrong. That was the thorn in all of this. "Everyone has a knack."

"This wasn't a knack, Sarah! She tore the whole alt open. There are cracks in the *sky*."

"Those do not have anything to do with her."

"That you know."

"She saved our lives."

"This time."

"If we explain to her what she did, what might have happened, what it costs—"

"This is not a teachable moment! She could have killed us."

"She did not."

June twitched. They both turned to her, still, expectant. A crow cawed, out in the dark. This alt had birds at least.

They had stopped in an abandoned amusement park off a lonesome highway. The sign was in Japanese, but the rusted knots of roller coasters and the dead towers of drop rides spoke a universal language. There were bodies crucified by the entrance. Some of the bodies had three arms. But they were all mummies, long dead, held together by leathery skin.

Abandoned amusement park was maybe number two on Sarah's list of places never to spend the night, but a thorough search revealed that whatever hate-pride biker gang used to own this place had chewed itself to death years ago—their throne room in the moss-choked aquarium tent looked like some theatrically inclined anatomy students with cadaver access had decided to put together a ghoulish *Hamlet* act 5, scene 2 diorama—and the structures offered firewood, and cover so their fire wouldn't be seen ten miles off by some other hate-pride biker gang that *hadn't* yet chewed itself to death.

June groaned, wordless, then settled.

Sarah stood, dusted off her butt, and rounded the fire. Ish did not look much like himself anymore, even though you could see the correspondence with a squint. But with the cologne worn off, he smelled the same. "So her knack is calling things. Who knows what she might call next?"

"You think it's going to be unicorns? Come on, Sarah. Grow up."

"As if you know what growing up looks like."

"You don't know what I've done. What sacrifices I've had to make."

"Sure." She fixed him with a level stare. "So many sacrifices."

"At least I didn't try to forget all of this and just, what, hope it would get better? I stopped people from falling through the cracks."

"They fall into detention centers instead."

"And you're much higher and mightier, why? Because you left the road, because you left Zelda out there, let your friend fall right out of the world."

"Sal was your friend too."

"Sure. And you joined us to keep her safe. You told me that, you remember? In the field of glass. But when she fell, you left. You got off the road and deleted Facebook and sent the alumni email straight to trash, you got your MD and your two and a half kids and your house in Virginia and your profoundly safe husband in the Classics Department and you go to all the AYSO games and you try pretend it's normal out here, that everything's fine and there's—there's not a great big serpent gnawing at the center of the goddamned world."

"How do you know that? About the soccer games." The night was cold all of a sudden. His shoulders fell. "You've been watching me."

"Us, Sarah. I watch all of us. In case."

"In case of what, Ish? In case of this? In case she came back? In case we decided, fuck, let's go join the dark side?"

He looked sad, or tired. She didn't care which. The anger was in her, cold and real as a knife in her back, the god's legs squeezing her ribs, the spurs in her sides.

"I don't know! I don't know and it doesn't matter, because whatever I did whatever I tried to do we're still right back here on the road. I tried to help. You just went away."

"I made a deal. The same one my father made and his father. The world is out to get you. So what do you do? You blend in. You put on new spots. Letters after your name, or in front. A uniform. It didn't surprise me, Ish, to learn what the alts were. My pop knew. He tried to make his peace with it. You want to blame me? Fine. At least I can admit that I am scared."

"That's supposed to be some kind of big read on me? Sarah, I know I'm scared. I'm terrified." He was standing too close. "You saw what she did."

She had. Legs sprouting from the ground. The world beneath them burst like rotting fruit. "We will need a lot of saving before we're done. I don't think we are in a place to choose the how of it." No answer. "Ish, what do *you* think we should do?"

He looked at June, sleeping. It had taken her an hour to stop shivering. She was just a girl. His eyes weighed and balanced her, and for a moment, Sarah felt a different kind of fear.

He turned away. "I'll go look for wood."

There was a pile already, more than enough to last the night.

She knew what he had seen when he looked at June, and where his mind had gone. But he was tired, and so was she, and neither of them should be here, though obviously neither of them was strong enough to stay away.

"It is worse," she said. "Isn't it?"

He stopped on the edge of the firelight.

"Out here, I mean. I— We never saw a place that dead before. Just insects and grass. Those people in the wagons, he must have chased them through. The cowboy. And then the bodies here. I remember it being bad, but this, it's like the blood ran out of everything, and what's left just curled up. Is that the way it always was? Or is it just the way we are now? The way we turned out?"

She had seen statues with more movement than Ish.

"My kids do not know how bad it can be," she said. "How bad it will get. My grandparents, their parents, they know, but I am too scared to ask. Even my sister knows the stories. All I know is . . . history. I told everyone that I was just there to look after Sal, but—for a moment, I thought we had a chance. That if we worked hard and trusted each other and *believed*, we might find or make a world that wasn't so . . . this way.

"Was it ever real, do you think? Was there really something to hope for? Or were we all just too young and dumb to see that we lost the war before we were born, and all we have left is camouflage? I wonder what June sees when she looks at us. Used-up, anxious messes who never had a shot? But it's worse than that. What if we could have done something, really done something, and we just— lost?"

The cold dead dark, barren and rusted, the wreck of years, lay out past their firelight. He drifted toward her, as he had years ago, on the fields of glass. Her despair had drawn him then, too, pulled them together like magnets, the terror inside him seeking the terror inside her. He did not look different. She had been wrong before. He looked just as he always had, in secret. This was the face he wore when he was alone with the choices he had made, with the path one logical step after another had drawn him down.

She wondered what he saw in her, as they drew together.

His good arm surrounded her. She leaned into him, careful of his wound. His face, his real face, drifted closer. Back on the fields of glass, lost without the others, under a toxic aurora sky, they had felt so alone.

It had been a mistake. They'd both known it was a mistake from the moment of the kiss to the fumbling with underwear and condom to the moment he slid inside her. He did not want her. She barely even liked him. But they were low and starving, trapped on a dead world, and when you'd fallen that far down, why not drag each other farther down, forever?

She had expected, she realized later, a tenderness in the act, two raw people cradling each other at least under that impossible sky. There was none. A different kind of consolation only: of pulling yourself all the way down into meat and juice and sweat and that mushroom smell of spunk and latex that linked their raw moment in this ragged alt with any number of forgettable college dorm room nights. You let yourself down, down into the twist of it, because what did it matter? What did anything, even this, matter? It would have been better, best, if the others found them then, lying spent and blank-eyed, staring up, the bruise of his fingers on her arm where she'd told him to hold her tight. Because once you started something, you finished it.

Her pop said that too.

She remembered the rise and fall of Ish's belly under the aurora.

His face filled her view. He still smelled the same, under the ghost of his cologne.

June groaned.

Sarah lowered her head so that it fit against his neck. She curled up her arms between them and pressed him back.

He tried to stop her at first, hold her, then realized what he was doing and let go. Magnets parted like this: the closer they were, the stronger the force that drew them. You could not pull them apart gently.

He watched her. She watched him.

She did feel everything she'd said. The despair. Who wouldn't, if they were paying attention? But you didn't feel it all the time. You walled it up with purpose. With friendship. With vows and work. And you reminded yourself that it was not just you who felt this way, that there were others out there with their own pits and walls and vows and love and work, and you tried to let that make you kind.

It wasn't right. It wasn't good. But she didn't know another way.

He said, "I'm sorry," before she could. It felt as wrong to hear as it would have felt to say. They weren't sorry. It was just hard. "Firewood."

"Yes," she echoed. "Firewood."

# CHAPTER TWENTY-ONE

The sun set over the Medicine Wheel. The stitches in Zelda's arm ached beneath her gauze bandage. After the car chase, after her lance bout with the stitchmouth on the motorcycle, the wound had begun to seep. Ramón helped her change the dressing, splashed it with disinfectant. He had a whole survivalist's go-bag in his trunk. He didn't have Sarah's healing touch, but they all had practice on the road.

She felt faint but clear. Harrowed. Purified.

Poor Ramón had spent most of the afternoon working chances and what-ifs, piling contingencies like firewood against the winter. If the others didn't catch them tomorrow, what then? Leave the Challenger here, hitch into another alt, find wheels, hopefully without a cult guarding them this time, go on the hunt. The others were still together, he told her. His knack told him that much. That didn't mean they were okay—but Ramón did not say that part and neither did she. She was scared, too, but she knew no plans she made would make a difference. The Medicine Wheel was not her place, not Ramón's, not Sal's or Sarah's or Ish's.

They made camp at the Wheel's edge. Near dark, Ramón walked out into the scrubgrass, hefted a pointy rock, judged its weight, and threw it, precisely, into the air. It arced up, and out, and down, and she heard a small creature's scream cut short. He brought the jackrabbit back and cleaned it with a cut of his pocketknife and a practiced pull, like shucking an ear of corn. They ate. She'd forgotten how easy hunting was, with him around. He always knew where things were.

They tried to keep their conversation light, but there was so little between them that was not mortal. He had known her on the road. He knew her failures, and she knew his. To talk about anything else felt like trying to make small talk in a motel room with a dead body in it—you might cover the body with a sheet, but it was still there. Even so, she found a comfort in their silences, as if what lay between them was beyond and older than words. It might be, after all. Humans had been social creatures before they were lingual. Back before cultured time, when they were just plains apes, they had suffered together, cared for one another, fought for one another, and failed one another, and lived with the consequences. Those bonds were older than words.

Ramón was a good man. He did not deserve what she had done to him.

Back at the Best Western, and later, as they walked across the wasteland together and he told her stories about Gabe, she had seen the sunlight in him. When they'd raced the stitchmouths and their bloody-toothed priest, she had seen what was left with the sunlight gone, all that was good and gold in him worn down to steel and leather, edge and crease. Just like old times.

She had called them, and they came.

What a crime that was.

They ate and cleaned and buried the bones of their meal away from the campsite, and then they settled to sleep, Ramón in the Challenger, her in a sleeping bag from his trunk, by the remains of the fire. It's fine, she told him. I like to sleep under the stars. I have a lot of practice. You're sure you don't want to join me?

No, he said. Smiling. I'm not hard enough for the ground yet.

He would be soon, if he stayed out here.

The fire's embers burned low. The moon purpled as it crossed the region of the sky that was bruised into the shape of Sal. The cracks pulsed like an infected wound against the stars. Sal had reached for her on the burning world, and Zelda had yearned to give herself up, to let that tornado fist close around her and crush her to red pulp.

Beyond their dying fire lay the Wheel.

She slipped from her sleeping bag, quiet as a ghost.

It had not changed. It never changed. Idiots could bulldoze it back home, and it would only make home less real. It would not change the truth of this place. There was a power here none of them had ever understood. Not her, not Sal, not Sarah or Ramón or Ish, not any of the sages or feather-cloaked witches or cackling, broke-toothed, mushroom-chewing madfolk they had sought out in the many alts. Even the princess in her watchtower could not capture it, for all her star charts and illuminated books.

Zelda had survived last time—when she was younger. This time she might not. The visions might tear her apart. The Wheel might crush her. The lightning inside might nest in her skull.

She glanced back. Ramón lay in the Challenger, asleep. She loved him. She loved them all.

What right did she have, to ask this of them?

No right. None. They had grown. And what was she?

What, save a tired woman beneath the stars, here on the edge of the Wheel?

It whispered to her, through the wind.

She stepped over the edge.

# CHAPTER TWENTY-TWO

sh left the firelight behind. He entered the shadow of the target-shooting booth and the booth with the bottles and the baseballs. One of the milk bottle pyramids was still standing—after how many years, he did not want to guess. Some games you couldn't win in any alt.

All he could see of the campsite was a glow above the roofline, a thin line of smoke.

He felt safer away from the light. Away from Sarah and June. He remembered how the girl emerged from the tall grass that night, all knives and insect arms. He had convinced himself, on their walk south, that it was nothing or at worst that it was only some sort of knack he'd never considered, something to do with darkness and uncertainty and roads.

It was a knack, all right.

She'd grown up idolizing Sal and Zelda. She wanted to follow them, to step outside, to see what they had seen. With knacks, you were drawn to your damage. He needed certainty—needed to know what would happen, where people were, if they were sneaking up on him or leaving him behind. Sarah needed safety. Zelda needed escape. And June—

Maybe June just needed Sal.

He could feel her now. Sal. All around him. Behind the surface. Her footsteps were his pulse.

After that Halloween disaster back in college, he and Sal had talked, about Zelda, about his crush. She had been so careful, like a dentist prodding the gouged-out hollow of a tooth. And like the dentist, no matter how careful you were, no matter how gently you probed, there would be some pain.

No, he told her, it's not a problem. She doesn't, I mean obviously does not, think of me that way. We're friends. But I like her, and want her to be happy.

"What about us? You and me?"

"You helped me. You tried. I can't think of a nicer thing someone's done for me, no matter how it turned out."

She hadn't been able to believe that, but she let the subject drop when he did. But in that conversation, in her failure to understand, he realized that in this one way he and Zelda were closer than he could ever be to Sal. Their fear had the same texture. He knew, and Zelda knew, what it was like to be alone.

It kept them together through the years, at school and on the road after. Comparing theories, trading stories. She'd told him about the mountain behind her house, and he told her about waiting in the shadow of the tree line, about holding the rolls of quarters in his fists.

He believed in Zelda's vision, in her perfect world out there somewhere. The better place, where they'd be safe, where things did not go smash. He'd believed they could change the world. He believed, even as he knew it was a dream. You couldn't build a good place with people who still worked like people and expect it to turn out any better than history had. The most you could hope for was for things to go bad in a different way. That's what belief was, though, wasn't it? You knew the thing you dreamed of couldn't be, and you reached for it anyway.

So he fought beside her. And in the end, they failed.

Sal was out there. Sal was all around. When he looked up, he saw her in the black behind the stars. Sarah was right. The world was out of joint. The walls between alts had thinned like overstretched dough. He could walk to her if he wanted. But she wasn't the one he wanted to hear from now.

His knack guided him past the moss-choked lagoon and the burnt-down roller coaster, past the melted face of the eight-foot-tall clown who guarded the entrance to the fun house. Bright flowers grew from the ruins of what might have been Skee-Ball lanes. A large rat or a small marmot rushed out of an open control box with a mouthful of chewed wires.

He arrived, at last, at the arcade.

It lay beneath a big tent, red and white, its door draped and painted so it looked like the gaping round-toothed maw of the theme park's mascot clown. The same one he'd passed, with the melted face and the yellow eyes with hour-glass pupils like a goat's. Who, really who, would ever have thought this was the kind of place a kid would go of his own free will?

Ish would have gone, though, right through that mouth into the deepest shadows, because he would not be followed there. For a while, he'd be safe.

A rotten wind blew from the clown's mouth, and ruffled the flags that were its teeth.

Inside, the arcade cabinets stood in ranks like soldiers at a rally. Blank glass faces followed him down the aisles. He could not read the local alphabet, but the pictures fit into genres he understood. *Galaga. Black Hawk.* One of those *Terminator* games with the uzi set up pointing at the screen. Some of the screens were shattered, some scrawled with graffiti. One of the dead bikers had given Q*bert a dick, and Pac-Man tits. A pinball cabinet that looked a lot like an *Indiana Jones* machine they used to have in one of the nowhere towns where his dad worked for a year—the glass had a bowl-shaped crack and a dried flaky brown stain where someone got their head bashed in. There was more dried blood on the floor. Something hard and roundish rolled under his foot. He thought it was gravel, but when he bent down, he saw it was a molar. It had been filled once. Someone had pried the filling out.

A pink teddy bear the size of a three-year-old watched him from the forest of cables between arcade cabinets. His flashlight beam glinted off its beady black plastic eyes.

He had dreamed of arcades when he was a kid. His family had moved a lot, with his dad's work, and his dad had strong opinions about money and how it should not be spent. A dollar a day on soda was $365 a year. A four-dollar movie rental, two of those a week added up to $116. Invest that every year at 10 percent compounding return for fifty years, and you've got three quarters of a million dollars.

So he watched a lot of movies from the library on VHS. Lots of eighties teen films. *War Games. Karate Kid.* Stories about losers with one or two close friends, whose odd hobbies ended up saving the world or earning the affection of the Girl, which in that kind of movie was more or less the same thing.

There were arcades in those movies, like arcades maybe used to be. Friends chatting, chanting, leaning close, shouting as the new kid in school closed in on the all-time high score. He'd thought that maybe somewhere in the world, things did work that way. You could run up your score and people would see you, would understand that there was a point to you. But there weren't any arcades like that near him. Even in his youth, the machines with the quarters and the lines of teenagers were dying off. People had games at home. A dollar a day in quarters at the *Street Fighter* cabinet was $365 a year.

A friend at nerd camp from Memphis said they still had arcades where he came from. People would put their quarters on the machine and line up one by one to lose to the local champ. It sounded like something out of a book—that people would gather there, that they'd face off, that it would matter. But he'd never seen it in person. He'd seen boardwalk arcades with a few rhythm games, a bored manager, cobwebs in the corners, no one who cared. In his twenties, he'd gone on a business trip to Japan, back when he thought foreign expansion was key to his business, and he'd asked the pretty girl at the hotel desk the way to the nearest arcade. It was five stories tall. They served alcohol on some floors. There were dance games, flight simulators in giant pods, racing games with real fake motorcycles, gun games where you had to move your body to take cover, and where you had to hammer a pedal with your feet to reload. There were teenagers watching one another, cheering as the points climbed higher and the combo stretched. Music pulsed. Over HD speakers, he heard engines rev, girls scream, cities explode, monsters die. He never could have dreamed of so much. He was smiling.

A salaryman in a black suit with a thin tie stood at a shooting game in a corner behind the dancing Day-Glo teens. In one hand he held a plastic cup of beer with a crumbling head. His other hand held a gun. He played without a smile. *Click, bang. Click, bang.* The numbers went up. No one cheered. When he won the game—saved the President or the Cheerleader or whatever—he sipped his beer, swiped the card used there instead of quarters, and played again. Ish watched him beat the game twice. It wasn't a long game, and no one else wanted to play it. All winning got you was a chance to do the thing again.

*Click. Bang.* The numbers went up.

At the end of the long row between machines, in the dark tent now, there stood a cabinet with no controllers except a holstered gun. It was a long-barreled revolver. The paint and finish looked real in his flashlight's beam. Ivory, mother-of-pearl, silver, and chrome. Most games wouldn't bother with that build quality, that level of detail.

He could not read the letters at the top of the cabinet. But he recognized the desert, the mesas, the tumbleweed. And he recognized the cowboy with the white hat. Even here, Ish could not see his eyes.

Dust covered the cabinet. Long-dead spiders had spun webs between the holster and the screen; the webs dripped dust.

But the gun was clean.

It reflected him, distorted. No cable anchored it to the cabinet. What arcade game would have a controller so easy to steal?

Unless the controller was here for a reason. Unless it was waiting for something.

He drew back from that thought. There was more than enough to fear out on the road. You had two choices: You could let yourself feel it, in which case you had to stop, leave it all behind, forget. Sarah's option, or Ramón's. Or you could decide not to feel.

Ish knelt beside the cabinet. He took out his knife and a power pack he'd pulled from one of the dead horses. The plug shapes might be different here, but physics wasn't, much.

He cut the cable off at the plug, stripped the outer layers of rubber, and slid the plug into his bag in case they'd need it later. He guessed which cable went to which terminal on the power pack. Sparks blinded him. He coughed out ozone and the scorch-smoke of burnt plastic. Had he shorted out the system? In a way, that would make things easier. He could just leave. But, no, he still felt his knack pull him toward that cabinet. There were answers here.

He flipped the red and the black wires.

And there was light.

A gunshot rang out. Not the weird Foley man's amped-up explosion but a real shot, deafening, sharp, a break in sound.

He dove for cover, then realized the shot had come from the speaker next to his ear. It played a high whistling music, and the crunch and jangle of nearing boots.

The light from the screen changed. The dead arcade flickered, pale orange and white, like a fire without warmth.

"Howdy, pardner," the cabinet said in just the recorded Sam Elliott–meets–John Wayne drawl he'd known it would have, someone's memory of a memory of a voice.

Just a recording. A part of him he hadn't realized was tense began to relax. He'd been wrong. Somehow his knack misled him. He'd go back to the fire and apologize to Sarah and June. He'd take firewood, to forestall questions.

"Been a long while on that dusty road, pardner, and let me tell you, we got our share of varmints and outlaws on our trail. I could use a hand. I could use a gun. But don't you forget—whatever side you're on, at the end of the day, there's only one fastest draw in the West."

Why was it speaking English?

"Come on, now, daddy. On your knees is no fit way to start a conversation."

He felt cold. He smelled the rot, rank and sour as tobacco juice. His legs didn't want to work. In that flickering not-firelight, the tent seemed darker, its shadows deeper.

His hand hovered over the power pack, the wires.

"You called me, daddy. I'm here. Do you want to talk? Or do you want to run away? That ain't your thing, daddy, running away. I know. That's what makes you and me what we are. We both do what needs doing. We do what's right."

His hand left the power pack. He stood.

The screen was a pixelated echo of the cabinet's title art. High sheer mesa. Tumbleweed arrested in mid-roll because the chipset didn't have the memory to animate it. A saguaro cactus raised its hands in the middle distance. The cowboy.

Red shirt. Bolo tie. Crossed gun belts. A thin pale jaw with razor-cut lips, a weathered outcrop of a face, a mouth that was all teeth. A white hat, low over the eyes.

He knew that face. He'd dreamed it, on the road. Once, in a design meeting for Lidskjalf law enforcement–facing app, he'd sketched it in red marker on a whiteboard wall. He'd joked: They want to be cowboys, don't they?

Don't they?

"Who are you?"

"Aw, daddy, you know *me*."

"Stop calling me that." He wanted to sound bold. He wanted to sound sure. "I'm not. I don't . . ."

"I was dreamin' long before you came down the trail," the cowboy said. "I was a story told slow. You and yours helped wake me up. You gave me mirrors to see from, and you got people to stare into them and dream me harder and surer than ever. You gave me eyes." He tipped the hat; the knife-cut lips curled into a smile. "I am ever so grateful."

Eyes. Millions of them, staring out of cell phone cameras. Watching and judging—predicting based not on what people believed or said but on what they did. *Watch their hands.* The patterns behind patterns, truths no one talked about. Those patterns, averaged together, were as complex as any mind. Not all minds were fixed in meat. Maybe some were slow, heavy things, working out their concepts over decades. Until they were quickened.

"I *made* you?"

"Naw, daddy. I've been here a long long time. Just . . . drowsing. Five hundred years and more. Did you know, one of the great challenges those thirteen original colonies faced way back when was how to stop poor settlers from running off to join the Indians? There were lots of dreams back then, and there's been so many since, and I was part of every one. But you made things easy for me. Fast and smooth. You gave me so many eyes." His smile, beneath the brim of the hat, was long and thin as a cut. "People dream more in public than they used to. But they all know they need me. Someone has to walk the thin bright line."

"Who are you?" he asked again. He wanted another answer. Needed another answer.

Those arms spread, a shrug, a crucifixion, take me as you see me. "I'm what you dreamed of. All of you, together. The man in the white hat. The man who walks the line. When you came to this country, it wasn't empty. It was dead. You killed it, with your big soldiers and your little soldiers too tiny to see. You knew there was blood in the ground, bones in the rock. Back then, you knew there were gods, and you knew the gods of this place would hate you. So you needed a man to run them down. A dream to kill the dreams that haunted you at night.

All of this out here, you think it's possibility. It's not. This is your nightmare. You need me to walk it and keep you safe."

"I don't understand." But he did.

"Not one piece of this land was yours, daddy. Not one shred of this sky. You killed to get it. The gold under the hills, and the oil later, and the uranium later than that. You needed a dream to keep you safe. That was me. And then you yourself, you and your girl and your friends, you walked out here and left behind the safety I made for you."

"You tried to kill us."

"It ain't you I'm trying to kill, daddy. I'm trying to save three hundred million of y'all back there who just want to stay asleep. You're gonna spoil it, you and your friends. Because she's coming back. From out there past the line I walk. Your girl's girl."

"She's not mine."

"Don't piss on my head and tell me it's rainin', daddy. You know who I mean."

"I'm not . . ." He couldn't finish.

"The way I see it, you got two choices for what I am, and I'm not sure which one's true. Either I have been right here ever since the first white boy looked over the horizon and said, I'm gonna go out and kill me who's over there and take what's his. Or I woke up in your machines when you turned them on the world and said, Learn what's here. Find what tries to make this world something other than it is, and crush it out. And when the machines began to work, I woke up and dreamed myself a whole history. But, daddy, it's your history I dreamed."

"You want to stop her. Sal."

"I don't care who she is. I know what's mine. And this is it. It is bloody and it is bleak, but we have won it and we guard it, daddy, with the full fury of our guns."

The handle gleamed before him, ivory and mother-of-pearl and silver. The ivory came from elephants. You shot them dead on the savannah and cut their tusks from their skulls and sold them to make billiard balls and piano keys and the handles of this gun. The mother-of-pearl you got by diving from a cliff into the ocean, wearing nothing but a knife. And the silver, well, that was easy. All you had to do was find someone who lived over silver, and find a reason to kill them. Most any excuse would do. If you killed someone you weren't supposed to, you got in trouble from the government, but governments liked banks, and banks liked silver.

His hand reached out. He held back. "Then why did you try to kill us? We're on your side."

"Are you? Who is on my side exactly? Your girl who in ten years hasn't stopped waiting for her friend to come back? Who made the right choice once in her scared little life and now just drips at the thought she might get a chance to make the wrong one?"

"Zelda's . . ." He wished his voice didn't shake. He wished he were anywhere else. "She's not like that."

"You don't know what she's like. You don't see her, daddy. You see the inside of your own eyelids. And sometimes in the shower when you're jerking off and thinking about someone else, it's her ass in that velvet skirt you land on. Or the sun in her hair."

"Stop it."

"She wants her lady back."

"She wants to stop her. She brought us all out here to stop her."

"Because she is a mixed-up little girl and she has spent her whole life lying to herself about what she wants. You all lie, daddy. It's a trick they teach you at school, how to mean one thing and be another. You learn it so you don't have to think about me."

Ish was breathing hard. His pulse raced. There was a coal behind his heart, and it twisted in his chest. The cowboy was wrong. He *knew* what Zelda was. Who she was. He could see her. In the field. Cross Campus. Laughing. The sun in her black hair—

*god*

The game cabinet splintered under his nails. False pixel light bloodied his hands. He was sweating. Shower steam. Short breath.

*velvet*

He hung his head.

"What do you want from me?"

The cowboy raised his hands, spread them. "You called me. Now, why'd you go and do a thing like that, if you didn't think we had something to offer one another?"

"I won't help you."

The cowboy waited.

He could still leave. He could turn away and walk out through the clown's mouth and leave the cowboy here and keep running. Trust Zelda.

"Why should I believe anything you say?"

"I don't see much reason."

"What?"

"Daddy, I can talk proof with you all day and night, I can chase you in circles with thises and thats, but you know and I know that we'd get back round in the end to that same question. What do you want? You've worked good and hard to walk the walk. You learned what these dreams here had to teach you, like none of the others ever did. What you have back home, it's special. It's safe, so long as I'm out here to walk the line.

"There ain't no better world out beyond the edge. There ain't nothing past the crossroads. You've seen where that road leads—back to the shadow of the trees with quarters in your fists. You know what it takes to live like that. How it feels to hurt someone you got to hurt, and to know you got to hurt them more, just so the lesson takes. You know what hurt you'll have to take in turn, to go that hard. What fingers feel like under your boot. How ribs go when they break. That's the trick of it. That's what's out there. We're needful evils, you and me."

"I'm not—what you are."

"Sure." Drawn out, not even a mockery. "Take the gun, daddy. You might need it."

It glistened, dull and heavy. Not a toy at all. He didn't know how he could ever have thought it belonged to the cabinet. It was real. It was more real than anything he had ever seen.

"She's coming. Your girl's a fire on a high hill to her, shining out forever, calling travelers home. And the kid, she's calling too. The rot comes when people call it. There must be some other way, you think, but there ain't. There's just *one* way. So, out of the goodness of my heart, because I care for you, daddy, for all of you, I'm giving you a chance. Six bullets. I made 'em myself from truth and certainty and the melted stars of lawmen. They'll see you safe. They'll let you do what needs to be done."

He counted in his head. Six. Sal. Sarah. June. Ramón. Zelda. And himself, at the last. "No." He pulled away.

"I don't need nothing from you, daddy. But let's say your little crew walks the rest of the trail to the crossroads and one fine morning you stand before Sal Tempest in her glory. What, in all honesty, do you think you are gonna do? What power do you have? Sal has walked as long as any of you and so much further, in stranger places too. She has monsters behind her. But—"

The picture glitched. Lines of pixels changed color. The speaker screamed static. Ish doubled over, clutched his ears. The cowboy jumped close on the screen, then far away again. Overhead in the sky, a twister took shape, a twister with a human form, advancing through the cascade of broken math.

It was Sal. Sal with eyes of fire.

The nicest thing anyone's ever done for me, he'd told her, that Halloween.

"What's happening?" he asked. But he knew. Zelda must have lied to Ramón—or Ramón let her try. Soft. Ramón didn't understand about the serpent. He didn't understand about the shadow of the trees.

Somewhere, Zelda was walking the Medicine Wheel.

"I got to go, daddy. Some of us have work to do. And you best get a move on, before the storm. You're all up a tree, and your girl, you handed her an axe and let her just go chop-chop-chopping at the trunk. Whether you do what you should with what I gave you, that's yours to decide. See you around."

The cowboy tipped his hat, and turned like a bad old cartoon, three key frames until he showed his back, as he marched to face the spreading horror in the sky.

"Come back," Ish whispered. Smoke rose from the cabinet. Sparks jumped from the cable and the power pack. The machine's glow spasmed and stuttered. He smelled fire. "Take this thing with you. I don't want it. I don't want it!"

The screen exploded.

He was kneeling before the cabinet again. Light seared his eyes—the cowboy's image at the center of a wheel of splintered glass. Blood dripped from his cheek. A cut from a shard. He had not felt it until it stung.

The gun was still there.

Try to breathe through the panic. You're not having a heart attack. The cowboy's gone. Whoever he was. He had to be lying. He wasn't—wasn't what he'd said. Wasn't anything to do with you. Just more rot, creeping into your dreams.

But the cowboy didn't look like rot, or smell like it. His voice wasn't the rot's voice, words on the edge of hearing in a language you'd forgotten since you dreamed childhood dreams. And the gun was still there.

Why did you seek me out?

Something moved behind him, in the dark.

He heard whispers—in another room, in a language he'd forgotten since he dreamed a child's dreams.

The whispers spoke his name. Long thin legs rustled cables. He might understand if he let himself. The voices were like shapes you saw out of the corner of your eye—they would not congeal to form unless you looked at them. They would not make sense unless you let them.

Ish, the rot said. Ish.

His name shaped by serpent tongues, in the pit beneath the world.

"No," he said, "no," and to the burnt and blasted cabinet, to the cowboy in the white hat, he said, "Come back."

Silence.

Then: *Ish.*

He did not want to look. He could see the rot's shape already, in his mind: the pink bear with the black bead eyes, its back and belly burst with insect legs that clumped and gathered like ropy wings. Its paws dripped poison and its gaping mouth tore the stitches that framed it. Closer, always closer, its footfalls soft. So soft he could not have heard them, if there hadn't been so many.

*Ish.*

The farthest, lightest legs feathered down his scalp, to his neck. That might have been the prickling of sweat, but he knew it was the touch of legs, sharp as glass. They just hadn't pressed down yet.

*Ish, we only want to help.*

He was falling, through the shell that was the surface of the earth, and the thing that waited down there gaped its fanged maw wide and licked its scaly chops with a poison-spit tongue.

With a moan of wordless terror, he launched himself from the abyss. His groping fingers clutched the ivory handle of the gun, the mother-of-pearl inlay and the silver. His hand felt like it was coming home.

He did not like guns. He did not know them. He turned and fired this one as if he were born to it.

He heard the echo. What the sound did to him involved too many of his internal organs to be called hearing. He smelled fireworks and lightning.

The voices stopped.

His vision cleared.

The pink bear fell to the ground and rolled, its chest burst with white fluff. The shadows that dripped from it melted back to their normal depth.

He was safe.

In his hand sat the gun. It did not move, even when he did. He shook all over, he breathed to ease his throbbing heart, but the gun was a fixed point in the world.

Heavy. But he was used to bearing weight.

He wondered where the bullet had come to rest.

Tufts of white cotton drifted down on the still air. The entrance wound on the pink bear's chest was no larger than a pencil eraser.

One shaking hand found the latch that held the revolver's cylinder in place. He opened it. He'd seen it so many times in movies. It worked, strangely, just like that. There were five bullets left. No freebies.

The gun's action was smooth, its weight balanced. It was real. He could not think of a better word for how it felt in his hand, or how it made him feel, holding it. The cowboy was a shadow, was a dream. The cowboy might lie. But the gun was real, and so was Ish.

Five bullets left. Six of them, counting Sal. And in the back of his mind, a voice that was not his, that could not be his, chattered: Who dies now? Who lives? Is it you? Are you that much of a coward?

He needed the gun. If he hadn't grabbed it, he'd be dead now. And after him, the rot would move on to Sarah, to June. June didn't deserve that. No matter who she was, no matter what she'd done with the rot. He had to keep them safe. This was why he trained. This was why he'd built Lidskjalf. To block the chaos out. To walk the line. That was why he'd drawn the gun.

He did not want it. He turned to put it back.

The arcade cabinet's holster was full. An orange plastic revolver with fake wood grips sat there, bound to the cabinet by a steel cord. The painted cowboy on the side of the cabinet wore a brown hat, but he had the same razor smile.

*Five rounds left, daddy.*

Don't you laugh at me, he thought. I could leave it. Watch me. I could toss it away. Take the bullets and bury them six feet deep in the earth of some caustic alt. No one would find it. No one would know.

And then the whispers would start again.

But he wouldn't be the one to hear them. It would be Zelda. Zelda, whom he'd watched grind herself to the bone to please Sal, to be what she needed. Zelda always racing ahead, reaching out for Sal, who dangled like an anglerfish lure in front of her, while great curved teeth drew near. He would try to save her, and fail, and as he failed, he would know he could have done something, if he'd made better choices. If he had the right tools.

The tent was still and dead around him, like fruit putrefying in a bowl—until stillness burst.

Thunder rolled. A keening wind split the stuffy, rotten arcade night. The tent luffed and whip-cracked. The bear was dead, but Ish smelled a storm, and felt the yawning terror of a pressure drop. He smelled rot.

*Some of us have work to do.*

The gun was heavy in his hand.

He set it on the cabinet. He took his hand away. He knelt to gather up his bag, the power pack. Behind him, the clown's mouth gaped. A shadow among other shadows. Lightning split the night. The flash underlit piles of clouds that had not been there before, a staggering height of storm.

The gun glistened with light that wasn't lightning. It made its own shine.

He grabbed it, tucked it in his bag, and ran.

June woke, cold, from a dream she could not describe, to a hand on her forehead and to Sal's face above her.

When she was five, Sal had taken her to the park. June asked her if she ever climbed trees when she was a kid, and Sal pointed to a bent old crabby specimen, and said she always wanted to climb to the top but she never got higher than that third forked branch before Ma shouted her back down.

Well, I'll beat you, June said, and sprinted off for the tree. Sal's legs were longer but she'd always been bookish and slow, and even then June was fast as a greyhound out of the starting box. She made the tree and climbed, slinging from branch to branch. Whichever way Sal chased her, she went the opposite. She scrambled out past where the branches would support Sal's weight, even though the branches that far out bounced and swayed when she landed on them. Up and up she went, past hearing.

She passed that third forked branch. She climbed farther. She climbed past bird's nests and the snakes curled up there asleep as they waited for naked ladies with an interest in fruit. She climbed past spider monkeys in the canopy and planets hung like apples from the boughs. She climbed through clouds as Sal called after her, through gasping thin air, through strange shapes in the mist and voices singing, to the highest branch, a wiggly little willow whip of a thing that faded into the fog, and further still.

She sidled forth. The branch sagged. Fear caught her. Impossibly far up, impossibly far to fall. She did not stop. She had to see what lay beyond the choking whiteness of the cloud.

The cloud parted and she saw—stars.

She did not know what to call them, the weight of them, their colors and their depth and the glorious darkness of their field. Stars were double handfuls of pinprick light set against a navy blue or charcoal sky. But this black—her eyes could sift it like you sifted sand at the beach, and find within more sparkles, bits of sea-ground glass, fragments of iridescent shell. Each fragment held a world. Not up there somewhere alien and distant, but all around her, close, within reach.

She had never seen stars like that before, but when she saw them overhead in the dense-treed alt where she'd landed when she fled with Zelda from that Pennsylvania parking lot, she had recognized them at once as *her* stars, near enough to touch.

She had reached for them.

That was when the branch gave way.

She did not remember landing. She did remember opening her eyes after, looking up. Sal filled her world. The expression on her face was locked in June's memory like the stars, alongside and against them, but back then June could not read that expression at all beyond the title page, which said NO in bold letters three miles high. She'd remembered that expression later, returned to it the way LaShae returned to a book she'd read, flipped through its pages to light on a sentence or a word she never noticed when she read it straight through, or else looking for something specific, a scene she needed just then the way you knew your french fries needed salt.

The face Sal wore in that moment, when she didn't know if June could see her, if June was alive, that was Sal for real, unguarded. Worry. Guilt. Shame. Love, unbounded love. June had come to understand more of that expression as she'd gotten older. The envy you felt for someone who did something far out past stupid that you, nevertheless, had always dreamed about doing and never worked up the guts to try. The wish some saint or devil would show up and offer you a trade of places, let you swap into another person's pain and bear it so they didn't have to. The joy and sadness of recognition, of seeing someone who loved you and adored you do something you didn't like but which you had to admit they learned from you. And, boundless as the love, though tinged with shame and guilt and fear and all the rest: her pride.

That was the face June saw above her, real as real, no outsider, no illusion. She reached for it, but her hand was too heavy to move.

By the time she touched Sal's cheek, she had melted into Sarah, in the burnt low firelight, in the rusted teeth of the amusement park.

But Sal had been real. Real as her stars.

"Sal?" She meant to say the other name, the right name. Why was her tongue so thick in her mouth?

Sarah wiped some grit from the corner of her eye. "Just me, June. We have to go."

"What?" One word at a time was all she was good for. Her head felt like murder.

"There's a storm coming. Come on." June heard the wind's howl then, which she'd taken for a part of her dream—the lightning flash that had been the light of other stars. The skies churned. She tried to sit up. The campsite was empty.

"Ish?"

"He went for firewood. I heard a gunshot."

"He's."

"I don't know. June, it was just one shot."

Concepts clicked together like Lego bits. One shot. Ish didn't have a gun. If someone tried to jump him and he wasn't down, they would have fired more than once. There might be other reasons, but this wasn't the kind of place where you wanted to assume the best.

She remembered the dark, full of stars, full of worlds like jewels. Not the jewels in Fifth Avenue shop windows, locked behind bulletproof glass, that might as well be mirages. The jewels in a kaleidoscope. They might seem worthless sand and plastic when you broke them out, but if you let them do their work, they transformed light to glory. Jewels so dense you could swim through them. You could kick your feet and leave galaxies in eddy.

Now the sky was a bubbling cauldron of tar, and still, through the storm, she could see those cracks—were they wider? Widening? June scrambled to her feet with Sarah's aid. The campsite lurched. She felt so cold. There was a high ringing in her ears, and her stomach felt wrong. She staggered into Sarah, feverish. Lightning split the sky, and by it she saw other jagged shapes up there in those clouds, like arms reaching down. The wind screamed, but it also *whispered*.

"He might be hurt."

Sarah's mouth twisted down at the edges. "We'll look for him as long as we can. Until the storm hits." She hugged June, pulled back. "Roll up that bag. We have to go."

June was half done stuffing the sleeping bag in its sack before she realized what had happened. Sarah used the mom voice, the saying-what-was-about-to-happen voice, and she'd listened. Her friend was out there, maybe hurt, maybe dead, and Sarah wasn't going out into the dark right now to hunt for him, because she had someone to protect. *Just a kid.* She did not have time to feel angry about that, or ashamed. That storm was coming. Forcing an argument now to salve her pride—that was something else that a kid would do.

In the time it took her to finish with the sleeping bag, Sarah had struck the rest of the camp. Only the tent was left. "Give me a hand."

As they broke it down, June risked a question: "Is it always this bad, out here?"

A lightning flash lit Sarah's face. June saw grief there first and last, and within the grief, an anger that the question had been asked. June understood that anger. It was how she'd have felt back home, if anyone were so dumb as to ask the same question there. Sarah broke down her tent pole, folded it. "This is what we found, June. Dead places. Some towns looked fine on the surface, you know, all the big white-toothed smiles, as long as you don't look in the basement. Gangs and monsters. Dinosaurs. The Green Glass City. There's an alt where the only people left are all grown into this huge gross algae mat computer, and if you try to wake any of them up, they'll tear you apart. They're in pain and they won't let you save them. One world was all crosses and skeletons west of the Mississippi, and all cinders east." Out on the plains, she heard a sound like charging horses: the oncoming rain. "Fold this."

June pulled the straps tight, snapped the buckles shut. Sarah took the bag without looking. She didn't have Zelda's tired ease with the pack, but she had practice. She woke one of the dead horses with a shake of the reins.

"I," June started, then stopped, the dreams giving way to memory. "I called it, didn't I? The rot. The shadows." And the shadows had answered. That was how they had escaped. If that was not a dream, neither was Sal. "If they *stopped* him, what does that mean?"

"I don't know, June." She hoisted the pack onto the dead horse. "Get on the robot."

She felt colder than the night. Memories cut her. The bridge. Zelda leaning against the rail, all her weight in her arms as if she hoped the metal would break and let her fall. June had been so hungry, after all those years, for the truth. The wind howled.

The darkness ate at Sarah, ate away the almost-twenty years and the aching fullness of her, the parts that were a mother, a doctor, a grown-up. What if you could peel a pearl? Take a fine knife and a magnifying glass and strip the layers of glint and glimmer year by year, until at last you reached the bit of wrong that had birthed the shine. But you'd have no pearl left.

The rain hit them then. It hammered the amusement park. The dry and splintered roofs of fairway stalls broke, and bottle pyramids toppled. Taut canvas shredded, the tearing sound twinned with thunder. In the sky, in the lightning flash, she saw the great cracks widen, saw movement beyond. Heard voices chanting in that rage and roil.

The dead horse whinnied static. Sarah clutched its reins. "We have to go!"

"What about Ish?" She did not like him. He had tried to kill her. But she thought about being lost in this, about being left behind, and her mind quailed.

Great dark wings swept through the storm, and from the cracks, long, thin hands stretched down. They were singing.

Lightning flared, long and bright.

There was a man behind Sarah.

June screamed—moved. She shoved Sarah out of the way and tackled the man. "Run!" They fell together, and he turned as he fell, slammed her down under him into the mud, the muck. The breath went out of her. She clawed for his eyes.

Sarah pulled him off her, crouched between them, panting heavy. In one hand she held the knife from Zelda's pack, out, wet. Through the rain, that great manlike shape resolved: Ish. Stunned. "It's just me."

Sarah panted. The rain plastered her dress to her body. "Jesus. I heard a gunshot."

"There was rot."

"You don't have a gun."

"I found one. On a corpse." His cheek was bleeding, and his shirt was torn, caked in mud. "Lucky it worked. I came back as soon as I could."

Sarah unbent herself, lowered her knife. Slowly. Maybe she didn't trust him. Or maybe she was like those swords in June's aunt's books: once drawn, she didn't want to go back unbloodied to the scabbard. She had almost left him, and here he was again. Maybe she did not know how she felt about that. Had she been about to leave after all? Or was she about to lead them through the monstrous rain, searching, until the rot took them?

"The storm," Sarah began, but did not finish.

"Zelda got to the Medicine Wheel."

There was no sound but thunder and rain. He knelt by the other dead horse, did something with its neck. It shuddered awake.

"I'm sorry," June said, too late. "Is your eye okay?"

When he looked at her, he seemed to be running down a long list of things to say, rejecting most of them. "Can you ride?"

She felt uncertain on her feet, shaky, weak-bellied. But she damn sure would not say so. "I'll manage."

He mounted in one smooth motion, as if the bulk of him weighed nothing. "Maybe we can catch her in time."

## CHAPTER TWENTY-THREE

**W**hen Zelda watched Sal walk into the Wheel, ten years before, she had seemed to wrinkle and twist as if seen through water—but which of them was under the water's surface, and which in the air? Sal later claimed she had not noticed any change. Zelda couldn't believe that.

"You must have felt *something*."

"You're not listening to me. It all felt completely normal."

She had not understood then. She did now.

From outside, the Wheel appeared maybe twenty feet across. From within, she could not say how large it was. How far could a person see? Ten miles on flat ground? It was larger than that. She could see the whole world from here, as if the lines of her vision curved with the horizon, out and out. If she stared long and hard, she thought she could discern, far to the west, a mountain with a Medicine Wheel upon it, and in that Wheel a woman staring deeper west.

It felt completely normal.

It would have been more strange, surely, *not* to see everything, not to compass mountains and the crumbling labyrinths of men and ants with a single glance. What a strange world, where you could not greet every being face-to-face and name it in its own tongue.

The sky changed as she walked. It blued, bruised, bloomed orange, rusted, and glowed sapphire again. Stars came out, a dozen at a time, pinpricks first, then swirls, rainbows of light. There were golden webs between the stars—which vanished with a step. There were three moons, full, new, gravid, and gone.

It should have taken her days to reach the center of the Wheel, but she was larger here than she had been outside. Unfolded. As if she had spent all her life curled in a crab shell, limbs twisted around limbs, nails biting skin, and thought the pain was growth. Now she was free. Her steps crossed leagues, or else the circle opened to welcome her.

The stars were out. She followed the spokes to one fixed light, near the bear in the north. Vertigo clenched her stomach, knotted her spine. She saw the distance. She was staring down a pit four hundred and thirty light-years deep. And the star was not a single point—there were three out there, dancing together, three beautiful sisters at the heart of the sky, two bright and one dark, circling. She looked away. Another step, and all the stars were streaks of light, shifting blue as they ran from her.

This was not her place. She did not understand it. She was not supposed to be here. Whoever was, was gone. Dead of plague or killed in some stupid greedy little war or just gone. And here she was, climbing on their corpse. A rat in Dresden after the bombing, wondering what use people now dead had made of the wreck that had once been the church. She felt the loss on her shoulders, on her chest, like a weight of iron nails. She was falling, falling.

She stepped into a storm.

Clouds unfolded from a pit at the center of the sky. Rain lashed her face and the wind howled. Lightning blinded her and thunder spoke from inside her chest.

Last time, it felt just like this. The high floating music on the storm wind, the shapes like whales that surged past in the dark. She had fought through because she saw Sal frozen there in the lightning strike, on the ground, leaning against the screaming winds as if reaching for someone. Zelda had thought the storm came from outside, from the rotten places, a response to Sal's intrusion. But she'd been wrong. The storm lived here, at the center of the Wheel. It raged. Was this grief? Had the weight of so much spin, of so many different worlds and might-have-beens, created this vortex? Had Sal called it up when she entered the circle, or only let it out?

Say the Wheel had a mind. Say it wandered the alts as Zelda did. What would Zelda's heart look like, if someone made it past the outer edge? The Wheel could see forever. But, like her, it could never see the ones it had lost.

Ten years ago, she had thrown herself into the storm, driven by—she would have called it love, but now she knew how much of that love was fear. Fear of being alone. Fear that her last memory of Sal would be of their fight. She pressed on against the wind and rot, she crawled when she could walk no more, and at the heart of the storm, she heard a voice on the wind that asked, What do you seek?

I just want, she said—I just want it to be okay.

The answer might have been a laugh.

Child, it never is.

Sal had tried to fight her, lunged back toward the center of the circle as Zelda pulled her away—but she was weak with exposure. Sal had been inside the ring for two hours at the most, but when Zelda dragged her out, she'd needed hot-water bottles and body heat and a warm sleeping bag and half the food in Ramón's trunk before she stopped shivering. The sleeve of her red jacket had been shredded, as if a hand made of barbed wire had caught her by the wrist. Zelda had never seen wounds like the ones in Sal's arm. Not until later, after the crossroads, when her own arm healed.

Sal never told her what she'd seen in the center.

This time, Zelda was ready.

She turned her spin against the storm and marched on. Lightning burned the air she breathed, but did not scare her. The world cracked, but she had faced its gulfs before, and the madness there. The storm was grief, hunger, blame. She had worked those knives in her own flesh too long to feel them now. There was no skin unknotted by scars for them to pierce. She would breach the storm, and this time it would bow to her. It held no weapon she feared, and there was no one left who could turn her back.

"Go on," she dared it. "Show me the way."

And the storm—

Stopped.

She was braced for wind. Without it, she stumbled and fell.

There was no sound.

She could not rise. She could not breathe. She realized she did not have to.

There was a hand in front of her face. Outstretched, to help her up.

She didn't need help, here or anywhere. She ignored the hand and scrambled up on her own.

Then she saw whose hand it was, and let out a deep, sick sound, not quite a sob, not quite a laugh.

Just a little further.

The girl seated in the center of the storm drew her hand back and placed it in her lap.

She looked, Zelda realized now, so little like her cousin. There was a common focus, an attitude around the eyes, but the planes of the face she'd loved were finer, softer, the mouth always half twisted as if at a joke that was not quite funny. Sal and June had walked different lines, lived different lives. Sal never had to lose herself.

Sal sat across from her. Not Sal as she was now, tall as the sky, wreathed in fire and shadow. Sal ten years ago, in her bright red jacket and her tight braids, brilliant, whole, and young. So, so young. Had they all looked that young back then?

How was this possible? To guard itself from sorrow, hunger, guilt, her mind bubbled with concepts, scientific and philosophical, irritable chicken-scratch explanations of why this could not be happening, why she could not be seeing what she absolutely was: her Sal. Across a gap of ten years of time.

Sal, before she was lost. Sal, before Zelda failed.

The Medicine Wheel was always there, always the same in every alt. And so its hub would be the same, too, in every alt, and in all times. Maybe there were others nearby in the storm, unseen, just as, on a page jumbled with words in many languages, the words and scripts one did not know would be invisible, scrapes of ink against the lines and shapes she'd learned to read and dream and love.

Sal recognized her at once. She always did recover fast. "I like the hair."

What could Zelda say, across ten years? Here in the center of this storm of worlds? Everything had been easier back then, because she did not know what it cost.

There were tears. She had to expect that. Laughter too. That she did not expect. "I thought you liked it long."

"It's beautiful long. I was glad when you grew it out again. But this suits you."

"I thought you came in here to find the crossroads."

"Is that what I told you? Or what I'm going to tell you? I should remember."

She felt as if she were twelve moves into a chess game against an opponent who was either much more clever than her, or making moves at random, and she did not know which. Some better version of herself would know what to do and how to do it, but that better version was not here. "We should make rules, I don't . . ." It was so hard to speak through her clenched throat, through the half-formed sobs. "I don't know what I can say that won't cause, that won't just mess everything up, I mean, *more*. Who knows what damage we can do. Maybe I just kiss you and all of a sudden I'm my own grandmother and—"

"Zelda."

Her name, in that mouth, was the only spell that worked.

With a movement of heart more than limbs, she found herself clutching Sal, and being clutched. She had not dreamed the strength of those arms. In ten years, she had found a strength of her own to match them. They breathed each other. Road dust and sweat and shea butter and Dr. Bronner's peppermint soap, and under that an aroma with no name but Sal. Young Sal. Vanished Sal.

Long fingers traced her hair back from her face, drifted down her shoulder to her arm, her wrist, the scars there. Her grip closed, and this time her hands were not claws. This time they did not tear.

"How long?" Sal asked.

She should not say. Every damn book she'd ever read about this sort of thing—about *time travel*, let's be honest—was clear on how much trouble she could cause by giving a straight answer. "Ten years."

"Am I . . ."

"No." She'd told June the opposite, and all their friends, and she had believed it herself until just now. Maybe she still did. "I don't know. You're . . . you're out there. Gone."

"Did I fuck it up?"

"No. I did."

"Are you sorry?"

She could not speak. She nodded once, wet, against her.

"Then I'll come back for you."

That, she did not say, is what scares me. "You can't. You can't last out there. It's . . . sharp. It's wrong."

"I'm sharper."

And she was. "I didn't get it," Zelda said. "I was just a kid and I messed up. I can't ever make that up to you."

"You get scared. I know. That's okay. Everybody does."

That's okay. As if ten years of torture, ten years of horrors in the shadows beyond the firelight's edge, as if all of that were a light price. But Sal didn't know what it meant yet. She hadn't felt it. She hadn't been changed. "What did you ask the Wheel?"

She looked almost embarrassed then. Down and away. "We've been on the road a long time, Zelda."

Two years felt like so long back then. That seemed strange to her now. "You can tell me."

"I started to wonder who we were, you and me, under it all—the road, the search. Who we'd be if we went home. If there was an 'after this,' for us."

She'd heard these words before, in a bedroom in Elsinore, in the days before it all went wrong. Sal had looked down as she spoke them, then back at Zelda, then down again, as if Zelda were the sun, too bright to look at for long. She'd been playing with something in her pocket.

"I had to see. I know you think I'm the one who's sure, who knows what's going on, but I'm as scared as you are. More. Different scared. What happens if I fuck up, what happens if you need me to be better than I am, but I'm just me after all? The girl I love—who's she chasing? Me? Or a shadow in her mind?"

Zelda sat up, pulled away. Sal looked at her with eyes that seemed older than twenty-three. But she wasn't. They had been children, back then. Sal was beautiful and strong and smart, she could outrace and outwit and outfight anything—she was the girl who had seemed the whole and perfect world to Zelda, eighteen and scared and fresh from home. But Sal was a kid. After a year on the road, she was just starting to understand the depth of the forces arrayed against her, and how brief and long at once was the span called "the rest of your life." She glanced around at her traveling companions and wondered, Can these flames shed the light we need to make it through the dark places?

Looking, closely, at Zelda.

At Zelda, who adored her, followed her, challenged her, and on some level neither of them could describe, needed her not to be afraid.

But of course she was afraid. They all were. You'd have to be stupid not to be.

Leave me, Zelda wanted to say. Walk out of this place and run far away and never think of me again, not once, let me die in your dreams, find someone whose skin isn't a suit sewn over barbed wire and broken glass. But that was her fear talking, and here sat a kid who, more than anyone, more even than June, deserved the truth.

"I have never stopped loving you, Sal."

"You started, though. Right?"

She was laughing, through tears. "What kind of question even is that?"

"A real one."

"Yes. I started. You're at the center of my heart. I feel like I've known you since grade school. I can't remember a day when you weren't there. It's been ten years since I saw you, and I still look over to the passenger seat to tell you things. I was never worth it. If you want my advice—"

"I don't."

That brought her up short. "You don't?"

"You don't get to talk yourself down in front of me."

"I've got ten years on you. I'm a better judge of character."

"You can tell me how you feel. Let me decide what to do about it. Trust me." The half grin again. She took Zelda's arms, held them at the wrists—and Zelda held hers, too, squeezing through the jacket to the flesh and bones beneath. "I love you. We're in this together. I won't let go if you don't."

It's not our choice, a scared woman railed inside Zelda's head. We're just passengers, and you're practically a child, and there is a great darkness out there, hungry and waiting to swallow us, and all the love in the world won't blunt its teeth. We had our test and I failed. Might as well have set it on fire. I let go. "I got scared," she said. "That's what happened. I got scared one night, and it got the best of me."

"I'm scared right now."

The eye of the storm was closing. Black swirling walls towered around them on all sides, flashing with lightning, with windowpane glimpses of other worlds. She held Sal close. Make this moment last forever, she prayed. Don't ask us to face what comes next, either of us, don't ask her to face my failure, or me to face what she's become. Don't leave me to the knowledge that she's changed, that I lost her, that even she could not live out there on the darkest road. Just leave me here, smelling her, leave us holding each other, just alive, like a sentence is when you close the book and put it down and never read the next.

The storm closed over them. Sal lurched backward, torn from Zelda's grip by Zelda's own younger self. Zelda clung to her, grabbed her wrist tight, with all her strength and the remnants of her spin, willing the world to shape. It almost worked. Sal's jacket tore. Her skin too. She felt Sal's blood on her hand, the only warmth in all the world.

And the cold wind caught her, and lightning crashed her down, and the world's only truth was black.

＊

The storm howled Ramón awake. He choked on his breath in sudden terror of the swirling, scouring wind that howled through holes the stitchmouths' spears had torn. The plastic bag he'd taped up to block the shattered window luffed and billowed, grotesquely biological. As he reached for it, the tape gave way and the storm tore the bag out. It flew like a witch into the choking wind and dust and rain.

Where did this storm come from? When he went to sleep, the sky had been clear to every horizon. And where was Zelda? There was no place to shelter up here, nothing at all on this alt's mountain peak save the Challenger and the Wheel. She had offered to take first watch. She should have seen it coming, should have warned him—

Oh.

The pieces assembled in his mind, and he hated them as they fit.

*I told you so,* the Challenger said.

Its voice was raw and mean. He ignored it. Rain hammered the windows. Wind roared through the gap in its body. And in a lightning flash, out there in the cutting dark, he saw Zelda lurch toward the center of the Wheel.

I told you so. You can't trust anyone out here, boy. Your feelings will only let you down. There are bones under every inch of this country. The road is a knife and knives are honest. You make believe you want to see, you lie to yourself that you want to know, but you'd rather live your cozy little fantasy with your farm boy by your side in bed, you'd rather have pancakes, and cream in your coffee, and baseball tickets once every while, than follow the road where it leads. She knows. She knows, and you're not fit for this.

He shivered. Wind rocked the Challenger on its wheels. Out here, wind leveled mountains and pitched houses twenty miles to shatter on impact.

That's the spirit, buddy. You and me, we're gonna ride the whirlwind all the way to Hell or Oz.

She went in without him. She left him behind. Of course she would. He'd left her. They'd abandoned each other at the end, in the parking lot of that Best Western where they'd all gathered ten years later as if the fact of their assembly could erase their rupture. They were not strong enough to keep going, and she was not strong enough to stop, and after ten years, he did not think he had made the wrong choice. What he did after, maybe that was wrong, until the moment he woke up on that beach, or the moment he met Gabe. But he had left her for the right reasons. And, look: there she was, unable to stop herself from running into the storm.

Why had he come back?

Because there was a world to save? The world was big and the world was always breaking. He came back because he knew the others would—and he came back because he knew that even if they did not, she'd go out there anyway. He remembered how she had looked at that Halloween party, marching across the courtyard to meet Sal. How, even bloody and broken at the end of the road in Montana, she would not let Sal go. She would throw herself at this chance to make up for her mistake. She would reach into a garbage disposal.

And he would stop her.

Because they were friends.

Another lightning flash, another glimpse. Zelda, hand outstretched, crouched at the center of the Wheel as if under an immense weight. She was bleeding. He reached for the door handle. Stopped. He remembered how they'd fought, Zelda and Sal, after Zelda pulled Sal out.

But she was screaming. He heard her above the wind. The Challenger bounced on its shocks. It laughed.

Hey, man. If the mountain's a rockin', don't come a knockin'.

"She needs my help."

She knows what this is. She walked the road when you ran away. What did you learn how to do, in the last ten years? You made a lot of money for people who already had enough to drown in, and then you left. Even your last-ditch, end-of-the-line, come-to-Jesus moment's wimpy. She learned how to survive out there. And she learned how to die. That's what you never got. Always so clever and so afraid. You know how to flinch. Stick with me, kid. We're vicious together. We're one bright needle at the vein. You think you can help her now? She's on her path. She wins or she dies. That's America.

How long had the storm lasted? Minutes that were hours. Time ran screwy in the alts. She was out there. He saw her in lightning strobes, bent, weeping.

She'd lied to him. She wanted to go in alone. She had not wanted him to follow her.

But then, Sal hadn't wanted her to follow either.

Another flash. She was down. The wind howled. Dust and gravel danced off the Challenger's windshield.

The next time lightning came, he could see only the storm.

That's that, then, the Challenger said. We wait.

He remembered Sal, torn and shivering after Zelda had dragged her free, too weak to do more than glare.

There was no light at all. The sand moved fast enough to take paint off the arrow grooves in the Challenger's hood. A pebble hit the windshield and carried off a splinter of glass. People died in this sort of storm.

He found the handle of the door.

A simp, a sap, an easy mark, that's you. The roadkill of the American Dream.

You have to go fast, not look back. Don't flinch, don't cry, just swing for the goddamned cheap seats. Your buddy knows. It's all just blood and more blood down here.

He stumbled out into the storm.

The first gust knocked him off his feet. He landed hard. His head bounced off the dirt. He heard the Challenger's door slam shut, lock. *Fine,* he thought. I made you, I will fix you, I can take you apart if I have to.

He found his footing. Stood. He pulled the neck of his T-shirt up over his mouth and nose. It helped. He could breathe. He still couldn't see.

He trusted his knack. Guide me forward. Lead me to her side.

One step at a time was all he could manage, but one step at a time was all he needed. With his hand shading his eyes, he risked a glance at his feet. He saw white stones in a line, somehow unmoved by the wind. A spoke of the Wheel. He had stumbled across the rim. Or else there was no rim really, and the spokes of the Wheel ran everywhere.

He followed it in. One step at a time. Each leads to the next. Tío, teaching him about cars, about restoration. You have to believe in the whole job. You have faith in it, in the shape you hold in your mind, in the feeling you want to have when it's done. But you can only ever do the thing one step at a time.

The wind cut through his jeans, his black T-shirt, his leather jacket. He might as well have been naked. His eyes burned. The Wheel spoke blurred. He realized he was bleeding, from small cuts in his arms and legs. Scoured by the dust.

What did he have faith in now? He had faith in himself once. In his power, or the power of his friends, to fix things. But there were so many things to fix, and fixing was a hard business. Other people can fuck up a car much faster than you can make it right. Besides—a lot of people seemed to think what they were doing was fixing, when in fact their fixing only made things worse. You bombed places to free them. You crashed an economy and blackmailed the world into making you richer. You killed people to save them. Fine.

He'd had faith in his friends—in young and brilliant things, in their eagerness as they set out on I-80, saying, "This won't be easy," but not yet knowing what *hard* meant. Even if the world was too big for him to figure, together they could find the answers. Zelda would know what to do. She always knew what to do.

He'd had faith in answers.

Where did all that faith leave him? Bleeding, in the dark, in the storm? What did you find when storm wind blasted your mountains down? What were the bones of you?

He believed it mattered. All of it. He'd seen too much to believe in a logic or justice the human mind could grasp—if there was a design to it all, a way the pieces fit, the consciousness that could apprehend it would look vast and utterly alien to his own, all wrong damn angles and higher dimensions, the kind of math professors said that even geniuses would understand for at most fifteen minutes in their whole career, and in those fifteen minutes the question was, how fast can you type.

But there was a gravity to it all. A direction. He had seen Zelda's eyes light up the first time she saw a dinosaur. He had kissed Gabe in Griffith Park with the whole city and the oceans underneath, while behind them in the observatory the great pendulum clock kept time. The lines converged. Not by accident, not by physics, but by—intent. Will. Care. Love.

His foot struck something heavy in his path, immobile and softer than a rock. He knelt. Zelda lay on the wet earth, curled tight against the wind, blood on her hands.

She weighed more than he expected, and she was cold. But she clutched him when he touched her, as if she could draw heat from him through her grip. Her legs could not bear her weight, but did some of the work. There would be time later to worry about her shallow, rapid breathing. For now, any breath at all was enough.

"You'll be okay," he told her.

She spasmed against him. He realized she was trying to laugh. She'd been bitten once by an alt-snake, something neither of them recognized. He tended her in the fever that followed, Sarah and Sal and Ish having been detained by some warlord somewhere. You'll be okay, he'd told her when she started giving him extremely detailed, extremely Zelda-practical instructions, for how he could sterilize a saw to amputate, for what he should do after that if she should die. *You'll be okay.* And she'd laughed at him then too. You don't know that. None of us know that. None of us know what okay even looks like.

That gross shudder of a laugh, more than anything, made him think they might get through this.

He'd turned himself around as he lifted her. Now he was truly lost. Except—there, beside his sneaker, ran a line of white stones.

He followed them through the dark.

There seemed to be other shapes near them in the storm, hunched, shuffling. He squinted, tried to make out details—two women, maybe, staggering together. He called out but they didn't seem to hear, if they were there at all.

He followed the stones. They seemed to lead him on for miles, unerring. It occurred to him as he walked that in every alt, one spoke pointed to the north star, but most seemed random. But this spoke was here, waiting for him.

There were many spokes, of course, and at the center, they were so close together you could easily stumble from one to the next. Simple to think of it that way. A comfortable explanation.

*Simple* and *comfortable* did not mean "true."

He walked the path, holding Zelda upright by his side. Time passed, and space, and finally the night.

He found himself on his knees, blinded by dawn. The sky was clear. The Challenger half covered in drifted sand.

He heard hoofbeats. There was no shelter to seek. The Challenger, ten feet away, might as well have been on Mars. He could not run. Could not walk, or stand. He was spent.

They rode with the sun at their backs up the long winding road: three figures on two dead horses.

He might have mistaken the two women, but out here in these starved and scoured alts there was no mistaking the bulk of Ish.

## CHAPTER TWENTY-FOUR

When Zelda pulled Sal from the Medicine Wheel, she was cold and shivering. They peeled away the torn sleeve of her red coat and wrapped the wounds in her arm. Sal stared up at them through delirium, through pain. Her fogged eyes found Zelda's face, her bloody hand reached out. Her fingertips were like ice, and she had to grit her teeth to keep them from chattering. But she seemed, somehow, happy.

They all wanted to get off this ridge—the storm had scattered their camp—but Sarah didn't want to take the risk of moving Sal tonight. So the others recovered what they could of their supplies and slept in the cars, rotating watch. Say this much for the ridge: you could see anyone coming a long way off.

Zelda stripped down to her underwear and zipped their sleeping bags together, hoping her body heat would warm Sal, that Zelda's skin would bring her back from wherever she had gone.

She lay awake in the tent beside Sal, smelling her. Usually Sal was a radiator in bed. Now she was ice. Her face still held that smile, which Zelda did not recognize and which scared her.

She could have lost Sal in there, lost her forever. None of them had expected the storm. Even as that scalpel wind blew sand in their eyes and drove them back toward the parked cars, she had thought, Sal has this under control. She knows what she is doing.

But none of them did. They had not known, when they set off for the crossroads, what they would find. Zelda had not known the risks when she crossed into the alts for the first time, or when she decided, back in Sal's bed in Ma Tempest's apartment in freshman year, to find someplace better, to find a way to make her magic circle real. To go out and out and out forever. Their adventures on the road, for all their ghouls and mutants and robot apes, felt just like adventures. She was scared only in the aftermath. Until today.

A year on the road, and they were no closer. A year on the road, and whenever they drew near to the crossroads, the alts broke to pieces and rot bubbled in. They had found so many decaying worlds. But you thought, just because you were on a Quest with a capital Q, that the Quest would have an end, that someday you would find the treasure or see the grail. That was how Quests worked. But the Quest was only in the mind, and they were really here. And she had almost lost Sal.

Zelda had watched her march into the Medicine Wheel, furious with her for taking that risk alone, but certain, deep down, that it would all work out. Sal was always one step ahead. Always first into danger, gallant and swift and sure. If there were a swordfight to be fought, Sal fought it. She was not tired. She was not weak. *Just a little further.* Even when she wavered in the Wheel, Zelda kept faith. She had grown up keeping faiths less founded on evidence. You practiced your faith in the calm so that when the storm hit, your roots were deep enough to weather. That's what Dad always said. She was not sure she believed in God anymore. She believed in this girl.

In the storm flash, Zelda saw her, not falling—saw her seated like Buddha, then fallen.

Zelda had not known if she was alive or dead. Dead seemed impossible. Sal's death would have shattered the mountainside. But this was how it happened. Sal could die out here as easy as a twig breaking underfoot. They were small, and the forces arrayed around them vast, and they had not reached the crossroads yet.

So she ran into the Medicine Wheel. Ish tried to stop her and she had clawed away.

Now she lay here, and maybe she had saved Sal and maybe she had not. When she went off to school, she had wanted more than anything to find her people, and to find someone who would feel about her as Sal did, someone she would break open for. Now here they were, side by side, and Zelda still did not know why Sal had walked into the Medicine Wheel alone, and she, Sal, was not saying. They were just kids, not heroes. Not even kids. They were men and women, and the forces awake in the world would pry them apart and crush them one by one. The night lay cold and heavy over her. Sal, dreaming, rolled onto her side. Her hand found Zelda's belly. Skin on skin should not feel like such a wall.

I'm not brave enough for you, Zelda thought. I'm not brave enough to look you in the eye and be weak and dumb and scared, which I always am and you never are. The crossroads is far away, and maybe it's not there at all, it's just something we need, something we made up. I'm pretending for you, I'm pretending to be worth you, and we can't see each other anymore. Why did you go out there? Why didn't you listen to me?

She saw a long straight road before them, its end in shadow.

In the night silence of high country, she heard the jingling of small silver bells.

At first she thought she imagined them. Their sound was gentle and clear, and did not belong in these rotting alts of creeping shadows and worn leather.

She held Sal's hand. She would never let it go. She sat up, reached for the zipper, and peered out.

Outside the tent, the night lay frozen clear, stars and moon midwinter perfect in a gelid sky.

She heard soft hoofbeats and the nearing bells, but saw no horse and no rider.

The sky above her gathered, like the tension before a thunderstorm. Her free hand rested on the knife she slept beside—but only rested. She did not take it up. She did not cry out.

In the center of camp, by the ashes of their fire, the air twisted, as it did when one of them was hitching in. But the others were all asleep.

In a confusion of the eye, among the tents and cars and ashes, there was a woman in white, upon a white horse.

She was not much older than Zelda herself. She seemed to be made of stuff the earth could not touch, from which all dye and mud and blood would slick away.

She turned to Zelda and fixed on her a wise and gentle smile.

"Do not be afraid," she said. "Long have I sought you, and we have much to do."

# CHAPTER TWENTY-FIVE

She had lost herself. She might be anyone, anywhere: beachside at Cape Ann and eighteen with her lover asleep beside her, or curled under a jersey sheet on her long thin dorm bed while snow piled against the windowpanes, or in her room at home where the morning wind swept through the mountain cedar. Knowledge of who and what she was congealed like matter forming from plasma at the beginning of the world. Bits of memory gathered into a life.

She remembered the Medicine Wheel. The ringing silver bells, the white horse, the princess. That had been so long ago, before she lost Sal, before she was the woman she was now, the woman she saw in the mirror, and still called—

"Zelda."

She opened her eyes, which were gummed with sleep. She pawed at them until she could see. Moving hurt. The light hurt, and her head hurt as it sorted the light, which she realized was after all quite dim, from patches of color into form and sense.

She lay under a quilt on a hard bed under a sod roof. There was a fire burning nearby, in a Franklin stove. Ramón sat by her bedside, his hands cradling an earthenware cup of something that smelled like tea. She searched his face for the scorn, pity, frustration she knew she would find there, but he was just watching her, kind and sad, and her waking mind was too unsure of itself yet to carve the scorn she needed to see into the face that was really there.

"I couldn't let you try the Wheel," she said. "I couldn't ask you to follow me. I was wrong to send the letters. You don't owe me anything."

He set his hand on her stomach through the quilt, and she welcomed the pressure. It kept her here, kept her from slipping away into other, easier times. "Zelda. We're not here because we owe you."

He helped her sit up to drink. Watching him reflected in the tea water was easier than staring into his brown eyes, which held none of the challenge or viciousness she wanted. She had failed. She had tried to make her failure good with one more sacrifice, and she had failed at that too. He went after her. Why? She remembered Sal, the sadness on her young face in the heart of the storm, and her faith, against Zelda's decade and all the evidence of her life accrued since. *We're in this together.*

Instead of why, she asked: "We?"

From a corner of the sod hut she heard a girl's voice, so like the girl Sal still was in her memory, and so different—the voice called her name, and then June was there, hugging her, and saying as they both cried, I'm sorry, I spilled your tea.

---

It was a one-room hut, lit by salvaged candles, a battery lantern from the Challenger's trunk, and crimson flickers of the stove's mouth. Zelda remained in bed with a new quilt while the old one dried, and a new cup of tea, unwilling to trust her legs enough to stand. Part of her shakiness was physical exhaustion, but the rest was joy.

The others had made it.

They had come through the alts, found Ramón by the Wheel's edge, and carried her away. Dragged the Challenger on chains behind their dead horses. They were here. Together.

Ish was quiet. Sarah seemed worn. June had a haunted air, and her shadow sometimes moved on its own. They had told their story, of the cowboy and the circled wagons. But they were here.

"We're with you," Ish said. "All the way."

"We have to fix this." From Sarah's expression, from the twist of her lips, Zelda could see she wasn't happy about that.

The memory of the storm whirled around her. Her skin felt tight. But they were together now. She had been wrong before, and weak. "We'll go back, then," she said. "Try the Wheel again. With all five of us, we can make it work."

Ramón looked away from her, and down. Sarah said nothing. Ish opened his mouth, almost spoke, stopped himself.

"We can," Zelda said, as if saying the words fast enough would make them believe. "We can use it. We can do it, together." Sarah looked embarassed. "What?"

Ish, to Ramón: "You didn't tell her?"

Ramón, his arms spread, defensive: "She just woke up."

"Tell me what?"

---

With one arm around June, she staggered from the sod hut into the burnt fields. Charred cornstalk stubble jutted from dead ground. A scarecrow remained, bloodlit by the red moon. That seemed to be all that the fire had spared.

Behind the scarecrow, the ground was cracked. So was the sky. It was the same crack—descending in three dimensions of roiling emptiness from the stars to plunge into alt-earth. Eye-sucking black beyond wriggled and writhed like the surface of boiling water, but when she tried to fix her gaze on what it was that moved, she saw only the dark.

More cracks webbed the earth and the western half of the sky. When they escaped the cultists and came to rest in that alt-7-Eleven parking lot, the cracks had been hairlines. There were more of them now, and wider. Stars were gone. Black bars fractured the red moon, as if it had been made from stained glass by a maniac. As she watched, the bars moved—or the moon did, behind and through them.

In the heart of the cracks in the sky, there was a gap. An unfolding vacancy. A black hole in the shape of a woman taller than mountains.

The others kept their distance. She heard them silent behind her.

"We can work around them," she said. "Climb the ridge on foot if we have to."

"The ridge is gone." Ramón's voice. "Half gone. In the storm."

"That's impossible. It's the Medicine Wheel."

"It's gone," Ish said softly. "It's wherever things go when they're beyond those cracks."

"What about home? Is it . . . like this, there?"

"I don't know," he said.

"What do you mean you don't know? We could sneak back to check. I don't have a phone. The cowboy wouldn't see me."

"We tried." Sarah joined her by the edge of the burnt field: colored bloody by the broken moon, arms crossed. "We can't find a way back."

Again, Zelda felt the cold of the Medicine Wheel, the cold between the worlds. "What do you mean?"

"You were far gone, after Ramón pulled you out. You needed medicine. I tried to hitch home. We got close, but we could not get there. When we try, the spin melts away, off into . . . that." She pointed to the gap in the sky.

"Sarah. Your kids."

Her eyes were bright and her face was set as a mountainside. "This changes nothing. I did not come here to half save the world. We will finish this, and I will go home." Then one corner of her mouth quirked up, in what on anyone else's face would have been a smile. "Let's go fast. I owe Evan enough child care as it is."

There was too much to say, and all the words were too sharp for her throat. "Okay." That would have to stand for everything she did not know how to speak. "This changes nothing," she echoed. It sounded weaker when she said it.

"What's the plan?" Ish asked. Tentatively. As if he didn't quite believe.

"We'll keep away from settlements. Supply caches in waste alts only. That should keep us ahead of the cowboy. We need wheels, though, and the Challenger's dead."

Ramón cleared his throat. "The dead horses can tow the Challenger as far as the Green Glass City. It's just on the other side of the wastes. Brigit's people owe us. We can use the garage there."

"If they're still there."

"They will be." That, at least, he looked like he believed. "And it's on our way. If it doesn't work out, we've only lost a little time."

"On our way," June said. "On our way where?"

Ish frowned. "Elsinore."

Zelda's memory recoiled from the place. Battlements, honed knives, tweezers heated in forge fire until they glowed, manacles, shadows like barbed wire, the princess beautiful in samite and gold, the princess dead, the queen falling from rot-soaked battlements. She wished they had another choice, any choice at all, but wishes only mattered at the crossroads.

June said: "That supposed to mean something to me?"

Could she tell the story? Could she explain the cold night after she dragged Sal from the Medicine Wheel? The princess moonsilvered, lighting from her horse, her feet bare, as if the world could not touch her, and her voice, silken after so many months of what she, Zelda, had thought back then was hard road, her silken voice saying, I seek what you seek. I, too, once walked the Wheel, and failed. But perhaps—with a blush, a glance away, and then a fierce turn back—perhaps we can aid one another. The princess felt like a dream then. She still felt like a dream. Perhaps she always was. "It's the place where everything went wrong." Which was a lie. It had gone wrong, she thought, a long time before. It had gone wrong when they first set out. Maybe it had gone wrong that first night, with the punch bowl. *Just a little further.* "It's where I lost her."

They slept after that. They tried. Eventually they managed—until Zelda woke in the dark and found June gone.

She was out by the burnt fields, hugging herself as she watched the broken moon, wrapped in shadows that wriggled like snakes when Zelda drew close.

Zelda stopped, raised her hands. "It's only me."

June glanced back, slumped, and the shadows slumped too. "You're not scared. Of . . ." She gestured down, around, at her shadows. "I thought you'd be mad. You stop the rot. And you stop people who call it. You said."

"Most of the time when I find them, they're ready to eat someone's face off. So that's a difference."

"She's out there." June looked up into the sky. She'd been crying. Zelda reached into her jacket pocket, pulled out a pouch of tissue paper, and passed it to her. "I know she is." And that was the why. The knack assumed a shape you needed. Sarah needed safety. Ramón had to know where to go. Ish had to know the lay of the land. And June—she missed her cousin. "But then there's . . . this." She gestured vaguely out, at the world, at everything. "I want to hear her. But I'm scared. She's been out there for a long time."

"I saw her," Zelda said. The words surprised her as much as they seemed to surprise June. "In the Medicine Wheel. Not her like she is now. Her back then. Ten years ago. Wearing that same red jacket. You remember."

"She wore that thing everywhere."

"You know she had us chase some biker king for, like, three weeks one time to get it back? Snuck into his camp while he was fighting off some raid by these robo-gorilla things. Definitely one of our worse-idea adventures."

"Where did it come from, anyway?"

"Goodwill."

"No shit."

She remembered trying on a straw boater in the mirror, taking it off with a moment's worry about thrift stores, head lice. Behind her: How do I look? A turn and then, no judgment, no pause to consider, that honest electric: *Perfect.*

"I liked the way it looked on her."

June leaned against her. The shadows between them parted like leaves. June's body was thin, whippy as a willow branch. Zelda tried to remember being that young. How weird to look at someone seventeen and think, I was never that young, and have the inner seventeen-year-old you still half believed yourself to be bridle and shout back—*Hey!*

June tensed beside her, a break in the stillness, as if she was about to say something, or ask a question.

"What?"

The moon bent low. Wind whistled over burnt ground. "Nothing." The moment passed, the question, whatever it had been, unasked. The sky yawned. A satellite crossed the Milky Way, broadcasting down, though no one was left to hear it crying in the dark.

# CHAPTER TWENTY-SIX

So this was it, Sarah thought: the road to the end.

They traveled for three days east from the mountains, from the cracks in the sky and earth. The dead horses strained to drag the Challenger down battered gray pavement.

She had known it would come to this. She did not have premonitions; she did not trust in dreams or prophecies or the whispers of gods or spirits or ancestors. When her sister invited her to celebrate, on those rare holiday visits back to the place she never could quite call home, she sat awkwardly at the fire's edge and watched, and listened to the songs with a soul that echoed their notes, and wished she might have been made otherwise, built to have faith in things she could not see. But she had known, as perhaps Ish and Ramón did not, what that letter on her kitchen counter meant, what it would ask from her, and how far she would have to go. This was not a college reunion. They had left a task undone, and in leaving, she had made a life for herself. Now, protecting that life meant following this road, all the way to the end of the line.

They would get through this, or not, together. So she reviewed them, each of her old partners of the road, these once-brilliant kids, and she reviewed herself, as she would a set of tools before an operation.

She was good at this, she believed: good at traveling and good at being afraid for her life and the lives of her friends, good at sleeping on cold hard ground and good at campfire cooking, good at saving their asses from any random damn scrap metal infection or poison thornbush they'd stumbled into. She had been good at it once, anyway, and the rhythm came back faster than she expected.

Every morning she shuffled through the pictures in her wallet. They were old, last year's Christmas photos. Susan insisted on cutting her hair short over summer, Alex got new glasses, and while those had not felt like big changes at the time, now she found herself looking, not at photos of her kids, but at photos of their past. They were smiling, Alex gap-toothed, the sparkling joy of kids who knew there were presents on the way. They did not know about the rot, about the end of the world. They did not understand their own history.

She had not meant to wait so long to explain it all to them, but she wanted them to grow up remembering a less painful world, even if that memory was not, strictly speaking, true—so they would know what they were trying to reach, the peace they were trying to bring. That's how she justified it to Evan, anyway. They'd talk about it tomorrow, she said. The right time always seemed to be tomorrow.

And now she was back on the road, and they were so far away.

The others found their own pace. When they stopped for the night, Ramón tinkered with the perforated mess of the Challenger. He couldn't fix it without spare parts and tools, but he could check the brake lines, the steering column, learn which hoses and belts he'd have to replace when they made it to the Green Glass City.

And after . . . She tried not to think about *after* yet. About Elsinore.

He tinkered. He hummed. He had his car, and his path.

Ramón was fine.

She kept her distance from Ish for a few days, unwilling to open that particular box again. Pandora caught hope in hers. Sarah caught shame. You could make mistakes when you were young, and move on. Everyone did. But when you moved on, your mistakes weren't unmade. The wrongness was part of the draw, part of why you made them, part of why her eyes at twenty-two drifted his way. Part of it.

There was a tight-wound spring at the core of him, which none of the others saw, underneath the fluff and the ill-timed jokes. He knew a bleak and bitter truth, even if he kept trying to ignore it. There had been a magnetism to his jerky, awkward resistance to that truth when they were young—a heroism in trying to deny something he knew the way he knew he had bones. She saw in him, back then, a courage that had nothing to do with her dad's, with the muscles and guns she'd grown up so comfortable beside, on a succession of military bases with an endless supply of boys pre-broken for her convenience. Ish, when they were young, could stagger bleeding from a brutal alt, one of those *Red Harvest* messes where they'd tried to save one girl and ended up with two withered old monster-men contorting their pet death machines against one another until the whole valley was soaked with blood, irradiated, and the girl dead—Ish could stumble out of that and say, I really thought we could save her, and, We'll do better next time, not with the optimist's ignorance but with the fierce conviction of a man trying to prove something. As though he were arguing, deep down, with his own gimlet vision of just how fucked things really were.

She could tell he did not respect the part of himself that was soft, the part that had been there inside before whatever happened to him had happened, and which lingered, deep down. She had wanted a piece of that hidden, remaining thing. She hungered for it. She imagined the softness in him as one of the sword-wielding mice in the Redwall books she used to love: a tiny creature in a dark cave, facing an immense and coiling serpent. Those books were so good precisely because you knew how that fight would go down in the real world, even if the mouse did have a sword: a motion in the dark, a snap, and done. But what more perfect hero could you imagine than a tiny furry thing, goofy, brave, idealistic against all evidence, and doomed?

Time had worn the soft bits of him away. She'd seen Zelda's shock at that, seen Ramón's surprise when he discovered the steel in Ish, as if the boy had worked some magic with his own body as a sacrifice to create this other hard-edged thing. But Sarah had always known it was there. She'd always known it was a matter of time before the mouse lost.

Perhaps she was wrong. Perhaps his little hero mouse was still alive. Hunkered down and shivering somewhere in the steel cage of him, tiny heart a-thrum. From time to time, she thought she glimpsed it. When they rigged the Challenger behind the dead horses in the morning, and she said they reminded her of the skeleton reindeer in *The Nightmare Before Christmas* and he sang a few bars—and the tune was off and warbling and imperfect, and she hesitated, wondering if that was the mouse she heard. *Are you still in there, buddy?* But when she turned to look, he'd receded again, if it was there at all—hidden under those composed features, the control that remained when the soft and interesting bits wore away.

Still, he seemed happy. Happy to have a goal, a path: the Green Glass City first, then Elsinore. Happy to wallow in the quest of it all. Happy, too, whether he'd admit it, and in spite of everything, to be here with Zelda.

And that left Zelda herself: haunted. Unwhole. But set on the road. Was she strong enough? What would *strong enough* even mean?

They made bad time. The dead horses could shift the Challenger on the interstate, but slowly. They crept toward the Green Glass City, away from the cracks in the sky.

One night, as Zelda was filling water bottles from a spring between two rocks, running the water through her filter pump, Sarah went to her. "You know the city will be bad."

"It might not," Zelda said without looking up. "Ramón's right. We left them in a good place. The drones worked. Brigit and her people turned back the mutants. They had food. Water."

"That was ten years ago. Look what ten years did to this place."

They had camped at this same spring before. Back then, green fields had stretched between the red rocks, dotted with flowers like poppies but with pointed petals. The grass was yellowed now, the flowers gray as ash.

Zelda kept pumping. She did not have to look. "There's been a drought."

"There used to be green out here. Real green. Have you seen any since we came through? Do you think there is a drought everywhere?" She sat on the rocks. Kicked a patch of earth with the toe of her boot. The wind caught an eddy of dust and spread it out in a thin line on the cracked ground. "Ish and June and I landed in a world with nothing but bugs. We never saw anything that barren last time."

Zelda didn't answer.

"It's all going sour. The life is seeping out. As if we are bleeding and cannot stop. We cannot even feel the wound. Do you really think we will get to the Green Glass City and find Brigit waiting with a home-cooked meal?"

"I know!" She didn't think Zelda had meant to shout. But she was tensed all over, from her diaphragm to the tips of her fingers, white-knuckled on the pump.

Zelda sat down hard beside the spring. "What do you want from me? I'm sorry. I said it ten years ago, and I've spent ten years living it. We were out of our depth. We still are. Yes, I think it will be bad at the Green Glass City. But there's no other way to get the parts we need. Yes, it will be worse at Elsinore. But that's the only chance we have. You knew that when you got my letter. And you didn't have to come. You shouldn't have."

She lowered herself beside her. The anger had rolled through and left her carved away, like the banks of a river after a flash flood. She felt tired. "No."

"You have kids, Sarah. Christ. And now you're stuck here."

"If the world ends, it ends for them too." Now the pumping noise had stopped, she could hear the gentle turn of water in the spring, under the cricket song. "You should have left her."

There was no question whom she meant: June, who'd been so quiet since the homestead; June, whose knack rippled around her at night. The girl they'd failed, as she had failed Alex and Susan, by not fixing everything before it became their problem too. "I tried to leave her," Zelda said. "She wouldn't let me."

"You're a pushover. You have to set boundaries with kids."

"She's almost the age we were when this started."

"She should be in school."

"When did school ever help us?"

Sarah hit that question like a bug hit one of those electric zapping paddles. Spark. She could answer it, of course. She could draw a line right from school to her MD to Evan to Alex and Susan and their comfortable house and all the things she knew too well what it would be like to live without. They wouldn't keep you safe forever, the mortgage and the diploma and the nice hospital job and the homeowners' association, but they let you tell yourself you were safe, even if you knew there was always another cowboy over the ridge. But Zelda did not have any of those things. And after ten years on different roads, they were both back here again, filtering water so they didn't puke themselves to death with some filthy stupid alt-disease before the monsters had a chance to kill them. "If not for school," Sarah said, "I would never have met any of you goofballs."

Zelda laughed at that, and Sarah smiled in spite of herself at the memory of Sal watching Zelda laugh—drinking in the rawness, the eagerness Sal and Sarah had both given up freshman year, when they forged their armor.

Sarah had told Evan everything. She never lied to him once. But she wondered if, with the house, the job, the lawn, the party decorations, she had in fact been playing the game she used to play with Sal, fashioning armor, pretending that she belonged. The game she confused with safety.

"I saw her, you know," Zelda said. "In the Medicine Wheel. I saw her on the other side of the last ten years."

There had been no doubt which *her* Sarah meant, minutes before. There was no doubt which *her* Zelda meant now. The name rose to Sarah's lips like water to the spring. "Sal." Once spoken, it sank beneath the silence, beneath the gathered dusk and time. The sound faded. But the pair of them, she and Zelda, sitting beside this spring in this dying land under the broken sky, were a more effective invocation of Sal even than her name. When they were last together like this, Sal had been just over the hill, arguing with Ish about the post office maybe, or the Civil War. All they had to do was stand and they would see her, or call out and she would come—frizzy, dusty, road-worn, real in her red jacket. Not the face in the storm. "June told me."

Zelda laughed at that. "She likes you."

"People tend to. Because I am nice." She let that sit between them. "What did *she* want?"

"To know if I loved her."

The night was very quiet. Fire crackled on the other side of the hill. "What did you say?"

"I told her that I did."

She looked north, where the stars were out. "And do you?"

"What do you think?"

"Zelda."

"Of course I do. I loved her then. I loved her when I—when I was weak. When she fell. I've loved her ever since. Alone. It does something hard to your heart. You wake up in the middle of the night in your back seat, and you hope before you open your eyes that the weight you're curled around is her, even if you know it's just your backpack." She looked up, eyes unfixed, and intoned: "I looked and I 'saw under the sun, that the race is not to the swift.'"

"Well. Fuck the sun, then."

She laughed, choked, laughed again, softer. "It's the only sun we got."

"Is it?" Sarah wasn't sure what she meant by that. The question seemed to be asked again, in deeper voice, by the desert, by the gray flowers, invisible now in the dark. Were there other suns? They had found so many worlds in the alts, but there was a sameness to them, a sickness she recognized. Power, fear, and control. Even when they found beauty, as at Elsinore, the beauty hid poison. The alts were bleeding out. There was a drought on everywhere.

There could be other suns. That was the promise, way back when, that had kept them on the road, all the way to Elsinore. All the way to the Crossroads. "If we live through this," Sarah said, "you will see her. At the end. Not her back then. Her the way she is now. What she has become without you."

"I know."

"Can you do that?"

"I think so."

"We have a lot riding on this for 'I think so.'"

"I can. We have to get through the Green Glass City first. Then the mountains. And Elsinore. I'll figure it out. We have time."

"Not as much as you think," Sarah said, standing. "The cowboy's after us. And he's closing fast. I can hear him."

She walked back to the camp alone. At the crest of the hill she turned back. Zelda sat beside the spring, head down, deep in thought. And behind one of the larger stones, invisible from where she'd sat—two glistening eyes in the dark, surrounded by a twist of girl: June, crouched to listen.

※

Sarah first heard the footsteps the day after the Medicine Wheel. Awake early— she remembered back in college being able to sleep till noon, but ever since Susan was born, she seemed to have a timer switch in her skull set for six, time to wake up and Be Mom—she lay in her sleeping bag beside June, watching the first gray of sunrise settle through the tent cloth on June's cheeks. Her sleeping bag rose and fell with her breath. Sarah eased into that gentle rhythm, unwound herself from the bad dreams that haunted her through the night, and almost even slipped back to sleep. But as she drifted off, she heard a second sound against June's breath. A rasp of sand on sand. Small rocks under boot-heels. Footsteps.

They were far away. She might have imagined them. They were sounds the mind shaped out of silence, the way the gentle ring in her ears in absolute quiet could, if she focused on it, rise and fall in pitch, gain tempo and other voices in harmony, multiply to a choir. But she had never heard footsteps before. The stride was slow, assured. The walk of a hunter. That was the cowboy's step.

She slipped from the tent.

She knew she should wake the others. Wake June. But she was angry. Furious. That he had followed her, that he lacked the decency to stay gone when shadows swallowed him up. Furious that he would play these games with her, of all people, that he would creep toward her so ineffectually, rather than just draw and shoot.

The camp lay still in the cold morning. The dead horses hunkered beside the Challenger. Ish slept on the ground, Ramón in the Challenger, Zelda at the edge of the firelight. She could see to the scoured horizon in every direction. The cracks burgeoned to the west, and mad whispers spoke through the wound in the sky. She wheeled, she wheeled, looking.

Her eyes had always been the keenest in the group. The others, she joked, were the real nerds. Sarah was an *athlete*; she grew up swimming. Moving from base to base, you learned to build a simple identity for yourself, out of points, like a constellation or an old comic book panel. Clear bold facts were easy to understand, and portable. If you were a swimmer, a Stephen King fan, if you wanted to be a doctor when you grew up, people would assume they knew you, and not ask more inconvenient questions.

That was how she'd met Sal.

She had been afraid, when she went off to college, though she'd not admitted it at the time. What would they make of her, the kids at a place like that? Would the tricks she had cobbled together from base to base work there?

After two weeks of confusion, in which she felt uncomfortable at the campus Native American Cultural Center, at the multicultural mixers, at the Party of the Right orientation (she'd thought of herself as "fiscally conservative" back then), it turned out that her base brat reflexes worked just fine. Better, even, than on base. So many of these kids had come to college with one main point to their identity, Being Smart, which didn't work now, because everyone shared it. They flailed for something new to replace it with. Meanwhile, Sarah could just un-pack Swimming, Stephen King, and all the rest, with a slight disappointment. She'd never thought of her self as a uniform before.

The drinking started after that. At the time, there didn't seem to be any-thing wrong with it. Pop never drank, not even champagne at New Year's, and he impressed his daughters with the virtue and value of that choice, so back in high school, Sarah had learned how. She was the prim, sober girl who would, when challenged, shotgun one of the bad beers that the cool-dad LT's son had brought to the party. If she'd put on the rest of her old uniform again, why not wear that part too?

At college there were parties in suites the size of homes, in frat houses with sticky floors, there were parties thrown by organizations, there were parties that started as someone's birthday and spilled out through the dorm entryway and developed their own gravity and momentum, while whoever's birthday it had been back at the start stood confused and crushed in the corner, wearing a silly hat, alone. Sarah went to all of them.

For weeks, every night, Wednesday through Sunday, she went out, then staggered home at one in the morning to the dorm room she shared with a girl she rarely saw, who kept her mess to her side of the line down the middle of the room while Sarah kept her creased sheets and hospital corners and her dusted desktop on hers. Sarah and her roommate had nothing in common, no more than she, Sarah, had anything in common with the kids at those parties. They all had nowhere else to be, that was all.

Those weeks were a blur in memory, their colors vivid and spattered: the cold rush of the pool at 6:00 a.m., the thrum of limbs through water, the squeak of her shoes on the DKE house floor, the tobacco-booze-body-spray stink of some hard-abbed lacrosse boy whose self-assurance melted when she looked him up, looked him down, shook her head, and walked away. The inner curve of a porcelain toilet, she could not remember where, they all looked the same. Hookah smoke. The word *Juicy* printed across the ass of sweatpants that preceded her into Organic Chemistry.

At three in the morning two weeks in, she was stumbling back to Old Campus, where the freshmen mostly lived, shoulder to shoulder with a girl she'd met coming out of someone's bathroom. The spike heel she'd found at Goodwill did something funny with the Elm Street pavement, and the girl whose arm was around her shoulders helped her stumble to the safety of a bench, beneath a streetlight that might have been the moon.

Catching her breath, with the world spinning back away from her, she asked herself what four years of this would do to her. She could not answer. It seemed like the whole thing might slip past, smooth, dripless, borne back and away like the drunken earth.

So she asked the girl by her side, Did you think it would be like this?

The girl said: I thought it might be.

Sarah said: Tell me something you've never told anyone before. Tell me something so true you can't say it in words, something so true it feels like a hole in you that's corked only by silence, something that if you say it you know you'll all go sloshing out of your own stomach. Tell me something that makes it worthwhile.

Don't you think, the girl said, that we should get to know each other first?

She looked, then, to her right, something in the tone of that voice made her look, and she saw that the girl beside her on the bench was her roommate. And she said, too shocked for anything more, her name: Sal.

We'll get through this, she said. Together.

They had. Until they hadn't.

And here she stood, in the stillness of the dawn camp, searching the flat razor line of the horizon, seeing nothing. No trace of a hat. No outline of a lean and rangy body. But she heard his footsteps and she felt him through her knack.

There was a wave approaching. Unhurried, but not patient. He was hungry and savoring the final moments of that hunger, like a man waiting for a bird to roast, so caught by the visions the smell excites—crisp glistening skin, yielding meat, the juice inside—that when the call comes to dinner, he turns reluctantly from the bird in his mind to the bird on the table.

But he comes to the table all the same.

She threw her knack against him, all her warding powers against the fact of his footsteps. Be still. Go away. Pass us by. She willed them invisible. She felt the void that opened behind her on that cold Elm Street bench. The empty space she could not name.

And the footsteps were gone.

They had not slowed, had not turned aside. Here she stood, still and mouse-small beneath the sky, one woman alone without a plan, who'd built a precious life for herself only to leave it all to walk one more time into the monster's teeth. Even though she knew her history. Even though she knew how stories with cowboys ended.

He was out there. Drawing near. He smelled her. Dreamed of crisp golden skin.

She stood, shivering, alone.

A hand touched her shoulder.

She jumped. Screamed.

It was Ish. Back from the dawn watch. No, he hadn't heard any footsteps. "Maybe it was me you heard?"

But he didn't wear boots.

"It's okay," he said. "Nerves. Me too." His hand sank, without seeming consciousness, to the bag he always carried now.

But it wasn't nerves. She heard the footsteps the next morning, and the morning after, louder. Each time she crawled out of bed and stood, trembling in her floral-print dress, a mom and an officer's daughter and a Lakota kid grown up, and herself, and spent what spin she'd gathered on the last day's ride to fend him off, to send him back.

So far, it had worked. But some days, she thought she heard him laugh.

When June asked her about the cowboy, that night, after Zelda and the spring, she tried to shrug it off. Tried to say nothing. But the girl was here, and trusted her, and deserved to know.

"Wake me up," June said when the story was done. "Let me help you."

"I will be all right." She heard her own exhaustion. "We will reach the Green Glass City tomorrow. Ramón will fix the Challenger. And then we will drive faster than he can follow."

"Sarah," she said. "Let me help."

She wanted to say yes. But yes was what she would have said to Sal. And June was not Sal. So instead, she patted her leg through the sleeping bag, said, "I will be all right," and closed her eyes and made herself sink into something not unlike sleep.

June slept lightly, as a rule. At home she'd wake when Ma got up in the night to use the bathroom, or when drunken party boys strolled by two streets over, banging a plastic bin for a drum to keep time for their songs. She woke near dawn the next day to find Sarah staggering back, bleak-eyed and alone, from the wastes. She moved as if her body were deadweight, a big old sandbag she had to shift by force of will.

Wind blew dry grass against dry grass, rock against rock.

Sarah had not woken her. She had gone to face the cowboy again. Alone.

When Sarah saw June standing by the tent, she raised her chin, a quiet salute, not quite hello. Her face had not aged overnight. Her hair was no more gray than it had been the day before. But June realized she was looking for something in Sarah's form and not finding it, and by not finding, it she realized how much she'd depended on its presence.

Dancers had a way of standing, even when they weren't doing anything you'd call a dance. LaShae had it: a composition of face and body, hips aligned, shoulders easy and somehow in exactly the right place, a pose that seemed effortless, a way of standing that made you want to believe the preachers when they told you people had been made by a wise hand, because if they were made, they were made to stand that way.

But it was a skill, standing like that. You had to learn it, to practice. It was different from relaxing. When LaShae slumped on the train coming home after a protest, she looked no different from any other girl.

Sarah had a stance like that. She was always ready. Even out here, where there were cowboys and dead guys and shadows and who could say what else— she had a look to her, a set of the shoulders, a twist of lips that was not a smile: Don't worry. I got this.

She wore that look so well June had mistaken it for her character—who Sarah was, how her heart was made. Seeing her now, weak, worn, trying by reflex to assume the posture, June understood. It wasn't that Sarah was faking. She was a mom, and a doctor, she had her whole family history to carry like an invisible pack on her shoulders, and when you bore a weight, you tried to convince the world you bore it easy. Now, too tired to manage the illusion, she still had to carry the weight, and with it the added shame of a magician who'd fumbled the rabbit from her hat.

June had never thought about it quite that way before—that Mom was another set of clothes you put on in the morning, like Doctor or Taxi Driver, that underneath it people were just naked, as she was.

Sarah said, *sorry,* and fell.

June caught her before she hit the ground, then helped her to the burnt-out fire, to the water bottles, to what was left of last night's meal. Sarah's hands shook as she brought the food to her lips. Even so, she did not spill a drop of water.

"He's gone," Sarah said. "For now."

"I can help you." She raised her hand. Even in daylight, shadows rippled between her fingers, in the creases of her palm.

Sarah guided her hand carefully down. She shook her head. The sun crept over the horizon, returning what color the dry world possessed. Zelda stirred in her sleeping bag, settled again. Sarah looked down into the water. "I should make coffee."

"You don't have to do this alone," June said.

"I do. I can. I will."

June had never heard Sarah angry before. The force of it pressed the breath from her. Her voice rose in anwer. "You don't have to protect me, Sarah. I've lost people. In a way Sal the easiest, because there was a mystery, so maybe I could get her back. She didn't just die like people die—someone gets shot by a cop, someone gets sick, someone gets their face blown off on the other side of the world for a country that does not give a shit about them. You can't carry all of this alone."

"I *know*." Sarah looked up at her, and June realized for the first time that she was the taller of the two. Sarah's rawness was gone. Her control settled between them like a door closing. "But I won't lose you too."

June wanted to apologize. To unsay. She hadn't realized until Sarah put on that mask again, just how rare was the trust Sarah had shown when she let it slip. And how much of a mess she, June, had made of that trust.

The loss covered her, pressed her down. She could not speak.

Sarah, slowly, rose to make the coffee.

━━━

June rode a dead horse behind Ramón, and Sarah slept in the Challenger. The desert fell away to either side of them, but the interstate bored on, across a high straight bridge perched on impossible pillars. June tried not to look down. When she did, she saw the plain far below ripple. It's water down there, she thought at first. We're over an ocean. But the patterns were wrong. Not rippling but wriggling.

She could not stop thinking about Sarah and her mask. The memory made her feel small and mean and sad. She wanted to help.

"Tell me," she asked Ramón, "about Elsinore."

"It's a bad story." Ramón shifted the reins to one hand. He kept his eyes on the road.

"I figured. They're all bad."

"Not all of them. The Green Glass City worked out okay."

"Where we're going now."

"We found it, the Green Glass City I mean, not long before the Medicine Wheel. Place was a mess. Mutants with mind-control worms hunting the few humans left. The alleys stank with rot. We hooked up with a young woman, one of the survivors. Brigit. Kid with a bow and arrow. Bright, fierce. For a while there, it seemed like every third kid we met had a bow and arrow. Weird. Anyway, we helped her restart the old security drones, clear out the mutants and the worms. We were feeling ourselves. It was good."

"And you're still not telling me about Elsinore."

He breathed out. "You don't want to hear that story."

"I do."

"It's a weird story. To start out, I mean: we didn't find the place. It found us. She did, anyway. The princess."

"Princess?"

"Castle and everything. Ermine robes, samite, cone hat. Wasteland nobility, a sort of postapocalyptic feudal kind of deal like you get out here sometimes. Knights on motorback. The king was dead. The queen remarried. In mourning, the princess watched the stars from her tower. And she saw them going out, one by one."

"Like the cracks in the sky."

"Worlds die bit by bit. This is the first time we've seen it happen to all of them at once."

"So what happened?"

"The princess knew her world was going down, but rather than sit there in her watchtower and take it, she studied. Looked for answers. She wanted to find the crossroads. That's not what she called it, but it was the same idea. She found the alts. The rot. She got as far as the Medicine Wheel, tried to walk it. Failed. Barely made it across the edge before she collapsed. But she knew there was power in that place, so she kept tabs on it. When Sal got further than she did, she thought, if we worked together, maybe we could go all the way."

"Did you?"

He nodded. "She had books, tools. With her, we figured it out, the path. We found spells, tricks. In the end, it was all set up. We were just waiting for the stars to be right. Then, when we were going to try . . . everything went to shit. Like it always does out here. The queen turned on us. Threw us in the dungeons. Sal was tortured. It was not good. We broke out. The princess tried to help us. She died. The queen cursed us, called on the rot in despair. The castle walls started growing arms and mouths. People got eaten from the inside out. It—well. It was rough. But as Sal and Zelda were running out, they saw the road take shape from the princess's balcony. They saw the crossroads. And they tried to get there."

"Jesus Christ."

He crossed himself. She couldn't tell whether he was being serious.

"And that's where we're going. The castle."

"It's the only place we know where the road's open. At least, where it used to be."

"Do you think it's still . . . cursed? Full of shadows?"

"We'll see."

"This is a bad plan."

"That is, you'll remember, what we told Zelda. But I don't think we have much choice." He nodded at the western sky, at the end of the world.

She changed the subject. Or maybe it wasn't a change, maybe there was only one subject left. "Sarah blames herself, for Sal."

He didn't say anything for a while. Metal hooves rang an even rhythm, mechanical, unchanging, dead as a gavel. "She couldn't keep Sal out of the dungeon. She couldn't keep her out of the mess with Zelda. She couldn't keep her from the crossroads."

She told him, then—about Sarah and the cowboy's footsteps. About how she left in the morning. About how tired she was when she came back. When she was done, he leaned over the neck of his horse.

"Sounds like her."

"We have to stop her," June said.

"How?"

"She's going to get herself killed. Because of us. Because of me."

"I'll talk to her," he said. "I can't tie her up or anything. But talking might help."

"Tonight. Do it tonight."

"Sure," he said. "Tonight. She'll be too hungover tomorrow to do much fighting, anyway. Once we get through that pass ahead, we'll come to the Green Glass City. There will be a parade. Feasts. Just you wait."

"Sarah said it would be bad."

"Sarah could be holding a full house and fold against the chance of a gut-shot straight. Look. We've been through a lot. It's not too much to ask, I think, that this one thing should break our way."

# CHAPTER TWENTY-SEVEN

They rode in silence through the Green Glass City.

When Sarah said, *It will be bad,* Zelda had agreed without believing it. She had been on the road long enough to know *bad* was the safe bet. But safe bets weren't certain. Surely somewhere would be whole. Surely somewhere things worked out. Why not here, in this city with its bottle-green buildings, its moss-colored windshields and emerald mirrors? They'd left Brigit and her people with the resources of a city to draw on, with the mutants chased into the wastes, with the remaining security drones at their bidding. If anyone had a chance, they did.

The city was empty.

Tarnished reflections flanked them down the boulevards. They could hear the wind. They could hear the clanking chains that pulled the Challenger, and the hoofbeats of the dead horses. Dry leaves rustled under trees that had, years since, outgrown the sidewalk gaps where they were planted, tearing open the concrete and the road with their roots. The leaves were bonfire orange, red, yellow, bone white. They had come to this world in autumn.

They heard birdsong. Their passage startled flocks of sparrows roosting in overgrown hedges. They swarmed up and away, with a sound like a curtain being torn. Zelda drew rein, wary. A splinter broke from the top of one sheer glass tower—it fell, pierced a sparrow—then the splinter spread bright wings, dipped low, was gone. The hawk's back had white eyespots like the coloring of a moth. What lived higher up even than those topless towers, that a hawk nesting there would evolve eyespots on its wings, a fake face turned always skyward?

One sparrow bled. The others fled. The hawk perched to feast. The silence was so deep her ears rang.

She had not expected a parade. She'd grown past the fool's need for ticker tape and celebrants, past any hope her small victories would ever be public enough for a festival. But she had not expected this quiet.

They had not left Brigit and her people safe. There was no "safe." New challenges would rise after Zelda and her friends moved on. But they had left them, she thought, with the promise of a life, and the strength to build one. There should be some trace left. Not this ringing, empty city.

Ramón, on the other dead horse, rode in grim silence. He seemed to hear a voice she could not, a voice that issued from the aching absence all around. June rode behind him. Shadows reached for her. Zelda turned away. It wasn't over. Not yet. They still had a road to walk. There was still a chance this would all turn out okay.

The empty road ended in a plaza and a palace.

The palace had been built to awe the people of an age when trains were new and human beings still walked down the center of the street: green marble, jade, and serpentine, its columns thick as redwoods, its lintel stones carved with scenes from legends Zelda did not know. Or else the carvings represented concepts, not stories: that four-armed hero fighting a beast with ten heads might be Governance, each head of the beast some social ill that seemed pressing at the time, like Poverty or the Ghibellines.

The palace still awed, not with height so much as with its ostentatious, labyrinthine sprawl in this city of skyscrapers. The wealth and power that, when this city was young and whole, had torn people from their homes and scoured all desire for parks and growing things from its downtown, that bought up shops and sent their owners scuttling to outer boroughs so in their place structures could be built so immeasurably vast that they seemed to have fallen from space, at obscene profit and with no end of graft and retainer and kickback for the relevant authorities. When the last of the old mayors fell and the mutants rolled in, they didn't burn the palace down. They respected its power. They occupied it, tore the faces off old paintings, decapitated statues and replaced the heads with clay models of their own tentacled leader. When Brigit's people cast them off, they moved right into the same spaces.

Zelda remembered their golden lion flag on the flagpole, a market bustling around the front steps. The smooth-faced stainless drones kept watch, with their pulsing, translucent, polymer hearts.

The market was gone. The tents had fallen and decayed. The flag hung in filthy tatters. Barricades were unmanned, weapons rusted. No carbon scoring, no craters, no bloodstains. No bodies. Not even bones.

There was no rot anywhere. No trace of rot. Only dust.

Three drones stood in the plaza before the broad front steps: sexless streamlined almost-human bodies, three-toed feet and three-fingered hands, their sensor suite eyes hidden behind blank reflective polymer masks. They did not move. She remembered their unsettling, even grace, and the strength of their thin limbs. She had shuddered when Ish entered the activation codes and the drones woke from decades-long slumber, and they understood what power they had called back from the blood-swamp of this city's past. She'd felt the joy as the drones answered to their call—but when the first one took its first step, she felt, beneath that joy, the dread.

In some moments, you could not deny the grinding force of history at work. Most days, you convinced yourself you were a single clearly outlined person with wants and goals and needs, like a character in a comic panel with a flat-color background, but from time to time your eyes opened and you realized your hands were not your own but wielded by a great groaning lurching process. You were the clockwork monkey atop a music box. If you could ask the monkey, no doubt it believed that it wanted to play the cymbals. That winding key didn't have anything to do with it.

She had wondered, several times since Montana, how it felt to wear one of the cowboy's white hats. If it felt anything like the way she had felt when that drone took its first step.

The drones kept still as they approached.

They circled the palace, past wind-tossed fallen leaves. Jade-black windows watched them. Zelda had a sudden impression that the palace was alive, an in-human giant buried to its neck in the city, staring at her with many blank eyes. Those emerald columns were its teeth. It waited for each new wave of lords and ate them each in turn, sucked their brains through small holes drilled in their skulls. It had outlasted the Green Glass City's first masters, and the ones who built the skyscrapers, and it took the mutants into its maw and ate them too. Why had Zelda thought Brigit and her people would meet a different fate? What did the palace care whose flag it flew, whose head sat on the shoulders of the statue on its throne? It was patient, and hungry. It laughed in architecture.

She wanted to leave.

She never should have led them here. Should have found another way, though there wasn't one, not with the Challenger wrecked and the cowboy steps be-hind. But even though she knew no other path for them to take, she found her-self wishing—even, almost, praying—that whatever swallowed Brigit and her people had also swallowed the palace garage where the oh-so-careful mutants tooled their rigs, where Ramón trained Brigit and her people to maintain the bikes and cars he fixed for them—the well-stocked, well-lit garage, all chrome and cream. Let it be gone, she thought as the dead horses pulled the Challenger down into the shadows of the palace's parking structure. Let it be looted, or overcome with cobwebs and rot. Let monsters dwell here. We'll move on. We'll make do. Better to flee the cowboy across the mountains, scrounging what parts we can from the wrecks we pass, than to let this palace eat us.

The underground parking structure gave her hope—empty, echoing, the lights long dead.

Ten years had not changed the way to the garage. When they reached it, she dismounted, and so did Ramón and June, to try the human-sized entrance before rolling up the corrugated steel garage door, which would clatter and alert whoever remained here. If anyone did. She hoped the hinges would creak, hoped the machines and parts inside were junk, and they could leave.

The side door opened soundlessly. The weak light that had made it this far into the parking structure failed within. You'd chain titans in this kind of dark-ness.

That was it. They could go.

Ramón flipped the light switch.

Light burst from the hanging lamps and blinded her.

When her sight came back, the garage was there. Well stocked, well lit, cream and chrome. Bays and bins of parts, mounted and well-tended tools. Not a trace of cobweb or dust. A drone stood silent in one corner. A crew might have just swept through in advance of their arrival, forewarned: Make it ready.

She wanted to run. She turned to Ramón. He wanted to run too. Even June seemed shaken.

But there wasn't another machine shop between the Green Glass City and the mountains. Sarah could barely stand. And the cowboy was following.

They had a choice. That was the thing about life on the road, in the alts. You had a choice. You took what you needed. And then you paid for it.

Ramón looked from her to June to the ruin of the Challenger, and back into the brilliance of the garage. "Let's get to work."

✦

If Ramón had been given a large piece of paper and told, draw up a perfect garage, list all the equipment you would need, the tools, design it for ease of use, efficiency, safety, make a spa for cars, natural caution would have stopped him from dreaming up anything so complete or perfect as the garage in the Green Glass City. When you caught a magic wish-granting carp, you had to stop asking for favors before it got mad and took everything back with interest—but you never knew where that line was. So you just asked for what you needed.

The Challenger rested, dead, silent, under the bright fluorescent lights. It had not spoken since the Medicine Wheel. Maybe the storm shook it. Maybe it was sulking from the indignity of chains. Maybe it was pissed at him for going into the storm after Zelda. *I didn't have a choice,* he thought. It did not answer. Its headlights were dull and milky as cataracts, its hide dusty, pierced by arrow and lance.

He did not understand the voice. He did not know what would bring it back, if he even wanted it back. If the voice had been there, it would have taunted him: Of course you want me. You need me. But a lot of people said things like that. I'm the only one who keeps you safe. I'm the only one watching out for you. You'll die without me. Just because someone said it didn't mean that it was so.

They didn't need the voice. They needed the car. And he knew what was wrong with the car. He'd found the holes that needed patching, the parts he could fix, the ones he'd have to swap. With this garage, and time, he could have restored the Challenger to working condition—made it better, even, than he had managed back at Tío's place. But they could not afford that time, and even if they could, he did not want to spend it here.

The quiet spooked him. The air was heavy. He dropped a wrench, and there were no echoes. He might as well have dropped it on velvet. The palace wanted stillness. It bore his presence like a tooth bore a drill.

The job, he'd estimated on the road, would take two days. He told them now: I want it done tonight. I'll need help.

No one argued.

He gathered the parts, told the others what to do. The Challenger came up on the lift; with the hood open and the torn bodywork suggesting teeth, it seemed like an anesthetized beast. He put his head in its mouth. And all of them were in the mouth of a still larger beast, the palace. And for all he knew, the palace itself was nested between the teeth of something even more immense. . . .

He was used to working while music played on someone's beaten old radio, used to men trading jabs with other men in the warm dry Valley air—complaining about their aches, their luck at cards, complaining about Dave Roberts or about their kids, all their groans radiating the sort of unspoken love that interior design shows on TV claimed people in Japan had for imperfect things. The men complained their love and slighted their happiness, and worked at ease together under the luxury of the sky. Here he was, without music, underground.

At least he had the others. Zelda and Sarah and Ish knew the Challenger from long ago, well enough that he didn't need to explain the difference between a fan belt and a timing belt. June had never driven a car until she rode with Zelda cross-country through the alts, had never looked under one's hood. For her, they were magic go-forward machines. So he made her his extra pair of arms—he could explain the basics while they worked, and she didn't need much expertise to hand him that wrench, no, not that wrench, the other wrench. Or: run this tube through a bucket of water and tell me if any bubbles come up. Or: put your hand here, hold this, and don't move.

They were five bodies in eccentric orbit, like planets around a black hole, slingshot from the Challenger to the tool rack and back. Orbits were, of course, harder to calculate the more bodies you had orbiting one another. That was the famous three-body problem: it was trivial to work out just how two objects in space would tug on each other, once you knew their mass and momentum. With more than two, the math tangled. You had to consider how each other body affected yours, every instant, and how yours affected them. It was common, easy, which meant wrong, to say: This planet orbits that star. In fact, the pull was reciprocal. Each planet tugged on the star, and on every other planet too. That didn't make much difference when the masses were so different as those of planets and stars. But take five complicated people and two or three great Absences—Sal, the Challenger, now Brigit—those differences added up.

Sarah was tired. Drawn at the mouth, all will and vectors. Her hands never shook. There was a muscle in her temple that stood out when the world closed in around her. Ramón wondered if she knew. She needed help, and that need drew Zelda toward her—Zelda, who needed them all together, needed them to be okay, her crew. But there was too much blood between them. And June noticed all of that, which twisted her like a screw.

Ish moved through all of this like a comet, bearing his shoulder bag and his tools, so careful that he seemed, for the first time since Ramón had met him on the roadside in Utah, bewildered, like a chess player who after following a promising line of attack looked down at the board and saw only bad moves. Go there, I'm dead. Go there, dead again. Whenever Zelda asked for a tool, Ish found it in seconds, before Ramón could draw his grease-slick arms from underneath the hood. Zelda thanked him, sincere, only for Ish to fly away again, busy with his own tasks. He was sensitive as a stripped nerve to her position in the room. And, for a different reason, sensitive to June.

Where did he, Ramón, fit in the tangle of orbits? Tugged every way and none, his path unpredictable to himself as the path of a knuckleball. He was, he realized, grieving. It was strange and wonderful to see his old friends together, back on the road—to be living with people who fit him like a key fit a lock. They were all still themselves, still the people who tried and failed together and limped away.

Wounds healed but scars remained. You learned to move and think in a way that did not hurt, even if that warped you. Maybe if they had all stuck together, they would have healed one another—knocked off the rough bits, filled the holes, learned a kind of gentleness they hadn't had to know when they were kids, because back then everything hurt less and what did hurt faded faster.

That's where the grief came from. He could feel a hollow in his life where they might have spent ten years together. But the versions of themselves that could have lived that way would never have split up in the first place. Those versions of themselves might never have needed the road enough to find it.

They might be broken, but they were broken in a way that let them do good work, fast. The day wore on, though the light did not change down here. The drone's shadow always held the same angle. The Challenger healed. He stepped outside once for air and was surprised to see the sun setting.

When they were all tired and stained, when his eyes ached from focusing on screws and wires, when his knuckles were bloody from some stupid choice or other—they gathered, and he put the key into the ignition, and the Challenger coughed awake.

They cheered. Ish hugged him, out of nowhere, and Ramón hugged him back and slapped him on the shoulder as if it were the most natural thing. They tested brakes and gears, did doughnuts in the garage. Fast work, and ugly, but it would serve.

They had done it. Again. It hurt, but they pulled through. His fear eased. Yes, it was bad. Yes, they were stumbling through a dangerous world. But they could fix it. They could solve the five-body problem. They could sort their shit out when they had to, come cowboys or monsters or rot.

It would work.

In the back of his soul, real or imagined, he heard the Challenger laugh.

After the others had gone to bed, Sarah lay awake, stared at the garage ceiling, and thought about the cowboy. About June. She should not have let June see her weak, that morning. She had felt ground to the bone after she turned the cowboy back, out there on the dry flats. But June trusted her. And Sarah had failed her. Again.

She needed sleep. She could not sleep. The cowboy was coming. Someone had to keep watch. She was so tired that the sound of his footsteps might not wake her. But if she did not sleep, when he came, he would find her frayed and shivering. He'd throw her aside with a laugh and stride past her and take June.

She heard footsteps in the dark—near, so near. She jumped up, tripped on her sleeping bag, tangled, and fell before she realized that she was not hearing the clack and grind of boots and spurs, but the *pad-pad* of sneakers. The figure approaching did not wear a hat, was, in fact, Ramón, carrying not a gun but a little ziplock bag half full of weed.

He had a pop-up battery lantern from the Challenger's trunk, and rolling papers and a lighter, and led Sarah out into the parking structure, where moonlight puddled on the exit ramp and concrete pillars stood like the truths of childhood. He closed the door behind them softly, holding the knob turned so the latch did not engage until he'd settled the door back into the jamb. They might have been teenagers sneaking out at night. With that thought, she almost felt like a teenager again herself, gangly and lean in a T-shirt in Berlin, hoping not to wake Pop, who could not sleep most nights and was always looking for someone to blame it on.

What a simple, strange, and terrible world sixteen had been. Great powers held her in their jaws. 9/11 happened one high school Tuesday, and she remembered coming home from class to find the whole base suddenly, violently Awake. As troops mustered and nations fell, she staggered through her own drama: a boy, a musician, another girl, everyday heartbreak that she'd known even then could not be the end of the world, because over there was the real world, really ending.

She'd met Ramón second to last of their crew—their circles were that different. He was funny—self-deprecating and light, focused on things few people at school really cared about, like cars and his own capital-*F* Future. He cared what happened to him after college, what path he'd take, just as she did, and for the same reasons—they didn't come from backgrounds where college was at all assumed, let alone the Ivy League, and this was a chance for them to build security, to carve a place of safety in a world that at best ignored you and at worst actively tried to make you dead. She wondered if they would have liked each other if they'd met in high school, whether they would have known each other at all.

"You looked like you could use a break," he said as he rolled the joint. His fingers slipped. He spilled some. "Sorry. I don't do this often these days."

"Hopeless. Here. Give." She took the paper and the baggie. Her hands knew the motion, just like his knew how to close a door without making noise. "You're so clean-cut now. Where did you find this?"

"It's the perfect garage," he said. "Wouldn't be perfect if there wasn't a little weed hidden somewhere."

"That's the, what is that, the ontological argument? For the existence of God? God is a perfect being, and one perfection is existence. It doesn't work, because existence isn't a property. A thing has to be in order to have properties. Did you bring a lighter? It's a tautology."

He passed it to her. "I'm happy to smoke my tautological weed in private."

"Just because your argument is invalid, doesn't mean we shouldn't subject your beliefs to empirical analysis. Retrograde motion still exists, even if epicycles don't."

"That's not the same thing at all. Who taught you logic?"

"I don't go in for your abstractions." The fire took. She drew smoke into her lungs. "*I* am a *physician*."

The weed hit her all at once, as though her bones had been connected by an elaborate web of tense wires that someone had, with extreme care, cut. Relief came in as breath rushed out. Tears welled in her eyes. She could not possibly have felt any real effects yet, but the cues were as strong as any drug. This taste, this feeling in her chest meant, You don't have to be on guard right now. It's okay. Uncurl. Relax.

She couldn't believe that. She had to focus. This was a mistake. She plucked the joint from her mouth, glared at the ember.

"June asked me to talk to you."

"Nice girl. It's kind of her to worry."

"I thought I wouldn't, at first. You've got this."

"I do."

"But then I thought some more," Ramón said. "And sometimes it helps to say a thing even if it could go unsaid. You don't have to fight him all alone."

"Who else is gonna do it, then?"

"Jesus, Sarah. We will."

"Sal was my friend."

"She was *our* friend." He took a long, slow drag. "Can I be an asshole for a moment?"

She watched him, disbelieving, in the off-blue light of the battery lamp, which made him look like some Force ghost in a cut-rate Star Wars. "Are you ever an asshole?"

He looked away when he passed her back the joint. "It's kind of an asshole thing to do, to say what you see when you look at someone."

"No one really knows what is going on inside themselves," she said. "At this point, I could use a hint."

"You need this to be your fault, because that way you're in control. That way, all of this isn't some whirlwind you're tossed in. It's a game you could have played better. We all tried, is the thing. We're all still trying. But at the end of the day, that's all we can do. We're not players. We're just people."

"We should be more than that by now." Meaning: It felt like we were more than that back then, it felt like we might actually change things, make a capital-*D* Difference. Back in college, didn't it seem like if you scrolled forward another ten years, we'd have all the tombs unlocked, we'd know answers to all the hard problems? She did not have to explain it, not to him. He nodded, and took the joint back.

"I don't think there's any way to be *more* than people. And there are lots of ways to be less." Smoke. Thought. "She's worried about you. June is."

"I am fine. I am just—doing the thing. It has to be done."

"Not by you. Not alone."

"She wants us to save Sal. She thinks that really can happen."

"You're not giving her enough credit."

"She's a kid."

"She's here. She's part of this. Just like the rest of us. She even has a knack."

"And what a knack. Jesus." The night softened and the little circle of light the battery lantern cast seemed perfect, as changeless and essential as the Medicine Wheel, binding the two of them together. "You don't know how much it hurts when I look at her."

"We all miss Sal."

"That's not what I mean. You don't have kids, do you?" He shook his head once, not with regret, only with the kind of puzzled expression people who had never given thought to the prospect of having children assumed when that prospect was raised. "I didn't think so. Someone else might not have shown me pictures by now. Not you. And you never asked for mine."

"Now I feel bad. Show! Show!"

She found, to her surprise, that she'd brought her purse out into the dark with her. Another habit. You learned so many of them—the soft rapid bounce to soothe the baby, the lift to your voice so they could tell you were talking to them, the periodic scans of the house when it was quiet, in case it was *too* quiet. You carried your bag with its ointments and salves, Band-Aids and tissues and needle and thread. And, always, the pictures. Most of them lived on her phone, but she carried a little leather wallet of printouts, because her father had. There it was, scraped by keys, stained by Alex's grape juice. There they were, inside.

Ramón made the right noises. For a while, the conversation was so normal the Green Glass City might have been a dream. He wanted to know about their favorite books (Susan's was *The Westing Game*, Alex kept rereading this Dog Man series and so far resisted literature that was not in comic form), he wanted to know what costumes they would wear for Halloween. She would have been happy to talk about them forever. But in the end, as he made their second joint, he said: "You're not her mother, Sarah."

"I know." It was easier to say, after talking about Susan and Alex. She felt like she had room to move. She wondered if Ramón's knack extended to conversations: finding the right paths. He had always been kind. "When we rode out last time, June was the age Susan is now. Now June's the age we were then—young, beautiful, confident, everything we thought we were. She has a knack. She's on the road. This shouldn't be her job, Ramón. We should have fixed it before she got here. And it just makes me think—ten years from now, this will all be even worse, and it's going to be Alex and Susan out here, finding their knacks, and then I'll really be a failure of a mom."

"That's not true."

He said it too fast to have spent any time weighing whether it was true or not. He was just saying it because it was one of those things you said. She held the ember up to the dark, watched it fade.

He asked: "Are your parents failures because they didn't leave you a perfect world?"

"I don't know," she said, then immediately felt bad about it.

"That's fair," he said. "I just mean—my mom and I, we have a lot of issues, but—all we can do is do what we can. And raise the ones coming up after us so they're ready for what they'll face."

"And yet you're here," she said. "Looking for the crossroads."

He kissed his teeth. "Yeah. I guess—we got to keep the whole thing going. So Susan and Alex and June have a place to stand when their turn comes." The wallet lay open in his callused palm: her son and her daughter. They'd taken forty shots to get one where Alex wasn't sticking his tongue out, but the shot she liked best was one with the tongue out after all. Susan was smiling but her dark eyes had that trace of suspicion, of the camera and the dress she'd been asked to wear for the photo. "I'm sorry I haven't met them."

"You will." She realized with shock that she meant it. "When this is over." She wasn't thinking *if*. "We should all have a cookout. I can host. No way Evan lets me out of the state again after this. I'll owe a month of solo by the time this is over. If I'm lucky."

"I thought it was a bad idea to keep score, in a marriage."

"There's keeping score and then there's a month of unscheduled solo child-care. I mean, Evan knows what I'm doing out here. He gets it. But he'll bring his mom in to help, and I mean, I love Joyce, but what's *she* going to think? You don't keep score. You don't do, like, arbitration, childcare default swaps. But you better keep track."

"Childcare default swaps. That's a scary concept." At her questioning look: "I went into finance. After we got back. For a while."

"Huh. How did that work out for you?"

"Made some money. I guess. I was depressed. It didn't seem like there was anything else to do. It's a strange world. You look at numbers—if the numbers are good, you are happy, and if they are not, you are sad. If the deal is done, it is good, and if it isn't, you work harder. It's a great way to spend your time if you don't want to feel anything."

"So what happened?"

"I had a fight with my boss. And a few coworkers. It got bad. I left. I woke up on the beach by Santa Monica Pier."

"What was the fight?"

"It was in November. A few years ago."

"Oh." She took the joint back. "It was a bad fight?"

"Not for me."

"I mean, I didn't think. We got into a lot of shit back on the road. More than most people ever see. And your knack."

He looked down at his hands. "I didn't touch them. I didn't have to. But I left afterward. The things that are wrong, no one person can fix them. Not even at the crossroads. I mean, shit, I lived in Calhoun College. You remember John C. Calhoun? 'Slavery is a positive good'? That motherfucker?"

"They renamed it, you know?"

"What? Really?"

"Grace Hopper College."

He shook his head.

"She's an admiral, a computer scientist. Invented—it's not really my field. I mean. The thing before the thing before COBOL. I think."

"We could look it up." He reached for his phone, by reflex.

"No reception," she pointed out. "Also, the cowboy."

He passed her the joint. "Seems like an improvement."

"You didn't hear about this at all? Aren't you on the internet?"

"Which internet?"

"Any internet."

"Not really. Baseball internet, I guess."

Eyebrows raised in admiration. "If I had a hat, it would be off to you."

"I've had enough hats for a while, thanks."

She choked on her own laughter. He slapped her back. "Like I'm fifteen again.

God." It was good to laugh. It was good not to think about June, about any of it. Then: "Did Sal ever tell you about that painting in the Corporation Room?"

"Zelda did."

"Someone got them to take it down, later. And I thought, when I heard that: We knew it was there. And we didn't do anything. We left it for someone else. It seemed easier to go hunting for the holy grail than to get the university to take that painting down. The kids coming up look around at what we haven't done, and they ask, What the fuck, Mom and Dad? They're right to ask. It was our job to fight for them. To keep them safe. And this is what we left them."

"She's not your kid," Ramón said softly. "But she does love you."

They had to sleep. They were tired and red-eyed, and she took those words with her back into the darkness, past the silent security drone, past the mounded sleeping bags. Held them warm inside her.

She had been wrong to try to save June from this. The girl had chased Zelda across New York, she had driven cross-country through the alts even though she did not know how to drive. She had not stumbled into this by accident. She had chosen it again and again. She chose them, too, the four of them.

June's sleeping bag lay beside Sarah's in the dark—the girl on her side, still.

Not asleep. Too tense for sleep. When June slept, her breath was heavy, easy. Awake, she kept still, kept quiet, kept watch. She was turned away, then, and pretending to sleep. Angry.

Sarah had felt her anger all day. June was not sullen, but there was an edge to her. Each tool Sarah needed, she found immediately and miraculously to hand, and water when she was thirsty, a chair when she grew tired, without June intervening once. When you were angry with someone you cared for, you sometimes did things for them, and made yourself invisible—not trusting your voice not to betray you. But your silence did, of course.

Someone you cared for. Ramón had said *love*. She loves you. In the dark, watching June fake sleep, she wondered why she ran from that word. She believed in love. She felt it fierce in her. But love could not be controlled. When you loved someone, you would die for them. You would march into unknown lands and stare down the cowboy for their sake. You might die. You might even, which was harder, live.

She loved Evan. She loved Alex, and Susan. She had loved Sal. How much love could a heart bear?

"I'm sorry," she told the girl. "I trust you. But I'm afraid." Whispers in the dark seemed louder than words in the light. "I don't want to be. But I am. And I want to keep you safe."

No answer.

She remembered what it was like to be seventeen and wrapped around a grudge like wrapping paper around a present, all that was soft and beautiful in you, memory, pity, love, all pressed into sparkly thinness around the shape and fact of your anger, the one true overpowering thing.

Her parenting instincts said: Let it be. Let her come around in her own time. You've opened the door and you can't make her walk through it before she is ready.

But Sarah was not June's mother. She was, maybe, an aunt—and aunts had different freedoms, and less power to hurt in ways that would not heal.

Anyway, maybe June really was sleeping, and she, Sarah, was being an idiot. More than once, sleepless with political fury and fear, she'd slipped off her skin and lain bleeding beside Evan, whom she'd thought was also awake, also silent, also bleeding, lain there for an hour only for him to shift in bed and snore. He'd been asleep the whole time. She'd laughed him awake.

She set her hand on June's shoulder.

Her fingers closed on something too stiff for a human body. Fear stabbed her, before her professional faculties caught up with her senses. This wasn't a corpse. Tearing away the sleeping bag, she found a knapsack, propped to suggest a body on its side, a shoulder. A bundle of clothes she'd mistaken for a head.

June was gone.

⋯

If you want something done, Ma liked to say, pray on it first, then do it your own dang self.

June didn't blame Sarah. Sarah was scared and tired and angry, and worried for her kids and June. On top of that, Sarah didn't trust June's shadows, didn't trust the road they'd lead her down. But June was on this road in her own right, not as a child or a student, and she would not let Sarah walk out to face the cowboy one more time on her own.

So she went hunting.

When Ramón woke Sarah in the garage, June was ready. The door closed behind them. She heard murmurs, laughter, a sob. She wondered if these old friends saw one another the way she saw LaShae—as someone who knew all the dumb mistakes you made, as someone just as strange as you but different. Sal's friends had all seemed like giants when she was six. Now here she was, in their lives and stories but not one of them. The cowboy had said: Ask Zelda what happened that night. She hadn't. She couldn't bear to. Not yet. Why?

Because you need them, the shadows whispered. You need her. Even now, you need them to be giants. Their height gives the sky meaning. But there is a sky beyond the sky.

Zelda shifted, mewed in her sleep as June passed. But she did not wake and June did not stop.

They would sleep, and she would fix this, in her own way.

She reached the door that led into the palace. Set her hand on the knob. She heard a whir like moth wings beside her ear, just as soft only farther away. She froze. Searched the garage in the dark. Zelda and Ish, both asleep. The Challenger still. Tools stowed. The drone dead silent in the corner.

It had not moved. Its faceless head rested at just the angle it had before. But she found herself hoping for the first time that day that the door to the palace would be locked.

It was not. It opened without sound. There was a hallway beyond. Clear and broad, with white tile floors, and swinging doors like they had in hospitals. She could not make out the colors—the shadows were too thick.

She stepped into the hall and thumbed her flashlight on.

The beam glinted off tile, off the metal hinges and fixtures of the doors. She saw no trace of dust or tarnish. The air smelled deep, like subway tunnels did after a storm. Why no dirt, if the place was abandoned? She remembered something, from grade school maybe, about how dust was dead skin. Maybe without people, there would be no dust. But what else might live here, now that the people were gone?

The door closed behind her with a click.

Reflex and fear sent her hand flying back to the doorknob.

Locked.

She'd checked three times before going through. It was unlocked each time. Wasn't it?

She could knock on the door. Call out. Wake the others. But then Sarah would know what she had tried to do. And Sarah would know she had needed help right away. Sarah would know, and tomorrow she would wake up to face the cowboy again. Alone. Because obviously she couldn't count on June.

June would come back and knock on the door when they were safe. When she'd chased the cowboy off by herself. Hell, when it was done, she could stride out the palace's front gates and work her way back around to the garage, fearless, conquering.

The doors off the hall led to storerooms piled with boxes of waxy green cardboard. Her flashlight beam startled nothing—no centipedes or spiders, no rats chewing insulation.

Tiptoeing in sneakers, she moved on to the door at the end of the hall.

On the other side: an office. She'd never been in an office but she'd seen them on TV and in movies: a warren of cubicles and conference rooms. They seemed to have been evacuated in a hurry. A book lay open on a desk, cobwebs over splayed and faded pages. She felt a stab of joy when she saw the cobweb. Something had lived here at least. But the spider was gone. How barren did a place have to be, that even the spiders starved?

Ramón had been so sure the Green Glass City would last. So confident that these people would welcome their saviors home.

That was one more reason for June to do this herself. She had never known the people who sat at these desks. She did not need them to be anything but dead.

She listened for the footsteps.

The shadows murmured in tongues she could not quite understand. They'd been with her ever since she cast the cowboy out—like the surf of an ocean hidden over the next hill.

If the cowboy smelled her, alone, in the dark, he'd come hunting. June knew his type. Knew the cold gaze of unseen eyes behind mirrored glasses, behind riot shields. He'd take a chance. One sheep at a time, that was how you took down a flock.

She would be ready.

But he wasn't here yet. So she passed through the dead office with its empty cobwebs and its teacups full of dried mold, and the heavy doors beyond.

An inhuman shadow loomed before her, arm raised.

June cursed, leapt aside—dropped the flashlight. It flared and died.

Darkness closed in. Crushed her.

Then she could see.

The hall—not a hallway but a hall, its ceiling as high as the big reading room in the New York Public Library, all marble and gold and brass and frescoes, the pomp of a young, rich city—the hall shaped itself around her in shades of purple and gray. There were vaults overhead, staircases and balconies, and in front of her, a statue, twice life-size, its raised arm holding a scepter, its original head knocked off and replaced with a cruder one made from clay. She could not tell and did not care whether the warped, sneering features were the artist's fault or the model's.

She could see in the dark. And with the light off, she could hear the shadows.

They were not murmuring anymore but clear and distinct, though far away. She didn't know the language they spoke, but knew that she could learn it. Beneath those voices, she heard a vast pulsing, a chord deeper than any instrument could bow, a song that filled the hall and could fill the sky.

June laughed.

She gathered herself. Shadows wreathed her, bore her up.

The headless statue, with its knobby scepter and its toga that she felt sure the people who really lived and worked here had not worn, seemed small, silly, a boy trying on his father's suit. It reminded her of that Greek story, the kid who took the reins of the sun god's chariot without the strength to guide the horses or the wisdom to know the danger.

The cowboy was here. But he had not revealed himself.

"You're scared," she told the empty hall and the statue with the wrong head. "You talk a big game but you're scared. Of me."

She heard boots on the stairs. Up, on the second floor, out of sight.

And she felt herself Seen.

The sense that she was known, pinned, stripped, revealed, it drenched her like a waterfall. Her knees buckled. Her blood roared in her ears. The voices quieted and fled. She had drawn the attention of something vast. It plucked her up, considered her. She saw herself reflected in its eyes, in eyes she'd never seen but could imagine as vast gulfs of nothingness, clear as holes: a child far from home, friendless, alone, in the dark.

It cast her aside.

The boots walked away.

*Oh no you don't*, she thought.

She chased those retreating footsteps up the stairs, through the high empty hall, through silent chambers peopled with the mannequin shadows of drones. He was always around the next corner, though his steps did not seem to hurry and she had made all-state track last year. Past paintings, sculptures, and drones, she chased him. Past defaced portraits and scarred murals. Down a winding stair and through a gallery of headless men.

You're running. Pass it off however you like, but still you're running from me. And I'm gaining. No horses here. No cops. Just you, and me, and the shadows. You don't scare me. We've got you outnumbered.

The voices were louder. Their song filled the hollows of her bones. Shadows slipped over her skin like snakes. The whispers were hungry.

The footsteps stopped. The hallway ran straight ahead to an open door. She could feel him in there—in the center of the room, his back turned, and no other exit. She was there already, every shadow a whisker, so much larger now than the limits of her skin. Was this how Sal felt in the sky, when she covered miles on legs made of storms?

I've got you.

She ran through the door.

It closed behind her.

The lights came on.

They flashed, blinding, from all directions at once. They tore her shadows away. She could not see. Her eyes were fire. Whiteness covered her nose and mouth. She sprang for the door, but it was not there—only more light, smooth and endless.

Her knees buckled. She could not breathe.

She fell. And she was lifted.

## CHAPTER TWENTY-EIGHT

They found her flashlight at the foot of the statue outside the office wing. June must have swiped it from the Challenger's trunk while they were working. Which meant sneaking off in the middle of the night had not been a sudden bad idea. It was a bad *plan*.

Sarah felt as if she were falling into a pit inside her own skin. She had tried to keep June safe—to protect her. But June was smart, smarter than Sarah. She knew there was no such thing as safe. She would not let herself be lied to.

That's two for two Tempest girls you've failed. Two for two promises you've broken.

"She's alive," Ish said.

"Where?"

His light cut the cave darkness of the green marble hall. So did the others', Ramón's flashlight and Zelda's. They were afraid, angry, concealing it better than she was. Better than she thought she was. Her cry had woken them—a gut-shot sound, more sob than scream. She was glad they were here now, for all the shame she'd felt when she tried to explain: She's gone after him on her own. Sarah knew that if she had not cried out, if her voice had not betrayed her when she found June's sleeping bag empty, she would have followed June into the dark without waking the others. She knew her own failings enough to recognize them. What she set wrong, she had to set right.

Ish stood beside her. She could not read him. He'd gone to that place inside where she could not follow. She pitied him, though that pity curled her like a fist—she felt him balanced now, teetering above a precipice, and she did not know which way he'd fall.

Two for two, with Tempest girls. Do you think you'll do better with your own flesh and blood? When you have even more chances to fail them, and they have even fewer guards against you?

"Ish," Zelda said, and her voice, always, melted him. "Where is she?"

His eyes softened. He was almost, again, the boy Sarah had known on those glowing fields of glass.

"Not far," he said, and led them, running, into the dark.

＞

June woke to pain. Coal fire on the back of her right hand. The wetness of blood. No way to retreat from that, no hiding in the dark water of her dreams. She thrashed, tried to pull away, could not. She was bound. Her eyes snapped open. Her eyes hurt too.

The room was light. Walls, ceiling, floor, all shone with pitiless artificial sun. She saw no door, no window, but she could not move, not even turn her head. There might be a door just behind her and she would never know. She sat in a metal chair. Two drones knelt by her side, with one hand each wrapped around her wrists and ankles. She had never seen the drones move, and they did not move now, no matter how she pulled against their grip. Other metal hands gripped her shoulders, her thighs, her flanks. They must belong to drones she could not see. She might as well be buried up to her neck in concrete.

She was afraid. There was a cut on the back of her hand.

"You look like her."

A woman circled into view: gaunt and knobby, all skin and muscle and bone. Scraps of clothing shaped her body: a sweat-stained and moth-eaten blouse, a leather jacket with all the color worn away, just a garment made of skin. Her blond hair hung lank and limp. She walked with a drunken sway. Her weight sloshed from foot to foot. In one hand, casually, she held a glass knife, its edge red and dripping. June's own blood dotted on the shining floor.

"She never mentioned a sister. I think she would have said."

"Cousin," June said when she could make her voice work. "I'm her cousin. You better let me go. There's people coming after me. You do not want to fuck with them."

"I know they're coming," she said. "We have time. Plenty. They're in the maze now. Lost. They should have known better."

"You're Brigit." She tried to see the skeleton before her as a hero, a leader, someone Ramón would remember with a smile. The woman lifted the glass knife. They made scalpels out of glass, she'd read in one of Sal's books, because it could get so thin—thin as a single molecule at the brittle edge. She never knew whether that was real, or just something the author of the book made up. Real or not, that was her blood on the knife. Blue eyes. Brigit had blue eyes in Ramón's story. She couldn't see the scarecrow woman's eyes at all.

"That," the scarecrow woman said, "was a long time ago."

"We're on your side. They helped you."

"They helped. Against the mutants." She clicked her tongue. "Against the half-men with the bubbling blood. They helped us win. They did. They woke the drones. It was a fight and we were beautiful together. And then they left. The shadows grew long. The whispers. My people would not listen to me. They would not hear the danger. They wanted to abandon the city, to leave it all behind. They were not grateful. The beautiful things we had here. The safety. What we gave them. They did not get it." Her voice rose and rose, higher, thinner, breaking. Her knuckles whitened on the blade.

"That's got nothing to do with me." June could not hear the whispers anymore. There were no shadows here. But she could still hear that single pulsing note, the deep music. If she could reach it—if she could call it to her—

There was, suddenly, a coal in her thigh. She looked down. That little glass knife wriggled in the meat of her leg. Buried to the handle. The scream came out like a flood, all her thoughts and will just a raft on the wave of pain.

Brigit's hand was empty. She had thrown the knife too fast for June's eyes to follow.

"Don't do that." Brigit swayed, her outline blurred by tears and pain. "Don't do that until I tell you to." She flicked the handle of the knife with her middle finger. The blade trembled in June's thigh and she gritted her teeth against the pain. Her grunt sounded animal even to herself. Brigit plucked the knife out like a seamstress drawing a pin. The tiny blade was deep red, dripping. A stain spread from the cut in June's jeans. Not a gush, just a slow seep. June didn't know much anatomy but she knew there was an artery there, or a vein, and if someone nicked it, you died fast. She'd been lucky. Or Brigit wasn't done with her yet.

Brigit said, "Play nice."

She wants to kill me slow. Or she doesn't want to kill me at all. Just to hurt me. The knowledge felt cold and clear. The cowboy had chased them, but the cowboy was a monster, just like the monster that tried to climb out of the Liberty Bell. This was a someone who had known Sal. A hero.

A monster at least had rules. A hero didn't have any.

They were deep underground. No one would save her. You asked yourself, sometimes, how it would feel to face death like this. You told stories. You tried to tell stories where you were brave. There was no way to know if those stories were true.

Brigit had said, *You look like her.*

June glared into her eyes and said, "Let me go. Or I'll make the shadows come for you."

There were no eyes in her face. What June had taken for silver makeup were metal threads like spider legs, stitching through the skin of her cheeks. They plunged under her eyelids, into the hollows there, into the meat and bone and brain. "They've tried," the hero said. "But I fixed myself. I can see them now."

---

They were lost. Zelda followed Ish and tried to ignore the clock ticking in her mind. The weight in her chest. I never should have let her come. I should have run further, faster. I should have been strong enough all those years ago to walk away, to walk out into the Hudson and never come back. I wanted to grovel, I wanted to beg forgiveness so forgiveness could be denied. I thought I owed her, I thought I owed Ma, but really it was about me the whole time. Like always.

A hand found hers—soft and strong. Sarah, gray-lit by the cast-off and reflected flashlight beams, raw and scared like Zelda was and for the same reason. That snapped Zelda into clarity again. She was making even this moment about her. If she'd fucked it all up from the beginning, if life was always going to skew in the worst possible way because she was ruined inside and spoiled what she touched, then there was nothing to be done, the situation was hopeless and failure was not her fault. But if that wasn't true, then there was still a way. A chance.

Their flashlights cut the dark. She assembled the palace's green marble and plush interior from the ribbons those beams revealed: a meeting room, a library, an office, a gallery hall, drones everywhere, statue-still. Carpet in many shades and patterns. Ish ran without tiring, following his knack, but now he had stopped.

"Closer?" she asked him, breathless.

"No." He didn't seem to notice they'd been running. "We keep passing her. Like she's moving." He looked so confused. "Zelda, I'm trying."

"I know." The palace was a maze. They'd chased mutants out of it, finding traps and half-eaten bodies left behind. If whoever had taken June knew the place, they could stay one step ahead forever—and kill her at the first sign of danger. But there had to be a way.

"I can do it," he said. So earnest, so true. She loved him in that moment. Loved that confidence. A problem to be solved. A problem like any other. He'd never heard Ma Tempest crying in an upstairs room.

But he was right, in a way. This was a problem. There were ways to solve problems. They didn't have time for a room-by-room search. June was here, Ish said. But she was moving.

Or they were.

She looked down. The carpet underfoot—she'd seen that grail-on-green pattern before, in the first room they'd come to when they climbed the stairs. "Ramón, check that door." She pointed to the nearest wall. That first room had been a foyer, and this was a sprawling executive office, with the kind of desk people used for photo ops. But when Ramón opened the door, she saw the staircase beyond, and the grand hall.

"What?"

But Ish understood, eyes wide. "The rooms are moving."

"Ramón, can you find us a way down?" She kicked the carpet. "Through the floor?"

"Down?" His brow wrinkled. "Down." The answer found him. She saw it in his eyes. "Yes! There's something—" He knocked over a lamp, scraped at the carpet with his nails, but there was no seam.

Ish's hand dipped into his trouser pocket and came out with a knife. Zelda had never seen the knife before—a wicked little curved blade like a talon, fat and hooked. The blade flicked out, locked—a practiced motion, like popping a Zippo cap. The blade danced in his fingers and he offered it handle-first to Ramón. Still a Boy Scout.

Ramón took the handle, but Ish held the blade. "Thank you," Ramón said, and Ish let it go. The knife flashed in Ramón's hand. Three long cuts, and a square of carpet peeled away. Beneath the floor was a maze of metal tracks, of the wheels and ticking gears that moved the walls. Inside that maze lay the seam of a trapdoor, hidden, its latch flush, mechanical—a last resort in case the system failed, never meant for common use, a service entrance into the grinding dark below. It took all of Ish's groaning might to shift the latch, but when it was free, the rising door revealed a long tongue of ladder, descending a black empty throat.

They shared a look, all four of them. They were here together. They were still the people who did things like this.

Down, then. Into the dark.

She propped the door with a lamp turned on its side, and with a heavy armchair. She was not surprised when, halfway down the ladder, the lamp slipped, and the door above swung closed with a tidy click.

*

"What do you want from me?"

Easier to ask it that way, to make this some pulp gangster moment, some *Godfather* shit, than to live in it here, now, in the coal and throb in her thigh, in the cut on her hand, in the steel grips that held her, with this woman who smelled like the smoke that came out of a light switch when you held it so the light turned almost-on. You are here, really here, with this woman who wakes people with a knife. Who gouged out her own eyes and replaced them with— that. Don't think how she did it, don't ask yourself, did she use tools, something like a shoehorn maybe or an ice cream scoop. Don't remember those little hook-toothed disks LaShae said the mortician stuck in her granny's eyes to hook the eyelids from the inside and hold them shut. She knew about those disks, LaShae, because, age five, she'd tiptoed over to the coffin and tried to peel her granny's eyes open, to see her one last time. They were mad at me for that, she said, even though I was the one who was really upset.

Brigit tilted her head left, right, like a bird.

"I see you," she said. "Soaked in rot. Dripping." Red dots on the white floor, June's blood backlit, luminous. "It listens to you. Just like they listened to it. My people. My family. I kept them safe, but still they heard the whispers past the walls. After all I did for them. They rotted. Ungrateful. In our beautiful city. After all we did to make it great. Like it was. Like it used to be. We could have kept it forever. But they betrayed us. Heard those whispers. Spread the filth. Whispered back.

"I fought it. The rot hates light, so I made lights. The rot hates certainty. So I made eyes, always staring, from the drones, from the lampposts. Wherever they whispered, I heard. I answered. I thought, an example or two will make it stop. Then they'll understand." The knife tended left, then right, ticking, a metronome. Blood drops patted on the floor. "They did not understand. I tried to save them. I tried to keep it safe. This beautiful city. I counted my people every day. I did not let them run. But they vanished. One by one at first, then whole families gone in a night. No bodies. Just gone. My officers left too. The ones I thought most loyal. All hollowed out. There were twenty of us. Ten. When there were five, I started to hear the whispers. When there were two left, my most trusted, we heard them clear enough to follow.

"We found the crack here. Hidden in the heart of our power. I turned away in horror—and when I turned back, they were gone, my final friends, my most true. I was alone. With the whispers. Look at it. Look."

June did not want to. She wanted to run away. She wanted to be home. She was not afraid of the rot, but she was afraid of this woman with her scalpel. The metal hands that held her face turned her head anyway, against all the strain of her neck. Those hands could break her spine with a flick, like opening a soda can. She fought them, fought the gentle cold fingers that coaxed her eyelids open.

There was a wound in the wall.

The Liberty Bell had a crack, a gap, a clean if jagged door between what was and what skittered, bubbled, and moaned on the other side. This was not a crack. A baby tore its mother's flesh sometimes, coming out.

The wound had a black line at the center, a hairline, so thin her eyes kept telling her it wasn't there. Around it, the wall was raw. Reddish and stretched like skin. Suppurated. Pulsing. Black legs, fingers, arms wriggled out from the black line to meet the light, and when they did, they withered to caustic gray. When she was a kid, she'd fallen, running, and tore her knee open on the sidewalk, bit her tongue, chipped a tooth. Stuck inside, healing—this was not long after Sal disappeared, not long after Zelda first came, bloody and crying, to their door—stuck inside, she fell into the habit of picking at the scab on her knee with a fingernail while she read Sal's books. Three weeks in, her knee was gross and seeping, liplike, puckered, wrong. The rest of the skin was smooth. She still had the scar.

June's eyes hurt when she looked at the wound, but the drones held her chin, her neck, forced her eyes open. She fought them. She thrashed. They did not notice. Her eyes watered, burned. It was sick, it was wrong. Let the wound close, or rip it open and finish it. Not this sick in-between. Her eyes had sharp edges. They carved the meat inside her skull. The light, the light with no shadow to hide in, no darkness to relieve. No shade, no shelter. Pitiless oozing constant light.

The drones let her eyelids go, let her head slump. She heard a large dog pant nearby. That was her. Someone's thigh on fire, bleeding. Hers too? She'd asked Ramón about Elsinore. He said Sal was tortured. She said sure, or oh, or maybe she said nothing. Had she heard his words at all? Not like she heard her own dog-wet heavy breath, in the darkness of the closed eyes she'd been given back. The eyes that were not hers now, because they belonged to someone else to give and take. So easy to say a word: *torture*. Easy to hear, or no harder anyway than other sounds. A word like a prison: a place you put things you didn't want to think about, a box you never wanted to open.

If June had a voice, she would have said, again, *What do you want?* Not like she would have said it in a movie, not defiant, not brave. She had to know what Brigit wanted, because she had to know what she had to do to survive.

She might have said it. She could not remember.

Brigit leaned in. "I want you to bring them back."

The halls were painful, certain white. When Zelda reached the floor, the lights came on, automatic and everywhere at once, walls and floor translucent panels of sunlight, as if she were standing on a screen. They wandered, blinking, until the afterpink cleared from their sight.

Ish remembered the place. "Drone control. It didn't look like this—it wasn't so bright back then. There should be a server bank down here. Surveillance."

Should be. "Your knack's not working either?"

A shake of the head, the fact acknowledged, nothing to linger on, just inconvenience. His mind, in love with problems and impatient with obstacles. "It's the light. The cameras. Too much scrutiny. I can fix it." Of course he could. He'd made this place—patched together the system's skeleton, tinkered with protocols until the old metal killers woke up and danced.

"Let's go," she said, and they went. Down halls, around corners, their footsteps echoless. She had to squint to see. In this unrelenting brightness, where could you rest your eyes? Ramón still carried his flashlight. Sarah had a wrench in one hand, and the flashlight June had dropped in the other. She looked like a hole in the shape of herself. Zelda reached for her. She pulled back by reflex, reproachful, jealous of the scrap of her own heart she was worrying. Zelda tried: "It's not your fault."

"She shouldn't *be* here." The cut went deep. Zelda flinched. But it was good. Sarah, angry, was proper as a slug of bourbon. If she was angry, she was fine.

The server room was as brightly lit as the halls, the servers themselves in blinking racks, webbed with wires, behind a glass partition. Someone had been living here. The surveillance console was lined with pill bottles, maybe scavenged from the pharmacy upstairs. Two of the bottles had been emptied onto the desk, their contents arranged in neat rows, tiny blue and purple pills like a calendar. There were knives in a row beside the keyboard, and gleaming surgical equipment. A vase of dried pale flowers.

Ish settled himself before the screens. The keyboard had an unusual number of keys, but that didn't bother him. Images danced as he commanded them: an empty surgery, its table mirrorlike; a drone storage bay, stalls vacant; a white room; a white room; a white room. With each click, certainty tightened its grip, and fear. She was too late. Failed again. One step further.

Wait. "Go back."

June, bound to a chair. *Bound* and *chair* were not the right words—the chair on which she sat was itself a drone, faceless, perfectly balanced, its heartbeat visible. The bonds that held her were other drones, their grips on her wrists, ankles, thighs, chin, skull more firm than manacles. Zelda had seen a drone leap from the plaza to the palace rooftop once, to catch a sniper. No run-up, just a gathering of pistons and a single jump, like in those old black-and-white Superman cartoons. They moved like thought.

Beside June, waking her with a swift clean scalpel cut to the back of the hand, stood Brigit. She had been so bright back then, so eager, the bold young girl they all, even Sal, had felt they understood, wanted to embrace, take home, ply with books and musicals and sushi, this hunter of old libraries, this visionary with her Disney Princess eyes and her bows and arrows and her bandolier of scrapwork blades. The hero. That was her. Changed, and still the same.

Behind her, on the wall, was the faint unmistakable wrongness of the rot.

She was talking. June was awake. "Where are they? Can I hear them?"

"Just a second. Wait. Yes. Here." He showed her the map on his third screen.

"Okay." Brigit's voice sounded clear and real over the speakers, as if they were in the room. She turned to go.

Sarah stood between her and the door. "Zelda. What's the plan?"

Right. She'd been on her own so long. You had to tell other people what you wanted them to know. "I'll save her."

"With all those drones in the room."

"Ish can shut the drones off."

"She'll know as soon as I try," he said. "I can't stop that. She's all through the system."

"That's why I'm going in. Just me. I'll distract her."

"She will kill you." Sarah barred the door.

"While she is, she won't be killing June. And once June's free, it will be two against one. This will work." She didn't know that. When she looked back on her life, she had to concede that she'd come up with a string of shit ideas. There was no time now for weighing and scoring probabilities. Zelda wished there were someone here better than her, some fierce lone wanderer who understood the secret ways of the world and could say boldly, This is how it will be. Someone who was not scared all the time.

But that person wasn't here, and she was. And June was tied to a chair.

"Come with me," she said. "In case it goes wrong." Please, she said with her heart. I know you love her too. Let me give this, if I have to.

Over the speakers, June screamed.

Sarah stood aside and opened the door.

✳

"You have," June said, then lost her voice, licked her lips, found it again. "You have to turn out the lights."

Brigit smiled coldly and drew closer with the knife. June realized she was aware now, always aware, of the knife, of the hand that held the knife, the angle of its edge. Her jeans were sticky with the blood. Hers. The coal, the pain, they didn't go away. They were facts for her now. "No," the knife said. "You want it. Like they did. The dark. But it's not for you. Force it open. Pull them back. Make them mine. Like they were. Do it now. Or I peel your leg. Like an orange. Thin strips, round and out." The knife drifted down to the dark patch on her jeans. Just a tap with the blade, not deep enough to cut. Not yet. The fabric sounded wet. Brigit wasn't here anymore. Just the knife.

"I'll try." Was she caving? Buying time to think of a plan? She didn't have one. She'd run off chasing the cowboy and here she was, she'd followed Zelda and driven half across the country into the alts and she was here, now, with the knife. Was there a difference between caving and buying time? You'd know if you caved. Wouldn't you?

The knife was there, against her thigh.

I can't do this.

She let her eyes drift to the wound in the wall. To the hairline of black, pure unstained black, that endured.

"I can't bring them back the way they were. The rot took them. The shadows. They're out there, changed. They're gone. You can't touch them anymore."

That was what Zelda would have said. Zelda fought the rot. She wanted to save the world. Maybe the world had been nicer to Zelda than it was to June; maybe that was why she wanted to save it. Maybe not. You could love a place that tried to kill you. You could love a family that hurt you. But the knife was in the world too. This chair.

When Zelda first showed her the alts, first showed her the edges of the world, June had, by instinct, reached out and called to Sal.

So she tried. *Help me.*

The wound—whimpered.

"I can see you," the knife said.

Could she? She could see June reaching for the shadows, but did she know what June had planned?

Brigit could hurt her, and make her afraid. And that fear would live in her, grow in her, rule her more fully than the knife itself ever could.

That fear was there already. It bubbled inside her like a spring. The knife sees. She knows. There's no part of you that's safe from her. Nothing she can't cut. If you test her, she'll prove it. She'll find some secret you never shared, because Sal was not around to share it with, and she'll cut an X across it and press down until all your joy weeps out.

"I'm trying," she told the knife, and silently, to the wound, to the shadows on the other side, she pleaded, again, *Help me*. I know she's hurt you. She won't let you go. I don't know if you can hear me. But we're in this together. She can't stop that. She can't cut it away.

The shadows twitched, in the rawness of the wall. Feeble, sticky lips parted by so slim a margin. Beyond, undeniable as the first fingernail of sun over rooftops at dawn, was the full and healthy dark.

The knife slipped through her skin. "Don't open it. I said. Bring them back."

She panted with the pain. "They need space to come through." The knife didn't know her thoughts. The knife could see only what happened in the world, not in her head. She could do this. If the knife gave her time. If the metal hands on her skull did not crush her like ripe fruit.

"They wriggled out. They can crawl home."

"I need time."

"What you need doesn't matter." The knife turned inside her. "You don't exist. You are an instrument."

God, it would be so easy to believe that. Imagine. If she weren't here. If she were just a body, a tool to be used and thrown away—could an instrument feel pain or fear? Could it dream? That's it, the knife inside her said. Yes. Collapse. Give up. No one would blame you.

Help me, she told the wound. Please.

There was a click. A door. She'd forgotten there were doors. The knife left her leg. The knife became Brigit again. It put on the mask of Brigit. A smile. "Zelda! I hoped you would come."

⤙

On the screen, they looked like ghosts to Ish.

"Let her go."

"We tried, Zelda. I tried so hard. You helped me build it and you trusted me to keep it safe. And I failed. I missed you. I missed you all. It's been so hard, to help them, to do what you would have done."

"Brigit. Put the knife down."

Ish was ready. His hands on the keys, the commands typed in to shut down the drones. All he had to do was push Enter. This was why you built systems, even bad ones for bad people. This was why you built them first and best and strongest. Because someone would. There were serpents gnawing at the roots of the world. There would be prisons. There would be towers and all-seeing wardens, there would be guards with cruel smiles and thick-soled boots. Who could think otherwise?

There would be kill-bots. There were kill-bots already, only with little human subroutines glued into their programming because it felt nice for generals to have compliant young uniforms to order around. These things would exist whether you built them or not. But if you built them, you had a measure, however small, of control.

Ramón bent over his shoulder, watching the screen. "You ready?"

"Of course." How could Ramón ask that? Ish had been waiting ten years for a chance to save her. He had not known when he built this system that one day he'd have to take it apart, but you never did know. You simply accounted for the eventuality. You made safeguards before you needed them.

He thought, for the first time in over a week, about Cynthia, in her black dress and heels, on his kitchen counter, reading. The long muscles of her legs, the arch of her neck. Was that really his memory? It belonged to another man, another life. Distance made that life seem golden. But it was his. She was his.

He'd built that life because he knew what was out here, because he had to be ready, because Zelda was on the road and Sal was working her way home through the rot. Of course Sal was. If you had Zelda, how could you give her up? He'd built his life in San Francisco because a serpent gnawed at the roots of the world. That life was a shell. This was real. He had to save them. Save her. He felt the weight of the gun. He carried it always. He slept with it. He wanted to grow used to it, to learn the weight of its possibilities. It was a tool. That's all. That was why he kept it. Tools gave you choices.

Brigit moved toward Zelda, knife out. He heard her clear over the speakers. "I tried, Zelda. We saved them. And they still left."

"This isn't you."

"You left, Zelda. You left, so you didn't see. You told me, way back when it all began, when it was just me and my bow and arrow and the five of you: Someone has to save them. And who else is there? We fought such a beautiful battle, and we won. But they did not stay saved. So I did what I had to do. Who else was there?"

This all felt wrong, shallow, hollow, like the shell he thought Cynthia had been, and his home and car and San Francisco. The alts were a dream. Here, beside him, stood Ramón, his best friend, the man he'd trusted, the man he'd taken an arrow for without thinking even after all this time apart—but Ramón, Sarah, Zelda, were not who they once were. Neither was he. He'd been living a dream of childhood, stretched over the now. Orbiting Zelda and helping her, silent, knowing what she needed before she even knew, as if by pretending that he still was the man he'd been ten years ago, he could roll back the years to that moment in Montana when he'd walked away, and make the other choice.

What was real? Ramón was real. Zelda on that screen. In danger. His hands on the keyboard. Sarah. The girl tied to the chair. The rot was real. The gun.

The serpent that gnawed at the roots of the world.

"June, don't worry. It's gonna be okay."

"Don't look at her. Look at me. Look at me!"

"It's the rot, Brigit. It has you. Let it go. Let the crack heal. I can help."

"You're wrong. I am clear. I have to save them, Zelda. You showed me how."

Ramón, by his side: "Do it."

Ish's own voice sounded wrong, like a recording of himself. "She's too close. Zelda has to get her farther from June."

"She's got a fucking knife, Ish. You've seen her fight."

He had. No mercy. No hesitation. When he saw her move the first time, against a mutant in a scrap-filled alley, he had recognized the expression on her face. He had been back in the shadow of the trees.

That was Zelda in there. She needed him to do this right.

The cowboy was wrong about Zelda. She wanted to stop the rot. Fix it. Save them. Even June. Zelda was good, and pure. The only good pure thing in the world.

"I know." Her voice shook. Was she crying? Zelda had seen Brigit as a hero, a shining girl. She always saw the best in people. "They left you. It hurts. But you can't get them back. You have to let her go. The rot's inside you now. Using you."

"No." There it was, the shift—from guard to predator. She stalked forward. "No, it's not." The clarity of that voice. "You, though. I see it all over you now. It's in your heart."

"Brigit—"

"They never can see when it's in them. I can cut it out and show you."

There. As Brigit moved on the screen, out of blade's reach of June, Ish slammed the alien Enter key. Shut it down. Kill the drones. Let June go. Save her.

Nothing happened.

Zelda screamed.

"Ish!"

It did not work. Why didn't it work? This was his system. He had made it. He was its god and father. COMMAND REFUSED, said the screen. Again. Zelda was down. So was Brigit—the knife torn from her hand. But she lunged, recovered it—up again, fast as death, a native of the shadow under the trees, and Zelda struggled to rise, bleeding.

Brigit's hand found the knife. No. No.

A wrongness caught her from behind.

On the screen it looked like a rope of static, old snowfall static like he used to see on cold Saturday mornings before dawn when he got the spare TV down and put up the rabbit-ears antennas to try to watch cartoons. A rope of *this is not right,* thin and writhing like a snake in pain, stretched out from the crack in the wall. Toward which June stared, as if in prayer.

She screamed as the drones began to crush her.

Ramón: "Ish, it's not working!"

He was still typing. Trying. There were other sequences. Other tricks. He had so many tricks. So many plans. So many layers to his wall. Measures of control.

COMMAND REFUSED.

COMMAND REFUSED.

COMMAND REFUSED.

*You see it, daddy.* That voice, in his mind. There. Reflected on the screen—a hat. He looked up—saw only Ramón. His eyes wide. *You see it, that rope on the screen. You think she's your girl. But the rot looks after its own.*

"It's not working." It was the rot, it was Brigit, it was the serpent. This was not happening. You said that, always, when the ground gave way, because you could not live and think, day after day, moment after moment, this *could* happen. Or: this *is*.

On the screen, the static broke. Brigit tumbled free, toward the knife.

"Ramón." He looked up. Scared. Weak. Alone. "I can't."

He was back in the shadow of the trees, back with the sound of breaking bones, with half rolls of quarters in his fists. Ramón could not help him.

But, after everything, Ramón was where he turned when he did not know where else to go.

At first, on that so-kind face, he saw only the emptiness of shock. He doesn't know what to do either. We're drowning. He is, and I am. You don't drown together, as a *we*. Even when there's someone else beside you, you both drown alone.

Then. As if from the heavens, a rope. Ramón's eyes widened. His mouth opened. Ish knew that face like his lungs knew air. An idea—too fledgling-wet for speech. The kind of idea that made you shove a friend away from the keyboard and say: Let me drive.

But Ramón didn't reach for the keyboard. He reached for a knife.

Ish scrambled after him into the server room, not understanding. The air in here was supercooled, iceberg core. Breathing hurt. If he could have taken these servers home, he'd have made more money than God. They put out demon heat but he was still wheezing from the cold. Ramón charged on, to the back, behind the racks of redundant iron that drove the drones, the palace walls, the lights. This wouldn't work. You couldn't just tear out a random server and hope things would break. There were backup instances. Failovers.

Ramón knelt, pried at a floor panel with numb fingers. Ish crouched to help him—use those muscles for something. Up! The panel tore free of its mount. Beneath ran a braid of thick armored cables, data, coolant. Power.

He lunged to stop Ramón—but the blade came down.

———— ✶ ————

June was losing it.

She'd held out longer than she expected. When the wound answered her prayer and stretched out one burning arm to seize Brigit, she'd expected a sharp, vicious crack as the drones tightened their grip—a sudden wet pop, a last awareness, maybe, of pain. But the knife was not done with her. It wanted her alive, obedient to its will. A tool to use as needed. So the metal hands closed, light and sure as a potter's, around her throat.

The sparks in her vision swelled to bright voids, a bright that was black, untouched by the surgical whiteness of the walls. The whispers were a rush of waves, of blood. Were those footsteps? Her heartbeat? Closer? Retreating? She felt that tendril she'd prayed for loosen its grip. She begged it to hold on. Just one more minute.

Losing it. Zelda rose, bleeding, unstoppable until she was stopped. June could not see her. But she knew her like she knew the knife.

*Sal. Please.*

The lights went out.

Now she could see.

The wound in the wall tore open. Shadow flooded out, choking rancid waves of it, held back by those lights for—years? She could not breathe. Shadows struck Brigit, and her body burst. Her glass knife broke. Zelda rolled away.

The drones' fingers went slack. There was air—somewhere far off. She groped for it. Choked on shadow.

She had climbed a tree once. Climbed through the clouds. And above them, singing, endless starlight. A realm like a flower, endlessly opening.

She reached out. Her hands were free.

If this was air, she had never breathed before. Her eyes filled with tears.

A hand found hers. Arms closed around her.

"June. Honey. Come on. Come back."

Not the voice she'd expected. Sarah's. Desperate. Needing her.

She couldn't stay. She had people back there. Back there, waiting.

She let Sarah draw her up.

＞━

Sarah staggered under June's weight, under the weight of the dark.

She could not see. She'd been in caves this black—on a class trip to a salt mine cave in Poland, where they turned the lights off, turned off their headlamps, and all of a sudden they weren't in a historic site anymore, weren't in tunnels workers carved with saints in bas-relief to make them homey. They were girls in a hole deep underground, and blind.

She heard great shaggy heavy things move around her, seeking. Her knack turned them away, made her invisible. Proper invisibility, too—not that "turning transparent" bullshit from Invisible Man movies. If light passed right through you without interacting, you couldn't see. Because seeing was what you called it when light met a healthy eye.

Her brain was chattering. That's what Evan called it when she got like this. Nervous, she jumped from topic to topic. I think you do it because, he said, and I know this is me trying to shrink you and that's shitty and I'm sorry, but because you don't want to feel what you're feeling.

Well, of course I fucking don't. What I'm feeling is terrible. I'm lost and alone and it's dark and I can't see, and there are huge shuffling groping hungry monsters all around and they're called history, and if they catch you, that's it. Game over.

But she had June. She thought she knew where the door was. She limped through the dark, feeling her way. The floor swayed. Was that real, or were her legs failing? Breathe. Breathe deep.

A hand caught her leg.

She screamed, kicked, lost her balance. Zelda cursed below her.

"Shit! Z, did I hurt you?"

A groan, another curse. There was blood on Zelda's hand. Sticky. She kept her other hand pressed to her side, her teeth gritted. She growled to her feet. "June."

"I got her."

"Help." Not a request. An offer.

"Zelda, you need—"

But Zelda groped her way around to the girl's side, draped June's arm over her own shoulder. "Go."

They went. She didn't speak—Zelda couldn't answer her, staggering, on her feet by will alone, June limp between them. Helping. God, Zelda never changed. Unable to stop, even when she should.

Sarah found the wall. Working her way along it, she found the door—slid her arm under Zelda's—took as much of her weight as she could. Two women, neither of them small. Her legs buckled. Fucking come on, Sarah. Get your *get* into it. You can swim the hundred in fifty-seven, you waste all those hours in fucking Mommy Pilates wearing Lululemon like the rest of the goddamned PTA, just get this fucking thing done.

One step at a time. Straight ahead. Through the dark. Even when you had to will every forward inch. Breathing deep. Breathing smoke. There was a fire somewhere. Maybe that was why the lights went out. Or the other way around. Had Ish done something? Or Ramón? She couldn't think. She coughed. Remembered fire drills. Keep your head low. She didn't have a scarf. She didn't have a free hand to hold one across her mouth, anyway. Keep moving.

Down fifty feet. A left turn. How long until the right turn? A hundred? They'd been running. Red emergency lights glowed from baseboards. She could see her feet. No more than that. "Z? Z, where do we turn?"

A groan beside her. She took more weight. More than she could bear. Her legs crumpled. It was all she could do to set them both down easy, to cushion their heads. Zelda: "Sorry. Just—just a second."

This kid. Lying next to June, Zelda seemed so—young. She was. Zelda was still doing the same things she'd been doing after college. No path to her life that wasn't this. No compromises, no Evan, no Susan, no Alex. No grocery runs, no mortgage, no life filled with random other humans who happened to share your shift, your class, your day care pickup time. Zelda didn't have any of that.

Sarah loved her. Loved June. Loved Ramón, and Ish. And she'd loved Sal. All those wonderful kids. Even herself.

"It's okay." She brushed her hair back from her face. "I'll take care of it."

She could drag them. Not together, but one at a time. Carefully. Down to that turn, past which the emergency lights stopped working. But if she remembered right, that hall dead-ended into the one that led out.

If.

Trust yourself. What other choice do you have?

She dragged June first, twenty steps straight down the hall. Went back for Zelda. Dragged her to June.

She had to stop then, pant. Recover. The air was heavy with smoke. She shouldn't be breathing. She had to breathe. Couldn't drag two women to safety without breathing. If—*when,* when she made it back, she'd get that personal trainer. The one she kept telling Evan she'd get. When there was time. They'd do. Sandbags. Fireman's carry.

She heard footsteps.

Boots.

Spurs.

Ahead. In the dark.

Fear closed over her like the ocean.

She gathered her knack around her like a cloak against the cold.

You can't be here. I refuse you. Stay away. Stay over the horizon, stay out there, chasing us, following. Don't be here, now. Please. Don't. I'm so tired. Just—go away. Let me be safe.

Let me be. Just pass by.

The footsteps, nearer.

I'll give you— What? What would she give? What did she have?

No. No more. She'd given too much. She would not bargain here.

The fear cracked.

She found her feet. Found her breath, through the smoke. The cracks spread, and rage seeped through them. Molten hot.

You want to bring it? Fucking bring it. Chew through poor Sean and that forest ranger and my parents and their parents and this whole country while you're at it. Go ahead. And at the end of all of that, you will not find me hiding. I will rip you with my claws and I will spit in your absence of a face. You talk a big game and you tell a big tale, but then you hide, you run for shelter behind your guns and walls and railway cars and your endless million dupes, but I know who you are. I name you fear and I name you poison and I will tear your balls off with my hands, and if you break my hands, then I will geld you with the jagged edges of their bones.

So come on, then. You and me. Let's go.

The footsteps slowed.

Stopped.

They were gone. And in the vast crackling silence, they did not come again.

She fell to her knees. Sobbing, laughing. Which was which?

She heard running feet, in sneakers. Flashlight beams. There were Ish's khakis, and there were his arms lifting her. She sagged into him. There was Ramón, his hand burned. The hallway darkness blushed with firelight. They carried one another out through the thickening smoke. Ramón found a door that opened onto the grand hall, which smelled of burnt insulation. The ceiling was sooty black. They ran through oven heat, past headless statues, through the office, through the clinic, to the garage.

The Challenger started on the first try. It roared like a demon, and its tires squealed.

Ish took one dead horse, Sarah the other, and they fled. She looked back as they reached a gallop: the palace burning, the clouds of smoke underlit by flames, the cracking sky, the Challenger and Ish and Ish's dead horse hell-colored with reflected fire. On her first night at college, the sky had been just that shade of orange.

When Ish found her back there in the darkness of the hallway, had she imagined that he was holding a gun?

# CHAPTER TWENTY-NINE

They crossed into dry fields where the only sounds were the curl of the wind and the high *tick-tick-tick* of grasshopper wings. Giant insect eyes glinted from the swaying grass, but so long as they kept to the road, none moved to approach. Ramón tried not to think about the size of the bugs those glinting eyes suggested. He flexed his burned hand on the wheel. The pain clarified.

At last the grasslands, too, gave way. They stopped in a rusted town near a green and greasy lake that spread to the horizon, where they found gas in an abandoned station full of rotting candy. A yellow Care Bear doll sat on the counter. June said it was watching her. Ramón tried to learn the names of every town they visited, but this one had only a single sign at the outskirts and it had been painted over with a scrawling messy word that made the rest illegible, so he thought of the place as Quarantine, Wisconsin.

They did not stay the night. Sarah, keeping watch while Zelda and Ish siphoned gas from the pump, thought she saw the cowboy's reflection in the tinted windows of what seemed to have been an adult video store, and Ramón himself heard bootsteps on crumbling pavement—but when he went to investigate, the street was empty. So far as they could tell, no one lived here. There were no people on the streets, there were no shops, no crops, nothing that would pass for food except for the gas station's moldy old Twinkies. (June: "I thought they didn't go bad." Ish: "Wait long enough, and everything does.") No people might mean no one for the cowboy to ride—but they knew he could ride bodies of the dead, and while those dead were fresh, no one wanted to test whether he could inhabit older corpses.

Besides, there were other signs Ramón did not like. Orange roses bloomed in front of a gray shuttered home across the road, a full glory of them, and roses did not bloom long without tending. Cars lay abandoned and burned out by the roadside, and there was enough broken glass to fill any apocalyptic lookbook, but some of the panes of glass here and there had been extracted with care and skill. Wood construction had been left to rot, but stone buildings—the library they passed on the way in, the city hall with its bare and rusted flagpole—seemed to have been torn apart, or mined, block hewn from block, like old Roman fortresses were when the locals a few centuries after the fall wanted to build a castle or a church. But they'd passed no churches, no castles, no new construction of any kind. The roads that stretched out over the fields had been blocked by wrecked trucks or masonry, but the roads that sloped down to the green, greasy lake ran straight and clear.

The lake spread foul and still to the horizon. He thought once that he saw something move beneath it—one huge twisting thing, or a body composed of many parts, the way a city would look from high up.

They drove until they could no longer see or smell the lake, and flickered through alts under Zelda's guidance. Some of the transitions were so fine he could tell they'd happened only by a slight shift in the color of sky. Near sundown, Zelda found their campsite: a circle of rusted cars standing on their rear bumpers, front wheels in the air. Some cars rested on top of the standing ones, creating shapes like croquet wickets, or doors from nowhere to nowhere else. They stopped in the ring for the night—a hill with a clear view to every horizon, and the cars for shelter and cover if needed.

"I saw something about this place on the internet," June said when they pitched camp. "Are we back home?"

Zelda said, "No. Ideas recur, that's all. Things at home have echoes in the alts, and the other way around. There's a man in the Inland Empire who's trying to build a mountain because God told him to. Who knows. Maybe he's right."

"We haven't seen anyone since the Green Glass City," she said. "It feels spooky. Like the whole place is haunted."

"It is," Sarah said. She looked around the group as if she expected one of them to argue.

"We're far out into the edges now," Ish said. "You can feel the rot. It eats away at everything. The ground gives way. It gets to you."

June frowned at him, but had no quick and easy answer. She just stood there, windblown, between rusting cars. Ramón didn't know what to say either. Sarah clapped June on the shoulder at last. "I want to walk a circle around this place. Keep me company?"

Those two were doing better, at least. June had started talking again. It took her three days, after the Green Glass City. She still walked with a limp.

Sarah was a good mom, whatever her thoughts were on the subject. Ramón wondered if she noticed the slight shyness in June's response, as if she were working her way up to something, or trying and failing to control an impulse she did not understand. Puppy love, or an honest crush. Ramón had seen it, felt it, many times. Acquaintance, friendship, helped you manage. Feelings were like water—if you let them flow, with maybe a little extra guidance here or there, they'd run pure and smooth and full of life. Stagnant, dammed, silted with regret, they would fester.

Ish sat close to Zelda that night, around the stove. They did not have the wood here for a fire, and even if they did, the hilltop was too exposed. Ish tried to make conversation with June, asked her about Ma, about school, about her art, and in the end she did relax and answer, though never for long. She sketched them around the fire, in a folio from her backpack, in charcoal: bold dark lines conveying weight and frame. She did not offer to show anyone what she was drawing, and no one asked to see.

Something about Ish's attempts to make conversation worried Ramón. The Ish he'd known in college was a tangle in his social instincts. He had weird edges, his gears ground against themselves. But he had learned how to hold a good conversation. He studied. He read books and took notes and each day sat down to compare his success and failures with the days previous, on whatever objective metrics he could find. This was how he sounded when he was trying.

Which might be fine. They were on a long road to an uncertain end. Why shouldn't he make peace with June?

And yet.

In the server room in the Green Glass City, he'd looked up from that console in despair. He'd dreamed of saving Zelda, and now he'd failed her.

Ramón woke early the next morning, though later than he was meant to. Ish had the night watch. He'd been supposed to wake Ramón before dawn, but when Ramón woke on his own, the sky was bluing, Ish's sleeping bag was empty, and he, Ramón, felt well rested and guilty.

He shook himself from his sleeping bag and picked his way through the camp.

Zelda slept near the fire. Her dreams had been bad since the Medicine Wheel—she didn't offer details, and Ramón's gentle questions had been gently rebuffed. Her attempts to share the tent with Sarah or with June had ended in sleepless nights and jittery days for all concerned, so she kept her distance.

Ish stood outside the car-henge circle, facing east, curling a large rock in his left hand. Ramón would not have expected the rock to be liftable at all, one-handed, but Ish finished his rep, tried another—got stuck halfway through. He growled, closed his eyes. Whatever he saw in the dark pushed him over the hump. The rock tumbled from his hand on the down-rep and he sat down hard beside it and rolled his left shoulder, testing the pain.

"I know," he said, low and bitter, without turning. "I should be resting."

"Are you okay?"

"No." He looked around at Ramón, and some of the edge left him. "There's not a lot of okay going around."

Ramón sat down and said nothing. Let him roll.

"I thought I was ready for this. To do what . . ." He didn't say *she*. "What we needed. I almost let her die. It's not getting better."

"The shoulder might. If you let it rest. I mean, Jesus, man, you saved my life. You're doing fine."

Ish smiled at that, or at something he'd thought, a private smile at a joke he'd never told. Ramón had liked those smiles. There used to be a lot of them.

Ish raised his chin, pointing. "I can't stop looking at them."

The cracks had eaten half the sky. They were spreading, the lines of wrongness growing together to create great gaps, pure absence. Sometimes he thought he heard the heavens creak.

Ish set his hand on Ramón's shoulder, as if to reassure himself it was still there. "Do you think she really wants to stop Sal?"

Ramón felt as if their conversation had been following what he thought was a straight path, when it was in fact only a straight section of a giant maze and now he faced an unexpected turn. "She wants to fix her mistake," he said. "And, you know, to save the world." He tried to make it a joke.

"But those could be very different things," he said. "She lost Sal. Wouldn't she do anything to get her back?"

"You think Zelda would turn?"

"I think if she—if someone I loved were out there, lost, even if I thought she was all the way gone, I could not stop myself from trying to save her. Even though I know what's out there."

"We don't," Ramón said. "It's beyond us."

"I know what's out there." He sounded like fresh gravel, or like the machine that ground stone to make the gravel. "So does Zelda. She's just trying to forget." He closed his eyes and let his head hang. "I was ten when I found out. I was ten and it was hard being ten. We just moved to a new town. We'd moved before. I was used to it, I thought. I was wrong. It got bad. I can't tell you how bad. There were kids who decided I didn't fit in. So they hurt me. Not just once. Every day. The teachers said I'd have to learn how to hit back."

"Fuck."

"I did. The worst of them, they'd gather at the edge of the playground, just in the shadow of the trees. That was their place, that's where they went when they wanted to be safe. So I waited for them there one day. I got rolls of quarters and I held them in my fists, because I'd read somewhere that it would help. Makes your hands heavy. You hit harder."

"Ish."

He kept talking, as if he were falling from a great height and to stop speaking would be to hit the ground. "I thought, you know, I have to hit them hard enough that it sticks. Most of them ran away when it started. There were three left. They say you just have to stand up to bullies. They don't go after people who aren't scared. But a certain kind of man, a certain kind of kid, needs to scare people to exist. If you're not scared of them, they feel like they're not there at all, and that terrifies them. So if you stand up to them, they won't stop until you break. To win . . . To win, you have to go harder than they can possibly imagine. It's just math. It started light. Scrapes. Shoves. Punches. The first bone broke. And it turned out that was just a line. Once you crossed it, you might as well go further. We went a long way out together. We lost sight of land. You ever see *Gattaca*? They talk about—swimming out until you know you can't make it back to shore. Once you're that far, you might as well keep going."

"What . . ." There were too many ways to finish that question. What happened? What did you do? "How did it end?"

"The kids who ran away got the teachers. By the time the adults came, it was over. Something like that, it can go a very long way in a very little time. Far out past sight of land. None of us could move. There was a lot of blood. Robbie never got his sight back in that eye. I don't remember everything that happened. Everything we did together. But—that's what's out there, Ramón. Past the firelight. It's just power and will. That's what's whispering to June. That's where Sal has been all this time. And whatever's true about the world back home—for all the ways it's fucked—it's not that."

Ramón felt anger inside him, sour and deep. "It is." He thought about the number of times he'd seen people argue that the Law was the Law. He thought about those woodcuts they put in public school textbooks about the slave trade, all those tiny silhouettes, featureless, laid neatly side by side like fish in a can. Illustrations didn't show the piss or shit or the stink of fear. He thought about Los

Angeles. "It's exactly that. Everywhere. Always has been. It just wears a mask in public. Some of the time. It's the monsters who put children in cages, it's the rallies and the raids. It's only a certain kind of person who ever gets to pretend it's not. What you're doing, whatever it is, you've helped them."

"I needed to shore up the wall. I needed their data. Their resources. Their contracts. I used it to stop the rot. To help her."

"What happened to you when you were a kid, that's fucked up. But, Christ, look at you. You're built, you're rich, you're white. You could pay some hard-working motherfucker union wages to hunt down all those kids who hurt you and beat them to death one by one with a lead pipe, and no one would blink. What the hell are you afraid of?"

He laughed bitterly and raised his hands to the gunshot glass sky. "What do you think?"

"It's not a choice between the cages and the rot. There are other ways."

"We haven't found one yet."

"So we keep looking."

"Is that what you did?"

That hit him. That burned him. He remembered the beach. He remembered those years he spent just making money because he did not know what else to do. "You're hooked on safety. I've never seen a junkie so hooked. Fuck, man, you used to learn how to lose."

In the silence, his anger passed. At last: "You're right," Ish said. The words were hollow.

Ramón put his hand on Ish's wrist, and Ish's own hand covered it. He looked east, where it seemed the dawn was always building but would never come.

"I remember when she told me about all of this—one day on Cross Campus. In golden light. It seemed impossible." Ish drew a breath. "A dream. I wanted it like I've never wanted anything. To go out, with her, into the unknown and face what we might find there. I was not afraid. For once. But we went into the dark. And we weren't strong enough." He took his hand away and rested it on the bag he always carried now. "Somewhere out there, we're still sitting on Cross Campus and none of this has happened yet. I didn't know what to tell her then. I don't know what to tell her now."

"Let it go," Ramón said. "You're friends. That's real. And if you try to make that what it's not, you're only going to hurt her. I think you've hurt yourself already."

"I want to help her."

"You are."

"It doesn't feel right, to let go. We're trying to save the world. Isn't that it? What's the world for me? There's the shadow of the trees. And that afternoon on Cross Campus."

"That's a small world."

"'I could be bounded in a nut shell and count myself a king of infinite space. . . .'"

"We're still a few days out from Elsinore. Give a guy a break, huh?"

The east was red and bright. Looking hurt his eyes, but he thought he saw thin cracks radiating out from the horizon, like the sun was a bullet hole in glass. He'd never seen them on that side of the sky before.

"Maybe," Ish said, "we should wake the others."

When they reached the camp, Zelda was sitting upright, legs crossed, against the car nearest the hillside where he'd been talking with Ish. Their eyes met. Hers were dark pools, still as the lake outside of Quarantine.

## CHAPTER THIRTY

They crossed the mountains and the wastes, day after day of blinding sun and parched bright ground, until at last, light-blind and weary, the desert gave way to rolling amber plains, to causeways over shallow seas, to the flat unfolding land at the continent's heart.

The cracks around the sun spread and deepened. Pressure gathered, the silence a nail might feel before the hammer falls. They were close, they were close. It felt like the weight and heat of a coming storm—but one night a thunderstorm did roll through for real, with lightning Zelda could read by and wind that rocked the Challenger, and when it moved on, the pressure was unrelieved. Greater, even.

The wounds in Zelda's side and arms were slow to heal. She took pills from Sarah's bag to dull the pain so she could sleep, but while they traveled, she brought the pain with her. This far out, she did not want to think what painkillers might do as she crossed from one alt to the next. Here, even the shadows of rocks writhed and wriggled when she was not looking.

She tried to talk to June, every night. Sometimes she succeeded. The girl was recovering slowly, from the Green Glass City, from Brigit. The wounds closed. The visible ones, anyway.

They watched a meteor shower together, after the others had gone to bed. They wrapped themselves in blankets and drank the last of Zelda's hot chocolate mix as the stars fell, or the satellites, or the alien spacecraft, June suggested. "Probably not aliens," Zelda said with some regret. "Never found any aliens."

"Never?"

"Nothing we were sure was aliens. Monsters, sure. But real extraterrestrials? Nah."

"That doesn't seem likely. No aliens anywhere."

"No aliens seems like the less likely option to you?"

"It's a big universe," June said. "How unlikely does life have to be for there to be none of it? And you've been through a lot of alts. Feels like you must have seen something."

"Maybe we're starting from the wrong seed." The hot chocolate was cooling. "The alts are paths we can see. Like dreams. When aliens show up, it's not really our dream anymore."

"Depressing. Think about that—stuck in your own dream. Breathing your own exhaust forever. Alone."

She found June's hand, held it. Up there, on the faintest edge of sight, another piece of sky fell. "Thank you for coming with me. We would never have made it this far."

No answer. She turned right.

Sal lay by her side, watching her with eyes jet black from lid to lid.

"Just a little further."

She woke with a start, a curse, spilled chocolate on the cold ground. June was shaking her—the same girl who had followed her from New York, with striking, normal eyes.

"How long was I asleep?"

"I don't know. Not long. You were talking."

"What did I say?" Meaning: Did I say a name? *Her* name? And do you forgive me if I did?

And there it was, the weighing look, the look that promised a question the rest of her could not yet phrase. "No."

They drank the rest of the chocolate together, alone, each in her own head.

Despite the tension, despite the cracks in the sky, she felt an excitement rise in them as they rode, as they gathered firewood, siphoned gas, trapped game, and huddled by the fire against high plains wind. They shared this—the hunger of a race dog for a metal rabbit. Years ago they had lost. They did not like to lose. They were not wired for it. Now their paths brought them back, and once more they stood at the gate, they saw the rabbit, and hunger wet their mouths.

They reached the Mississippi River again and for the last time, and followed its broad ramble south. The flat gray-green roll of it reminded her of granite cliffs out west, of the underground blocks of accreted island ranges thrust up by relentless tectonic pressure into light. The river carved its way atop the oldest land in the country, in the continent: the deep American craton, what America was millions of years ago, when the West Coast ended at Wisconsin. She had wondered in her years on the road whether that mattered, the age of the rock through which the roads were made. There was no one to ask. They'd set out on this quest without a wizard to guide them, finding the rules as they went. To do that, you read, you listened to jazz records or to the blues, you argued about hip-hop lyrics, you danced and you watched dancers and you listened to poets and storytellers where poems were still read and stories still told. Sometimes you caught a glimpse, you caught a hint that others knew what you knew, that they had dreamed the path you now walked, or walked it themselves for a while.

The Mississippi. Twain's river, carving the country in, well, in twain. On the surface. Go a few hundred feet down, and it wasn't one single country at all, but a jigsaw of melded rocks. All simple answers belonged to the surface. Deep down, South and North were gnarled and intermeshed. And on the surface, there was the river, the great fat gnome viewed from orbit, his hat on the Minnesota border, his gut swollen with Iowa, the curved boot-tip of Louisiana with a New Orleans buckle. Memphis and barbecue and blues and that one Marc Cohn song and across the river in Arkansas the Jonesborough storytelling festival, where one fall Zelda had seen the broad-winged storyman called Brother Blue, who could not have been there, who had passed away the year before, and yet there he was, streamers trailing from his spread arms as he spun in sunlight. Call it a revolution.

The *City of New Orleans* kept the river company on its journey south, and the Southwest Chief paced it back and forth partway. This deep in the alts, the tracks ran bare and lonesome, but if she put her ear to the rails, she could hear them, hear the whistle far off through the cracks.

They passed the gutted wreckage of a steamboat. She could not make out the name. The paint had flaked off and the boards were rotten through, the great hooped wheel a lidless eye. It might have been the *Sir Walter Scott*. Foul shadows moved in its skeleton. They rode on.

It had seemed like a young river back when she was a dumb kid. No pyramids here. No Viking longboats plied it. No kings fifteen hundred years ago had carved their poems into its flanking cliffs on their way to legendary battles. No ancient gates to the underworld opened nearby. The river could boast a handful of novels—a form whose name meant "new." Some songs. Blues and pop and rock. Big wheel keep on turning.

But of course there had been stories, there had been thousands of years of history. She just did not know them. Legends and myths, jokes and tall tales and memories, stories for children and stories old women told to other old women, a whole ecosystem of breathing, fluttering, bright-plumed stories ancient before the first Viking touched this continent. And none of them were hers. The people who scouted the roads she traveled now had done their best to wipe those stories out. They failed. The tales survived, in their own language sometimes, or emigrated to others, adapted and transformed, local fauna taking shelter from the invasive species that had no natural predators yet.

But to Zelda, the river held its tongue.

Sarah and June stuck together. Ish trained and stretched, much as his mending shoulder and cracked ribs would let him, until finally Sarah told him, in no uncertain terms, as a doctor, to slow down, rest. For once, he listened. Ramón worked on the car—asked June for help, and Ish. He explained each length of hose as he replaced it, each bolt as he tightened it. The systems were old, the parts were simple. Modern technology was more efficient, he admitted. You couldn't work on an electric car this way. But you can see what each part does here, you can understand why it was made and how it works, which means you can love them.

At night, June sketched by the fire. They had not seen a trace of the cowboy for days. June still did not offer to show her drawings. You learned to honor little privacies, on the road. But one night as Zelda walked past her shoulder, she glimpsed the page out of the corner of her eye—all four of them rendered there, not memories anymore but human weight in charcoal on rough paper.

---

The next day, just after noon, they saw Elsinore.

It loomed from a hilltop over the barren land, peaked and rusted, bristling with useless antennas and surrounded by the fallow overgrown remnants of the fields and towns it used to rule.

Even at this distance the building seemed restless. Alone on its hilltop, swollen with battlements and silence, it brooded and chewed old grudges, more tumor than structure, its defenses heaped need by need and hunger by hunger over the centuries as it clawed its share of flesh from the countryside.

It had been built on a crime. Its teeth were broken and its ramparts burned in sieges, its halls blood-soaked murder, its dungeons painted with screams. As they approached, Zelda tried to remember if it had looked this awful on that first day, when they followed the princess home. Had she understood what this place was, what it meant? Or was she taken in by grandeur and pennants and by all the stories she had ever heard about what a castle was, and about the kinds of people who lived there?

There, the princess said, pointing with an arm clad in samite, there stands my tower.

Zelda had hoped, against all her own experience, that in ten empty years the rot in that place would have ebbed like the tide. She knew better, but she hoped anyway. Even at this distance, the stone bubbled, and the windows moved when she was not looking.

They could do this, she told herself. They had gathered spin. They were together, and if they were together, anything was possible.

Even this.

"Where did the people *go*?" June asked as they passed a church, its windows gaping, its Saint Andrew's cross fallen down. "We've seen bodies, but not enough. Even if everyone who lived here died, other people would move in, wouldn't they? Ruins don't stay empty. People use them—for stones, if nothing else. And fields are fields. We read *East of Eden* in school and, like, half that book is about how hard it is to get anything to grow anywhere. So if these are good fields, why isn't anyone farming?"

"They're gone," Ish said. "The rot took them."

She watched him out of the corner of her eyes, and kept quiet.

They traveled for an impossible distance to reach the castle. It perched on a grand hill at the end of a long low valley. The road was gone in some places, trapped in others. They had to wheel the Challenger around broad pits and torn asphalt.

With every passing mile, Zelda's fear grew. The air was storm-tight. That this castle, out of all the bleak horror houses and lifeless fortifications in hundreds of barren alts, should be the gateway to the end felt like a cruel joke. It had been an end to her before—or a semicolon, connecting the road with the disaster of the rest of her life. Here she was again, barely wiser, much older, much worn.

She had a chance, at least, to fix her mistake.

Even that prospect cast shadows. Fix it, and what then? Who would she be without that mistake? If she reached the crossroads and walled out the rot, what would be the use of her back home, a witch after the end of magic, a warrior after war, stuck in a dying world without the power to change anything? Maybe banishing the rot would cure the other ills of her world, or let them cure themselves. Maybe the planet or the country could right itself. Or maybe people would just keep fucking one another over, as people always did. Nobody ever needed a supernatural motive to be a dick.

There has to be something better. She'd said that to Sal, so many times, before the end.

***

"We'll be there tomorrow," Ramón said after dinner, near the fire, as darkness gathered.

"So that's it." Ish sat cross-legged on the ground beside him, staring into the flames. "End of the line."

They had passed through a light rain that afternoon, and while looted ponchos kept them mostly dry, the chill lingered. "It looks like we beat them here. Sal, the wiggly unpronounceables, and . . . the other one."

Zelda remembered the grove behind Mona's house, back in Tennessee. "Let's not get ahead of ourselves."

Ramón poked the coals with a long stick. Sparks rose. "Long way up to the watchtower, once we get inside."

"We should clear the building," Ish said. "Floor by floor. Make sure nothing sneaks up behind us."

"Can't do it. You remember that place." Ramón glared across miles at the watchtower. So close, the destination had him in its jaws. "The dungeons alone would keep us busy for days."

"We could split up? Cover more ground that way."

"Are you nuts?" June looked up from her sketchbook. "Split up? I thought y'all were supposed to be nerds. None of you ever played Dungeons and Dragons? Don't split the party. Jesus."

"This isn't Dungeons and Dragons," Ish said.

"Ramón *literally* just said there were dungeons."

"You didn't worry about splitting the party back at the Green Glass City," Zelda pointed out.

"Yeah, and a woman stuck a knife in my leg. Makes you think."

"She has a point," Sarah said. "We should go in and straight up the main stair."

Ish, chewing seared rabbit: "The queen had a secret passage, didn't she, up through the library?"

"That sounds like a great place to get trapped and eaten alive."

He swallowed. "Good point."

Zelda watched the fire dance. "The way to the crossroads opens at high midnight. That's what she called it. When the moon's highest. I think our odds are better if we go in by day, fortify, and wait. The light's on our side. I don't trust that place at all, but especially not after dark."

June asked, into the silence, "What then?"

Zelda breathed in slow. "When the path opens, we walk it. We get to the crossroads. And if we make it there, we wall away the rot."

"Along with Sal. And whatever else is out there."

"And save the world," Ish said.

"Some world."

"You prefer the ones we've found out here? Poisoned earth. Dead guys, and guys way worse than dead. We've never found a place that I'd call better."

"Better for you, maybe." Her pencil scraped paper. She set it down.

"Would we have found a better place, really?" Sarah, soft. "If you want to find something in the alts, you have to be able to see it. Picture yourself there.

Evan plays these monster-killing games on the computer, to relax. But there's a Fire button a lot more often than there's a Don't Fire button." Her face twisted as though she had just tasted something sour. "It sounds dumb. Sentimental nonsense. 'What if they threw a war and nobody came?' But that is the point, isn't it? It is hard to even think *better* in a way that does not make me flinch." She waved to the empty fields, the broken sky, the wastelands through which they had passed. "This is . . . easier. Sick, but easier."

"You look under every rock in this country, and there is blood." Ramón wore the same fixed vicious expression he sometimes had while driving, as if the road might vanish and he would plow and pave a new one by force of will and wheel. "What did we expect to find out here? A healing spring?"

"I would have liked to find someplace that was not settled. Someplace Columbus was not a prick, someplace white folks kept their promises. Crazy, right." And Sarah put herself away. The rawness gathered, folded inside her, stored, and what remained was serious, practical. A doctor's trick? A parent's? Or something she had learned growing up? Sometimes you had to be something other than a feeling woman. Zelda wanted to stop her, to shout: *No, don't do that, don't do what you think you must!* "As bad as our world gets, as bad as it is, there are billions of people who live there and mostly just want a good night's sleep. And two of them are my kids. So we will do what we have to."

June considered her hands, considered the earth, considered her sketchbook. Glanced from Sarah to Ish to Ramón to Zelda, then back down. There was a maze inside her, a maze or a labyrinth. Zelda wondered which it was. A maze had dead ends. A labyrinth always led you centerward. "All the power in the world just to keep things like they are. I mean. I guess."

Zelda was tired too. "The world is dying. And we have a responsibility. We don't know what we'll find at the crossroads. We've never made it that far. Maybe we can save Sal, along with everyone else. Maybe we'll find Ramón's healing spring." She didn't want to say those words—she didn't dare to hope. Maybe that was what Sarah meant. You had to see it before you could find it.

"I am glad we're here together." Sarah said it all in a rush, looked away from the fire, embarrassed. "I mean, maybe we are all about to die, but it sure beats my ten-year college reunion."

Ramón looked up, no longer fixed or vicious—just himself, tired, kind, surprised. "You went to yours?"

"Evan's idea. We brought the kids up to New York, did the *Hamilton* thing. The reunion was actually okay, I guess. The five-year was worse. Everyone pretending they had any idea what they were doing, all the bad old crushes seizing a last desperate chance. One guy in the hall outside our room ended up shouting at his ex through a locked door for an hour until the cops showed up. I am glad I went, though. I did in fact have some friends in my year, as unlikely as it may seem. Did you go to yours?"

"To the five-year. Sort of." He blushed, looked down. "That thing you said about crushes. I found one the first night. Apollo. We didn't get out much after that."

"Good for you."

"I loved what I saw. Everyone seemed more relaxed, five years out. They all knew what their damage was. We could understand each other and we knew how rare that was." He scanned the circle. "What about you guys? Fess up. Anyone else go?"

"I," June said without looking from her sketchbook, "am seventeen."

"The five-year was Series B," Ish said. "The ten-year, I was busy with election stuff. I didn't realize the reunion was going on until it was too late."

Ramón's brow creased, but Zelda could tell he didn't want to fight. "What about you, Zelda?"

"I tried." She surprised herself with the confession. "Walked into New Haven. Got a slice of pizza at A1. You remember the woman who sold roses outside Au Bon Pain? I used to buy them for Sal. She was there, selling. I asked myself what I would do if she said hello, if she asked me where Sal was. Or what I'd do if she saw me and didn't ask? Or what if she didn't recognize me at all? And what if one of you was there? So I got a doughnut at the Yankee Doodle and left. Just walked away."

"Jesus."

"This is better. I don't do well in large groups."

"Sure," Sarah said. "Better. Apocalyptic errand. Six or seven fractures, countless contusions and lacerations, and zero showers between us. Drinking something nasty we looted from an alien 7-Eleven." She raised a bottle. "All we're missing is a speech from the dean and some school songs."

"From the tables down at Mory's," Ish tried. He had a high tenor, cool and wavering in the night. "To the place where Louie dwells."

"The hamburger guy?"

"I don't think so? Maybe?" He broke off. "Anyway, how does it go after that?"

Sarah sang: "Ashes, ashes, we all fall down."

"Pretty sure that's not it."

"Something something Whiffenpoofs assemble, and um there's another bit," Ramón hummed, "and then 'We are poor little lambs who have lost our way, baa baa baa.'"

The notes settled. Sarah frowned. "That cannot possibly be how it goes."

"I swear. Except the parts I made up."

"Bright college years," Zelda tried. "With something rife—"

"Pleasure."

"Really."

"Is it actually 'rife'? Isn't 'rife' bad? Gotham City is rife with crime and iniquity? Can you be rife with pleasure?"

"I am certain that's how the song goes."

"We," Sarah said, "are not doing the alma mater proud. Five thousand a cappella groups on campus plus the Glee Club, you'd think one of us would be able to get through a song in one piece."

"I'm telling you," Zelda said, "it's 'rife.'"

"Don't look at me, I am *still* seventeen, and I did not go to y'all's weird school."

"It was a good school. We all went there."

"Y'all, three Bushes, that drunk Supreme Court guy with the calendars—"

"He went to the law school." Ish.

"That makes it better?"

He shrugged.

"All I'm saying is," said Sarah, who had been trying to say it for some time, "you'd think that at least one of us would know one school song."

Zelda shrugged. "I still say it's 'rife.'"

Ish: "I tried."

June laughed.

Ramón looked down.

"Go ahead, Ramón."

"It's not a school song. It's just one I heard at school."

"It's better than 'rife pleasures.'" But Sarah was enjoying the needling, and Zelda was enjoying being needled.

"Fine." He hummed a note. The night stilled.

He sang. His voice was soft and high, and he sang as if he were alone, but each of them heard it like a confessed secret. When he was done, no one spoke for a long time. It seemed that even the fire had knelt.

"Jesus," Sarah breathed.

"Was that Paul Simon?" Ish sounded as if he were guessing, but he didn't guess about things unless he was certain.

"It's the last verse of 'The Obvious Child.'" He prodded the fire with a stick, and sparks flew up. "I didn't know that the first time I heard it. I wasn't even listening. It was a Duke's Men concert, freshman year. We were in the Berkeley Dining Hall, that big dark space with the wood and chandeliers. It was September and it was too hot and I'd never seen an a capella concert before. I was in a T-shirt and sticky, and up onstage there were these beautiful guys in tuxedos, singing. I didn't know what was going on, where I was, what any of this was supposed to be. They were good singers. I knew some of the songs. Not most. I was lost. And then this guy steps up to the mic, near the end of a song I hadn't been listening to. The tempo changes, the rhythm vocals back off, and he sings—that.

"His voice was so clear and so cold and high. I felt like I was looking at us all through the wrong end of a telescope, the dining hall and the guy and all of us together. We felt so far away. I don't even know what the rest of the song is about, but that part . . . It's about being older, I guess. Not old, not yet. Older. Being there, and all of a sudden realizing you are, and not knowing how you got there. It wasn't just the song. It was the song and the night and the boy who was singing—he was a boy, really. We all were. Kids. I heard him sing and I knew that he was so young, and I was so young, and there were years ahead of us, decades, this huge pit of time, if we were lucky enough to live it. I *knew* that all at once. I knew that we were children and that we weren't anymore, and we'd never be again. I was remembering us, even when we were still there."

None of them wanted to go to sleep, after that or ever.

They talked for a long time while the fire burned low, wandering through stories, interrupting one another, shifting around the fire as the wind chased smoke this way and that, until at the end of the night they had all found their original spots again. The stars were out, and if they stared into the fire crouched low against its coals they did not see the sky broken overhead.

# CHAPTER THIRTY-ONE

A t the end of the night, the men drifted off to bed. June slumped over her sketchbook, snoring softly. Zelda and Sarah communicated with their eyes. They lifted her and, draping her arms over one shoulder each, sleep-walked her to the tent.

Zelda lay awake under the strange stars thinking—about bright college years and about whether you could be rife with pleasure the way a house was rife with termites, worked all through with something that was not yourself, eaten away hole by tiny hole until you crumbled. She thought about Ramón, singing, and about her glimpse of June's sketchbook before she closed it and slid it into the sleeping girl's backpack, along with the charcoal that had fallen from her fingers.

A drawing from life, the artist not pictured. Old friends gathered around the campfire in the dark. But there were five figures around that fire, and there should have been four.

June's imagination must have played tricks, or her fancy drove the image. Or they had changed places as the night wore on.

But she, Zelda, could not remember looking to her right. Not once, all evening. With couples, you didn't have to look, because you knew she was there, like how you knew you still had eyeballs, or your ankles were where you left them.

Had she felt a gentle pressure on her arm?

She was alone now, in this campsite surrounded by her friends, so near the place of her greatest failure. Even regret deserted her. She had to do this—for the future, for the millions upon millions back home. She had to reach the cross-roads, and fix what they had broken.

But when she tried to picture all those millions, she saw only actual persons. Mona in Tennessee, weeping in the glen. Ma Tempest, graven in solitude, working her herbs in her apartment of carvings and masks. The woman in the Pennsylvania rest stop, with her card and her hostel beds. Sal, in the Medicine Wheel. All of them reaching out. There has to be something more than this.

She fumbled in the pocket of her battered jacket, and pulled out a folded piece of paper. It was stained and crumpled at the edges, dimpled and smudged, bloodstained, its creases frayed to lace. She had kept it as whole as she knew how.

She unfolded the drawing.

Travel and time had passed their hands over the image, blunting the scalpel edge of June's memory to expose the truth behind the story June told herself—their curve on the bed, each to each, the tender gap between their hands. Sal looked at her, needed her, and Zelda wanted, needed to look back. Their bodies inclined together, drawn by gravity into the hollow that parted them. But Zelda's gaze was turned away, to the window, to the future.

Back then, as everything went wrong and the trail opened in the sky, she had gripped Sal's iron ring in her hand and heard a voice, and what she had to do was clear.

She needed that voice now. She had to hear it. She had to be sure.

When the voice came, it was not the one she had expected.

"I wondered if you had taken that."

She had not heard June approach, but she was not surprised to see her: her bare arms goosefleshed in the night, the gold coin at her neck glimmering. Shadows around her curled and shifted, though she seemed calm. Her knack betrayed her, like a big cat's tail.

"You should be asleep," Zelda said.

"So should you." She settled down beside Zelda and touched the face of the woman in the drawing, the woman she'd remembered her to be.

"How did we measure up?" Zelda asked.

"Better than I was afraid you might. You know. Eight out of ten."

"That's fair." It was hard to speak. "I don't think hardly anyone's better than eighty percent at being themselves."

"We've got so many other people to be, I guess."

"I stole it," Zelda said, "because it was wrong. You drew it like it was this beautiful clear thing and that's not how it was at all. That's not who we were. I never—I tried to give myself to her, I tried to give everything. But I was always scared."

"She loved you."

"I know. I wanted to deserve it. Her."

"You did."

"I loved her. But that's not the same thing as deserving."

The light shifted in the sky. The broken world was laughing, and its laughter was not kind.

"Zelda," June said quietly, carefully, like a cardplayer laying down a hand long held to their breast, "what happened?"

June's fingers lay on her face in the drawing that was more true than she remembered. June's eyes were clear and brown, almost black in the night. Zelda wanted, not to lie, but for the truth to be otherwise. But that voice in her was small and frightened, and her love was great. And love demanded honesty.

━━━━

They had just come back from a true eyeworms-and-cannibals motherfucker of an alt, with, barely, all their fingers intact, and the golden astrolabe the princess said she needed. She gathered them on her balcony and said, her face fixed in perfect radiance, *We're ready.*

Zelda had expected, after the blood and dirt and terror, to feel relief at those words, but she did not. On the balcony, drinking the castle's cold blue wine with the countryside spread out beneath them, she wanted to do this forever, to just go and go, from one adventure to the next, struggling but never failing, hurt but never broken. No one wants a good book or a good life to end. But she squeezed Sal's hand and remembered that night in the Corporation Room. They were not here for the adventure. They were here because things had to change. They could just wander in the dark forever and let the rot get worse, hopeless—or they could take action. More than action: they could take control.

She remembered her grip on Sal's hand and the glow on the princess's face. She had tried, so often in the years after, to remember Sal's expression.

They were young and strong. They had their knacks, and after two years on the road, they knew how to help one another and how to fight. They had the princess and her books and tools, her equations and incantations, her certainty. Astronomical alignment was the final key—the cross-quarter day in August should be enough to open the way, the princess said. And once opened it would not be closed again.

It was almost time.

That night on the balcony, tipsy with wine and with the prospect of success, of transformation, Sal suggested: Why don't we take a break before the main event? The Fourth of July is coming, back home. Go. See your families. Enjoy the fireworks. We'll meet back here afterward, to do this thing.

They understood. They'd all been near enough violence by then to get what she was saying, even if, being young and lucky, the actual prospect of death seemed unimaginable to them—as unimaginable as failure.

So they went home. Even Zelda.

"But Sal didn't," June said. "We never saw her that Fourth. I would have remembered."

"I know." Zelda frowned. "I'm trying to tell the story."

"Okay. Go on."

North Bend was the kind of small town the Fourth of July was made for. As a kid, Zelda had not known everyone in the parade herself, but *everyone* knew everyone. This friend from church or that friend from school was the grandniece of the Shriner driving the little yellow car. And every year the balance of the town community chest come summer went into gunpowder and fireworks for July, for the display on the edge of the lake where the college kids went kayaking. Her church went every year, and the youth groups sang songs and passed a guitar. She'd wander, she'd sing, trade jokes, win a handstand contest, sneak a taste of a beer Cindy MacPhearson swiped from her dad's fridge in the garage and make a face. She liked it all. There were things she could not be in public, sure, but wasn't that true of everyone?

Sal found her in the woods by the lake near sundown on the Fourth. Below, the party on the lakeshore was in full swing. A giant beach ball bobbed through the crowd, batted away whenever it chanced near rest, never quite allowed to settle. Lee Greenwood's "God Bless the U.S.A." played over loudspeakers. Zelda had been remembering the first time she heard that song, in the fall of 2001, as she felt, for a moment, an electric charge—a sense of possibility, a sense that this horror might lead people to joining hands, extending love, bringing peace. Surely the Second Coming was at hand. Now, to the ears of her soul, the song sounded like a balloon rubbed the wrong way. It offered the wrong answer to the wrong questions. The last decade left her feeling bruised and naive, and hadn't much improved the song. That was what she had been thinking, when she looked left and saw Sal crouched beside her.

Zelda hugged her fiercely as a drowning woman might hug her rescuer, and laughed and sobbed at once.

Zelda had meant to go home. She had. She kept in touch with her family all the time she was on the road, through emails from library computers, through postcards and a P.O. box she rented in Chicago, never telling the whole truth, just, I'm traveling, I'm with friends. She did not exactly lie. She'd even been home for Christmas, drinking hot chocolate while the winter drizzled gray outside and talk turned to snow, to weather.

When she reached North Bend this time, she thought: I should tell them everything, about Sal, about the road, about where I've been and what I mean to do. I don't want to lie to them anymore, not even through silence.

She had walked up the long winding drive to the little house in the woods against the slope, which seemed no smaller than she remembered because it had always seemed small. A spotted hound dog tore across the yard after a squirrel, and she stopped short. She did not recognize the dog. The dog looked nothing like Goof. Her father called from the backyard.

By the time he caught the dog and looked up, looked over—Zelda was gone.

She camped. She was good at camping by now. She haunted the woods. She haunted her family, followed them without their knowledge from home to school, to church, and back. She fed the dog squirrels she'd trapped, so he wouldn't bark at her. She watched her mom and dad rock on the front porch, reading, and wished she could have something that easy. One afternoon, the pastor visited. She remembered him as a young man. He was still young, but he'd trimmed his hair short like some men did when they started to bald. She was a ghost. She remembered the thing that lived in the woods, that killed Goof and hunted her, but she felt no whisper of it now, never felt herself observed. The hunter had died or moved on, or hunkered down and hidden inside her heart.

She would leave. She would do what needed doing, and come back, and then she would tell them everything and be whole.

"Come on," Sal said when Zelda was done trying to explain. She held out her hand. "I want to see the fireworks."

The grill smoke smelled of cedar and seared meat, and the loudspeakers sang about hearts and how they don't forget. The crowd rolled around them. Kids Zelda didn't recognize played Frisbee and tossed foam footballs. The youth group circle passed the guitar around. Sal grabbed two burgers from the buffet, nodded thanks to the cook, who worked at Zelda's school but whose name she did not remember. The burgers tasted good. The night was warm, and fireflies slipped in and out of glow in the swimming pool air. A swarm of grade school kids chased a girl with streaming blond hair and a sparkler held high. Night covered them and stars sidled out, and hand in hand they belonged here.

The loudspeakers played "The Star-Spangled Banner." Zelda held Sal's hand close. The whole beach stood, singing. Zelda noticed Sal wince. Zelda was holding her torn arm too tight. She eased her grip but Sal held her just as tightly, despite the pain.

Zelda leaned in. "Thank you."

"I'll never let go," Sal whispered back.

They kissed as the music crested and the crowd cheered, and it might have been for them.

"Zelda?"

She hadn't done anything wrong. Still she pulled back. There behind them stood Cindy MacPhearson, every inch herself—bubbly and eager and bright, the kind of girl who would have been queen of an enormous Texas football school with as little effort as it had taken her to rule North Bend's hip-pocket equivalent. Zelda felt time pop like elastic—she'd last seen Cindy when they were both eighteen, and for sure they'd aged since then, but it didn't feel that way. Or were they still fourteen and competing to see who could make the grossest faces after sips of her dad's skunked beer? Some of Zelda's nightmares started just like this, a kiss, a question, a face from the past. Never Cindy's face, though. She hadn't thought of her at all.

"Omigosh!" And all of a sudden she was being hugged, and—"I didn't know you were *home*, I thought for sure someone would have said *some*thing—and please, oh gee, I'm sorry Zelda, introduce me!"

Sal's eyes wide, her eyebrow up and Spocklike, her face extremely schooled. This wasn't how the nightmares went. This wasn't how they went at all. She must have *seen*. That had been the whole moment. Not hiding, and for once no fear.

"This is Sal," she said, on autopilot. "My. Sal." Words didn't work, and neither did her tongue.

Sal did laugh at that, held out her hand. "Mine too. Nice to meet you . . ."

"Cindy!" Without beat or hesitation. "Zelda, I just saw your dad and he didn't say one word about you, and I mean I have never known him not to hint when there was a surprise and—does he know you're *here*?"

"We just got in. I couldn't find him in the crowd." She felt as if she'd been backing away from a cliff only to tumble down a pit she hadn't known existed. Why was she lying? Why had she come here?

"He's right over there." Cindy waved and shouted: "Hey!" And the man with more white in his hair than there used to be, the man who'd tried and tried to teach her Greek so she could read Euclid and the New Testament, turned her way.

Behind and above, fireworks exploded.

Zelda pushed, with all her spin and all her fear, at the skin of the world, and with her Sal slipped through, and they stood alone beside a dry lake under a shattered moon, and Zelda was breathing hard. "I'm sorry."

"I love you," Sal said, as if it were easy, and then: "Let's go save the world."

So they went back.

Much later, she would ask herself what were the signs she missed at El-sinore, the whispers in plush corners, the dirty looks ignored, whether the haze of threat that lingered over her memories of the castle in those final banquet days had been there in fact, or was only memory's foreshadowing, now that she knew what would happen next. Even after two years on the road, most of her experience of conspiracies still came from stories about them—and stories were meant to communicate what was happening to an audience, while a real con-spiracy depended on everybody save its actors living like goats in a farmyard, ignorant of knives until they fell.

The truth was that they had enough on their minds. They came back healed, chastened, staggered, renewed by their visits home. The princess welcomed them; the castle made ready to celebrate their local version of Lammas. And they made ready, in their own hearts, for the crossroads.

(She did not want to tell this next part. She did not want to tell any of this.)

The night before it all went wrong, she woke in the darkness and, when she realized sleep was lost to her, stared up at the painted ceiling of stars in the cham-ber they shared. The future lay beyond those stars, ahead, outside. The future and the end of the road.

"You're awake."

Sal's voice startled her. She lay under thick blankets, curled by Zelda's side.

"You too," Zelda said.

Sal sought her hand under the covers and squeezed it with a fierceness Zelda had never felt before. "We're really going to do this."

It was not a question, but the words lay over a void, a gaping uncertainty packed with tangled questions, unvoiced because after two years on the road they were unthinkable. "I'm right here." She tried to lend Sal's body warmth and strength, to hug it into her. But Sal just lay there, and Zelda felt her strength tumble into the void.

She did not let go.

A question emerged. "What do we want, Z?"

"I want you." She nuzzled her neck.

"Then why are we here?" Sal wriggled away, sat up, blankets rolling off her like water. She took the void with her, and Zelda lay blinking through sleep and vertigo, trying to prime her mind for a conversation she was not ready to have. "Why do we need the crossroads?"

"To fix things. You know that."

She turned from the window, back to her, in the dark. "How do we know we can?"

"You're . . ." She couldn't fit the word *afraid* and Sal in the same sentence. "You're worried."

Sal shook her head. "I'm not saying how do we know things have to be fixed, I'm saying how do we know *this* will do the fixing. We've traveled through the alts for a long time, and we haven't found anyplace better than home. I don't mean, like, better at making killer robots, I mean a place that's *better*. Less about cults and kings. Even here—I like the princess, sure, but do you think the people out in her fields would say that? Out here, where we should be able to find *anything*, there's just death and colonies and collars.

"Maybe we're only seeing these places because they're the only ones we know how to see. We can't find better alts, because we're so stuck on how things are back home, that we can't think it any different. But we don't even really know what home's like, what it *could* be like. We know what we've seen, and little enough of that, and what we're told. It's like we're trapped inside someone else's dream."

"We see the rot."

"But what *is* it? We saw it the first time we went for the crossroads, and it scared us—but why? Is it evil because it tried to stop us from changing everything? Five college kids who don't know the inside of their own heads?"

"It eats worlds. Stars disappear."

"And where do they go? We just know they're not here anymore. Rot's our word. What if it's like . . . inflammation? Or two tectonic plates meeting—one way of being and another—and one of them knuckles under for a while only for pieces of its rock to burst back up further in. We don't know what the rot is or what else is out there. We don't know what we're doing. We think that if we were in charge, we'd be able to fix the world—but we can't come up with anything better. It's our heads that make the monsters."

"What are you saying?"

"I'm saying we should admit what we don't know."

"The crossroads are opening, Sal. One way or the other."

Her eyes glittered in the moonlight, earnest and sure. "Let's go to them, then, and *keep* going. See what's out there. Past the rot, past the fear, past anything and everything. Together. Let's find out. Or . . . let's go home. And see what's really there, and what we can do, until we can find a better way out here, and *then* come back. Let's lead everyone out, everyone who's ever hurt, everyone who's scared when there's a knock on their door. All of us, together, not just five people who think they're special." She screwed her eyes up tight, shook her head. "I'm getting this wrong. All this philosophy class shit. It's easier to talk about power and fuckin' metaphysics than it is to . . ."

She trailed off. Zelda waited.

Sal reached for her jacket, folded with the rest of her clothes by the side of the bed, fished something from a pocket, and offered it to her: a ring of black metal.

"I love you, Z. And I want to walk together, forever. Under all stars. If you'll have me." She held out the ring.

"Sal." Then: "I don't know what to say."

"Yes, maybe. Or: I love you. If you want."

"I love you." It was an echo, wondering. The castle's stone walls seemed thinner than a shell. She took the ring, her fingers clumsy, her chest tight. She did not slide it onto her finger—just left it in her palm, black and cold and heavy. What did forever look like? Who was she, to say anything was forever?

"That's a start." Sal sounded—sad, poised. Patient.

"We could be dead this time tomorrow. I could hurt you."

"You won't." There was a light in her, a warmth. No performance, none of the old pirate bravado, the duelist's strut. She was raw and glowing. "I've seen it. Ten years from now, you'll still be you, this woman I love, right here. And you will love me back. That's all that matters to me. Whatever happens in the meantime."

She kissed her then, like the sky breaking in thunder. She kissed her and she said, *under all stars,* and she pressed her down, and they were hungry for each other, and afterward they slept.

With the ring clutched tight in Zelda's palm.

———

She looked across to June. "Do you know what happened next?"

"Ramón told me. He tried, anyway. I didn't follow it all."

"We didn't either, and we lived through it. They came for us while we were sleeping."

June shook her head.

Zelda tried to make her understand. "It would be easier to explain if you'd seen the castle up close, before it fell. All velvets and tapestries, jewels and secret passages, bright fires and revels and assignations. They lived in gold and silver; the vizier prayed to a magic mirror. They were queens and kings and lords, they carried knives and used them. They were predators in human skin. It was beautiful and it was a bear trap. I thought the princess was different, but I'm not sure I was right. She wanted knowledge, and truth, and the power of the crossroads. Just like us.

"The queen, the vizier, the others, they knew about the rot. They knew the stars were going out. They heard whispers through the cracks in the world. They knew the princess was on the verge of gaining power and they knew we were her allies."

"How did it happen?"

"Like it does anywhere. They grabbed us. The trap snapped shut. We tried to escape. Poison and blood. Duels in the hallways. Blood ran down the stairs." She was surprised that she could say it so flatly, that she could recount the terror of that night as if she were reading off a shopping list. But what other way could she tell it? "I didn't . . . I didn't experience it like time. Maybe that doesn't make sense."

"It does."

"We did what we had to. But when I think back, I remember how scared I was. I remember Sal's weight, when we got her out. She was barely able to walk. We tried to escape, but we kept getting lost in tunnels and passages I'd never seen before. When did the walls start to move? When did the shadows wake up? There was blood on my hands. The princess, dying, told us to go. I remember a duel in the Great Hall. I remember Ish killed someone. So did I. I must sound like I'm crazy."

"No."

They could see the rotten castle still, miles off, dark and swollen as a boil.

There was too much darkness of the wrong character gathered there. The cracks Sal left in the sky sucked at their vision, but the castle repelled it.

"I've seen things go bad," June said. "It's the same shit all over, I think."

"You sound like Sal."

She said gently, "I didn't mean, 'How did you get caught?' I mean, what happened at the very end?"

"At the very end?" She laughed wetly. "We ran. The queen threw herself from the battlements. The princess was dead, the sky was breaking open, and the walls were eating people. I ran. I got Sal out."

"And then?"

"And then I looked up."

⸻

They'd set guards around the Challenger, of course, in case the witches and traitors managed to escape. The rot ate two of the guards, ate them right out of their boots. The third stood his ground and did his duty, until Zelda dropped him. Later she wasn't even sure what she had done. Heart attack? Aneurysm? She thrust spin into him and he crumpled. She stumbled past his body and heaped Sal into the Challenger's passenger seat.

Sal was out of it. The cut at her temple had opened again. She kept her eyes shut tight, against the pain or against the world. But as Zelda straightened, Sal grabbed her hand, hard. The iron ring on Zelda's finger cut into her skin, and creaked against her finger bones. Sal had always been the stronger.

Behind them, the castle was dying. Stone walls could not contain the screams. Somewhere, stained glass shattered.

The light changed.

Zelda looked up and saw why.

Writhing fractures broke the sky into shards of cloud and star. The moon was high. And there, from the princess's balcony, ran the path.

The black-flower road, straight and clear through silver fields.

She had done it. There it was, after all their journeying. The path to the crossroads.

She was afraid.

Sal clutched her hand.

"Sal. Sal, look."

Her eyes were glazed with pain. She shook her head, turned away.

They had to go now. The castle had fallen. The princess was gone. The rot soaked through the grand halls like blood through a towel. They had failed. There would be another chance.

But there was the road, right there, leading from the princess's balcony. This could be as close as they ever came. The princess was gone. All her books and tools and secret knowledge, they would fall into the rot.

How much longer could they bear this road?

Let's go beyond it, Sal had said. Or let's go home.

Zelda remembered that first night in Sal's bed in the Bronx, a million years ago, when she had felt so naked to the world. She was scared, alone, exposed, and hungry, desperate as a woman in free fall for some ledge to clutch no matter how sharp, for a rein on the world, for things to have an order and a place. For control. A hand across her mouth or around her throat.

They would go home themselves, two years out of college. No more school, no more magic. Back to the world. The world was cold and if she did not rule it, it would rule her.

*We're trapped inside someone else's dream.*

She wiped sweat from her forehead. The ring was cool in her palm and she clutched it tighter.

She loved Sal. She trusted her. She was afraid. She realized—she had always been afraid. It wasn't even her fear. It was something she had breathed in, like a miner filling her lungs with stone.

Escape, she told herself. Leave this charnel house of kings. Go home with her and wear the ring and love her and work beside her and let that be enough. Build what you can from there. Even though it scares you.

But there was another voice inside her, calm and sure.

You know what's out there and what's back home. You know what's real. Darkness and pain, pain forever. It will close around you both like a mouth and swallow you. Do you think it will go away? The world is changing, girl, and love ain't but a slim reed to lean on. You got to find safety. You got to take care of her. Of you and yours. You got to finish what you started. She thinks she loves you now. But will she when the wolves come close?

*Yes,* she told her voice. *Yes.*

Then she'll throw herself between them and you. She'll do what she has to, and she will die, and that will be your fault. Just like today. She don't look so good. She's fading. And this is your fault. You led her here. You with your puppy crush on that girl in white, and the hunger you can't name. You did this, and it's on you to make it right.

*No.*

You can't have it both ways. That ring right there, it's forever. That ring right there, it's a door out of childhood. No games, no magic circles, no pretending what's true doesn't matter, that you'll be safe and cozy. That's the rest of your real and natural life, and if you're strong enough to make it that far, at the end one of you dies first. You want safety? You want to carve out a little hole for yourself, or for the two of you? You get one chance. There it is.

The long black trail, and the crossroads.

———

She stopped. She could not speak anymore. She should have hidden, she should have lied. The moonlight was cold outside.

"So you left."

June's voice was still and clear.

"The voice," Zelda said. "I heard it in my dreams." She sounded pathetic. But then, the truth was pathetic. "I heard it on the rooftop in Montana. I don't know if it was him, or if when he speaks, we hear the language we use against ourselves."

June said nothing.

"I left the ring in her hand. I passed Sarah, running from the hall—I told her to watch Sal. I told her I was going back for Ramón and Ish. I fought my way up to the balcony. The rot tried to stop me. It took—I don't know how long I fought to reach the top. Some days it feels like I'm still there, climbing, losing blood, just . . . losing. The castle walls crumbling about me. But my feet knew the way. I made it to the balcony. To the road. And I began to walk."

It went well, at first.

The silver land was a mirage only until you entered it, silver only while it was a mirage. Once through, she saw with double vision. It was night. The hills and hanging moss were green gold and gray under the moon. An owl called. Overhead, among the trees, huge, quiet shapes slid by on mighty wings.

The road was black beneath her feet; beneath the flowers, it was wet like tilled earth, and where the moonlight fell, she thought the wetness red.

Lightning flickered across the sky, bright enough to green the darkened hills. The lightning bolts were stuck overhead, pale, throbbing wounds. She could see farther here than should be possible, and miles and miles distant lay the crossroads.

Cracks opened in the ground. The road split beneath her. White lines of lightning widened in the sky as if something were trying to break in.

Sal was on the road behind her, gaining fast.

How? Sal was bleeding, she could not run straight, but her eyes were open and her legs were longer than Zelda's and she was faster, she was closing, with a determination that scorned pain, fear, and death.

Zelda would learn later, as she and Sarah screamed at each other in the parking lot in Montana, that Sal had come out of her daze to find the ring in her hand, staggered to her feet, and run into the castle after her. Sarah tried to stop her, but Sal decked her, right through Sarah's knack. Unstoppable, always. Sarah and the others tried to catch up with her, but by the time they reached the balcony, the road was in tatters, the sky a roil. They did the only thing they could: they chased after them in the Challenger, following the black-flower trail through the sky.

"Zelda! Wait!"

She couldn't. This was the path. She had walked so far already.

Keep going. Almost there.

She looked back.

Sal ran after her. Where she stepped, cracks spread through the sky. Through them Zelda saw, down below, far, far below, the flickering rawness of the earth.

Long spindly legs of shadow reared up from the cracks. Sal was so near.

Don't stop. You made the hard choice once. You couldn't make it again.

Sal didn't understand. It would be better this way. Once she reached the crossroads, once she made the world right, they could be together without rot, without shadows, without fear. They would be safe. She would make sure of that. You could give up anything in trade for that. You could give up your soul. You could give up your own name.

At first glance, the pits that opened in the road went all the way down to the hard earth far below. Then, between instants, they became gaps into deep and writhing space, into somewhere her eye could not taste nor her heart accept.

You're close.

She had to make it. Their whole life together, she'd been one step behind Sal, but now she could do this—for them. For her.

She did not know how long they ran. Hours, minutes, weeks. Forever. She was still running. And there lay the crossroads.

Her legs were lead. Her lungs fire.

She heard a scream.

---

"I tried to catch her," Zelda said. "She had fallen into one of the cracks. The legs, they had her, pulled her down. I tried. I caught her hand." She was crying. She breathed it in, tried to master herself. She'd said this much. She had to say it all the way. "I was so scared. I loved her. I wanted her to think I was brave."

"You caught her."

"And she looked at me."

---

Sal's eyes were wide and shining and full of roiled black from lid to lid.

She dangled over the void. Legs wire-thin and strong caught her, cut her, dragged her down. Zelda's grip alone held her suspended, anchored to that path in the sky. Sal laughed, wild, hysterical, as though she had finally seen the joke of the world. "Zelda. It's beautiful here."

Horror gripped Zelda. Still, she pulled, muscles straining, arms and back and legs. She would not let go. She could not.

But Sal sank her arm deeper into the blackness and dragged her down with inhuman strength. "You don't get it. It's not our dream. But we can wake up from it."

Her skin tore. Blood ran down her arm, her wrist. Her fingers slipped.

"Zelda. Look at me!"

Her teeth were long, were sharp, were fangs. Weren't they? Was that darkness after all, was it insectile and many-jointed with inhuman geometries, or was it something else, deep and black and clear as night? Were those screams, or song?

She was being pulled down. She could not hold herself back.

"All those empty worlds. Where do you think the people go? They left him, Zelda. They left him and they're waiting out there. They're waiting for us."

Her own grip on the bloody earth was failing. Her nails tore. A finger popped out of joint. She screamed. She could not stop screaming.

"Come on, Captain Kidd." Her eyes of many facets, so many tongues in that gaping mouth—or was it her still, Sal, her Sal, desperate earnest and golden-eyed? "Just a little further."

"And then she fell."

"It was the blood," Zelda said. "Just the blood. Slippery. She didn't let go." It was true. No matter how she relived it, no matter how deep her self-loathing, it was true. It was the blood. "And she fell. The road broke open beneath us and I fell too. Not into the dark. Sometimes I wish I had.

"They found me in Montana, half dead, nine days after Elsinore. I hadn't been lying there that long. I think we were on that path for a long time. Time is different out there, or distance, or both. Or it's all in our heads. Ramón thinks he almost caught up with us. But the Challenger burned. So that was one more piece of us I'd broken.

"I told them everything. I told them what Sal said, about abandoning the road or going into the dark. I told them I was scared, and that the rot took Sal and she fell. And they left me.

"And they were right."

She couldn't look at June. She didn't think she could bear it. "It was my fault. I lost faith. Or I couldn't make her understand. Or I didn't trust us. What's out there now, what's taken her and cored her and eaten her, it marked me." She took the ring from her pocket: simple black iron, cold to the touch. "I told you the truth back in New York, as much of it as I could. And then I saw that picture on your wall. I never meant to lie to you. But I have. I lost her. I'm sorry."

In the silence that followed, she could not bear to look over at June's face, only out into the silver lie of the road, the dream that draped the land.

She imagined what June must be feeling, what she had every right to feel. Sorrow, rage, betrayal. A need for revenge. If the girl offered her poison, she would drink it. Or Zelda could follow the old queen's example and fling herself from the battlements. Just step out into the air and fall.

Speak, she willed her—prayed to her, never looking up. Command me to destroy myself. Scorn me and curse me. I broke the world with my fear. I opened cracks I have spent ten years mending, and that work will never measure up to the depth of my crime. My sin. Pride, the first and final, the illusion that in all the world I was alone.

I held on with all my strength. But still I set the ring in her hand, and left her.

Get on with it. Curse me, and I will die.

June kissed her on the crown of her bowed head, and wrapped her, shaking, in her arms.

Zelda did not understand. She flinched from the touch as she would have from a blow. She pulled into herself as if June's skin burned. She had never imagined a cruelty like this.

The embrace broke and she heard June laugh, an Easter Sunday laugh. You found the stone rolled back, and the tomb empty.

"Z. Don't you get it?'

June glowed in the moonlight. Around her, the shadows writhed. Her face, her figure radiated certainty. As if they'd been puzzling over a problem all this time, trying every normal complicated path, filled pages with notes and the air with chalkboard dust, and she'd just found the sheer elegant three-step proof. And Zelda, her hands coated with chalk dust, still didn't understand.

"We're wrong, Z. Wrong this whole time. They left him, she said. You heard his voice, in the courtyard, on the trail. The cowboy's voice. Z, we've been thinking that our world was the real one, the right one. But it's not. It's not real, it's not right. It's not even ours. It's his."

"You don't know what you're saying."

"I do. Zelda, it's okay!" She was weeping, with a fierce joy. "What's out there, past the last exit, it looks scary to us because *he* can't bear it, because he can't *be* there. There's no place for him. If you'd only ever had salt water, would you trust the taste of sweet?"

Her logic was wrong. Skewed. This wasn't what Zelda had been afraid of, but—it couldn't be true. Not possibly. "There are monsters, June. I've seen them. I've saved people. I've sealed cracks."

"The monsters grow in people, when they've seen what's outside. Some of them want to get out, but . . . there are big men in prison too. People who weren't anything before they went inside. How do you think freedom feels to them? Don't you think they'd kill it if they could? Wouldn't it drive them mad?"

She remembered the grove. Mona.

*It hears me.*

"No."

"You saw her, Zelda. Just for a moment, you saw the other side. What it could be like. He's crouched in the heart of our world dreaming we need him, but, Zelda, his dreams are so small. We could be so much more. He can't let that be true. All the shadows he casts are barren things. Hollow things. Without life or joy. He chases life and joy from them."

"June. June, stop."

She walked from the ashes toward the castle, trailing shadows like the train of a black silk gown. "I saw it, Z, that first day on the bridge. She touched me and I saw. But it wasn't right, it wasn't the way things were, so I unsaw. I got it wrong. I should have trusted. She's out there, Z. She loves you and she misses you. She's coming back to rescue you. And I'm going to help her."

Zelda lunged for June but a great whispering wind threw her back. June raised her arms, spread wide like wings. She was mountain-tall and mighty.

"Come with me." She stretched out her hand.

It hung between them, the offer, the space. The gap in time and worlds. Could June be right?

Zelda grabbed her and tried to pull her close, wrestle her down.

Shadows seized her then from behind, glass-splinter arms of rot curling round her and forcing her back, peeling her fingers away, even as they bore June up, her expression beatific and sad, merciful. The rot had her. Zelda had to fight, had to push through, but she could not fight the wind from beyond the worlds. Her spin melted. Her muscles froze. June was walking now, through the air, through a tunnel of shadows, toward the castle, and the sky creaked like river ice beneath her feet.

"I'll fix it," June said. "I'll make it right."

Shadows closed around her, and she was gone.

The talons that held Zelda melted away. She fell to the packed earth, bleeding, panting, slick with sweat and horror. The earth gaped beneath her. What had she done? She failed, always and forever. The world was deep and cruel, and she was always losing.

But, in that moment—what had she seen, reflected in June's eyes?

There were voices around her, shapes—not the mad whispers from beyond, but human voices. Sarah and Ramón, and Ish, helping her up, and Sarah saying: "What happened?" and meaning: What did you do?

There came a crack and a flash. Storm clouds boiled all along the horizon. The lightning left afterimages against the stars, and they did not fade but deepened, inverted, digging trenches in the sky. After so many years, the end of the world felt just the same. Whispers rose on the storm wind. She stood, with their aid. Sarah, unsure, her face barren. Ramón determined and scared. Ish alone seemed ready, like a prisoner for the axe. Had he known? Had he been right to know? She held his gaze, she reached for his arm.

"I lost her," she said. "She's going to the crossroads. To let them in."

# CHAPTER THIRTY-TWO

The Challenger screamed through the dark beneath an opening sky, and the dead horses galloped with it.

Zelda's grip whitened on the reins. The castle neared. Silver lights and twisted thorns of shadow played around its battlements as the cracks spread wider. The immense heap of stones seemed to stretch and breathe. Its black and broken windows watched them come.

Ten years of decay had not softened this place. Plates of steel armor had rusted off the outer walls to reveal bullet-pitted brick. A great dish antenna lay cracked in half beside the barbican. The gates were a mouth of curving fangs, and as they neared, she thought for an instant the whole awful place was about to swallow them, gulp them down its throatlike halls to stomach dungeons where they would be acid-burned and pulped and torn apart. As they crossed the lowered drawbridge, a fanged porcullis made of dripping rot and shadows swept down to bar their path.

The Challenger roared ahead, crimson lights blazing, and the shadow-teeth tore and broke on its paint. The car skidded, screeched over the spot where the queen had fallen. Zelda galloped after, and Ish, and then they were all there, at night, in the courtyard they had left so long ago, at the toes of the immense and rough-hewn keep.

Lightning lit it monochrome. Sal had thought the place looked too medieval Europe to have possibly been built here—some millionaire's folly perhaps, bought and carted over block by block from this alt's Old World, then seized by whichever local family did the skull-crushing hereabouts when society fell apart. Or else this castle was here because they dreamed of castles, even in a country where there were none.

Here, in the Great Hall past the doors atop that lion-flanked staircase, Ish had killed a man, to save Ramón's life. There was the queen's window, and far overhead, rising above the rest, was the slim, peaked tower and the balcony where the princess had watched the stars.

Zelda had spent ten years running from this courtyard, from the strange lights in that starless sky, from the road that led from the princess's balcony to the crossroads. She had no choice now. She had left choice behind long ago.

Wind howled. She clutched her jacket close. The keep loomed, its parapets and the towers of the curtain wall like the fingers of an immense, malformed hand. At any moment, it might close into a fist.

The night was a wilderness of keening winds and rolling thunder and grinding, breathing stone, but they stood within the cacophony as if inside a bubble of time. Ramón's gaze was haunted. Ish's massive hands were tight-balled into fists. Sarah looked unsure. She loved the kid, Zelda knew. She had heard the fight, some of it. Zelda had tried to tell them what June said, tried to make sense of it. If they could catch up with her, maybe they could explain. Maybe they could talk her back from the edge.

*She's coming back to rescue you.*

The past did not go away. If you went back, you would find it waiting.

It would be different, tonight. This time she wasn't the one who ran, the one who spoiled it all. They were together. That would make a difference.

Or would it?

Zelda had told June everything, even the parts she had spent most of a decade not telling herself. The full story of her crimes and fears, and her great crushing weakness at the end.

June had listened, and judged, and what she said was: You're wrong. You don't understand what's happened to you. You don't understand the story of your own life. You have lied to yourself, or worse, you believed a lie that was told to you, about who you really are, about what you have come here to do.

June was wrong. She had to be wrong. She didn't know. She had not seen Sal fall into the dark.

What scared Zelda the most, here in this courtyard again, as the sky opened again, was the irrepressible spark and flower, the warmth in her chest. Hope.

Not hope that they could do this. Of course they would try, they would give themselves and break themselves and grind themselves to powder in the attempt. They were strong enough for that. It might not work. But if it could be done, they could do it. This was what they were made for. They were strong, and they had no other choice.

Unless they did.

That was the hope, that was the pernicious lightness in her chest, the bird in the cage of her ribs. She might be wrong. She might have been wrong all this time.

But if she let herself believe she might be wrong, she could not be the way she had to be to win, to beat June and Sal to the crossroads. She would fail, be just another victim, just another crumpled woman in history's teeth, the thing she'd promised herself, in that bed in the Bronx in freshman year, that she would never be.

No, she could not hope. She could not be wrong. She had to do what she had to do.

She scanned the others.

Ish alone seemed ready. Scared, his eyes reflecting the light show in the sky—but ready.

"What's the plan?" he asked, looking at her.

She licked her dry, cracked lips. She did not want there to be a plan. She did not want this to be happening at all. They had meant to sneak through the crime of this place, waking as few of the things that slumbered here as possible. Now the stones beneath her feet were breathing.

But there was no other way.

"The castle is awake," she said. "We have to go through. All the way to the balcony, to the road. Ish, Ramón, we'll need you to find a path through the dark.

Sarah, help me fight." She drew her knife. It wasn't much against a living castle, but holding *something* made her feel better. "Let's go."

The great double doors opened easily, as if they had been waiting. Beyond lay the night-drenched hall. The throne was empty, the tapestries moth-chewed and faded, gold thread noblewomen and unicorns clouded by time and grayed by shadows. Ramón's flashlight danced over the empty chamber. Half was lit silver gray by the moon through the eastern windows, and by the lightning of the gathering storm, while in the other half, darkness coiled back from his flashlight beam.

The doors slammed shut behind them like a coffin lid. The screaming winds of the courtyard gave way to silence and whispers.

Ramón took a deep breath of dust and age. His hands were shaking. He heard the Challenger's voice, distant but clear.

This is it, kid. Your time. Your place. You've run and run, but this is where you belong, here in the dark, in the monster's mouth.

He had to find a path. That was all. Find a path that wouldn't get them killed.

He tried to remember this place, both as it had been ten years ago, torchlit and alive, and to remember it through his knack, as it was now.

Behind the throne and to the left, a narrow stair rises, concealed behind a tapestry, twisting, twisting, toward the watchtower, the stair of servants and spies. It won't take us all the way, but that doesn't matter. Once we're past the keep's Great Hall, the walls are wormed with passages and tunnels left by a century of plotters. All we have to do is get there, keeping out of the shadows. Stick to the path moonbeams and your flashlight make, to the brilliance left by the lightning. Don't step in the dark.

His hand tightened in Ish's—he glanced left, tried to meet his eyes. Ish looked away but in that second he'd seen what Ish could not hide: the haunted look others mistook for confidence. In a way it was, but a sick kind of confidence, not faith in himself or in his friends, but in his vision of the world, in the shadow of the trees.

"You're not there," he said. "It isn't then."

Ish turned to him, surprised, his soul suddenly bare. "Thank you."

They would get through this. They had to. They would reach June, break her out of her trance. Save her. Together. He squeezed Ish's hand, and for a moment, he thought he must have imagined it, the man behind those eyes was the man who'd sat across a chessboard from him and, not knowing what he was doing, moved a pawn.

"One step at a time," he said, and Ish said back: "One step at a time."

They led the way, hands linked, along the paths their flashlights traced, toward the throne.

*Stop*, Ramón's knack told him, and he stopped.

He could not see the thing at first: it slithered away from his gaze, a swelling in the tar-thick shadow opposite the windows of the Great Hall. But he knew it was there, the rot-serpent, tall as the vaulted roofs, rearing with many mouths all fanged and gaping, unseen only because his terrified mind refused to gather the shreds his senses reported into a single shape.

"Ramón." Zelda's voice, behind him. Unsure.

"Keep to the light." Such a thing could not exist, not even here, not even now. Its own weight would pulp it. If they skirted the moonlit sections of the hall, if they darted across the shadows pillars cast, they could make it. Halfway there now. Closer. Almost.

Storm clouds closed over the moon, and the hall went black.

His flashlight fell on what should have been a stone floor before his feet, but instead of illuminating, the beam sank into cave-pit nothingness.

There was no path, his knack told him, no path at all, not forward or back. There was only the night.

The shadows gathered underfoot. Anywhere he stepped, he would fall through and keep falling. This was the world, and it ate you up, it ate even your grave, it left you nothing but an empty room and the working of great meaningless machines.

Sweat rolled down his forehead, stung his eyes.

"Ramón." That was Ish. "I can't see."

He heard a hiss, loud as a roar—a sweep through the dark, the crash as rotten furniture burst to splinters, as skeletons left ten years back for beetles to pick their flesh away were crushed now, dust at last as the serpent rushed toward them. Ramón recoiled in panic, lost his balance, almost fell, almost fell forever.

Ish's blunt grip held him bruising-tight. He would not let go. Then, around him in the dark, he felt Sarah's knack, her power shielding them, not with its usual careful plaiting of coincidence but with the raw weight of her refusal to let them die.

The serpents's teeth glanced off stone, drawing sparks.

He found his footing. Unseen, the serpent recoiled in the darkness, ready once more to strike. Could Sarah hold out a second time?

"Close your eyes." Zelda's voice—and as he did, he felt her knack at work around him, her will picking at tumblers, saying not what the world could be but what it was, carving shadows back. He felt a path take shape—not a true path, not yet, but the promise of one, the possibility. "Get ready to run."

"Zelda, I can't see."

"I'm working on it." Her voice was tight. He felt her spin coursing, not out but up, into the storm.

And the lightning came.

You never saw it like this on the coasts, or else so, so rarely. This was a midlands storm, not a crack or a flash of lightning but a sheet, filling the sky, bright enough to read by, miles of lightning, brilliant and unforgiving.

He could see. For this illuminated instant, the hall was dead and empty. There was no serpent. There was a path before him.

He ran, pulling the others along, battered by the roll of thunder—he ran past the throne, through the threadbare tapestry—and as the lightning died, as the thunder still roared, they were through, upon the winding stair.

Zelda slumped against the stone wall, panting. "I'm fine." Sarah supported her weight, managed even in the tight stairwell to wrap one arm half around her. Zelda said: "I can do this." She looked ragged and her eyes refused to focus, but he recognized that look, that set of her shoulders, from a long-gone Halloween. Her will set against the world. Even against herself. "Let's go."

They climbed. In this narrow space, free of the Great Hall's greater shadows, they were stronger. Their spin pressed the walls into shape, confirmed that each turn of the stair existed before they reached it. Their flashlight beams were the prows of an icebreaker against the dark, their will and their spin the engines that pressed them on.

The rot battered their defenses, but found no gap. They climbed step by step, working the world into being. There was no place in their hearts unfilled with certainty. They could do this. Ramón knew the rot, but he knew the kid too. June. She was strong, but she loved Zelda and Sarah. They would get through to her. They'd make this work. The four of them together, there was nothing they could not do.

And then, at once, the flashlights went out.

The darkness crushed them.

Ish felt it happening before it happened, and made one of those choices that passed so quickly, it did not seem like a choice at all.

The flashlights died. Shadows slammed down, parting them, all of them from one another—and he saw Ramón crumple, fall. Ish jumped toward him and covered him with his body.

The darkness hammered down. He could not see. The shadow's weight was immense. He might have been lying on top of Ramón at the bottom of the ocean, with whales and giant squids wrestling above, so far down not even starlight that darted unfazed across ten thousand million miles of space could reach them, here in the dark of teeth and the deeps of time. Ramón was there. Ish could feel him struggling to breathe. Ish struggled too. His bones creaked. This was the brute weight of shadow, and he knew, as none of the others did, just how thin was the shell of the world, how crumbling, how soon it would give way beneath this weight and he would fall.

A serpent gnaws at the roots of the world.

Ramón groaned.

Ish tried to remember futures from this point. A second ago as they had climbed, his mind had fizzed and popped with kaleidoscopes of chance, a blinding confusion of branching paths, depending on where he set his foot, but now those memories were silent, and there was only weight.

Here they were again, he and Ramón, alone, and neither of them knew what they were doing. They could die here. That was one thing you could do, in the shadow of the trees: you could curl up and let yourself go. He had loved those first weeks with Ramón, at college, knowing no one else, loved the freedom of them, the joke, the lie of trying again and again and letting yourself be bad at things, failing without consequence. They had left all of that behind so long ago.

They could not fail. He could not let Ramón fail, or Sarah; he could not let Zelda down.

He gathered himself and lifted against the world.

It was impossible. Nothing could shift this darkness. His knack did not have Sarah's strength, or Zelda's; his mind and magic and muscles were all equally useless here. He would stay down until the ground gave way and the serpent's mouth was all his world.

But that was how it always felt, before the weight began to move.

His hand twitched, groped for the bag he carried.

He clutched the gun.

With a great shuddering groan, he heaved to his feet. The weight pressed down, but he stood. He could not see, but the fact of the gun was in his hand.

Ramón lay still beneath him. Ish reached down, and with a great creaking roar, lifted him to his shoulders. Ramón's weight added to the world's was not enough to notice.

He tried a step. Staggered. Think of anything but the weight.

The gun in his hand was cold and true. The gun was his certainty, his path. One step at a time.

He thought of roads.

People liked to think they lived in a world built to their scale. They crossed and crossed the country and one another, broad and straight, and sized for giants so that brains evolved in bodies which could in ideal conditions process a world at, what, ten miles an hour, could make meaningful decisions at eighty. They liked to think they knew how the pieces fit together. They were wrong.

If you were smart, you didn't challenge them, just sold them the right to dream the dreams they wanted at the scale they wanted, which kept them busy while you turned to face reality. The cracks in the world. The serpent underneath.

Roads: a network. Not a network. A net, laid over the body of the land. Pressing into her skin. Crosshatching her softly parted lips. Holding her down, lest she wake and rise.

*You used to know how to lose.*

Ramón said that to him. He thought Ramón would understand—you couldn't afford to lose, not here, not in this country. You have to win and win and win because the alternative waits with gnashing teeth. Because there is a serpent.

Someone has to walk the line.

He climbed one step, another. He could not make it all the way to the tower. Not alone. Where was Zelda, where was Sarah? He had not reached for them when the darkness came down. They could have handled this together. They could have found a way. But there was a voice in his head saying, no, saying, this isn't something you solve by holding hands and singing, don't try to Care Bear Stare your way out of this shit. This is the serpent. They did not understand when you tried to tell them. They did not listen when you warned them about the girl and her shadows.

He could not make it on his own. He did not know how.

Ramón would know.

Set him down. Wake him, or try. He's still breathing, he's still there. You could win through together.

But that was another lie, wasn't it? He had tried to tell Ramón the truth, tried to explain to him why he did what he did, why he needed power and why it found him and what the stakes really were, and Ramón had no answer, or he had tried to answer, but all he could say was that Ish's world was small, which was the whole point, the world might look like a big large easy place where you could live as you pleased, but really it was so small, it was a postage stamp, all this great weight pressing down on you, and you could choose to be crushed or you could choose to walk the line.

The gun was . . . not glowing. There was no light here, from within or without. But he could see it clearly just the same, the fact of it shaped out of the endless dark, a truth he could cling to. Don't trust your eyes. Don't trust anything. See by the gun.

There was a path before him in the dark, narrow as a blade. He remembered it. He took a step, and it was easier, like carrying the moon would be easier than carrying the earth. Another.

What was time? What was turning, rising, and falling? The path was all he could see, the line in the dark, and he followed it. He did not try to remember the future or the past. There was no use choosing where to go. The path carried him.

When he reached the end, he fell to his knees and saw.

He knew this room. The vizier's sanctum, his strange shrine, where he knelt and made sacrifice and prayed to the blank stare of his black mirror. The drapes were torn and mouse-chewed, the drawers out and the floor strewn with dully glinting keys. Gems lay in shards, and paint was stripped and gold dented. But there, still, was the black mirror framed, illuminated, and wreathed with wires atop the altar.

He laid Ramón down and stared up into that mirror, into his own reflection.

The mirror flickered. Within, there was light.

"Hello, daddy."

---

Sarah climbed, and Zelda climbed, each one's arms laced around the other's shoulders, through the dark, up the stairs they could not see. The weight took her breath away, but with their four legs and two backs, with Sarah's knack pressing the danger aside and Zelda's making sure of the stairs beneath their feet, step by step, they climbed through the dark.

Vision was not the only sense. It was not, after all, light that made the world.

Sarah did not know where Ish or Ramón might be. They were beyond her reach, parted in that instant when the flashlights died. Ish had jumped toward Ramón. That was something, she thought. That was hope. Little enough to go around.

She had lost June. She had lost again. Ish had told her the signs and she had ignored them, because—why? Because she loved June, and because June loved Sal, and Zelda, and all of them.

Foolish. People are only walls you set up against inevitable time. You lose, that's the truth of it. You lose and you lose and you lose, over and over again, world without end. That's why Pop would burst from his bedroom shouting, wide awake in the middle of the night, when you'd sneaked into the kitchen to get a drink of water—because he knew the truth, and he tried not to tell you, tried to make you live the lie he'd lived himself because that was the only way he knew to survive. But when he held back from speaking, he drowned you out with his silence. It was a silence that took up space. Grown people, solid, with their own shapes and lives, would not notice the silence, but the unformed, the not-yet-fixed, the children, found themselves channeled and carved, curled into the hollow that silence left. Talk about anything else, she had learned, without ever being taught, talk about anything else but that. Stay quiet. Stay still, unnoticed. If they see you they will come for you, so be unseen, perfect, careful.

She was alone, the silence told her, and she had believed it until that moment on the Elm Street bench, when she met Sal. When Sal was lost, she had believed it again. Wasn't that the staggering truth of them all, the secret silence of her house and cul-de-sac? She was alone, she was alone, she could not speak, and Evan and Susan and Alex, who were with her always, lay atop that loneliness.

She was tired of it.

Here was Zelda with her now. And here was Zelda ten years ago, too, bleeding and scared in that parking lot in Montana, after she lost Sal, lost everything, and Sarah had lost it too. She had seen in that instant not Zelda-the-rival, not Zelda-the-girlfriend who never understood what she had in Sal, but a reflection: another woman, harrowed and unsure.

That was her, in the Montana parking lot: seen, shattered, raw. To touch that image would be to make it real.

So she left. When they had needed one another most, she left. They had been together in that loss and she turned away. She'd told herself so many times over ten years that back then Zelda did not have a plan other than to keep battering her head against the world. She told herself that Zelda was an arm that had been broken and set wrong. But you told yourself things over and over only because you did not believe them. You said the Pledge of Allegiance day after day in school.

She could have stayed. She didn't have to go along with Zelda's mad plan, no, but she did not have to leave either. They could have found a way out of that parking lot together. They could have helped each other. But to touch your reflection was to own it as yours.

Ten years later, she found that letter on her counter.

Step by step, by step by step. Four legs, two backs. She could not see, in this dark, except through memory, and while memory lied, memory was in some ways clearer than sight. It carved false and incidental facts down to the truth on reflection, to the truth of reflection. She saw Zelda not in this moment of climbing stairs but in collage, Zelda over their years together and apart, Zelda glimpsed and Zelda remembered: how she looked in pain, how she looked teeth gritted and striving, how she looked in love.

It's not enough, Sarah thought. But it's all we have.

How could she say all of that, back here again after so long, climbing this tower in this darkness? How could she speak the words? How could she speak at all, beneath this terrifying weight?

"You got harder." She had to breathe after three words. "In the last ten years. Or I got softer."

"I love you," Zelda said back.

Only will and main strength kept Sarah on her feet. She tasted salt, which was not sweat. She saw June again, June in the Best Western lobby, June in starlight, June that morning after she asked to help, the morning Sarah sneaked from the tent without her anyway, because she thought there was no other way. She saw Susan back at their kitchen table at home, so fixed on problems, and she saw Alex's fierce riot in answer to any rule.

They climbed. Floor by floor. So close now.

"She's a good kid," Sarah said. Meaning: June.

From the depths, from the dark, Zelda answered: "Do you think she's right?"

The castle might have cracked beneath them. Zelda was always so sure of her path—because she had to be, because anything else was terrifying. Yet here was Zelda, just like Sarah, unsure.

"I don't know." They were the only honest words that came to mind. "I think we might be wrong."

The shadows broke and they stumbled onto the balcony.

After the long dark climb, she reeled to find herself in the open air, atop the tower and beneath the churning storm-ragged sky. Gravity seemed loose, a suggestion. The wind might catch her and spin her away.

Once this place had gleamed with the brass and chrome and lens glass, worked by the princess's own hands, machined and polished and ground to an elegance unimaginable in this lush and decayed alt. Now the metal was lightning-blasted slag, scaled with rust, the glass in fragments, reflecting the million horrors of the world. It had lain, like them, scoured too long.

At the balcony's edge, before the storm, stood June.

She turned to them, her eyes full black from lid to lid.

"Good," she said. "You're just in time."

# CHAPTER THIRTY-THREE

Whata had Zelda thought she would find on the princess's balcony?
There were shadows and thorns, there was the rot and the storm
and the voices, the screams and whispers on the wind, and the deep,
deep dark. She was ready for all of that. This is how the story goes,
she had known that since childhood. The dragon comes and the world catches
fire.

She was not ready for June, at the balcony's edge, to turn from the path taking shape in the sky.

Her eyes were dark, and shadows rose around her like spider arms or wings, diffusing through the air like a drop of ink in clear water. There was monstrosity enough.

But there was also the girl.

June was not lost. She had never once been lost.

As Zelda stared at her, she could feel her own mind working, great systems of which she was only vaguely aware, churning to make a monster out of June. There were so many reasons to fear. This was the end of the world. This was the end of the world. Wasn't it?

There was that bird in her chest again. Hope.

Ten years had led her here, with Sarah by her side, all the way back. Those same years led June here, too, and she was calling out to the night.

"June, you can't do this."

"No," June said. "*You* can't. You can't let yourself see. There's too much that's not *you* in your head. But I can show you, if you let me."

Sarah and Zelda traded glances and ran for her. The demon wind pressed them back. It screamed across hundreds of miles of dead land and weed-choked fields. The lightning set them all on white-gold fire, changed the ruins to glory. Then it faded and the night smashed down again.

Zelda fought forward through the dark, step by step, side by side with Sarah, felt Sarah's knack and hers, this can't be happening, don't let this happen, trying to stand against the demon wind of *yes*.

The moon broke through the clouds. Silver and right. High midnight.

She felt an unbearable tension in the storm. The clench of a jar lid before it opened.

The wind stopped. They staggered, sprawled. Zelda scrambled to her feet.

The path took shape.

Beyond the balcony's edge, the storm clouds spread, parted, then knit together. In moonlight and starlight a new land took shape, an airy, spreading country of silver gray, of great black trees with fruit that glittered stardew. Through that strange country ran a path, a road of flowers blacker than black, into which the light poured and was lost.

The road, the land, the trees, they were at once there and not, like the hologram superheroes on cards Zelda used to get in cereal boxes. Turn your head just a little, and the clouds were clouds and the gaps between them empty air. But if you stood in the right place at the right time and held your heart at the right angle like a skipping stone, the road would bear you.

There, at the end of the black-flower path, lay the crossroads. She could not see it, but she heard it whisper to her, the same old wily questions. What do you want? And: What will you give?

She had seen it just like this, ten years ago. In that instant, time seemed to touch.

The years between now and then fell like a blade.

The sky cracked. Black lighting flashed and stuck and turned the long, silver trail bright green. Spin poured out from June, twisting into the world. Zelda felt possibilities bloom and wither and shift beneath her like a melting glacier.

Another crack. A third.

The thunder seemed to go on forever.

At the limit of sight, striding toward them, toward the crossroads, massed like a mountain above the world of clouds—was Sal.

Not the monster in the clouds. Not the demon she had run from all these years, the shadow of her own mistakes.

Just Sal herself.

Older. Wiser. A touch of storm gray in her hair. Sal, tall and strong and coming home.

There was her smile, still and always the smile at the joke of the world, but it was not cruel. What Zelda had seen as legs, as claws, as tentacles before—deep underwater, if you opened your eyes despite the burn and looked up, you saw bodies ringed with arms of light. This was light, too—the light of a darker, stranger sun.

It was her. Really her.

Zelda saw her only for a moment, before the horror closed in again and replaced that vision with holes in the sky, the tentacles, the waves of shadow and eyes of flame, the angles that were wrong. But she saw and she could not deny the seeing. She could not will this truth otherwise. The cage of her ribs cracked.

"June."

*She's out there, Z. She loves you and she misses you. She's coming back to rescue you.*

How did you know whether you were seeing or unseeing? How could you trust a world that lied to you about itself, about its past? About Sal? A world that told a lie so convincing even Zelda believed?

But that was no lie. She could not see it now, could not see Sal behind the terror in the sky, any more than, underwater, she could see a shape ashore clear and right-angled. The ripples between them were not the truth.

*All the shadows he casts are barren things.*

She fell to her knees and wept.

"It's okay," June said. "I'll fix it."

The girl stepped out onto the path.

✳

"You ain't doing so hot, daddy," said the figure in the black mirror. "If you don't mind me saying. I gave you the gun. I told you to watch the girl. And now the sky's opening. Damn shame."

Even now, he could not see the cowboy's eyes.

"It was a free gift. No strings attached." The tongue that tasted the cowboy's lower lip was white as a fingernail. "How did it turn out, with your girl? Did you save her life? Did you make her quiver?"

"Stop it."

"We walk the line, daddy, because so long as the world's there, we can take the things we want from it. You build a garden wall to keep the peaches safe. But now that wall's coming down."

Ramón twitched on the floor beside the altar. Moaned. His eyelids flickered. Coming around.

"We can still stop her," Ish said. "We need your help."

The cowboy shook his head slowly. "You don't get it, do you? There ain't no *we* in this. There's just you and me. You're alone out here, daddy. All alone. One by one, they're giving up."

A great crack shook the tower. Thunder was his first thought, but that sound was deeper than thunder, deep as memory. He had heard that sound before, the night it all went wrong. There had been cracks in the sky and in the earth, like lightning bolts that lingered. As if the world were an egg and its shell was opening. He heard the rising wind inside the castle walls, the high and shrieking wind of whispers.

"Let me show you. You're far away now, I don't have many eyes round here and the girl ain't exactly helping, but let me see what I can do."

The cowboy's image in the mirror flickered, and he saw the balcony, the princess's balcony, and June standing at the edge, and Sarah fallen, and a monster in the sky. He saw Zelda on her knees, staring over the edge of the world. Tears in her eyes, but no horror there. He remembered that look, that awe, from the way his heart used to twist when she looked at Sal when she thought no one else was watching.

He had never seen her this naked.

"You're lying."

"Do I lie, daddy? To you? Have I, even once?"

He could not speak. He could not answer. He bowed his head and looked away and screwed his eyes shut. A tear burned his cheek.

A touch, featherlight and hard with calluses from long and bloody work, lifted the tear away. And a voice whispered in his ear: "That's all right, daddy. We can do what needs doing. We have enough rounds left."

"Ish?"

Ramón was sitting up, staring at him with hazy and unfixed eyes, at the mirror, at the cowboy, at the gun.

No time. No time to explain, no time to waste. He had tried, hadn't he, and Ramón didn't get it. You had to walk the line. Even when it hurt you. Even when it hurt the ones you loved. Because without the line, there was only the serpent waiting.

The gun flashed out. It moved his hand. That's how it felt.

Its stock hit Ramón in the temple and he crumpled.

Ish looked down at the unconscious body of his friend, and at the gun, and at his hand that held the gun.

He didn't understand. They didn't. He'd be fine. Ramón. Probably. He could not comprehend the danger.

*Make sure of it,* the cowboy told him. Was that the cowboy's voice after all, or just the voice inside his head?

He remembered Ramón's doubt, when he pushed that pawn back in freshman year. I don't know how to play. *Me neither.*

---

Ish lurched from the shrine room, down the hall. There was no weight now, no darkness, only the pure draw of the gun. There was the line. It was always there, just where you had to go. It ran before you. There were no decisions to be made, only the line, only the world and the saving of it.

He rounded the final corner and breached the curtains, and there was the balcony, just as he had seen it in the black mirror vision.

Sal a demon in the sky. Sarah fallen. Zelda down, weeping, and June, June as he'd always known her, ringed with shadows, robed in spider legs and crowned with thorns. June, on the path.

At the crossroads, you could wall them out. Or you could invite them in.

Chaos. The shadows at the edge of the trees. The war of all against all.

Someone had to walk the line.

A serpent gnaws at the roots of the world.

There was June.

The gun raised his arm.

The wind screamed. It laughed. Babbling mad voices.

His sights found the back of her head. Nothing existed but that. The back of her skull. His need.

The trigger.

The gun kicked his hand.

But June did not fall.

His aim was true. But: dull, in the flash of lightning, smaller than you might ever imagine, stuck in midair, was his bullet.

Sarah stood between him and the girl.

---

Cold high wind whipped Sarah's dress about her legs. She stood with hand outstretched, trembling at the balcony's edge above the long fall. June was behind her, walking toward Sal, toward the monster in the sky. Zelda was on her knees. And there stood Ish with that fucking cowboy costume gun. The barrel smoking.

He had tried to shoot June.

And she, Sarah, had stopped him.

The bullet fell. It bounced off the balcony and spun to the courtyard far below.

Sarah had never stopped a bullet before. You could make a gunman miss, make their weapon jam or misfire, you could screw them up in so many different ways. But there had been no time for elegance. She'd seen him, the gun, the muzzle, and the girl.

She'd grown up around guns and she'd had the rules screamed into her since she was old enough to pry open a cabinet door by herself. Never point a gun at someone you don't want to kill. Not for a photo, not for a joke, not if you hold the magazine in your hand and removed every round yourself. Never rest your finger on a trigger. Never place your finger on the trigger at all, unless you want to make the gun do its work, which is killing. You did not fuck with those rules. That was how people got dead.

So her first reaction to seeing him with that gun raised was fury—because Ish was breaking the rules. Didn't he know that was how people died?

Then the gun spoke.

And she stopped the bullet.

How dare he? How fucking *dare*? Even with the rot and the crossroads and Sal in the sky—how could he have raised that gun? He didn't know Sarah would stop him. Even Sarah hadn't known herself that she could.

Blood and spin rushed in her ears, her heart a stampede.

He had meant to kill. She could ask how and why, but those questions only papered over what mattered more than anything: that he had raised the gun, taken aim, pulled the trigger. That strange hard structure, that form she'd felt buried inside him, emerged from the lake of his mind, serrated, dripping. As it unfolded, moonlight glinted off its bolo tie.

Ish stepped from the shadows into the balcony's weird silver light, and she saw a pale halo around his head—the afterimage of a cowboy hat.

She heard footsteps through the scream of the wind. She heard the jangle of spurs.

Had she scared him off in the Green Glass City—or had he simply drawn back, waiting, biding his time until he was welcomed in with open arms? They welcome the cowboy when they get scared. They talk a good game, they may turn from him for a while, but in the end, fear takes them and they call him down. She remembered Ish's face, in the light of the crystal fields. She wondered how long the cowboy had been speaking to him, how long he had lived inside. How long he'd hated what he thought was his weakness, when in fact it was the part of him that was still him, the brave and tiny mouse, not this old hand-me-down monster.

Face me, you asshole. Not her. Not him. Let them go. Face me. We're the ones with history.

Time ran slow. Her heart was rabbit-fast, and still oceans of silence spread between the beats. In that silence, in the infinite time between contractions, he spoke: *Darlin', I have history with everyone. What you and me got, that's special.*

She stood her ground. Spin howled through her. Her will was a castle all its own. *He's not you. He's not yours. Not really. He's a sad kid, and you warped him as he grew, but you're just a goddamn shadow, and your time has come. You can pull that trigger, but how many bullets do you have left? Not one of them will touch her.*

She met Ish's eyes. She wanted him to be what he had been in the crystal field. She wanted him to be everything he might have been, if he were not so goddamned scared all the time.

She wanted Evan, and Alex, and Susan. She wanted to be home. But she had to be here now.

Time was coming back. Ish's gun hand shook. *No,* the cowboy said. *I can see that.*

The gun spoke.

———

Sarah stumbled back. Her mouth gaped: red, shocked, bowed around the blackness within. There was a new flower on her dress. Spreading fast. She sat down hard.

She had always tried to save them. Even Ish.

He had walked with her in crystal fields.

*I'm sorry.*

This wasn't right. This wasn't right. He was supposed to save her. Save Zelda. His hand had moved. He had done—

*What was needful. You did what was needful.*

That voice was not his, but it was inside his head. Didn't that mean it was him, really? It was him, it was what he'd willed, it was what he'd invited in. Sarah fell. Sarah was still falling.

The girl, June, turned back and saw. Her mouth opened. A scream? A cry? Was she still human enough to cry? The wind tore her words away, but he could not hear the wind either. He heard his own heartbeat. He was underwater. In a weighted suit, you didn't float, you just fell and fell, into the dark.

How could he have done it?

But he had.

When she turned, the girl, June, saw Sarah, bleeding, fallen, and took her mind off the path. The path that was nothing but intent.

The black-flower road parted beneath her feet like a cloud. She fell.

Zelda lunged for the balcony's edge—straining, straining, to catch the girl.

The path was before him. The trail to the crossroads. The path was breaking up, torn by the storm wind, but it was still there.

At the far side, drawing closer, summoned, ringed in nightmare: Sal.

She was coming. He had not stopped the girl in time. Sal was coming, with the serpent and the rot, she was coming and she bore with her the shadow of the trees.

This was all her fault. She was the one who had stepped wrong, she was the rot's champion, walking home from far outside the circle of firelight, that tiny human patch of reality where squares had four corners and the angles of a triangle added up to 180 degrees. Walking home and bringing the many-angled horrors of elsewhere with her.

Sarah was bleeding. He had shot her. If he had done that, he had to go further. He had to go all the way.

He could reach the crossroads first. He could stop her. Fix this. Change things. And if Sal and the serpents and all the powers of darkness stood against him—well, someone had to walk the line. The world was mad. But the gun had its own logic, and that, he could trust.

He ran to the balcony's edge. Jumped. It was easy. He'd cleared farther distances in his workouts back home.

The black-flower road lay underfoot. Ahead: the crossroads. Sal.

There was still time.

Three bullets left. A job to do.

# CHAPTER THIRTY-FOUR

In some moments, time itself seems sick.

Zelda struggled to her feet. She had seen Sal in the sky, not the Sal of ten years past but Sal grown. She had seen Sal walking toward the crossroads, summoned by June from the space beyond possibility. The vision lasted only for a second, but she believed it. Not the way she believed in Jupiter or asteroids, but the way she believed in air.

And then.

Ish shot Sarah. Sarah fell. June turned, cried out . . . and slipped from the path.

Zelda believed that too. Even though it was all too much. Even though if she were God, she would have unwilled these things, cast them out of a working universe.

She flung herself across the balcony. Sprawled, she skidded to the edge and strained in the dark with her hand, with her knack. The fall was three hundred feet straight down to the courtyard. But it's possible, it's just possible, let it *be*—

June's hand found her wrist and clung. Zelda's arm jerked in her socket. Pain shot up her shoulder. The girl's weight pulled her down, pulled her head and shoulders over the edge. Flailing, Zelda caught a balcony pillar. It held. Wounds opened in her wrist, in her arm.

Cobblestones spun far, far below. Ten years ago, the queen had called the rot, then thrown herself from the battlements. They'd seen her fall.

Now, still alive, wide-eyed, grateful, afraid, dangling from Zelda's grip, was June.

"I've got you," Zelda said. "I've got you."

The balcony was crumbling. Her arms were agony. Sarah's neat stitches pulled in her side.

She was not strong enough to pull June up. June's feet kicked empty air.

Don't let go, she ordered herself. You'll think of something. You always do. Just. Don't. Let. Go.

Another hand joined hers around June's wrist, and with a roar, as thunder cracked and rolled, they were lifted. June cleared the edge.

They tumbled back onto the balcony, into Ramón.

They lay panting in a bloody heap. June beside her, dazed, her shadows gone, just a girl again, a girl who was not dead. Two people, not dead. Three. Ramón's face was a mess. There was an ugly, swollen cut on his temple, blood mixed with sweat, he was gulping for breath, his gaze unfixed. "Oh God." Zelda heard her own voice. It might have been a prayer. It was the only thing she could say. "Oh God. Sarah."

She tried to rise, but she was slow, she was old. June was up in an instant, as if she'd never fallen in her life. "Sarah." June scrambled on all fours to where Sarah lay, propped against the banister. She shook her. "Sarah, wake up."

Sarah's eyes were closed. The blood on the front of her dress might have been a strange, creeping flower.

Zelda remembered their walk in the cemetery, back in college, when this all started and Sarah did not believe about the alts. She remembered the cemetery gates and the lidless winged stone eye and the inscription, THE DEAD SHALL BE RAISED. The pair of them, trapped together in that coffin. The sly smile later when she revealed the skull she'd lifted on their way out.

Please.

Sarah's eyes fluttered open. Her lips twisted. "Don't." A dart of tongue. "Don't. Shake me."

June hugged her, but pulled away when Sarah gasped in pain. "Are you—okay?" Her face wet with tears, unsure even of the right words.

"I've been shot. So. No." Her bare toes twitched. "Looks like he missed—you know. I can. You can move me. I think."

"Z." Ramón's voice. "What do we do?"

Lightning cracked the sky again. The path was breaking up, the silver world shattering. By the weird light, they saw Ish on the path, with his gun.

A white hat on his head.

Running for the crossroads.

Zelda looked back at Ramón. She knew without asking where the wound on his face had come from. She felt furious, a profound trembling pressure inside her, enough to break bones—hers, Ish's, anyone's, everyone's. There should not be a bone in all the world without its marrow running out. But Ramón looked . . . cored. Ish had been a long time walking away, and the whole time, he'd tried to believe they were still side by side.

Zelda looked away. "Sarah needs a hospital."

Sarah stretched one hand up and Zelda knelt, caught it. "He shot me, Zelda. He tried to kill her. Stop him."

"I won't leave you."

"Get over yourself, Zelda. Go." She slumped back, exhausted with the effort.

Ramón's hand was on her arm. He said nothing.

And out there, Ish marched toward the crossroads.

June was shaking, was a girl again. No, that was wrong. She had always been a girl. There on the edge of the balcony, summoning Sal and breaking the world apart, she had been a girl then too. They were all themselves. They were every monster she had ever found, and every darkness.

Right now June's shadow was thin, weak, normal as anyone's. She'd spent all her power calling Sal, and Sal was coming, and Ish was walking out to meet her with that gun in his hand and the cowboy in his head.

"Save her," she told Ramón. He nodded.

June's eyes were on hers, wet. "Z."

A prayer was a kind of question.

Who are you? What do you want? What will you give up?

She found her feet.

Beyond the balcony's edge, the path lurched and chopped like a sea in storm.

It was drifting away. If you didn't hold your heart just right, the black-flower road was only empty air, three hundred feet above the courtyard stones.

She ran. She jumped.

She landed on her feet, on the path. Blood seeped through the soil between her toes, and the black flowers brushed her ankles.

The crossroads lay before her, and the bobbing dot of Ish's white hat.

Sarah moaned when they lifted her, and kept her eyes screwed shut. She said nothing Ramón understood. Her legs buckled. Her arms clutched them tight. The balcony swam around him, and a drum pounded in his head, the same drum he'd heard when he tried to stand up back on the altar room floor, after Ish— After. But he could keep his feet. He could drive. He'd taken worse hits. He'd just been younger then.

They staggered downstairs. Sarah whimpered with each step. But June helped, and as thunder rolled, they found their way from the tower to the main floors.

Stone dulled the roar of the weather outside. The castle shook.

He heard footsteps.

Boots. With spurs. Drawing closer. From down the hall. From the altar room.

The footsteps quickened from a walk to a jog. A run.

"He's between us and the stairs," June said.

Ramón's memory and his knack bubbled up a path, an instinct. Maybe, a chance. "Come on."

The staircase from the queen's chamber down to the library was narrow, but the door could be locked from inside the passage. They stumbled through the dust and broken mirrors and wrecked silks to the moth-eaten unicorn tapestry, which had always bothered him, a symbol of purity in this place of poets stripped naked at knifepoint.

Okay, maybe that blow to the head rattled him more than he'd thought. Keep it together. Focus. If the passage still opens at all.

It did.

Ramón yanked the door closed behind them, felt the latch engage. They were locked in the dank, shadowy stairwell. Down, down. Behind them, he heard muffled boots on thick green carpet, then—an earsplitting crack. A hole opened in the hidden door. A bullet sent stone chips dancing off the walls. But the latch held, for now.

Timber cracked behind them as they tumbled into the library, then down a passage to the throne room, down the grand stair to the courtyard. To the Challenger, waiting, its black paint reflecting now white, now blue, now every earthly rainbow color as the path to the crossroads twisted in the sky. Sarah was heavy against his side, limp weight. Just limp. Not dead. Not yet. He popped the passenger seat forward and helped June lever her into the back. Sarah was breathing. Still. Her eyes tight shut. Her skirt was all red, her belly.

That was bad. He did not want to think how bad.

He had to get her to a hospital. That was all. Past the storm and the cracks and the rot and the cowboy. He could do that. He could drive. He'd been driving all his life.

June was shivering now, shrunken. She was a kid. She was so many other things, but she was a kid too. Like him. We never stopped being kids, whatever else we became. He took her shoulders, looked into her panicked dark eyes. "Keep pressure on it." That was the right thing to do, wasn't it? He should have studied something else. What had he studied? Applied math. Applied to what? Not this.

June scrambled into the back seat. He slammed the door, *Dukes*-slid across the hood to the driver's side, opened the door, and—

There, at the top of the stairs, stood the cowboy.

And he did not miss.

But Ramón's knack lay in finding spaces. Parking spaces, gaps in traffic, clear paths to walk. Spaces, he hoped, where bullets weren't.

He ducked forward, then leapt back. A bullet winged off the stone behind him, another at his feet. Then he was inside the car. Gloved in leather. The chrome skull on the shifter pommel grinned.

It spoke to him, in the engine's roar, in the thick tongues of gears and the whir and tick of belts and the squeal of tires finding traction. He'd almost forgotten what it sounded like, that scorn, that voice, older than time, more real than he was. He'd started to think it was a dream.

You tried this before, the Challenger said. Didn't I tell you? You can't run from it. You can't save anyone. You can't escape the blood.

The engine roared. His hands and feet did their dance.

He screamed away across the bridge and out into the night.

Behind him, the cowboy ambled down the grand staircase to the dead horses. He snapped his fingers and one rose. He mounted it with a smooth and easy single motion.

Its eyes shone red. His spurs gouged troughs in its metal flanks.

The cowboy rode after.

---

Zelda ran through silver green.

The sky was cracking, and the ground beneath. The world was ending. It was always ending, and it never stopped.

The wind was full of whispers and all the whispers spoke her name. The blood of the black-flower road seeped through her shoes. The wind smelled of moonlight and fresh-mown flowers and earth, but those scents were not enough to hide the blood.

There was Sal, ahead, drawing near, as she had drawn near on the road behind, all those years ago. The night Zelda failed. Was June right? Could there be a world outside this one, a world beyond the deserts the cowboy had sucked dry? What other chances were there? What other dreams?

She had seen Sal, for an instant, in the sky.

Really Sal.

She ran faster.

The world changed.

———※———

The winds tore at Ish. The ground burned beneath his boots.

Just one step at a time. That's how you reach the crossroads. Same way you ate an elephant.

His boots? He was wearing sneakers. Wasn't he?

The place itself abhorred him. It pressed him back like the wrong pole of a magnet. The gun was so heavy and so hot. But he needed it. He had used it, he was right to use it. It hurt him to use it. That's how he knew that it was right.

In the flicker between one footstep and the next, he was somewhere else.

His boots caught on grass and he stumbled, righted himself, and looked around in shock. He was in a Georgian courtyard at night, redbrick walls and white windows, a steeple against a purple-orange sky. And the courtyard was full of—

Monsters, his brain supplied, and then, children. Neither. Three zombies with red Solo cups, arms wrapped around shoulders, swaying, singing. Vampires with greasepaint skin and gods and someone dressed as a faun, wearing stilts— Dressed as. These were costumes. A girl in short shorts and a tank top, with garter belt pistol holsters and knee-high boots, strode away in a huff from a guy wearing a leather jacket and Goodwill's best approximation of a fedora. It was all so bright and clear and distant, as if he'd flipped binoculars around to see the world the wrong way. They were talking but the voices came through cotton. Somewhere, many people were failing to rap to "Lose Yourself."

He knew this place. He had been here before. The Halloween party. Timothy Dwight courtyard. Fourteen years ago.

He still held the gun.

This was a trick. He knew what the path to the crossroads was. He had seen it from the Challenger, the shattering black trail, the endless lightning, the boiling rot. Or it was not a trick. Of course the path would push you back, of course it would confuse. Your will was your vessel through the alts, your soul was the tiller. Your memory shaped the path.

When he looked down, he saw the black-flower road beneath his feet.

Which meant—

He saw Zelda then, through the crowd, and she saw him. She was doubled: at once the woman she was now and the woman he had known, though they would have called each other boys and girls back then, at once in jeans and flannel and Frankenstein makeup and her beaten bloody jacket and her ragged sneakers and her ten years of scars and dust.

Fourteen years ago. Face-to-face. You built walls around feelings like this. You made bargains and agreements. You placed money in escrow, you signed elaborate contracts, because you could not let what you felt blind you or bind you from the bare truth of the world, from what had to be.

He reached for her. His hand still held the gun.

Zelda ran.

She was always faster at the start. She reached the gate that led out to Temple Street before he did, clanged off the heavy iron, and staggered out into the marching band chaos of Halloween. He chased her. His footfalls, hammering concrete, echoed through his legs. She was racing down the Temple Street sidewalk now, dodging a frat pack's naked run by veering into the road, into honking slow traffic, and always she was on the black-flower trail, and he was after her.

Black lightning flashed in the purple-orange sky. He cornered too fast, slipped, almost fell into an oncoming Buick. There was Sal, tall as forever, beyond the eggshell of the sky. This was not the past. It was now. Or it all was now, time all folded up inside or on top of itself, inside him. And there was Zelda, running toward her.

Caught between two rocks, two monsters. In the shadow of the trees. He trusted Zelda. But she was—she was wrong. About Sal. Misled. She had been wrong back then, too, she had not seen what was true about the world, even about this strange slice of it.

He had to convince her. To put things right.

(The light on her hair.)

It wasn't that. It was the principle. The shadow of the trees. The serpent that gnawed at the roots of the world.

(Velvet.)

The path cracked underfoot, all along its length. He leapt to one side without thinking. They were on Cross Campus now, and the fire jugglers and the dancers and the idling gods and the happy weirdos with their foam swords did not seem to notice that the world was broken in half and waterfalling blood down into the gap, into the mouth of the hungry earth. Zelda was on the other side of the gap, Zelda was still on the road, still running.

Side by side. Always. Wasn't that what he wanted? Always what he wanted—running with her, side by side, to do the work the world needed—

(A net, pressed against her lips)

There were voices, mad voices, whispers. Promises. Temptations. Surrender. Give in. It's not too late. Open your eyes. Put down the gun.

He would never surrender. You could not surrender, in the shadow beneath the trees. He had to do this. He had to save the world.

He gathered himself and jumped.

---

Blood rained on the Challenger. Ramón gunned the engine, turned on his wipers, and drove like hell.

Sarah moaned in the back seat—good. She was still there. June was talking to her in a calm, low voice. He didn't recognize the words. They weren't English or Spanish. Sarah seemed to recognize them, though. Reached up. Touched June's face.

Focus. Do your job. Get them home.

Alts flickered into other alts outside the window, pivoting on details. The color of a sky, the texture of the road, the smell of exhaust, you could pivot on anything if you were good and fast and smart. He drove through lava fields and fields of crosses. He drove through jungles and on cracked paths along glacier cliffs. And always, behind him, the cowboy neared.

Dead horses couldn't run this fast. But he was gaining. His bullets winged pavement, creased the Challenger's side. When the cowboy shot all six, he reloaded easily, unhurried, one-handed, his other hand sure on the reins.

This is it, the Challenger said. All along, I told you. You peel back the skin and fat, and all you find is blood.

He needed a hospital. He needed a road to one, a path home.

There. With a hard left, he pulled them onto an interstate ramp. The ramp ended in a jagged gap in this alt, but one alt over, the road ran clear and easy under stars that were not—

"Ramón!"

June's shriek. He ducked. His window exploded. Glass, stinging, and the dull impact pain of a deep cut near his eye. God, he hoped it was *near*—

There was a cowboy on a motorcycle, even with his door.

He jerked the wheel sideways, trying to ram the cowboy off the road, but the bike peeled away. The cowboy's spurs rang sparks from the pavement. Ramón blinked blood out of his eye. Where had the cowboy found a motorcycle? But, no, there was the cowboy in the rearview mirror, on the dead horse. There was more than one.

He wanted to ask Ish what to do. The wanting hurt.

He'd seen despair on Ish's face, as he raised the gun. But he'd still raised it. *I failed her,* he had said after the Green Glass City. I can't fail her again. They'd met failing, at auditions, at tryouts. They'd made a game of it. They'd tried to fail at something every day, back at school. Wasn't that the point of the thing? But he understood now, as he remembered the wild ice-field bleakness of Ish's expression back at Elsinore. For Ish, the game of their freshman year wasn't to test his limits but to convince himself that failure could mean something other than death.

Ish had spent his life fighting something. And he had lost.

Sarah needed a hospital. Ramón had to find another path home, free of cowboys.

Off the interstate. Down. There—a road sign not quite unlike the ones that welcomed you to Mississippi. Almost.

Sirens behind him. A squad car peeled out from cover. The Challenger's rear windshield exploded. Behind the squad car's steering wheel sat a man in a big white hat.

It's blood, and more blood, no matter how hard you pretend it's otherwise. No hope. No healing. You push up against the edges here, and they'll cut you. But at least it's honest.

He turned hard, then swerved to avoid a cowboy standing in the middle of the road, gun raised, a ghost in the headlights. A muzzle flash. The Challenger almost tipped. He spun the wheel. He leaned. The car landed the right way up. And—on. Faster.

Run from it all you like, kid. The truth's not going anywhere.

Zelda ran through the shattering past.

She ran past the ghosts and gods, the vampries and the beautiful young things and the dude in the SPERMATOZOA SWIM TEAM CHAMPION T-shirt, none of whom seemed to notice as Cross Campus tore apart, one half creaking up and the other creaking down into the night. Not one of these kids knew where they were or what was coming. The black-flower road bled and she trailed ruddy footsteps. She glanced over her shoulder, saw Ish gather himself and leap across the superhuman gap, stumble around a Frankenstein juggling fire, and run after her, hat on his head, gun in his hand, past a knight in shining armor.

How could she be here again? There was a girl, bangled and bare-midriffed as a belly dancer, there was a Neo kissing an Agent Smith on the corner outside Durfee's. Zelda ran across traffic and cut through a marching band, scattering brass and horns. Somewhere there was Sal in her orange body stocking, her tail and cat ears and her tall boots, sword at hip, crying. Somewhere there was Ramón, flaunting, tempting gods, and Ish himself, softer and kinder and sadder, in that strange vampire getup with the banjo. Somewhere, maybe right now, she was staring at her own reflection in the dorm mirror, ready to cut off her hair.

The crossroads waited. Why had the path led her back here? She ran past the children and wished she could take them, each of them, by the shoulders and scream. Where were they now? Out in the world, like her? Wondering what had happened or what path they'd chosen or if they had any choice at all, wondering if they'd fucked it up, wondering what their place was? Were they chasing the crossroads? Was the crossroads chasing them?

A horn, a screech of brakes; she jumped, rolled across the hood of an oncoming car, caught the ledge of the Elm Street sidewalk as it broke off and reared overhead. With a kick of her legs she made it up over the cliff, back on her feet, racing down the black-flower road, and somehow Ish was still behind her, tireless, gaining.

*We don't know the world enough to save it.*

She ran as if running itself would be enough. She'd been running like this for ten years, hoping the next step, the next turn, would take her to the end of the line. She could not breathe. Her heart ached from pounding. Where? Where did it all lead?

Through Saybrook, through Branford, past hockey girls in Care Bear onesies, up to York Street. They did not see the lightning in the sky. They did not know the world was breaking open. But it was. The world was always ending, not somewhere else over the horizon but right here, right beneath you, and you did not know how to look. You were ending it.

Left on York. Past the small brick building where the Christian Fellowship met. Where she was still arriving, now, always now, in her knee-length dress and her sensible braid and her rainbow pin, thinking she knew what defiance was. Thinking she was ready.

Where did it lead?

Then she saw, and knew, and could not gather breath enough to laugh or cry.

✦

Ish was bleeding and sore. He'd torn his hand catching the rising Elm Street ledge. Cut his forearm somewhere, and a thin line of blood ran down to his grip and made the gun sticky and hot like a living thing. But he could run.

Yes, he could run. All that training, all those predawn days, because there was a serpent that gnawed at the roots of the world, because you had to be stronger, faster. Because you knew that all your success, all your wealth and striving, meant there were people out there who had to work harder and fight more and they wanted what you had, and you, without the left-hand luxury of a world that would make you hard on its own, had to build yourself twice as hard to match them. Muscle for strength. Sprints because so much muscle left you deadweight, made you food for the serpent.

Zelda lived on the road. Zelda was hard. She could have made her money, she could have bent that uncompromising mind of hers to remake the world. But she was not that person. She was always running ahead, trying to catch something he could never see. But she was fast on her feet. Was she running toward, or away? Was he?

He remembered the sun on her hair.

No distractions. Just run.

On the straightaway up York, he was catching her. Closing. Faster.

The black-flower road unfurled ahead of her, straight down the sidewalk, up the steps, toward the A & A Building.

It had some other name, but he'd never heard anyone say it. The structure towered at the edge of what he always thought of as the campus. The university owned other buildings farther out, but they were disguised, they looked normal. The A & A Building was smaller than the huge fake Gothic edifices, it was smaller than the baroque rocket of Harkness or the library or the gym, but the bleak fact of its huge spans of brutalist concrete and vertical glass ribbons made it loom. The style did not apologize, did not pretend it belonged to some quaint antique power structure that had horribly fucked peasants three hundred years ago. The A & A Building was real, was honest, was now. You could snap your fingers and pour tons of concrete in a year and make a building that would outlast bombs, if you did it halfway right. This is the power, if you're willing to hold it. If you're willing to give up.

He had hated the building. Ramón hated it. Everyone they knew in school did, or said they did. He wondered if they understood, if he had understood, down deeper than words, what it meant, if even then they were afraid.

The black-flower road led to a side door, to a stairwell. She'd need an ID card to get in, but of course there was her knack. She reached for the handle, yanked it open, and was through.

He slammed into the concrete, grabbed the handle, pulled, knowing it was futile. The handle crumpled. The door burst off its hinges and clattered to the breaking sidewalk.

He did not ask questions. She was ahead of him. Racing up the concrete stairs. He climbed after her.

His heart surged in his chest. He felt sick. He was gaining, steps at a time. Heartbeat, his own footfalls hammering through his shins. Go faster. There was another sound, too loud to be a sound, a concussion wave like standing too close to a bomb blast, over and over.

Footsteps.

Sal wreathed by tentacles, Sal become a monster in the sky. She had helped him. She had been there in the autumn courtyard, gold and red with maple, she had been his pretend love, she had trained him and they had laughed together and that should have been the start of something. He saw Ramón sprawled on the floor in the altar room. He saw Sarah.

Sarah, falling.

What was at the crossroads? What were they running for, after all this time? What had he been running toward, ever since? Who was waiting for you? What was the secret at the heart of the world?

Eight stories up and he was only steps behind Zelda now. He could smell her. She was slowing, tiring. Faster. Go faster. Ahead, the rooftop door. She hit it first, though he was steps behind.

He tumbled through.

Blood in his mouth, in his eyes, panting, he stopped, gulped air as he anchored his gaze in the dust beneath his boots.

All was—still. A crystal pane. A glass-fresh lake at sunrise.

The crossroads was a flat and quiet place. A rooftop, that was all, with a chain-link fence to one side, and all the towers and palaces of the world spread out beneath. Marching through the sky behind that chain-link fence: Sal.

There, across the gravel, stood Zelda.

And the cowboy.

---

Ish was bleeding, Zelda saw. Out of breath. Just like her.

She said his name.

He looked at her as if fitting puzzle pieces together in his mind. For all his mass and strength, the gun in his hand seemed to drag him down.

The cowboy stood, hands easy at his sides, near his holsters. One holster, she saw, was empty. His hat still hid his eyes. He was smiling.

"Leave," she told him. "Get out. This isn't your place."

Her words sounded thin and hollow. The air was so still, as if the breaking apart of the campus below, the cataclysm of the sky, even Sal, approaching, were just painted figures. As if this was the only place in the world that mattered. As it was. This was what they had searched for. The place where you could do what had to be done. The place where things could change.

"Of course it is," the cowboy said. His voice was unchanged after all these years. She remembered it inside her, in the courtyard, standing over Sal. It was a sound more in her bones than in the air. "You want me here, you and daddy, in that warm little scared-mouse heart of yours."

"Listen to him," Ish said. "Zelda, he's right."

She looked at him, shaking, bloody, sweat-slick. They had met in class. She'd been a week into her freshman year, so stuck on proving herself—being smart, being clever, asking the good questions. After the first class, she went for coffee with him, and ordered hot chocolate, and realized forty-five minutes into the conversation that she wasn't pretending. That there might be people here she could love, without having to impress.

And he had loved her.

And now he was wearing that stupid fucking hat.

"I know what you want," the cowboy said. "And I can give it to you. You want things fixed, whole. You want what comes after the world is saved, you want the monsters beat and you want to be quiet, and comfy, and home. All you have to do is ask for it. You're here. What you want, you can make. Nice white house, picket fence, helicopter pad? Warm girl in your bed? She'll even look the same." His mouth a cut, a scar, a smile made from blood.

"I want what's real. I want what's out there." She pointed past the chain-link fence Sal first taught her to climb, out to where the monsters thronged in the sky.

The cowboy shook his head, just once, a slip of that hat from side to side. "You don't want that. Look close."

She stared into the monstrosity, into the whirl and chaos, into the darting batwinged forms and ropy shadowy arms and teeth, into the terror shape that was and was not Sal, and tried to see the vision she had seen before, the vision June had shown her on the road, the woman Sal had grown to be, out beyond the limits of what Zelda could imagine.

*I love you. We're in this together. I won't let go if you don't.*

With the cowboy's voice in her ear, she could not see it. There were only teeth and claws, only the rending awful terror of powerlessness, and she was afraid.

Zelda was tired. She was alone. She had walked such a long road. And at the end, if she took this final step, there was just more road on the other side. He knew that, and he knew her. He was inside her. He had been inside her all along. Keeping her safe. He had been there in Sal's bedroom, that hot wet autumn when Zelda realized she had stepped outside the magic circle, when she felt the realness of the world crush her like a mighty fist. Ten years ago, she had not been strong enough, and she had only worn down since.

"What's out there ain't easy," he said. "It ain't kind. And once you step over the line, you can't ever come back. There's still time. We can save the world and it does not have to hurt."

"I can't," she said.

"Zelda." Ish, his voice raw and unsure, rife with hope. "Zelda, listen to him. We don't have a choice. You know what it's like. You know how bad it can be. We can make a difference. Don't you see? This is our chance. We can fix it."

Fix it. She saw Sarah fallen, gutshot, bleeding. She remembered holding Sal's hand, gripping it tighter even as she slipped out, beyond, into the thorns where Zelda could not bear to follow.

*What do you want? What will you give up?*

She understood.

"This place isn't power," she said. "It's a wound."

His eyes said that he did not understand.

"We wanted . . . *I* wanted to be safe. I wanted control. Infinite worlds, don't you see? And every one poisoned."

"Because of the rot."

"Not because of the rot. Because of us. Because this is the only way we know how to see. We could have gone anywhere and done anything, but we always come right back to power and control. And him. We carved him into us because that is what we thought the world was. But we don't have to keep carving." He didn't believe her. She could see it in his eyes, wide, staring. He wanted to but could not. "I won't."

She flung those words against the cowboy, wishing they felt like a battle cry, like a standard. *Non serviam.* I will *not* be bound by his small and broken worlds, by the crumbling, bloodless edges of his worn-out imagination. But her heart was a hummingbird in her throat, and she was trembling, and she did not know what came next.

"Well," the cowboy said, "from where I stand, that leaves you in some trouble."

His hand sank to his belt.

He smiled that crime of a smile.

"Two against one."

Zelda did her best to smile back. "Are you sure?"

There were ten cowboys behind Ramón now on the road, no, make that twelve. And two more from the side road. Fourteen.

"I can't lose them!" he shouted. He thought he was talking to June.

Of course you can't, the Challenger said. They're more real than you are. The cowboy beats you, overwrites you, overlays you. You're just a shadow, as far as he's concerned.

He hadn't heard anything from the back seat in a while. Maybe it was lost in the roar of wind through his shattered windows, his perforated roof. His world was dread and speed and the road beneath his headlights. "Sarah?"

"She's not moving, Ramón. She's still got a pulse. She's breathing. She needs help."

"She needs a hospital. She needs home. But the closer we get, the more of him there are."

"Because he lives there! Don't you get it? Home is his place. It's where he comes from. The roads are his roads."

She needs help.

But there is no help, the Challenger said. No help. Just blood, and him.

Ramón felt engines inside his head, churning, driving hard, as they did when he faced a problem or a proof on paper. There was something here, something deeper.

No help. No healing.

Why don't we, he had asked as a half-bitter joke, why don't we ever find a healing spring?

*The roads are his roads.*

His knack churned. Paths unfolded.

To get the right answers, you have to ask the right questions.

He tightened his grip on the wheel and thought of Gabe.

Zelda said, *hospital.* But after that, she'd just said, *save her.*

Wait, the Challenger said. Just—wait. What are you doing?

"Trailblazing," he said, and turned hard left, off the road and into the dark.

           ➤

They stood on the A & A roof, in the stillness beneath the churning sky.

The cowboy did not move. His shirt fluttered in a breeze Zelda could not feel. Ish was heaving like a horse after a race.

She felt her spin, the great pool of it gathered in their long journey from the Green Glass City, all against this one attempt at the crossroads. She had spent much on the long climb to the balcony. But there was, she thought, enough left to foul one shot, to spoil even the simple mechanism of an old cowboy's gun.

But there were two guns. Two men in hats.

Her eyes flicked from Ish to the cowboy and back.

Could she split her spin between them, try to foul both at once? Risky. The cowboy was damn certain of his piece. Only one bullet had to find her. Those guns would not need a second shot.

Sweat rolled down Ish's forehead. There had been whipped cream on her hot chocolate, that first time after set theory, with sprinkles. What did he have? A cider, she thought. A cider with cinnamon.

She remembered sitting across from him one afternoon on Cross Campus, under the sun, young and easy, talking math. Happy to be alive.

"It's not too late," she said.

The cowboy's hand came up.

           ➤

It's not too late.

It was. It always was. The cowboy was moving, his gun infallible. Ish had only one memory of the future and this was it, forever and ever, Zelda on the rooftop bleeding, Sarah bleeding, the gun in his hand. That was how it had to be.

This was his job. He'd taken the gun. Even if he couldn't remember putting on the hat.

The cowboy's hand came up.

He remembered Cynthia, in her black dress. The long, worked muscles of her legs.

Sarah. Sarah was the one who had told him about Florence after the revolution. You hired a sheriff to keep order. A nobleman, because your soldiers would not follow a man of common birth. At the end of a year, you took them to the wall, gave them a bag of gold, and told them to leave and never come back, or else you would chain them in a dungeon and kill them slowly. Because you could not live in chaos, but you hated tyranny.

He loved Cynthia. He loved Zelda. He loved Sarah and he had shot her.

Someone has to walk the line, daddy. There are wild things out there, and it is up to us to break them. You know how it is, in the shadow of the trees.

I do know how it is, he thought. I know how it is. And ever since that afternoon, some part of me has lived there, where the bones break, where the fists rise and fall. It is in me, that truth, in deep. Its roots around my heart.

*It's not too late.*

There was only one path. The future was a straight, unbroken razor line, and his role to walk it.

The cowboy's hand came up.

Ish tried to move. His arm weighed a thousand pounds. It was so easy to look at her. So hard to point the gun anywhere else.

Don't fight it. This is what you want, what you need. Remember. A serpent gnaws at the roots of the world.

He stood, again, always, in the shadow of the trees. But there were other worlds than his. Ramón and Sarah, Zelda and Sal. Cynthia. He had failed them, but they were real. More real than the trees, more real than the serpent, more real than the cowboy.

He had been afraid so long. And this was power.

His arm weighed a thousand pounds. But he woke at five o'clock every morning and walked into the lemon-scented room with his racks of weights, and lifted.

Over time, you get used to feeling like you're about to die.

Zelda raised her hand.

The cowboy's gun went *click*.

Ish screamed as his hammer fell.

—✦—

Zelda ran to Ish.

He lay on the rooftop, bleeding from the chest, his eyes wide.

She had thrown her spin against the cowboy, spoiled his first shot, and hoped. And then Ish's round took the cowboy in the chest. The cowboy moved snakefast, even then. The gun came up again, around.

Where the cowboy had fallen, there was no body. He never had one, she thought. Just a hat, and a gun.

She had not heard the cowboy's second shot. But he must have fired again, the sound hidden by the thunder of Ish's gun. Unless—Ish was wearing the hat, and somehow—

Ish did not move. That was all.

She knelt. She closed his eyes.

Had he known? That look on his face—the final look—not surprise. Understanding. He had won. Not at first. He had lost so many times, lost his whole life to fear and need, and he had hurt so many people. But at the end, for an instant, he understood. Then he was gone, and she was here.

She was crying. Not for him, not just for him.

Now the rest was up to her.

She rose.

We might have been brothers, she thought, Ish and me. We fought the same battles. We nursed so many of the same wounds. And we both, from fear, did things for which there can be no forgiveness. None we dare seek, and none that we deserve. What comes, comes through grace, or not at all.

We came here wanting power, and a kind of chain that we called freedom. We found each other.

The fence stood before her. Every breath here weighed whole lives. The silence failed. The stillness was always an illusion. She faced the howling storm, and the rest of her life, and the end of the world.

She was weak and worn and alone.

Sal marched toward her, tall as clouds, made of shadow and flame.

There was so much healing before them, and weeping and true valid rage. And after that, so much work to do.

Before her was the fence, and beyond the fence—what lay past the crossroads? What was on the other side of the world you thought you knew?

She slipped the iron ring onto her finger.

Just a little further.

She dug her fingers into the chain, said, "I love you," and began to climb.

As she climbed, the woman in the sky seemed smaller. No—not that. With each link, with each toehold and each pull, Zelda unfolded. She was light, she was tall—the world behind her such a small corner of what might be. As she grew, she saw differently. The shadows and flames folded in, or opened out.

Sal did not grow less. She was, as Zelda had seen her, as she had always been: beautiful.

One final twist, and Zelda landed, hard, on the other side.

She fell to her knees. They hurt. She used to be young.

There was a hand on her arm, lifting. A voice she had not heard in a long time, a voice she had never stopped hearing.

"Took you long enough."

# CHAPTER THIRTY-FIVE

The Challenger, trailing a fender and shreds of its left rear tire, tore through a blackberry bush and down a steep, wet hill to crunch to a stop against the great leaning stump of an old oak tree.

The airbags deployed.

When Ramón fought himself free, ears ringing, dazed, blinking packing powder from his eyes and coughing it from his dry throat, he found, to his shock, that he was still alive. Which, naturally, led his attention to other matters.

"June!"

"The fuck did you do that for?"

"Get her out, come on. Help me." He took Sarah's shoulders. June took her legs. She was so limp. Her dress was so wet. This couldn't work. It had to.

The night was close and cool, alive with tree frogs and crickets, with warbling insect song, with birds. The trees that ringed the lake were tall and fat and full, sequoias in council, trees before trees were. They had age and wisdom and a bearded respectful hush. In their branches, shadows moved, and not only shadows. The branches themselves twisted against the wind.

He was observed.

"She needs help," he said.

"I know she needs help. What are we doing *here*?"

"I wasn't talking to you."

The branches drew back. He was permitted.

"Come on." Together they brought her down to the water's edge.

"Where are we?"

"I don't know." He dipped his hand in the water. "For once. I just don't. We're off the road. We'll have to find our own way back."

"With Sarah?" She looked around. "I can rig a stretcher, maybe. Salvage from the car for cords and seat belts to use as rope. If—" She cut off. He heard what she would have said: *If she lasts that long.*

"Just give me a second." He tipped the water into her mouth and pressed her jaw closed. He thought he saw her swallow. She was so still.

No. It couldn't go this way. He had found the place. He'd left the road. He'd asked.

It had to make a difference. It had to matter.

"Ramón." June's voice, still. "The stars."

He looked up.

"There are more of them."

There were. And more, in all the colors whose names he had ever forgotten. And still more. And some of them were moving. He remembered Christmas songs. Shepherds and angels.

"Aliens." Not his voice. Not June's.

He looked down. Sarah was smiling as if fresh-woken from a bad dream. There beneath her sodden and blood-soaked dress, through the ruined hole where he could not bear to look before, lay rippled brown skin, scarred but whole.

"She did it," June breathed.

He felt them open all around, through the shadows of the trees—not roads but paths. The stars along the other spokes of the Medicine Wheel. The secret ways to other worlds, drawn back and hidden. Open and waiting. Lands beyond the cowboy, beyond the border, beyond all borders and any map.

There were so many stars up there. He'd wanted to see them all.

"What now?"

"Now," June said, "we go home. And we get them ready."

## CHAPTER THIRTY-SIX

Sarah drove her family north along I-95, when it was safe.

They had spent a long time inside. Out on the open road, the sky felt unimaginably big, bigger even than she remembered. It felt like it went on forever. It did, in a way. But the forever you could see from here was just the beginning. The kiddie pool of forever. It was the easiest part to see. When you understood that there was something else beyond—that was when you realized just how much work there was to do.

They stopped only at gas stations. She never went in; she paid at the pump and sent Evan in with the kids if they needed snacks or drinks. Sometime in the last two years, she'd turned chatty. She'd make small talk in the checkout lane these days, at the coffee counter, like an old person in a movie. She made small talk now, at the pump. People looked at her out of the corner of their eyes when they learned where she was bound.

She smiled at them.

It was funny how people repeated themselves. She received the same advice, five times, on how to skirt around the city, which you could do if you didn't mind going a few hours out of your way, or if you wanted to be extremely careful, you could head up toward Albany and then east on the Mass Pike. Or, if that's too much—just stay on the big road and drive right past. Once you're north, you'll run into outbound traffic, so get ready for the wait. It's better than the alternative.

Oh no, she told them. We're going to the Bronx.

She watched her rearview mirror all the way. Alex bucked against his seat belt and sang along with the radio. Susan read. She'd brought a tote bag so packed with books that she could barely lift it.

The road behind them stayed clear.

She didn't know what to expect. The papers and TV news said everything was fine, everything was normal, people were back to work, the stores were open. They said *normal* a lot. You didn't have to say something so often if it was true. She'd heard whispers on the internet. Stories about new streets, about places that hadn't been there when the world closed down, about doors that had been always shut, but were open now. About statues that walked. Someone saw the lions on the public library steps stand up, shake their manes, do that big cat stretch, and settle back down.

Back home in Virginia, people shared these stories at the parties everyone was having in their backyards these days. She'd been to more barbecues in the last two months than in the five years previous, even if you didn't count the years inside. The storytellers were always laughing, like, can you believe this stuff, like, everyone went crazy cooped up for so long, I know *I* sure did. They laughed it off. The New York stories, they told. The Virginia stories—the tree that caught fire but did not burn down, the sunrise choir, the lights in the woods, the dog lost for ten years who came back wagging and and lolling its tongue, not a day older—the Virignia stories, they didn't tell. They did not tell the stories that had happened to them, personally.

She didn't blame them. She knew what was going on, and she wasn't sure *she* believed.

Ramón had emailed directions and Sarah copied them onto the back of a worksheet Alex had brought home from school. The directions were precise as poetry. Turn left at the dog. Go until the sorrow hits you. Right at the McDonald's.

Wherever she went, the road was clear. New York and its environs might have been a maze built just for her.

Not a maze. A labyrinth. In a labyrinth, all paths lead to the center.

They had to park six blocks out. There were too many people. They filled the streets—tall and short, young and old, hair all different colors and architectures, speaking six languages or sixty, singing, singing. She smelled barbecue. A girl Susan's age walked through the crowd with a basket of cookies, offering them to anyone. Susan took a cookie, and before the girl could go, Susan chose, carefully, a battered book from her tote bag and offered it to her.

It was a party, it was a festival. It was not quite the Fourth of July.

On and in. Sarah had expected her cane to be a problem, and it was, and so was her leg, but not in the way she had thought. It was just the usual hassle. Her shoulder hurt if she used the cane for too long, and even though she'd shopped around to find a comfortable grip, it did bad things to her wrist and rubbed at her palm. She'd taken to wearing a glove on that hand. Plus there were all the cascade aches of her body accommodating itself to the injury.

Even magic healing springs, it turned out, had limits. You could come back. There was that power in the world, in your friends, in your love. But you came back different. What was broken might heal, but could never be *un*broken. You could not undo, but you might mend, and grow again.

There had been no winter this year. They laughed about it on the television, when they told stories about how everything was back to normal. Somehow you could laugh at anything on television.

You could not undo. You could, perhaps, advance.

Her cane was a hassle, but only the usual hassle. The crowd opened for her like water. Evan was tense at first, ready to protect her, sweet, but he eased as they proceeded, like a knotted muscle under a healer's hand.

They reached the place.

People flowed up and down the stairs to Ma Tempest's apartment, but they made a path for her. A young man helped Susan with her books. She'd given away half of them during the walk from the car. Alex looked around as if the walls were made of gold. Maybe they were.

There was a grill on the roof. There was a party up here—no, a group. They had purpose. Young women with binoculars scanned the skyline. Twinkling out there, among the water tanks and spires and antennas, Sarah saw flags, flags of many colors, rising and falling. The city, talking to itself. They reminded her of flowers. They reminded her of spring at her grandparents' home, bursts of color mapping the dry plains.

The women read the flowers on the roofs and called out codes.

"Fire at 138th and Canal. Anyone have a medic?"

"I know a guy."

The flags on the roof's edge danced and others echoed the message.

"Madison's sending food, thanks for the help."

"They say to save room."

June was there, among the girls with the binoculars, answering questions, deciding. She turned, saw Sarah, and for a moment she wasn't a leader. She was almost a kid again. She ran to Sarah, hugged her. Sarah rocked back on the cane, laughed, winced. June righted her, apologized. "No, it's—it's fine."

There was so much to tell.

At the roof's edge stood Ramón, and his man, the blond—Gabe, that was it. And Ma Tempest, seated, hands folded, waiting. Watching. Sarah thought she had been doing both for a long time.

"You got here just in time," June said. "Can't you feel it?"

She felt something. But she had been wrong before. "What happens now?"

June shook her head. "It's happening already. It's been happening. It'll keep happening, and I guess we'll all just learn how to ride it." She looked at her, weighing. "You scared?"

There were too many ways to answer that question. She chose the honest one. "I used to be."

June's face broke in a smile. At first, Sarah thought it was her words that caused it—some joke she hadn't realized she was making. But, no—June was rigid, one finger raised, as if straining to a sound only she could hear through the rooftop jumble and hive. "Hold up."

Everyone stopped talking. The flags stilled. June's smile beamed. Sarah heard it then, in the quiet: the rap of knuckles on wood. A knock on the olive door, far below.

June ran to the roof's edge, leaned over, way out, and shouted down. "Come on in. Come on in! It's open."

*Somerville, MA*
*Nov. 20, Cambridge, MA*

## ACKNOWLEDGMENTS

About eight years ago, I looked at a blinking cursor in an iTunes playlist title, and typed "Songs for the Highway Kind." It wasn't the first step to the book in your hands, but it was far from the last, and as I press the play button today for its final run 'round the bases as an active project playlist, I'm moved to gratitude for everyone who's walked with this book a little while on its way.

When I was a kid, my parents were both teaching high school, and family used the long summers to head off in a Plymouth Voyager for months at a time, crossing and re-crossing the country, sleeping in Walmart tents. We never ended up in any alts to the best of my memory, but sometimes we might as well have. Without those trips, and the dreams they seeded, this book would not exist. So thanks, Mom and Dad and Hal—I spent a lot of those drives reading rather than staring out the window, but something did sink in.

I'm used to writing further-out fantasy, with wizards and time travelers and such, and it's strange to cut closer to the bone, even in the unreal reality of these Unprecedented Times. I was a southern kid at Yale; I've had a Saybrook College bottle opener on my keychain since 2002. Maybe it's because I know many of these places, streets, apartments, restaurants, stretches of road, that I feel compelled to say, you won't find these people in any alumni register, you didn't go to most of these parties, and you won't find North Bend on a map—though you could, for a while, way back when, hop the chain link fence at the top of the A&A building to see what lay on the other side. What's here, and what I remember, has suffered a sea change. Timelines and details have been smudged a bit throughout.

The portrait Zelda and Sal see in the Corporation Room is real, and hung there until 2007 in our alt, when it was taken down due to the efforts of a student activist. You can read the full story on the *Yale Daily News* website, Feb 7, 2007, "University to retire 'Racist' portrait." The portrait can still be seen on the Yale Center for British Art website.

Thanks to everyone who read some version of this book. My memory quails, but names that stand out include Vlad Barash, Bo Bolander, John Chu, Anne Cross, Seth Dickinson, Lara Donnelly, Amal El-Mohtar, Dan Jordan, Matt Michaelson, Stephanie Neely, Victor Raymond, and Rebecca Roanhorse. Thank you all for your support, your criticism, and your patience while I growled my way through crises both in the world and in my head, on the way to an elusive final page.

Ish's sketch outline of Florentine history was first related to me by Ada Palmer; as with all else here, inaccuracies are my own, where they're not the character's.

I'm grateful to my agent, DongWon Song, who gave me the extremely helpful, if at the time terrifying, advice, when he read what I thought was a revised version of a first chapter, to just carry on and rewrite the entire book from there. It was the right move. I don't know that I could have made that call on my own.

Melissa Ann Singer, editor extraordinaire, and Rachel Bass, and senior publicist Desirae Friesen, championed this book throughout its journey at Tor. Eliani Torres went above and beyond as a copy editor, drawing my attention to many infelicities and flaws of memory. Lauren Hougen proofread the typeset manuscript, and Megan Kiddoo (production editor) and Heather Saunders (interior designer) transformed a comment- and strikethrough-laden word document into the beautiful, hefty, typeset home defense implement you (may) be holding at present, as well as its no-less-handsome digital version. Artist Sylvain Sarrailh and designer Russell Trakhtenberg took the seething dread I felt while writing this book and smelted it in the star-forge into the perfect cover. Thanks also to Jim Kapp, production manager, and to Andrew King, Becky Yeager, and Angie Rao for their hard work on marketing, advertising, and creating extremely rad social media and ad graphics.

Finally—thank you, all of you, for being on this road with me. There's no clear path to where we're going, and the road may seem dark, and without end. But let's walk it together with care, and kindness, and strength. One step at a time. Just a little further—and further still.

## ABOUT THE AUTHOR

MAX GLADSTONE is a fencer, a fiddler, and the winner of the Hugo and Nebula Awards for *This is How You Lose the Time War,* co-written with Amal El-Mohtar. A two-time finalist for the John W. Campbell Award, he is fluent in Mandarin and has taught English in China. He is also the author of the Craft Sequence of novels (a Hugo Award finalist), a game developer, and the showrunner for the fiction serial *Bookburners.* Gladstone lives and writes in Somerville, Massachusetts.

maxgladstone.com
@maxgladstone